Praise for Jack Whyte

"To read Jack Whyte is to surrender to a storyteller of the old school. His writing is firmly rooted in the basics of good storytelling: strong characterization, effective plotting, and excellent writing. It helps, of course, that his stories have their origin in one of the greatest stories of all time, the tales surrounding King Arthur and his court at Camelot."   —*Quill & Quire* on *Clothar the Frank*

"Whyte avoids the clichéd trappings of the Arthurian myths with careful attention to historical detail…. The muck and mire, the casual violence and deep-seated political intrigue will be surprising to readers more accustomed to, and expecting, the pomp of traditional accounts of Arthur."   —*Toronto Star*

"Eschewing the fantastical and the miraculous, and opting for a rational and workmanlike approach, the author conveys the believable exposition of a well-bred warrior's upbringing and early manhood. In his tale, Whyte weaves historical fact and folklore together with an accomplished and bardic verve."   —*Edmonton Journal*

"From the building blocks of history and the mortar of reality, Jack Whyte has built Arthur's world and showed us the bone beneath the flesh of legend."   —Diana Gabaldon

"Perhaps not since the early 1970s, with Mary Stewart's *The Crystal Cave* and *The Hollow Hills*, have the Roman Empire and the Arthurian legends been intertwined with as much skill and authenticity."

—*Publishers Weekly* on *The Skystone* (starred review)

PENGUIN CANADA

THE EAGLE

JACK WHYTE is a Scots-born Canadian who has been around long enough by now to have done most of the things he ever wanted to do, and all of those seem to have been connected, in one way or another, to storytelling. His novels on King Arthur have been translated into a number of languages and are sold worldwide, a fact that Mr. Whyte finds gratifying and astonishing at the same time. Having brought his Arthurian cycle to a close with *The Eagle*, he is now deeply involved with a new project, a trilogy of novels examining the rise and fall of the Knights Templar. The first of those, *Knights of the Black and White*, is now available from Penguin. Jack Whyte lives with his wife, Beverley, in Kelowna, British Columbia.

the Eagle

JACK WHYTE

PENGUIN
CANADA

PENGUIN CANADA

Published by the Penguin Group

Penguin Group (Canada), 90 Eglinton Avenue East, Suite 700, Toronto, Ontario, Canada
M4P 2Y3 (a division of Pearson Canada Inc.)

Penguin Group (USA) Inc., 375 Hudson Street, New York, New York 10014, U.S.A.
Penguin Books Ltd, 80 Strand, London WC2R 0RL, England
Penguin Ireland, 25 St Stephen's Green, Dublin 2, Ireland (a division of Penguin Books Ltd)
Penguin Group (Australia), 250 Camberwell Road, Camberwell, Victoria 3124, Australia
(a division of Pearson Australia Group Pty Ltd)
Penguin Books India Pvt Ltd, 11 Community Centre, Panchsheel Park, New Delhi – 110 017, India
Penguin Group (NZ), cnr Airborne and Rosedale Roads, Albany, Auckland 1310, New Zealand
(a division of Pearson New Zealand Ltd)
Penguin Books (South Africa) (Pty) Ltd, 24 Sturdee Avenue, Rosebank, Johannesburg 2196,
South Africa

Penguin Books Ltd, Registered Offices: 80 Strand, London WC2R 0RL, England

First published in a Viking Canada hardcover by Penguin Group (Canada),
a division of Pearson Canada Inc., 2005
Published in this edition, 2006

1 2 3 4 5 6 7 8 9 10   (OPM)

Copyright © Jack Whyte, 2005

LIBRARY AND ARCHIVES CANADA CATALOGUING IN PUBLICATION

Whyte, Jack, 1940–
The eagle / Jack Whyte.

Sequel to Clothar the Frank.
ISBN-10: 0-14-305164-4
ISBN-13: 978-0-14-305164-0

I. Title.

PS8595.H947E199 2006   C813'.54   C2006-901877-4

Visit the Penguin Group (Canada) website at **www.penguin.ca**

Special and corporate bulk purchase rates available; please see
www.penguin.ca/corporatesales or call 1-800-399-6858, ext. 477 or 474

To my wife, Beverley, who, after more than a quarter century of living with the Res Britannica, has mixed feelings about cleaning out the vaults and moving on to other fields …

AUTHOR'S NOTE

Although this is a stand-alone novel, capable of being read without knowledge of, or reference to, anything that has gone before it, it is, nonetheless, a sequel to *Clothar the Frank,* and it chronicles the events of Clothar's life in the aftermath of his meeting and befriending Arthur Pendragon, High King of All Britain. The story features many of the same characters and places involved in the previous book, and that means that much of what I wrote in my preface to *Clothar the Frank* is no less relevant and appropriate here than it was there.

Be warned, then, that readers familiar with Clothar and his previous exploits will find much of what follows here to be familiar, but I have chosen to repeat it for the benefit of new readers who are not familiar with the fifth-century world of which I write.

I have said before that, in approaching this story, I was forced to come to terms with a few historical realities that bore heavily upon my vision of how the legend of King Arthur came into existence. In my mind, the entire story revolves around the Arthur/Guinivere/Lancelot triangle, and everything that occurs in the legendary tale is attributable to the humanity—and the human weaknesses—of the King himself, the dysfunctional nature of his marriage to Guinivere and their joint attraction to the brilliant foreign warrior known as Lancelot.

But Lancelot's full name is Lancelot du lac, Lancelot of the Lake, and it is a French name. Lancelot himself, the legend tells us, was a French knight who crossed the sea to England expressly to serve as a Knight of the Round Table at King Arthur's Court. Well, even making allowances for legendary exaggeration, that simply could not have happened in the middle of the fifth century, because in those days England was still called Britannia and the land now called France was still Roman Gaul.

Not until more than a century later, when the Anglo-Saxon invasions of Britain finally came to an end and the tribes called the Angles emerged as the dominant force, would Britannia begin to become known as the land of the Angles—Angle land, and eventually England. By the same token, Roman Gaul would not become known as France until much later, when the invading Franks finally established their dominance over their arch-rivals, the Burgundians. Over time, the Frankish territories became the land of the Franks— France—while the Burgundians remained in their own territories of Burgundy.

Reputedly wonderful horsemen, the Franks are the people generally credited with bringing the stirruped saddle to western Europe, and from the time of their first appearance in the Roman Empire, along the Rhine River in the third century, they had a reputation for being blunt spoken and utterly tactless, probably because their original tongue contained few of the subtleties of Latin or Greek. Be that as it may, we still use the term "speaking frankly" to denote directness and an unwillingness to mince one's words.

Clothar, then, is my interpretation of Lancelot. Academic opinion indicates that the name Lancelot probably developed from the Latin word *lancearius,* a Roman military denomination that was probably similar to the European lancer regiments of the nineteenth century. In Clothar, I have posited a Frankish horse warrior who, as a close and trusted friend and companion of the High King, Arthur, earns himself an undying reputation as an archetypal hero, the character who will be called Lancelot centuries later by French storytellers who have heard of his fame and his exploits but have lost awareness of his real name.

Language

The major difficulty any author faces in writing historical fiction is that of language, because language is constantly evolving and we have no real knowledge of how people spoke and sounded, in any language, hundreds of years ago. We cannot even comprehend how people from different regions of a tiny country like Britain were unable to understand, or speak to, one another as recently as a hundred and fifty years ago, but the truth is that people from Yorkshire, from London and from other regions of the country spoke dialects so different from each other that they were, in effect, completely different languages. I have chosen to write in standard English, but even that is a relatively new development, since the language was only "standardized" in the nineteenth century. Before that time, there was no orthographically correct way to spell anything.

Most of the characters in my stories would have spoken in the ancient Celtic, Germanic and Gallic tongues—tongues that are completely lost to us nowadays—while the major characters, the kings and leaders, may or may not have conversed in Latin. And in those instances where people of mixed tongues met and mingled, they would have spoken the lingua franca of their time, although the real lingua franca—literally the language of the Franks—had not yet come into common use. But throughout history, whenever people of mixed tongues and races have come together to trade, human ingenuity has quickly developed basic, fundamental languages to fit the needs of the traders. In Africa in the eighteenth and nineteenth centuries, that language was Swahili. In Oriental Asia, it was Pidgin. We do not know the name of whatever trading language was dominant in fifth-century Europe, but I have chosen to call it the Coastal Tongue, because the coast was the interface point for most traders.

One unusual word used quite widely in this book is *Magister*. It is a Latin word that has given us our modern words *magistrate* and *magisterial,* but it was a word in common use in the Roman army in the fifth century. It appears to have had two levels of meaning, and I have used it in both senses here. The first of these was the literal use, where a student or pupil would refer to his teacher or mentor as Magister (Master), with all appropriate deference. The second usage, however, resembled the way we today use the term *boss,* denoting a superior—officer or otherwise—whose status entails the accordance of a degree of respect but falls far short of the subservience suggested by the use of the word *Master.*

the
Eagle

ONE

1

"Chariots."

The word apparently made no impression on the man to whom I had spoken, so I said it again, raising my voice slightly, despite the absolute silence, to make sure that he could hear me. Again, however, he chose to ignore me, his attention focused on the layer of whiteness that ended at the threshold of the cave that sheltered us. It had started snowing early that afternoon, tiny, individual flakes blown on a chill wind, their appearance unsurprising beside the sudden, harsh reality of the drop in temperature and the wind's strengthening bluster. But the snowfall had increased steadily ever since, so that now, a mere two hours later, the entire world had turned white, and the leaden clouds overhead were already leaching the light from the day, creating a premature dusk.

"What about them?" It was a dismissive response, and he kept right on talking, ignoring his own question, as though by merely acknowledging my reference he had dealt with the chariots in full. "This snow does *not* appear to be passing us by, my friend. It looks as though we might have to bring the horses inside. We could be here for the night." Arthur Pendragon, nominal High King of All Britain, squinted at me in the darkness of the cave with snow-dazzled eyes. "That means we will have smelly lodgings, but well sheltered, and at least their body heat should stave off the worst of the chills, in the absence of firewood." Stooping to avoid banging his high, crested helmet against the low ceiling, he moved inside to where I sat with

3

my back securely in a corner of the wall. He placed his long, sheathed sword carefully against an outcrop in the cave wall where it would not fall and then nudged my outstretched foot with his toe. "Move over, unless you want the entire floor for yourself."

I made room for him, and he eased himself down beside me, then bent forward awkwardly, tugged the heavy war helmet from his head and placed it on the floor between his upraised knees. That done, he sighed and leaned back, scrubbing at his short-cropped hair with the palms of both hands before turning to peer more carefully into the depths of the cave that sheltered us, his dark, yellow-flecked eyes narrowing in concentration as he tried to penetrate the gloom back there. He was two and twenty that year, but looked older than he actually was, his face lined prematurely with the strains of leadership, and somehow, in spite of our relationship as High King and Frankish Outlander, he had become my dearest friend in the four years that had passed since my arrival in Britain at the age of sixteen.

"It's dark back there," he grunted, and I did not contradict him, for I already knew the cave was both long and deep. We were seated in the day-lit area before the cave swung to the right, about five paces in from the entrance. Beyond where we were sitting, the darkness became absolute. Across from us, the corresponding angle in the wall was sharper, a knife-edged projection of stone jutting outward to form a flat-sided baffle that concealed the widening of the cave from anyone looking in from outside.

Past the corner formed by the flat-edged rock, the place widened to become more of a cavern than a simple cave, although it was pitch-dark back there. I knew from my first casual exploration that the roof was high enough to permit a tall man to stand upright, because I had done so and been able to stretch my hands above my head. I also knew there was a well-used fire pit in the middle of a spacious floor, because I had blundered into it, falling forward onto my hands and coming perilously close to twisting my ankle. One outthrust hand had landed on a smooth fire stone, and after I straightened up I had lobbed it into whatever lay in the darkness ahead of me. The pause that followed, and then the sounds as the stone struck the wall and fell to the floor, told me that there was more than sufficient space for men and horses beyond the limits of my vision.

Arthur turned back to me in the fading afternoon light. "It's not exactly a bedchamber in Camulod, is it?"

"It's dry," I responded, "and it's large. There's a fire pit, too, so it'll warm up, once we drag some dead wood up here."

His face wrinkled into his familiar half smile. "Up here from where? And did I hear you say 'we'? Are you suggesting that the chosen Riothamus of Britain should go out foraging for dead wood? That he should slide and slither down a mountain in a snowstorm and then fight his way back up again, dragging a tree trunk like a common charcoal burner? Is that what you are trying to tell me?"

"No, not at all, Seur King." I wrapped my cloak around me more securely, shutting out the chilly draft that was gnawing at my legs.

"What is that?"

"What is what?"

"That word … that expression you use when you address me as king. You could be calling me nasty names, for all I know."

I thought hard, wondering what in the world he was talking about, and then I laughed. "Oh, you mean *Seur*!"

"That's it. What does it mean?"

"Nothing dire, rest assured. It is a term we use at home in Gaul. A term of respect used in addressing a superior, as in Seur King, or Seur Something-else. That's all. And sometimes we use it as a personal gesture of honor, when we are dealing with someone who has no royal rank, for example, but who is otherwise admired as a clever or a noble man. Like Merlyn, for example. I might call him Seur Merlyn in speaking to him, or perhaps even Seur Caius."

"Aye, very well. Now, what were you saying, before I interrupted you? You had made some kind of unacceptable suggestion … a hint, if I remember correctly, that I might think seriously about toiling like a common charcoal burner."

I shrugged. "I was suggesting nothing, other than that you should, perhaps, think in terms of fuel, rather than of firewood, and that there are large amounts of it down below us, quite easily accessible. We could take our horses down with us and let them pull the load up—the snow's not deep."

"Not yet, but give it time."

"Hmm. No need. It will *take* all the time it needs and wants, Seur King, heedless of whether or not we choose to give it any. Most important of all in this discussion, however, is the self-evident truth that I, as a loyal retainer and faithful companion, might well go down there alone, as you propose, and do what needs must be done. But the storm is worsening, as you say, and I might only be able to make one passage. Thus, it seems to me that if you would prefer your kingly arse to stay warm all night long, instead of having it freeze to the bones in the darkest hours, you might consider it worthwhile, for once in your life of slothful privilege, to set aside your *dignitas* and concern yourself with simple comfort and survival."

"You mean I should come with you—share the labor—work like a common clod?"

"Did I say that? Aye, I suppose I did. But think of it as sharing the warmth afterwards, rather than the labor beforehand."

"Put like that, I admit the notion does have a certain logic to it." He scratched his chin. "Slothful privilege. You know, you're the only man in Britain who would dare say such a thing to me, in such a way."

I could no longer keep my face straight and grinned at him. "Aye, I know. You keep telling me so. But that, as you are always pointing out, is because I'm nothing but a foreigner, lacking the proper awe of your status and stature."

"Status *and* stature? Both in one breath? That's clever, Clothar, that's very good. You always manage to redeem yourself just short of the executioner's sword." He glanced again towards the back-lit entrance and its curtain of swirling snow. "Damnation, I swear it's getting worse. Even God has no respect for my situation here." He sighed dramatically. "Well, I suppose we had better go and see to it. No point in sitting here idling while things worsen. Come on, then, up you get." He rose quickly to his feet, giving the lie to his earlier act of weariness, and held out his hand to pull me up.

"How do you feel?" he asked then, all traces of levity gone as he leaned forward to peer closely into my eyes. I had had a deep-seated headache earlier in the day, probably caused by over-tiredness born of little sleep in the previous three nights, but it had abated steadily as we traveled and now my head was clear. I reached down for our helmets and clutched my own under one arm as I held the King's out to him.

"I'm fine now. But I'll feel better when I'm warmer."

Our horses were ground-tethered just outside the cave, still saddled. We brushed the melting snow off our saddles and remounted, then made our way down the slope to the wooded area at the bottom.

Within an hour we were back inside the cave and had a healthy fire crackling between us, its light sending shadows dancing high on the vaulted ceilings at the very rear of what had turned out to be a huge and ancient cavern. I was conscious of the melted snow steaming gently around the periphery of the fire pit. It was snowing harder than ever outside now, the swirling flakes agitated by a keen, biting wind that had sprung up just as we put our horses to the upwards slope of the hillside. Each animal had dragged up a large, rope-tethered bundle of dead branches, and we had scampered uphill beside them, clutching their bridles and slipping and sliding on the treacherous slope.

Once back at the cave, our first concern had been to light a fire, and I had spent some time attending to that, working carefully in a corner far from the gusting winds, plying flint and steel against dried moss and wood shavings until we had a flame that would not go out. As soon as we were sure we could leave the fire to burn safely on its own, even though it was not yet as alive as it ought to be, we off-saddled and led our animals into the rear of the cave, where we rubbed them down and left them with their nose bags on, contentedly chewing on a double handful of oats apiece while we

busied ourselves in the main cabin, seeing to our own comfort.
Arthur wielded my battle-axe expertly, chopping our hard-won fuel
into manageable pieces while I laid kindling for a second fire, this
time in the shallow pit inside the cave that had been well used for
the same purpose frequently in the past. I then carried the live coals
from the first fire, over in the sheltered corner, to ignite the main
one. The wood we had found was dry and well seasoned, so it
burned almost without smoke, and the little smoke that there was
drifted straight up and disappeared into some kind of natural flue in
the overhead rock.

Warm and reasonably comfortable now that our work was done,
we sat with our saddles bracing our backs, eating cold rations
together in companionable silence, aware, because we had checked
carefully to be certain of it, that no hint of our fire could be detected
from the darkness outside the cave.

I could tell from the expression on Arthur's face that something
was troubling him and I knew him well enough by now to know, too,
that whatever it was, it was far from being a casual, passing annoyance. I said nothing, however, knowing from four years of close
friendship with the man that he would speak when he was ready.

Finally he sniffed and folded the remains of his meal into a
square of cloth before stuffing it back into the leather scrip at his
waist.

"Chariots, you said. What about them?"

I knew better than to comment on the fact that more than an
hour had elapsed since I last mentioned them. "I've never seen a war
chariot before. Thought they were used only by the ancients. But I
counted nigh on a score of them out there this morning, and they're
impressive, dangerous-looking things. Where would Horsa's Danes
have found such things here?"

"Here?" Arthur's lips turned down in doubt. "They might not
have. I've never seen any here. They probably brought them over
with them when they came." He picked up a heavy section of branch
and thrust it deep into the flames. "They break down easily enough
for shipping, despite the solid look of them. Wheels and axles come

apart and are easily stowed, and the bodies are no more than strips of hammered leather, woven over sturdy frames. They'll stack one atop the other. Those Danes riding in them today could have brought the things over years ago—no telling when—and the horses could have been stolen from anywhere. These great Roman roads of ours have reversed the wheels of time, providing causeways to permit our enemies nowadays to put their weapons to the best use they can make of them, with little peril."

"But they look unassailable, Arthur, and most of them had blades attached to the wheel hubs. They will cause havoc among our horsemen when they join battle, with their weight and bulk and speed."

The King pursed his lips and nodded agreeably, looking remarkably unperturbed, it seemed to me, considering the gravity of what he was acknowledging. But as I was about to learn, he knew more than I did about this topic.

"Aye, they might," he said quietly, "were they ever able to reach our horsemen. But they won't be." He brought both hands up in front of him, arms extended, and mimed the actions of pulling a nocked arrow back to his ear. "No chariot builder, here or anywhere else, ever thought to encounter a weapon with the strength and accuracy of our Pendragon longbows, Clothar. You wait and see. My bowmen will kill every single charioteer before any of them can come within a quarter mile of our ranks. No gamble involved, either, my friend—at least, not on our side. An attacking charioteer, whipping his team straight forward towards combat against us, is a dead man. I don't care how gifted or skillful he may be, or how much he weaves and wavers in his approach. Sooner or later, simply because he is steering a chariot, he will have to turn it around and steer it straight towards us in order to attack. And then he will die, before he ever comes within striking range of us. You wait and see."

Twice in that little address he had told me to wait and see, and I grinned. "I might have to." I waved towards the now-dark cave entrance behind us and beyond our sight. "If the snow keeps falling out there, we won't be able to move, let alone fight a battle tomorrow, so the wait might be a long one before we see anything."

I estimated we were about three, perhaps four, miles distant from our army, an hour's ride in normal weather, but we had not anticipated the snow coming so early or so heavily, and now I found myself wondering if we could reach our encampment at all, with darkness falling so quickly. We had left our forces camped in a valley to the south that morning, while we rode up into the hills to spy on the enemy formations heading southward towards our position. We had been playing cat and mouse with them for a long time now, remaining ahead of them and keeping out of their sight until we could find a suitable spot in which to bring them to battle on our own terms.

Arthur shrugged as well as he could beneath armor and cloak. "We may not be able to move, but neither will they, Clothar. Neither will they. Our enemies and their chariots will be immobilized."

"Hmm."

"What d'you mean, 'Hmm'?" He turned and frowned at me. "Do you think I'm wrong?"

"No, not at all."

"Then why do you sound so doubtful?"

I spread my hands, palms upward. "I'm not doubtful, Arthur ... It's simply that I detect a hint of doubt in you yourself." I held my hand up now, to prevent the angry retort I knew would spring to his lips, and spoke before he could deny what I had said. "A hint, I said, the merest hint, and shapeless, I will admit ... but a hint nonetheless. I sense a doubt in you, my friend."

"Then damn you for having eyes too sharp for your own good. Now look to your own affairs and talk about something else."

"And how might I do that, my lord? My affairs are all your affairs. I have none of my own and nothing else to talk about. You know that."

"Then find some."

"Of course. I shall. Immediately. As soon as the snow stops," and with that I set aside the remnants of my own meal and pushed my saddle backwards, away from the fire, then stretched myself out to sleep on the opposite side of the fire pit from him.

2

There was no anger in what I said or did in response to Arthur's terseness; we had been friends now for too long for any kind of pettiness to come between us. But Arthur always had much on his mind, far more so than I, and that was only right, since he was the High King, with priorities and concerns the like of which I never had to imagine, let alone grapple with. And so I had quickly learned, on the infrequent occasions when his concerns caught up with him and made him less than normally communicative, that the best thing I could do for him was to leave him alone to think a situation through and work out his own solutions. There had been times, too, when, in order to make it possible for him to do that, I had gone so far as to shut him off from other people, fending off and even threatening anyone who sought to interrupt his thoughts, and pointing out that he was the High King after all and had a need to be alone sometimes, simply to think.

I was almost asleep, drifting in that half world between waking and dreaming, when he spoke again, and I had to shake my head to clear it. I turned as far as I could towards him, hampered by my blanket and twisting my neck around until I could see him. "What did you say?"

He had been holding a forked twig, twirling it between his finger and thumb, and now he flicked it into the fire at my back, out of my sight. "I said we should not have lost Eleron today. That was bad."

I made no attempt to answer immediately but struggled instead to sit up, making heavy work of it by pulling and tugging at the blanket that restricted me until it finally came free, allowing me to move. Arthur watched in silence as I hurriedly organized myself, sitting upright and then reaching to throw fresh fuel on the fire, which had died down. I was thinking furiously, knowing now at least a part of what was troubling him, but floundering still, unable to see why this one thing should disturb him so deeply. I knew he hated losing men—any commander did—but Eleron had not been killed. Or rather, he had not yet died.

Eleron was one of our brightest and youngest officers, a brilliantly gifted cavalryman whose like I had seldom seen, even among my own people in Gaul. That afternoon, in a skirmish with a roving group of bandits that should never have occurred had our own guards been properly distributed, he had taken an arrow in his chest, just beneath the cage of his ribs. The shot, hard fired, had burst right through his cuirass, penetrating multiple layers of boiled and hammered leather that should have deflected the arrow's point like solid iron. But the leather at that point in his harness had been imperfectly prepared, brittle and weak where it should have been solid and resilient, and the arrowhead had cracked it and plunged through, its impact lifting young Eleron bodily from the saddle and throwing him backwards over his horse's rump to land on his head.

The medics had all been poring over the lad within moments, but no one knew if Eleron would survive, and the five interlopers had all been shot down and killed before anyone had a chance to think of questioning them, so it was not known, either, if their presence there at that time had been accidental.

I wiped the last remnants of the gathering sleep from my eyes with the heel of my hand. "Eleron's not going to die, Arthur. We haven't lost him, not completely."

He pursed his lips, gazing at me through the smoke that was rising now from the new wood. "He will not ride with us against the Danes, tomorrow or next week or whenever it is to be that we can meet them. So we have lost him, Clothar. And that is one loss too many, after so long."

I knew what he meant. It was already October, and we had been on campaign without letup or release since the middle of March. Our losses had not been particularly heavy, but their cumulative leaching had been discouraging. We had fought five separate enemy forces in the past seven months, three of those being substantial armies of more than a thousand men, and we had beaten all of them. But each of those defeated forces had withdrawn to some form of refuge afterwards, to lick its wounds and heal itself, whereas we had moved on to deal with the next threat, with no time to heal or to reinforce our strength, absorbing new casualties on top of those that had gone before in other fights. That situation was made worse by the fact that we had won all five of those victories within a mere four months—an astonishing feat that we had only been able to achieve through a once-in-a-lifetime combination of good weather, wonderfully fortuitous timing and a series of geographical coincidences that placed us on three occasions within easy reach of foes who knew nothing of our nearness.

By the end of the fifth battle, we had felt invincible and believed that God truly was watching over us, and precisely at that time we had received authoritative information that Horsa the Dane was on the march from the eastern territories of the Saxon Shores at the head of a great army and was making his way westwards across the breast of Britain, directly towards our victorious army.

Horsa was now the paramount chief of all the Danes in Britain who had been clients and landholders of King Vortigern before Horsa killed him and usurped his lands and title. Arthur believed the Danish leader to be the most dangerous of all his enemies, a beacon luring all the disaffected and dispossessed elements in the province the Romans had called Britannia.

Flushed with our successes until then, we had quickly agreed to support the King in a bold attempt to stamp out this enemy while we could, and we had been playing a complex game for three months since then, attempting to lure the Danes within striking distance of our cavalry without alarming them or alerting them to our presence here in this rocky-hilled region so far away from Camulod.

We had been falling back before them for weeks now, proceeding with great caution and hiding like timid deer as we tried to lure them into a trap we had devised, but the constant and unrelenting need for caution and secrecy had been wearisome and tedious, and our soldiers—warriors first and above all else—were rapidly losing patience with such interminable prudence. They wanted to fight, to bring matters to a head and have done with delicacy. And then had come the infiltration of our camp today and the attack that struck down Eleron, and hard on the heels of that, this snowstorm that now threatened to make all our careful planning worthless.

Lost in these thoughts, I suddenly saw that Arthur was staring at me, waiting for me to say something, and I looked away from him, casting my eyes about the shadow-filled walls of the cave. His sword still stood where he had leaned it, my own weapon, less visually impressive but no less lethal, standing beside it. Finally I turned back to him and spoke the words in my mind.

"It's not simply the loss of Eleron, Arthur. There's more to whatever is upsetting you than that. Eleron is only one man—a good one, certainly, and he might yet live to become one of the best of us, but he is still only one man, and I have the feeling your concerns are more widespread than that."

He rose to his feet, throwing his blanket over his shoulders as he did so, and walked away, towards the mouth of the cave, where he leaned against the wall and stood staring out into the blackness at the whirling snow. I followed close behind him and joined him in the doorway. The wind had died, and for a spell we stood together side by side, gazing out at the snow and listening to the death-deep silence beyond the threshold. So quiet was the night in front of us that we could clearly hear the hiss of sap in a piece of the wood burning behind us.

"The men are losing heart, Clothar. I can feel it."

There. It was out in the open now. It was a starting point, and one that I could address, for I had been thinking about that very point for some time now—for months, if the truth be told—and I had almost brought the matter up to him before this. Now, instantly, I was glad I had said nothing earlier, because the correct words had only now come to my mind and to my tongue, upon hearing him say what he had said.

"They're only human," I murmured.

He cocked his head slowly sideways, looking at me askance. "That is … profound," he said, his voice dripping sarcasm. "Have I given you any indication of expecting them to be otherwise?"

I held out one cupped hand to capture a large snowflake. "No, you haven't. I know you know they are human."

"Thank you, for that."

"But they don't think *you* are, not quite."

He frowned, but said nothing, clearly thinking about what I had said, and I left him standing there in the entrance while I went back into the cavern to where his sword stood propped against the rock. I picked it up by the middle of the sheath and held it in front of me, conscious of his eyes on my back, and then I spun and tossed the weapon towards him. He caught it easily.

"There is your problem, and also your answer to what ails you and your men."

He gazed at me for long moments, hefting the sheathed weapon in his hand and looking from it to me and back again. "Clothar," he said eventually, his voice pitched so low that I could barely hear it, "I've told you before that you're a clever lad, but I have absolutely no idea of what you are talking about, so that must make me very stupid."

"No, not at all, master King. You don't know what I'm talking about because you have never *thought* about what I am thinking of."

"Which is …?"

"Magic, Arthur. Invulnerability."

"Explain." He would no longer give me the satisfaction of seeing him at a loss for understanding. I smiled.

"Your men, all of them, saw you endowed with that magic sword you're holding now. They saw it come into your possession miraculously, on the day of your coronation, when you drew it from the stone."

"That is ridiculous. There was nothing miraculous involved. It was mere mummery, designed by Merlyn for effect, no more than that."

"Then it was wondrously effective. It worked better than well, for it convinced the world."

Arthur glanced sideways at me, as though to gauge the strength of my belief, then shook his head in terse denial. "Not the world,

Clothar. The watchers there, perhaps, those who saw it." He raised the sword up in front of him so that he held the cross hilt at the level of his eyes, showing it to me as though to prove a point. "But this is what they saw that day: a sword, no more than that, and much like any other, save that its blade is different. It's an extraordinary sword, I'll grant you, but there is nothing magical about it. It was made by my own great-grandsire, Publius Varrus of Camulod, a sword maker, and it has been in my family's possession for decades, long before my coronation."

"Aye, so I've been told, by you. But no one else, other than your relatives, had ever set eyes on it before you pulled it from that stone. Is that not right?"

"Aye, but what of that?"

I shrugged. "I wasn't there, so I don't know the truth of it, but I've been told you drew it from the altar stone itself, in front of thousands of people, in the great theater there by Saint Alban's Shrine."

"Aye, I did, but it was no—"

"And when you drew it forth and brandished it above your head, the clouds parted and a beam of light from Heaven itself shone all about you. Is that not true?"

"Aye, it is, but even there there's no ma—"

"No magic, my lord?" My interjection left him open mouthed. "Is that what you were going to say? No magic? No miracle?"

Arthur stood there, nonplussed by my obstinacy and frowning at my insistence in this matter, the rising flush of blood in his cheeks evident even in the light from the flickering fire. But then he drew a quick breath and opened his mouth to speak again, and once more I cut him off before he could utter a word.

"Nigh on ten thousand people watched you do what you did that day in Verulamium, Arthur. They saw the bishops place the golden coronet of kingship upon your brow and name you Riothamus, High King of All Britain, and they all heard you swear an oath to use your military might to defend all Britain and the Christian Church against the foreign invaders who were even then marching against you."

He was gazing at me, smooth faced and wide eyed, waiting for me to finish, and I pushed right ahead.

"They saw you swear your oath upon the cross that stood before you on the altar. You grasped the cross through the purple Lenten cloth that covered it, and then they saw the bishop behind you call upon Heaven for a sign that you were justly chosen. And upon his call the clouds above you parted and the sun shone through, bathing you in golden light as you drew a sword—this sword—out of the altar stone.

"Ten thousand people saw that, Arthur, with their own eyes. And would you now tell them that what they saw was trickery? That they saw no miracle that day, and that the clouds would have broken open anyway, precisely when they did?"

"They would," he whispered, "they would have opened as they did, even had no one been there."

"But everyone *was* there, Arthur, and they saw the heavens open in a sign that had been called for. And they saw you raise a shining silver sword the like of which had never been seen."

"No! It was not like that at all!" His voice was huge, angry with denial of what he knew to be the truth, but mine was, too, as I shouted louder.

"Yes! Yes, Arthur, yes, it was! They saw their Riothamus crowned and blessed with a bright and magical sword, and that is why your men think you are more than simply human!"

He blinked in shocked disbelief, and then he reared up, one upraised hand clutching the sheathed sword as though he would strike me down with the hilt of it, and I saw the rage swell in him and be checked, held and forced back down with an effort of will that was clearly visible. He stood there for long heartbeats, drawn up to his full height and filled with a massive, bated breath, teetering on the edge of fury, and then he suddenly seemed to sag. The tension and the rage drained out of him. He dropped his chin on his chest with an audible snort, then tossed the sword into his other hand and reached across to lean it where it had been before, against the wall of the cave. He looked down at the fire then, and moved directly to sit on his own saddle, where he bent forward and threw a few short lengths of fresh wood onto the embers.

I remained where I was without moving until the first tongue of new flame sprang into life, and the King pointed to my own saddle, across from him.

"Sit, man, in the name of God." When I had done so, he looked at me sidelong again and blew out a long exhalation between tightly pursed lips. "Now ... I know you had no thought of provoking me to anger, Clothar of Benwick. And I know you are a Frank, and therefore unaccustomed to speaking in subtleties. But then I also know that, providing you speak slowly, you can speak Latin fairly well, and even understandably at times, despite the outlandish tortures you inflict upon your vowel sounds ..." He wrinkled his face into a wizened mask. "So tell me, slowly, if it please you: why are we having this conversation and what does it concern? Can you explain that, clearly?"

I nodded. "You are concerned about your men's mental conditioning ... their morale. You are fretting about their well-being. They, on the other hand, see you as being invulnerable. I see an opportunity to relieve your worries about the men, and to enable them to share your gift and profit thereby."

"What gift?"

"Your invulnerability."

"You're mad. I'm no more invulnerable than you are. You know that. You've seen me bleed. Damnation, man, you've *made* me bleed!"

"True, my lord. But we are not speaking of truth here. We are speaking of perception."

"In God's name—"

"No, and let us leave God out of this discussion for the time being, at least. I say we can allow your men to share your gift and I am correct. We can pass on your magical endowments, from you to them. Hear me out, Arthur, please." This was to stem him, because he had begun to rise again, but now he subsided once more, albeit reluctantly.

"You make no sense, Lance."

"No, not to your ears at least, King Briton, because you have not yet allowed yourself to hear what I am trying to say. Now will you listen to what I have to tell you? And before you say no, try to recall the last time I wasted your time." I paused, giving him opportunity to respond, but he said nothing and so I continued, this time in more deliberate and measured tones.

"Some time before we left Camulod this spring, I heard Merlyn use a word that I had heard used once before, by Bishop Germanus. I recognized it when I heard it again, but I did not understand it when Merlyn said it, any more than I had understood it when Germanus used it. I asked Merlyn what it meant, however, and he told me, and we talked about it for a long time after that. It's a wonderful word, Arthur; a word of power but not an obvious one. I used it a moment ago and you took no notice."

"What word?"

"Perception."

"Perception. That's your word of power?" The King nodded, his brow slightly wrinkled. "It means appearances, I believe. Why would you call it a word of power?"

"Because of the way Merlyn spoke of it and explained it to me. He believes it to be powerful, and so did the blessed Germanus. But it doesn't mean appearances … at least, that's not all it means. It means the way people see things, Merlyn says. People's perceptions can govern how they behave and even how they live their lives. He says perceptions can influence a man, or a group of men, or an army, or even entire peoples, to change their ways of doing things and adopt new beliefs and new ideas." I paused to let that sink home, and then I concluded, "Perceptions—the way people perceive things—can shape destinies, my lord."

"Are we back to 'my lord' again? I like not the smell of this. Where are you leading me, Lancie?"

"To here and now, no further for the present. But in the here and now I will challenge you to think upon perceptions."

"Hmm." The King stared into the fire's heart as he plucked pensively at his upper lip, but finally he peered upwards at me beneath raised eyebrows. "Proceed then. Let me hear this challenge."

"Very well." I leaned back and made myself as comfortable as I could. "Imagine, if you will, that the perceptions held by your soldiers are all true. Rightly or wrongly, they perceive you as being invulnerable, protected by the shining, unearthly beauty and power of the glorious blade you call Excalibur, the sword you pulled from God's own altar stone.

"They perceive that, as long as you retain possession of that blade, as long as you hold Excalibur and wield it, you will lead a charmed life, unable to be injured. Of course that is nonsense, and I believe that as much as you do, but that is what *they perceive,* and that perception, in and of itself, can be invaluable to us—to you and to the entire realm of Britain.

"How so, you ask, and so you should. Imagine this, for a moment, Arthur. Think seriously about it, not as something to scoff at as soon as I am finished but as something that you may legitimately put to use for the good of everyone involved." I took a deep breath and moved on.

"It's becoming more and more likely we'll be here all night and there will be no battle tomorrow morning. But there will be a battle soon, Arthur, one of these days. Visualize the gathering, if you will, before you send your leaders to their stations. All of them will be there, awaiting your instructions. And they will all be watching you, admiring you, probably thinking to themselves that after the battle, when it comes time to tally up the butcher's bill, they might well all be dead but you will still be seated on your horse, your armor unsullied, your skin unblemished, your very life protected by the shining blade you wear …

"Now … Imagine this. Imagine that tonight, on the eve of battle, you were to gather all your leaders close and tell them that you are aware of your good fortune in being so blessed. Not only that alone, but you tell them that you have devised a way to share your gift with them.

"You tell them all the story of your vigil on the night before you claimed the crown—of how you cleansed yourself in the holy ritual and were then purged of all sins by the attending priests, then spent the night awake and in prayer, preparing to go forward with the rising sun, in purity and as a penitent, into the sight of God, seeking his blessing and enlightenment.

"Tell them all that, and then tell how you accepted the gold corona of the Riothamus onto your brow, and the shining purity of Excalibur into your hands …

"They will enjoy the hearing of such things directly from you. All of them will, even those who were there to see it for themselves. But they will all wonder, too, what this tale could possibly have to do with any of them in person. Then you tell them that you have decided to share your gifts. You cannot share the high kingship, for that is a task for one man only and a fearsome, daunting burden. But you can share your other attributes, and, given they are properly prepared, shriven and purified, penitent and prayerful after spending the night in a waking vigil, you may share with them the mantle and the aura of the power vested in you through Excalibur. If they come to you in the veil of dawn, properly prepared and spiritually cleansed, and kneel before your feet in loyalty and humility, you will bless them with the power of the sword by laying its bare blade upon their shoulders, one, and then the other, encompassing their head so that the aura of this peerless, shielding weapon lies over them. Then, when they rise again, they will be transformed. Because they will be perceived, by their peers, and in their own eyes just as firmly, as being different, being altered … being more than they were before …

"*Perceptions,* Arthur."

He looked hard at me then, his brows contracted in what might have been the beginnings of a frown, although I knew it to be no more than a sign that my friend was already beyond contact, sinking deeply into one of his frequent periods of intense concentration. I had engaged his full attention with my talk of new things to ponder and I knew he would have no more to say to me for some time. He would think through everything I had told him, considering the pros and contras of every aspect of each point he could identify, and when he had satisfied himself that the topic could hold no fresh surprises for him, he and I would talk about it further.

3

The silence that followed was long but comfortable, requiring nothing from either of us, but nevertheless I found myself focusing intently upon a need to sit motionless, not even daring to glance sideways at him lest I interrupt his thinking. I knew that was ridiculous, because in the course of four years of close friendship I had come to know that once Arthur Pendragon had immersed himself in the analysis of some problem, nothing short of a physical interruption would induce him to abandon the process. Even so, and fully aware of the lack of need to do so, I kept my eyes directed straight ahead, gazing steadfastly into the fire and showing nothing of what was in my mind as I waited for Arthur the King to decipher whatever was in his. Looking back on it, I can never remember enduring another silence as long as that one was. But as we sat there in the utter stillness of the night, we heard, from outside, the muffled thump of a falling body and a stifled curse.

Arthur was on his feet almost before I could react, and there is nothing wrong with my own reflexes. But as I started to leap upright, he was already there, leaning forward, one hand outstretched to stop me from moving, the other raised to his lips signaling silence. He shrugged the blanket quickly from around his shoulders and threw it to me, then twirled his hands around each other in a signal for me to lie down and wrap myself in it as though asleep. As I fumbled with the cloth, shaking its folds loose, he reached down and retrieved my long dirk from where it lay by his saddle, then lobbed it to me before he stepped swiftly to collect our swords. His own dirk, which was really a Roman *gladius* short-sword, swung in its sheath by his right side. He turned back with the two long swords, moving swiftly for such a big man, and quickly shifted his saddle sideways and threw our two horse blankets over it to make it look as though it might be a sleeping man. He propped my sword against the end of the bundle, where its cross hilt could be clearly seen against the embers behind it. Then, again signaling me to be silent, he quietly unsheathed Excalibur, dropped the empty scabbard against the wall and moved swiftly to stand motionless behind the sharp corner where he could not be seen from the entrance to the cave.

He had not managed to be completely silent in his hurried movements, and so for the first few moments after he grew still we scarcely dared to breathe, waiting for an alarum to be raised and for a crush of bodies to come charging into the cave, alerted to our presence. But the moments lengthened without disturbance, and eventually we—or I, at least—began to think we might have escaped detection. I raised myself cautiously on one elbow, preparing to rise to my feet, but Arthur was both more cautious and less trusting than I, and he waved me back down. I subsided, my senses straining again, thinking he might have heard something new.

It had occurred to me, of course, that whoever was out there might be from our own army, but without absolute certainty of that, neither Arthur nor myself would have dreamed of endangering ourselves by taking even the tiniest risk of discovery. And so we waited there in the darkness, our heart rates gradually returning to normal as the time passed.

An ember settled in the fire close by my head with a soft crushing sound, a whispering puff of powdered ash and a small display of bright-burning sparks that rushed frantically along the charred and blackened surface of some of the sticks in the fire pit like scurrying ants, before dying into invisibility. I watched them, fascinated with the way their image remained bright against my eyelids when I blinked. There was no possibility of the embers being seen from outside the cave, I knew, but if anyone came inside there was equally no possibility of the dying fire going undetected.

As that thought came to me, bringing a clear vision of a featureless man standing with his head tilted back, nostrils flaring widely as he sniffed at the cave entrance, I heard stealthy, muffled movements right outside the cave. Once more I froze, holding my breath, and this time was rewarded with the sound of a low-pitched voice muttering in a harsh, guttural language that was unlike anything I had ever heard before. Whoever the man was, however, he was still outside the cave, and the odds were favorable that he might be alone, for no one had answered him. I threw my mind back to the sight of the snow outside when Arthur and I had stood there looking out a short time earlier. The heavy, blowing snowfall had covered all trace of our earlier movements by that time, so there was nothing out there to betray our presence. No blemishes of any kind marred the perfect, wind-smoothed layer of snow fronting the entrance to the cave. I looked over at Arthur then, wondering what was going through his mind.

He had propped his long-bladed sword carefully against the wall since I last looked at him, and now he held his unsheathed shortsword loosely by his side. His left hand was still extended towards me. Its fingers spread in a peremptory signal for me to remain where I was, but all his attention was focused intently on the sounds, or more accurately now the silence, beyond the outthrust shelf that concealed him.

Then came the sound of a single, hesitant footstep on the bare ground inside the entrance and Arthur waved his hand at me in an unmistakable command to lie down, quickly. I lowered myself instantly, knowing I was within moments of being seen by the intruder. My face in the crook of my bent arm, I heard him come forward slowly into the cave and then stop with a sharp intake of breath. There was another long moment of utter silence, and then a rush of footsteps as he ran rapidly towards my "sleeping" form, evidently hoping to put an end to me before I could move to resist him.

I swung around and away, hard, pushing myself up into a sitting position just in time to see Arthur step smoothly out of concealment, pivoting on his left foot and grasping the running man by the back of the neck, pulling him around and off balance towards him as he thrust upwards with the sword in his right hand, the entire strength of his body uncoiling behind the blow. The Dane—for there was no doubting his identity, even in the dim light of the dying fire—died instantly, his chin snapping downwards to his chest and the breath leaving his body in a grunt as the lethal blade of the gladius slammed through his sternum to the hilt and ruptured his heart. Arthur held him upright, hunching his shoulders and bending his knees to accommodate the man's weight as he spoke to me in a hiss over his shoulder.

"Make sure he's alone. But be careful. Don't show yourself."

I moved close to the entrance, bending low to the floor to avoid being seen by anyone outside, and when I was sure it was safe to do so I crept slowly closer to the mouth, to a point from which I could see all there was to see. I scanned the scene outside carefully, then went back inside.

"He was alone. Only one set of tracks out there."

"Well, that's a blessing, at any rate. He's a heavy whoreson, and I didn't want to let him fall in case he made a clatter and brought others running. Here, take his shoulders while I get his legs. We'll lay him over there, against the wall."

When we had done that, and Arthur had retrieved his gladius— no easy feat, since the dead man's flesh had had time to clamp itself around the blade by then—I began to rekindle the fire.

"I wonder who he was. A Dane, obviously, but I wonder what he was doing up here."

"Looking for us, I should think. Or at least looking for anyone who's not supposed to be up here when Horsa's down below. But whatever he is, he's a clear signal that there will be no more sleep for us tonight, or warmth, either. You'd best put that fire out completely. This fellow's here because he smelled the smoke some- where close by, and I doubt that he came all the way up here alone." He thought about that, then added, "Mind you, if there had been anyone with him at the time, he wouldn't have arrived here alone, would he? Perhaps he was separated from the rest of his group and didn't want to shout to them for fear of alerting us. In any event, if he did bring company with him, then they're going to come right in here looking for him, following his tracks. And that may be sooner than we think, rather than later."

Arthur was now gazing about him as he spoke, his eyes taking in everything there was to see, and although he kept talking, it was clear his thoughts were focused elsewhere. "So, young Lancie," he mused. "We had best be preparing to welcome whoever is out there. And let us both hope fervently, my spear-throwing friend, that our silent companion there is one of a small scouting expedition and not an outrider of Horsa's main army."

I nodded, agreeing with him and at the same time amused, against all logic, by his personal name for me and the way he sometimes talked to me. Whenever he was deep in thought, distracted by the points of a decision that had to be made, he would speak to me as though I were a babe in arms, a mere tyro in whatever was occupying us at the time. It was a harmless thing, a quirk of who and what he was, and in a strange way a signal of his high regard for me. I had quickly grown comfortable with the name and accustomed to the way he talked to me, but there were times when it would suddenly seem both novel and amusing to me, for less than two years separated us in age and we were roughly similar in experience and fighting skills. He was the better bowman, certainly, but my lance-throwing skills inspired both awe and reverence in him.

Most of his warriors called me simply the Frank, disdaining to sully their tongues with my foreign, alien-sounding name, while others referred to me as the Thrower or the Spearman or even the Lancer. This was no more than normal usage, for it was not the custom in Britain in those days for men to call each other by their given names. Every man I knew, except for those who were kings and lords and singular men of power like Merlyn, had a working name, bestowed upon him by his fellows. Arthur had chosen to call me simply Lance, and more often than not he added the ubiquitous Gaelic diminutive "ie" to the end of it, so that, to him alone, I became "Lancie."

I was ready to smother the fire with a large, flat slab of stone but he stopped me again, bidding me put it down and leave the fire alight while he thought further on the matters facing us. Obediently, I sat down and stirred the embers up again, dropping small pieces of fuel into their redness until a small new flame sprang up among the coals.

"Very well, then, Lance, build up the fire. I know what we have to do."

I twisted around to face him, intrigued and alerted by the new tone I heard in his voice. Sure enough, his eyes were glowing with the enthusiasm that had quickly become both welcome and familiar to me in the time that had elapsed since first we two met. When Arthur Pendragon's dark, yellow-flecked eyes lit up and sparkled as they were sparkling now, it meant that he had made a firm decision and was prepared to act upon it.

"Rebuild the fire, high as you like. We're going to need it. Besides, why in the name of God should we be cold simply because we might be facing death? Now, help me carry our visitor over here and prop him up by the side of the fire as though he's enjoying the warmth. We'll wrap him in a blanket, too. That will cover the blood and make it look as though he's nodded off to sleep by the fireside. Once he's settled, you and I will take turns watching from the cave entrance, and as soon as we see his friends coming, we'll come back in here and wait for them. We'll set ourselves up at the back of the cave, behind the horses, depending on how many of them there are. Six or fewer, we'll let them come right in and then shoot them as they enter. Any more than that, however, we'll have to shoot as many of them down as we can from the entrance and then go out and fight them in the snow."

"Why let six come in but not seven or eight?"

He looked at me as though my question had surprised him. "Because we can deal with six. They'll be blind when they come into the light, out of the snow, and we'll be waiting for them with drawn bows. Three each, we can shoot them all dead before their eyes adjust to the light in here. Any more than that, however, and we'll risk giving them time to recover and retaliate, and we might end up killing ourselves for lack of space. With six or fewer, we're better off where we are. As long as we stay here inside the cave and wait for them, there will only be one set of footprints coming into the entrance. We'll have the advantage of surprise, and they'll look to their friend first, to share his fire, never thinking to see us."

He paused then, looking back towards the entrance. "Any more than six, though, and this place becomes a death trap for us. Once they know we're here, we will have lost any advantage we might otherwise have had; they'll be able to sit outside and wait for us to come out—which we'll have to do, sooner or later—and then pick us off at their leisure. So we'll saddle our mounts now, ready for anything, and then we'll settle down to watch for guests arriving. Then, if it turns out that there are more than we can handle easily, we'll ambush them from the doorway, picking off as many as we can before they withdraw out of range. After that, as soon as they do withdraw, we have to follow them, on horseback, giving ourselves all the advantages we can, although that might not be much, with all this snow on the ground. But if we are to die here tonight, then I, for one, would rather do it on my horse, out in the open where I can swing my sword, than in a stinky, dark old cave where there's no room to fight and where I could be cut down by any sneaking coward who can crawl up unseen behind me with a dagger. What say you?"

What could I say? I asked myself. I agreed with him whole-heartedly.

4

They took no pains to keep themselves concealed as they came, and that was fortunate for me, because by the time they eventually arrived I had committed the unpardonable sin of falling asleep on watch. It was the sound of a voice shouting in the distance that shocked me into wakefulness, and I sat frozen for a moment, unsure of where I was or what time it was, and then awareness returned and still I sat there, stunned into immobility by the enormity of my own dereliction. I glanced about me hurriedly and was relieved to see that I could not have been unconscious for more than a short time. The scene was exactly as I remembered it: a scattering of clouds directly over my head, against a sky that would be bright blue once the sun was up, and a complete lack of shadows, as the morning mist still hung intact above the distant hills and thus there was no source of direct light.

I had nodded off for a few moments, nothing more than that. I sighed with profound relief, looked carefully around the scene before me one more time, and then I cleared my throat softly before flexing my shoulders and preparing to stand up. And then the shout came again and I realized that this was a repetition of what had startled me out of my doze in the first place. I rose quickly to my knees, bracing my elbow against the wall and leaning forward to peer down into the ground mist that shrouded the bushes on the hillside below. The voice had come drifting up from there, I knew, but I could see nothing. It came again as I knelt there: the long, winding shout of a searcher hunting for someone who was lost.

"How far away?" Arthur had come up behind me unheard.

I shook my head. "Your guess is as good as mine. The mist down there muffles the sound and makes it impossible to tell where they are. But making a noise like that, it's plain to see they don't know we're up here."

"Yes, they think they're all alone, which means they're either truly stupid and deserving of all the grief they encounter, or they've already searched this entire area thoroughly and found nothing ... no sign of our people. Which means, upon further thought, that we are both higher up and farther north than we thought we were."

"That's a pleasant notion. I knew we shouldn't have followed that damn streambed up into the hills when we did."

Arthur grunted. "Aye, well, you'll recall there was something like a profusion of Danish warriors close by us at that time, leaving us little room for choice. But anyway, it's too late now for plaints, young Lance. You ought to have spoken more insistently at the time."

"I did, don't you remember? But you said you were the king and overruled me."

The High King of All Britain cocked his head and looked at me from narrowed eyes. "That's right, I did, didn't I? I knew there was a reason for our being here. Ah well, keep looking. Let me know as soon as you see or hear anything new."

He went back into the cave, where I could hear him moving about, but he returned a short time later to crouch beside me. "Anything?"

"Nothing new, but the voices are coming closer."

"Hmm. Here, have some of this."

I took what he was holding in his outstretched hand. "What's this, and where did it come from?"

"It's food, from the dead man's scrip. I'm sure he won't be needing it. It's very good, too. I had some when I first found it. It's salted beef, I think, wrapped in bread. Very tasty and too fatty to be venison. And the bread seems to be coated with some kind of fat drippings. Try it."

I did, and it was truly delicious, setting my stomach juices churning instantly and reminding me of how long it had been since we had enjoyed a really good hot meal. I devoured the food in great bites, chewing it lovingly and exulting in the salty tang of it on my tongue.

"That idea of yours, about sharing the power of the sword … did you discuss it with anyone before you mentioned it to me?"

My mouth was full, and so I merely shook my head.

"You did not mention it even to Merlyn?"

I heard the disbelief in his voice and so I swallowed quickly. "No. I've never mentioned it to anyone. I've only been thinking about it from time to time, whenever something spurred the thought in me, and I hadn't even put those thoughts in order until I spoke of it to you last night."

"Aha! We have company. Below us to the right, on the edge of the tree line there. And there's another of them, back among the trees to the left of the first one."

I scanned the distant tree line and found both men just in time to see another movement between them as a third man stepped forward into the open. All three stopped there, their eyes sweeping the slopes above them while they waited for the rest of their party, three more men, to catch up to them, so that all six pairs of eyes were soon sweeping the slopes in our direction.

"Will they be able to see us?" I asked.

"Not unless they have the eyes of eagles. They're looking up at us, focused over our heads. They'll never see us standing here, and if by chance they should, they'll take our heads to be rocks on the slope. It's a good five hundred paces from here to there and they're looking up. Now what we have to do is wait and see if they'll come up. It will be a hard climb from where they are, and if they can't see any signs of their friend's having been here, they might not feel inclined to be too inquisitive. He didn't come upon us from down there. He came along from the side, and he must have been up above us to begin with, in order to have smelled the smoke from our fire, because the wind was blowing the smoke up the hill, not down."

"How do you know that?"

"It's obvious. Look at the way the snow has drifted. It's all blown that way, drifting up the slope of the hillside and into the entrance here, piled against that one side." It took only one glance to show me he was right. "They're moving again, but I don't believe they're coming up." He was right again, and we stood side by side and watched them as they picked their way across the hillside below us, to disappear eventually behind the swell of the hillside down on our left, on their way directly towards the next wintry stand of stark black, leafless trees.

"What now?" I asked then, betraying my Frankish ignorance of British weather. "Can we leave?"

Arthur's grin was rueful. "No, not yet, I fear."

"Why not? We can ride the other way, away from them."

"We could, and we could probably ride free. But we would have no guarantee of anything. The simple appearance of safety isn't worth the risk. We have to stay here, for at least a few more hours." He clearly saw the incomprehension in my eyes, because he waved at the ground outside the cave. "The snow, Lancie, the snow. It shows the tracks of everything that moves across it, even the wind, if it blows strongly enough. As soon as we set foot outside this cave and into the snow, our presence here will be clear to anyone who comes along later—and not only our presence here but our trail to wherever we go next. As long as the snow endures, we will be pursuable to anyone with eyes to follow our pathway. There's no hiding it."

"And so we stay here?"

"Aye, until we are either driven out or are able to ride out upon our own terms. We have no certainty that those hunters out there will not double back or that they won't take a higher route and find the tracks left by their friend." He watched my face as I digested what he had said, and then he spread his hands. "It is inconvenient, but there is no way around the situation."

The hunters did double back. We heard them again within the hour, and it was immediately clear that they had scaled the hillside and were now coming directly towards us, following their dead companion's tracks in the snow. Fortunately, they were still convinced they had the entire mountain to themselves, and so we had plenty of time in which to prepare for their arrival. We concealed ourselves at the rear of the cave, strung our bows, set out our arrows and waited for the enemy to come to us.

Although we could understand no word of their language, we could tell from their approaching voices that they were excited about finding the cave and their companion's tracks leading into it. They came spilling into the interior, making no attempt to be quiet, their shadows darkening the fall of light from the entry, and then they fell abruptly silent and stood hesitant and wavering, just at the angle of the corner, blinking in the sudden darkness as they waited for their vision to adjust to the change from bright sunlight to almost complete darkness.

Our first two volleys took down four men before the remaining two realized that they had walked into a trap and flung themselves back towards the daylight outside. I dropped my bow and seized one of my lances as I charged after them and burst out into the sunlight only to realize that we were now the blind ones. I stopped just beyond the threshold of the cave and squeezed my eyes tight shut, hearing the strange, slithering, powdery sound of someone trying to run through deep, heavy snow ahead of me. Even through my closed lids, the bright light was almost unbearable, and I brought my left hand up to cover my eyes. That felt better, but I knew I had to find my vision again, and so I opened my eyes slightly, squinting through a tiny gap between my fingers. I could see someone running through deep snow to my right, and then I turned my head slightly to my left, keeping my hand in place, just in time to see another running man throw up his hands and disappear in an explosion of snow.

I closed my eyes, reaching into the scrip at my waist with the ease of long practice to withdraw a throwing cord, which I wrapped firmly about the butt of the lance I now held in my left hand. When it was securely in place, I wound the other end about the index finger of my throwing hand, the right one, and balanced the forward length of the missile gently in the open palm of my left. I opened my eyes as cautiously as I could and peered towards where I had seen the man on my right. The light was less painful now, less violent, and the man was still there, and still running, bounding down the steeply sloping hillside with little concern that he might fall. I had no doubt that he was anticipating the thump of an arrow piercing his back. I saw more movement then, to my left, and saw Arthur leaping after the other man, lifting his long legs comically high as he ran through the knee-deep snow. I made my way forward until I could aim and cast my lance.

I knew as soon as I released it that it was fairly launched. As far as I know, no one has ever managed to describe or define the sensation of feeling, right from the outset, that a given shot is good. This shot felt right. The lance soared high, its shaft revolving as it flew, as indicated by a tiny circling movement of the butt end, and then it stooped and fell, perfectly, swooping downwards to take the running man precisely at the base of his neck, between the shoulders. He went down headfirst and disappeared from sight, covered by a cloud of upflung snow that slowly settled down upon his unmoving form and then turned bright red.

Arthur was standing a score of paces to my left, gazing down into the snow on the slope beneath him, and I called to him, telling him I had to collect my lance. He paid me no attention, and I left him there, picking my way carefully down the slope, with its treacherous mantle of snow concealing all its hazards, until I reached my fallen quarry and pulled my spear from his back.

On my way back up, I traveled sideways, using my spear as a walking stick and making my way gradually up towards where Arthur still stood silent, looking down the hill. I could see now what he was staring at. The man who had been running from him was still upright, but he was buried to the armpits in what was evidently a snow-filled hole. Arthur's long Pendragon arrow had transfixed his upper torso, and the snow around him was stained deep red with his life's blood. I reached the man and leaned forward to pull him towards me, but he would not budge.

"No hope of getting this arrow back," I shouted up to Arthur.

"Aye," Arthur's voice came back to me. "Don't even try. Come back up here, and let's be on our way. Too many dead men around here now for my liking."

Later, riding down the lower slopes of the mountain, our horses picking their way carefully now that the steepest slopes were behind us, I looked up at the sky and commented that the snow had passed and the temperature seemed to be rising. Arthur glanced at me sidelong and responded with something that I thought at the time was completely out of character.

"We left seven dead men up there, Lance. Has it occurred to you to wonder why?"

"I know why. They would have killed us, had we not killed them first."

"Hmm. Then mayhap I asked the wrong question. Do you know *how* we left seven dead men up there?"

"Do you mean how were we able to? Because we took them by surprise. Caught them unawares."

"Aye, perhaps that's so. But we were only able to do that because of the snow. The early snowfall changed everything. It changed the look of the entire world and it changed those men's attitude to being in the mountains. It changed their perception of danger and risk, completely."

"Oh, not again, my lord. If it please you, no more perceptions! Am I to live with perceptions now for evermore?"

Arthur, however, made no acknowledgment of my mock horror. "I cannot answer you on that, my friend," he said in all seriousness, "but your observation has proved remarkably accurate in the case of those men. Their perception of safety destroyed them. They were lulled by the gentle whiteness … the seeming softness and innocence of the first snowfall of the year … and it cost them dearly."

I felt vaguely unsettled. "What are you saying, Seur King? What are you telling me?"

"That we will not let appearances betray us, as those Danes did …" He fell silent, leaning forward in the saddle as he gave all his concentration to guiding his horse along the steeply sloping stony bank of a narrow, dangerously winding streambed. The horse hesitated, gathering itself, and then launched itself towards the other bank, its hooves scrabbling momentarily for purchase before it gained solid earth. Arthur's body adjusted easily to the movements, even as my own did moments later, and soon we were riding side by side again. Arthur, however, seemed determined to be grave and serious this morning.

"I learned a great deal last night, Clothar, and even more this morning. We are going home now, today, you and I and our army. This snow may disappear within the next few days, but then again it may not. It might lie on the ground until next spring. I have never been fond of entrusting myself to the vagaries of the weather, and I learned today that I have no wish to commit my followers to the foolish and uncountable risks of winter fighting in heavy snow. They have been on the campaign trail for far too long this year and they have earned some peace of mind and an opportunity to take their ease for a while without fear of being attacked. We will winter at home, now, as sane men do, and ride out again come spring."

"What about Horsa?"

"What about him? If he is mad enough to keep his army out here in the dead of winter, then he deserves whatever may come his way. In the meantime, we will send out scouts from Camulod to search for him at winter's end, and if he is still here, we will hit him early in the spring, before he has time to reorganize his army, let alone anticipate our arrival. But that is wishful thinking. Time will make that deliberation for us.

"In the meantime, we are going home to Camulod, and you and I are going to talk much more and much longer about this notion of yours for protecting my men. It sounded ridiculous and fanciful at first hearing, but I thought much on it last night, and now something is telling me your strange idea might just be sufficiently nonsensical to appeal to the people I most need to please. But if we are going to do it, we must do it well, and properly. The matter of the vigil you suggested must be defined and finalized, and with it all the preparations for the ritual. And we have not yet spoken of the ritual itself. It is a ritual we are discussing here, is it not? Do you agree?"

I did agree, of course, because I always agreed with anything that made sound, solid common sense, and after that we rode in silence for a long time while each of us pondered what we had discussed.

5

We were still thinking about it the following morning, when we were challenged by the first of our army's outlying guards, and when, less than an hour after that, we breasted one steep rise to see our army stretched out before us, the thought of ritual was still uppermost in both our minds. It was a pleasure to behold our force from such a vantage point, because notwithstanding the fact that we could field twelve hundred horsemen at any time, our encamped army yet looked disciplined and serviceable. Our infantry was drawn up in the center of the vast square, its accommodations laid out exactly in the classic Roman marching camp format that had been in use for more than a millennium, with the headquarters unit and the officers' quarters in the very center. Around the square periphery of the infantry camp, the tents of our various cavalry contingents were neatly arranged in numbered ranks, the horse lines interspersed among the various squadrons' barracks so that they were well removed from the infantry quarters, offering no threat to the smooth functioning of the central camp, yet sufficiently close to where they were needed to be instantly available, saddled and ready to move out within minutes of an alarum.

We had always, since the earliest days of Camulod, called our cavalry formations by the ancient Roman names of *alae* and *turmae*—or alas and turmas, as the ordinary soldiers spoke—simply because we had not yet found better words for them in any of the local tribal languages and Latin was still sufficiently common to everyone to be useful. Nowadays, however, change was afoot and the language used by the ordinary Camulodian troopers had changed with it. Hardly anyone referred to an ala nowadays, although the word *turma* was still widely used. The word most commonly in use to describe the ala formation today was division, and it made sense, because the size of each cavalry ala in Camulod today was half what it had been in the early days. Instead of being a thousand-unit organization, our alas had been divided in two, so that each half contained approximately five hundred mounted men, distributed among twelve or sometimes thirteen turmas, each turma containing from thirty-five to forty horsemen in two twenty-man squadrons.

In the camp we were looking at now, there were two cavalry divisions, split in turn into halves and laid out so that they extended outward from the walls of the main camp. Half of one division lay quartered on the west side of the encampment, while the other half lay to the north, and the other division was similarly laid out on the southern and eastern sides. These two divisions had been working with each other for many years and called themselves the Hammers and the Anvil, because of the fighting techniques they had developed, which involved intricate, complex and fiercely disciplined maneuvering, frequently at high speeds, to trap whatever enemy they were fighting between their two forces, and thereafter crush them.

As we sat watching from the crest of the hill, admiring the peacefulness of the scene, I, at least, was conscious of the irony involved in the peaceful contemplation of the beauties of an armed camp.

"How many of your commanders will you include in the first ceremony?"

"What ceremony? Oh, you mean the idea with the sword ..." Arthur sniffed, his eyes fixed on the distant view. "All of them, I suppose ... all of the senior commanders, anyway. There's no other option, is there? I've already said that if it's to be done, it must be done properly. Care and diligence, Lancie, care and diligence."

From far ahead of us, down in the area fronting the armed camp, came the long-drawn, winding note of a military war horn, signaling that we had been seen and recognized. Arthur winked at me as the sound died away. "Well, at least the guards are awake. Shall we go and bless them with our presence?" He spurred his horse, and as I followed down the hillside close behind him, I noticed the first drifting flakes of fresh snow on the strengthening wind.

6

That first snowfall was not the harbinger of winter; it was winter itself, fully fledged and implacable. It snowed without respite for four days and then the temperature dropped like a stone, freezing even the swift-flowing brook that was our water supply. We huddled miserably in our summer-style encampment, shivering in the biting cold that made mockery of our fair-weather campaign clothing, and waiting for a break in the onslaught, for the first hint of warmth to return and permit us to escape down into the more temperate lands below.

On the sixth morning, the sun rose into a sky of bright blue, with masses of broken cloud being scattered by warm winds. The cold snap, in what seemed a miraculously brief transition, was over, but our relief was short-lived. The previous coldness—which had at least been dry—was immediately replaced by even greater misery as the snow began to melt and icy water soaked into clothing and the fustian backing of chain mail, turning men's hands and feet into frozen lumps of pain that they could not escape. What point in stamping your feet to restore warmth when the very ground on which you stood was ankle-deep in freezing slush?

Arthur, who had been highly aware since he and I returned from the mountains that we really did not know where Horsa's army was encamped, issued orders immediately for our army to break camp and move out. Much of the preliminary work had already been done in anticipation of a withdrawal; everything that was not immediately necessary for our survival had been dismantled and loaded into the wagons, and our livestock needed only to be saddled and marshaled. By mid-morning the tents were folded and stowed, and what little work remained to be done had almost been completed. We would be on the march before noon, but as Arthur looked at the slushy, mud-churned wasteland created by our presence there, his expression was deeply troubled. I nudged my horse over to where he sat staring at the ruined ground, out of earshot of the small group of senior commanders who waited upon him.

"It's ugly and it's obvious, Arthur, but there's nothing to be done about it, is there? The only alternative to leaving it like that is to stay here and freeze, waiting for Horsa's Danes to stumble over us."

"I know, and you're right. But I hate to ride away leaving such an obvious trail behind."

"What difference does it make? Even if Horsa finds it, he won't follow us. We are too many for him and that will be obvious from the size of the trail we leave. He'll know we've been here, and for

some time, too. His people will be able to judge how long simply
by looking at the refuse pits and latrines. But Horsa will assume,
because he is who he is, that we knew nothing of his presence in
this region."

"He might still follow us home to Camulod."

"He might, but I doubt it and I don't think you believe it any
more than I do. Horsa is no fool. Nor is he a hothead. He's a natural
strategist when it comes to battle and tactics. You know that. We've
been watching him for months now, trying to tempt him into a trap,
and he's as cagey as an old bear. Bad-tempered and ungovernable
he may be in his rages, but he is not foolish or impulsive when it
comes to endangering his men unnecessarily in the field, and to
follow us to Camulod would involve too many risks for him. We're
a long way yet from Camulod and we'll be riding through friendly,
allied territory all the way. To follow us openly for all those miles,
through terrain that's as hostile to him as it's friendly to us, would
make him a far bigger fool than I believe he is. Besides, we're no
more than a score of miles from the great north road, and once we're
on that, no matter which way we turn, anyone can follow us simply
by staying on the road."

The beginnings of a smile twitched at the King's lips. "Very
well, Master Lance," he said, "I will bow to your logic and your
beguiling tongue, and should they follow us in fact, we'll turn
around and smite them." He pulled himself upright in his stirrups
until he was standing, and nodded to his commanders, all of whom
were watching him intently. "You, young Bors. Ride to Bedwyr on
the opposite side of the camp, if you will, and pass the word to him
that we are prepared to move out on his signal. He is to give that
signal when ready, since he is in a better situation to judge the right
time than we are."

Bors, who had matured greatly in the four years since our
arrival in Britain and was now confident in and thoroughly deserving of the position of respect he had earned for himself among
Arthur's commanders, brought his arm up smartly in a clenched-fist
salute and wheeled his horse away.

Arthur turned back to us. "The rest of you come with me to a spot where we will not be overheard. I have things to say that are not for the ears of our soldiery."

For the next half hour we sat in our saddles—far more comfortable and much warmer than standing on the ground with frozen feet—and listened to our King as he talked about his ideas for winter training in Camulod and his plans for the campaigns of the following year. Of course all of it was tentative at best, for the entire gamut of priorities could be set at naught by one unexpected attack from any direction or by a threat from a serious adversary. Lacking those exigencies, however, Arthur was planning far ahead in the hope of being ready for battle come spring, no matter what might occur. From time to time he would ask one or another of us for our opinions on a particular point, and twice he threw a topic open for general discussion, and I was pleased to see that everyone appeared to understand the set priorities in each case and to have a firm grasp on the criteria surrounding their own roles.

The discussion was winding down when we heard the trumpet flourish that was the signal from Bedwyr for our exodus to begin, and I moved away with the other commanders to find my own unit and oversee the disposition of my forces. Everything seemed chaotic at first, with no real sign that the general congestion might ever be resolved, but as the time passed steadily by and the line of the outgoing column grew longer, it soon became apparent that there was a method at work within the chaos, and as the rank and file of our infantry finally came together and began to tramp away in good order, the milling mass of mounted men in the center of the marshaling ground gradually shifted and sifted itself into the regular lines and formations of the rear guard that would protect the lengthy column ahead of it. This was my command, the rear guard, seven forty-man turmas of the Anvil division, minus a few casualties incurred over the summer. At last count, just before arriving in this camp, we had mustered two hundred and fifty-seven troopers, with an additional complement of twenty-one junior officers—fourteen squadron leaders and seven turma leaders—plus myself and my three troop commanders, making an overall count of two hundred and eighty-two combat-ready bodies. A full score of those were already deployed and had been so for several hours, ranging backwards into the hills behind us, alert for signs of any approach by Horsa's Danes. They would remain out there for another two hours, I estimated, before they began to fall back towards us, and they would keep moving vigilantly until they caught up with us.

In the meantime, in acknowledgment of the possibility that enemy insurgents might be able to penetrate our screen of scouts without being detected, another two full turmas would spread out in a mile-wide semicircular formation behind us. The remainder of my division, four and a half turmas, would escort the rear infantry formations, containing our best veterans. These infantry detachments were actually the basis of the traditional rear guard, and in the event of an attack they would draw themselves up in battle formation, facing rearward, giving the main body of the army time and opportunity to react to the threat. My cavalry would work with them in that case, but until an alarum was raised, my horsemen flanked the marching men on both sides and spread out behind them.

We had been moving for about four hours by the time the word came back to us that we had reached the main road and would be camping for the night in a meadow that ran along the road, and half an hour later I handed over control to my three subordinates and left them to the task of getting our division settled for the night, while I went to inspect the setting up of our camp.

It was completely unnecessary for me to inspect anything, and I felt vaguely guilty for even saying such a thing to myself. The simple truth was that I wanted to be alone with my thoughts for a short time. We had had no word of any enemy activity. My rearward scouts had caught up to us more than an hour before we reached the road, and none of them had seen a single sign of Horsa's forces anywhere on their patrols, so I was beginning to believe with some conviction that the Danish war band would not find our tracks at all. But I was not completely at ease, nor was I totally assured that we were safe from detection. There was an illogical quality to my concerns, I knew, since we outnumbered Horsa's force by nigh on three to one and he had no horses. He could not have won against us even were he to arrive blown on high winds stirred up for him by his people's high god, Odin. But knowing that changed nothing, and recognizing the truth of it made no difference to the substance of my unease.

The evening was pleasant enough, with roasted goat meat and freshly baked bread, and our enormous bonfires robbed the night of its chilliness, but I was loath to go to my cot afterwards, and when I did I slept poorly, tossing and turning and expecting to be hauled out to repel an attack at any moment.

The night passed without incident, however, and we made good speed the following day, the warmer temperatures and the multitude of passing feet and hooves having stripped every trace of snow from the surface of the road by the time we came trudging along at the rear of the procession.

We saw not a single hint of any alien force at any point along our way, and five days later we were within sight and sound of our home in Camulod.

7

The colony was agog by the time we reached it, and after an absence of so many months, the celebration of our homecoming was an epic event that lasted far into the middle hours of darkness.

At one point that night, I took a walk around the perimeter of the fortress, to demonstrate an official presence and to keep an admonitory eye on the festivities of our off-duty troopers. When I returned to the great hall, I noticed immediately that Arthur had left his place at the head table. A quick glance around showed me that he had not simply moved to another spot, and so I went looking for him, making my way casually among the throng while I scanned the alcoves and shadowed recesses that lined the main walls. The evening was far advanced by that stage, and many of the revelers had passed out where they sat, facedown at their tables and snoring into their food. Search as I would, however, I could see no sign of the King, and that surprised me, for there were several visiting dignitaries—lesser kings and chiefs from other parts of Britain—who, I could see, were still *compos mentis,* and I would have wagered that Arthur would not simply abandon them to their own company. That would have been unwise and in some cases, insulting.

A movement in the gallery above the main floor caught my eye, and I recognized Arthur standing up there in the deep shadows. I recognized him by his height and the breadth of his shoulders more than anything else, because the shadows were dense and the light was very poor. The gallery on which he was standing was the most recent addition to the hall, added at the whim of one of the Council who thought himself something of an architect and had had a dream of providing a platform for musicians and bards that would raise them above the throng sufficiently for everyone to be able to see and hear them, and would have the additional advantage of opening up clear space in the room at floor level. The gallery was reached through a flight of sturdy steps running up the exterior wall of the building and I made my way to it, slipping easily and unnoticed through the main doors to the outer courtyard.

When I reached the top of the stairs I found the door ajar and the interior masked by a dense, heavy curtain of black cloth, designed to keep the light from streaming into the gallery. Arthur's voice came to me from behind this barrier.

"Come inside, Clothar. I saw you notice me."

I pulled the curtain aside and stepped into the gallery, seeing Arthur's shape silhouetted again, this time against the brightness of the hall below. He was leaning against the wall with his back to me, gazing down at the revels. I stepped forward to join him, moving slowly so as to avoid any sudden movement being seen from beneath.

"What are you doing up here?" I asked him, using no formal address since we were alone.

He made no answer, his lips pursed in thought. Then, just as I was beginning to think he would not speak at all, he said, "I'm watching my guests ... or one of them, at least. And I can see him better from up here, looking down on him, than I can see him down there, looking him in the eye."

"Which one? And why do you need to watch him?"

"Pelinore," he said, naming one of the northern kings who had recently pledged allegiance to Pendragon and the Camulod Companionship, as Arthur's new vassals and allies were being called nowadays.

I scanned the room below and quickly picked out Pelinore, deep in conversation with one of the most durable of Arthur's veteran supporters, King Derek of Ravenglass, in the far northwest.

"He is a hard man to read, that one, and I don't know whether to trust him or not," Arthur said. "Derek says he's fine, and Merlyn says I should trust him, but for some unclear reason of my own, I have my doubts."

"How so? Derek's a fine judge of men and I have never known Merlyn to be wrong on such things, either. If both of them say the man is trustworthy, then it seems to me he must be worth trusting."

"Do you think so? I might, too, except that Pelinore has brought a daughter with him, for my ... consideration."

"Your consideration ..." I allowed that to hang without comment. "As a wife, you mean?"

"Aye, what else? The man is a king in his own right. He is hardly likely to offer me his favorite daughter as a concubine. That would make him look like a panderer."

I thought about that for a moment, then smiled. "But isn't that what he is doing? Pandering to your need for a queen?"

"You believe I have need of a queen?"

The question caught me off guard. I shrugged what he termed my Gallic shrug, spreading my hands and holding my elbows close to my sides in a way that I knew amused him. "Why not? You're a king, but you're a man, too, and a man needs a woman, whether it be as wife, consort or concubine."

"Do you?"

I repeated my gesture. "No, but then, as you so often point out, I am exceptional. I am a Frankish Outlander and there is much of the priest in me. Besides, I have never known a woman, and I have no intention of changing that. Not yet, at least."

From the room beneath us came an angry shout, followed quickly by the crashing of an upset table and a clamor of voices. I leaned forward and saw two struggling men being dragged apart from each other by their companions. It was that time of night when tempers often flared, but Arthur's rules about fighting in his dining hall were clear and unequivocal. A man's anger might last overnight on unusual occasions, but the most violent of murderous impulses tended to be forgotten after seven days of bread, water and strict confinement in the holding cells. I watched the two antagonists being frog-marched out of the hall amid jeers and howls of laughter, but Arthur had not even moved to look at the fracas and he spoke next as though nothing had occurred.

"You are a fortunate fellow then, Lancie ... doubly fortunate in that you are not a king, and therefore no one really cares whether you have a woman or not—queen or otherwise. I, on the other hand, am, as you astutely pointed out, a king, and therefore I should have—must have—a queen, according to some."

"What *some*? Who has been telling you that?"

"Merlyn has, for one. Is that not so, Merlyn?"

"Yes, my lord King, that is so."

I spun on my heel, almost losing my balance, all my superstitious fears of Merlyn and his supposed sorcery conjured up on the instant by hearing his deep, resonant voice beside me in what I had thought was a place that was empty save for myself and Arthur. Even so, I failed to see the old man at first, robed and cowled in black and seated as he was in the deepest shadows in the corner. It was only the pallid whiteness of the hand he extended, palm outward, to soothe my obvious fright that showed me where he was, and I immediately felt foolish for having demonstrated my sudden, childish fear so unmistakably. Merlyn, however, was accustomed to having people react thus to his presence and he spoke quickly to put me at my ease.

"Pardon me, Clothar," he said. "The fault is mine. I should have known that an old man in black robes, sitting in a corner black with shadows, would not be seen or suspected here. Forgive me, my Frankish friend."

I collected myself quickly and begged his pardon for my own lack of observation and my ill manners in having ignored him, and the awkward moment passed. Finally I glanced from him to Arthur, and then back to Merlyn.

"The King seems ill pleased with your advice, Lord Merlyn."

"Aye, he is. But for my sins I am his counselor, and as adviser, it is my duty to dispense advice on matters I deem to have import. This matter of a queen, in my consideration, has great import."

"Aye, in your eyes, perhaps. Not so in mine." Arthur's voice was tight with tension, but Merlyn ignored that. He merely sat and stared at the High King, his student and protégé, and I saw the whiteness of his eyes flicker within the cowl that shrouded his head as he blinked.

"You must marry, Arthur," he said eventually, "like it or no. The welfare of your realm demands and requires it. Without a queen to share your life, you will continue to be seen by many as no more than an upstart warlord with no legitimacy. With the mere presence of a queen, however, you will give the lie to all such calumny and will be perceived as a man of integrity and strength—a man in search of permanence. A queen will bestow upon you the appearance of solid strength, and a wish to establish and rule a united and peaceful civilized kingdom."

I recognized the truth of Merlyn's words as he spoke, even as I recognized Arthur's unwillingness to accept them, and to avert the outburst that I knew was coming I turned back to Arthur.

"Have you seen this daughter of Pelinore's?"

He threw me a withering glance. "Of course I've seen her. Don't tell me you haven't. I can't even walk to the latrines without tripping over her."

"Ah! Ugly, is she?"

"No, damn it, she is not ugly! To some people she might be highly attractive ... she is well made and she has wealth and power for the offering, involving security and support as an ally of Pelinore. But she has no attractions for me. None of them have. None."

"Nary a one, eh? How many have there been?" Knowing that he was not going to answer me, I turned to where Merlyn sat watching. "Master Merlyn, you are our resident sorcerer. Can't you put this poor fellow out of his misery?"

The black shape in the darkness of the shadows stirred, as though it were shaking its head, and when the words came they were slow and distinct, almost drawling in their delivery. "No, Seur Clothar, I cannot. The misery, you see, is of the poor fellow's own concoction. No one else would ever recognize it for what it is in the eyes of our Riothamus. They, being ordinary men, would see nothing but good fortune in having fair women pining to take care of them and to be taken by them, but our High King sees naught but jeopardy and peril in such things—entrapments strewn around and about him by scheming women anxious to possess his soul."

"Where's the Pendragon? Where is the High King? Why is he not here? Are we abandoned by our host against the laws of hospitality?"

The rough-toned, belligerent voice came up from below, loud and drunken enough to silence much of the din in the hall, and even before I could begin to react, Arthur was already at the balcony railing. He threw one leg casually over the rail and sat astride the barrier, raising his voice to overcome the other man's.

"Padraic, you brazen Eirish trumpet, lift your eyes and look above yourself for once! I am up here, talking with the messenger who could not make himself heard over the noise of your snoring down there—not without shouting into my ear for everyone nearby to hear, and some messages are ... delicate." His pronunciation of the last word dripped with salacious overtones, implying that the King had secrets that concerned women, and it evoked a great shout of raucous and appreciative laughter from his bleary-eyed audience, many of whom had been wakened by the shouting.

Padraic Mac Athol's voice came right back at him, loud and unrepentant. "We were talking, you and I, and had not done. Then I turn around and you are gone. What kind of trickery is that?"

"Trickery? And you turned around and lost me, is that it? We spoke last, you and I, nigh on an hour ago, and in the middle of a word you spilt your beer, fell forward into your platter of food and started snoring. So I moved on, thinking you had grown tired of my company."

There was a moment of silence while the crowd digested that, and then they broke into a roar of delight, and as the crescendo swelled, Arthur swung his other leg over the rail and launched himself into the air, flawlessly catching one of the heavy ropes that anchored the massive candleholder above the center of the enormous room. He swung there for a moment, looking down on the heads of the startled crowd, most of whom were still screaming in approbation, then dropped effortlessly onto one of the tables, landing easily, with knees flexed, among the debris of the meal that littered the tabletop, before bounding down to the floor and making his way through the revelers to the head table, where he seated himself and bent his elbow around the neck of his friendly tormentor.

Merlyn had stood up and come to my side while this was going on, and now he said quietly, "That was a fool's gambit. He could have broken a leg." He spoke in Latin, a far more subtle and dexterous language than the Coastal Tongue we had been speaking until then, and I knew that the change from one language to the other, with its increase in nuances, was not insignificant. We had progressed to more important topics now, but I was ignorant of what or why.

I responded to his comment in the same language, my Latin fluent and effortless. "Perhaps so, Master Merlyn. But at the moment you spoke, I was thinking that it was an inspired thing to do. He turned a moment of potential criticism into a small triumph. Quick thinking, and an eye for the right thing at the right time."

The cowled head nodded, slowly and deeply. Even at this range, his face was completely shrouded from sight. "I agree, and when I was your age I would have applauded. Old age brings with it a certain ... reticence ... a tendency to shun physical risks that is unknown to younger men. And I am old, nowadays, it seems." He shuffled away, back towards his shadowed corner, speaking over his shoulder to me as he went. "Tell me, if you will, about this idea of yours concerning the sword and sharing its power."

"You have heard about that?" I could not conceal my surprise and pleasure that Arthur would have brought this matter to Merlyn's attention so soon, on the very day of our return, but before the words had fully left my lips I regretted them. One of the first things I had learned about Merlyn Britannicus was that he never wasted words and he never stated the obvious. Once again, however, his graciousness saved me from embarrassment.

"How could I not have? Arthur came to find me as soon as he had dismissed his army and turned them over to you and the others. He could not wait to share your idea with me, said it was the most innovative and exciting thing he had heard in the entire duration of the campaign. And so I closed all doors and shut the two of us off from everyone for more than an hour while he told me everything you had proposed. And I will tell you without guile that I listened throughout, with never an attempt to interrupt him.

"You think his move there was inspiring?" The black-cowled head nodded towards the railing and then turned back to me, allowing me to see the pallor of white skin deep within the sheltering hood. "This idea of yours might well inspire all of our people to great things. It is a truly inspirational notion. But Arthur could not tell me enough about it to satisfy the fire he lit in my mind in such a brief time. He has the enthusiasm, but not yet a complete understanding of what must be involved. And so you and I must talk, and discuss this idea with a view to making it a reality." He paused, motionless, and I could visualize his lips pursed in thought. "But not here," he resumed. "I can't hear myself think. Will you walk with me to my quarters? We can talk there both in quietness and in privacy."

We left the small gallery together and made our way down the steep outer stairs in silence, each of us immersed in his own thoughts, and neither of us spoke until we had arrived at the long, wooden barracks building that housed Merlyn's few possessions. It was a single-story building shared by eight senior garrison officers, and Merlyn's quarters, sealed off from the main part of the unit and with a private door for his personal use, took up one entire end. He held the door open for me, waving me inside, and I stepped into a room lit by the flame of a single candle of fine beeswax. I had been there before, but not often, and so I was unsurprised by its Spartan appointments; it contained nothing but a cot, a work table, two chairs and a shelving unit made of planks supported on boxes. I knew that there were two coat pegs in the wall to my left, and I debated taking off my cloak, but then I decided to keep it on, since there was a bite to the air that night.

"Sit, please, and pardon me while I provide us with more light." I did as he bade me while he lit four more candles from the flame of the first, placing each in turn where its light would do the most good. Finally he was finished, and he came back to the other chair, but stood there, hesitating as though seeing me in some strange light that I myself could not see. Once again, I felt a stir of shapeless, superstitious fear eddy about the small of my back, but it was a fleeting thing and quickly banished by Merlyn's next words.

"Tell me," he said, his expression unchanged, "about this title that you have, this ranking … this word by which I addressed you when I first spoke your name this evening."

"What word is that, Master Merlyn?"

"This *Seur*. I call you Seur Clothar because I know it is the Frankish way. What does it mean?"

I spread my hands wide, indicating my ignorance, and mystified why such a simple little word should suddenly assume such significance. I had been using it ever since I came to Camulod, although probably not often, but no one had ever remarked on it before, and now both Arthur and Merlyn had challenged me on it.

"Why, it means nothing at all, as far as I am aware. It is merely a form of address among my people, nothing more. Do you have nothing like it in your tongue?"

"Not at all, neither in the Latin we are speaking now, nor in the Coastal Tongue, nor in any of the languages spoken by our various tribes. I only know it from having met and spoken with several of your fellow Franks, over the years, and all of them seemed to use it constantly. Many of them even applied it to me. I assume it to be a term of respect?"

"Oh yes, it is, very much so."

"Explain, please. How is it used? How earned, and awarded?"

I had to stop and think deeply before I could answer that, because the silly, short little word and its explanation grew more and more complicated as I sought to grapple with its meaning. Merlyn sat and waited, and although I could not see his eyes, I could feel him watching me intently.

"Well," I began eventually, "in the first place ... its most obvious meaning ... it implies respect, as you say. It is the term any of my people would use in speaking to someone older and more ... *distinguished* is the word that is in my mind here ... more distinguished than they are. And yet, even that's not accurate. An apprentice speaking to his master would certainly call him Seur, as would a peasant speaking to the man who owns the land on which the peasant lives. But then, a merchant, too, in dealing with male customers of his own rank and status, will frequently if not always call them Seur. And so will a tavern keeper, in speaking to certain of his patrons—although certainly not to all of them. The distinction, therefore, is not always one of simple rank or standing or possessions ... Is what I am saying making sense?"

"Oh yes." Merlyn's voice was very soft. "I find it fascinating."

It crossed my mind to wonder why he should be so fascinated with a single word, even if it did represent an idea, but by then I was myself fascinated with finding an exact definition that would tie down the nebulous thoughts teeming in my mind. In the end, however, I had to throw up my hands and admit defeat, unable to arrive at a satisfying, let alone definitive, answer.

"I confess, Master Merlyn, I can tell you nothing more than I have already. It is a word, no more than that, a term that is used in honor, and in recognition, of many different things ... many attributes ... But why should the word interest you?"

"Curiosity, no more than that for the moment." He raised his right arm and exposed his outstretched hand as though brushing the matter aside. "Back to your sword idea. We must apply ourselves to the structure of the ceremony involved." I heard what he had said but I lost awareness as he continued on this new track, for it had struck me forcibly—I had no idea why now, after all the time I had known him—upon seeing his right hand outstretched, that I had never seen his left hand. I looked now at the arm by his left side and saw the extreme length of the sleeve that covered it. The shape of his hand there was plainly discernible, but the material of the long sleeve draped over it completely and hung down far longer than any sleeve I had ever seen on anyone. The right hand was disfigured, its two smallest fingers twisted and claw-like, and I remembered the story of how Merlyn, during a war fought several years before I myself arrived in Britain, had fallen into a fire in his enemy's camp and had been badly burned trying to rescue the severed head of his brother Ambrose from the flames. That he had been disfigured in that incident I had no doubt; I had seen the scar tissue on his right hand. I had heard other tales, however, of darker explanations for Merlyn's concealment of himself from ordinary eyes. People spoke in hushed, dread-filled whispers about his being a leper, the most feared of human creatures.

I had always found a grim kind of humor in that, for the plain fact was that among ordinary folk, Merlyn, without the blight of leprosy, was already, in his own right and by his own contrivance, one of the most feared of human creatures: he had deliberately made himself appear to be a sorcerer, using people's fear of the black arts and their practitioners to ensure that he would be left alone to do what he must do, without interference by petty meddlers.

I suddenly became aware of silence and saw that Merlyn had stopped speaking and was now waiting for me to respond to whatever he had said or asked me about.

There was no point in attempting to disguise my inattention. "Forgive me, Master Merlyn, my mind was miles from here, distracted by foolish thoughts, and I did not hear your question."

The white, disfigured hand withdrew into its sleeve. "I asked no question. I simply stopped talking, noting that your mind was elsewhere. There is nothing to forgive in that. It happens to me all the time."

I attempted a smile, feeling my face flush, but he continued, "I had been saying that Arthur mentioned something about a vigil, to be undertaken by the participants on the night before the ceremony. Can you tell me why you would propose such a thing, and what prompted the thought?"

"Aye, Master Merlyn, I can and I will." I went on then, for some time, to tell him what had been in my mind when Arthur and I spoke of this; how Arthur himself had spent the night before his coronation in prayer and contemplation under the guidance of Bishop Enos of Saint Alban's Shrine and the other bishops who would consecrate the following day's ceremonies. His vigil had been a ritual cleansing, so that the new king would be shriven and properly prepared to participate in the solemnity of what was to be a unique and portentous event, the first event of such stature in Britain since the advent of Christianity and the first coronation of a Riothamus since antiquity.

It seemed only fitting to me, I explained, that if the events we were discussing were to be carried out at all, it would be in the interests of everyone involved to mark their importance by establishing some similar form of preliminary and preparatory ritual to be followed by the participants before the actual ceremony.

"How important should these matters be?" Merlyn asked me.

I had to school my face to conceal my surprise that the answer should not be self-evident to him. I told him, however, that I felt very strongly that a ceremony of this kind, a new and unprecedented rite, deserved to have all the solemnity and sense of occasion that we could possibly bring to it. "Even if that means—and I believe it *should* mean—bringing in at least one and possibly several bishops to sanctify the proceedings and to envelop them in the mantle of the Church's sanctity."

His shrouded head nodded slowly several times, and then he sat back in his seat, raising his right hand again to pull his cowl even farther forward over his face.

"Enos is dead," he said. "He died last spring. Word reached us at midsummer. His place has been taken by a man called Anselm, whom I have never met. He did not attend the High King making. But by all accounts I have received, and I have been at pains to find out all I can of him, he seems to be an able bishop and a worthy man. I agree with everything you have said. This plan of yours could be the making of Arthur's best designs. So I will write to Bishop Anselm, explaining what it is that we intend to do and inviting him to visit us for the occasion or, failing that, to send another in his stead. Before I can do that, however, we will have to name a time and a place for the occasion, whatever form it might finally take.

"But now, and with that foregoing point in mind, I must ask you what might seem to be a foolish question: what is it, exactly, that we intend to do in this? It seemed to me, listening to Arthur at the outset, tripping over his tongue at times in his enthusiasm, that although the idea was good—the thought of extending the protection of Excalibur's supposed magic, the apparent gift of invulnerability, to the King's captains is greatly attractive—yet the realities of life and the godlessness of battle must set it all at naught from the moment when the first man sustains a cut or a wound of any description. The perception of invulnerability is no more than that, a perception, for of course there is no such thing as invulnerability. Even Achilles had his fatal heel."

I was listening closely, but while he spoke I stood up and crossed to where one of the candles was sitting in a strong draft, guttering and flickering noisily and blowing its flame to one side, where it was melting the protective rim around the bowl of the wick. I moved it out of the draft and turned back towards Merlyn.

"I have been thinking much the same thing for several days

now. There is no such thing as invulnerability. So why should we even consider this course of action? And yet, Master Merlyn, I am convinced that we are doing the right thing here. I cannot tell you why—not quite, not yet—but there is nevertheless a vastly pleasing rightness to the thoughts going through my head. We are discussing a new and exciting idea, and it has to do with the perceived power of the King's sword, Excalibur. But even more so, it has to do with the King himself, and the tasks he has set himself, and with the qualities of the men he has assembled to help him in those tasks. By honoring these men in this way, we will be exalting them, elevating them, rendering them finer and better than they formerly were, and setting them apart from the common herd. We will—or Arthur will, as High King—endow the participants with something new, something noble and fine—"

"Founding and establishing a new order."

"What did you say?" I managed to gasp eventually.

"I said we would be founding and establishing a new order. Isn't that what you are describing? And isn't it what you reminded me I had promised to do when first you came to Britain, to found a new order to the greater glory of God?"

"Yes," I said, still astounded by what he had said. "Yes, it is, and it was, but ... but it was not my task to do it ... to come up with the idea ... That was to be your responsibility."

"Fortunate, then, that I have the intellect and am responsible enough to recognize a brilliant idea when I hear it, and incisive enough to act upon it then, even though it be not mine."

I was still gaping, my head filled with memories. "Bishop Germanus ... I remember he said ..." I cleared my throat and shook my head to clear it. "I remember asking Bishop Germanus what form this new order should take, and being astonished that he should have no idea, no slightest thought or opinion on the matter. He said to me then that when the time came, God would supply the inspiration and everything would fall into place naturally."

"And it seems he might have been correct. So, what will you call this new order?"

"I … I have no idea. I'm not even sure that this will *be* an order. There are, as I said earlier, no more than a handful of men involved."

"Aye, in the first ceremony, but once you elevate those, once that has been done and been seen to be done, every eligible man in the armies will want to enjoy the same status. And having elevated and honored your first inductees to the order, how will you distinguish them?"

"What do you mean?"

"I mean, quite simply, that this rite, this ceremony, whatever final form it may eventually take, will, as we have already agreed, set its participants aside from their fellows and mark them as very special people. How, then, will you mark that? What must we do to ensure that no one ever loses sight of the truth that these men have undergone a singular and life-changing ceremony? For that is what this will do to them. Their lives will never be the same again. They will have gone into the ceremony as one man, and emerged at the other end as a completely different person. How will you mark that, so that no one can doubt it?"

"I have no idea."

"I do. You give them a title—one that no one else can use."

"You mean, like Legate?"

"No. Like Seur."

I could *feel* the uncomprehending look on my face. "Forgive me," I said. "I don't understand what you're saying."

"I am saying that we will endow each man with a title that will mark him as having been raised to prominence by the High King under the protection of Excalibur. And we will take that title from your language, not ours, since your tongue has a very specific word that none of ours has. And that word is *Seur*—a term of respect and honor. Thus, when a man like Bedwyr is received into the order, he is awarded the name and title Seur Bedwyr, and he will be set apart and known by that name and ranking forever after."

"Seur Bedwyr …" I repeated it after him, slowly, rolling the sound of it around my tongue, savoring it, testing it. "Seur Bedwyr …

Seur Clothar ... Seur Perceval ..." I could feel his eyes on me, waiting for my opinion. "I like that," I said. "It sounds right, feels right. Do you think it will work?"

"You mean, can we make it work, so that people will accept it? Aye, I think it will work easily. Arthur will like it, too, and so he'll make it work. It's a new word, a new title, but the people will take to it because it will describe a new kind of warrior, a champion, recognized and honored by the High King. It will work, you wait and see."

8

The catalyst to all the various ideas that had been teeming in our minds on this matter of the King's new order came while we were campaigning in the north and east that summer, more of a progress than a war campaign, in truth, in that we were parading our military strength for all the kings whose lands we visited to marvel over, and to let them consider, and sometimes reconsider, their commitment to Arthur's leadership. We had been ready, in the spring, to deal with Horsa's host, but he had vanished with the snows, and so we had set out to make the best of a promising start to the new year by demonstrating our readiness to our allies. Most of the kings and chiefs, faced with our military strength, did not have to dig too deeply to find reasons for befriending us, and once agreement had been reached or found, Arthur proved himself to be a Magister in fact, an adept in the skills of enlisting loyalty and friendship while doing nothing to lessen or diminish any king's hold on his own lands or people.

The few exceptions who perceived us as threatening, or even invading, enemies and chose to make war on us were quickly dealt with and deposed, their places filled by others more inclined to moderation and compromise.

On the day in question we had approached the great Roman fortress of Deva, home for four hundred years to the Twentieth

Legion, the Valeria Victrix. Deva, safe behind its mighty walls, was now a prosperous trading and farming community of more than four thousand souls, and we had come there to visit its king, a man called Symmachus whom I had met three years earlier, during my stay in Verulamium with the venerable Bishop Enos. Arthur had high hopes of aligning Symmachus with our cause of unification, but Symmachus had been cool to several earlier approaches by intermediaries and I had reservations about the likelihood of his undergoing a change of heart, even face to face with Arthur.

I had not liked Symmachus when I met him in Verulamium. In fact I had found him remarkably easy to dislike. He was cold and aloof, disapproving and inimical and completely without charm, all of that disregarding the fact that he believed, utterly without reason, that I had designs on his elder daughter, Cynthia.

Notwithstanding my concerns over the warmth of our welcome, however, I had been looking forward with more than a little anticipation to meeting the king's remarkable younger daughter again. Maia was skinny and long legged and self-contained without being in any way like her elder sister, and even at twelve or thirteen years old she had been, and she remained, the only person I ever met who could cast my throwing lances properly with natural ease.

Both Arthur and I were destined to be disappointed in Deva, however, for Symmachus and his retinue, including his wife and daughters, were not in residence that summer. They had gone again to Verulamium, to offer prayers there at the Shrine of Saint Alban, where they had conceived a child, another daughter, on their first visit. Unwelcome as the news of their absence was to us, I did not find it particularly surprising, since the king's two eldest daughters had been born to his first wife, long since dead. The first visit he and his new queen had made to Saint Alban's Shrine, when I met them, had been for the express purpose of enlisting the aid of the Blessed Alban in their endeavors to have a child of their own. Now they had returned to petition the saint's additional intercession in the matter of a son and heir.

We learned all of this when we stopped before the main gates of the massive fortress to make ourselves known to the guard commander. A small party of us—Arthur, myself and Tristan, Perceval's younger brother who had accompanied us to Britain after serving for years as a mercenary in the pay of Rome, accompanied by our squires and a ten-man mounted escort—had ridden in advance of our army, to avoid giving rise to any alarm over our approach and to allay any hasty impressions of our intent being less than peaceful.

We had been held there, however, in front of the closed gates, to await the arrival of the officer, who finally emerged, looking distinctly flustered, to inform us that there was no one there of suitable rank to receive us.

"Then we must simply regret a lost opportunity," Arthur responded, "and will leave immediately and bother you no further. When King Symmachus returns, pass on the word to him, if you will, that we were riding by his lands, on our way homeward to Camulod from the north, and decided upon a whim to offer our respects. A misfortunate piece of timing, but such things occur and there is little to be done about them. May I ask your name, Captain?"

The man's face was a study in indecision, for now that Arthur had announced his intention to leave immediately, the hapless fellow was at once concerned over whether he had done the right thing in refusing us admission to Deva. Flushing deep red now, he cleared his throat and told us that his name was Gardolf, Chief Captain of the Castle Garrison. Arthur inclined his head and put the man's mind at ease again.

"Our thanks to you, Master Gardolf, for your courtesy, but may I ask one more consideration of you? I have an army at my back, but it is disciplined and well behaved, far from being a rabble. It is also an army happy to be going home unbloodied for once. Is there some place nearby where we might quarter them for the night? We number a thousand and a half, so we need space for men and horses, and ideally a source of running water. We will gladly pay in coin for the privilege of using such a place, and will be gone southward in the morning."

To the captain's credit, he did not even consider accepting Arthur's offer. He frowned slightly, thinking, and then his face lit up in a smile. "I know the perfect spot for you, my lord King," he answered. "Less than two leagues directly to the south of here you will find an abandoned farm. It sits in a broad mountain glen, close to the main south road. The villa was destroyed nigh on twenty years ago by raiders in from the shore, and the landowner was killed, with all his family. It has lain empty since, for it's too far from any source of help should raiders come again. But it will suit you well. The fields are overgrown but they are large and spacious, free of heavy trees, and there's a river there, with clean, sweet water."

We thanked him and took our leave to rejoin our army, and less than two hours later we arrived at the place he had described.

Arthur sat watching as our squadrons filed precisely into their appointed places for an overnight camp and dismounted, and while the infantry contingents set to the preliminary work of laying out the encampment, our troopers attended to their mounts immediately, before going to join the foot soldiers in their labors. When everything was solidly under way, the King swung his horse around and beckoned me to ride with him, and I rode beside him in silence until we reached the ruined shell of what had once been a magnificent villa. We dismounted and went into the open ruins of the atrium, where a rubble-filled fountain still stood in the center of a hub of intersecting pathways that had once led to the various parts of the great house. The pathways themselves were of fitted slabs of stone, each slab hexagonal, the work of a master stonemason, but many of them had been torn up and broken, and the entire surface of the place was littered with broken shards of marble, masonry and clay roof tiles.

Arthur walked slowly forward, his nailed boots grating on the rubble, and lifted one foot to rest it on the lower rim of the fountain as he looked about him, his elbow resting on his upraised knee.

"D'you know what a Vandal is, Lancie?"

"Aye, my lord, they are a tribe from the eastern marches of the Empire. Flavius Stilicho was a Vandal."

The King snorted, half laugh, half curse. "Aye, he was. But Flavius Stilicho was a very enlightened Vandal, his family civilized by hundreds of years of Roman living. In the beginning of things, when the Vandals first appeared on Roman soil, they became famed for depredations like this …" He waved his arm about the atrium. "Wanton, destructive savagery, ruination and defilement for the pure love of creating chaos and havoc. The reputation they earned for themselves will never be forgotten, for whenever cultured men see violence and destruction on this kind of scale, they will recall the Vandals." He looked around him again. "The people who did this must have been remarkably like those Vandals of old. Have you ever seen such devastation? This place was beautiful once, so why was it destroyed?" He straightened up, gripping his waist in his hands and arching his spine backwards, easing the kinks caused by a long day in the saddle.

"I spent much of my early childhood in a place much like this, among flowering gardens. You know it—the Villa Britannicus. No one lives in it now—not permanently, I mean, for we use it as guest quarters, as you know, and the gardens there today grow vegetables where once there were flowers. But when I was a lad it was still in daily use by the descendants of the Britannicus and Varrus families." Again he looked about him, turning in a complete circle this time to scan everything he could see. "This is what we are fighting for, Clothar—places like this, and for the right that people in this land have always had to *build* places like this, and then to live in them in peace." He shrugged, flexing his shoulders this time. "Well, that may be an exaggeration. Before the Romans came, the people here lived in huts of clay. But that was five hundred years ago, and there have been houses like this in Britain for the past two hundred years, and if we fail to stem this rising tide of incoming Saxons, they'll all end up in ruins like this one. Walk with me, my friend. Seeing this kind of blasphemy inspires me to deep anger and a greater resolve to do what I have to do."

For the next quarter hour we walked among the ruins of the ancient house, mostly in silence, with Arthur pausing every now and then to indicate something he wanted to bring to my attention, and while I was looking into a tumbled pile of stones that had once been a smithy—the rusted anvil stuck out through the rubble beside the nozzle of an archaic bellows—a small, unexpected shape caught my eye. I went forward to retrieve it and found it to be a plain wooden box.

"What is it?" Arthur asked as I picked it up. He had come to stand at my shoulder, and I shook my head, holding the box out to him.

"I don't know. A box of some kind. It's hinged. And really old, I think."

"*Really* old, there's no doubt of that. Look, you can see it was varnished once." He was picking with one thumbnail at the patina I had thought was ingrained dirt, but he quickly used both hands to prise the lid open and then stood rapt, so that I had to lean forward to see what he had discovered. It took me some time to make any sense out of what I saw in its blackened interior. The box itself, from front to back, was the breadth of my hand, and about two-thirds of that in depth, and I guessed that its measured length would be slightly greater than the same hand from mid-wrist to fingertip, but all I could see of its exposed contents was a blackened mass that appeared to be hopelessly tangled upon itself. Arthur knew what he was looking at, evidently, and he grunted deep in his throat and turned the container upside down, allowing the mass to drop into his open hand before he stooped to lay the box on the ground at his feet. He pulled what he held apart and showed me one piece in each hand.

"Spurs," he said, and I recognized them immediately as he tossed one of them to me for my inspection. As it thumped into my hand I was surprised by the unexpected weight of it. "These were someone's pride at one time," he continued. "Solid silver, and finely wrought. Look at the workmanship, the engraving. It's hard to see, under all that tarnish, but there are words there … Look, I was right." He had drawn a knife from his belt as he spoke and used the point to make a tiny scratch on the metal, exposing the bright silver underneath. I held mine up to my eyes, peering closely at it in the sunlight.

"You are right." I held the spur closer, squinting to make out whatever was stamped into the metal in tiny letters that were blacker than the blackness surrounding them. "Looks like a name ... I think it's Petrus something ... Yes, it is. Petrus Trebo ..."

"Trebonius?"

"Aye, that's it. Petrus Trebonius something or other ... Cinna! Now there's an ancient name, Cinna. Petrus Trebonius Cinna. I wonder who he was."

"He was a senior officer in the Twentieth Legion, according to this spur. And he was a knight, an Equestrian, in rank."

I blinked, all awareness of my companion's regal stature forgotten. "How do you know that?"

He peered again at the spur he held. "Hold on, there's something else here, on the other side of the shank, but it's not very clear." He turned his back to me, holding the spur up to catch the maximum light, and for a moment there was silence. I turned my own spur over, but I could see no writing on the other side of it.

"Claudius," he whispered then. "Claudius Imperator. This thing was made during the reign of Claudius Caesar, Clothar. Do you know how long ago that was? Five hundred years. Or close to it. It was Claudius who built the fortress here at Deva, to house the six thousand men of the Twenty-second Legion."

I nodded. "That's almost too long ago to imagine. You didn't answer my question. How do you know this fellow was a knight?"

He grinned and held up the spur, pointing with it at the one I held. "Because of these. They are far from ordinary. Commoners and even patricians wore iron spurs ... Well, perhaps wealthy patricians might have owned golden ones, but only knights owned silver spurs. It was a jealously guarded privilege. Silver spurs were the symbol of the rank and status of an Equestrian, and the conferring of them was a great honor dating from Republican times, before the Caesars. It signified that the wearer of the spurs had distinguished himself in the service of Rome and was entitled to own a horse that was fed and stabled at the expense of the State." His face became solemn and he looked down at the spur he held, tapping its pointed end against his other palm.

"The truth is, Lancie, that the creation of the Equestrian ranking was something of a revolution within the Republic. It marked the beginning of the middle class, a new order of society, because before that time, there were only two possibilities governing a man's station in life—two classes. You were either a patrician, born into one of the original founding families of earliest Rome, or you were a common citizen, a plebeian, the nominal equal of the mob, no matter how hard you worked or how much wealth you might pile up. With the creation of the knightly class, the Equestrians, all of that changed within a short space of time. A new order of society was born." He looked at me again, his eyes wide. "Are you *hearing* what I am saying, Lancie?"

"I think so, but I don't see the connection to the new order we have been discussing. Were these military men?"

"You tell me. What do you know of Roman history?"

"Not much of the early history, apart from what I learned as a lad in school." I thought back to my early days in Auxerre, trying to recall my lessons. "Aye, they were. All men were in those days. Farmers in time of peace, they were expected to turn out to fight in time of war."

"Which was most of the time. Thirty-five years they were expected—no, they were obliged—to fight, from the age of majority at sixteen until they were old men of fifty-one. After that, those who remained alive were free to stay at home if they so wished. But Rome had no standing army at that time. That would not come into existence for nigh on five hundred years, under Gaius Marius. And they almost never used cavalry. The soldiers of the Republic were farmers who had been trained to fight in the manner that would one day conquer the world for them. Standing side by side like rocks in a streambed and defying anyone and everyone to come and beat them face to face."

"So why the conferring of spurs and State-fed horses?"

"As an acknowledgment of honor. These men were heroes, but most of them were ordinary citizens and far from wealthy enough to own and feed a horse. The gift of the spurs and a public horse entitled and enabled them to take their pride of place and ride in public parades and spectacles."

"There must have been very few of them, then. How could they become a class?"

"By emulation. As the State grew wealthy, which it very quickly did, a community of rich merchants soon came into existence. All of them were plebeian, for patricians never soiled their hands with open commerce. The new riches were owned by shopkeepers, traders and brokers of varying kinds, and as they amassed their fortunes, they grew hungry for distinction from the common mob. And so, being as rich as they were, and corruption being what it is, they soon began to buy advancement by the only avenue open to them: they became Equestrian knights. In such cases, of course, their knighthood was conferred without the attendant State-fed horse, but they were all rich enough to care nothing for that. They were happy to provide their own horses, so long as they could hold the rank and ride in the parades."

"Hmm. That sounds neither distinguished nor admirable, so why are you so excited about the order?"

"Because it was *there,* Clothar. It *existed.* Look at these things! Ugly old discolored spurs, black with neglect and unused for hundreds of years, their leather straps perished beyond repair, as though they were made of ancient, ill-formed wood; their former owner dead and lost to history, and their entire significance lost to the world today, fallen into disuse and oblivion. Yet were we to take the time to polish them and replace the perished straps with new leather, they would be magnificent again, as bright and beautiful as when they first were made, and people would admire them."

"And so? Forgive me, Arthur, but I'm not following you."

He clasped his hands together, cupping the old spur between them. "Suppose, purely for the sake of supposition, that we were to reinstate the Order of Equestrians under another name. And in so doing, suppose we were to issue silver spurs in open tribute to men of established honor and integrity. What would you think?"

"An order of knights, you mean."

"An order of knights, each man raised to the order by the rite that you first thought of, the benediction involving the laying of Excalibur upon the candidates' shoulders, and confirmed in his rank by the privilege of wearing the silver spurs of knighthood that he has earned."

"That sounds impressive, given that it be properly done."

"It will be, I promise you that."

"Where would you begin? Who would qualify, and how?"

"The how part is easy: through prowess, military and otherwise."

"Otherwise? What does that mean?"

"Integrity; loyalty; propriety; devotion to duty; admirable conduct in the man's own life, setting an example to others. There is no lack of qualifications to fill the 'otherwise' category. And I would start with my own leaders, as I have intended from the outset. Each man among them is a trusted friend and an able, tested and tried commander of men. You yourself would be among the first, as would your two friends Tristan and Perceval. And some of my own dearest friends have been at my side since boyhood without ever flagging in their loyalty and love: Bedwyr, Gwin and Ghilleadh prime among them, although there are several others, the current commanders of the forces of Camulod."

"How many in all?"

"Eight, each of them an able general today. Their elevation to the order will simply acknowledge their honor and their contributions to Camulod."

"So you are including the infantry commanders."

"Of course I am. They all ride horses much of the time. They are entitled to the spurs."

I held up my hands in surrender. "You'll get no argument from me on that. And eight is a good number for a beginning, but others will be clamoring for admission once the significance of what has happened here starts to become plain. Merlyn believes that, and so do I."

"And so do I, and that is as it should be." The King smiled, and this time I saw him as the King, and not simply my friend Arthur.

"Let them clamor, and let them swarm, for the greater the competition for admission, the higher will be the standards set for those who qualify. We will begin with my chosen eight, all of them legate generals of Camulod. Thereafter, we will fill the ranks of their subordinates with officers qualified to take their places when the time comes, and as our armies grow and expand in size, we will have a ready stock of well-trained, highly qualified commanders."

"But—"

"But what, my friend?"

"Two things, my lord."

"Start with the first."

"I am no legate general of Camulod, nor are Perceval and Tristan."

He smiled again, and his voice was soft when he answered, "You will be, all three, once you wear the silver spurs. You are qualified in every other respect. Your second thought …?"

"Will every member of the order be an officer?"

"Why is that important to you at this time?"

I cleared my throat before being blunt, despite knowing I had no need to fear any consequences. Arthur had that kind of presence; a man tended to think twice before demurring to anything he said or thought as King.

"It seems to me you might lose many an opportunity for greatness if qualification for entry to the order is confined to those of … a certain station."

He looked at me calmly, one eyebrow rising high, one corner of his mouth rising in concert with it to form an ironic little smile. "A certain *birth* and station, you mean, do you not? How well do you know Dynas?"

"The quartermaster? Not well, personally. But I know he is a wonder at what he does."

"Well, that's an encouraging beginning. He is the best I have ever known. Cultivate him, Lancie, for he will be your quartermaster in the years to come, and your very existence in the field may hinge at some crucial point upon the love he bears for you as his commander. Dynas's parents are but simple people, hardworking but penniless, and he began his life in the service of Camulod as a kitchen pot boy, the lowest of the low. How far think you he might have risen if his abilities had been affected or restricted by his station in life?"

I had no reply to that, but the King continued speaking, waiting for none. "There, in the case of our worthy and invaluable Dynas, lies the answer to your conundrum. Birth and station will have no place in the determination of what might make a man eligible for advancement into the order. Acceptance, in and of itself, will determine nobility and worthiness. Can you see it, Lance? All the members of our order riding out together—a gathering of warriors equal in prowess though not necessarily in rank? And the silver spurs alone will set a man apart from the ruck of commonality."

"What about a sword?"

A long pause followed as he considered my question, then he cocked his head in a familiar mannerism. "What do you mean, a sword? I don't understand your question."

I drew my spatha, the weapon I had taken from a dead friend's saddle, and which had been worn by Cato, my old teacher, for most of his life. I held it up before my face, in the vertical salute to the King, then pointed with it to where Excalibur hung by its belt from his saddle horn. "This," I said, "and that one of yours."

He looked from me to my spatha and then back into my eyes. "A fine weapon, but I still don't know what you mean. Explain."

I turned my weapon over, looking at both sides of the blade as though expecting to find spots of rust. "I've been thinking carefully about swords for months," I said. "About how they are made, and where and when. There are very few sword makers in Britain, outside of Camulod."

Arthur nodded. "Agreed, that is true. The Romans left no trained weapons smiths behind when they departed. But we have always had our own smiths in Camulod, since the days of Publius Varrus, so why should whatever point you are driving at be important, other than in our being thankful to have our own resources?"

"Because I think the day will soon arrive when no swords at all are being made in Britain. And those being made here now are heavy, clumsy things of limited use. If I am right, and I believe I am, then anyone owning a fine sword in years to come will be more powerful than all his neighbors ... and if you are to be High King in truth, it will be to your advantage to have all your men well armed."

He was frowning now. "My men are all well armed now. They all have swords."

"Aye, my lord, they do, but all their swords are different, from man to man. I am thinking still about your new order. Each entrant will be raised to the order by the ceremony involving your own sword, Excalibur. What if we presented each new member with a special sword, modeled upon your own and made personally for each man by your own master smiths? My sword is fine, as you say, but look at it beside Excalibur and it pales to insignificance. It does not have the size or strength, the width and length of blade, or the strength or balance to be even remotely comparable to your weapon."

"Are you suggesting that we should duplicate Excalibur?" There was the merest hint of a bemused expression about his eyes, and I shook my head in denial.

"No, my lord, not entirely. In the first place, from what I know of the sword's origins, that would be impossible. But there is yet the possibility of copying its size and something of its strength. That could be done without impairing the original in any way."

"But that is already done. We have many swords in Camulod that match Excalibur in size today."

"Many, perhaps, my lord, but not enough. Besides, the swords I speak of would be made specially for your Knights Companion—perhaps incorporating a design to mark them as such, but certainly using only the very finest of metals, and manufactured by the very best craftsmen among your smiths. They would not have the silver shining blade, but they could be of our best tempered iron and have a burnished brightness in themselves, gray though it is. And if it is

Excalibur that makes you invulnerable, as your men believe, then in this gifting of a sword like it, you will be giving each man a shade, a share, a portion of your own power."

"Good thoughts, Lance. I like that, yes. I will give instructions for the first eight swords to be put into production as soon as we return to Camulod, each one made to measure for the knight who will wield it. And I liked that other suggestion, too … what did you call them? The Knights Companion? I like the sound of that. Where did you find that name?"

I blinked, surprised yet again by his ability to notice and focus upon things that to others would be inconsequential details. "I didn't find it, my lord, I learned it in school in Gaul—or I learned part of it. The personal cavalry of Alexander the Great were called the Companions, and the name came back to me but moments ago, when you were talking of how your knights would be ordained. Each man of Alexander's Companions was selected individually, some of them from the ranks, and their company was the single greatest elite group of ancient times, and thinking of that, the conjunction of Knights Companion simply came into my mind."

"Well, never stop thinking, Lance. You have found the perfect name for our new order: the Order of Knights Companion to the King. It sounds imposing and magnificent, don't you agree?"

I did. And thus the order had been named, endowed with a symbol and armed.

9

The first knighthood ceremony made an indelible impression not only on those who were admitted to the Order of Knights Companion but on everyone who witnessed it in any capacity. Arthur and I had talked, that day we found the spurs, about a simple ceremony, conducted with dignity but nonetheless lacking any great complexity, and at that time we had been more than content to think of it as being just that: solemn and ceremonious yet unpretentious. But the simple ceremony expanded to become a ritual as people who became involved with planning it grew increasingly enthusiastic about what the event portended and what it signified. It took on a life of its own, evolving and growing from day to day even though none of us really knew what we were doing or what would become of our efforts. From the King himself to Merlyn, and from me to the assorted bishops who would officiate at the induction, there was a blissful ignorance of what all our planning and our efforts would produce, and yet from the very outset each of us knew, without the need of verification by others, that something unique and extraordinary was taking shape in Camulod.

My own belief in the rightness of what we were planning never wavered, because the original idea had felt sound from the moment it came to me, but when the time had passed and I found myself walking in procession with my fellow initiates on New Year's Eve, filing into the chapel of Camulod in pairs through the clouds of precious incense that wafted behind the bishops preceding us, I felt the small hairs prickle on my neck and arms and I shivered in anticipation of what we would achieve this night. The bishops prayed for grace on our behalf, intoning sonorous and solemn wishes written specially for the occasion, and we were placed in order, all eight of us, throughout the tiny chapel, my own place being assigned last, behind the altar. And then we were left alone, with the light of only one long eight-hour candle, to stand in prayer, at attention and in full armor, and prepare ourselves for the following morning's ceremony.

I cannot remember ever having spent a longer night, for the temptation to sleep grew stronger as the night elapsed and the candle guttered, making the only sound in the air for most of the time, save for the occasional rustle or clink of mail as someone shifted his weight against the fear of losing his balance and falling over. I tried to pass the time by praying, but praying ceaselessly for hours on end is more than merely difficult, it is impossible to anyone who has not learned to do it over the long course of years and dedication. And so I spent much of the night merely thinking, examining my life and the people who had taken part in it since my birth. I remembered all of them, trying at first to keep them numbered in my head, but that was futile, and so I settled for merely recalling them with pleasure, for the most part, although there were those from whom I gained no pleasure and never had. But those were very few and even they helped the time go past. The candle burned down and expired eventually, leaving us in darkness, but no one spoke a word until the chapel doors swung open and the light of the new day spilled in.

The rest of that morning's events were grand, the proceedings slow and solemn, yet at the same time exciting and stimulating. There was no doubting now that something of great significance was happening here. But when the moment came for me to kneel at Arthur's feet and be touched on each shoulder by the shining length of Excalibur's magnificent blade, my throat swelled up and I came close to tears, utterly entranced by the reality of what this signified. Arthur, our King, the Riothamus of All Britain, had become much more, I suddenly understood, than the mere man he was. He had become the embodiment of all that his people—including me— dreamed of and believed in. He had become the living symbol of their hopes of freedom and a life of dignity, and in their eyes and in their minds he had become both invulnerable *and* invincible, and the magical impossibility of all of that was captured and symbolized somehow by the impossibly silver, glittering purity of his magnificent sword, a gift bestowed on him by Heaven's light at the moment of his coronation, its appearance witnessed by thousands of his people.

And as the solid weight of that shining blade rested for a moment on my right shoulder, then was raised and moved over my head to rest again on my left, I shivered, imagining I felt a liquid yet intangible *something,* a presence of some kind, forming about my head like a shining helmet. It was a momentary, fleeting image, but it was one for which I was completely unprepared, and it left a memory tingling in me, filling me again with gratitude and the urge to break down and weep.

Moments later, I rose to my feet and looked about me, seeing the smiling faces everywhere and the nodding heads that expressed approval and satisfaction with a thing well done, and I turned and bent forward at the waist to look along the line of my companions. There were eight of us—Gwin, Ghilleadh, Bedwyr, Gareth, Perceval, Tristan, Sagramore and myself—and none of us would ever be the same again. We were Knights Companion to the Riothamus, and that Riothamus, Arthur Pendragon, was approaching us again, accompanied by a retinue of others, all of them festooned with equipment.

He stopped before each of us in turn and greeted us as Companions and equals, and then he presented each man with the sword and silver spurs designed for him in person. The spurs were practical and beautiful, of solid silver, a memento of this occasion, a symbol of the ancient origins of knighthood and a signal of advancement duly earned and deserved. The sword, equally beautiful and even more practical, was each knight's badge of office—a personal gift from the King, made to fit each knight's size and requirements and modeled after the King's own sword, in acknowledgment that the aura of invincibility embodied in Excalibur had been passed on, in spirit and intent, to the possessor of this blade.

I know we left the ceremony that morning and moved on to other things for the remainder of the day, but I have no recollection of anything beyond taking the spurs and sword from Arthur's hand and looking him in the eye, returning his smile before I bowed my head and saluted him. On a hundred occasions since that day, however, I have looked back on it and acknowledged, quietly and to myself, that it was the best day of my life.

TWO

1

It had been another long campaigning season, and I was eager to have it over and done with so that I could take my men and go home to Camulod. We had earned a few months of comfort and relaxation in friendly surroundings, free of the constant tension of trying to anticipate and forestall attacks on any and all fronts. No snow had fallen yet, but the looming winter was already a reality, ushered in by days of heavy, wind-driven rains that leached all the energy from my men and myself.

Nothing could have been more attractive to me that night than the idea of going home, and it occurred to me the same kind of thoughts must have been going through the mind of Knut One-Eye, the man I was watching now as he lounged back in a deep-cushioned, hand-carved wooden chair that four of his men had carried close to the roaring fire in front of him. But he showed little sign of awareness of any need to hurry. He held an enormous drinking mug in one hand and I could hear the bellow of his laughter even over the roaring of the fire and the raised voices of his companions, most of whom continued to sit and sprawl around the open-ended square of tables in what had, until mere hours earlier, been the great hall of Ushmar, the self-appointed king of the nameless northwestern territory surrounding the fort that the Romans had called Luguvallium, the westernmost point of the great wall that Hadrian had built to keep the woad-painted Caledonians out of Britain.

Ushmar and his people had managed to maintain the fort remarkably well since taking it over soon after its Roman occupants left, although they had neglected the original stone buildings of the military headquarters and its attached administrative center, allowing them to deteriorate sadly, simply because his people were not comfortable with such airy, spacious rooms, preferring the dark and noxious smokiness of their own hand-built hovels. Apart from that, however, the major fortifications were secure and in good repair, and the garrison who had manned the place had enjoyed living conditions far better and more comfortable than those available to their neighbors in the remainder of Ushmar's little kingdom. Unfortunately for all of them, however, the fort's single but fatal weakness, tragically unnoticed by the king or any of his followers, was that most of its defenses had been built to withstand an assault from the north. Knut One-Eye's raiders had crept up on the place from the rear, from the southwest, and had overrun the few guards without any difficulty. The fort had fallen quickly after that.

That my men and I were there at all was sheer coincidence. We had been patrolling nearby, displaying our cavalry and its strengths to our newest allies in a neighboring kingdom to the east of Ushmar's, ruled by a warlord called Connlyn whose eastern territories were bordered by an indefensible area occupied by strong enemy forces, mainly Saxons. More than a year earlier, Connlyn had visited Camulod, uninvited and unannounced and purely on his own initiative, offering his friendship and loyalty to its young Riothamus in return for a promise that Camulod would come to his aid as an ally in the event of a threatened Saxon invasion of his northern lands. I had not liked the man on first meeting him, nor had I warmed to him since, but I could not deny that his overture of friendship was an astute move, demonstrating the northern king's foresight and preparedness.

Arthur had thought so, too, and had seen the advantages to himself and to his cause in accepting Connlyn's proposed loyalty and support. And so he had welcomed Connlyn into the growing cadre of his loyal adherents, gently turning aside the reservations of myself and others of his followers and advisers. Connlyn had come to Camulod of his own free will, his offer of alliance unsolicited, our leader pointed out to us, and he had done so at an opportune and useful time, when Arthur had need of being seen to attract adherents from distant regions. It mattered nothing that the offer was self-serving; such was the way of kings, who must constantly bear in their minds the welfare of their people, who depended upon them and upon whom they themselves depended in turn. His gesture had been noted by others like him, Arthur assured us, and he would hear no more ill talk of our new ally. Besides, he had asked us, his eyes shining, did we think he was insensitive enough not to have noted the things that concerned us, even before we brought them up for his consideration? That had been the last mention of anything negative about Connlyn, and in truth nothing more had occurred to make any of us remember it.

This year, as part of my campaigning activities, Arthur had sent me on an extended sweep to the far north with my First Cavalry Wing, leaving the Second Wing in the hands of Perceval. Our purpose in going there was to demonstrate Camulod's goodwill by providing a show of force in Connlyn's region, but while we were there word came of a strong raiding party to the southward, led by a Saxon chief called Knut One-Eye whose name and reputation were well known to Connlyn's folk. The raiders were reported to be skirting Connlyn's territories, following his southern border but heading directly towards the lands of his neighbor to the west, a king called Ushmar. It was a development we could not ignore, irrespective of King Ushmar's reported disdain for us and for anything to do with Camulod, because a Saxon presence in his neighbor's lands to the west would isolate Connlyn's domain between two enemy territories.

I had first heard Ushmar's name one night shortly after my arrival in Connlyn's own fort mere weeks before, when Connlyn himself told me that King Ushmar had known of his journey south the previous year and had disdained to join him in acknowledging Camulod's sovereignty, claiming to have no trust in anyone from the Southland, as he called it, and to have no need of any swords but those of his own warriors. But at the same time he had not tried to discourage Connlyn from going on his mission. I had immediately asked why, sensing a potential danger from this unknown and previously unheard of Ushmar, but my concerns were laughingly set aside by my host and his assembled captains. Ushmar, they told me, was not overburdened with brains when it came to long-term planning, and tended to be timid about setting foot outside his own domain. He called himself a king, but it was a matter of jest that he had no single jot of kingship in his nature. He was a petty warlord and no more than that, Connlyn himself told me, a warrior brave enough in battle and adept at spilling blood for his own ends, but he was afraid of taking risks when they involved any threat, real or perceived, to his own power.

At the time, however, listening to what was being said in Connlyn's hall that night, it seemed plain to me that in reality this Ushmar was not at all what my host and his advisers thought him to be. My interpretation of the very things they laughed about was totally opposed to what they saw. In my view, Ushmar was a very clever man who cared nothing for what Connlyn and his people thought of him. He plainly saw Connlyn's domain as a buffer, protecting him against invasion of his lands from the east, and I could not believe that Connlyn and his people were unaware of that. Nor could I believe their blindness to the clear truth that their despised neighbor had accurately calculated that any additional strength Connlyn might gain from his overtures to Camulod would be advantageous to Ushmar without committing him to a formal alliance.

This, then, was the man we had ridden to protect, albeit unwillingly. We had made a two-day forced march towards Luguvallium, leaving soon after the tidings of the Saxons reached Connlyn's court. But by the time we arrived, Ushmar's stronghold had already fallen and all its defending warriors had been slaughtered, overrun on Knut's initial attack, with only Ushmar himself and a few others taken alive and held captive. They would have been better off had they died in the fighting, because Knut One-Eye's horde were savages and had reveled in torturing their captives and finally burning them alive. We had passed their charred corpses on the way in here.

Now I stood on the narrow wooden floor of a storage loft, no more than two paces deep, that had been laid along the rafters at the gable end of the great hall, high above the riotous crowd below. Looking down between the roof beams, and ignoring the over-worked servants who were plying the revelers with drink, I had counted upwards of eighty men before their movements made me lose track of my tally. There were no women in evidence at all, not even captives, which struck me as being very strange, but I had too many other things on my mind to think about that for the time being. Most of the men below were drunk by now, sated on Ushmar's stores of potent beer, and none of them had any inkling that I was up there watching them.

Penetrating Ushmar's stronghold, now Knut's, had been ludi-crously easy and made easier by the fact that after eight days of downpour the rain had stopped the previous evening, permitting us to travel that day dry clad and dry shod and fit for battle. Now, outside in the quiet night, all of Knut's unwary guards were dead and my men surrounded the hall; any drunken reveler unfortunate enough to go outside to relieve himself would be swiftly dealt with before he could raise an alarum. Knut, swollen with the power of a new victor, had not given a moment's thought to any possibility of being attacked himself within hours of his triumph here, and he was about to pay for his hubris.

I did not have a massive force at my disposal, but it was a full expeditionary patrol, powerful enough to be highly visible and intimidating when necessary, and far and away large enough to swat Knut and his raiding party like a cluster of flies. My cavalry troopers numbered six score, plus officers and remounts, and a complement of two full centuries of infantry, with an additional half hundred of Pendragon bowmen accompanied by two wagons filled with arrows, bows and bowstrings. I could have ended this simply by having my trumpeters blow a call outside, then slaughtering Knut's warriors as they poured out of the building, but I had sound reasons for not doing that. I had no wish to kill every man below. I wanted most of them to survive, to witness what was about to take place and then to spread the word of what had happened to Knut's raiders.

I moved back to the opening under the eaves that I had used to enter the loft, and leaned out to look down the length of the ladder that rested against the wall. Below me, I could see Bors's pale face looking up at me. I fumbled for the length of thin rope that hung from my waist and tugged on it in the prearranged signal, and when Bors's responding tug came back immediately, I began hauling the rope up, hand over hand. It was light work, because the only thing tied to the other end was one of my long throwing lances, too long and potentially awkward to carry with me when I first scaled the ladder. When I had it safe in my hands, I untied the rope from my waist and dropped it down to Bors before moving back into the loft. Behind me, I knew, six of my best bowmen were already climbing the ladder.

Hefting the lance gently in my hand, I stepped forward carefully until I was as close to the edge of the loft floor as I could go without risking being seen from beneath. Little enough chance of being noticed, I knew, but there was no sense in being foolish; the vacant eye of some lolling drunkard might be attracted by a hint of unexpected movement among the roof trees. I had already selected my angle of attack and now I verified it with a quick review. My cast would be downward between the rafters, and accuracy was everything since, because I was standing where I was on the floor of the loft, there appeared to be more wooden beams ranged in front of me than there was space to permit a clean throw between them, and my lance was long and light. The merest hint of contact between one of the beam edges and the butt of my spear would destroy my shot.

Listening to the stealthy footsteps of the bowmen now ranging themselves at my back, I resisted the urge to turn and tell them to be careful; these men were all veterans, the best of my best, and had no need to be told what to do. I contented myself with holding up one cautionary arm to forewarn them, and then I busied myself in wrapping the long leather throwing thong in a tight spiral along the feather-light shaft of my lance, then slipping the first finger of my throwing hand into the small anchor of the launching loop. The tip of the weapon, a three-sided needle of tempered iron with a thumb-thick butt hollowed to hold the narrow end of the shaft, was three handspans long, twenty-three thumbpads or inches as we counted size in Gaul, and it would skewer anything it hit.

The shaft was painted white, an idea born of Merlyn's wish to identify each of Arthur's commanders clearly to everyone who met them. Gwin's color was green, a pale but vibrant hue produced by boiling a variety of plants and weeds; Ghilleadh's was the blue of a summer sky and no one other than Merlyn himself knew whence it had been obtained, although he had taught the secret of its preparation to the armorer Gannon, whose responsibility was the preparation of such things; Bedwyr had laid claim to the rich red dye that Gannon produced through some alchemy of his own; the saturnine Sagramore's color was black, because he thought it suited his personality; and Arthur used two colors, the only one in Camulod to do so: his own Pendragon red on a field of yellow gold. Perceval and Tristan, the two friends who had accompanied me from Gaul with my young squire, Bors, had both chosen to continue to wear my colors for the time being.

I realized that I was woolgathering and sucked in a deep breath, pulling my thoughts together. It was time. I hoisted my weapon, my bent elbow flexing slightly as I tested the balance of the missile, and concentrated on my throw, visualizing the arc of flight, out and slightly upwards over the first four beams and then down, cleanly between the fifth and sixth and onward to where Knut One-Eye sprawled backwards in his great wooden chair before the fire. Useless to throw the thing straight down, for that would annul the effect I wanted to achieve. I wanted its flight to slant as gently downwards as it could, so that Knut's people would see it flying and not know instantly whence it had come. One last time I asked myself, despite my knowing the answer, if it might not be better, safer, simply to have one of my bowmen shoot the lout below. It would, and again it would not. An arrow would bring certain death, but no one would mark its flight. The spear, however, properly delivered, would convey a lesson; an effect, an example and a demonstration of punishment that no simple, hard-shot arrow could achieve.

Behind me, my men were motionless, probably holding their breath in anticipation of what was about to happen, and I did not need to look to know that each of them already had an arrow nocked to his string. I drew in my breath slowly and stepped forward into my throwing stance, and as I did so Knut uttered a mighty roar and pulled himself to his feet, weaving there, with his tankard hoisted high above his head as he demanded the attention of everyone in the hall. As a relative silence fell and all eyes turned to look at their leader, I launched myself into my throw.

It was perfect, and the launching thong unwound with a gentle whishing sound, spiraling the hurtling shaft into the silent, spinning flight of its flawless arc. I held my own breath as I watched it go, knowing it was the best and most difficult cast I had ever made, exulting to see it soaring exactly as I had wanted it to, then dipping gradually to angle easily and cleanly through what now appeared to be an impossibly narrow space between the two rafters I had selected as its most suitable entry into the space beneath. As it swooped downwards its spinning, snow-white length reflected the lights from below, and I dropped to one knee, craning sideways to watch it arrive at its target.

People saw it. For a timeless instant the surprise of everyone there was palpable, its suddenness evinced in the utter stillness of caught breath and arrested motion. And then the missile struck. Even Knut had seen his death approaching and had frozen in shock, his eyes beginning to flare wide a hundredth of a heartbeat before the slender point took him in the center of the chest, piercing his bullhide cuirass as though he wore nothing at all and throwing him violently backwards off his feet to crash into the seat he had just left as the length of the slender, lethal blade shattered his heart and emerged from his back with sufficient force to pin his already lifeless body to the back of the chair.

For a long moment no one on the floor below was capable of movement, but then someone howled a curse and the entire crowd was instantly thrown into panic. Apparently no one had seen where the lance had come from, and no one thought to look up above their heads, but once the initial surging movements of panic began, chaos erupted. As I had expected, however, Knut's closest associates surged forward to surround his corpse, and although I could hear nothing of what was being said, I knew they would soon be accusing one another of treachery. I stepped back and waved my bowmen forward, pointing at the gesticulating throng of enemy leaders that now surrounded their former chief, and as I moved quickly then towards the rooftop door on my way down to ground level I heard the snapping thrum of bowstrings as they began to launch a deadly storm of arrows.

Bors was waiting for me at the bottom of the ladder, holding the bridle of my horse, my long white war cloak with its great red Pendragon blazon folded over his arm and another white-shafted throwing lance thrust point first into the ground beside him to support the shield that leaned against it. I shrugged quickly into the cloak, threw it swirling over my shoulders with a swing of my arms and secured it with the broad clasp at my chest before flipping the sides away to hang down behind my back. I swung myself quickly into the saddle and settled my feet in the stirrups before donning the heavy war helmet that hung by my saddle bow and finally taking the lance and shield Bors was holding up to me. I spent several moments adjusting the throwing thong he had already wound around the spear's shaft and inserting my finger into the throwing loop, and then I grunted my thanks to him and raked my spurs along the horse's belly, sending him forward with a leap and a mane-tossing jerk of his head.

Tristan was waiting for me in front of the hall's main entrance, with a formation of four fully armored mounted men, one by his side and three behind him, all of them helmeted and wearing the white cloaks that marked them as mine. In front of them, a knot of my infantry, arms linked for strength and leverage, blocked the entry doors firmly with their mass against the panicked efforts of the men inside to throw them open.

I took my place at the point of the arrow formation of mounted men, dipping my head to them as I arrived, and they saluted me solemnly and formally. The wide main doors were broad enough to accommodate three horsemen riding abreast, and our six-man close-packed arrowhead formation would sweep the crowded threshold clear of bodies as we entered. I settled my helmet firmly on my head, then raised my shield in the prearranged signal, and our men leapt away from the doors, allowing them to spring open.

By that time we were already in motion, and the rabble who now began to spill out through the open doorway found themselves unexpectedly confronted by an advancing mass of solid horseflesh. They barely had time to arrest their flight, pushed forward by the men at their backs, before we hit them and flung them bodily back through the doorway to sprawl in every direction. Many of them were screaming, injured and badly damaged by the hooves and bodies of our war horses, which were trained to kick out at and maim anyone they encountered in action. In mere moments we were inside the main hall and I was scanning the crowd from my vantage point high on my horse's back.

I saw Knut's heavy chair, with his body still spiked to its high back, and in the same glance I also saw a giant with a forked beard who had climbed up on a table and had just then loosed an arrow at me. I bent forward in my saddle instinctively, sweeping my shield up in an arcing swing to catch and deflect it, but it was hard-shot, and the force of its impact knocked my shield arm up and away from my body and sent me reeling off balance, for I had already begun to push myself up to stand in my stirrups, gauging my own aim, and the unexpected impact almost unhorsed me. I dropped quickly back into my seat, fighting to stay in the saddle as the weight of my helmet dragged ferociously at my swaying head, and fervently thanking my old horse master Tiberias Cato for the years of training he had dedicated to teaching me how to ride without reins and how to adapt my body and my balance to any eventuality. It took me mere moments to readjust, and by the time I rose up again to throw, the giant who had shot at me had barely moved.

I threw almost without aiming, except that hours of daily practice over long years of training had assured me of being able to hit any target within range of my weapon. He saw the lance coming for him and snarled, flailing at the projectile with his now-useless bow, but he mistimed his effort and his sweeping bow stave barely grazed the shaft, deflecting it down so that he took the point in his belly instead of his chest. The blow was no less fatal, but now he was gut shot and would die slowly and in agony unless he was lucky enough to find someone to dispatch him. He teetered back on his heels and bellowed at the top of his lungs, and then he grasped the spear shaft tightly in both hands, ripped it out of his body and raised it above his head to hurl it back at me. I watched in amazement, too stunned even to think of drawing my sword, but before he could throw he died, his temples shattered by a long Pendragon arrow that snapped his entire body sideways to fly whirling from the table.

I was waiting for the trumpet blast I had ordered, and it came instantly, the brazen noise of it completing the stunning effect of our attack. Everywhere I looked, men were ceasing to move, gazing about them wild eyed and fearful. I saw that my bowmen had obeyed my instructions and spread inward to right and left of the doorway so that they were now ranged all along the walls of the vast chamber, bows fully drawn, arrows threatening the huddled crowd but holding back. My infantry, too, were pouring through the rear doors of the kitchen, herding the terrified staff against a wall there, away from the enemy forces where they would be safe from any but the most accidental harm.

Even so, beaten as they were, some of Knut's men were still defiant. One bearded monster with a pendulous gut, who had been blinking and looking about him in confusion, suddenly uttered a grunt that swelled rapidly to a roar of rage as he swung a massive, two-handed axe above his head and charged towards the men guard-ing the doors. Two of his fellows joined him, gripping their swords in both hands and adding their voices to his as they ran to catch up with him. I counted nine clear bowshots as all three men went down in death before they could come close to the door, and that was the end of any resistance.

I kicked my horse forward in the sudden silence, allowing it to pick its own way through the sullen throng of still-armed men and the litter of overturned furnishings, guiding it gently with my knees towards the grotesque figure of Knut One-Eye, still pinned by my lance to the back of his great chair by the fire and surrounded by the piled corpses of his captains, all of them bristling with long Pendragon arrows. When I reached him, I bent forward from my saddle and grasped the white lance shaft, then braced myself strongly in my stirrups before jerking the weapon free and holding it up in front of me as I slowly wheeled my horse around, careless of the bodies I might trample. As soon as he saw me turn thus, a man called Lanar, sent with us from Connlyn's stronghold to serve as interpreter to the enemy should we require one, stalked forward looking neither to right nor left and climbed up onto one of the tables left standing close to me. Beside him, equally expressionless and matching him pace for pace, marched the young but white-headed man called Albinus, aptly named and newly appointed squire to Tristan, bearing my personal banner: a great red dragon rampant on a spotless field of snowy white. Albinus stopped by my right hand, slightly ahead of where I sat, and turned to face the crowd. I paid neither of them any attention, intent upon scanning the watching faces all around me, faces that were, almost without exception, gazing at the bloodstained weapon I was holding aloft.

"I am Clothar," I declaimed in oratorical Latin, "Captain of Camulod and Knight Companion to Arthur, King of the Pendragon Federation and Riothamus of All Britain, and this white spear is the symbol of my status and of my displeasure. I offer you a choice, here and now." As the crowd gaped at me, plainly having under-stood not a word of what I had said, Lanar repeated my statement in their own tongue, his voice deep and vibrant, and I watched their eyes grow wide. I knew there were no matching words in their primitive tongue for the sonorous titles that had rolled so grandly from my mouth, but I had discussed this with Lanar before our attack and he had memorized the titles, knowing what my intention was. Now he incorporated the titles I had used, and among the unintelligible gibberish he was spouting, the Roman words stood out like sparkling gems. But I saw that some of what he said evoked response from his listeners. Even here, it seemed, the Saxons had heard of Camulod. As his words died away I saw one or two of them begin to gather themselves, preparing to respond, but I carried on before any of them could, raising my voice even higher to override their murmurings and hearing my own voice thunder in my ears, distorted by the confines of my heavy, visor-flapped helmet. I turned in my saddle and waved the spear upwards to indicate where more than a dozen of my bowmen stood looking down from above the rafters, and even through the helmet flaps I heard the hiss of indrawn breath as men looked up and saw the death above them.

"Look about you. My men are everywhere. You can choose to die here and now, with those who have already gone down, or you can listen and depart this place alive, taking your weapons with you. Your choice, but one to be made now, on the instant. Lay down your weapons, or die."

Again Lanar translated, and in the hush that followed his speech this time men looked at one another in the hope of finding guidance and leadership. But all their leaders were already dead in a tangled mass of twisted limbs on the floor around Knut One-Eye.

The silence stretched until one man, perhaps more fatalistic than his fellows, perhaps more cowardly, spat viciously and threw his sword to the floor. The clatter of its fall acted as a signal, and the air filled with the sounds of clanking metal as discarded weapons fell upon each other throughout the hall.

As the sounds died away the bowmen above me and around the halls relaxed and lowered their arms, easing their muscles from the full draw but keeping their arrows nocked and ready.

"Bors," I said, and my squire came forward leading a detachment of men who set to work collecting the discarded swords and axes, and as the weapons were swiftly gathered up and removed I spoke again to Bors, this time in our own Frankish language, telling him to have his men next clear away the broken tables and create enough space for me to move about without having to dismount. I turned to Lanar and reverted to Latin. "When Bors has finished clearing some space tell them they are under my protection and have nothing to fear. Then tell them to line up, shoulder to shoulder facing me, where I can speak to all of them without shouting."

I watched as the captured enemy warriors shuffled reluctantly into position as Lanar had instructed them. They were sullen, but there was more curiosity than truculence in their faces now. I waited patiently until they were lined up, and then I hooked my shield to my saddle bow, against my left leg, tossed my lance to Bors and reached up to unfasten and remove my helmet, which I hung by the chinstrap from its saddle hook before I scrubbed my cropped head with the palms of my hands, enjoying the coolness of the air against the perspiration on my scalp. The room was almost completely still now, and I felt every eye in the hall upon me, my own men no less intrigued to hear what I might say than my prisoners were. I counted fifty-eight captives, all of them facing me in a single, ragged row.

Slowly, moving with total deliberation and completely aware of the effect I was creating, I shook out the folds of my cloak from behind my shoulders, pulling its front edges to drape its whiteness around me and over my arms and clasped hands, covering my slung shield and helmet. That done, I looked slowly along the entire row, meeting a few eyes but dwelling on none.

"You should all be dead by now," I resumed, and Lanar translated as soon as I had spoken.

"You have earned death by the harshness with which you meted it out to Ushmar and his men. I dislike torturers and see no merit in burning enemies alive. But for now, I choose to give you your lives, solely so that you can deliver a message for me. A message from Arthur Pendragon of Camulod, Riothamus, High

King of All Britain ..." I saw no fault in hammering the sonorous title home and I watched them take note of it yet again.

Once more I waited for Lanar to finish and I gave them plenty of time to absorb the words before I continued. I was in no rush to end this and I wanted no error in their memories of how they had been treated here and what they had learned this night. At length, when their attention had returned to me, I spread my arms wide, holding the edges of my wide cloak so that it hung from my extended arms like white wings. "Look on my back."

Slowly, using my knees to guide my well-trained horse, I turned until they could all see the great red dragon of Pendragon spread across the shoulders and back of my cloak, an exact replica of the beast on the standard held by young Albinus, and when I felt they had all taken sufficient note, I returned to face them, lowering my arms. When I began to speak this time, I spoke slowly and clearly, pausing frequently, allowing Lanar to keep up with me easily.

"You and your kind have come here to this land to raid and pillage, thinking the people weak and easy prey. Go back now to your camps and tell your fellows that they are in error. And tell them that they will pay with their lives ... all of them ... if they continue with this madness.

"You have wakened the sleeping beast that guards this Britain, the red dragon you see upon my back. Pendragon is its name and Arthur, the Lord of Pendragon, the High King of this land, is its keeper. I know not what your name may be for this land in which you now stand captive. Nor do I care. But we who live here call it Britain, and it is *ours*—the home of the red-scaled, red-toothed avenger called Pendragon." I indicated Albinus and the standard he held so proudly.

"Beneath this banner, stirred into fury by the brutality and savagery of your attacks on peaceful people—and by your lust to conquer lands to which you have no rights—new laws have been proclaimed in Britain, and new armies levied to enforce them.

"Armies," I repeated. "Mark the word and heed it. Legions. Not shapeless mobs of greedy, bloodthirsting rabble like yourselves.

Legions, trained in the Roman ways, with Roman discipline but with a purpose Romans seldom showed.

"And our legions are mounted, on trained horses the like of which your world has never seen or known. Trained horses, and trained men. Disciplined. Angry. Vengeful. And committed to the destruction of raiders and thieves like you and your stiffening slaughterers on the floor there, together with all they represent." I waved dismissively towards the sprawl of bodies at my horse's feet.

"Knut One-Eye there met a simple end, far better and more swift than he deserved. And you yourselves have met reprieve. But if you ever face the dragon's men again you will perish, every last one of you. Our armies will reap you like hay and our cavalry—our mounted troops—will scour you from the earth. Our bows will shoot you down from afar before you ever find the chance to fight with us."

I looked from face to face among them now, meeting them eye to eye.

"That is no idle threat, uttered in bluster. Believe me, and be warned. This force that holds you here is but a small part of my own legion, and as you can see, all of them wear the white of my standard. But what you see is but the smallest part of what we can bring into the field upon an instant's notice … one tenth of the legion I command. Camulod has other legions, led by other Knights Companion to the High King, and every one of them a match in strength for mine. And thus, if you have one spark of wit or intellect within you, you will know I make no silly threats in what I say. I make a promise: draw our ire again and we will come in thousands and destroy you. Tell that to your masters and your fellows.

"We will return this way within the year and we will come in strength that will appall any of you still foolish enough to be here. We will approach you from the east, through the territories of our friend and ally Connlyn, and from the southwest and the south, and we will sweep the territories you hold now, raining death in storms of arrows and obliterating all sign of you from our lands with mounted force. You may fight. That is your choice. But if you do, you will surely die. Go home and spread that word. You have one year to shake the earth of Britain from your feet."

I paused to let those words sink home, aware of the utter lack of movement in the hall, and then I told them that they would be confined that night under guard but would be released, still under guard, the following day, their weapons returned to them on the southern borders of the neighboring kingdom governed by our friend and ally Connlyn. That said, I dismissed them into the custody of Tristan and called Lanar to me. I thanked him for his able assistance and then silently passed him two gold pieces that were warm from being held in my hand. His eyes lit up and he nodded, but neither by word nor gesture did he indicate that anything had changed hands between us, and he showed not the slightest temptation to glance down to see what I had given him. I winked at him and nodded back, then followed Bors to the quarters he had found for me.

2

He had chosen a small single room for me, the former Roman paymaster's office I guessed, judging from the table-like counter fronting a small shuttered window in the interior wall, and I was grateful to see Bors had had it swept and cleaned and well lighted with half a score of fine candles before setting up my traveling cot and table. There was fresh hot water in a steaming ewer and cold in another, and the hanging leather bag spread and suspended in the collapsible frame of my wash basin was freshly waxed and ready for my use. The travel boxes containing my personal possessions, including the enclosed armor tree given me years earlier by Germanus, had been neatly placed along the wall opposite my cot, and a sheaf of white-painted lances leaned in a corner, ready for my use. By the time I awoke tomorrow, I knew, the two lances I had used in the fight tonight would have been washed clean of blood and dried carefully against rust before being returned to the sheaf. I yawned and stretched, looking forward to being freed from my armor.

Before Bors even had time to start on the first buckle, however, I heard a discreet cough outside my door, and Powys, the commander of our Pendragon bowmen, blocked the opening with his bulk, leaning into the doorway almost apologetically. Before the attack, I had assigned him the task of searching the fort and its buildings from top to bottom as soon as the fighting was over.

"Your pardon, Clothar, but we have found—"

"Women," I said, cutting him short as I recalled my earlier thought on this. "You found Ushmar's women." Powys blinked at me in astonishment. "How many?"

"Aye, women … and children." He was frowning. "Two score or so, mayhap half a hundred. No more."

Powys was far from being a youth. He was a Cambrian Pendragon veteran in every sense of the word, and his beard had grown grizzled as his body thickened throughout decades of service to Arthur and to his father, Uther, before. He was the only one of my commanders who called me directly by my name at all times and never addressed me by any outward title of respect, but I cared nothing about that and was content to have it so, for such was this man's reputation that had he held me in any disdain at all he would have made the fact abundantly clear long since. Instead he respected me as a man and accepted my Frankish differences with a tactful tolerance that he showed to few others. In his dour, unforgiving, xenophobic eyes anyone not born to the Pendragon clan was bound to be an inferior being, but I had somehow measured up to his stern, judgmental criteria and won a form of mildly reluctant yet ungrudging acceptance. He may not have accorded me the honorific titles others did, but he stood solidly behind me. Now he stood waiting, knowing I had more questions.

"Where are they? Are they in good condition? Have they been abused?"

"Abused?" He almost chewed upon the word, searching his mind for a meaning that would be acceptable to me. "They look healthy enough. None of them have any wounds to speak of. They were shut up when we found them, confined in a darkened room beneath the floor of one of the buildings, but I can't say they have been abused … Then again, I am not sure they would know what abused even means. They were Ushmar's women, after all …"

"Aye, I take your point. Fifty of them, you say. How many children?"

"Half a score, but all of them well grown. No brats or sucklings. And from the wailing of the women I would guess there might have been more before the attack. If you want my opinion, I'd say they were kept alive to serve as slaves—sold among the Saxons, I mean—and so Knut's people did not damage them too much. For all I know some of them may have Saxon seed in their bellies, but that's to be expected."

"Aye, well, there's not much we can do for them, I fear. Set them free and feed them, Powys, and my thanks for doing this. Tomorrow we will offer them the choice of staying here or coming with us to Connlyn's lands. I imagine most of them will want to come with us, since their men are all dead, but some of them might have families nearby and might choose to go to them. In the meantime, feed them and find some place for them to sleep without being bothered by our men." I noticed that his frown was still in place. "What? Have you something more to tell me?"

"Aye, I do. There are others, found in another room, above the stairs. An elder woman—rich, judging by her clothes and where she was being kept—and a clutch of younger serving women."

That caught me off guard. "A wealthy woman? You mean a woman of high birth, here? Who is she?"

Powys shrugged, an eloquent gesture. "High birth? What's that? As for her name, your guess will be as sound as mine. She speaks a tongue I've never heard. But she is old and frail … agued and not too strong, save for her tongue. That bites like a new rasp, and you don't need to know what she is saying to know that."

"Have her brought to me, Powys." My mind was racing, wondering who this could be, but I was unprepared for Powys's answer.

"Nah," he grunted. "I can't do that. I'd have to carry her and she would claw me to death along the way. Best you come to her."

He meant it, I could see, and I sighed and turned to where Bors waited. "Give me my helmet, Bors. I must go and find out what is going on here. Wait for me. I will not be long gone. And send someone to fetch the interpreter, Lanar. I may have need of him again."

3

"Magister! Stand to!" The warning shout was followed immediately by a stamping of booted feet and the rattle of weaponry as the guards at the top of the stairs became aware of my approach and jumped to formal parade stance. I kept my face expressionless as I climbed the last few steps and stopped, facing them, my helmet cradled in the crook of my left elbow. Beside me, Powys stopped, too, and I ignored him as I ran my eyes over the guards, knowing well that his head was half turned towards me, his right eyebrow quirked in the half-scornful, half-evaluating mannerism I had come to know and accept over the past few years.

The reason for my refusal to look at him was a personal one, born of my own insecurity because I had not yet grown accustomed to being addressed as Magister. It was a title I had extended to every leader and teacher I had ever admired, and the thought of having it applied to me was vaguely discomfiting, making me wonder every time I heard it how people could be so blind that they could not see how young and unqualified I was for such a title and ranking. The sole exception to this rule was my squire, Bors, who was genuinely uncomfortable with calling me anything else and whose junior position enabled me to accept his deference. Apart from that, however, within the privacy of my own mind I was yet a student, learning every day and in every area of my endeavors, and I had far to go, I knew, before I might accept the title uttered by so many voices older and more experienced than my own. In Powys's case, moreover, I suspected that he knew the truth of things only too well, and kept that wee half smile of his in acknowledgment of his own tacit assessment of my abilities. I cleared my throat, trying to empty my mind of the thought, and went into my inspection persona.

The guards looked magnificent, and deserved my acknowledgment as their commanding general, irrespective of my discomfort with their regard for me. They were impeccable, wearing the standard uniform of my infantry troops: heavy black knee-high boots of highly glossed sandaled leather with thick, iron-studded soles; knitted woolen leggings beneath the boots, covering their feet and calves and keeping them warm; snowy woolen tunics that reached to their knees and were worn beneath traditional Roman legionary armor of layered and shaped iron plates; and armored kilt straps made for them by our own smiths in Camulod. They carried long spears and light, strong shields, and sheathed swords and daggers hung from the simple black leather belts around their waists. They were identically helmed, in the Roman fashion that had barely changed in a thousand years, and each wore a white cloak bearing the badge of his rank if he yet owned a rank. Four of these men wore no badges, each of them indistinguishable from his mates, and the decurion in charge carried a single miniature red dragon sewn on the left breast of his cloak.

I returned their crisp salute and told them to stand at ease, my ears already adjusting to the sounds of whispers and hurried movement behind the double door that stood partially open at their backs, and when a stillness signaled that my audience within was waiting and prepared, I nodded again, this time to the decurion, whose name, I remembered with amusement, was Plato. But before I could move, I heard footsteps on the stair behind me and turned to see the man Lanar approaching.

He was a strange fellow, this Lanar, small and unprepossessing in his appearance, slightly hunched of back and walking with a pronounced limp, but I knew something of his history and did not let his strange posture affect me. He was a former cleric who had spent many years as a prisoner and slave of the Saxon invaders in the east, Connlyn had told me, and they had abused him sorely, breaking his bones and leaving him to heal himself. In consequence he hated Saxons with a vitriolic fire, but he spoke a number of their languages with great fluency and had been educated in Latin prior to his capture by the heathens. I found him erudite and amusing, with a wry sense of humor and a well-developed sense of his own failings. There was nothing pompous or pretentious about him and I had found it easy to like the man. When Connlyn had recommended him to me as being potentially useful in any dealings I might have with the Saxon raiders, I had accepted him immediately and had arranged with Dynas the quartermaster to supply him with new clothing to replace the rags he had been wearing. Now he stepped confidently towards me, smiling and saluting me in the style he had observed my troopers use.

"You have need of me, Lord Clothar?" His Latin was rippling and flawless.

"I may have, my friend. We have some well-born women here, I am told, and I have not yet met them, so I may require your skills. Then again, however, I may not. That will depend upon whatever tongue they speak, so if you will wait here, I shall call upon you within moments. And if I do not do so within a sensible time, you will know that I can converse with them without need of translation."

"I understand, my lord."

I nodded in thanks to him and stepped forward into the room that held the women, noticing that Powys remained behind, closing the doors at my back with unexpected courtesy, whether in consideration of me or the ladies inside, I knew not.

"And who might you be? Another bandit, no doubt."

The woman who spoke the words was regal. The word occurred to me immediately upon my setting eyes on her. She stood against the wall ahead of me, in the shadows on the far side of the imperfectly lighted room, six women drawn up in front of her in such a way that I could not see her clearly at a single glance. But she was tall, and there was no questioning her *dignitas*. She held her head high and proudly, as though she were looking down the length of her nose at me. Such was her presence that I looked at none of her companions, intent only upon seeing her clearly. Powys had said she was old and frail, but nothing that I had seen or heard to this point struck me as being accurate in either case. Perhaps, I thought, the woman speaking was an impostor, one of the other women set to disarm my suspicions and conceal the other's real identity. But then I realized that I would recognize the oldest woman immediately and I looked from face to face, seeing that all of them were undoubtedly too young to be thought old in the sense I was seeking.

"Well, man? Have you no tongue?"

The words were in flowing Latin, and the tone of voice was even more imperious than before. I returned my gaze to the speaker and bowed from the waist, as deeply as I could wearing full armor.

"Pardon me, Lady. My name is Clothar. Clothar of Ganis, born in the Frankish lands across the Narrow Seas from Britain. But I am known today as Seur Clothar of Camulod, and I am here today in the stead of Arthur Pendragon, King of the Pendragon Federation and Riothamus, High King of All Britain."

"What kind of foolery is that? Britain has no high king." The voice was withering, its contempt undisguised, and I felt my back stiffening, goaded immediately to think that this woman was indeed a gimlet-tongued shrew, as Powys had opined. But I restrained my urge to snap at her ill-natured tone and contented myself with correcting her gravely and clearly.

"Ah, Lady, but it does, and that high king is Arthur Pendragon, duly proclaimed and crowned with the corona of the Riothamus by the assembled Christian bishops of Britain, and acknowledged by a growing multitude of regional kings and rulers throughout the land. May I be permitted to ask your name?"

"My name is no concern of yours, just as your master's pretensions are none of mine. All you need to know is that I am a sister to a neighboring king, Connlyn of Southwall, and I was taken captive on my way to visit him at his insistence."

"At his insistence? Then being so insistent, did he not send an escort to see to your safety on the road?"

Her entire body seemed to stiffen and grow taller as she reared up, radiating outrage. "Curb your insolence, fellow, for I'll have none of it. How dare you speak to me in such a tone? And who are you to make such presumptuous insinuations?"

Stung again by her unrelenting hostility, I snapped back at her in my best parade voice. "I presume nothing, Lady. You came at your brother's summons, by your own admission, and you are here, a captive hostage, being held for ransom. I merely wondered how that could have happened."

My response seemed to give her pause, because she fell silent for a moment, and when she spoke again her voice was measurably less offensive, if no less haughty.

"My brother was, and is, unaware of my arrival," she said. "He and I have not met for many years, but he sent messengers to find me, bearing word that he has matters of great import to share with me. The men evinced enough urgency to convince me, eventually and against my better judgment, to come south to meet with Connlyn. I brought an escort of my own, but we were waylaid by the vermin belonging to the creature Ushmar and my men were outnumbered and overrun. My women and I were brought here, to await the payment of a ransom before being killed."

I frowned. "Before—? That makes no sense … If the ransom were paid, why would—?"

She interrupted me as though I were a simpleton. "Ushmar fears Connlyn, and so he could not let me live, even were the ransom paid. He was to deal with Connlyn through others, intermediaries, keeping his own identity unknown to Connlyn. He would never risk being discovered as the abductor, and therefore the only course open to him would be to kill me and my women as soon as he had no further use for me."

"Further use? Such as what?"

"Having me send witnessed word to my brother ... or sending a fresh-cut finger bearing one of my rings, to demonstrate that I was still alive. I could think of a dozen uses he might find for me during his negotiations, but they are all beside the point, since he is dead now and I am alive.

"Then the others came today, the Saxons, and you came after them, hard on their heels. We may be captives, but we are neither deaf nor blind. You will free us now from our captivity and deliver us to my brother in Southwall."

I stood blinking at her, bemused by her arrogance and by her high-handedness. Queenly she was, beyond dispute. But pleasant she was not. I fought to keep my voice level and courteous.

"You are correct, Lady," I answered, "I will. But only because we will be going that way tomorrow. I know your brother. I was a guest in his house when word came to us of this raiding party of Saxons, and we came at the forced march to stop them. I spoke long with Connlyn during my time with him, however, and he said nothing to me of expecting you, or of your failure to arrive. He made no mention of any sister, or of an abduction, let alone a demand for ransom."

"That is because he knew of none of them." The voice remained clipped and aloof, unmoved by my knowledge of her brother. "Ushmar took us less than a week ago and he had not yet found time to put his foul plan into effect. As for my brother Connlyn, he knows nothing of my coming. I sent his envoys home with a refusal and only after they were gone, months ago, did I change my mind."

I was incredulous, and said so with a question. "But ... Pardon me, Lady, but this makes no sense to me. Why would you not inform him of your coming? Surely you could have sent riders on ahead to warn him you were on your way through dangerous territories? That seems like simple common sense, if nothing else."

A long pause followed my outburst, and then, somewhat to my alarm, the woman stepped away from the wall at her back and made her way slowly towards me, seeming to glide between her women, who immediately moved aside and seated themselves on the long bench along one wall. Although I could see seven piles of bedding on the floor to my left, there was only one chair in the entire room, a plain, ungainly thing of hand-hewed wood, and I had not the slightest doubt the lady, whoever she might be, would have long since appropriated it for her own use.

As she came closer, I began to see that she was indeed far older than my previous distant view of her had revealed. She was in fact far advanced in age, her hands betraying her even if nothing else might. They were thin of skin, spotted and slightly palsied, their individual bones clearly defined, and the phalanges of her fingers reminded me of the sections on my bamboo lance shafts. She was old indeed, although I would not have been able to guess at her years. Her face, too, was gaunt and deeply lined, but flashing eyes and high cheekbones gave evidence even to my youthful gaze that she must once have been a handsome beauty. She held her head high as she walked, and her neck, despite being wrapped in an obscuring silken veil that also covered her hair, was long and slender. Her eyes were a pale and faded blue but still lovely, sparkling with their own inner fire, their whites only slightly dimmed by long years of looking out on life. She saw me taking stock of her and stopped abruptly, drawing herself up even straighter than before, but then she came on until less than an arm's length separated us.

"Carrein," she said, in a voice completely different from the one she had been using, "bring me my staff."

One of the women against the wall rose up immediately, took a long staff from where it had been leaning in a corner and brought it directly to her mistress. It was thick as the base of my thumb and taller than the lady was, but she took it effortlessly and held it with ease in her bony, fragile-looking hand. I stared at the thing, never having seen its like before. It was bark-clad, but the covering was smooth and polished and clearly of great age. The bottom tip seemed to be encased in bone, and the upper end had been seamlessly inserted into a broad, curved and deeply hooked handle of some kind of horn that was carved into fantastical shapes and patterns. She saw me looking at it, and when she spoke again it was in the placid but imperious voice she had used to address the woman Carrein.

"It is called a cruik," she said. "Our shepherds use it to hold and manage sheep." And then, unbelievably, she reached out with it and placed the hooked end about the back of my neck, which was too thick to permit her to catch me completely. "The cruik itself is used to hook the sheep by the neck and hold them still for other ministrations, and it is generally a plain working tool made from the horn of a ram, boiled to softness and then shaped to size. Mine is a special one, since I am queen, and therefore it is carved for my pleasure."

I did not know what to do about the hook around my neck, and by the expression on her face I knew she was enjoying my uncertainty, but then she gently pulled my head down to where she could speak softly to me.

"I may have misjudged you when you first came in. You appear to be a reasonable young man, well bred and well intentioned, now that I see you near. My old eyes are not as keen as they used to be in seeing things from afar." She paused, and then continued in the same mild voice. "I did not send word of my coming to my brother because he and I have never been close, and there was never any familial love between the two of us. The truth is, I am not, and have never been, disposed to trust him fully. He has always been self-serving and ambitious, to the detriment of everyone around him, be they family or strangers. And so I thought it better to arrive in his domain unannounced. That way, I thought, he could have no time to prepare any … special arrangements for my arrival.

"Oh, he would not harm me," she said quickly, seeing the alarm in my eyes caused by her last words. "Nothing like that would ever cross my mind, or his. I have no fears for my safety at his hands. But knowing him, I cannot quite believe he would not use me to his own ends and solely for his benefit. Hence my unwillingness to give him time to prepare whatever he might have in mind. Do you understand what I am telling you, young man?"

I nodded awkwardly, and she released me, allowing me to straighten my back as she lowered the bony tip of her staff to the floor. I fingered my neck as though still feeling the closeness of her cruik and managed to summon up half a smile.

"What would you have of me, then, my lady?"

"Nothing, Magister, other than safe conduct to my brother's house. The guards I brought south with me are all dead now, and all my possessions taken by that loathsome king."

"Then they must all still be here somewhere, my lady. As you yourself have said, Ushmar has had neither time nor opportunity to dispose of anything in the week since he captured you. I have my men searching the entire fort now, and everything they unearth will be laid out for my inspection come morning. You may come with me, if you so wish, and reclaim anything of yours you may identify."

She bowed her head slightly. "Thank you, that is most generous of you." She glanced away to where her waiting women sat, their eyes downcast to give us privacy. "My women have eaten nothing since noon today. Think you your men could find them a bite of something?"

"Of course. There is food in the kitchens, still hot from before we arrived. I will have some brought up to you immediately. And I will find you all some more suitable place to sleep."

She looked away again, towards the piles of bedding. "No, there is no need of that. It is too late and we are here for only one more night. We will make do as we have these past nights, if you will but see fit to leave your guards outside our door. That will be a pleasant change, enabling us to sleep the better for knowing they are there."

"They will remain, my lady, and you may sleep sound. Now, if you will pardon me, I shall go and make arrangements for some food for you. Sleep well, and I will come for you in the morning." I hesitated, then indicated the piles of bedding. "Is that bedding your own?"

"Do you mean did we bring it with us? Gods, no! It was ... supplied for us, and will suffice for tonight, but we will not be taking it with us when we leave. How far is it to my brother's place?"

"Not far. We should be there by nightfall on the day after tomorrow, all being well. In the meantime, we will issue you with cots and clean bedding from our own stores. And before you ask it of me, I will send your brother no hint that you are traveling with us."

She smiled for the first time and rapped me lightly on the shoulder with her cruik. "Excellent. You have impressed me. What did you say your name was?"

"Clothar of Ganis, my lady."

"Ah, yes, and that is in Gaul?"

"It is, my lady."

"You are far from home, young Lord Clothar. Sleep well."

4

I did not sleep well, which was unusual for me. I had difficulty sleeping at all, in fact. Troubled by the need to think about the coming morning, I lay awake most of the night, dozing only intermittently, and I was wide awake when Bors came to my room as ordered, long before dawn. I saw the approaching light of the candle he carried, one hand cupped around the flame as he eased into my room quietly, lest he disturb my rest before he needed to.

"I'm awake. No need to creep about," I told him, startling him into almost dropping the candle.

I threw back my blanket and rousted myself out of my cot, swinging my feet to the chilled stone floor and fumbling for the woolen stockings that I had foolishly and peevishly discarded during my restless night. They were my one Frankish concession to the bone-chilling, clinging damp of the long British nights, when my feet seemed at times to turn to lifeless lumps of ice. "How long till dawn?"

"An hour, Magister, as you requested. Seur Tristan will be here soon, as will Powys, Anacis, Morgan and the man Lanar." Bors finished lighting the last of the candles in the room and returned quickly to the door, where he stooped to retrieve the ewer of hot water he had left outside before entering.

"When did you tell them to be here?"

"At first light, Magister."

"No, I mean when did you pass the word to them?"

His surprise at being asked such a question was evident on his face. "Last night, Magister, as soon as you retired."

"Have you had any sleep?"

"Enough, Magister."

"I doubt that," I said. "Here, give me that and prepare my Germanus armor." I took the ewer from him, enjoying the heat of it and uncommonly aware of the predawn coldness in the room, and as I poured the steaming water into my basin and began to wash the sleep from my face, I heard him moving about behind me, opening the doors of my parade armor case and removing the magnificent equipment given me years earlier by my old mentor. It fitted me perfectly nowadays, and I had brought it with me on this campaign solely to wear it in Connlyn's presence, to remind him of whom I stood for and the power I represented in visiting him, but the previous night I had decided to wear it again today, to create the same impression upon these Saxons before releasing them. By the time I finished drying myself, Bors had spread a fresh suit of clothing— tunic, underwear and knee-length breeches—on my bed and was buffing my brown boots again, though they had known no speck of dust in weeks.

I dressed quickly, enjoying the feel of the fresh, clean clothing, and as I fastened a narrow belt about my waist and bloused my tunic over it to bring the hemline to the proper height above my knees, Bors stood ready with my almost weightless armored corselet, ready to assist me with the underarm buckles that were difficult to reach. Once it was all in place and adjusted to our mutual satisfaction he held up the white cloak that completed the costume, its rear and shoulders heavily worked in embroidered gold wire depicting the crest of the House of Germanus and the imperial arms of Rome, and I stepped into it, shrugging my shoulders until it hung comfortably and then leaving it to Bors to drape the gorgeous garment to best effect. When he had done, he stepped back and looked at me critically, his eyes missing no single detail of my appearance. By the time he nodded, finally, in approval, I was smiling at him.

"You know why I am wearing this today, don't you?"

His eyes were still studying his work, and he dropped to one knee to straighten a buckle on my ceremonial greaves. "Of course, Magister. To show the Saxons what they are dealing with: the power and the skills."

"The wealth, you mean."

"No, Lord, much more than that." He finished with the buckle and stepped back, one critical eyebrow still raised as he looked me over yet one last time. "The power is what matters. The power in having the skills and the ability and the craftsmen to manufacture armor like this, garments like that cloak and weapons such as those you carry. Wealth can purchase such things, but the ability to create them is what makes the difference between thinking men and savages."

I looked at my young squire in astonishment—he was no more than two years my junior, but that meant nothing—and then I smiled inwardly, delighted by the maturity of his analysis and recalling several other times when he had amazed me by his insight.

"Hmm. That had not occurred to me, but you are absolutely right. Enough now of this fussing. I am as well turned out as I could be. Go you now and find the others and bring them here if they are ready. It is early yet, but I am set to make a start."

"Aye, Magister." He left without another glance at me.

Young Bors had come a long, long way since first we had arrived in Britain, fresh from Gaul. Then he had been a raw recruit, willing enough but more than a little rebellious. He had also been inclined to feel sorry for himself over the tribulations life had already thrown at him. He was resentful of authority and newly out of school, in need of harsh training and discipline, and committed to my personal care by Tiberias Cato and by Germanus himself. Faced with the trust entailed therein, however, he had quickly lost all semblance of the surly lout he had been pretending to become, and in the five years that had since elapsed, he had been eager to absorb everything Perceval, Tristan and I could teach him. In the doing of that, he had become a fine man while remaining unaware of how he had changed. He did not know it yet, but I had recommended to Arthur that he be included in the next batch of admissions to our newfound Order of Knights Companion to the King, and I was looking forward with pleasure to telling him about his coming elevation when the time was right. By the end of this year, Squire Bors would be Seur Bors, blessed and exalted by the regal salute of having the King's own sword, Excalibur, formally laid upon his shoulders, his status, responsibilities and rank ratified and affirmed for all to see by the silver spurs he would wear proudly, the public acclamation of his knighthood.

I was standing by an open window, watching the lightening sky and thanking God for holding back the rain for one more day when Bors returned a short time later, leading Anacis and Morgan, my two infantry commanders, and followed closely by Powys and Lanar. Tristan, who held overall command of my two cavalry squadrons, arrived mere moments later, apologizing for his tardiness. I glanced back to the window, where the glowing dawn now exposed a cloudless sky. This morning's work, as I now envisioned it, would be pure dramatics, a spectacle worthy of the hippodrome. But it was necessary, and would have been impossible to do properly in the pouring rain of the previous few weeks.

I stepped away from the window and explained the day's agenda to them in detail, satisfying their understandable curiosity about the morning's unusual events by giving them a short explanation of my reasons for what would be done and then quizzing each of them in turn to be sure they really knew what I required of them. I then dismissed them to make their own arrangements and issue their own necessary orders while I turned my attention to a hot porridge of ground oats that Bors had brought for me. It was sweetened with fresh, thick cream and liquid honey, and on the first delicious bite I discovered I was ravenous.

As soon as I had eaten, I donned my helmet and made my way to the battlements overlooking the eastern approach to the fort, intercepting a passing soldier as I went and telling him to send Dynas, my quartermaster, to meet me on the walls.

Dynas was one of my greatest assets, a natural clerk and records keeper. Barely literate in the accepted sense of the word, he nevertheless had an uncanny affinity for lists and numbers and a merchant banker's understanding of accounts and inventories; all this despite the fact that he had risen through the ranks of our catering staff from being a pot boy at the age of nine and had never known a day of formal schooling. Not a thing within his far-reaching administrative realm escaped his notice. He could tally our entire resources on a weekly basis and carry every scrap of the information that was entailed in his mind, ready for regurgitation upon demand without a moment's hesitation. He knew everything that could be known about our disposable assets in men, horses, equipment, armor and weapons, as well as in transportation, remounts, saddlery and tack, commissary stores and all the general sundry and ancillary goods in our possession. And he was as trustworthy and honest as a man could be, despite holding a position in which he could have enriched himself. Dynas was that greatest and most fabulous of treasures, a pearl beyond price, and I cherished and honored him by treating him as a friend and equal, which made him unique in the eyes of his peers and his subordinates.

I heard him clumping towards me in his trooper's boots as I stood surveying the scene beyond the walls, and I held up my hand to stay him. His footsteps slowed, but he came right up to my side and leaned forward to see what I was looking at, bracing his hands against the top of the wall.

"You're looking very lordly in all your finery this morning, Master Frank. What's going on?" He seldom called me Magister or any other title, save on formal occasions.

"Our prisoners. We'll be treating them to a display of Camulod's power."

Dynas said nothing to that, content to watch and try to figure out for himself what was happening. The prisoners were being led out of the eastern gate in two files, each man attached to his neighbors behind and in front by a long line that had been threaded between their bound wrists. They walked awkwardly because of the ropes, but without difficulty, holding their bound arms out to one side and flanked by files of armed guards who shepherded them through the gates and down the gentle grassy slope to where a parade ground and training area had been flattened out hundreds of years before. The surface was grass-grown now, but in Rome's time, no more than fifty years earlier, it would have been bare, hard-beaten earth, in use every day. The downwards slope from the east gate ended on a grass-covered ramp that had once been a reviewing stand, and there, according to my instructions, the guards would seat them in a row, facing the parade ground.

"We found a lady being held here. She will be returning with us to Connlyn's court. She is his sister, but I don't know her name. Just call her 'my lady' when you speak to her. Ushmar, the king who died here yesterday, abducted her and stole all her possessions. I think we'll find they are all still here. Did Powys deliver all the stuff his men found last night when they searched the place?"

He nodded. "Aye. It's all laid out in the great hall waiting for you."

"No time for that. Is there anything there worth keeping?"

"In your eyes or in mine? There's much of worth, and there are treasures, too. Booty. This whoreson was a hardworking thief. He could never have amassed so much in precious metals and jewels otherwise, living in a place like this."

I grinned at him. "You'll have no argument from me on that. Sift what we've found and pick out whatever you think would be of value to us in Camulod, but before you do, take the lady to where you've laid everything out and allow her to take back whatever she lays claim to. We are not thieves, and some of those goods are hers. And even if she cheats, we'll not be much the poorer for it.

"I'll also need you to take charge of everything we can find here that has wheels. One cart, at least, to carry the weapons belonging to these people below. I promised they would have them back when we release them."

Dynas turned his head to see if I was twitting him. "That's generous," he said. "Some might even say it was stupid."

"Some can say whatever they like, my friend. These are important messengers for Camulod's affairs. That's why we'll be presenting a show for them today. I want these men to take the story home with them … and if I turn them loose without weapons, they won't survive. The local folk around here have no great love for them.

"A few more things: the lady has five serving women with her, which means we have six high-born women to transport. She is old, and they can hardly be expected to walk at our speed, so we'll need carriages for them. I'll be surprised if their own vehicles are not found safe in one of Ushmar's buildings. If so, they'll be detailed in your report from whomever Powys assigned to do the tallying. If they are not, you will have to improvise.

"And last of all we have a number of women and children taken as slaves by the Saxons. Some of those may have kin nearby and wish to stay with them, but all their men are dead and so it's reasonable to assume that half of them at least will have nowhere safe to go, and so we'll take them with us to Connlyn's lands. His people will be glad of them. Hard-worked men can always find places for women in their lives. But that means more transportation for you to supply. No need for it to be luxurious, in any of these instances. Farm carts will do if you can find nothing finer. So be it they have wheels that revolve." I reviewed my mental list of points. "I think that's all. Any questions?"

"What's happening with the door there?"

I looked down to where a squad of infantry surrounded a sturdy hand cart, manhandling it down the slope behind the prisoners and struggling simultaneously to restrain its weight and to balance the enormous ancient door of solid oak that rested upon it. I had seen the door the previous night, sagging from a broken hinge in the open entrance to the *praesidium,* the military headquarters building of the old fort. Now I grinned as I became aware of Dynas watching me.

"I have a use for it. You'll see."

"Right. Now, about the booty. Do you mind if I keep the very finest jewels for myself? I have a weakness for glittering stones."

I smiled at him. "You can have one—your own choice, so be it you show it to me to protect yourself against any accusations of theft. My gift to you. And if you find any clay or wooden ones, you can have all of those as well. Now I have to prepare. Go you and earn your bread."

He nodded, smiling slightly, then marched away without another word, moving as though he had been born and raised on a parade ground. I watched him go with a smile of my own. I had no slightest expectation that he would claim a single jewel for himself, but if he did, I had already given him my blessing.

5

The spectacle that unfolded less than an hour later on the overgrown parade ground outside the fort of Luguvallium verified my hippodrome analogy. I had only twice been in a hippodrome, as a boy in Germanus's city of Auxerre, but I could still recall the air of pomp and unreality that had marked the dramatic spectacle presented there, and it seemed to me that these events today were little different.

I knew, for instance, that the decurion in charge of our prisoners had demanded that they produce their smallest man, and that the man in question had been selected previously by our own guards and positioned deliberately at the very end of his file, so that his tethers could be undone quickly and without difficulty.

I had not been present at the time, but my orders had been precise and I could visualize the uncertainty and apprehension among the captives as the terrified fellow was led forth and made to lie flat on the enormous door from the praesidium. The thing was the height of two men, and he had been placed with the midpoint of his shoulders precisely on the center line and the top of his head no more than three handspans, a foot and a half, from the upper edge of the door. Another of my men had then come forward, this one a carpenter from the wagon master's crew, and had traced the supine man's outline roughly with a cake of carpenter's chalk, then drawn a line beneath the fellow's feet, the same distance from his soles as his head was from the top of the door, before releasing him to rejoin his fellow prisoners.

The carpenter had then laid down his chalk and proceeded to apply a coat of whitewash to the entire door, from the baseline he had drawn, up to the top, stopping only at the edges of the outline of the lying man so that when he had done, the prisoner's shape stood out black against its broad, white background.

The next step in the spectacle had been taken by a squad of men with mattocks and shovels, who had quickly dug a deep, narrow pit in the ground at the left end of the row of watching, now-snickering prisoners and sunk the bottom end of the painted door into the hole, anchoring it there firmly by filling in the trench. The door now stood upright, the shape at its center visible to all the prisoners.

As soon as this scene was set, I nodded to the four trumpeters watching me, and as the brazen sound of their horns rose on the air, I heard voices shouting commands behind me, followed immediately by the sounds of marching feet as our two infantry formations, a hundred men to each, moving in columns eight men wide and accompanied by their officers, tramped out of the fort through the east gate, their hobnailed boots rising and crashing down in unison as the drummers marched ahead of them, sounding the cadence.

As the last rank of marching men went through the gates, I gave the signal for the cavalry to ride out through the north gate in a long column, two riders abreast, where they would swing around eastward and back to the west in a wide three-quarter circle to face the assembled prisoners, spreading out into a solid, disciplined line of horseflesh and armored troopers as they advanced. Powys and his fifty bowmen went out through the east gate at the same time, making their way in ranks of five down to the right of the seated prisoners until they reached the end of the parade ground opposite the standing door and two hundred paces from it, where they formed up in a block five men wide and ten deep.

One last glance around showed me that Dynas and his people were hard at work, marshaling our train of vehicles and preparing to evacuate the fort. I waved to Dynas himself, who stood watching us, then nodded to Bors and Lanar to accompany me, the former bearing my standard, and kicked my mount forward to overtake the marching bowmen, placing myself at their head until we reached the parade ground, where I turned away and rode, followed by my two companions, until I reached the center of the seated line of men and swung my horse to face them. The other two ranged their horses on either side of me, Bors on my right. I had timed my arrival perfectly. Tristan and his cavalry came to a halt fifty paces behind me, and the infantry had already regrouped themselves smartly into a three-sided formation, flanking the prisoners with fifty men on either side and a hundred more lined up two men deep behind the captives' backs. There was not a sound to be heard as I sat gazing at the prisoners, most of whom looked decidedly apprehensive, twisting backwards against their bonds to eye the silent ranks behind them, then turning back to me, plainly wondering how and when I would give the order to slaughter them. I gave them time to absorb every detail of my appearance, and then I removed my helmet and spoke, while Lanar translated my words fluently.

"Some of you will have convinced yourselves by now that what happened to you last night was mere bad fortune, that you could have won against us had the fates given you but a hint of warning of our coming. You are wrong. Look about you as you did last night, after the fighting. Then you saw bowmen ranged along your walls and up among the rafters, and your leaders were already dead, with more than a score of your comrades. But you saw few of the soldiers who surround you now, and fewer horsemen, for they remained outside the hall, unneeded, while we took you.

"Unneeded, I said. But they were there, and ready." I raised my hand in a prearranged signal, and the horsemen behind me began to move in a tightly disciplined pattern that was part of our standard training technique in Camulod. None of the men seated on the bank knew they were watching a simple drill, however, and their jaws dropped as our mounted troopers, moving inward at a tight-reined walk in two arcs from a six-man group that formed an immobile center, crossed and recrossed their ranks in perfect symmetry, wheeling and weaving among themselves with never a word being uttered and never a horse touching or obstructing another while the six men who had remained at the rear rode forward slowly side by side through the moving mass until they were within a few paces of where I sat, at which point they split and arced away again, back whence they had come, followed by the others, still wheeling and veering through one another's ranks until they had all returned to their original positions and again sat facing their audience. It was a daunting display of rigid discipline; doubly so, I knew, to this fierce audience who had never known such constraints.

One of my officers, standing behind the prisoners, nodded to me when the cavalry line was still again, and without looking rearward I kneed my mount and led Bors and Lanar to where the bowmen stood at the side of the field. And then my horsemen lowered their spears and charged forward, bending over their horses' necks and developing seemingly unstoppable momentum as they came. The prisoners, convinced they were about to die, began to try to scramble to their feet, crying out and fighting their bonds. But at the precise moment when one more pace would have brought both horses and troopers crashing into the struggling men, Tristan raised his arm in the awaited signal and the entire line came crashing to a halt, a solid wall of muscular horseflesh and spear-bearing armored men within two paces of the edge of the field.

For long moments they remained there, as steam rose from their horses in the morning air and some of the cowering men in front of them quaked in terror. Then they wheeled their mounts, again in concert, beginning from both ends of their line, and rode back to their starting point. I spurred my horse forward immediately, alone this time, but wheeled away from the watching line before turning to face them again. I had no need to speak this time; no need for a translator. I simply raised my hand and Powys growled an order to his bowmen.

They came forward at the run, five abreast and spacing their lines three strides apart, Powys behind them counting cadence, and when they had covered fifty paces the front rank stopped, nocked arrows to their bows and fired at the black shape on the door that was now a hundred paces distant. Then, not even looking to see the results of their shots, they broke immediately to their right, allowing the next rank behind to pass them. Ten times in succession this occurred, within the space of mere moments, until all fifty men had fired their shots and stood in reverse of their original, their front rank now at the rear. The effect produced was awe-inspiring even to me, who had seen this spectacle many times.

The door was made of ancient time-cured solid oak planking, six thumb widths thick from front to back, and many of the arrows had penetrated it completely, their points, and in some cases the entire arrowhead, protruding from the back of it. Now the prisoners were rousted to their feet and brought forward to see what had been wrought here. The black figure in the center of the door had taken the mass of hits in the chest and torso, the arrows that lodged there forming a solid-seeming, greatly splintered mass of shattered shafts and dangling strips of fletching. Four shafts only of the fifty fired had missed the mark, and those had plainly been deflected, their points lodged at strange angles in the wood, outside the target's edges.

When I thought they had looked for long enough, I had them herded back to where they had been sitting and waved to Lanar to join me again.

"I promised you your lives and weapons, and you shall have them. But take back this word to those who await you: remain here in Britain, and you will know the wrath of Camulod." As Lanar repeated my words I turned away to face the decurion in charge of the guards and told him to have the prisoners ready to move out

within the hour, and then I rode back to the fort, accompanied by
my faithful Bors, to see how our evacuation was progressing.

6

"Seur Clothar." Tristan's quiet greeting as I reached him bore only
friendship, no hint of irony.

"Seur Tristan." I returned his smile.

"That was an impressive display this morning for our Saxon
guests. Think you it achieved what you were hoping? Will they be
impressed enough to tell their friends to stay away?"

I had ridden back all the way from the front of our procession,
now almost half a mile behind me, checking to see if everything was
as it should be, and had reined in my mount when I came level with
Tristan, who rode at the head of the rear guard. I grinned now,
turning my horse to ride in step with his before answering his question, knee to knee with him so that I could keep our words between
the two of us and safe from the listening ears of the ever curious. It
was the first opportunity either of us had had to speak with the other
since leaving Luguvallium three hours earlier, and I was glad to take
a pause, knowing that everything from front to rear in our long train
was moving smoothly.

"Who knows what will impress such men?" I said. "But I think
they might bear the word to others. I'd wager they took note and
will not be too swift to return to any place where they might meet
us face to face again. And I think they will warn their friends."

"They'd risk being scorned. Their kind fear nothing human."

"Aye. Well, they might learn to. As for the scorn, you're right.
Many of them will say nothing, trying by silence to deny how
soundly they were whipped. Men are always tempted to make more
of what they did than of what they failed to do. But there will be
some who pass the word to others that they trust, to whom they pay
respect."

"So you believe, despite all you know of these Saxons, that they will stay away from this day on?"

I looked sideways at him and grimaced. "Away from where? Men have to go somewhere. My fondest hope is that it be whence they came, but that is a hope, nothing more. And anyway, what 'all' do I know of these Saxons? These are the first of this particular kind that I have ever seen, so I know nothing of them. They are but men, Tristan, and Saxons but a word we use for them to mark their kind as enemies. They are of many races. Their only commonality is that they all come from beyond the seas.

"I'd be a fool to hope they stay away from this day on, but hesitation would be another matter. That I would welcome. I would have them hesitate before they come again so brashly, and when they come I would have them … apprehensive."

"Then they'll come in strength."

"Aye, and in strength we will meet them. That would be our good fortune and a blessing from God Himself. Their strength lies in numbers, they believe, and they have numbers. But they are scattered all along the eastern coasts and they need time to gather anything more than a few boatloads. Then, given that time, they will come back at us in strength. Look there." I pointed to where a hawk was stooping down the sky, dropping like a stone, its sudden fall from the high spaces signaling death for some small creature out there. Tristan had seen it, too, and we watched as it struck a fleeing bird, the impact sending feathers whirling in the air as hawk and prey fell to disappear behind the trees.

"That's what we need, Tris. That kind of strike. The Saxons are wrong in their belief of strength in numbers. A thousand of us is an army, horse and foot and bowmen; a thousand of them is but a thousand men and a few horses, all in a single mass that we can hit and crush, the way that hawk took his meal. But these few score we will release today know they have seen a new force brought against them, and they will talk, I promise you. And if that talk yields but a moment's pause or a day's grace before their next attack, our folk throughout these lands will have that much more time to live in peace before the fire, and before havoc comes again to visit them. I have to get back to the van. I've been gone too long. Is everything well back here?"

Tristan smiled, merely touching one open hand to his forehead, lips and breast before wafting it gently outward, bidding me go in peace with a gesture I knew he had learned from the nomads on the other side of the world, during his mercenary days.

I passed back down the length of the column towards the front at a canter, nodding to those whose eyes I happened to catch as I rode by and leaving the rest to watch my departing back. Half of the hundred infantrymen of the second division marched in ten ranks of five men each directly ahead of Tristan's rear guard, enough space between their rear rank and Tristan himself to allow the dust of their passage to disperse, had this been summer. In front of the rank and file, two of Morgan's four junior officers rode, turning in their saddles from time to time to check that all was well behind them. Ahead of them were our prisoners, in ranks of four now, still roped in files and shepherded by guards on both sides. Morgan himself, commander of the hundred, rode in front of the prisoners, at the head of the second half hundred with his two remaining officers, and ahead of him the enormous and cumbersome quartermaster and commissary wagons that were Dynas's responsibility lumbered like landlocked galleys.

The First Infantry division marched ahead of those, split into fifties as were their comrades of the Second, but in front of them moved a catchall assembly of vehicles, gleaned from the buildings of Luguvallium and carrying the surviving women and children of the abandoned fort. Next in line from those, the six former hostages rode in their own redeemed carriages, the only conveyances in the entire assembly that had been designed for comfort. Then came my own cavalry detachment, forming the vanguard. Powys and his bowmen were our scouts, as always, ranging the countryside ahead of us in a wide half circle, searching for danger.

"Master Clothar!" The summons, imperious and unmistakable, rang out as I cantered by the lady's carriage. I reined in and drew closer.

She was holding one flap of the leather curtains back with one hand, leaning forward to look at me. "I am aware you have concerns to see to. But if and when we stop tonight for rest, I would be obliged were you to spend some time with me, discussing certain matters."

"It will be my pleasure, Lady," I said, dipping my head. "We will be stopping soon to eat and rest for the night—a few more hours, no more. My scouts are already looking for a suitable spot, large enough and safe enough, with ample fresh running water for our needs."

7

That night, for the second consecutive time after meeting with Connlyn's nameless sister, I lay awake again for hours, unable to sleep because of my turbulent thoughts. Something was troubling me, and that I could not identify what it was annoyed me intensely and fed upon itself. Eventually, accepting that there would be no rest for me that night, I got up and went outside, dressed only in tunic, boots and leggings and wrapped in the blanket from my bedding. The guards greeted me quietly, surprised to see me astir without good reason in the middle of the night, for I was known as being able to sleep deeply anywhere and at any time once I had decided sleep was in order. I spoke to none of them, however, and went directly towards the nearest campfire, where I stirred the embers into flame and threw on fresh fuel. Then I went back and fetched my folding camp chair from my tent, and sat watching the new wood catch fire as I brought my mind to bear on my meeting with the old woman the previous evening.

It had been an interview rather than a conversation; I had no doubts at all about that. I remembered the point at which I had become aware—regrettably not soon enough—that I was being subtly and skillfully probed for information that I could not, would not divulge. The realization had shaken me. I was being exploited, I suddenly knew beyond argument, for purposes I could not even begin to guess. And yet, despite this new awareness of a need to be careful in what I was saying, I had nothing at all on which to base the vague but real sense of unease that now gnawed at me; only shapeless misgivings and the apprehensive tension that twisted gently but disquietingly in my gut.

It had been a long discussion, serene and courteous, the lady gracious and showing me no hint of the querulous distemper and disdain with which she had attempted to dismiss me at our first encounter, and in truth I had felt no discomfort of any kind at first, or for a long time afterwards, in answering the many questions she posed to me.

It was only towards dusk, with the evening shadows stretching long against the setting sun, that I sensed strongly that there was more to this nameless woman, more behind her curiosity, than had been apparent to my unsuspicious eye up to that point. She had asked me a specific question about the ceremony surrounding the King's bestowal of knighthood on my brethren of the order, and I had answered her as I would any other who asked such a question casually, describing the ritual solely at its most public and visible level and blithely claiming no knowledge of the inner workings of such things—a lie, but one with which I felt no discomfort. I professed mildly to be but a simple knight, elevated by the King himself for his own regal reasons. Some of those reasons, I opined as an explanation in afterthought, had apparently involved an impression he had formed of me as the result of several fortunate experiences I had had in battle.

That, I now recognized, was when I felt the first stirrings of alarm, because the lady clearly had no intention of accepting my demurral. I sensed it quickly from the slightly impatient way in which she turned aside my answer, almost brushing it away contemptuously as she rephrased what she had asked me before, making her question this time far more specific and more focused, insistently digging deeper to acquire information that I had no wish to share with her, nor with anyone else. I began to review the entire conversation that had gone before, wondering what I might have unwittingly disclosed.

We had found the night's camping spot within an hour of my having spoken to her earlier that afternoon, but almost two more hours elapsed before our camp was properly set up and settled to my satisfaction, the horses tethered and brushed down before being fed, and our legionaries' tents neatly arranged in Roman order. And by that time, in the ancient tradition of all such camps, the cooks had done their work and the aromas of roasted meat and fresh-baked bread had the saliva flowing in our mouths.

I ate with my officers as I always did, and then I wandered through the camp for a while as had become my habit, exchanging greetings with whoever caught my eye, and making myself available to any soldier who might seek me out, wishing to speak with me. Tonight there had been none of the latter, and I ended up making my way to the lady's quarters, as I had promised, where her serving women were busily cleaning away the remnants of their meal. As I approached, Lanar the translator was leaving, and we exchanged nods and smiles as we passed each other. And for the next hour and more the time passed most pleasantly for me.

Now, gazing into the watch fire's flames, I carefully went over the earliest stages of our encounter, looking for something, anything, on which to fasten a beginning for the strangeness, but there was nothing. The lady had bidden me be welcome—disarmingly so, since I had been more than half expecting the same aloof displeasure she had shown me the night before—and had called for one of her women to bring wine, laughing at the expression on my face and then explaining that there had been half a score of small amphorae of wondrous wine from Gaul hidden in bolts of cloth among her stolen stores, and that, miraculously, they had survived their brief captivity undetected. They were intended as a gift for her brother, but she had broached one of them this evening, to celebrate her deliverance, and was now delighted to share the joys with me, a Frank who would appreciate the beauty of the wine.

I did, too, despite my normal distaste, for this wine was magnificent, almost a royal purple in hue and smooth on the tongue as silken bedsheets must be on the body of a king.

We spoke of trivialities at first, the kind of small talk strangers always exchange with one another, but then she went on to tell me that Lanar had been telling her what little he knew of Camulod and its young king, Arthur Pendragon. She had been impressed by what the translator had told her, she said, and went on to apologize for her initial behavior at our first meeting, when she had disputed the existence of a Riothamus and sneered at the notion of a high king in such an unheard-of place as Camulod. In none of this, thinking back on it carefully, could I detect any hint of wrongness.

"Tell me about this king of yours, this Arthur," she had said, and then held up a warning hand. "But not, I beg you, about his prowess in war. I am prepared to accept that he is a paragon, else he would not be what he already is, but I truly have no interest in such things. My interest, as a woman, lies in the man himself … Does he have a wife?"

"No, my lady, he does not." I smiled at the thought. "Although not from lack of trying on the part of others. There are kings and kinglets all over Britain who would dearly love to see their daughters wed to him, and thus to Camulod, purely for the power such a marriage would entail. But Arthur has no wish to wed."

"No wish? How so? That seems … strange. Is he … unmanly?"

Now I laughed aloud, warmed gently by the wine. "You mean, does he prefer men to women, boys to girls? No, Lady, by the Holy Cross, there is nothing in Arthur Pendragon that could be thought unmanly in any sense of the word."

"Pendragon … Whence comes that name? It sounds strange."

Something clicked in the back of my mind at that, some flicker of awareness, but I ignored it.

"It is his family name, rooted in Cambria, a large mountainous region in the west of Britain."

"I know of Cambria, young man."

I nodded, accepting the mild rebuke. "There is an association of allied clans there, all of them called by different names, but paramount among them is Pendragon, and the clans now call themselves the Pendragon Federation. Arthur is their king and has been for years. And so his father was before him."

"And this father ..." Again the merest tic in some part of my mind, an awareness of something; a tone of voice, a fractional hesitation, something there. Again I dismissed the unformed thought as she continued, "What was he called?"

"Uther, my lady. Uther Pendragon. And his mother was Queen Ygraine of Cornwall."

She frowned, as though trying to understand. "This was Uther's wife, the Queen of Cornwall?"

"No, Lady. Not his wife. But she was Arthur's mother."

"I see ..." But it was plain from her tone that she did not.

"It is a long and complex tale, and I am not the one to tell it, my lady, since I was not yet born when those events occurred."

"Hmm. So why is your Arthur so unwilling to be wed?"

I remembered an evening when Arthur had told me something of the tale of his lost love, and I chose my next words with care, for no other reason than respect for his having confided in me.

"He had a true love once, when he was very young, and lost her. I imagine he is ... deeply unwilling to expose himself to such a thing again."

"What was her name, this woman? Who was she? Do you know?"

I shook my head. "I know only that she was young. It seems to me her name was Morag, and that she came from somewhere in the north, beyond the Wall, as you do."

"And the loss has soured him?"

I held up my palm. "Forgive me, my lady, but I know only what I was told on one occasion and that was little enough. It would be foolish and blameworthy of me to speculate."

We were silent for a time after that, before she began to question me about Camulod and the newly formed Order of Knights Companion, and innocuous as her questions were at first, I was surprised at the extent of her knowledge, aware that she could not have gained all of it from Lanar. By his own admission, Lanar had known little or nothing of Camulod before our arrival in Connlyn's stronghold. Whence, then, had she gained this information, I wondered. I had tried immediately, instinctively, to steer the conversation away from there, asking her yet again by what name I ought to call her in conversations such as this.

She looked at me strangely, plainly aware I wished to change the topic, then smiled a tiny smile, mysterious, it seemed to me. There had been a time when such a question from a young man might have held all kinds of connotations, she told me. But that time had been long decades earlier and now she was old and frail, with nothing about her—including her name—to incite the interest of any young man. I had been calling her "my lady" and she had found nothing lacking in that. Then, just as I was thinking she would say no more on the topic, she looked me in the eye and smiled the same smile again before telling me that I could think of her as Judith. It was the name she had taken upon her confirmation as a Christian. I was mildly surprised, for Judith was a Hebrew name. I recognized it from my studies at the Bishop's School. But I said nothing of that, and merely thanked her graciously for her confidence.

She immediately returned to questioning me about the knights and the ceremony surrounding their elevation to the order. Were they in any way considered heirs to Arthur? I thought that a strange question, but it was one that I felt free to answer openly with a flat denial. Arthur had yet no heir, I told her, and until recently had had no need of one, since the kingship of the Pendragon Federation was conferred by the acclaim of the clans and depended not on birth but on prowess. Only when he became Riothamus had the matter of succession become important, for there had never been a high king in living memory, had never before been such urgent need for one. Times and needs had changed, now that we were facing a rising tide of invasions. The prime function of the new Riothamus was to weld the teeming peoples of Britain into a single, effective fighting force that would repel the invaders. Before I left Camulod, I told her, there had been talk of appointing a successor to the King, should anything befall him, but the matter had been unresolved by the time I set out to come north.

She sat musing after hearing that, then nodded slowly. "So there might be another set in place already, ready to take the place of your young King ..."

It was not quite a question, but it set me wondering immediately why this woman would even remark upon such a thing. She had told me plainly at the outset that she held no interest in the military affairs of men, yet here she was, an hour later, openly considering the overtones attached to Arthur's untimely death, God forbid that such a disaster should be allowed to happen. What was going on? Why was she so curious about Camulod? I dismissed that thought as being misleading even as it occurred to me; everyone was curious about Camulod, I had discovered. But why was she so intent upon learning about the structure of the King's new order—a structure that did not yet exist in entirety, I reminded myself, since there had been but one ceremony to this point, the one in which I myself, along with Tristan and Perceval, Gareth and Sagramore, Gwin, Ghilly and Bedwyr, had been admitted as the Founding Brethren of the order.

I decided, then and there, to distance myself from this apparent interrogation and give myself time to explore, as much as I could, whatever was bothering me about this situation, and in order to do that, I knew I needed to be alone and away from the Lady Judith or whatever her true name might be. I finished the wine left in my cup and rose to my feet to leave with a show of reluctance, thanking my hostess for the wine and the pleasure of her company but pleading pressure of work and too little time in which to accommodate it, which was not entirely untrue, and within moments I was on my way back to my own quarters, having given her no cause, I believed, for any misgivings about my behavior.

Now, my eyes dazzled by the fierceness of the heart of the fire, I heard the familiar sounds behind me that signaled the end of a watch and the changing of the guard, but I did not look up until the old guard had departed and silence had settled again. Shortly afterwards, however, I heard the tread of boots approaching me and crunching to a halt behind my right shoulder, and I turned and looked up to where the night guard commander stood at attention, waiting for me to give him permission to speak. I had to squint my fire-blind eyes to see him clearly. His name was Lucius Quinto and he was very young, the scion of one of Camulod's oldest families and newly promoted to the rank of officer trainee. From what I had seen of him to this point, he seemed willing, industrious and conscientious.

"Yes, Lucius, what is it?"

"Your pardon, Magister, but one of the guards told me you have been sitting here for more than an hour. Do you need anything?"

"No. Couldn't sleep tonight, so I came outside to think … That is a commander's lot, you know. You'll find it out yourself, one day. Never enough time to think during duty hours."

He nodded. "Yes, Magister. Can I bring you anything? Water, or a flask of wine?"

"In the middle watches of the night? My thanks, lad, but no. Get you to bed. You don't hold command rank yet and you need your rest."

He saluted smartly and I watched him march away before I took my own good advice and rose and carried my stool back into my tent, then fell asleep upon my cot without being aware of lying down.

8

The next morning, after what seemed no longer than an eyeblink of sleep, my mind was more at rest. I was satisfied that my previous imaginings had been wild and willful, and so I determined to waste no more time fretting over any of it.

We struck camp at dawn and were soon on the road south again, and as soon as we were clear of Ushmar's former lands and not yet into Connlyn's I released my prisoners and returned their weapons to them as promised, confident that they would cause us no more trouble.

We reached Connlyn's stronghold the following day, and although he professed astonishment to see his sister among our small train—we had left the main body of our men a mile or so behind to make camp in the same place we had used before—his reaction rang false to me, and I had the distinct feeling he was willing no hint of what he really thought to show upon his face. He greeted us cordially and thanked us for escorting his sister, but offered no explanation for her presence in Ushmar's camp, nor for her journey southward from beyond the Wall. Puzzled, but reluctant to have him think I might wish to pry into his affairs, I made no comment other than to inform him that we would be leaving in the morning, to return to Camulod. He invited us to dine with him later, and so I decided to wait until then before delivering my report to him. There was no doubt in my mind that his sister would have her own version of the tale to tell him, and I resolved to match whatever I might have to say that night to the questions he would ask of me.

In the event, Connlyn had few questions about the Ushmar affair, protesting only that he was mightily relieved to know that we had unburdened him of the problem of the marauding Saxons. Listening to him, I might have believed that he was genuine in expressing his regrets over the death of his neighbor Ushmar. Knowing what I knew, however, I was hard pressed to conceal my dislike and anger when he proceeded to tell me a tale about Ushmar's having rescued the Lady Judith from bandits a few days before our arrival. The whole implication in what he said was that had we not arrived when we did, his sister would have been taken by Knut One-Eye and his men, with unspeakable consequences. That was true, but it was not the entire truth or even close to it, and I could not understand why he would evade the underlying truth when he had nothing at all to lose by acknowledging the whole of it. Instead, in suggesting by his silence that his former neighbor had been honorable and that his intention had been to return the lady safely to her brother, the man was insulting me, obviously supposing that I did not have the wit to discern his falsehood. Plainly, his sister had said nothing at all to him about having told me the truth of what happened, and that, too, was mystifying to me.

I found I had no taste for Connlyn's food after listening to his mouthings, and my companions were surprised when I rose early from the table and made my excuses, saying I needed to see to the disposition of the details of the morning's departure. My unexpected announcement meant that they must leave, too, but I found the idea of interrupting their dinner to be more easily digestible than Connlyn's food, or his transparent lies.

I had no smile for the Lady Judith as I took my farewell of her that night, and she had none for me. She gazed at me intently as I stood over her, and her face betrayed nothing noticeable to anyone else who might have been watching, but the merest flicker of her left eye and the set of her mouth left me in no doubt that she knew exactly why I was leaving, and when she inclined her head in acceptance of my explanation and extended her hand to me, I felt a message in the pressure of her fingers over my own.

"My gratitude is yours, Seur Clothar. Fare well upon your way south and be vigilant, aware of all you see and hear in your travels."

I strode from the hall wondering what she had meant by those last words.

When I returned to camp, I called for a general muster and announced to the assembled army that we would be returning directly home to Camulod in the morning, with no more diversions along our route. The men were jubilant, cheering me and obviously more than simply glad to be going home with not a drop of blood spilt during the campaign, and they broke camp with commendable alacrity and precision the next day, eager to move out even before the sun had risen.

I, however, had yet to make my formal farewell to Connlyn, and little as I wished to, I made my way back to his stronghold accompanied by a single squadron of troopers from Tristan's cavalry division as soon as I had given the remainder of my forces the order to move out. This was a task that would not take long, and I would happily have avoided it altogether had it not been for my responsibility as Arthur's official representative. I could not risk offending an ally by riding off without a word of explanation.

I left my mounted escort outside the gates and made my way to the large, ill-lit chamber where I knew I would find Connlyn conducting his morning affairs, but I was more than a little surprised to see him already in conversation with his sister as I approached, and I hesitated just outside the room. They were speaking a language unknown to me, and I assumed it must be some tongue from north of the Wall, but there was no mistaking the hostility in their confrontation.

As I stood there, almost hovering, just beyond their sight, reluctant to interrupt them, the Lady Judith snapped something that sounded full of angry contempt and turned on her heel to stalk stiffly away from her brother, her head held high. He watched her go, and he was plainly unused to having people treat him in such a manner, for it took him several heartbeats to respond. Then his voice cracked like a whip, repeating one word several times, singly and distinctly, amid a series of others. His sister ignored him and swept out through a side door without looking back, leaving him almost spitting with rage.

I knew I could not stand there another moment without risking being seen, and so I backed away cautiously for several steps, until I was sufficiently far away to move forward again, almost stamping my feet then to be sure that he would hear the approaching sounds of my boots ringing on the floor. This time I marched straight up to the doorway and addressed him, and he swung violently around to face me, obviously not having heard my arrival despite the noise I had made. Lines of fury were stamped deep between his brows and deeply etched on each side of his clamped, lipless mouth, and I had no doubt that had I been anyone else, he would have savaged me for daring to approach him. As it was, he had to struggle to control himself, while I gave no indication of seeing anything amiss.

I went through the formalities of confirming our departure and thanking him for his hospitality, and I informed him that I would be sure to deliver his fondest and most loyal regard to the Riothamus on my return to Camulod, and then I waited while he composed himself sufficiently to mouth the appropriate responses. I thanked him one last time for his gracious treatment, surprised to discover that the words did not stick in my craw, and asked him to extend my best wishes to his sister. When he nodded to me in acknowledgment, his face finally settling into its normal lines, I saluted him with the clenched fist of our Camulodian troopers, my knuckles rapping sharply against the left breast of my cuirass, then I bowed deeply, spun away and marched smartly out of his sight.

And there, as I turned the corner to approach the outer doors, I marched almost full tilt into Lanar. He was glad to see me, I could tell, for he had no time to dissemble, and I apologized for jostling him in my haste and told him we were leaving immediately and that my escort was awaiting me. He began to walk beside me, and for a few paces we exchanged affable farewells and trivialities. We reached the main door and were squinting in the bright light of the new day, and as I thanked him again for his excellent services, I recalled the word Connlyn had spat so repetitively.

"One last question, my friend," I said, "for of all the people here you are the man most likely to know. I came across a new word, and it is in my mind like a piece of verse, refusing to let me rest even though I know not what it means. I am well nigh certain that the word is *morgas*. What tongue is that, and if you know that, what does morgas mean?"

He gave me a look as if he suspected me of gulling him. "Morgas? It *means* nothing, my lord. It is a name, no more than that. Morgas is the name of Connlyn's sister."

That stopped me in mid-step, and in a flash I knew that I had nothing to fear about Lanar's discretion or his loyalty to Connlyn.

Lanar had been dressed in rags when Connlyn offered him to me, and there had been no discussion between the two men of any willingness on Lanar's part to be so used.

I reached into my scrip and withdrew the tiny leather bag that held the remaining eight gold coins of the ten I always carried with me against need. Lanar already had the other two in his possession.

"His sister. I did not know you knew the lady."

He shrugged. "I don't know her, Lord Clothar, I merely know of her, and little of that. But the lady is his sister and that is her name."

I reached out with the hand that held the little bag of gold coins and felt his fingers close over it, feeling the heft of it, and I saw the satisfaction in his eyes.

"Walk with me a little, Lanar, and tell me what little you know of her."

THREE

1

Camulod was different when we returned from that first visit to Connlyn and my encounter with his enigmatic sister. The guard turned out to welcome us as we approached, but both Arthur and Merlyn were missing, which was the first thing I discovered. Arthur's absence would be brief, the Captain of the Gate told me. He had gone hunting two days earlier and was expected to return at any moment. The Lord Merlyn, on the other hand, had been away on one of his journeys for months and no one knew when to expect him back.

Merlyn's absence, I knew, was to be expected, for he spent less and less time in Camulod nowadays, maintaining that he could form a more accurate, better-informed overview of what was happening in the outlying regions of the country by visiting the people and hearing for himself what was going on. Arthur encouraged him, for the King, too, believed that.

I turned over my command to Tristan and left him to dismiss our troopers and make whatever arrangements might be necessary for their temporary dispersal, while I went to the stables and exchanged my tired mount for a fresh one before exercising my returning commander's privilege by making my way directly down the hill again towards the Villa Britannicus and its superb bath-house facilities. When I arrived there I lost no time in shedding my armor and the clothes in which I had been traveling. Bors would be close behind me, I knew. He had gone straight to my quarters upon his return, to fetch a complete set of fresh new garments for me, under- and over-clothing that had not been washed and rewashed and then folded up in campaign chests for the previous half year. I bathed slowly, making the full progress from the tepid pool to the hot pool, then sweated in the steam room until I thought my bones might melt. I emerged from there streaming with sweat and steaming in the coolness of the outside air, and then, willing myself not to think about it before I leapt, I plunged directly into the icy-cold waters of the *frigidarium,* and then pulled myself out and lay down on a stone plinth, wrapped in warm, thick towels, where I submitted myself to the rejuvenating pummeling of one of the villa's masseurs.

By the time I emerged from the masseur's cubicle I felt like a new man and Bors had tidied up the mess I'd left for him and was ready with a complete change of soft, warm clothing. No armor! It was grand to be back at home. I thanked young Bors and sent him on his way to his own personal freedom, telling him that I would not need his services until the following morning, and then I went outside to saddle up and return to the fortress. It was there, returning through the villa courtyard on my way from the stables, that I first noticed a surprising number of brightly dressed young women, many of whom were staring at me unabashedly and giggling among themselves.

Puzzled at seeing so many women where I could not remember having seen any before, and aware that I knew none of them, I merely nodded a silent greeting to the largest cluster and then kneed my horse out through the gateway, where I put spurs to him and galloped back the mile or so to the bottom of Camulod's hill before tightening the reins and climbing the wide, winding approach to the gates at a more sedate pace.

I had barely entered the gates when I became aware again of an amazing number of young women about the place. I swung away in some confusion and directed my horse along the interior perimeter of the walls, avoiding all of them and looking around me in the hope of seeing one or more of my friends.

I followed the unmistakable sounds of wooden practice swords to find Ghilleadh and Bedwyr belaboring each other in one of the small garden spaces that had been created here and there within the fortress in recent years. Their heavy weapons were moving so swiftly that my eye could not follow individual sweeps, perceiving only blurs of motion among the ringing cracks of wooden blades smashing together, and their concentration was intense, each man focused completely on his fast-moving opponent. It was Bedwyr who saw me first and jumped back from the contest, grounding the point of his weapon as he did so, so that Ghilly checked himself, grunting on the point of delivering a mighty backhanded slash, and looked over his shoulder to see what his opponent was grinning at so foolishly. And Bedwyr might well grin, I knew, for he had not been faring well and was glad to see me. He was red faced and sweating and short of breath, none of which surprised me, since I had frequently found myself in much the same condition, face to face with the redoubtable and indefatigable Ghilleadh.

Among us all, Ghilleadh was far and away the strongest and best swordsman, with lightning-fast reactions and immense strength in his arms, shoulders, hands and legs. He might seldom have much to say, but he was prepared to fight and win at any moment, upon demand. And he was one of the best loved among us, despite the fact that every one of us had frequently spent days recovering from some of the bruisings he had heaped upon us.

Now he grinned at me, no sign of any kind betraying that, mere moments earlier, he had been locked in quasi-mortal combat with the breathless Bedwyr. "Lancer," he growled. "You're home. Good. Take Bedwyr's sword and show us what you learned while you were away."

I held up my arms in surrender, claiming I was too fresh off the road to do anything strenuous, and slid down from my saddle to embrace both of them. It was then that I asked about all the young women I had seen.

"All after Arthur," Ghilly grunted.

"After Arthur for what?" I asked, but he merely raised a dark, saturnine eyebrow and directed his attention to a loose strap on one of his greaves, and so I turned to Bedwyr. "What's going on?"

"Marriage proposals," he replied, his grin as broad as ever. "Treaties and alliances in the making. We have six power-hungry kings and their breathy, eager daughters here in Camulod right now."

"Six? There's more than that. I've seen scores of them, and I have only been here for mere moments."

"No, six of them only are suitors for Arthur's hand and kingdom. The others are all like us, ladies companion, just as we are Knights Companion—cousins and sisters and aunts, all in attendance upon their mistresses. But it makes for interesting mealtimes in the Hall, believe me. Aside from the women, there are more bards and musicians here today than I can ever remember having seen in one place before. Not to mention all the tumblers and acrobats and players."

I looked back again to where Ghilly stood, his face a blank mask. "And you, Ghilly. Do you think you might find yourself a wife among all these beauties?"

He cocked his head. "Aye, if I grow old and doddering before they all leave. I want no wife, man. I'm not a farmer, hungry to acquire land—nor am I a king, seeking profit in being wed to someone who can help me. I'm a soldier. I live free and that's all the life I need. My needs of women are few, and easily looked after whenever they arise, without the encumbrance of a wifely tongue. God save us all, but you can have any willing would-be wife who sets her eye at me, Lancer. I'll have none of them."

"And what about you, Lancer? Could you be tempted?" Bedwyr was smiling gently now.

"Tempted? Aye, mayhap. Any man can be tempted. But I have not yet come close enough to any single one of these brightly colored creatures to see a face, let alone be tempted. I was thinking about other things, to be truthful—like finding something cold and plentiful to drink. Where should I look for that long, cool draft?"

"To the kitchens! They broached a new barrel last night. Come on, Ghilly. Put your sword away and resign yourself to drinking beer in pleasant company instead. Mayhap we'll find a woman there for you who seeks no wifely voice."

The kitchens, which occupied an immense area indoors and out, were probably the only place in Camulod that day where a man might sit without seeing a shining woman somewhere in his field of view. There were several young females around us, truth to tell, but they were all local girls, working, and hence, to our eyes, invisible, intent as they were upon the feeding of several thousand people that night.

The new beer was excellent, smooth and sweet with none of the pungent bitterness that had been noticeable in several batches the previous year, and the three of us sprawled in comfort at an outside table, talking idly about the things men talk about after being released from work and duties. Bedwyr had drawn his duty in Camulod that year, the prime and most sought-after posting for all of us, so his summer had been very pleasant, with nothing untoward threatening his easy existence. Ghilly, on the other hand, had been riding the boundaries to the south and west, and had had several clashes with bands of raiders, a few of them large and powerful parties. But he had outmaneuvered, outfought and defeated all of them and returned home some days before me, with the loss of only fourteen men and a score of horses. He was fiercely proud of his men's fighting abilities, which was not surprising, since he was known as the strictest taskmaster in Camulod and his men were constantly on the training grounds when they were not out on patrol.

Merlyn had been absent for most of the campaigning season, no one knew where, and Arthur, they told me, had spent the entire summer dealing with emissaries from various parts of the country, cementing relationships and negotiating new alliances far and wide.

I shook my head in wonderment. "I find it hard to believe that, faced with all these beautiful women, he would take the time to go hunting."

"Believe it. He didn't simply go, he *escaped*," Ghilly muttered. "They drove him out. You know Arthur. Sees more beauty in an antlered stag than in a herd of women. But he's the one being hunted here, so he hid. I'd do the same. So might you."

"I doubt that," I said, smiling. "So who are these six kings offering their daughters for a panderer's fee?"

Bedwyr answered me. "It's a fat fee, Lancer, for any panderer, be he king or beggar, to have a daughter wed to the High King. You can see how great they fancy the stakes to be when six of them turn up here at the same time, all with the same thing in mind. It's keeping Arthur on his toes, I can tell you, trying to be polite to all of them and keep them all smiling and give offense to no one. It's a thorny path. There are times when the tension around here is thick enough to smell, and it's a wonder to me that they haven't all been at each other's throats by this time."

"Who are they, these people?"

"Well, there's Pelinore, first and foremost, from up in north Cambria. But Pelly's a known quantity, a good fellow, a staunch friend and a strong warrior. He'd make a powerful ally, with a formal treaty, but he's a formidable one as things stand, without one. Unfortunately, his daughter's as ugly as a hammer-headed horse. Plainest one of the lot, and heavy, too. A *big* girl. Then there's Cyngal, from the southeastern end of Eire. He has a strong fleet of galleys and a lovely daughter, but I don't think Arthur's interested in an Eirish alliance, not right now, when he can have the same size of fleet from Annar, who's king on the Island of Mann. But he also doesn't want to alienate Cyngal, so he'll tread softly there. Annar is here, too, and his daughter's name is Anna. Prettiest one of the bunch, I think. But I knew Annar as a boy and he has always been an ignorant lout, loud mouthed and violent and not afraid of treachery if it suits his purposes. I wouldn't trust him to look after my interests, were I high king. He's too fond of himself, by far, to have any fondness left for a rival, even if he calls him an ally and pretends to kiss his arse.

"Let's see now, that's three of them. Who else is there? Aye, there's a fellow called Einar, an Anglian from the Saxon Shores area, near the old town of Colchester. Can you believe that; an Outlander Anglian? But his people have been settled over there in the east for nigh on a hundred years now, it appears. And here he is, suing for alliance with Camulod."

"And his daughter?"

Bedwyr shrugged. "Attractive, I suppose, if you have a liking for white hair and white skin and pale, washed-out eyes. Her name is Hilde, or Hilda, and she's comely enough, but she's no competition for Annar's Anna, and that's the truth."

"Who else? You're still missing two."

"Aye, I know. Let me think. There's an evil-looking animal called Lachlan. He comes from Cambria, too, far to the north, beyond Snowdon. Big fellow, dark faced; always scowling and muttering to himself as though he suspects everyone of planning to jump on him and kill him. But he's here, and his daughter looks as though she might be a prize. Tall, black haired with blue eyes, wears yellow gowns all the time. And the last one's Kilmorack, from smack in the center of Britain. His stronghold is the old Roman fort at Venonae, although they call it something else now. From the way he speaks of it, it's a real fortress, and he has the men to hold it against all comers. His daughter's the youngest of them all. Barely twelve years old, but she'll be beautiful someday."

"So why has he come here? If he and his holdings are so well entrenched and defended, why does he need an alliance with Camulod?"

"Because he's clever, and I believe he's trustworthy. He can see what's happening. The Saxons are growing stronger every year, and he's wealthy enough and strong enough to hold them off for now, but that can't last forever. The men he has now are all he has. Every one that gets killed weakens him. And the Saxons keep coming, more and more of them every year."

"Hmm. You're right, Bedwyr, he is clever. I've been in the same situation he's in, in Gaul, where every man lost to us was a catastrophe that couldn't be remedied. It's an unpleasant reality to have to face, but it sounds as though this Kilmorack intends to do something about it. How does Arthur feel about the man?"

"Same way Bedwyr and I do," said Ghilly. "Positive. Hopeful. Man's a natural ally for us. Thinks the way we do, fights the way we do—hard, smart, determined. He's an able commander."

"So you think Arthur will wed his twelve-year-old daughter?"

"Nah!" Ghilly's scornful dismissal was close to being a laugh. "No need. Those two are friends now. Natural allies, as I said."

"Venonae, you say his place is called?" I glanced at Bedwyr. "I've never heard of it, either."

Bedwyr smiled. "No more had we before he turned up here, but it's been there for hundreds of years, he told me, built by Suetonius Paulinus, the Roman governor who ruled Britain at the time of Boudicca's rebellion, back when Claudius was emperor. I have a feeling we'll come to know it better, now that Arthur has met its king. Pour me some more of that beer."

We sat there, drinking and talking in desultory spurts, until we were interrupted by the clear sound of a brass horn, quickly followed by three more.

"Arthur's back," Ghilly said, standing up. "Let's go."

2

The King, whose face was now unexpectedly concealed by a short-cropped beard, was glad to see me, but despite the genuine pleasure in his welcoming smile, I could tell that at least some of his gladness stemmed from reasons and reactions similar to Bedwyr's when I had appeared to save him from Ghilly's punishment earlier that day. He was unarmored, dressed in hunting clothes that set off his immense physique, his only visible weapon the great hilt of Excalibur that reared above his shoulders from the sling at his back. He had a large party of hunters with him, more than a score in all, counting his own armored escort, and six of them were obviously his regal visitors, a fact I would have discerned from their clothing even had I not seen Pelinore among them.

Arthur had not really escaped, I realized then; he had merely escaped from the ubiquitous young women, a development their fathers would have accepted readily enough, given the consequential opportunities they might have, or might make, to plead their own causes in the course of an enjoyable hunting expedition. I could see that he was tired, and I felt a surge of empathy; there could be no pleasure in being constantly surrounded by a host of opportunistic parasites, I surmised, particularly when their common motives set all of them at odds with another.

My eyes sought out Pelinore again and I felt a twinge of guilt for having thought of him, even fleetingly, as a parasite, for he was no such thing. The others, however, I did not know, and I was content to hold my disapproving judgment of their motives until time and events should show me I was wrong.

Which of them would be the man called Kilmorack, I wondered, the one Ghilly and Bedwyr had warmed to? And then I saw him and knew him instantly. Something about him set him apart from his companions. He was younger than all of them, I estimated, by at least five years and possibly ten, and there was an easiness in his face and manner that indicated—to me, at least, knowing what my friends had said about him—that he had fewer concerns over his dealings with Arthur than the others had. That was pure conjecture on my part, but it felt right.

"My lord Riothamus," I said, bowing and using Arthur's full title as he slid down from his horse and came towards me, his arms extended to embrace me.

"Seur Clothar. You are a sight to gladden a man's soul. When did you return?" He flung his arms about me in a great hug and then, without waiting for my response, he released me and swung around to face the hunting party, one arm still about my shoulders. The group sat, watching us with varying yet uniformly unreadable expressions on their faces. "My lords, you have all met my two

Knights Companion here, Ghilleadh and Bedwyr, already, but now I would like you to meet another of their Brotherhood. This is Seur Clothar, freshly returned with his army group from an extended patrol of the northlands below the Wall. Six months at least since we saw his smiling face around here, and it pleases me greatly to welcome him home." He looked down to smile at me, half a head taller than I was, then looked back to his guests and continued speaking. Although he addressed himself to everyone in general, I knew he was really speaking to the six visiting kings.

"Seur Clothar and I, as you will appreciate, have much to discuss after so long a separation ... matters that I assume he will wish to share with me without further loss of time, and so I must ask you to entertain yourselves for a few hours while I pick my commander's brain for the information he has gathered since he left us. I will rejoin you all tonight in the Great Hall for dinner, but for now, fare ye well. As you already know, we have a fine bath house in the Villa Britannicus, where you are all staying, and its facilities are yours to enjoy. You are welcome to steam and sweat and wash away the residue of your exertions of the past few days, and if you are anything like me, you will marvel at how well our masseurs will ease and soothe your aching muscles after your bath. Seur Ghilleadh and Seur Bedwyr will look after any other needs you might have for the time being. Come now, Seur Clothar, walk with me and tell me all that I need to know of your adventures in the north."

He kept his arm about my shoulders and his head close to mine for the length of time it took us to walk to the end of the courtyard and turn a corner that took us out of sight of his guests, but in all that time he said not a word, and I knew this was a charade, giving an impression of our being deep in conversation to those watching our departing backs. As soon as we had turned the corner he stopped, and he raised both arms to scrub at his eyes with the heels of his hands.

"Thank God for your timely arrival, Lance. I swear by all the ancient gods, had I known that this kind of futile nonsense would be involved in being High King, I would never have consented to being crowned. Sweet Mother of God! There is never an end to the demands of some of these people … and the task of placating them and pampering their vanities and follies would make the ancient Sisyphus volunteer to push a bigger boulder uphill with his nose, rather than assume the task of looking after them. It really is beyond belief how petty these men are."

"Are you including Pelinore in that, my lord?"

"No, I am not. I am not even including all the others, but Pelinore is only one of them through circumstance. He came here with his daughter Rhea in search of self-protection. Clearly he had word that some of the others were coming, sniffing for whatever they could gain by proffering their daughters to my kingly lusts, and so he chose to come, too, in order to keep an eye on developments and assess the ambitions and propensities of his fellow kings. As for Rhea, she and I have been friends for many years and there is nothing of physical attraction between us. Pelinore knew that when he came. He merely brought her along as protective coloration. No, Pelly is not one of the buzzards."

"And Kilmorack, is he one?" Arthur's eyebrows shot upwards in surprise at my mention of the name, and I explained, "I don't know the man. Bedwyr and Ghilly told me about him this afternoon, while we were drinking beer together."

He looked at me for several moments before responding. "They like him."

I nodded, and he nodded back. "I do too. And so will you, once you meet him. Kilmorack is a fine man, exactly the kind of ally we need. But we have agreed, he and I, without even discussing it, that there will be no need for me to marry his young daughter to cement a treaty. He loves the child too much to use her in such a way, although he came here prepared to do so were it necessary. For my part, I would never consider marrying a child. Where were you drinking this beer you spoke of?"

I grinned at him. "In the kitchens … well, outside them, at a table in the shade."

"Lead on, then. Take me there, but choose a route by which no one will see us. If I have to force another smile today I might go mad and kill someone."

We met no one on the way, and sat down at the same table I had been using earlier. No one said a word of greeting to us, but the news obviously went immediately to Curio, the majordomo of the kitchens, that the King himself was sitting outside, for he came bustling out mere moments after our arrival, wiping his hands on the long white apron he always wore. "My lord King—"

Arthur cut him off with an upraised hand. "Forgive me, Curio, but I am in retreat from all the world, else I would not usurp your premises. But I need both privacy and anonymity, for a spell, and my friend Seur Clothar suggested that this might be the most suitable place in all of Camulod to fit my purposes. He also tells me that, aside from your natural courtesy and discretion, you have some excellent beer. Might I have some of that?"

Curio bustled away, almost overwhelmed by the King's graciousness and compliments, and returned moments later with an enormous jug of fresh-drawn beer, two large mugs of fired clay and a wooden platter of cold meats and cheese, freshly sliced bread and a container of precious olive oil. After he had departed for the second time, no other member of his kitchen staff peeked out at us or emerged to disturb our colloquy. The small enclosure was ours alone, for as long as we wished to remain there.

I was hungry, having eaten nothing since breaking my fast before dawn, and it was plain to see that Arthur was, too, and so we sat in companionable silence and simply ate, until nothing was left on the platter but a few scraps. Arthur leaned back then and drank deeply from his mug, belching softly as he lowered it again.

"You're right. The beer is excellent. So tell me, how was your time in the north? Did you encounter any problems? And was Connlyn surprised to see you?"

"He was, my lord, and he seemed pleased—"

"Enough of that nonsense," the King interrupted. "I have been 'my lorded' nigh to death these past weeks. You'll please me more by calling me plain Arthur when we are alone, you know that."

"Very well … Arthur. As for problems, we encountered none that we were not equipped to deal with."

"Did you lose many men?"

"Not one. Not a single casualty, although we ran into a band of Saxon raiders near Connlyn's land. We took them on and thrashed them, but we were lucky not to sustain a single wound."

He held up a hand to stop me before I could go further. "Excellent. But unless you have something urgent to tell me, I would prefer to wait and hear your full report when I am in a better frame of mind for listening."

"No, then. There's nothing urgent enough that it can't wait."

"Excellent again. Now tell me this instead: how loyal are my Knights Companion?"

I stared at him, my mug half raised to drink. "What does that mean? You know their loyalty is unconditional, my lo—" I stopped myself, and lowered my mug slowly to the table. "You will never find any loyalty greater, no matter where you search, or for how long."

"Aye, I know that, Lance. But that is not exactly what I meant, so I suppose the question was too vague. What I really meant to ask was, will they do anything I ask of them?"

Still mystified, I spoke more brusquely than I might otherwise have done. "Aye. They will. All of them. Even if it means their deaths."

"What about death in life?"

"Arthur, I have no idea what you are talking about."

He smiled beneath the beard, but his thoughts and his unfocused eyes were obviously fixed on something elsewhere. "No matter, I was merely wondering if they would marry for me, were I to ask it of them."

"*Marry* for you?" I laughed aloud, drawing his gaze and laughing again at having discovered the way his thoughts were drifting. "You mean, would they unburden you of the need to choose a wife from among your supplicants? Aye, they might—some of them at least. Nevertheless, there are but eight of us, Arthur, and only three of us here, and you have six young women panting for you here and now. And not only the legitimate kings and chiefs but every petty bandit strong enough to proclaim himself a king has a herd of daughters. There must be scores more of them all over the land. And honestly, I doubt if many of those here now would settle for less than the King himself."

"Not even for the King's closest and most trusted friends? I think you might be wrong there, Lance. Even their fathers might see an advantageous match in being kin by marriage to a legate general of Camulod."

"Aye, but ..." I was struck by a sudden insight. "It won't stop until you've made a choice, will it?"

He sighed, deeply, and I heard regret and unhappiness in the sound. "No, it won't, Lance. And I seem to be the only person in all this land who wants me to make no choice."

"None at all?"

"Absolutely not, although that is for your ears alone. I have no interest in marrying anyone, not even for the so-called sake of my people. Besides, I can only make one choice, and that choice, in its commission, will alienate everyone else. But no one seems able to see that, not even Merlyn.

"By making such a choice—and everyone seems bent on having me do it—I will be setting all my plans back to naught, perhaps irremediably. All the work I've done to date, all the negotiations and the planning, all the cajoling and the threatening and the treaty building could be destroyed simply because I have to choose a wife from among a throng of jealous, ambitious competitors. Two of these people here today, Annar of Mann Isle and Lachlan of north Cambria, I will swear to you now, will withdraw their support from us immediately if I don't marry their daughters. And I may not do that, for even as High King I cannot marry two of them. One wife at a time is all the Church permits a man, and that applies to kings as strictly as it does to other men. Were I to choose one of their daughters, the other would march off and terminate or violate our treaty. This is a situation in which

I find myself impossibly beset, Clothar. I cannot win, no matter what I do."

"So what will you do? I have the feeling that you have decided on a course of action, but I can't guess what it might be."

"Inaction, Lance, not action. I have decided to do nothing—to make no choice and yet contrive somehow to leave my options open. But now I have to find some way to send all these importunate petitioners back to their home lands with their pride intact and their daughters' dignity perceived as not having been insulted. The doing of that—if it can even be done at all—will entail an exercise in diplomacy worthy of Imperial Rome. In honesty, I do not even know where to begin."

"You have already made a beginning. Deciding to have none of these women or the treaties their fathers offer in exchange is a beginning."

The face beneath the beard twisted in what might have been a rueful smile. "But no one knows, Lance. I have not yet told anyone."

"So tell them now. Call them together tonight—before or after the evening meal makes no difference—and tell them your decision and explain your reasons clearly: that this matter of a royal marriage is a weighty one and too important to this realm of Britain to be taken lightly, without deep thought and time to consider the matter fully. It is a thing you must discuss in full with your advisers, and take their considerations into account before making such a decision. And it is true that many of them, most notably Merlyn, are not here at this time. Be open in admitting that you have no wish to offend anyone among them, but point out the potential for ill feelings here and now, with only six of them present, out of all the scores of kings and chiefs from one end of this land to the other.

"Play the Riothamus role, the role of the high king—it is yours, after all—and explain your responsibilities as you perceive them. Then tell them that when you do decide to take a wife, you will do so as High King and will inform them all at the same time. We already know they won't like this, but if you tell all of them at once, when they are all together, they will have no choice but to accept it equally. As things stand, some of them probably think you'll choose in their favor over all the others, because such is the self-delusional power of kings. But in choosing not to choose, you return all of them to an equal footing, the subordinate position that is truly theirs. Some of them might be angry, but none will dare do anything openly to offend you."

He said nothing, but his facial expression stated quite openly that he did not have my faith in the reactions of all six of his royal guests, and so I took up the issue before he could say anything.

"Think about it, Arthur. Think about it as the High King, not as Arthur Pendragon. What can they do? Threaten you in front of everyone else with their displeasure? That would give you ample reason to come down on them with all the force at your disposal."

His brow furrowed slightly. "How so?"

"How so? Because if any one of them were stupid enough to threaten you with consequences for taking this stand, he would be stating openly that he considers himself your superior and expects you to take note of his displeasure. But none of them is Riothamus, Arthur. You are. That is your greatest strength: you were crowned Riothamus by the bishops of the Church in front of a gathering of kings and chiefs from all across and up and down the land. Use that *dignitas* properly, and the few who might be angry enough to renege on their promises of loyalty will be afraid to do so openly, then and there, because the others will immediately close ranks with you against them."

He made a wry face. "Aye, then and there perhaps, but what about afterwards?"

"Arthur, if any one of them intends treachery, he will be treacherous in his own time. You cannot control that. But handle this present dilemma decisively, and you assert your dominance *and* the power of the Riothamus. You seize the chance to show potential rebels the unified strengths against which they will risk rebelling. Pelinore and your new friend Kilmorack will stand by you in the doing of that, and their combined strength is not a thing to be ignored by anyone. How many of these six are you concerned about? You mentioned two of them who might renege on their promises, but are there more?"

"No, I think not. Only the two of them. The two others, Einar and Cyngal, seem straightforward enough for my liking, and I believe they will cause us no problems. Cyngal seeks alliance here in south Britain because of his seagoing fleet. He needs the reassurance of being able to land his galleys for shelter and repair along our shores without fear of attack."

"Will he settle for a treaty without a marriage to his daughter?"

"Aye, he will. He but brought his daughter in the hope of using her were such a thing needful. He will sign a treaty without that, because a treaty is more important to him than to me at this time. Alliances across the sea have no real benefit for us the way things stand today. The distances are too long and the weather threats too hazardous.

"Einar the Anglian, on the other hand, has no ships at his disposal, but he, too, needs the assurance of aid should his people and their lands be threatened or invaded. He and his people are Christian. His father and mother were named Cuthric and Cayena, and they became friends of both Merlyn and your mentor Germanus when the good bishop last came to Britain. That was nigh on ten years ago now and Cuthric and Cayena have been dead for some time, Einar told me, both of them killed in a raid. Einar is king of his people now, appointed to the rank by the people themselves. Prior to that appointment by acclaim, he had merely followed his father as headman of their community. So now he is a king, but I have no true knowledge of the size of his holdings or the strengths of his followers. One thing I do know, however: he poses no threat to Camulod or to me. Therefore I am inclined to trust him." He smiled at me, teeth gleaming from the depths of the carefully trimmed beard that I found so disconcerting. "I am inclined to trust you, too ... your judgment in this, I mean ... It makes sound sense and I am grateful."

"No need." I waved away his gratitude, slightly embarrassed by it. "When did you grow the beard?"

He scratched at the growth covering his chin. "In the spring, soon after you left, I suppose. I was traveling almost every week, and it was easier to let the whiskers grow than to undergo the fuss of shaving every day. Now that I am home for the winter, I intend to shave it off again. You disapprove of it? I rather like it."

"It makes you look older."

"That is a benefit, my friend, not a liability. Most of the kings with whom I have to deal are graybeards, far older than I am. You will have to find a more substantial plaint than that before you can sway me."

He was laughing at me, I knew, but I merely shrugged my shoulders and spoke my mind. "Beards are not to my personal taste. I like to see a man's face when I am talking to him and I find beards to be like masks. They cover much that should be open. They suggest a wildness to me, too, a lack of civilizing influences."

Now he did laugh aloud. "Ah, is that the loyalty you were describing earlier? The unrestricted, unconditional kind? You find me suddenly untrustworthy, unreadable because I choose to wear a beard? A *mask*, Lance?"

His words stung. "I was speaking of beards and the men I have met and disliked who wore them, Arthur. I meant no word of it to apply to you."

"But how can that be? I have a beard."

I was thinking of my long-dead cousin Gunthar, the most evil man I had ever known, and I could see his face floating in my mind, taunting me, with the blood of his slaughtered brothers clotting in the thick beard he wore to disguise his lipless mouth and his empty, soulless, ever-shifting eyes.

"It must be the Roman Gaul in you, Lance," Arthur continued, his tone bantering. "More Roman there than Gaul, however. Did you not know the Gauls invented beards? That's why the civilized, clean-shaven Romans called them barbarians—because they wore *barbas*, beards."

"Aye, and they never bathed." I strove to make my tone as light as his, seeing no profit in bringing up Gunthar's name and thereby gifting him posthumously with acknowledgment that he had ever lived.

Arthur's face sobered abruptly. "The mask effect is a nonsense, Lance. Clean-shaven or bearded, the man himself remains unaltered. Hair on the face is natural, all men have it. It is the removal of it that is an affectation—in my case this year, an inconvenient one. I was traveling constantly throughout the spring and summer, but I was not formally under arms. I was a visiting dignitary, making my rounds and at liberty to grow a beard if I so wished. And I so wished. And I have enjoyed the beard, and the free time it has afforded me, not having to scrape my face every morning.

"Had I been riding with an expeditionary force, however, growing it would never have crossed my mind. Under arms, the enforcement of mandatory shaving is part and parcel of discipline and uniformity: the need to do it every day takes up time that might otherwise be used for mischief, and it gives the men a common cause for complaint and harmless muttering. It also increases and enhances uniformity. Lastly, it separates the disciplined army from the barbarian rabble. But I shall bare my face tomorrow, to avoid causing you further pain."

I sipped my beer slowly before changing the subject. "May I ask a question, Arthur?"

"Of course."

"It is a personal question … you might not like it."

"Then it will not be the first such question you've asked me. Since when have you become so reticent?"

"It is … It's in my mind that you have absolutely no wish to marry … to marry anyone, I mean, not just one of these six maidens. Am I correct?"

"You are."

He gave no sign of wishing to add to that, and I shifted my weight and cleared my throat. "Why not? Am I permitted to ask that?"

"You are permitted to ask anything, Lance. I told you that. Whether I choose to answer you or to ignore your questions is another thing altogether. But let me ask you a question, by way of answering yours. Have you ever been in love?"

Had I? I had known several women, most of them young girls, but really very few, and none of them had caused me any loss of sleep or shortness of breath, or any of the other symptoms I had grown to believe were caused by being in love. I shook my head slowly.

"No, I don't believe I have. But perhaps I have and simply was unaware of it. I suspect I might not know I was in love, even if I were. We had little room or time for such things in the Bishop's School."

"I believe you. Now you listen to me and believe me, as your friend if not as your king. You, Seur Clothar, have never known love. If you had, you could not possibly bleat such nonsense as has just emerged from your mouth, because the experience of being in love alters everything in what you had previously known as life. Once you have experienced love, my friend, nothing can ever be the same again … including you yourself."

"Why? How?" I suddenly felt both ignorant and foolish, a boy in school again, but I could not resist asking. "What does it do to you?"

"I've told you, it changes the world, but I cannot tell you how. No man can do that, for each man's world, before he loves, is his own and known to him alone. Only after he has fallen in love can any man recognize what he once had, and know that what it was is gone beyond recall or recapture. Your time will come, Lance, and when it does, you will remember this conversation and understand what I meant."

I was unable to think of a single thing to say, but there was no need to say anything, for his brow was furrowed with concentration, and it was obvious from the halting way his words eventually emerged that he had never tried to put these thoughts into mere words before.

"I believe …" He stopped and considered, then began again. "I have been taught, Lance … without ever having received a lesson in any such thing … that love is a divine gift—a benison direct from God Himself and created for the beatitude, the ennoblement, of mankind … That sounds very grand and exalted, even to my own ears, but is no less true for being so. And I have been taught, by the same voiceless teachers … people like Merlyn and others who have taught me by example … by the very lives they live … that there are many kinds of love, apart from the love of men and women. I have come to see that nothing in this world is more powerful or more important than …" Again he hesitated, searching. "Than what? Love is the word that comes into my mind, but it is not the word I need …"

He waved a hand as though to silence me, but nothing could have been further from me at that moment than the desire to speak and interrupt what I had recognized to be a new level of intimacy in his confiding in me.

He thought for a time and then smiled uncertainly and continued, his tone almost apologetic. "Bear with me, if you will—I find this difficult. Philosophy has never been a strength of mine, much to the despair of my boyhood tutors, and I have never tried to explain these things before, even to myself … You know me, Lance, as well as any comrade can. You know how I am, how I think. I deal in real things and seldom in anything more abstract than a strategic battle plan. And battle plans, as you know well, are designed to be revised and improvised upon as soon as the first exchange of blows has neutered them …

"Now … I was talking about love, and the lessons I have learned—" He stopped abruptly and uttered a sound that was part laugh, part snort of disgust. "Lance, the thoughts in my mind right now as we speak are so strange to me that were I to hear them spoken aloud by one of my own commanders, the mere utterance would be enough to make me doubt his competence."

I hesitated before I said, "Then perhaps it would be better not to voice them."

"No! I need to look at them, out in the open. And it seems to me that I could not do that better than with you. You are the only one I can talk to about this. Your ears are open to me. Merlyn's are blocked by who he is. He is more than twice my age and he sees things as my father would have seen them had he been alive today. But I don't *need* my father's outlook on the world, nor do I need his solutions to the problems that beset him in his youth. Everything is new today. Everything is different from the world my father and Merlyn knew as boys and young men, and my role—mine alone, Arthur Pendragon's role of Riothamus—is one that no man has ever had to play before. You are my friend, Lance, and I need you, in this situation, as I have never needed any man. Will you listen?"

I attempted to smile easily. "You do not even need to ask that, Arthur."

"Then pour us some more beer. It seems to ease my tongue."

I poured the last of the jug's contents into our two mugs, and then we both sat silent, sipping slowly, each immersed in his own thoughts. Finally Arthur set his mug down and sat back.

"Let's be about it, then. Set me upon the path. Tell me what you have heard."

I sucked air audibly between my teeth, searching for a starting point. "You have no wish to marry. That's where we began, and then you spoke of love, and life lessons, all of which you said were concerned with love in one way or another. Then you grew frustrated with the word 'love' because—"

"Responsibility. *That's* the word that was eluding me. Because we use it all the time, but we never think of it as having anything to do with love. Yet it has everything to do with it. Love *is* responsibility, Lance, in all its aspects. Think of it, and begin with marriage.

"When a man falls in love and takes a wife, he takes responsibility, for her and for the children he will sire on her. Now we all know that many men take none, but they are not worthy of the name of men. True men, men of goodwill, assume responsibility for wives and families, and everyone expects it of them.

"Now look at yourself and your brethren, my Knights Companion, all of the legates general of Camulod. All of you are filled with love of each other and I believe you would willingly die for one another, which makes your brotherhood unique. And all of you are filled with love of what you do, and that entails further responsibility, for the duties with which you are charged, and for the men you command. Look at Ghilleadh. His men think of him as a slave driver, and in some ways he may seem like one, even to us. But Ghilly's concern is all for those men of his. He feels a personal responsibility for their welfare and their lives. He lost fourteen on his last tour, and was distraught. He named every one of them in his report to me. That is love, Lance, and it entails a responsibility, an integrity, that is wholly admirable and commendable.

"I love my father, although I never knew him. To be more accurate, I love the memory of him as it has been disclosed to me through others. And that love, more akin to reverence, I admit, keeps me aware of my responsibilities to him, to what he was and what he represented: nobility, fearlessness, and a commitment and dedication to his own duties and responsibilities in Cambria that surpassed all else in his life.

"Now think of Merlyn, my uncle and my cousin both, and his love for me, which I have never doubted. Think how seriously he takes his responsibilities … to the point at which he sometimes makes me impatient, if not angry with him. And your own favorite teachers and tutors when you were a lad in Gaul, did they love you? Perhaps you may not think they did, but ask yourself this: did you love them? And if so, why? Because they showed their love for you by executing their duties as your tutors with absolute responsibility, making you the man that you became. Who was your favorite teacher, apart from Germanus?"

"Germanus was my mentor, not my tutor. My favorite teacher was Tiberias Cato, who taught me to ride and to fight and to throw the lance. And yes, before you ask, I loved both of them, although I doubt I knew it at the time. Now that they are both gone, I know how much I love and miss them. And their sense of responsibility— for me and all the others in their charge—was absolute."

"There you have it then: love of man and woman, love of man and man in brotherhood, filial love and paternal love, and the love of duty, all of them involving, *demanding,* the faithful and unflagging pursuit of fulfillment of responsibilities. There is only one love that I have missed, and that is one that no one ever seems to think about or acknowledge ..."

"And what is that?"

"Love of one's homeland. This Britain that we live in. I love it, in addition to all the other loves I have mentioned. And I feel—no, I *am*—responsible for it.

"I am High King of All Britain, even though such a Britain does not exist, save in my own mind and dreams. It did exist, once not so long ago, but it was not a land in the sense I mean. It was a mere province, ruled by Outlanders who ruled the world. It was no more than a small and unimportant part of an enormous whole, which is why they abandoned it." He paused again.

"We talk, I talk, Merlyn talks about this realm of Britain. You spoke of it yourself mere moments ago. But there is no realm, Lance, not in reality. I have no realm. What I have is a chaos of voices—the voices of small kings and scattered kingdoms—each one clamoring louder than the next in the hope of gaining some advantage over all his neighbors, something that will set him ahead of them, something that bears not the slightest likeness to the wishes of the next man trying to make his voice heard.

"And surrounding them, threatening all of them, is the menace of invasion by the Saxon hordes. Oh, they all love to talk about the dangers, but the plain truth is that as long as the threats are confined to other people's lands, the other kings are all content to ignore them and concentrate only on their own little concerns, their own agendas. And there are scores of these little kings, Lance, perhaps hundreds. So here I am, High King of All Britain, and I cannot even count the number of lesser kings within my so-called realm with any kind of accuracy.

"But I can dream, and within that dream lies my responsibility.

"I dream, my friend, of what my title Riothamus means ... of what it really entails ... the hard reality behind the fine-sounding name. I dream of a Britain united, one people, unified under one monarch and protected as securely under the rule of law as they were when Rome governed here. My task in life, the sole task for which I have been bred and trained, is to achieve that unity, consolidating all the clans and tribes and little kingdoms of this land into a single force that will withstand and throw out the Outlanders who seek to take our Britain from us. That is my duty, my responsibility, and it demands all the love and dedication that is in me. And my greatest fear is that I may not have sufficient time to fulfill it."

"And so you feel … you cannot take a wife."

"Precisely. A wife, at this time, would hamper me with responsibilities I cannot afford to undertake. I have too much else to do, and too little time in which to do it. It will require all my effort, single-mindedly, to achieve even the half of what I have to do."

"So you will never marry."

"No, that may change. Nothing can last forever and I will probably be forced to marry at some point. People expect it of me, to sire an heir. But when I yield to that necessity it will be out of duty, not out of human, man-for-woman love, and it cannot be now or in the imaginable future."

"But what if you meet the woman God intended you to meet … for we are taught He has a mate for each of us … what then?"

He turned his face away from me, inhaling deeply and then expelling the breath forcefully. "I have already met her, Lance, and lost her, long since. The bishops tell us that we have but one soul mate in life, one love for all time, and that any subsequent love we may find is but a misplaced shadow of what might have been. I had such a love, once. I have known my soul mate. Her name was Morag. I told you of her once before. I was sixteen, and she was younger, but we were in love. So deep in love that I have never recovered from the loss of her. And lose her I did, simply because we were so young that no one could believe that we were old enough to love in such a way. And so we kept it hidden from the world, fearing that what actually happened might occur. Less than a month I knew her for. Less than a month, but we enjoyed a lifetime in those weeks. We slept together and knew each other carnally, despite our youthfulness. No one ever knew. I was afraid of being flogged, had we been caught, for I was a mere stripling boy, not yet a man, and she was a guest in Camulod, niece to a visiting queen.

"And then one day she was gone. I watched her go, and I was desolate, but I believed she would come back to me. It had been promised by her aunt, and by Merlyn ..."

"And you never sought to find her?"

"They told me that she died within a year of returning home ... I thought I might die, too, when I heard that. I wanted to. But I lived on and no one ever knew or suspected what was in my soul, the despair and the emptiness. How could they? I was but a boy, too insignificant to be regarded as a person, too young to be a man or to dream of love."

"Obviously you still think of her at times like this."

His beard twitched. "At times like this? There has never been a day since she went home that I have not thought about her. And no woman I have ever met has stirred me as she did. I will never forget her, Lance. She was my love. The one love of my life. Of course, now that I am a man, people would think me mad were they to hear me say such a thing, because, of course, I was a mere boy at the time, and therefore ..."

I sat quietly, waiting.

"And so I say nothing. It is all part of who I am, and what I have become, and it is no man's concern but my own ... save that you now know about it too ...

"But if I am correct in equating love to responsibility, then I must accept the love of God apparent in the responsibility he has laid upon me to be High King of this Britain in fact, rather than merely in name, and I am grateful not to be distracted by any fleshly love." He looked me in the eye. "Do you think me foolish?"

"No, on God's name I do not. But I had no idea ..."

"How could you? No one does, not even Merlyn." He sat straighter in his chair and clapped his hands together. "So, if it please you, your opinion on my ravings?"

"No ravings, Sire," I replied, feeling the need to acknowledge the awe I felt. "The honor you have done me here is more than words can deal with, and I am inspired by what you have described to me in this vision of Britain. My life is yours, henceforth, more than it was before, which is not even possible. But now to my devotion to your person and your rank, I add complete and utter dedication to your quest, your dream and your ideal."

He gazed at me, his mouth invisible beneath the beard, then nodded his head slowly, three times. "So be it, then. You approve of my designs, my wishes?"

"Without reservation, my lord King."

He rose to his feet and extended his right hand, and I knelt and kissed it.

"Come you, then, and walk with me until we are beset with visitors. And accept my thanks for your patience. You have eased my mind more than I could ever begin to describe."

No more Lance and Arthur, we walked from the kitchen yard as High King and Knight Companion.

3

"Morgas, you say?" Merlyn had straightened up as though slapped at the mention of the name. "Are you sure her name was Morgas?"

"Aye, as sure as I can be."

"No, Clothar, I need more than that. This is important. How can you be so sure?"

"Because I was told it was so by someone who had no reason to lie about it—someone whom I had no reason to distrust. I asked him what *morgas* meant, thinking it to be a word with some meaning in whatever language Connlyn and his sister were speaking when I overheard them arguing. He told me it was a woman's name, no more than that—the name of Connlyn's sister."

"Hmph." Merlyn hunched forward again, his right hand disappearing beneath his enormous hood as he pinched his chin between thumb and finger. He had arrived back the morning after my own arrival, and this was the first time I had spoken to him, unaware until I met him unexpectedly by the main gates that he had been back in Camulod for three days by then, all of them spent in seclusion with the King. The regal visitors had all departed Camulod on the morning of his arrival, their business here concluded by Arthur's announcement the previous night that he would not yet be choosing a bride.

I had spent the intervening three days settling in again for the winter and supervising the hundred and one chores that had accumulated during my summer absence. My chain mail was badly rusted, for one thing, its leather lining dried and cracked and its thin padding rotted beyond repair after years of campaigning in all weathers, and I had to make arrangements with the smiths to have another suit made for me.

On the morning of the day I met Merlyn, I had risen at dawn and spent the day alone, practicing since first light with my Gaulish hunting bow and with my throwing lances, recapturing and refining my skills with them both afoot and on horseback, so that by the time I returned to the fortress in mid-afternoon, my back, arms and shoulders were tight and aching with fatigue. The unexpected sight of the King's black-clad senior counselor, however, filled me with a rejuvenating surge of pleasure and I made no attempt to disguise it.

Merlyn returned my greeting with equal warmth and told me he needed to speak with me, and then he steered me to his quarters with one hand on my arm above the elbow, his grip firm and strong. Once there, he poured each of us a cup of wine before beginning to question me closely on my recent expeditionary visit to Connlyn's territories.

He listened in silence to all I had to tell him, until I mentioned the name of Connlyn's sister, eliciting this sudden lively interest, and now, seeing him so deep in thought, I questioned him more directly than I had ever dared before, for he had told me mere moments earlier, to my great pleasure, that I had earned the right to speak to him as an equal, as plain Merlyn, without titles or honorifics.

"You know the name, don't you? It means something to you. Who is she?"

"I know the name, yes. It is … familiar. And yet it's but a name. How many women named Paula do you know, here in Camulod?"

"That is a diversion," I replied. "Paula is a common name—there are three serving women with that name in the officers' section of the dining hall—but Morgas is not. I had never heard it before."

He made that "harrumphing" sound again. "You are right, the name is … unusual. That is why it disconcerted me."

"Then you do know her?"

"No, I do not. But I heard tell, once, of a woman named Morgas, long ago …" He fell silent again, this time for a long time, and when he spoke up again, his voice musing, it was more to himself than to me. "No, it could hardly be, surely …" Then, abruptly, he was speaking to me again. "Tell me about this one, the woman you met. You say she was old. How old?"

I shook my head. "How would I know that? She was … she was simply old, no longer young. Someone's grandmother."

"Whose grandmother? She has grandchildren?"

"*Anyone's* grandmother, my lord." Old habits are hard to break, and the term of respect came to my lips without volition. "I was but trying to convey her agedness. I heard her say nothing of grandchildren, and Lanar made no mention of any."

"Hmm. What did she say to you?"

Yet again I had to shake my head, aware of how ignorant I must seem in the face of his need to know these things. "Nothing memorable. We spoke of trivial things most of the time. And yet she seemed … somehow strange. There was something about her that unsettled me, something in the way she questioned me, although I have long since given up trying to determine what it was."

"Questioned you about what?"

"About nothing that I have been able to identify as being uncommon or peculiar … I feel stupid, speaking this way, admitting ignorance time after time as though I am a complete ignoramus, but I've grown used to that feeling since I met that woman. That's what I mean when I say she unsettled me. I had the feeling she was probing me for information, but there was nothing I could tell her in response to her questions that could have been of any import to her."

"What about what you could *not* tell her? What could you have told her, think you, that might have been of value to her?"

"Again, I have no idea. She asked only vague and general questions."

"Questions about *what*?" The impatience in the old man's voice was clear-edged.

"About Camulod, about the knighthood ceremony, about Arthur."

"What about Arthur?"

I waved my spread hands in frustration at my inability to be more clear. "Nothing that any other woman would not have asked. What kind of man is he, does he have a wife, that kind of thing. General, as I said, and born of female curiosity. Nothing that was intrusive."

"What then of Camulod and the knighthood ceremony?"

"The same. She had no interest in the military aspects, only the spectacle and panoply of the thing, although she wondered if the knights could be Arthur's heirs."

"Heirs? Are you sure of that? She asked about Arthur's heirs?"

"Aye, and I told her he had none. Master Merlyn, this has clearly upset you. What am I failing to understand here?"

He sagged backwards in his chair. "Nothing, Clothar, nothing at all … at least nothing that I myself am not equally confused about. Did she tell you any of her history?"

"No, I told you, she did not even tell me her real name. She told me I might call her Judith."

"So you know nothing about her other than her name?"

"No, I know a little more than that. The man Lanar told me all that he knew of her, although that was not much. She was married to a king in the west of Caledonia, by the sea, a place called Gallowa. His name was Tod. Tod of Gallowa."

"Did she have a son?"

"No, she had but the one child by this Tod, a daughter. Why is this so important, Merlyn? Who was this Morgas that you knew?"

"Later, I will tell you later. For now I require to know this daughter's name."

"I can't tell you that, for I don't know. Lanar knew only that there was a daughter who had died far in the north, on an island called Orcenay, where she was wed to the governor."

"Orcenay is ruled by the Northmen."

"I know. This governor was appointed to his post by the Norweyan king, who was his father's brother." I had to stifle a strong urge to ask him again why this should be so important. Merlyn was notoriously close mouthed about the King's affairs, and took his role as principal adviser to the Riothamus very seriously. I knew he would tell me anything he thought it important for me to know, and beyond that he would say nothing, and since I could do nothing to alter that, I bit down on my question.

It had grown dark in the room in the short time we had been sitting there, and the single lamp burning over the open fireplace had begun to cast a yellow glow. Merlyn swallowed what remained of his wine and then was on his feet, opening a cupboard against the wall from which he produced a number of long white candles, which he thrust beneath his left arm. He immediately lit one from the lamp's flame and then he moved about the room, lighting the others one at a time, using only his right hand, and anchoring each of them in small puddles of molten wax spilled from their tops. He lit eight, bathing the room in beautiful white light, before he blew out the single lamp.

"I hate lamps," he said then. "Smelly, smoky things. But I love the light of candles made from bees' wax. It is pure and unearthly, almost liquid in its beauty, don't you think?"

He did not wait for me to agree with him, but stooped to the corner by the fireplace, where he gathered up a small, tied bundle of dried rushes from a basket half-filled with them and held one end of it to the flame of the nearest candle. Then he crouched before the hearth and, when the rushes were burning fiercely, he thrust them into the heart of the waiting pile of logs.

"Hate the cold, too," he said, still crouching, gazing into the rising flames. "Worse as I grow older. The winters are bad for old bones like mine. They bring out all the aches and pains you never think about in summer."

Then, with his back to me and his cape concealing everything I might otherwise have seen, he reached out with both hands to warm himself. I have seldom experienced any urge as strong as the one that hit me then, making me want to rise and move sideways to where I might be able to see his left hand, the one he always kept hidden. But of course I did not move, and he eventually stood and retrieved his cup, then crossed the room to refill it from the jug on the table by the wall.

"More wine?"

"Aye, half a cup, if you will." I stood and crossed to him, and as he began to fill my cup I said, "I am free of duties tonight. Nothing to do but think." He stopped, surprised, I thought, then raised the jug again.

"Then hold it up." I did so, and he filled it almost to the brim. "Thinking is thirsty work, my friend, and dangerous. Sit, sit."

I returned to my chair, taking care not to spill anything as I sat down again, and by the time I looked back at him he was leaning against the wall by the hearth.

"That is close to being the very last drop of the last shipment of wine we received from Gaul, two years ago. Too long. And who knows when or how we will find more of it?"

He drank, and although I could not see into the shadows beneath his hood, I sensed from his posture that he was rolling the wine around his tongue, savoring it. His next words, however, drove such thoughts out of my mind.

"We heard rumors, long ago, that Uther had sired other sons than Arthur ... that there was another heir." I sat motionless, aware that I was hearing confidential matters. "Nothing ever came of them ... the rumors, I mean ... no mention, ever, of another claimant to Pendragon blood rights. Not to Uther's blood rights, at least. And so the rumors died away and were forgotten. Nothing to do with Camulod in those days, you understand. Uther was king only of the Pendragon Federation in Cambria. I was legate commander here in Camulod, a post I took upon the death of my father, Picus Britannicus, and Uther was my cousin. My father and his mother were first cousins."

He fell silent and shifted his weight against the wall. I raised my cup and sipped cautiously, afraid of distracting him from his thoughts and feeling a stir of anticipation roiling somewhere inside me. I had heard only bits and pieces of soldiers' talk of Uther Pendragon, dead now for more than twenty years, and indeed I knew next to nothing of Merlyn's own younger days. All that I had heard was barracks hearsay and, I was sure, greatly exaggerated. What was emerging here was the truth at first hand, and I wanted more of it.

The room was almost completely dark now, the shadows held at bay only by the flickering firelight and the steady white light of the candles. Merlyn bent at the knees and placed his cup carefully on the floor in front of the fire, then pulled his chair close to the hearth before picking the cup up again.

"Bring your chair over here, to the heat. It occurs to me that you are still a newcomer to our land, so you will know little or nothing of what I want to talk to you about. I will have to give you the background, if you are to understand the rest of the story."

I drew my chair up close beside his own and felt the welcoming warmth of the fire against my bare, outstretched legs, and we drank from our cups at the same time. Merlyn clearly felt no need to look at me as he was speaking, and I accepted that and simply looked straight ahead, into the fire, knowing that were I to turn to look at him I would see no more than the side of his black hood. He continued speaking, his voice, deep and sonorous, emerging clearly from behind the heavy cowl.

"I have to begin with the days before Arthur was born, years before these rumors I spoke of earlier. In order to understand my reaction to the rumors, you need to know something of who and what I was in those days, and it is something I never speak of nowadays. The birth—Arthur's birth—was something completely unexpected by me. And when I found out about it, it caused me great … concern. Concern, and much grief, for it forced me to look into my own soul, and to evaluate and judge what lay in there, much of it unknown and unsuspected.

"We were not close at that time, Uther and I, for I had cause to believe he had done me great wrong." He stopped, for the space of several breaths. "Let me be open with you—nothing veiled and nothing left unsaid. I believed at that time that my cousin Uther, who had been my closest boyhood friend, had murdered my wife and with her my unborn son."

I went rigid in my chair.

"Aye, you may well be shocked. Imagine, if you can, how I felt about it, my family murdered, and more than a little knowledge in my mind of certain things that pointed indisputably, it seemed to me, towards Uther Pendragon as their murderer. I had no means of proving what I suspected, nor of disproving it, and there were indications of both guilt and innocence on Uther's part, according to how one viewed the circumstances. I was the grieving widower, and thus my view of them was … jaundiced."

He bent forward and took up the poker, stirring the fire listlessly for a while before he continued. "I now believe I was mistaken. No, I know I was. Uther had no knowledge of the events involving my family. But the outcome of it all, again because of circumstances, was less tragic than it might have been. God knows the way Uther died was tragic enough, but he died in battle—in a minor skirmish at the end of a long war—and by God's mercy I had no hand in it. And yet, that said, the truth is that I went alone in search of Uther Pendragon with every intention of killing him when I found him. He was campaigning in Cornwall at the time, in a just war against an abomination of a creature called Gulrhys

Lot, who styled himself King of Cornwall, and no matter how I tried to catch him, Uther always managed to remain one jump ahead of me." He sighed then, a deep, gusty outpouring of breath.

"That may have been the worst, most deeply regretted journey I ever made, for Lot was crushing Uther's forces by sheer weight of numbers, exhausting them by throwing mercenaries against them from every direction until he finally caught them in an indefensible position against three advancing armies. I was following behind throughout all the defeats, trying to catch up, driving my horses beyond endurance and finding our slaughtered soldiers, both Camulodian and Pendragon, lying like bloody windrows on the ground at every step. I missed the final battle, coming to it only after everything was over, but a strong contingent of our army had managed to fight their way out of the trap—thanks to a subterfuge of Uther's—and were making their way home to Camulod when I met them." He hesitated, looking, I thought, directly at me. "You know Donuil Mac Athol."

I nodded, immediately envisioning the affable and enormous Eirish Scot who had welcomed us on my first visit to Camulod, five years earlier.

"Aye, well Donuil's sister, Deirdre, was my wife. It is a long, sad and strange tale, not needed here, but the strangest part of all of it is that Ygraine, the Queen of Cornwall and spouse of our greatest enemy, was sister to both of them.

"Uther and Ygraine had met some time before, and Ygraine was with Uther now, having fled her brutal husband, Gulrhys Lot. They had fallen in love and he had sired a son on her, although I did not learn that until later." Merlyn sucked in a great breath and straightened up in his chair. He lifted his cup to his mouth but then lowered it without tasting the wine.

"In my madness at the time, I could taste my vengeance on my tongue and rode after Uther, refreshed by the thought of having him almost within my grasp. But even when I found him he had eluded me. I found him on a sandy spit of land by the sea, fighting over a beached boat and surrounded by dead and dying bodies, men and women, and the killing continued as I drew closer, until we two were the only ones left alive. I challenged him to fight me and he took off his helm, and I recognized him, but this man was not Uther.

"He had killed Uther earlier that morning, he told me, and had stripped him of his armor out of need, not out of any desire to plunder. Uther was a giant of a man, and so was Derek of Ravenglass, the man who slew him."

"Derek of Ravenglass?" The name dumbfounded me. "Are you talking about the same man who was at Arthur's table on the night you and I talked in the gallery? He slew Uther and you permitted him to live?"

Merlyn shrugged and spread his arms. "In conscience I had no other option. Bear in mind what I said about my own search that day. I had been looking for Uther in order to kill him, believing he had killed my wife and child. I had had murder in my heart that day, but Derek had not. He was a warrior at war, who had fought and killed an enemy according to his duty, without malice. He had stripped the corpse solely because his own armor was rusted and battered and almost useless after years of warfare and Uther's was the only equipment he had seen that would fit him comfortably. But he had no notion of who he had killed, no idea that he had killed Uther Pendragon, the Cambrian king."

"So you did nothing."

"Nothing. I had no wish even to fight him, let alone kill him. I had seen enough of killing by then. I allowed him to leave."

"Wearing Uther's armor?" I could not keep the incredulity out of my voice. The black-robed figure beside me remained immobile.

"Uther was dead. He had no need of armor. The victor needed it. He was a mercenary without friends, alone in a warring land, and I had met him years before and believed he was a man of honor. And so I sat there on my horse and watched my cousin's killer ride away ...

"But as I sat there that day, I heard a sound behind me, and found one of the women still alive but fading fast. She begged me to save the child, to save Arthur. But there was no child, and I thought she was raving. She died there, as I knelt beside her, and I recognized her and knew she was the queen, from the deep red color of her hair and her resemblance to my own dead wife. And then I heard an infant wailing in the boat that was drifting out to sea behind me. I swam to it and pulled myself aboard, and I found the boy, with Uther's personal seal on a thong about his neck."

Another long silence followed that, and I sat waiting, enthralled by the picture he had painted for me with his words.

"Believe me, Clothar my friend," he went on after a time, "I experienced a lifetime of change in the hours that followed, alone there on that little boat with the child. My earliest impulse was to kill the boy, in retribution for my own bereavement. It was the sheerest impulse, born of rage and grief and frustration at Uther's death by any hand but my own and the survival of his breed when my own had been stamped out, but when it came down to doing it I was incapable of harming the child.

"Instead, I adopted him and raised him as I would have my own unborn and unnamed son. And the result of that you know. I brought him home to Camulod and made his education and training my life's work ...

"Which brings us full circle, to the woman Morgas and the rumors of another heir to Uther. Arthur was still but a child at the time the rumors first surfaced. But I was his guardian, and the possibility there might be substance to the whisperings sent me searching for a root cause. Believe me, I searched high and low and far and wide. But I found nothing.

"The only thing I did discover, from Huw Strongarm, one of Uther's own Cambrian captains who had been present at the time and was close to the king, was that when Ygraine and her women had first been taken by our forces, they had played a game in order to safeguard the queen's true identity. One of them, a haughty, fair-haired beauty, had pretended to be Ygraine, and Uther had sequestered her in his own tent, separating her from her companions.

"Huw was of the opinion that Uther might have bedded this woman, although he could not be positive. Uther had been very discreet, even in the midst of his own army, in his own command tent. Nevertheless, Huw remembered thinking at the time that the two of them must be frolicking together in the night … he said the woman's smug self-satisfaction was too noticeable to mean anything else.

"But Huw did not know the woman's true name. He thought she was the queen, Ygraine. And by the time he discovered the truth, she had already gone. Greatly perplexed by what he saw as his own lack of perception—for he had thought nothing of any of this for years, until I questioned him about it—he then referred me to others who had been there in the king's camp and were yet living, and I spoke to all of them. It was one of those, who had been briefly wed to another of Ygraine's women before she died in childbirth, who was able to recall his wife's speaking of a woman called Morgas, who had been the first to be sent away from Uther's camp. That was the only time I ever heard the name, and I was never able to find out what became of the woman—and believe me, I tried diligently. But whoever she was, she had vanished, never to be found or heard from again.

"If what Huw Strongarm had suspected were true, it seemed to me conceivable that this woman Morgas might have borne a son to Uther. But Arthur came of age in due time and nothing was ever heard of any other claimant to Uther's paternity, and so I set my fears aside. Only now do I see that I never thought to search northwards, beyond the Wall.

"And now you come to me with word of a woman called Morgas, come out of the north beyond the Wall. And now you know why I reacted as I did when you named her. And since you know everything there is to know about the matter now, I will ask you again: can you think of anything, anything at all, that you have not already told me about this woman?"

My mind flicked quickly through memories, and then I shook my head. "No, except I may not have mentioned that when I first met her, I thought she must have been very beautiful at one time. She was old, but she held herself very proudly, and the planes of her face were very pronounced. At the distance from which I saw her first, in fact, almost hidden in the shadows behind her women, I thought she was much younger than I had been told she was. She is … impressive."

"'Proudly,' you said. Would you describe her as being regal? Queenly?"

I smiled. "Strange word, queenly, but yes, I would. She *was* a queen, in Gallowa."

"Right, but I am wondering if she might have pretended once to be a queen in Cornwall."

I could only shrug and spread my hands, but he did not see either gesture.

"Tell me about this brother of hers, this Connlyn."

"You probably know more about him than I do. You met him when he came here last year to offer the alliance."

"That is beside the point, my young friend. I asked you for *your* impressions of the man. I already know my own."

"Very well, then." I finished off my wine and said exactly what was in my mind, determined to return the same kind of open honesty that had been extended to me. "He sets my teeth on edge. Don't ask me why … We already know he is astute enough to have weighed the pros and contras of approaching Camulod before we could approach him. And then he acted decisively. That tells us he has foresight, and he is astute, and has trust in his own convictions. That it also means he has his own reasons for doing what he did, and they are probably more self-serving than anything else, is irrelevant, in terms of being a negative. Connlyn is not a king in name. He would prefer to have us see him as a simple warrior, a captain, or at worst a warlord. But he is a king in all respects save that, and he rules his territories effectively … at least as far as I have seen.

"We went directly to his stronghold, one of the old Mile Castles along the Wall itself. A barbarous-looking place, but strong and easily defensible, and well garrisoned, in numbers at least. I had no opportunity to see or to test the quality of his warriors. Our troops were quartered in an area some distance outside his walls that had been cordoned off from his own people. We were not prisoners, nor did we even feel discomfiture, by any stretch of the imagination. In fact the strangeness of it all did not occur to us while we were there. But we were not quite at liberty to roam as we pleased. And my own official party, some twenty of us, were accommodated in much the same way, although within his castle walls. We were made welcome—we were feasted and entertained, and our counsel was sought and appeared to be taken seriously—but we were not taken outside the main defenses at any time during our visit. It was all so smoothly accomplished that I did not really realize the extent of his manipulation until we had ridden out of his lands and were well on our way south.

"After the raid on Knut One-Eye, we rode directly back to Connlyn's castle, but we stayed only briefly. We were there, we had been able to assist him, he was grateful, and then it was time to leave again. It was Dynas who made a comment on the road south about not having seen many of the local clansmen, and that observation, innocent as it was, prompted me to think more carefully about the entire experience."

"Hmm. So what are you telling me? What does that mean?"

I clapped my hands together and bent forward to replenish the fire. "Merlyn, if I knew what that meant—if I could interpret it—then I would be an adviser to the King."

When I straightened up again he had turned to face me, and I saw firelight reflected in one eye within the gloom of his hood.

"You *are* an adviser to the King, Seur Clothar. You are a Knight Companion and a legate general of Camulod. How could you not be aware of the concomitant status of adviser?"

I sat blinking at him. "I had not thought of it that way."

"Think of it that way from now on, for it is the truth and your sworn duty. Now I will ask you again, as a fellow adviser: what do you think Connlyn's failure to show you his realm might have meant?"

I thought for no more than a few heartbeats this time, seeing more now than I had seen before. "Well first, I don't believe there was any failure involved at all on his part. He did not fail to show us anything. He was successful, for he clearly had no wish for us to see or learn anything of substance."

"Including the extent of his realm."

"We know its extent—" I stopped myself. "From east to west, at least. What are you suggesting, Merlyn?"

"His stronghold, his central defensive position, is a Mile Castle along the old Wall. Isn't that what you said?"

"Aye, it is."

"It seems to me to be a strange location for a stronghold. It is hardly central, no matter the strength of the place or the strategic or defensive advantages it offers. What kind of warrior, or warlord for that matter, positions himself with his back to the wall before any hostilities have begun?"

"Sweet Jesu! I didn't think of that! You mean his territories could extend into the north, beyond the Wall?"

"That is exactly what I mean. And if that is the case in fact, he had more than ample reason to keep you and your people well fed and entertained and disinclined to be too curious about what lay outside his walls. It also throws a different color of light upon his eagerness to be our ally."

"I don't follow that."

"You will when you examine it and what it means. You have already pointed out his forethought and his capacity for seizing opportunity when it suits him. What lies beyond the Wall?"

"Caledonia. And the Painted People ... the Picts ... the Caledons ... whatever they are called nowadays."

"And why was the Wall built in the first place?"

"To keep them out."

"Right. And why was the Wall abandoned?"

"Because it couldn't keep them out."

"There, you see? You follow me perfectly. Now one more little leap, perhaps two. If not all of the Caledons are above the Wall, what follows then?"

"Some of them are below it."

"Aha. And whence came Morgas, Connlyn's sister? And perhaps even Connlyn himself?"

"From north of the Wall. From Gallowa."

"Well, from north of the Wall, at least. We cannot be sure of Gallowa. Morgas was wed to the King of Gallowa. We know no more than that. Now, let me add one more thing for you to think about. We may have grounds here to suppose Connlyn has made alliance with the Outlanders from Caledonia, which means he will have provided them a base within Britain ... a base from which they could move southwards with impunity, into the heartland. If that is so, why do you suppose he might come seeking alliance here with Camulod?"

"In order to—" I stopped, already glimpsing the appalling possibility lurking at the edge of my imagination. "Wait. Wait ... Let me think this through ..."

Merlyn sat silent, allowing me the time that I had asked for.

"He was specific, very clear about his needs ... the quid pro quo underlying his offer of support for us in the northland. He wanted us to ... He required a promise, unequivocal, from Arthur, that Camulod would come to his aid in the event his territories were threatened or invaded from the lands held by the Saxons on his flank, to the east of him."

"Correct. Now, let us carry our supposition one step further. If he were to be invaded, would we go to his assistance?"

"Of course we would. Arthur's promise binds us."

"It does. Now describe for me the corollary to that."

"I don't understand."

"Think about it. You understand 'corollary'?"

"Of course." I fell to thinking, and it did not take me long to provide his answer. "The corollary is that were he not to be invaded, we would have no reason to go there."

"No reason at all. Well done, Seur Clothar. We would have no reason at all to go there, or to visit his lands, particularly since we know him to be a voluntary ally and a willing supporter.

"You said we know the extent of his realm to the west and east. To the west of him lies the kingdom until recently ruled by Ushmar, is that not so? I wonder who rules there now, since your departure." He held up a hand to stifle any response. "Does it strike you as strange, or in any way peculiar, that the raiders who hit Ushmar from those eastern territories—the raiders you encountered—should have skirted the southern edges of Connlyn's lands on their way to Ushmar's?" Again he held up the peremptory hand. "And would you think it impossible for a man, a king, to bring northern Outlanders in from one side for his own purposes without considering the advantages to himself in forming an alliance with the equally savage Outlanders with whom he must live shoulder to shoulder in the east? Think about it.

"And think, too, about this: he expected no expeditions from Camulod this year, but you turned up unexpectedly, on a goodwill visit with a strong, mounted, highly mobile force. And so while you were so providentially there, might he not have decided to provide you, with short but sufficient notice, with a small sample, at first hand, of the kind of threat under which he and his people live? Convenient, eh? And the incidental benefit of that was the fortuitous removal of a potent and dangerous rival from his western borders, and the opening of more land for him to pre-empt.

"If all of that were true, instead of being mere conjecture proposed by me out of boredom here in Camulod, Connlyn might now command a block of lands and men stretching halfway across Britain below the Wall, a solid, strategic and tactical base for a confederation of his own, his other allies, the Saxons and the Caledons. Nothing to the south of him could withstand a concerted advance from such a position, particularly with us sitting safely down here in Camulod, trusting him and leaving the way clear for his attack. What think you of that?"

The tiny hairs on my arms and neck were standing erect in a rash of horrified gooseflesh. "In Jesu's name, Merlyn," I whispered, hearing the awe in my own voice, "I think you have dissolved an alliance and issued a call to war."

He laughed, a surprisingly rich, deep, ringing sound. "No, I have done no such thing. I have merely raised suppositions, Clothar. Conjectures, as I said, to give you an object lesson on how a conscientious adviser to the King must approach his responsibilities. Men are not all as good as you would wish to have them, my young friend. Few are, in fact. The majority of men walking this earth are venal and self-serving, their ambitions constrained only by their own inadequacies—their lack of intellect and their inability to plan and achieve their ends. The few of those who do possess such intellect and skills make fearsome enemies, unless they are stamped upon before they can emerge from the egg.

"Arthur Pendragon, I am grateful to be able to say, is molded from another clay altogether. I saw that in him when he was a toddling infant, too young to dissemble. He is unique; incorruptible and, thus far, invincible. It is our task—yours and mine, I mean—to make sure he stays invincible and that his principles remain inviolate, and for that reason alone we must scrutinize the acts and motivations of other men remorselessly, looking for base metal everywhere, even among the most noble-seeming. These arguments I have made against Connlyn's integrity may well be specious and empty, all of them. But they might also be true. In either event, they suggested themselves to me, and I would be at fault if I now failed to examine them for truth and content.

"Together you and I have developed an excellent case to present to our King … a case against an untested ally. That is as it should be, for we can take nothing, and we can allow the King to take nothing, at face value. The situation in the north obviously needs to be investigated. Connlyn needs to be investigated, his loyalty and trustworthiness determined in a realistic manner. Tomorrow we will speak to the King, and he will ponder our suppositions and come to a decision. In the meantime, you and I may share this last cup of wine and then sleep well, knowing our duties have been well discharged this evening."

4

The King did, indeed, ponder over the information Merlyn and I presented to him the following morning, but he did not make a decision before consulting his captains. It was one of Arthur's most appealing and inspiring virtues that he believed implicitly in the strengths and ability of his eight newly created Knights Companion. Seeking our opinion on important concerns was not something he did for effect, or to create a mere impression of depending upon our input. He truly believed in the usefulness of open discussion for the common good.

His great-grandfather Publius Varrus, one of the co-founders of the colony that had grown to become Camulod, had initiated the idea, in the earliest years of the colony's existence, of forming a governing council much like the ancient senate of Republican Rome, a council in which every man's voice would be equal to that of any of his peers, and Arthur had decided long before the knighthood ceremony that the men to be honored there, and whose loyalty, honor and abilities had earned them their advancement, deserved greater recognition and acknowledgment than the mere endowment of spurs, swords and titles. How better, he had asked Merlyn and the assembled Council, could he acknowledge such men than by giving them a similar equality of voice and purpose to the Council itself, but specifically in the military and defensive affairs of Camulod?

Thus, Camulod now had two governing councils, the first of them continuing the duties that had concerned it from the outset: the administration of the thriving community that had become Camulod today, numbering close on five thousand souls, discounting the military personnel, who numbered more than eight thousand above that.

Not all of the ordinary residents lived in Camulod itself, of course. Many of them were farmers, occupying the villas and buildings that were scattered about the colony and working the thousands of acres of rich farmland that kept its citizens and soldiers healthy and well fed. Many more were artisans—smiths of all kinds, blacksmiths and weapons makers predominant among them. But there were also masons and builders, cobblers and bakers, farriers, and herdsmen to look after the needs of our huge herds of horses and other livestock. There were barrel makers and tanners, carpenters and charcoal burners, weavers, butchers and cooks and an army of others dedicated to the daily, mundane tasks that a society such as ours depends upon in order to function smoothly. Most of the smithy crews lived within the fortress of Camulod itself, but the other craftsmen and artisans were scattered widely throughout our holdings, on the farms and in satellite villages and towns like the neighboring Ilchester, that we had garrisoned and fortified for the housing and support of our troopers. All of these people and the regulation of their daily lives fell under the jurisdiction of the main Council of Camulod.

The military affairs of the colony, now officially the Kingdom, was the responsibility of the Council of Knights, with Arthur himself as the presiding guide and Merlyn serving in the capacity of chief adviser to the King. At their first assembly soon after their elevation to the knighthood, the King had made it clear how he intended to proceed from that day forward, and how he would expect the brethren to embrace and live up to the expectations and demands that he would now formally place upon them in recognition of their altered circumstances and their elevated ranks. The eight knights had all been his closest brothers in arms prior to that time, continuously schooled over a period of many years—with the notable exception of myself, Tristan and Perceval, the three newcomers from Gaul—in Arthur's uniquely equestrian theories on strategy, as well as in his battlefield-perfected tactical practices, but they were also able administrators, each of them accustomed to the responsibilities of commanding large numbers of men in both peace and war.

Henceforth, he informed them, they would all be legate commanders of Camulod, each in permanent command of his own battle group. Each battle group would be identified by its own colored standard, and its group commander would carry that standard blazoned on his personal shield. Further, each battle group would have a strength equal to half the complement of the existing armies of Camulod, which were four in number. The creation of eight smaller battle groups, he had explained, would give each unit greater flexibility by increasing its ability to deploy its forces in a short time, while leaving all of them free to act with other battle groups when necessary. Now each group would have five hundred cavalry troopers, a full thousand infantry and a hundred bowmen with their great Pendragon bows of yew wood and their long, deadly, lathe-turned arrows of ash wood. The bowmen would be mounted when a battle group was on the move, mainly on their own shaggy mountain garrons, and when they were not fighting they would function as scouts, the capacity in which they had come to excel over the years since Pendragon and Camulod first made alliance. In battle, however, they would fight on foot, in serried, lethal ranks the equivalent of siege artillery.

Arthur then dictated the primary responsibilities of a legate commander in times of peace: those not on campaign, on patrol or on garrison duty, which in recent years had always kept one full army far away in Cambria, would meet together every fifteenth day to discuss affairs common to them all. They would also, at such times, deliberate matters of policy and advise the King on how best to proceed for the good of the kingdom, and thus was born the concept of the round table, at which every man's voice was equal.

Of course it was an ancient system, dating from the earliest days of the Roman senate, and the governing council of Camulod had used it since the days of Caius Britannicus and Publius Varrus, the colony's founders, but for some reason, the idea of the King's new Knights Companion convening regularly to assist the King in governing captured the imagination of the rank-and-file troopers, and within a short time the occasions when the Knights' Council met were always treated with great solemnity by the entire community.

The day of our submission regarding Connlyn was such an occasion, and only Seur Gareth, patrolling with his army group in his home in Pendragon Cambria, was missing from the Council.

No one spoke until Merlyn and I had finished presenting our thoughts and our summation of what our suppositions might entail. When everything had been said that we wanted to say, the King, more solemn than he usually was—and he never brought levity into such advisory sessions—asked us several pointed questions and then fell silent, absorbing our answers.

"This woman Morgas," he said at length, looking at Merlyn. "Could she be the same woman my father knew in Cornwall?" None of us missed the significance of that word *knew,* with its overtones of possible consequences.

Merlyn shrugged. "She could be, my lord King. She would seem to be the proper age, or thereabouts. Your father, had he lived, would be more than sixty now and the woman Morgas known to him would probably be younger, although I know not by how much. The woman Seur Clothar met would appear to be older than either of those, but Seur Clothar himself acknowledges that he could not assess the woman's age with any hope of accuracy. Yet the name is … uncommon. I had only ever heard it once, before Seur Clothar brought back word of meeting this Morgas."

Arthur sat silent, mulling upon that. "Merlyn is an uncommon name, too," he said eventually. "Limited to you alone, I believe. And so is Arthur, for that matter. And then there is Seur Clothar himself. No one here had ever heard his name before, when he first came to us." He turned to me. "Tell me, my friend, did you know other Clothars in your home in Gaul?"

I nodded, smiling. "Aye, my lord, more than a few. Mine is a common name, where I come from."

"Yet unique and alien where you are now." He looked back at Merlyn. "Common in Gaul, unheard of here. This sister of Connlyn's comes from above the Wall. Where did your Morgas hail from?"

"I have no idea, my lord. We have no way of knowing that."

"And does it not follow that, as Clothar is a common name in Gaul, Morgas might be as common where she came from?"

Merlyn merely inclined his head, agreeing without words, and Arthur shrugged. "So be it. Since we cannot know, we will waste no further time in fruitless guessing." He nodded then, in agreement with himself, and turned to look around the gathering.

'Well, brethren, what think you of the matters we have listened to today? Have you heard enough, or is there something one of you might wish to ask or add?' No one answered him, each member of the group deep in his own thoughts, and then he nodded again. "So be it. Now, bearing in mind that nothing that has been said here is known to be true, let me ask you this. Does what you have heard this morning *ring* true?"

"Aye, it does. All of it." Ghilleadh, the speaker, was the most taciturn of all of us in that room, known by everyone there never to speak simply for the sake of hearing himself talk. His deep, rumbling voice, accepting the possibility that Merlyn's assessment might be accurate, made the others nod in agreement, and then Perceval spoke up.

"True or not, my lord King, it needs to be looked into. And quickly. And there's the problem. How do we look into it without causing unnecessary friction? It's a long way from Camulod to the Wall, and much of the journey is through hostile, unknown territory. Anyone going up that way at this time of the year had best be well backed up with men and equipment. Too few of them, and they could be wiped out on the way there or back, just for being unlucky enough to encounter the wrong people or the wrong weather conditions. For that matter, too few of them and they could be wiped out by Connlyn himself, if what we suspect is true and he finds out we know. And yet we can hardly send an army group up there without good reason, for we could lose a valuable ally if it turns out that we are wrong and he has been open and honest with us all along. We need to think carefully on this, my lord, and proceed with caution. Not out of fear, but out of tact."

Arthur nodded. "I agree. Does anyone else have anything to say about that?"

Gwin spoke up then, and as usual I marveled at his way of speaking. He was Ghilly's brother and the son of Eirish Scots, but in his youth he had spent much time among Arthur's people, the

Pendragon of Cambria, and had absorbed, perhaps unconsciously, their distinctive way of speaking, the lilt and cadence of their speech, and because of it he pronounced his own name in a slurred drawl as though it should be Gawain, rather than plain Gwin. He cleared his throat now and rubbed his chin with the palm of one hand. "We cannot really do anything about this until next year, can we?" he said in his slow drawl, chewing on every vowel so that everyone had to listen closely to understand him. "It's winter now and we've already had a few snowfalls. Up on the higher ground, the snow will be blocking the passes. Little profit in sending anyone out into that."

"You might be wrong there," Ghilly growled. "No one would expect us in wintertime. And the snow could cover our advance."

"Aye, and leave our tracks behind for all the world to follow," Gwin snapped back. Not normally an impatient man, he rose to his feet now and started to pace the circular space in the center of the group. "What I'm thinking, Arthur—and the rest of you lads—is that, come spring, we'll be into another year. Don't laugh, it's not a jest, obvious though it sounds. Another new campaigning season. Don't you see? People will be expecting us to be out and about, visiting other parts and checking up on how people survived the winter, as well as guarding against threats from any direction. We could send an army group up then, as part of our normal dispersal, that is all I'm saying. But if we send any kind of force up there now, before we have to, we will be asking for trouble."

"We're *looking* for trouble, Gwin, that's why we're talking about this." This was the first time Bedwyr had spoken.

Gwin spun to face him. "Looking, aye, but not *asking* for it! There's a big difference, Bedwyr boy. What I am saying is that by going back up there now, this year, we will be warning this Connlyn fellow that we suspect something. He is not a fool, we know that already, so why make ourselves look like the fools by warning him when we have no need to?"

"We can't afford to give him the time involved," Bedwyr responded.

"*What* time?" Gwin barked. "What time would we be giving him? The winter? What can he do in the winter? I will tell you what he can do, boyo. He can do nothing more than any of us here can do, and probably less. He might plan, and scheme, and make himself ready to move south as soon as winter breaks, but what of that? We can do the same thing here in the southwest and be ready before he is. If he does march, with his Saxons and Caledonians, then our way will be clear when we arrive at his walls, because he will not be expecting us." He returned to his seat. "There's all I have to say, Arthur, for what it is worth."

"It is worth much, Gwin—sound common sense, and valid. And it points to, but does not resolve, our problem. We have to decide what we are going to do about this, my friends, and then we have to take steps to make sure that it is done. This Connlyn is not some minor irritant that we can safely ignore or postpone investigating. So we stay here in this council until we are in agreement."

The decision we came to was that I, as the only one with any knowledge of Connlyn's region, would return northwards in the springtime with two army groups, my own and Ghilleadh's, and that we would approach Connlyn's territories from the westward, along the Wall. Once close enough to our target, but far enough removed for our main party to remain undetected, I would ride on ahead with a smaller group, composed mainly of Pendragon bowmen under the command of the veteran Pendragon commander Powys, and discover what I could about the situation in the kingdom that had been Ushmar's. When I had secured that information I would govern myself accordingly before moving on to see whether there was any abnormal activity in Connlyn's domain. The details of the expedition would be worked out during the coming months, but the commitment had been made.

FOUR

1

That night after the conference about Connlyn marked my first return to regular duties after my homecoming, and it remains in my memory after all these years because it was the night my second-best cuirass disintegrated while I was putting it on.

Armor wears out. It is not a thing that people who never wear it think about, but it happens, and it happens quite frequently. Faced with such a statement, those same people who never wear armor might think that the reason for the failure is the abuse the equipment undergoes in battle, but that is not true. Armor is worn constantly, but it is seldom subjected to battle conditions. Three fights, three fully armored, hand-to-hand encounters with a hostile enemy in the course of a single year, would be unusual enough to be greatly remarkable, but even then the damaging results of blows from weaponry would be minimal, since the material, when all is said and done, is armor, expressly designed to absorb and deflect blows.

The truth is that most of the deterioration that affects it and every other part of a soldier's equipment, be he foot soldier or cavalry trooper, is caused by weather. Rain, snow, frost, humid air and mildew are all notoriously destructive of iron and leather.

I had just delivered a suit of mail the previous day to the smiths, to be melted down because its very fabric was choked with so much rust that, despite all young Bors's efforts to keep it clean, it had simply become unwearable. I could not blame Bors, for it was not his fault. He could burnish the exterior of the links for hours a day, but the damage was all done by the accumulation of rust between the tiny individual pieces, where no cleaning tool could penetrate. A new suit of mail would be ready for me the following day, after being adjusted to fit me as closely as was possible, and in the meantime I felt safe enough. There was no need for a mail coat on garrison duty in Camulod itself.

Now, a mere twenty-four hours after surrendering my rusted mail to the smiths, I lost my leather cuirass, too, at least until it could be mended. One of the straps at my waist broke just as I pulled it to its tightest point to insert the tang of the buckle, and the piece tore off right at the edge of the breastplate, leaving a too-short stub I could do nothing with and a yawning, unsightly gap at my side that I could not disguise, no matter how I tried to cinch my belt about my waist.

Cursing, and rebuffing Bors's wordless offer of assistance, I tugged at the buckled straps and finally threw the whole cuirass down to clatter on the floor at his feet. He stood watching me, his expression noncommittal, and it crossed my mind that he was growing more clever every day, because there had been a time, not too long before, when he would have tried to assume the blame for the failure, which would have earned him the rough edge of my tongue for his folly. Tonight he simply stood and waited for me to make a decision. He knew the importance of what had happened. I had another cuirass, but it was old and battered, its leather torso scarred and scratched beneath its lustrous polish by too many years of hard, everyday use. Normally I would have asked for it immediately, but tonight was different.

My men had been at liberty for the past four days. At sunrise, they would muster again for duty for the first time since coming home. There would be sore heads and queasy stomachs among them after the previous night's carousal, the last of their liberty, but they would be on full parade, drawn up for my inspection on the first morning of their new tour of duty. They did not yet know where they would spend the winter, although they knew it would be close to home, possibly in Camulod itself but more likely in one of the outlying garrison towns. They were well aware, too, that their duties over the next few months would be easy compared to the unrelenting tension of being constantly moving on campaign, far from home and assistance should such a need arise. They would learn their fate at dawn, after I had completed my formal legate's inspection, and they would be uncomfortably aware, from past experience, that the examination they were facing would be meticulous and merciless.

That dawn inspection was the reason for my reluctance to wear my old, battered campaign armor. Each and every member of my army group would be sparkling with glinting metal and polished leather in the dawn light, having spent hours throughout the previous four days in preparing their gear and equipment for the scrutiny I would subject them to in that parade, for they knew that woe lay in wait for any man found guilty of the tiniest omission or neglect in his preparations for legate's inspection. The slightest speck of rust or mildew found anywhere on a soldier's gear or on a trooper's saddlery would condemn the miscreant to a week in the cells, and hard labor on the ever-growing curtain walls would be the lot of anyone found guilty of more serious transgressions. Knowing that, and visualizing the efforts they had made, I could not bring myself to inspect them wearing my own old campaign armor. They might think nothing of that, too afraid of my disapproval to take note of what I myself was wearing, but I felt I could not betray my own standards.

The solution, of course, reposed behind me, still enclosed in its portable traveling case: the magnificent suit of imperial ceremonial armor that Germanus had passed on to me, which he had worn as commander-in-chief in Gaul, during his ten-year campaign against the rebel Burgundians. With its burnished leather cuirass and kirtle of armored straps, all intricately sculpted and embossed, and sumptuous with studs and bosses of pure gold, and its great, high crested helmet and matching armlets and greaves of polished bronze inlaid with gold, the costume was magnificent, but I only ever wore it when I was abroad, representing Arthur and the *dignitas* of Camulod to kings and other men of power in Britain. I was enormously reluctant to wear it in Camulod, for even the King had nothing that remotely compared to it in splendor. Arthur himself found that amusing, I knew, for he cared nothing about such things, but that knowledge did nothing to decrease my reluctance to flaunt my outrageously ornate finery among my own.

On this occasion, however, I knew I had no choice, and mere moments later I was standing motionless, my arms outstretched at my side as Bors cinched the underarm buckles tight and then tugged at my tunic until he was satisfied that the garment was evenly kilted above my knees. As he knelt to place and fasten the heavy greaves over my sandaled, knee-high boots, I stifled a surge of impatience. I knew that he could adjust the bronze leg shields more easily and comfortably than I could now, simply because I was already wearing my cuirass and could not have bent from the waist to fasten the ankle straps without great difficulty. He finished quickly and unfolded the thick, richly embroidered cloak that went with the uniform, then fastened it about my shoulders. He stepped back and surveyed me from top to bottom before nodding in approval.

"You're ready," he said.

I had only ever seen myself once dressed in this suit, and at the time I had been too small to wear it properly, still several years away from developing the frame that supported it today. Even so, its opulence had taken my breath away. It fitted me to perfection today, but there was no mirror of polished silver in Camulod large enough to show me my reflection the way the massive, flawless surface of the man-high mirror on the wall in Germanus's home had shown it to me. It occurred to me, as I remembered that mirror, that it was the single most impressive artifact I had ever seen, even more magnificent in its splendid purity than the armor it had reflected that night. Some ancient silversmith must have worked for many months, if not years, to attain that impeccable surface of polished metal, for it was as flawless in its perfection as the motionless surface of a woodland pool on a calm evening.

I grunted, realizing I was woolgathering, and saw Bors looking at me. "You'd better go and get yourself armed now, too. I'll be here when you are ready." He nodded and left the room, and I walked to the small window and peered out into the predawn sky as I focused myself upon what I had to do. My horse would be ready for me when I went out, but other than using it to ride down the winding road to the parade ground at the bottom of the hill, I would have no need for it in the course of my inspection. The infantry detachment and the Pendragon bowmen would all be afoot, and the cavalry troopers would, too, on this occasion, standing by their mounts to allow me to examine them as thoroughly as I might wish.

The Pendragon bowmen were scouts, rather than regular soldiers, and they were Cambrians, not Camulodians, so they were not subjected to the same degree of scrutiny as the regular troops, but they were none the less my responsibility and in my charge, and so I exerted a certain discipline over them, to which they responded without demur. Soldiers or not, their weapons depended upon the care lavished upon them, and as a bowman myself—although my Gallic bow was a far cry from being as powerful as their Pendragon longbows—I knew what to look for in inspecting them. I would not merely examine their bow staves; I would examine arrows picked at random from their quivers, testing them for straightness and smooth fletching, and I would test the condition not only of their strung bows but of the extra bow strings they carried in their scrips, unfolding some at random and running my thumbnail along their length to test for fraying and for too much dryness.

I bent forward into the window opening, listening intently, and could hear the sounds of my troopers passing by my quarters on their way to the parade ground. They were on the opposite side of the building, so I could hear no voices and there were no sounds of shuffling infantry feet, but the clinking of hundreds of ironshod hooves on stone was unmistakable and carried clearly on the still, predawn air. Too soon, then, I thought, for me to be outside. My presence among them before they had time to make their way down and assemble in their formations would unsettle them.

Resigning myself to waiting until Bors came to fetch me, I took off my cloak and made myself comfortable, leaning against the sill

of the window and watching the slowly paling eastern sky as I
allowed my thoughts to drift back to the strange conversation I had
had with Arthur two days earlier about love and the responsibilities
it engendered and entailed. It was something I had never thought
about until I heard him put it into words, but listening to him speak,
I had realized that he was absolutely correct and had captured my
complete agreement—in everything, that is, except the matter of
love between men and women. That was *terra incognita* to me.

Thinking back on what he had said about how God had created
one woman, one true mate for every man, and how having found
and lost his, he had no further interest in meeting another, I shook
my head in troubled disbelief. How could he be so sure that the girl
Morag, whom he had known for less than a month, when he himself
was but a boy, had been *the* one God had intended for him? And
then I had the truly disturbing thought that he might have been
mistaken, might have misinterpreted his great loss and his solitary
grief over the tragic death of the young woman. He had lain with
her, he said, and she had been his first and only love.

I had no doubt of his sincerity in what he said, but there was
doubt within me now, none the less, and it was the first doubt I had
ever felt about my King. That perturbed me deeply, for until that
moment my faith in Arthur, in his leadership, his abilities, his vision
and his wisdom had been absolute. I had never known him to be
wrong in anything. The King was far from being an ordinary man,
in any sense, but he was less than himself in this, it seemed to me
now, since even I, virgin that I was, had heard it said time and again
by men whom I respected and admired that there is first love, which
a man never forgets, and then there is true adult love, a different
creature altogether.

At that point, standing there by my window, I knew that Arthur
must be wrong, that he would love again. As Riothamus, High King
of All Britain, he would be forced to wed someone, someday. He
had admitted as much to me, confessing that he would have to yield
to the wishes of others at one stage or another. But that admission
had troubled me when I heard it, for it seemed to fly in the face of

everything else he had said. How could he marry in conscience, I had wanted to ask him, without accepting full responsibility for the woman he would wed? For surely it seemed to me that any woman marrying a king—and especially such a king as Arthur—would want children of the union. How, then, I had asked, could Arthur deny her that, withholding the love to which she was entitled as his wife and queen?

And of course the answer came to me now, armed as I was with my new and blinding insight. He would live up to his responsibilities and he would not deny his wife a family, for although one of the main reasons for such a marriage might be purely the political union of his new wife's part of the country with Camulod when it was important enough and all other measures had failed, the primary and paramount reason for such a union must be the breeding of progeny—an heir to the kingdom. It would be an absolute duty that he owed to the people, assuring them of continuity in what he had achieved for them—an end to the anarchy that had prevailed in Britain since the Romans left. And Arthur Pendragon would always place his duty above all else, including his personal preference. That sudden conviction reinforced my certainty that, no matter what the King believed at present, he would someday come to love another woman.

I was beginning to feel extremely foolish, standing there by the window in my military finery, prepared to inspect an entire army group of two thousand men, yet reduced to grappling with the mysteries of love and procreation like a boy not yet old enough to achieve erection. I was acutely aware, more so than I had ever been, that I had never experienced any kind of deep feelings for a woman, with the sole exception of my mother's sister, my aunt Vivienne, whom I had revered as my mother. Yet such feelings hardly qualified as the kind of love Arthur had been speaking of.

Why then, I asked myself now, need I fret over what Arthur had told me? Arthur appeared to have everything worked out in his mind, and he would not allow himself to be rushed in whatever he decided to do. I steadfastly refused to allow myself to reflect on what he had also worked out wrongly in his mind concerning the girl Morag, concentrating instead on what he had done right. He had avoided giving offense to any of the six kings who had come offering him their daughters, handling the difficult task of refusing all of them with great skill, and word of that refusal, and the stated reasons underlying it, would spread out and give him some time in which to breathe—and plan—before the next such circumstance arose. And it would also give him time, I thought smugly, to meet his destined mate and find love again.

A discreet cough behind me broke my train of thought. Bors was back.

"The men are assembled, Seur Clothar."

I was astonished now at the silence outside, for I had not noticed the sounds of my troopers' passage dwindle away and I had no notion of how long I had been standing there. I swung about quickly and snatched up my cloak and helmet from where I had laid them, throwing the heavy, folded garment over my arm and cradling the helmet against my cuirass before following Bors wordlessly out into the courtyard, where I found Tristan already mounted and waiting for me, accompanied by Ghilly and Bedwyr in full armor.

"I'm surprised to see you two here," I said to the latter pair. "Have you nothing better to do?"

"Better than watching a gilded Gaul inspect an army of Britons? What would that be?" Bedwyr sat grinning down at me, mightily pleased with his own wit.

I handed my helmet to Bors, swung my cloak over my shoulders, then took the helmet back and settled it onto my head while Bors saw to the cloak's fastenings. When he stepped back, I looked back to the others. "Very well, my friends, if you care to waste your morning on such doings, I'll be glad to instruct you both on the niceties of command inspections." I pulled myself up into the saddle and took a moment to settle myself comfortably, spreading my cloak to best effect and adjusting my long sword so that it hung easily, slanted between my shoulder blades so that its tip lay against my mount's right hip and the long, two-handed hilt projected above my left shoulder for an easy draw. When I was satisfied that all was as it should be, I closed the flaps of my helmet and put spurs to my mount, and the others fell in behind me. It was first light, and the eastern sky was brightening rapidly with the promise of a fine early-winter day.

2

I always loved the hollow sound of hooves in the early morning on the cobblestones between the gateway towers, and this morning was no exception. I was at peace with the world, happy over my newfound insight into Arthur's future prospects and more than content to have my closest friends flanking me as we rode out through the gates to inspect my men, drawn up in flawless formation far below. I was aware that above our heads, on the tops of the guard towers, the lookouts were gazing down at us and in all probability taking careful note of my finery.

My enjoyment, however, barely survived our egress from the gates, because as soon as we were out in the open, Ghilly stood up in his stirrups and pointed away to our left.

"What in the name of God is *that*?"

As I turned to look I heard Tristan answer, "Fire!"

Flames were leaping in the dawn shadows, and I knew at once it might well be the Villa Britannicus, the family home of Caius Britannicus, the founder of Camulod. Shouts were coming from all directions now, and from the parapets above came the clamoring of a general alarum as a guard beat an iron bar against the sides of a hanging iron triangle. I swung immediately to Tristan.

"It may not be the villa but it's close to it, and whatever it is, we need to put it out. Quickly, Tristan, get down as fast as you can to the bottom and bring the entire group at the double. They can't see anything yet from where they are. Keep them in formation, but waste no time … this could be anything. It might be an attack, it might not. But take no chances. Go! We'll meet you at the villa."

As Tristan galloped off down the steep road, I turned to the others. "We'll be quicker if we cut down the hillside, straight to the villa, but it might be a rougher ride than we bargain for, in this light. Are you with me?"

All three of them, Ghilleadh, Bedwyr and Bors, had set spurs to their mounts before the words were out of my mouth.

It was a dangerous ride, as I had predicted, but the light was increasing steadily by then, making it progressively easier to pick our route as we descended, and the leaping flames in the distance grew brighter and higher every time I dared to raise my eyes from the ground ahead to look at them. By the time we reached level ground, about halfway to where we were going, there was no doubt in any of our minds that it was the Villa Britannicus that was burning. It could not be anything else, for there were no other buildings out there. I was praying as I rode that the fire might be confined to one or other of the outbuildings and that the villa itself might be safe, and I knew my companions were hoping the same, for the four of us were riding knee to knee, standing in our stirrups and leaning forward over our horses' ears to coax the maximum speed out of them.

We met the first fugitives when we were less than a quarter of a mile from the main gates of the farm, a scattered trio of servants, running madly in the direction of the fort to raise the alarum, and even as I saw the blood that covered the face of the leading runner I heard his voice raised, shouting the one word I would have least expected to hear: *Saxons*!

Saxons in Camulod? The question had barely formed in my mind before I heard Ghilly's bellowing response.

"How many?"

He had already aimed his horse directly at the running man and had shouted the question at the top of his voice, to make himself heard over the thunder of our hooves, and I swung my own horse in that direction, straining to hear the man's response. But instead of answering, the fellow threw up his arms protectively and sank down in terror, dropping to his knees at the sight of two armed horsemen bearing down upon him and surely believing he was about to die. We both reined in our mounts at the same time and came to a trampling halt, one on either side of him, and Ghilleadh leaned down from the saddle, grasped him by the shoulder and pulled the unfortunate wretch to his feet, not ungently, where he stood blinking up at us through the smears of blood that covered his face, his eyes flicking from one of us to the other and his elbows still held defensively in the air. He was very young and very afraid. I spoke to him before Ghilly could.

"Put your arms down, lad, we're not going to hurt you, but we need you to tell us how many men are in there. How many Saxons?"

His mouth moved, but nothing came out at first, and then he found his voice. "I don't know, my lord, but there's a lot of them. They're everywhere, but mostly inside the house by now. They killed all the guards when they first attacked."

"How long ago was that?" Ghilly's voice was harsh; the guards had been his men.

The fellow blinked again. "Not long ago, my lord. Just before first light. They came out of the dark, with arrows first, I think. All the dead guards had arrows in them."

Bedwyr and Bors had joined us now, and the other two running men had stopped to listen, breathless and panting heavily.

Bedwyr spoke up. "How did you escape?"

"I just ran, my lord. Didn't stop to think about it. I was in the kitchens when I heard the shouting and the noise of fighting at the front, and then I smelt smoke and I jumped out the window and ran out the back gates. And then I thought I'd better run to Camulod and raise the alarum."

"How were you wounded?"

He blinked up at me in confusion. "Wounded? I'm not wounded."

"There's blood all over your face."

He wiped his palm across his brow, then stared in awe at his reddened hand. "I don't know. I fell, I remember. Against a wall, by the gates."

The four of us exchanged glances. There was clearly nothing more to be learned from this one, but I tried once again, looking at the other two men and including all of them in my next question.

"We still don't know what we are facing here, so think hard, all of you. How many Saxons did you see? Have you any clear idea?"

"Aye, lord," said one of the others. "I know my numbers, some of them, anyway. I counted four score of them before I left my hiding place and ran. But I could have been wrong. There might have been more, might not. They were running about all over the place, so it were hard to count. But there's too many of them there for just the four of you."

I nodded. "There's help on the way. Now get you to Camulod, and when you meet my troopers, tell them we are under attack and need them here. Go now."

They ran off, together now, and I turned to Ghilleadh. "Four score of them?"

He shrugged. "Could be more," he said, aping the speech of the other man, "might be less. But they won't be expecting horsemen. Let's make a start. We're fully armored."

I swung my horse around and looked back the way we had come, but there were only the three running men in sight. It was almost full daylight now. I unhooked my cavalry spatha from its place by my saddle horn and tossed it to Bors, who had no blade, and then I drew my long sword.

"There's only room for two abreast through the gates. You and me in front, Ghilly. Bedwyr and Bors behind. Form up on me as soon as we're inside, and come where I lead, four abreast and knee to knee. Ghilly on my right, then Bors, then you, Bedwyr. And be prepared for anything. We won't have time to debate our course once we're inside, so I'll pick the biggest target I see as soon as we're through and we'll hit them hard. Let's go."

We were inside the gates within moments, riding at full gallop, and I remember being aware that my three companions were in their assigned places. Then I saw a press of alien bodies surrounding a two-wheeled farm cart, throwing booty from the villa into its high box, and I wheeled directly towards them, standing upright in my stirrups and wishing I had a shield as I aimed my sword blade like a spear at the nearest man.

They did not see us coming until we were right on top of them, and by then it was too late for any of them to react. Our charging horses scattered them like chaff as we thundered along the side of the cart from rear to front, and I caught one fellow, who had been standing gaping at us from the top of the piled booty, with a full swing, feeling my blade bite deep as I swept by him. By that time, however, our line of four had been split by the press of bodies, and I was alone. I saw an entire line of men, most of them carrying plunder, stretching from the cart all the way back into the main house, and I turned my horse towards them, mounting the rise of seven steps that led from ground level to the garden level above. Even as I turned, however, I was aware of burdens being cast aside and weapons being drawn, and the long line coalesced into knots of determined men brandishing weapons and crouching in preparation to meet me and whoever else came with me.

After that there was chaos. I have no memory of dismounting, although it was futile to remain horsed in such a fight, when the horse could not help its rider in any way, hemmed in and trapped in a narrow space. I remember being back to back and shoulder to shoulder with Ghilleadh, swinging my sword with savage enjoyment of the knowledge that my back was protected and no one could come near me from the front because my blade was longer and sharper than any of theirs. And then Ghilly was suddenly gone, the pressure of his back no longer there against my own, and I heard the ringing clatter of his blade as it fell on the stone slabs of the pathway.

I swung around immediately and there he was, on all fours, fighting to stand up, but blood was dripping viscously to the ground from somewhere beneath his helmet. I jumped to him and straddled his back with my legs, sweeping one bending fool away with my blade and then chopping backhanded to sever the arm of another.

I could still hear swords ringing, so I knew at least one of my companions was still alive and fighting, but I dared not take the time to look about and locate the sounds. Something hit me hard across the back and I stumbled clear of Ghilly as I swung around and killed the upstart who had tried to take me from behind. And then Ghilly was on his feet again, his own sword in his hand, and for a moment there was no one facing us.

"Over there," he cried. "Bedwyr."

I looked where he was pointing and saw Bedwyr and Bors hard set in the far corner of the atrium, surrounded by a large number of men who were hampering themselves by being too many and too close to one another. Ghilly and I hit them from behind and carved our way through the mass, climbing over corpses until we were side by side with our friends, facing a much reduced number of enemies, few of whom seemed eager to come against the four of us combined.

Our relief was short lived, however, for our attack from the rear had merely weeded out the press, leaving those who remained with more room in which to fight. The first to move against us was the biggest man there, a wild-eyed giant with a gigantic broad-headed axe. He swung the thing aloft with a roar and leapt towards us, aiming, I believe, at Bedwyr, but before he could come close enough to chop at anyone, young Bors flew at him and drove his long spatha into the fellow's exposed armpit, then fell away to his right, twisting and pulling two-handed at his blade like a lever so that the giant screamed in agony and fell forward at my feet, gurgling and spitting blood. I finished him off with a hard chop to the exposed back of his neck just as the entire crew of them surged forward again. I took one blow to the head that came close to knocking me senseless, and I reeled uselessly for what felt like a long time, but suddenly there was a broad back in front of me as Ghilleadh returned the service I had extended to him a short while earlier.

And then our friends arrived, Arthur himself bounding through the main gates at their head, mounted on the enormous chestnut horse he called Colossus, and in what seemed like the blink of an eye the entire courtyard was jammed with mounted men and the Saxons were in full flight, most of them running back into the main house in the hope of escaping from the rear. I was still reeling, leaning on my sword as I regained my breath, and I saw Arthur dismounted and dashing in pursuit of them, wearing only the lightest of leather cuirasses and brandishing Excalibur. But he was alone, with no one behind him in support. I shouted a warning to Ghilly and began to run after Arthur, only to find him crouching a few paces inside the entrance of the atrium, his back to the decorative fountain in the center as he waved Excalibur's long, shimmering blade in front of him, daring the three men who faced him to come against him.

My arrival startled the three and they began to run, but Arthur leapt towards the one nearest him and cut him down, turning his back in the process towards the second man, who changed direction in mid-step and swung a heavy hand axe at Arthur's back. I was not quite fast enough in my scramble to intercept him and did not have time or room to swing or stab, so all I could do was throw myself forward, hitting him with my shoulder as he swung and knocking him off balance, deflecting his blow so that only the flat of his blade hit the King's shoulder and glanced off. I spun quickly, regaining my balance before the axe man did, and dispatched him with a single overhand blow that almost clove him in two. Arthur, however, had been struck down by the force of the axe blow and was kneeling slumped, his head hanging, clutching his right shoulder with his left hand as he groped clumsily with the nerveless fingers of his right in search of the hilt of Excalibur, which was lying on the ground in front of him.

I heard a scuffling behind me and spun again to see a bowman no more than six paces from me, taking aim at the King's undefended back. Too far away to reach him in time to save Arthur, I leapt backwards, frantically trying to find and shield the King behind me, and as I did so I saw the raider loose his arrow. I remember nothing else.

3

The next time I set eyes upon the splendid cuirass that saved my life that day, I experienced mixed reactions. I gave thanks, first of all for the random chance of the broken strap that had led to my donning it in the first place, for had I not been wearing it I would most certainly have died. No other armor could have withstood the full force of a war arrow loosed from so close a range. I owed my life, I knew, to the plaited, resilient weave of thin blued-metal straps layered beneath that burnished, ornately molded leather exterior.

I gave thanks, too, for the skill and pride and excellence of the unknown master craftsman who had fashioned the thing, long decades earlier in some unknown corner of the Roman world, for the arrow had struck cleanly in the center of the chest and rebounded, its viciously barbed head destroyed by the force of the impact.

Ghilleadh and Bedwyr and Tristan brought the missile to the sick bay to show me, as soon as the medics pronounced me well enough to receive visitors, because they were amazed by the damage the war head had sustained—it was smashed and twisted beyond recognition—but they were even more astonished that my magnificent cuirass appeared to be undamaged.

My entire body was a mass of pain, my ribs so sore and bruised that I could breathe deeply only if I gritted my teeth, but I sent Bors to bring the cuirass for me to examine, and I was as surprised as my friends were when I saw that what they had said was true, for I had been sure that I would never be able to wear the armor again after such an impact. The underlying structure of the cuirass appeared to be intact, without a dent or any other signs of warp or distortion. Only the exterior gave any hint of what had happened to it, for there was a fresh, ragged-edged gouge now on the gleaming leather surface, to match the older scar from decades earlier when the cuirass had saved the life of Germanus under similar circumstances. The new gouge, however, was deeper than the old, for it had split the leather, and the dark gleam of the underlying metal weave was exposed. Thinking back to when I had heard the story of the first scar, I remembered my skepticism about the details of the force involved in that incident, but now I knew there had been no exaggeration. The cuirass was almost magical in its resilience and strength.

Afterwards, when my friends had withdrawn to their duties and I was alone again with time to think, I experienced regret and a strong sense of nostalgia, remembering my old mentor's affection for the armor he had given me and for his own expressed regret over the dulled and much-polished scar that was the only blemish on the entire costume. It had saved his life, he told me then, and as such, the old scar was a badge of honor, a wound received in combat, but he would have been happy to find some way of repairing and concealing the damage done to the leather. And then he had asked me to be careful with it, and to avoid putting any more scars on it, and I had solemnly pledged to do so.

He had been smiling when he extracted my promise, however, and I had known with complete certainty that, given a choice between saving my life at the cost of the armor or saving the armor at the cost of my life, the latter option would never have occurred to the old man. Now I consoled myself with imagining the pleasure Germanus would have taken in knowing that his gift had, in fact, saved my life beyond dispute.

That brought me to consider the fight itself, and the truths underlying it, truths I had not yet heard or guessed at, since less than a day had elapsed since the morning raid, and no one yet understood much of anything about it. I realized immediately, however, that this could have been a catastrophic encounter, despite the relatively small enemy numbers involved, because it had taken us by surprise and Arthur himself had been placed in a very real jeopardy that would rarely have been equaled by a formal battle situation. The surprise element alone would cause major repercussions immediately, for it exposed a glaring deficiency in our security, and that made me feel compassion for Ghilleadh, since the army group responsible for the undetected penetration by the hostiles was his.

That the deficiency had gone undetected for years before the attack meant nothing in this instance, for the responsibility as legate in command was Ghilly's alone. The Saxons had reached Camulod, and, irrespective of the type of loophole they had found to penetrate our defenses, that was simply neither acceptable nor defensible.

Nor did it matter that the "Saxons" were not Saxons at all. They were enemies and they had penetrated the heart of our territories. I knew, because Tristan had told me, that they were Danes, from the eastern coastal territories we called the Saxon Shores. But how they reached Camulod and what had brought them there was still unknown. We had taken seventeen prisoners, however, and Tristan had told me they were being questioned. I knew they would be deprived of sleep and food or water, but they would suffer no physical torment at the hands of anyone in Camulod, and sooner or later, driven by their very humanity, their need for comfort and an end of confinement, they would tell us what we needed to know. They had no reason *not* to tell us. They were raiders, marauders bent on spoils and plunder, not soldiers bound by discipline or loyalty to any but themselves, so they could protect their own skins without fear of betraying any grand scheme.

The prisoners held out in silence for three days, by which time I was on my feet again, and then they lowered their defenses and spoke openly and readily. It turned out that the reason for their three-day silence had been loyalty to their own, the companions they had left behind at the coast to guard their boats. The arrangement had been that, were they not back within seven days of having left, their companions were to stand off to sea and wait for three days more, then sail home with the word of their deaths.

The tale they told when once they began to speak was a tragic but sadly laughable one, a farcical affair of futility and frustration. They had left their home base early in the spring, with a small fleet of four galleys containing a hundred and a half men, intent upon rounding south Britain, Cornwall and Cambria and raiding across the sea into Eire, for it was commonly known in their eastern lands that a twenty-mile-wide belt of uninhabited and therefore worthless territory stretched the length and breadth of the coastline of Britain, created as the result of decades of fierce and incessant raiding from the sea by their own kind.

Upon their arrival in southern Eire, however, they had fallen subject to a rain of troubles. One of their galleys had been lost at sea, mere days after making landfall, when it was swallowed up in a dense sea fog off one of the coastal islands and then swept onto a hidden ridge of rocks along the shore. They had lost more than half the ship's complement in that episode. Less than a month after that, having abandoned their initial landing place because it generated nothing in the way of plunder or rewards, they sailed southwestwards for two days and landed again, only to be surprised immediately by a large war party of local clansmen who were on their way to raid a neighboring clan and stumbled across the Danish raiders. In that encounter, too, they had sustained heavy casualties.

Their next affliction had been a plague of some kind, a pestilence that decimated them, with one in every three men falling sick of a virulent, pustulous fever and one in three of the stricken dying within days of falling sick while the others lingered in excruciating pain for weeks. By the time the wretches had recovered from that, the summer was over and the autumn already showing signs of degenerating rapidly into winter, so they had embarked once again in their three remaining ships, all three seriously undermanned by that time, and put to sea just in time to be caught in the first of the winter storms that ravage the seas around Britain every year. There, in that chaos of winds and waves, one of their ships had rammed another full in the side and sunk it. They had counted themselves fortunate in losing only three men, for the two vessels had remained locked together long enough for the crew of the stricken ship to clamber to safety aboard the other.

Two days after that, they had limped ashore on the marshy fenlands to the north and west of Camulod, near to the great tor of Glastonbury, but far enough removed from it to have no idea that the tor was inhabited, albeit only by a colony of anchorites. There, in desperation, they had left a small holding crew of twenty men to guard their two remaining galleys while the rest of the force, fewer than three score as opposed to the originally reported four, proceeded to strike far inland, in the hope of finding a town or a village and being able to salvage something in the way of plunder to make up for the disasters they had undergone. They had found nothing for three days, but had avoided being found themselves, more through blind chance than good judgment, it transpired, and just as they were about to turn homeward in defeat, they had found the well-tended outlying fields of our colony, and had soon discovered the Villa Britannicus itself.

Their blundering misadventures immediately became legend among our soldiers, for our men could not understand how any fighting group of any kind, or of even rudimentary competence, could venture to attack a wealthy target like the Villa Britannicus without first taking elementary precautions and making an effort to discover how safe or how dangerous it might be. That the Danes' spies failed to notice that all the guards at the villa were under strict discipline, wore uniform armor and were equipped with superb weaponry seemed beyond belief to our troopers, and that their scouts could spy out the land without noticing a garrisoned fortress with upwards of two thousand men less than a mile away was nothing short of ludicrous.

That was, however, exactly what had occurred, and there had been nothing sinister or premeditated in the way they had been able to make their way into our heartland. They described their journey inland to us, for at least they had been wise enough to take note of the directions they must follow to win back to their ships, and a large scouting party of my own troopers was dispatched immediately to seal the route. It offered little solace to Ghilleadh, however, to know that by merest chance and in the face of incalculable odds, these witless dolts had managed—flawlessly yet in complete ignorance—to thread a needle no one had known was there.

Our sole consolation after the debacle was the knowledge that the weakness in our safety net had been identified. Never again would we be taken by surprise from that direction. Arthur refused

Ghilleadh's claim of responsibility for what had occurred and exonerated him completely, pointing out in the Council gathering of knights that followed the event that no matter who had been legate in charge of the home army on that tour of duty, the result would have been the same. No one had known the flaw in our defenses was there, and thus no one could have anticipated what occurred. And as it was, he pointed out, we had been fortunate even in our misfortune, for my group had been assembled for that morning's inspection and was able to respond immediately to the alarum. We had sustained no major casualties other than the guards who were slaughtered in the predawn attack. Only a few had been injured: four troopers slightly wounded in the skirmish and eight of the villa's servants beaten by the looters in attempts to make them betray where the most valuable goods were kept.

Apart from all of that, however, the summation was that the enemy had been routed quickly, the damage to the villa had been only slight and confined mainly to the farm and storage buildings within the compound, and nothing of any value had been taken or destroyed.

The only contentious matter remaining was that of the seventeen prisoners and what to do with them. We could not simply set them free to return to their home on the Saxon Shores, for they had no way of getting there now, except by traveling on foot across the breadth of the country, plundering and killing to support themselves the entire way, and, once arrived home among their own again, they would be likely to return against us, seeking vengeance. Nor could we easily keep them as prisoners in Camulod, for our system had not been designed to accommodate prisoners on any large scale. And seventeen hostile and potentially lethal aliens was a large scale. We had detention cells, but they had been built to house the occasional criminal or malcontent and were capable of containing a maximum of ten men, if they were all crammed in together, so they were useless in our present contingency. And of course the solution of simply killing all of them out of hand was beyond consideration, although several voices were raised in favor of that solution.

Arthur deferred judgment on the matter, dividing the seventeen captives for the time being among the outlying garrison posts and guard posts, each of which was equipped with a cell in which a prisoner or two could be temporarily lodged under guard.

None of us could have guessed then that the situation would be resolved swiftly and efficiently in the following month by the arrival in Camulod of an old friend and ally of both Merlyn and Arthur, the Scots admiral called Connor Mac Athol, who was brother to the adjutant of Camulod, Donuil Mac Athol, and who would take all seventeen prisoners to serve on his galleys.

The episode of the raid on the villa was consigned to the past, its lessons learned and acted upon, and the only recurrent reference made to it thereafter was by our garrison soldiers and troopers, who would never be able to bring themselves to believe that any military force could be as hapless and stupid as our invaders had been.

4

"Do you remember our visit to Chester last year?"

Arthur was riding slightly ahead of me and had paused to wait for me as I attended to a loose binding on the shaft of one of my throwing lances, where the tightly coiled thong of the leather hand grip had begun to unravel. I decided the repair would take more time than I had then and replaced the defective weapon in the hanging scabbard behind my saddle.

"That was two years ago, Arthur, closer to three," I answered. "The time we found the silver spurs."

"Was it that long ago? I suppose it was, now that I think of it. Anyway, as you say, we found the spurs, but you may also remember that we did *not* find the man we went to visit. What was his name? The king there, your friend from Saint Alban's Shrine."

"Symmachus. He was no friend of mine. He couldn't stand the sight of me, in fact. Thought I had designs on his witless, self-engrossed daughter. Disgusting woman, too much like her father for my tastes."

"Ah! That's right. What was her name?"

"Cynthia, a completely spoiled brat. She treated poor young Bors like dirt, just for being smitten with her. Used him like a slave and couldn't make him miserable enough to please herself, although she never tired of trying. I ended up detesting her mainly for that."

"Was she comely?"

I shrugged and kneed my horse forward. "Comely? No, she was beautiful. That was her problem—too beautiful for her own good and too stupid to know that surface beauty is worthless if there's no substance inside to back it up. I was glad to see her finally ride away with her priggish father. Young Bors recovered soon after that ...

"I liked her stepmother, though, the king's wife. Demea was her name, and she was pleasant and harmless—and young, too. Symmachus was besotted with her, and for good reason, I thought. She was the only one of the brood whose company was even bearable, except for the younger daughter, Maia, but she was just a girl child who was trying very hard to be a boy."

I reached behind me and selected another lance, and held it out to him. "Here, try this one. See the stump there, ahead of us, the one with the sapling growing up out of it? Ride past it on the left, at about twenty paces, and let's see how close you can come to the sapling."

He broke away from me immediately, wheeling his horse around and to the back, kicking it into a canter as he went and taking it in a wide circle around the open space surrounding us, increasing his speed steadily and raising himself in his stirrups until he was almost standing, reins held loosely in his left hand, his right outstretched, balancing the long, tapering, needle-pointed javelin I had given him. Then, when he reached the farthest point of his looping turn, he swung his mount inward and galloped straight towards the rotted tree stump with the parasite sapling growing from its moldering corpse. As he charged past me his eyes were slitted in concentration, and I watched his arm draw back, his body angling into the cast, and then the smooth arc of the throw as he launched the weapon. It missed the sapling, but barely, and it was the best cast he had made all morning. He reined his horse in, rode over and collected the thrown javelin, then came back towards me, smiling.

"Getting better."

"Aye," I said, nodding in assent, "that was a good one, no denying that. Had that sapling been a man, he would be dead or badly injured now. Out of the fight, certainly. You're getting better. But you're getting older, too, and you're doing that faster than you're getting better."

His only response was to whip off one of his gloves and throw it at me. It was a gesture normally perceived as a deadly insult and a challenge, but I caught the glove, laughing, just before it hit me and flung it directly back at him. He caught it easily.

"Why can't you do it like that?" I said. "You threw the glove perfectly. What's so different about throwing the spear? It's not much heavier. That's the lightest weapon you'll ever throw, other than a knife, and you're deadly accurate with one of those."

We had set out that morning to visit the farm master Dougald, who had been injured in the Danish raid the week before, but it was a pleasant, almost balmy day and we were in no great hurry, so we had spent hours practicing casting the javelin from a charging horse along the way. Arthur was fascinated with my lightweight javelin and its use, but the truth was that I was still the only one in Camulod who could use the weapon easily and skillfully. Arthur was the closest to me in performance only because of his obstinacy—he had spent countless hours in dogged practice and his efforts were bearing fruit—but he would never be better than adequate and he knew it. That I could laugh openly at his determined attempts spoke highly of our easy friendship, but I would never have thought of doing so when anyone else was around. Now he sniffed disdainfully.

"I am not sure I really want to learn such an outlandish, Gaulish method of fighting after all. It occurred to me as I threw that time that, even in the casting, I was preparing to swing aside and flee. That is hardly the proper conduct for a king, or for any of his knights ... or so it seems to me now."

I laughed outright. "Absolutely not, Seur King. Far better to go charging straight ahead and die gloriously when your throw goes astray and your target chops you down. That takes real dedication to the ideals of bravery."

He looked at me evenly, his face expressionless. "You know, Seur Frank, you have absolutely no notion of the proper deference to a king. This would be a good time to scrape and bow and toady, in the hope that I might forgive your unforgivable insolence and allow you to continue living."

"Aye, it might, Seur King, but then again it might not. Apologies are tiresome and weakening and you would think me sick were I to change from the way I am. Are we to sit here arguing all day?"

He looked about him and then tossed me my javelin. "Perhaps not. It might rain. Come on, then. It must be less than a mile from here to the Villa Varo."

We rode on, now beginning to penetrate the fertile lands of the villa, with its extensive fields that had been under cultivation for longer than anyone could remember. Quintus Varo, the owner of the estate at the time of Caius Britannicus's first notions of creating a defensible enclave here, had been a close friend of the family Britannicus, related to them by marriage, and although his own family had since died out—there were no Varos left alive anywhere in Camulod—the villa and its lands had been an integral part of the colony since its beginnings and was now the agricultural center of Camulod, with all farm planning and implementation organized and coordinated from the villa itself.

"So, Master Pendragon," I asked as I caught up to him, riding knee to knee beside him. "What prompted you to bring up Symmachus back there?"

"Merlyn thinks he is important, and so I have to think seriously about him. I've never met the man, but you have. Would you trust him?"

I knew that he was not asking lightly but was looking for my real evaluation of the northern king, and that forced me to be judicious. I took so long mulling over my opinions, however, that he turned in his saddle to look at me. I shrugged and spread my hands, letting my reins fall slack.

"That is a complex question, Arthur, and in truth my answer would have to depend on what it was I was trusting him to do. To look to his own interests, definitely. To keep his own counsel and guard his own back, surely. To alienate and try to intimidate everyone who comes in contact with him, absolutely. To be disdainful, unfriendly and aloof at all times, beyond a doubt. In all of those things I would trust him without reservation and beyond any possibility of uncertainty. But none of those is likely to inspire you, is it? So I must look at what I think you really mean. Would I trust him to be a staunch ally?"

The King gazed at me, waiting patiently.

"Well, as far as a simple alliance goes, I might be tempted to, providing I was sure he knew the alliance would be to his advantage above and beyond everyone else's. But staunch? I think not, because the strength of his conviction would rely upon his perception—and there's that word again—his perception of how strongly that same advantage weighed in his favor. As soon as that changed, his intent and commitment would change with it.

"But your question was more pointed, wasn't it, more specific? Would I trust him? Would I trust him implicitly to be true and steadfast in backing me up and supporting my plans and strategies for building a Britain united under me were I Arthur Pendragon?" I shook my head. "No, Arthur. I would not. Because that kind of trust, the kind of trust you are looking for and will be bound to rely upon, depends entirely upon honesty—honest, open friendship and respect, and mutual confidence, good faith and goodwill. I don't believe Symmachus deals in such things. I don't think he has the capacity for friendship, or even for plain dealings. He is arrogant to the point of utter folly. His eyes are ever focused upon his own interests and he has no time or patience, and even less willingness, to consider the needs or the design of any other than himself."

The King shook his head, his mouth twisted into a wry smile beneath his close-cropped beard. "You know, my friend, my only wish for you is that along with showing me proper deference and respect as your High King, you might some day learn to say what you really think, instead of beating the bushes endlessly with vague insinuations. So, you dislike the man."

"Dislike him? That is neither here nor there. I said I would not trust him. And that is what you asked me."

"It is. It is indeed."

"So why the sudden concern with Symmachus? He is a local king, no more than that."

"He controls Deva. That is why. Merlyn distrusts him, too, as deeply and instinctively as you do, but whereas you would appear to discount him, Merlyn sees him as a menace and a danger. That fortress of his was built to hold six thousand men, and it has grown since first it was built. If Symmachus wanted to, he could fill it up with enough men to cause us great heartache. And therefore Merlyn thinks I should pay court to him."

"By the Christ! Not to wed his daughter, surely? She would drive you to despair within a year, Arthur."

"No, not at all. No weddings are involved. I would do it merely to make myself and Camulod appear amiable to him."

"Useless. A waste of time. You've already done that more than once, and he has shown no response. Even after you went out of your way to meet him that time, going knocking on his gates, he made no acknowledgment of your visit."

"True, but—" A terrifying sound erupted from the other side of the rise we were about to crest. "Shit! What in God's holy name was that?"

I was already spurring my horse towards the soul-chilling sounds, knowing exactly what they were and hoping, in spite of my sudden fear, that the cause would not be as bad as it sounded. But as I crested the rise I knew immediately that it was worse. At the bottom of the hill, against a background of the buildings of the sprawling villa, I saw three people being confronted by a very angry bear that had already downed another of their party. All three were standing stock-still in terror, and the bear was taller than any of them, erect on its hind legs and swinging its extended arms at them, although they were at least fifteen paces from it at that time. But fifteen paces, to a charging bear, is no distance at all. The beast would cover it in the blink of an eye, and I was still two hundred paces from being able to intervene.

"Shit!" the King roared again from behind me. "That's Dougald. Fly, Lance, fly!"

I dropped my reins across my horse's neck, giving him his head, and he responded as trained, breaking immediately into a run that within a few paces was a full, free gallop. I steered and controlled him with my legs alone, adjusting without thought to his movements and using both hands to prepare a throwing lance from the quiver at my back. The first one I pulled out was, of course, the damaged one I had been working on and I threw it down to stick in the ground, hoping that Arthur would collect it in passing. I pulled out another, trying not to think of what would happen if my horse set one foot wrongly in this downhill plunge, and set about coiling the throwing thong around the shaft. That is not the easiest of tasks on a fast-moving horse, but for that reason alone I had practiced doing it a thousand times and more, and now, when I needed to do it swiftly and cleanly, all that training proved itself.

I was on level ground already and had covered more than half the distance between me and the bear and it had still not lowered itself to charge. I took up the reins again in my left hand, gently, still allowing them to hang loose lest my horse misinterpret the signal and break stride, and I stood up in my stirrups, extending my arm backwards for the throw as I counted the bounding leaps that were devouring the distance between me and my target. The bear was large, but the distance separating us was still too great for any hope of accuracy and I knew I would have only one chance. If my throw went wide of the mark, the animal would not even be aware of it, and whatever was destined to happen might occur before I could prepare another. And still, as my count reached twenty, nothing had changed. The scene before me was as motionless as a setting of statuary.

But then one of the men saw me coming and his nerve broke. He shouted aloud and turned to run, and in the blinking of an eye the bear was down on all fours and charging after him.

In less than twenty paces the enraged animal overtook him and smashed him to the ground, where he flopped and rolled like a child's rag toy. The bear sped past him and stopped, reared up again with another bowel-loosening roar and spun back, and at that moment the fellow's two remaining companions began to run, too, one of them straight towards me and the other away from me.

The sight of two fleeing figures appeared to confuse the bear, because in the act of launching itself at the man on the ground, it reared up again, its head swinging from one side to the other as it attempted to decide which of the two fleeing creatures deserved to be chased down first. Then, perhaps because it saw my movements, too, it charged after the woman running towards me and screaming for help. But now the beast presented me with the worst of targets, its thick skull, held low in the need for speed, protecting it from a chest shot.

Cursing, I swung my horse out and away, hoping the woman would not veer to follow me. More than thirty paces yet separated me from the brute when I saw the best shot I was likely to be offered and threw instinctively.

I knew as soon as I released it that the cast was good, and better than good. The lance leapt forward like an arrow from a full-drawn bow and flew true, and I thundered past the lumbering animal, amazed at its single-minded swiftness and appalled at how close it was to pulling the woman down. But just as it seemed the woman must die, the lance struck home, its two-foot-long needle-pointed head penetrating cleanly between a pair of ribs.

The bear's reaction might, at any other time, have been comical to see, but I was to realize that only long afterwards. As I reined my horse in hard, bringing it to a quivering, snorting, stiff-legged halt, the woman fell headlong, and at the same moment the bear spread its front paws and skidded to a stop, its rear end sliding on the grass. And then it sprang erect and twisted violently sideways, snapping its teeth in rage and straining to reach the missile that had pierced its side. But it failed, and it continued to spin, ever more slowly, until it fell over on its back, its legs kicking spasmodically and a froth of bright blood erupting from its mouth. It was dead within moments of being hit, and so close was it to the quarry it had been pursuing that its blood was splashed all over the woman's skirts and bare legs.

Before I could begin to move again, Arthur reined his own horse in beside me, breathing hard as though it had been he and not his mount that had done all the running. "By the sweet Christ, Lance, that was a throw! You must have pierced both heart and lungs. Now I know why you laugh at my efforts. Is the woman dead?"

I shook my head. "No, I think not, unless she died of fright. The bear never touched her."

"But look at the blood!"

"It's the bear's."

"Well thank God for that. Check her for injuries while I see to Dougald and the other fellow."

Knowing that the crisis was over, I finally took the time to heave a deep, rich breath and looked about me, clenching my fists against the reaction that I knew would soon have me trembling, and forcing myself to concentrate on what was happening around me. People were running towards us from the villa now that the danger had passed, and somewhere among them, I presumed, was the surviving fellow who had fled. Arthur was riding towards the man who had been already on the ground when we first saw them. In his right hand he held my discarded lance. I took another deep breath and swung myself down to look to the woman.

I had not even known she was a woman until she screamed and I noticed her running with raised skirts. I knelt beside her, feeling for the pulse at her throat. I found it immediately, strong and regular, and I knew there was nothing greatly wrong with her, but I found myself unwilling to remove my fingers from her neck. It seemed softer and warmer than anything I had ever felt before. She was young, perhaps twenty, perhaps slightly older—I was no judge of women's ages. And she was comely, her closed eyelids almost translucent in their whiteness, the brows above them a deep reddish brown to match the red sheen in her disordered hair, and her skin young and supple, with no trace of lines or wrinkles. A good, very pleasant face, with a wide red mouth and full lips that I felt sure must laugh easily. And still I held my fingers to her throat, feeling the warmth and the beating of her pulse.

She opened her eyes suddenly, looking directly up at me, and then tensed, as if preparing to scramble away. But then she lay still, staring at me. I began to take my hand away, but she reached up quickly and seized my wrist, and brought my spread fingers back into contact with her neck.

"You killed her."

The accusation startled me. "Her? Who is *she*?"

"The bear."

"Oh, the bear. Yes, the bear is dead."

"Where are her cubs?"

I shook my head. "I saw no cubs, Lady, only the bear."

"Two cubs. We frightened them, came upon them suddenly, and they called for her. The mother came running, and my father—" She started up, spinning in place and looking about wildly. "Where is my father? Is he dead?"

"Hush, Lady, I can see him. The King is with him. They are picking him up to take him inside and the King is talking to him, so he is alive."

She had become still again and looked at me from beneath arched eyebrows. "The King? The King is here? Then who are you?"

"My name is Clothar, Lady. I serve the King."

"Clothar? The knight, the one they call the Frank?" She seemed flustered, almost afraid, and I smiled at her.

"Aye, and sometimes the Lancer, depending upon who is speaking. But that is who I am, Lady."

Now her eyes flared, angrily, I thought. "I am no Lady, my lord Knight. My name is Elaine."

"That was my mother's name. Elaine of what, my lady?"

"Elaine of what?" She laughed, although what emerged was more like a snort of exasperation. "Elaine of here, my lord Knight. Elaine of this villa, this farm. Now help me rise. I must see to my father." She stopped in the act of reaching for my hand, her head straining, her nostrils twitching. "What is that *smell*?"

I smiled again, and pointed to the dead monster at her back. "It's the bear, my lady." She turned to look and then suddenly gasped and started in a great leap, throwing herself towards me until she crashed into me, knocking me off balance so that we both fell sprawling and I ended up with my hand beneath her skirts, the back of my fingers against the soft fleshy heat of her thigh. I snatched my hand away and scrambled to my feet, feeling the heat flaming in my face, but she appeared not to have noticed, keeping her gaze fastened on the dead animal behind her as I helped her up from the ground. Only then did she turn to look at me, her eyes wide with fear.

"Was she that close to me when you killed her?"

I could only shrug, still embarrassed about touching her bare thigh, and I said the first thing that came into my head. "It hasn't moved since."

She blinked at me, then looked down. "Your hand is bleeding."

I jerked my hand—the guilty hand—up and looked at it, feeling my face flaming again. "It's not my blood, Lady. It's the bear's. It's all over you, too."

She hoisted her skirts sufficiently to allow her to see that what I had said was true, and then she shuddered and looked into my eyes, her expression unreadable, before turning away. The small crowd that had gathered was now moving back towards the villa gates, and among them they carried two stretcher biers. I saw Arthur standing by our horses, watching me. So did she.

"The King is waiting for you," she said. "Will you bring him inside?"

"Aye, I will, if he will come."

"Then come you, too. And—"

"And, Lady?"

"I have not yet thanked you, for my life."

I managed to find a smile. "To see you alive and well is thanks enough, my lady."

"Aye, well ... Perhaps." One corner of her mouth twitched upwards in what might have been the beginnings of a smile, but then she turned away again, and spoke to me over her shoulder. "I must see to my father. Come inside and ... wait for me, if you will."

I was still watching her retreating back when Arthur pulled his mount to a halt beside me, leading my own horse. "A fetching lass, our Elaine, eh, Lance? You'll come to no harm from having saved her from a ravening beast, unless she turns you into one yourself."

"Who is she?"

"Dougald's daughter, although she's not his daughter. He and his wife, Martha, adopted her when she was still suckling. Martha wet-nursed her when her own mother died, and the child never left them. Now she is Dougald's entire life, since Martha died five years ago. We'll go inside for a while, see if there's anything to be done for Dougald."

The woman had passed out of sight beyond the villa gates, and I looked at Arthur now for the first time since he had joined me. "What mean you, to be done for him? You expect him to die?"

The King laughed. "Dougald? Not this year. He's badly cut up, covered in blood, and his face has been mauled, but it would take more than a swat from an angry bear to kill that old boar. No, I simply meant that he will have the best of care, and most probably with no need of help from us. But I want to be sure of that before we leave him, because he is a jewel beyond price, the best farming mind in all of Camulod, and perhaps in all of Britain. Besides, I'm thirsty, and I could eat something, and I can see you're thirsting, too, although not for beer. Mount up. Let's go inside while I try to phrase exactly what I intend to say about that throw of yours when we return to Camulod. Gwin and Ghilleadh and the others will think me a liar when I tell them. Here." He handed me the lance with the unraveled grip and I turned to look at the other one, now firmly clamped in the dead bear's flesh.

"I have to get this one out first. Shouldn't take long. I'll join you when it's done."

In fact it took me a long time to free the lance, and Arthur had vanished into the villa by the time I finally managed to wrest it from the dead beast. In the end, with the help of a couple of brawny farmhands and after much pulling and pushing, trying to release the pressure of the dead flesh around the shaft, I had to tie a rope around the butt end and use the weight of my horse to drag the weapon out of the wound. I was grateful to retrieve it and carried it to a nearby brook to scrub as much of the blood from it as I could. I had too few of them to sacrifice any and they were irreplaceable.

5

The Villa Varo had settled down by the time I eventually arrived there. The injured men were already installed in separate rooms, their wounds being tended by the farming community's resident physician, and there was little for Arthur and me to do but wait for whatever information was to come from the two sickrooms. Someone had brought us beer to drink in the meantime, and Arthur spoke with several of Dougald's closest subordinates while I stood close by the door to the atrium, listening to what was being said behind me, but watching and waiting for the woman Elaine to reappear.

The bear, I heard them tell Arthur, had become a familiar sight close to the villa buildings in the past few years, foraging for food and scraps. She had been little more than a cub herself when she first appeared, and until today she had shown no signs of aggression.

I heard Arthur call out to a young man, about my own age, whom I had noticed earlier, standing alone and pale faced in one corner of the room where we had gathered, and ask him to tell us what had happened. He turned out to be Dougald's son, Luke, half-brother to Elaine, and he had been the third man, the one who had escaped the bear's attack.

According to Luke, no one had had any thought of bears today as Dougald led his three companions away from the bustling villa to where he could speak his mind without being overheard. One of the trio, a man called Jonas, was the headman of a village half a day's march beyond the borders of the colony, and he had been paying court to Elaine for some time. He had come that morning to make an offer of marriage to Dougald, and it was to negotiate and finalize that offer that Dougald had led him away outside the villa gates. Elaine and Luke, who had no voice in the negotiations, had followed along simply because Elaine herself approved of Jonas and his offer and none of the participants anticipated any difficulty in arriving at a settlement. In walking and talking, however, Dougald had led them right to where the bear's cubs were playing unseen in a copse of trees, inadvertently cutting the cubs off from their dam and frightening them into crying for her.

Barely aware of what they had done, Dougald and the others had been caught in the open when the sow came charging through the bushes that had concealed her. Before any one of the four humans could even move, she had been among them, and Dougald, the person closest to her cubs, had been the first to attract her rage. The others had stood frozen, utterly drained by terror and incapable of moving either to help Dougald or to flee.

Jonas had been the first to run, as the sight and sound of my approach broke the spell that had held them. The bear had struck him down savagely, but had not mauled the man beyond that point, thanks to my intervention. How badly Jonas had been hurt by that single ferocious, mutilating blow now remained to be established. He was alive, Luke told us, but that was all he could say.

My first reaction to hearing this tale was anger, but it would take me hours of thought before I realized that it was jealous anger. The primary thought in my mind at the time was that this stranger, this outsider Jonas, had come into Camulod from beyond its borders and endangered some of our residents. That I was thinking of only one of those residents was a mere detail that I did not allow myself to recognize. Perhaps because the events had taken place so soon after the unprecedented Saxon raid of the week before, I immediately stepped into the center of the room and demanded to know how any outsider could have such easy and casual access to our most important farm.

The question earned me strange looks and wide-eyed stares. Jonas was an outsider in name only, I was told. His village was prosperous, well run and, thanks to its proximity to our borders, virtually a part of Camulod itself. Our troopers visited and policed the place irregularly, making sure that no problems ever arose there. The village housed the finest weavers, carpenters and leather workers in the region, their products highly valued within Camulod and essential to the supply and maintenance of farm equipment, and as a result its craftsmen and artisans were free to come and go between their home and Camulod whenever they so wished.

As I listened, learning more than I had sought to know, I was aware of Arthur watching me from where he sat, and I felt my ears burning with the knowledge that, were I to look, he would be wearing that private little grin that I had long since come to recognize as a signal of his seeing things that others had missed. I knew that beyond a doubt, but I did not look at him, because the confusion in my own breast was telling me that I myself did not know what it was that he was seeing in me this time. Instead, I merely nodded in acceptance of what I had been told, and then stood silent, my chin sunk on my chest, until the physician came in to deliver his report to the King at first hand.

Both men would live, he told us. Dougald had been knocked unconscious by the bear's attack, and that had probably saved his life, since the bear had clawed him only twice before abandoning his inert body. One of those two blows, however, had gouged out the old man's right eye and broken his nose. Grave injuries but not life threatening, so long as they remained free of infection. Jonas had sustained only one blow, but the power behind that had been massive. His shoulder had been dislocated and his upper arm bone badly broken, and the physician suspected that several of his ribs had been broken, too. Jonas, it seemed, would not be moving at all for a long time, but when that time eventually elapsed, he would probably be returned to full health, little the worse for his unfortunate encounter.

I had not even noticed the woman Elaine come into the room, but suddenly she was standing by my side, slightly behind me, listening as the physician ended his report. I actually smelled her presence before I saw her, and the unexpected awareness of her nearness brought the hot blood rushing again to my face and ears. But before I could suffer any discomfort over my blushes, Arthur was speaking to her, asking her about her father. We had just heard a full report on that from the physician, but Arthur wanted to hear the daughter voice her own opinion.

"He has lost an eye and his face will be badly scarred. But Strabo here has sewn the wounds tightly shut, so they should heal cleanly. Half blind as he will be, my father will still be able to function as he did before. Had he lost an arm or a hand … well, a one-armed farmer is a man half dead. So …" She drew herself erect and pursed her full, red lips. "We will make the best of it and think ourselves fortunate it was not worse."

"And what of Jonas, your betrothed?" Arthur hesitated. "He is your betrothed, is he not? Or had that still to be decided when the bear attacked?"

Elaine shook her head, glancing at me briefly, her eyes expressionless. "No, it was arranged. We are betrothed. The marriage bargain is settled, the bride price agreed upon. We will be wed when Jonas is himself again." She frowned. "But that will take some time. Jonas is badly hurt—not like to die, as you know, but crippled, none the less, for the time being and likely for months to come."

"Aye," Arthur said gently. "But those months will pass, Elaine, and when they are gone, you'll scarce remember they occurred, believe me."

"I believe you, my lord." She turned her head from Arthur to look at me then. "And you, my lord Clothar. I have not yet had the time to thank you for your aid, nor have I now, except to take the time to say that I am grateful. Will you not return when there is time, to allow us to express our gratitude?"

She seemed completely unaware and unconcerned that there were others there listening to her words, but then she caught herself and turned back to Arthur. "Forgive me, my lord King. The knight is in your service. I had no right to—"

"If anyone has such a right, Elaine, you have." Arthur was smiling at her. "I will need to be kept informed of your father's progress, and since I have no other whom I trust as fully as this man here, it seems only reasonable that he should be my messenger. What say you, Seur Clothar? Will you serve me in this?"

I could only nod, incapable of taking my eyes from the tiny pulse throbbing in the woman's neck. "Yes, Magister," I said, managing to sound calm despite the rapid fluttering in my breast. My reward was another glance from Elaine's unreadable eyes and the hint of a smile at the corner of her wide, red lips. The King turned away and led the conversation in another direction, and as he did so the woman Elaine inclined her head very slightly towards me and moved away, back to her duties, and my eyes were filled with the way the stuff of her gown clung to her swaying hips and buttocks.

FIVE

1

Every man in my army group was happy when we drew home duty in Camulod itself for the winter, and in consequence my own duties were comparatively light at that time. I quickly fell into a routine of making snap inspections of outlying guard posts each night and spending every morning on my administrative tasks, which left me free to do as I wished for the remainder of the day. In consequence, and by no means accidentally, I spent much time at the Villa Varo in the days and weeks that followed the bear's attack, outwardly conscientious in my duty to ensure that the King was kept well informed on the progress of his master farmer.

I made no attempt to delude myself, however, about my real purpose in going there every second day. The woman Elaine intrigued me, and the more I came to know her the more admirable I found her to be. Her brother, Luke, who should have shouldered her father's duties when Dougald was struck down, was amiable enough, but completely unsuited to any managerial responsibility, and so Elaine, who was eminently suited for the task, had assumed her father's workload immediately and wholeheartedly, working from dawn through nightfall on the affairs of the villa farm and of the larger agricultural community that was Camulod. Watching her in admiration as she went about her day, I discovered just how intricate the colony's agricultural affairs really were, and how greatly every element of our lives depended upon the smooth running of the farms that nurtured and fed us.

Like all my fellows, I had previously thought of Camulod as a
purely military community composed of knights, cavalry troopers
and infantry squadrons, all of them existing solely to further the
interests of the King, and secondarily the territories we watched
over. Had anyone asked me prior to that time to name the colony's
single greatest asset, I would instantly have specified our vast herds
of horses, since I relied upon those absolutely as a commander of
cavalry. Only now, thanks to my personal interest in Elaine and
what she did every day, did I begin to appreciate that, without
Camulod's farms, our herds could not have been as prosperous as
they were, nor could our soldiers and troopers have enjoyed the
magnificent food and the luxurious amenities that they took for
granted, for even the furnaces that fed the central heating
hypocausts were fueled by coal mined on one of our own smaller
farms, where a long, rich seam of the substance surfaced on an
open stretch of heath some distance behind the Villa Varo and
extended for more than half a mile, into a hillside that had been
excavated to great depths.

On my first visit to the farm, two days after the incident of the
bear attack, Elaine and I had unwittingly established what was to
become a routine between us. I asked for her as soon as I arrived
and was taken to where she sat in her father's dayroom, half hidden
behind a pile of documents of assorted shapes and thickness. She
was sitting with her head bowed, one hand supporting her chin as
she studied a document on the tabletop in front of her. Surprised to
find her there, and unsure at first of what she was doing, I was
astonished to see that she appeared to be reading, and was then
unwise enough to ask her if she *could* read. She raised her head and
looked me straight in the eye, and for long moments she did not
respond, merely fixing me with a gaze that I could not interpret, but
which told me immediately that I had erred. I have never forgotten
that moment, or the sense of foolishness that set me blushing again.
I had ridden hard to reach the villa, my heart racing with the anticipation of seeing her and my head full of the things I wanted to say
to her, but the mere sight of her, sitting there at her father's work

table, had unmanned me to the point of being reduced to asking a single, futile and offensive question.

Finally, her face still wearing that same enigmatic expression, she raised her other hand and wiggled the pen it held. "Aye, Seur Clothar, and I can write, too. Can you?"

The truth, as I soon discovered, was that she had been as well educated, perhaps even better educated in certain things than I had been, by a twin brother of Dougald's now-dead wife, a wise and learned cleric who had fallen ill while visiting them and had completely lost the use of his legs thereafter. From that day forth he had lived on at the Villa Varo, loved and cared for by his sister Martha and her husband, Dougald. He had survived for ten years, in constant pain and unable to move beyond the single room that had become his entire world. But he had accepted his suffering as a penance, and in restitution for whatever sins he had ascribed to himself, he made it his life's task to encourage and develop the talents he had quickly discerned in his bright-eyed niece. Elaine was only five years old at that time, but by the time the old man died, soon after her fifteenth birthday, she had become the best, indeed the only, educated person on the entire estate, able to speak and write fluently in both Latin and Greek and possessing a well-rounded knowledge of both mathematics and computation. Little wonder then, I thought, that she should be capable of doing the work she did, and the awareness of her astonishing capabilities, coupled with the sheer pleasure I found in her forthright and effortless conversation, merely added to the attractions I found in her.

Both injured men were progressing well, she told me on that first visit, but she herself had no time to stop and talk to me that day. She apologized again for the inconvenience of time constraints, but nevertheless invited me to sit and wait for her if I so wished, after which, she suggested, we might go to the kitchens and find something to eat while we talked. I sat down happily, more than content with the opportunity to sit quietly and simply look at her as she worked. And work she did, for more than an hour, while I sat drinking in the pleasure the mere sight of her gave me.

She looked up several times on that first occasion and caught me staring avidly at her each time, but she seemed more amused than annoyed by my gaze and rewarded me each time with a tiny smile that I interpreted as appreciation for my patience. But then before I could say anything, she would take up yet another piece of vellum or parchment, or more often a waxed tablet filled with columns of numbers, and focus her entire attention upon that. And when she eventually completed that day's tasks, as promised she led me to the villa's large kitchens, where we ate crusty, fresh-baked bread with bowls of thick, delicious soup from a huge cauldron while we talked of many things, but mostly of the myriad tasks involved in running a farm. She talked, for the most part. I was content to listen and watch the expressions that animated her face, changing and shifting constantly with her enthusiasm and passion.

I discovered very quickly that she had been helping her father with clerical records for years, and that she had in fact designed and implemented many of the record-keeping procedures used on the Villa Varo. And now that Dougald was incapable for the time being of handling his duties, she had taken over the entire organization of the affairs not merely of the Villa Varo but of the other ten villas and lesser farms that made up the colony's holdings. She had assistance, certainly, and in plenty, but she herself was the major conductor of operations overall, trusted and looked up to by the managers of all the farms because she had a comprehensive understanding of the working priorities governing the dairy herds, the feed herds, the sheep cotes, the swine and cattle breeding programs, the herds of deer on the various estates, the arable lands, the fallow and grazing lands, the crops that were harvested, the grain and root vegetables that were stored in various locations, and the condition and capacity of the three mills the colony owned. She even knew the number of hives in each of the honeybee colonies that were scattered in clearings among the wooded sections on each estate, and she could tally to the last bale the amount of raw wool that was sitting safely under cover, waiting to be processed into clothing and blankets.

By my fourth visit, I had become comfortable in her company and was able to converse openly and spontaneously with her, with no fear of embarrassing myself. I had also, by that time, absorbed enough of what concerned her to be able to talk intelligently with her about her most pressing concerns. By my tenth visit, some two weeks after that, I knew enough to be able to start making suggestions on how she might enlist extra help, for example during harvest time, by tapping the resources of our military forces, where commanders were constantly on the lookout for ways to keep their off-duty men usefully employed and out of mischief.

It was on my twelfth visit, the twenty-sixth day after our first meeting, that she threw me into confusion again. My presence had long since become a commonplace at the villa, so that I would go directly to the stables to unsaddle my horse, and then make my own way, unaccompanied, to find her. On that particular day, I walked into the dayroom and found Dougald himself sitting at his table, fast asleep. His face was still bandaged, although not heavily. His empty eye socket was covered by a leather patch tied around his head, and the entire expanse of his forehead was discolored with livid bruises. I backed out of the room quietly and went looking for Elaine, a distinct chill in my belly making me acutely aware that I should have been *expecting* to see Dougald up and about by this time. That I had not expected it was a sign of how involved I had become with Elaine, rather than with reporting upon the old man's condition to Arthur. I saw now, with disconcerting clarity, that I would soon have no valid reason for continuing to visit the villa.

Elaine and I never spoke of Jonas and his injuries. He had been returned to his own village in a wagon less than a week after being mauled, and I had not seen him since. Nor had I allowed myself to think of him, since the very thought of his recovery must entail thoughts of Elaine's forthcoming marriage. And Elaine never mentioned his name in my hearing in all that time. It was as though the two of us had formed a pact of silence on the subject of her betrothal, her commitment, to Jonas.

That thought was an unsettling one, and yet nothing had occurred between the two of us that anyone could have described as being unbecoming or improper. We had become friends and we behaved as such, mingling freely with others when we were together, and including everyone nearby in our conversations and activities ... except, of course, that the feelings I had for her were far more complex and disturbing than those of any other friendship I had known, so that I had wondered on several occasions if I might be in love with her. That idea was a frightening one, in some ways, for I had no criteria by which to gauge or even recognize such feelings, other than vague hints and formless mutterings from others and a mention of unspecified but dire changes from Arthur when he spoke of his lost love. I had never known a woman, and there was a fear, somewhere deep within me, that should I ever come to know one, or, God forbid, to fall enamored of one, it might prove the undoing of me in ways I could not even begin to guess at, let alone understand. I certainly felt changed, I knew, and perhaps even in the manner that Arthur had described as the result of love, whereby nothing seemed to be as it had been before. And so I fretted sometimes and agonized often in the privacy of my own thoughts. Of course, I said nothing of this to Elaine herself, and I assumed, with the folly of all young men in dealing with women, that she had no idea of how I felt.

I found her in the byre that day, kneeling on a pad of straw, feeding a calf whose mother had died, and she looked up, smiling, as I entered.

"You sounded just like Justin, clomping across the cobbles there, except that his boots were less solid than yours."

I stood close to her, admiring the deft way she was handling what looked to me a difficult task. She held the tiny calf's head firmly beneath her left arm, securing it with her elbow while the calf sucked voraciously at one end of a short tube of animal intestines, the other end of which, clutched firmly in the fingers of Elaine's left hand, encircled the narrow spout of a small metal funnel containing milk. In her right hand she held a wooden jug containing what was left of the milk, and as I watched she poured the last of it gently into the funnel, from where it traveled down the short tube and into the mouth of the hungry calf. It was an ingenious device, and when it finally popped from the small animal's mouth I saw that the end on which the tiny creature had been sucking was tied off tightly with a piece of cord and had been pierced several times above the knot with a needle, to permit the milk in the tube to be sucked out much as it would have been from the mother cow's own teat.

"Who is Justin?" I asked idly. I had never heard the name mentioned before.

"Who *was* Justin, you mean. He was my husband." She was not looking at me, her attention focused on the calf as she fed it the last of the milk in the funnel, and so she did not notice the effect that information had on me. Instead, she set the feeding apparatus aside and stroked the now sated calf's poll. "There, young beastie, all fed up. Would you take her for me and put her in that stall, please? She's clean. I washed her just before I fed her."

I hoisted the calf up, grunting with the effort, and was glad to have my back to Elaine as I carried it to the straw-lined stall she had indicated, but when I turned around I saw her still kneeling in the same spot, gazing at me with a bemused look as she brushed a stray lock of hair off her forehead with the back of one wrist.

"What's the matter?" The hint of a frown ticked between her brows. "You look strange. Is something wrong?"

I shrugged, suddenly unsure of myself. "I didn't know you had been married."

The frown vanished and she smiled and sank back onto her haunches, twirling the stray lock of hair between her fingers and tucking it back out of sight as she shook her head. "Ah," she said wistfully. "No, of course you didn't, and how could you? But that is not even the start of it, my friend. The sum of what you do not know about me would shock you beyond your belief. You know my name, and my father's name, and where I live, and you know you like me and I like you, and you know, too, that you have never met anyone quite like me before, a woman who can read and write and keep an accurate tally of strange things, and even act like a man in areas where few women ever venture. Here. Help me up and walk with me a while. I'll tell you anything you want to know about me."

She reached out a hand and I pulled her to her feet, and she smoothed her skirts and smiled at me again, her head cocked to one side. "What else is troubling you? It can't be that little thing. Justin has been dead these four years and more. What is it?"

"I don't really know … except that you are right. I thought I was coming to know you, but I'm not … and I want to."

"I see." Her eyes narrowed, searching my face. "And what else? There is more than that, surely."

"I saw your father. He's asleep at the table in his dayroom."

"Aha, now I *do* see. And so you foresaw an end to these visits of ours, is that it?"

"Aye, something like that."

"Aye, indeed … Well …" She gathered up the feeding apparatus and took it to a table between the stalls, where she placed it carefully, lodging the funnel so that it could not roll off and fall to the floor, and then she walked directly to the door of the byre, beckoning with her fingers. I followed mutely, blinking my eyes against the harsh glare of the early-winter afternoon, and she led me to the open parapet of the villa's renowned well, right in the center of the main courtyard. She bent forward and peered down into the depths of the well shaft, which was as broad across as my outstretched arms, and she spoke almost absently, still without looking at me.

"So when my father is well, Jonas will be well … perhaps sooner, perhaps later. Is that what you were thinking?"

"Aye, it is."

"And what would you have me do?"

"Do?" Her question left me at a loss. I could only shake my head. "Nothing, I suppose. There is nothing you can do, nothing to be done …"

She looked at me now over her shoulder, and her voice sounded different somehow, almost amused and yet not so. "Oh, but there is, or there might be, and were you anyone but you, you would name it. But you are who you are, and so I will accept what you say. There is nothing to be done about any of it."

She stood now, leaning back against the low wall and crossing her arms beneath her breasts, unwittingly thrusting them into prominence, I thought at the time, so that I had to make a determined effort not to gawk down at the soft fullness of white flesh revealed in the square-cut neck of her bodice.

"You know this can't continue, don't you?" she said. "You and me … this attraction between us. It won't work. There can be no future in it. Jonas is to be my husband and I agreed to the bargain. I will not go back on it now." She stopped suddenly. "Tell me, when you come here from Camulod, do you always follow the same route?" I told her I did, by the shortest, most direct path, and she nodded, unsurprised. "Will you come again tomorrow instead of the following day, now that my father is mending and growing stronger every day?"

"Aye, if you wish me to."

"I do, but on the way I would like you to do something different for me. You know where the pathway splits beside the great oak that stands alone in the water meadow? Take the right fork tomorrow and follow the path around behind the forested hill. It will still bring you here, although it will take you longer to arrive, but look about you as you travel and take careful note of what you see. I will not tell you what to look for, or where, but we will talk of it later. Will you do that for me?"

Of course I said I would, and she pursed her lips into a pout, her arms still folded beneath her bosom. "Good," she said, after a silence. "Go you home now, then, and before you sleep tonight think upon this: I will be married to Jonas, mayhap within the month. That must happen. We are betrothed, he and I. After that, I may remain here for a time, working beside my father until he is strong enough to work alone again. But after that I shall move to Jonas's village, as his true wife. You and I may never see each other again thereafter. We could, perhaps, with no one the wiser, and it

might be—would be—pleasant for a time. But it would be treachery of a kind and it would destroy whatever we might find together.
I will not permit us to do that to each other. Nor would I do such a
thing to Jonas, who is a decent and honorable man and deserves an
honest wife. So, will you think upon that and face it as a knight's
burden?"

Unable to do otherwise, I told her I would.

2

Intrigued by Elaine's request to take a different route the following
day, I was tempted to ride home that way after leaving the villa, but
something warned me not to, and I was able to convince myself
quite easily that I didn't even know how or where to find the alternative route from this end of the journey. So I rode directly home,
my head filled with thoughts of Elaine's beauty and with fears of
losing her and the friendship I had come to cherish in such a short
time, and by the time I arrived back I had grown so despondent that
I was almost at the gates before I noticed that Camulod had received
unexpected visitors during my absence. There were strange warriors
everywhere, clad in garish, outlandish clothes and bristling with
weapons. They were peaceable enough, lounging at their ease
around campfires outside the main gates, and none of them showed
any signs of hostility, but none the less I forgot all about my own
troubles as I made my way to the guardhouse to find out who these
people were.

They were Scots, I was told. Mariners. Merlyn's old friend
Connor Mac Athol had come a-calling.

Connor Mac Athol had become a legendary figure during his
own lifetime, a one-legged admiral commanding a fleet of war
galleys that patrolled the seas around the Dalriadic Isles off the
shores of Caledonia and kept his people safe from the depredations
of pirates and enemies. Connor of the Wooden Leg, they called him,

and although I had never met the man, I had heard tales about him that seemed to defy belief, save that I knew beyond dispute that his exploits were real and that both Merlyn and Arthur valued his friendship highly.

I knew, too, that even though he and his clan were Outlanders, originally from Eire, his entire family was strangely connected with and involved in Merlyn's life and in Camulod's affairs. I had heard from Merlyn how he had once been wed to one of Connor's sisters, Deirdre, and another of his sisters, Ygraine of Cornwall, had been Arthur's own mother. Yet another family member, Connor's younger brother Donuil, had been captured by Merlyn and held as hostage to his people's good behavior decades earlier. Prisoner and captor had become close friends, and Donuil Mac Athol had chosen to remain in Camulod when his captivity ended, serving for years as adjutant to Merlyn Britannicus and as such entrusted with running the daily military and administrative affairs of Camulod. An old man, now, Donuil was the first man I had met on coming to Camulod, and he was the father of my fellow knights Ghilleadh and Gwin, who were thus Arthur's cousins.

Donuil had always been the tallest, strongest man in Camulod, and although he was now grizzle bearded and elderly and beginning to stoop under the weight of his years, he was still a giant and was, like his brother Connor, a prince in his own right, a younger son of Athol Mac Iain, the forward-sighted King of Scots who had led his people to migrate from their inhospitable holdings in Eire and to establish themselves in the Caledonian islands that men were now calling Dalriada. King Athol had died decades before I arrived in Camulod, and his descendants now ruled in Dalriada, and Connor of the Wooden Leg was still their guardian and defender.

Connor was meeting with Arthur and Merlyn when I arrived, and I had no wish to interrupt them, but I met Donuil as I was walking back from the stables—he had been out seeing to some minor thing— and he ushered me in ahead of him to meet his brother and to deliver my report on Dougald to Arthur. They were deep in conversation when we entered, and I could tell that, whatever they were discussing, they were treating it very seriously. More than anything else on that occasion, brief as it was, I remember being amazed by Connor Mac Athol's youthful appearance, for I knew he was older than Donuil by a number of years, yet he looked a decade and more younger. He rose to his feet when Arthur called me by name, and came striding to meet me, his wooden leg thumping solidly on the floor with every step. He greeted me amiably and with great formality, telling me he had heard wondrous things from his friends Arthur and Merlyn about my abilities and prowess. He then invited me straightforwardly to join their colloquy. It was very flattering, but I knew they had personal and family matters to discuss that would mean little to me, whereas I had pressing matters of my own to see to, so I declined as graciously as I could, making my excuses and going about my own duties, leaving the four of them to return to their discussion. It had been nearly six years since Connor Mac Athol had been in Camulod, I knew, and I wondered idly what had brought him back.

They rode out again while I was inspecting my troops shortly after daybreak the next morning, the King on horseback, accompanied by a ten-man squad of mounted troopers, while Merlyn rode with Connor in the two-wheeled wagon the Scots admiral used for land travel. All three of them acknowledged me and my men in passing, but did not stop to linger, and that displeased me not at all, for that morning inspection marked the end of my current twelve-day spell of duty, leaving me with a two-day rest period ahead of me, and so I was able to leave for the Villa Varo earlier than I normally would, under the threat of rain from heavy, sullen clouds. The now-familiar excitement and anticipation of seeing Elaine again bubbled in my breast as it always did when I set out, even while I knew this might be my last visit.

It was cold enough for snow, although it was still only early November, and a biting wind cut right through my clothing, so that I rode muffled in my heavy woolen foul-weather cloak, my sword securely thrust into the quiver of lances hanging from the rear of my saddle in case of need. I took the right fork by the lone oak tree as Elaine had directed and from then on found myself in territory I had never visited, riding eventually through dense woodland on a narrow, twisting path that rose steadily through a steep-sided ravine with a fast-flowing stream at its center. When I reached the top of the climb, however, the land flattened out dramatically, and I was soon riding through thinning trees on a plateau I had never suspected was there, and a short time after that, no more than a quarter of a mile from the top of the ascent, I rode into a place of great beauty, with a narrow lake stretching to my left, and came to the first of a long series of lush, tilled fields on my right, many of them bearing the stubble of the recent harvest and still awaiting the plow. The pathway widened there and became a rutted roadway, showing signs of recent traffic, and I followed it until I came to a long, low-set and shuttered farmhouse, set off from the road and surrounded by outbuildings. I stopped in front of the place, allowing my horse to crop while I sat gazing into the farmstead, looking for signs of life and seeing only my own breath emerging as vapor in the chilly air.

Nothing moved anywhere, and the buildings, although they were in good repair, showed no signs of being inhabited. There were no geese, cattle or animals to be seen; the pathway leading to the house itself was overgrown and grass was growing among the thatch on the roof. The place had clearly been uninhabited for some time, possibly for several years.

That realization troubled me more than a little, for these were Camulod holdings, where nothing was ever permitted to go to waste or to lie unused when it might be put to good purpose. But then, in a flash of enlightenment, I was sure that this must be what Elaine had intended me to see. It had to be, I reasoned, as I had seen nothing else of note along the entire route I had followed, apart from the sedge-lined lake in the distance, and my sense of direction told me I could not be far from the Villa Varo itself by this time.

Curious now, I dismounted and led my horse towards the house, seeing that it was solidly and soundly built, of thick logs, and that the small windows were tightly shuttered. The door was heavy and secure looking, too, even from a distance, and as I approached I could see that it had been made from only two fitted slabs of smoothly planed wood.

A spatter of raindrops hit my face, blown from the side, when I was some ten paces from the house, and then, without further warning, a torrential downpour erupted, the deluge crashing straight down and obscuring my view of the building. Cursing, I covered the remaining distance in a running jump and lunged for the doorway, turning to flatten my shoulders against the wood and gain whatever shelter might be there in the tiny space, but the door swung inward as I hit it and, unbalanced, I reeled backwards, cursing aloud again.

It was pitch-black in there, and I smelled smoke, and the last thing I saw was my horse, directly outside, its ears pricked forward in comical surprise at my disappearance. Then the heavy door swung slowly back into place, shutting out the gray daylight and leaving me in total darkness. I had regained my balance quickly, but even before the door swung shut I knew that I was not alone and my reflexes took over, my mind flaring with the instant, urgent awareness that I was wrapped in my heavy cloak. I swung around and dropped to one knee, flinging out my right arm to rip the heavy woolen folds from where they were draped over my left shoulder, and as my knee hit the floor I snatched the dagger from my belt with my left hand. The blackness was stygian, not a glimmer of light to reveal either shape or movement, and I bent forward quickly, switching my dagger to my right hand while making myself the smallest target I could offer, my chest against my upraised knee, my blade held low and pointing upwards, waiting for whatever might come at me.

"Put your blade away. I'll light a lamp."

The voice stunned me, leaving me gaping into the blackness, incapable of moving. The sound of the downpour hammering on the roof was thunderous, and I listened to it for what seemed like a long time, clutching my dagger as though it were a lifeline, before I could even attempt to speak.

"Elaine?" My voice was close to being a croak. "What are you doing here?"

"Waiting for you."

"In the dark?"

"No, I had a light. I blew it out when I heard you coming, because I thought it might be someone else … I didn't expect you so soon. I only recognized you when you came flying through the door."

I thought I could detect a smile in her voice but still I could see nothing, and then I heard a scraping sound and a square glow of red light sprang into existence. Elaine was holding a small portable clay fire box filled with embers. Before I could move, she spoke again, her tone now absolutely matter-of-fact, betraying no awareness of what I must have looked like, crouching foolishly on the floor with a naked blade in my hand.

"I was sitting there thinking about going outside to wait for you, when I heard you coming towards the door. I didn't really expect you to arrive for another hour at least, but I was afraid you might ride by without stopping, and I wanted to be sure of catching you." She straightened up and closed the lid of the fire box, to protect the lively flame she had stirred up inside it, then walked away towards the fireplace, carrying it carefully in front of her. "That said, it's fortunate that you arrived when you did, otherwise you might have had to swim up the streambed on the hillside. Your poor horse is drowning out there, however. Why don't you take him around to the stable at the back and make him comfortable? Mine is already in there. I'll have this place brightened up by the time you come back. Go."

I stood up, fumbling to replace my blade in its sheath, then hesitated. "How did you know I had drawn a blade?"

"I heard you. It is a very distinctive sound."

I wrapped myself in my cloak again and moved without another word to do her bidding, thinking to myself as I dashed out into the leaden downpour that I had never met a woman like her in my entire life. Even my aunt Vivienne, regal as she had been, might have taken second place to this young woman, for Elaine acted and spoke as a man would. More than a mere man, in fact—she spoke as a commander of men, decisive and self-confident, issuing orders, advice and instructions to all about her, myself included, without the slightest trace of hesitancy. And yet she was overwhelmingly feminine and radiantly beautiful.

It was only as I stood beside my horse in the stable, wondering whether to unsaddle him or merely to tether him for the time being, where he could share some loose hay with Elaine's mare, that I started to smile at what I had been thinking. There was not a single man in Camulod, with the exception of Arthur Pendragon himself, who would have dared to speak to me as she had, and I had obeyed as immediately and unthinkingly as one of my own troopers would have, hearing an order from me.

What was going on here, I asked myself then. What was she doing here? It was a mystery I knew I would never solve by standing out here in the stable. The only way to find out what she wanted was to go back inside and ask her. I had not the slightest doubt that she would tell me. I removed my horse's saddle and brushed him down very quickly.

The rain had not slackened by the time I returned to the house, but the single room was bright with welcoming light by then, and I closed the door behind me and looked around as I shrugged out of my wet cloak.

"Did you close the stable door?" She was moving past me as she spoke and I stepped aside and watched as she quietly lowered the heavy wooden door bar into its slots.

"Yes," I said, not trusting myself to say another word until I had some kind of understanding of what was happening here.

"Good. Give me that. It's soaked." She took the cloak from me and spread it out to hang from two pegs behind the door, and I watched the way her body moved as she spread her arms and stretched up. She was wearing clothing I had not seen before, a long, loose, full-sleeved pale green robe over a white ankle-length shift, and her feet might as well have been bare, protected only by lightweight, delicate-looking sandals that struck me at once as being far too flimsy for weather like today's. Her outer robe was girdled by a thick rope of twisted dark green yarn that emphasized the shape of her as she stretched up and forward, spreading my cloak evenly, but as she turned back towards me I swung away to look around the room, afraid that she might see my lewd thoughts reflected in my eyes.

Apparently she saw nothing. "I know you have questions to ask me," she said, moving back into the room. "I can see them in your face, but before I'll say a word I insist on being comfortable, if only for once. So put your helmet on the table over there and take off your armor."

A fire blazed in an open stone hearth built into the corner to the right of the door, and a large table stood against the wall on my left, flanked by a sideboard with shelves on one side and a tall, plain-fronted cupboard on the other. A smaller, low table sat in front of the fire, angled towards the center of the room, with two padded, comfortable-looking armchairs, one on either side of it, facing the fire. A fat, buttery candle, made of wax from the Villa Varo's own beehives, burned on that table, another on the high mantel above the hearth, and a third, much larger than the others, was set on yet another small, purely ornamental table by the head of the large bed that was pushed against the rear wall, covered with thick furs spread over heavy, floor-length woolen blankets. I placed my helmet carefully on the table between the chairs but made no move to take off my armor. Elaine sucked air sharply through her teeth and came to where I stood, her eyes scanning my leather cuirass and the heavy ring-mail coat beneath it.

"Lift your arms. That metal's cold and heavy and you'll be chilled. Silly to keep it on indoors, since we are unlikely to be attacked here." I obeyed, and she busied herself for several moments unbuckling the straps at my left shoulder and beneath the arm, so that I could remove the entire device from my right as one piece and set it upright on the floor. Then, as she stood watching, I loosened the straps holding my ring-mail coat, shrugged out of it, and bent to undo the straps behind my knees before loosening the belt that held my mailed leggings in place about my waist. They fell to the floor with a heavy clatter, and I was left standing in my knee-length undertunic, my woolen leggings and my boots.

"There," she said. "Doesn't that feel better? It must, if only because of the weight you don't have to carry."

It did, but I was far from comfortable, feeling unaccustomedly vulnerable. I was still at a loss as to what was happening here, but I knew it was important and I was beginning to suspect where it might be leading. My heart was pounding wildly with anticipation but I was far from being confident enough to assume that what I thought might be happening was in fact the truth, and so I avoided her eyes and her question by bending down to brush my fingertips lightly over the tabletop. There was no dust.

"Whose house is this?"

"Mine." She moved away from me to sit in one of the padded armchairs. "This is where I lived with Justin. He built it for us before we were married, eight years ago. He was a woodworker, a carpenter and wagon builder."

I had half expected that, my own eyes having told me that her familiarity with the place could not be accidental, but the words still jarred me. I looked about again, taking more careful note of the furniture and its construction this time, seeing now that there was nothing here that was crudely or poorly fashioned. Even the floor was made of fitted, polished wooden planks, and I remembered the thump with which my knee had hit it when I dropped down, thinking I was going to be attacked.

"A wooden floor in a log house," I said.

"No, a wooden floor in a carpenter's home."

"Of course." I looked at her again. "What happened to him?"

"Nothing dramatic. He died, quietly and sadly. He woke up one morning feeling sick, grew worse by nightfall, and was dead within the week. Congestion in the lungs, Strabo told us, brought on by a chill when he fell through the ice on the lake out there, the week before. He was close enough to the edge that the water was still shallow, so he could stand up, but he couldn't climb out, because of the ice, and so he spent almost half an hour in the water before we found him and pulled him out." She shook her head, gently.

"It was awful, the speed with which he sickened. By the end of the third day he couldn't catch a breath without coughing, and it sounded as though his chest was full of phlegm and ripping apart. And then he was dead and I was a widow … Three years, we had been married. I was eighteen. I couldn't live here after that, but I couldn't abandon the place, either. It had been my happiness."

I cleared my throat. "You had no children?"

"No. Justin was older than I was, much older, and he had been married before, for more than ten years, without siring children, so we knew from the outset that he was incapable of fathering a child."

"How could you know that?"

She looked me square in the eye. "Because he traveled to Cornwall once, to build wagons for a king down there, and was gone for more than half a year. When he came back, his wife was quickened … with child."

"Oh." I pondered that for some time, not knowing how to respond appropriately. "So what did he do?"

"Nothing. He had no need. He arrived home in the middle of an outbreak of pestilence. His wife was already sick of it and died soon after, but before she died she miscarried. Justin learned much from that experience."

"I see … and then he met you, after that?"

"No," she said slowly, smiling. "He had always known me, ever since I was born. Justin was my father's closest friend. I grew up liking and admiring him, and when I reached marriageable age, three or four years after the death of his first wife, he chose me. It was a warm and loving marriage, but not one of fire and passion. We were very happy."

I looked at the interior of the small house from a new perspective now. "Will you live here again, then, when you marry Jonas?"

"No. I told you that yesterday. When I wed Jonas I will go to live in his village. He has a big house there, the headman's house, much grander than this. Come, sit here beside me."

She indicated the empty chair, but I was not yet brave enough to approach her so closely, and so I continued my inspection of the room, this time becoming aware of the pile of cut logs by the fireplace and the glory of the newly lit fire. I pointed. "Was that fire ready in the hearth?"

"Yes. I built it last night."

"You were here last night ... Do you spend much of your time here?"

She shrugged. "Not now, not for three years, other than stopping by occasionally to make sure everything is still well. I brought food and beer for us, too. We'll eat later, after we have talked. Now, will you come and sit by the fire and take off your boots? You are always wearing armor, dressed for war. I've never seen you without it until now, and it makes you intimidating, difficult to talk to. I want to talk to you today as a man, not as a knight and a soldier."

I nodded slowly and went even more slowly to sit in the chair across from her. I felt the heat of the fire on my face as I sat down, my head aswim with the knowledge that she had planned this meeting the day before, if not earlier.

"I really wish you would take them off ... your boots ... unless you feel uncomfortable here?"

She let that hang in the air, part question, part suggestion, and I quickly shook my head in denial. "No, not at all. I'm not uncomfortable ..."

"Merely confused? Wondering about all this?" She grinned at me, a flash of pure mischief, white, even teeth gleaming behind those wide, red lips. "I'm not surprised. New directions always give rise to confusion."

My insides were jangling with awareness of her nearness, separated as we were by only the low, narrow table, and as I settled into my seat I could smell the warm scent of her.

"Here, let me help you."

Before I could say anything, she was kneeling on the floor at my feet, tugging at the leather lacings on my high boots, and the sudden intimacy of her posture brought my heart leaping up into my throat, threatening to shut off the flow of my breath.

"I can do that," I protested, leaning forward, but she shook her head without looking up.

"Easier for me, now that I'm here."

My face was now within a foot of her bowed head, and the fresh, warm scent of her filled my nostrils and sent the blood rushing to my loins, so that I felt light-headed and horrifyingly aware that I did not dare sit back again, for fear she would see my condition. How could she not see it, I thought. My arousal was huge, undeniable. And so I remained as I was, bent forward, red faced and mortified. If Elaine was aware of my embarrassment, however, she gave no sign of it and continued working at my laces until she was able to kneel upright and pull off my boots, after which, grinning again, she pulled off my stockings, too.

"There now, isn't that better? Your feet are freezing." I felt the heat of her hands around the arch of my instep, kneading my right foot, and her touch, instead of inflaming me further, somehow brought me back to reality as I realized that my feet really were icy. "Stretch your toes to the fire and wiggle them. You'll feel like a new man once they warm up."

I did as she suggested, feeling the heat stinging my bare soles, and grateful that her eyes were on my toes and not on any other part of me. She rose to her feet then, using one arm of my chair for leverage, and placed three logs on the fire, pushing them down into the burning coals with a heavy iron poker, before crossing to the bed to gather up one of the fur pelts. She threw it into the corner by the fireplace and lowered herself gracefully to sit on it, with her back against the wall and her feet tucked out of sight beneath her robe. She gazed up at me from there, and I was gratefully aware that my riotous blood had receded and I could sit upright again without fear.

"You are a strange man, Clothar the Frank."

"What makes you say that?" The response was automatic, because I was lost in the beauty of her face, reveling in the way she was looking at me as avidly as I at her. Some small part of my mind was aware, I recall even now, that she was really not as beautiful as some of the young women I had seen in Arthur's castle—the planes of her face were too strongly angular for that—but there is an ancient saying that every man creates his own beauty, and my eyes were full of Elaine and had been empty of anything else for weeks. Her answer to my question, when it came, was indirect.

"Perhaps because you saved my life and seem to have no need of being thanked."

"But you *have* thanked me, several times."

"Ach! I've spoken words of gratitude. But those were all said to a king's knight, not to the man who came flying to my rescue. There is a difference, you know. This is the first time you and I have been alone together, speaking to each other. No, wait, before you say anything, I know that sounds silly, but it's the truth. Think about it. You have always been an official visitor until now—the King's own envoy, a cloaked and armored, helmeted knight visiting my place of work in search of news of my father. And I have always *been* at work, no matter where we were or what we were doing, and always with other people nearby, if not actually with us, people who listen and overhear even without meaning to. You and I have been together, if you will, in each other's company, but we have never been truly alone, and all we have ever talked about is my father's health, and farming and agricultural matters affecting Camulod. True?"

"True, but what makes you think there is no one around to see or overhear us now?"

That won me another fleeting smile. "Because no one knows we are here and the door and windows are all tight shut. But even more, because I am my father's deputy, so I issued instructions and allocated duties yesterday that would ensure no workers come anywhere within miles of this place today. And I did that because I wanted this time with you, to talk to you like this, alone."

I nodded. "That is very ... pleasing ... but you know, now that I think of it, I never found what we talked about before to be displeasing."

"I know, and that's why I say you are a strange man. Most other men I know spend all their time trying to amuse me, to lure me away from my work, into dalliance, wasting my time. You never have. You are content to sit silent and look at me, or to walk with me and listen to what I have to say, and even to assist me at times, and your visits, every second day, have become the high points of my life, so that I find myself impatient and short-tempered on the days between."

"And yet you told me yesterday that those visits have to stop."

"I know that, too, but let me finish what I have to say." She was looking at me through slightly narrowed eyes, her head tilted to one side. "May I continue?" She saw my nod and returned it, then waved a hand to indicate the room in which we were sitting. "I told you I've been unable to abandon this house, because of the memories it holds for me. But now I have to leave it, and with it all those memories, to go into my new life with Jonas." She saw the widening of my eyes and quickly raised her palm to stop me from speaking. "Forgive me, I know you don't want to hear that, but it cannot go unsaid …" She turned away from me, looking sidelong at the fire. "I received word yesterday, before you came, that Jonas is almost mended. He is up and about and regaining his strength daily, and he sent word to me that he will be coming here within the week." She turned back to me, looking directly into my eyes. "Once he does that, I won't be able to see you again, Clothar. I could, I know, but I will not. There's too much pleasure in it, and it would be unjust, and wrong."

I spoke through the lump in my throat, afraid my voice would betray my anguish. "What's wrong with knowing pleasure?"

"Nothing, and yet everything, because it begs for more, and I don't think I would be strong enough to deny myself."

I started to speak but she raised that hand again. "I know you think of me as being as strong as a man. I've seen it in your face, in your eyes, the admiration and the … affection. And in many ways, not counting my appearance, I suppose I am like a man. I was brought up to think like a man, to accept responsibilities and shoulder duties, to use the skills God blessed me with, despite my being a woman, and to be unafraid of hard work—men's work. But I am a woman. And I have never had the slightest doubt that while you are in awe of my abilities as a manager of men, and as a records keeper, in your eyes, and in your heart, you see me and desire me as a woman."

She looked at me searchingly, and I felt the color rise to my cheeks again. "I know you have wanted to touch me, to reach out and kiss me on many occasions. I've seen that, too, every time. And I know that among the things that have held you back from doing so are your own basic decency and goodness and your sense of the duty you owe to the King as his messenger."

That latter part was true, and I acknowledged it mutely as she spoke, for the thought had more than once occurred to me that were I to succumb to the urge to lay myself at this woman's feet as I longed to do, my usefulness to Arthur and perhaps even my sense of duty and responsibility must surely suffer. But far more strong than any such consideration was the simple, visceral fear of attempting to engage her that directly and being rejected, perhaps even spurned or, even worse, deflected with pity. That, more than anything else, was what had encouraged me to keep my hands clasped behind my back most of the time in dealing with Elaine.

She was looking closely at me, her head tilted slightly to one side in a mannerism I had come to know well, and now she waved an open palm, as though trying to come to grips with something that eluded her. "But there's more to your restraint than that, isn't there? You have this strange … I don't know what to call it, but it is almost like … an *awe* of me, although that's a silly, foolish word for what I really mean … Perhaps you feel that way because of what you see me do daily, or because of the way I behave in handling men … workers. But most of all it seems to me that … that *thing* … that awe—I don't know how else to describe it—springs from the way you believe I *think*. You are afraid of offending me because of that, because of what you think I might be thinking. And that is silly. You can never *know* what or how I am thinking at any time, Clothar. You can't. It's impossible. And most of the time, when you believe it most, what you *think* you know is wrong. Help me up." She reached out a hand and I pulled her to her feet, rising with her until we stood face to face.

She reached up and I felt her fingers brush against my cheek. "You're blushing, and I knew you would. You always do, and I love that. You are the most gentle man I know, Seur Clothar of Gaul, and it always amazes me whenever I hear someone speak of you otherwise, because I cannot imagine you being as violent and formidable as they say you are in battle. You have never shown me that part of you."

"And never will, I hope," I said, winning another smile from her and glowing inside with sheer joy as I felt each of her fingers separately caressing my cheek and lingering there while she continued to gaze at me.

"I have a gift for you," she said eventually, her voice, barely audible, a caress in itself. "A parting gift ... for both of us, in truth." Her thumb touched my lower lip, pressing gently, pushing it out of shape and to one side, but when I moved my head to capture the questing thumb, to kiss it, she moved it away quickly to trace the line of my jaw instead. "A gift of gratitude," she continued, her eyes fixed on my own, "but also one of gratification, which is not at all the same thing ... because while I hope it will please you, I know the giving of it will please me and leave me in your debt again ..." She took her hand from my face and loosened the woolen rope of her girdle, and let it fall noiselessly to the floor as she reached out to take both my wrists and pull them to her waist, beneath her outer robe, pushing gently downwards until my open hands had come to rest against the swell of her hips, and as my fingers flexed involuntarily, feeling the warm, yielding softness of her body beneath the thin shift, she raised her arms and swayed towards me, pulling my head down and opening her mouth to my lips.

I have no memory of how long that first kiss lasted, but I have never forgotten the wonder of it, for it was the first true kiss of love I had ever known and I was lost in the magic of it, overwhelmed and swept away by the voluptuous softness, heat and clinging intimacy of her moist, warm underlip and the probing, wet, demanding tongue that invaded my mouth and my very soul like a living creature. By the end of it, we were both shaking and gasping, struggling for breath, breaking apart for only a moment before starting all over again, and my hands were filled with bare, smooth flesh. My own clothing was all open and undone, hanging about me where she had stripped away lacings and bindings to uncover and lay her cool hands on me, and I was thrusting against her blindly, seeking friction, hoping to achieve I knew not what, standing as we were. And then, without having seemed to move, we were against the bed and falling to the piled furs, where we struggled frantically to discard every scrap of clothing and be naked, body to body, flesh to flesh, without breaking our soul-drowning kisses.

Elaine was panting, shuddering in her urgency, but no more so than I was, and I found myself on my back as she rose up and straddled me, pinning me with one hand on my chest and telling me to wait while she guided me with the other, and then suddenly, slowly, but with more appalling speed than I had ever known before, she sank down on me, engulfing me and hurling me instantly into an ecstasy that I thought might tear me apart as I lost any vestige of control and simply exploded, emptying myself helplessly into her as she cried out, once and then again, and fell forward against me, cradling my head and seeking my mouth again with her own.

3

Later, much, much later, long after the fire had died and we had burrowed for warmth beneath the coverings on the bed, long after the noise of the rain on the roof had faded and disappeared, when we had both been emptied of desire and finally sated, we lay together entwined, content now to simply hold and touch each other, lips nibbling tenderly, hands moving constantly but without urgency, exploring the wonder of each other's body. I was drifting in that mindless state that welcomes sleep, blissfully aware of the warm, smooth body nestling in my arms, when Elaine suddenly gave a leap beneath me, thrusting me away from her so that I reared backwards, alarmed.

"The candle! It's going out! Let me up."

I raised myself on my elbow as she threw herself away from me, rolled out of the bed and scampered into the darkness. Wide-awake now, I heard fumbling noises, then a dull clacking as hard objects rattled against each other, and then she was back, flying towards me and clambering right across me to the other side of the bed. As I turned in astonishment I saw her, bent forward from the waist, huddled over the guttering candle on the table there, and only then did I realize that the room was otherwise completely dark. She held a new candle in each hand and was holding both wicks to the dying flame, her concentration complete, and even as I watched the guttering flame flicker one last time and die, I saw a new pinpoint of light as one of the wicks it had touched caught fire. Reverently, almost fearfully, Elaine held the new candle on a gentle slant, turning it slowly, willing the flame to grow, and when it did, she released a pent-up breath, tilting her hand further to drip beads of hot wax onto the tabletop before setting the candle end carefully and deliberately into the cooling liquid. She then lit the second candle from the first, and only when it, too, was securely anchored in its own little puddle of wax did she begin to laugh.

"Have you any awareness of how close we came to being caught with no light and no fire?"

I shook my head, uncaring, fascinated by the sight of her breasts in the candlelight.

"That was an eight-hour candle … which means we have been rutting in bed like demented animals for almost that long. Eight hours!" Her voice softened. "But it may have been the most wonderful eight hours of my life. I have never been loved like that, my lord Knight."

"Good." I reached out and grasped her around the waist and pulled her back and down as I kicked the coverings away from between us. "Neither have I, so let's do it again." She fought me this time, laughing and struggling, kicking her long legs wildly and coming close to making her escape until she felt my renewed hardness pushing against her, and then, for another while, the world went away again.

Later still, she slipped out of bed and moved, naked and golden in the candles' light, to the nearest window, where she raised the bar of the shutters and pushed them wide before leaning out and inhaling the night air deep into her lungs.

"The rain stopped," she said.

"It stopped hours ago, I think."

"Everything always smells so fresh and clean after the rain. It's one of my favorite scents. Come and see the stars. The clouds have all gone."

I joined her at the window, feeling the coolness of the night breeze blowing in against my warm skin, bringing me out in gooseflesh, and I slipped my arms around her, my left arm hooking about her neck to fondle her right breast as I slid my other hand down the warm curve of her belly, pulling her buttocks gently into the hollow of my groin and kissing the top of her head. She snuggled back, fitting into me perfectly.

"When do you have to be back on duty?"

I squeezed her gently. "I don't. Not tonight, nor tomorrow night, so we can stay here till then."

I felt her shoulders stiffen slightly, but she made no response other than, "Are you hungry?"

"Of course I am. Can't you feel it?"

She reached behind her, bowed her body out and away from me, and slapped at the hardness that had been prodding at her. "You're worse than a randy ram."

"Not *worse than,* woman, *ready as.*" I was incredulous at my own ease in being able to say such things now. All my awkwardness and hesitancy, all my virginal uncertainties and fears, had vanished sometime during the burning of that eight-hour candle. Her hand came back, angling me upwards to lie along the base of her spine as she pushed back against me, and then she folded her arms over mine. "Randy, ready, both admirable at the proper time, but I was talking about food. Are you hungry?"

"I don't know. I haven't thought about it. What time of night is it, anyway?"

She pulled away from me and leaned out the window, craning her neck to look up at the sky. "I can't see the moon, but it's still well short of midnight. We lit the candle soon after noon, so it can't be far beyond the ninth hour by this time." She pulled the shutters together again and replaced the bar before turning around, still within the circle of my arms, to pull my head down to her mouth. But then, too soon, she placed both hands against my chest and pushed me away.

"It's cold in here. There's kindling by the fireside, and fresh logs. Bring one of the candles over here and light us a fire while I bring us something to eat."

Lighting fires indoors had never been covered in my training, but I quickly found that anyone can light a fire in a hearth, given sufficient kindling and fuel, along with a burning candle. There are disadvantages to attempting the task while naked, however, and that had not occurred to me until the kindling started spitting sparks, several of which landed on my skin and sent me scampering out of range. I heard Elaine laughing behind me and turned to find her grinning at the sight of my scuttling nakedness. She held a tray piled with bread and cold meat and a large wedge of cheese.

We ate on the floor in front of the fire, sprawled on furs I had brought from the bed, and I discovered to my delight that she had brought a tiny bottle of precious olive oil and a bowl of other unexpected delicacies with the normal food: partridge eggs, hard boiled and shelled and then preserved in some wondrous vinegary pickling mixture. They were delicious, like white, tart grapes sprinkled with salt, and I ate all of them. And as we ate, we talked, although as usual it was Elaine who did most of the talking while I listened, this time in growing panic and reluctance.

She was determined to make me understand and accept that we would never see each other again after this night, and I was equally determined to convince her that we should and must, and at one point I must have told her that I was in love with her—in my rutting confidence I was convinced of it by then, I know—although I have no recollection of saying the words. I remember her reaction, however, and it struck me dumb for a while, because I had no effective way of countering the argument she brought against me so forcefully.

"That was a silly thing to say," she said, sitting up abruptly and sounding suddenly furious. "So please don't say it again."

"Say what again? What did I say?"

"That you are in love with me. That is nonsense. You cannot possibly be in love with me. My God, man, you barely know me."

I was stunned by her anger and the strength of her reaction to a comment I had barely been aware of making, but she was into her stride by that time, and not to be reined in. "We have only known each other for a matter of weeks, you and I. Don't you know that it takes years, and sometimes decades, for love to grow between two people? Love, *real love,* is founded upon common understanding and usage and respect and admiration. Love does not just *happen.* It has to be nurtured."

"Now *that* is nonsense," I responded, stung in my own pride. "I have been falling more and more deeply in love with you since first I saw you running from that bear. I didn't choose to do it. I had no choice in the matter. I saw you and I was thunderstruck."

She relented at that, turning to face me with wide, soulful eyes and reaching out to cup my cheek in her hand, her voice suddenly transformed from fury to tenderness. "I know you were, my dear. I was there too, do you recall? And we were both thunderstruck by the same bolt of lightning. But that was not love, dear man, it was desire, and because it was not satisfied at once, it grew into a raging fire. And thus you think you are in love with me, but what you are is fascinated by me. Do you know what that means, *fascinated*?"

I did not. I recognized the word, of course, but I had no slightest idea of what it meant. It was not the kind of word people used in ordinary speech, so I sat for a moment, frowning and fretting as I tried to define it, and more than a little annoyed that Elaine plainly knew the word well. Finally, however, I had to shake my head. "No. What does it mean?"

She grinned, and quipped: "The fact that you don't know it means that you have spent too much time at your Bishop's School in Gaul, living among holy men. Think about the ancients, Clothar, and their temples. Those enormous symbols you see everywhere on them." She used both hands to draw the symbol she was describing in the air.

"The *fascina*!"

"Yes, exactly. The fascina."

I knew what she was talking about because I had seen the device many times in my travels in Gaul, usually as a large, decorative element on very old public buildings. You did not need to be educated at all to recognize such things for what they were—representations of male genitalia, erect phalluses with testicles—and they were commonplace enough to have become so stylized over the centuries that no one ever thought about them consciously anymore. Thinking about that then, looking at the play of firelight on her skin as she spoke, and listening to what she was describing, I felt myself generating my own version of the symbol, and she looked down and pointed.

"There, you see? That's a perfect example of what I mean," she said, her cheeks dimpling in a smile. "That is the reality behind the symbol, that thing rearing up in front of you, and that's where the word *fascination* comes from."

I felt myself flushing with inexplicable shame and embarrassment, but she did not notice, so intent was she upon proving her contention. "You are in that condition constantly around me," she said. "And I have enjoyed every minute of knowing that, and knowing that you were unaware I knew. And as a woman, I can think of nothing that might please me more, so do not misunderstand me, for I am not complaining ... But that is not love, Clothar, not *real* love. It is carnal lust ... natural, sensual, perfectly healthy desire, and although you are obsessed by it now—and that delights me—it will fade eventually, as all such things must, and you will move on to other things and other desires. In the meantime, however, you and I are free, for the time being, and brief as that may be, to enjoy each other to the full. Love, however, is not for us. We do not have the time for that."

I had not spoken a word since she began to talk about the fascina, and now I found myself beginning to grow angry, for what I was hearing was, to my ears, a condemnation, or at least a dismissal, of what I was feeling deep within me. I was still very young and it would require the passage of many years before I would grow wise enough to see that what Elaine was saying that day had little to do with me and my feelings of love for her. Had she allowed herself to countenance the thought of loving me then, she would have felt bound to act on it, and that would have meant an endless concatenation of consequences affecting many people. Had she permitted herself that day to think that love, real love, was there between us, she might never have been strong enough to do what she knew must be done.

By that time, of course, we had drunk most of the beer she had brought with her the previous night, and it was a potent brew. I had never been much of a beer drinker and I disliked the taste of wine, even diluted, so I had never formed any kind of resistance to the effects of strong drink. On that occasion I can only attribute my reaction to the beer to my sudden release from all the inhibitions that had controlled me until that afternoon. I was completely at ease in the company of an unclothed woman, a beautiful woman with whom I was utterly besotted, and therefore the effects of what I was drinking took me unawares, because although we were talking about things I didn't want to accept, we were also being highly intimate, kissing and caressing and nibbling and teasing at each other in the warmth of the fire as we talked, our hands managing to generate magical effects upon each other, frequently to the severe detriment of our conversation.

After one such delightful interruption, while we lay smiling in the afterglow, Elaine dismissed our entire conversation to that point as having been unimportant. She was lying with her head cradled in the hollow of my shoulder, idly twisting some of the hairs on my chest around one of her fingers, when I heard her say, "Of course, none of that matters anyway, when you look at the realities surrounding us."

I lay still for a moment, going over what she had just said, and then asked, "None of what matters? What are you talking about?"

She pushed herself up until she was propped on one elbow, looking down at me. "All that we've been talking about. Love and lust and the complications of it all. It's not important, in the face of the reality."

"What reality? I don't know what you're talking about."

"Us. Our reality ... we have none. When this is over, when we are ... done here, you and I will never be able to meet each other like this again. Unless things change beyond belief."

This took me unawares, and before I could say anything in protest, she drew away from me and rose to her feet, then crossed to the bed and wrapped a blanket about her shoulders, covering herself completely. She sat at the foot of the bed, then, from where she could look down on me and deliver her opinion more forcefully.

"You are a king's knight, Clothar, and there is nothing else in the world that you would rather be. We both know that, and we both know that it is the way God intended you to be. But because of that, your life is not your own to command, or even to control, and neither you nor I would wish it to be any different. Is that not true?"

I nodded, and began to speak, but she cut me off before I could say a word.

"Of course it is. Your duty and your loyalty are to the King before all else, sworn and dedicated to his service alone and forever. But you are a soldier, too, Clothar, a legate of Camulod. That carries its own burdens of responsibility and duty."

"Aye, it does," I said, finally managing to find a space into which I could speak. "But none of these duties—not all of them together at one time—bars me in any way from loving you, or from taking you as my wife."

She moved from the bed now, coming to kneel in front of me, and bent over me as I lay by the fire. "Perhaps not," she answered, her voice sad and soft, "but it bars me from taking you as a husband." She stretched out her hand quickly and laid her fingers against my lips, to prevent me from speaking.

"I have a life of responsibilities too, you know. And I know you do know it, for it was that knowledge that attracted you to me in the beginning. I am a farmer's daughter, Clothar, bound to the land I live on. And that is no apology. My duties, and my *sense* of duty, are every bit as important to me as yours are to you. Both of us were born and bred to duty. But my duties, as a working woman and a loyal wife, tie me to one place. To be what I must be, to be true to myself, I need a simple, predictable life ... continuity and permanence." She increased the pressure of her fingers against my lips, smiling gently down at me.

"You, on the other hand, are driven to opposite extremes, Seur Clothar. You are incapable, by nature and conditioning, of remaining in one place for any length of time. That would kill you. You are a soldier, and a mounted one, which is even worse. Your most important requirement is the ability and the need to travel far and fast at a moment's notice, whenever your duty requires you to."

By that point I was looking up at her stupidly, feeling the effects of too much beer fogging my mind, and incapable of finding any words to contradict her even as she watched me narrowly, plainly expecting resistance, but when she saw that I would say no more, she sighed and shrugged the blanket off her shoulders, then lowered herself to lay her breasts against my chest and wrap her arms about me. "You tell me I am beautiful, Clothar, and I know you mean it and I love hearing it, but sitting up there, looking at you, I could see that I have never known anything or anyone as beautiful as you are."

Time passed, and a long time later she stirred against me, flexing her long legs against my own. "Someday," she whispered, her arms clasped about my neck and her mouth against my ear, "if God is cruel enough to take another husband from me, I will welcome you back into my arms and to my bed if you still wish to come, but only for another wondrous interval like this has been." She said no more, had no need to; her body spoke for her.

4

"Clothar, I have to go," she said much later, wakening me from a light sleep. "It must be close to dawn. But before I go, will you answer me a question that might strike you as strange?"

"Hmm …"

"Of all your friends among the King's knights—and not counting the King himself—which one do you admire most?"

The unexpectedness of her question brought me fully awake, for I had never thought about that before and I had no idea why she would ask me such a thing. Asked by anyone else, I would have said I had no favorite among my friends. Each of them had his own skills and abilities, his own charms, his own particular attributes, and all of them were admirable. But this was Elaine who was asking me, and so I lay still for a while, thinking about each of my friends in turn.

She was lying beside and atop me, in the crook of my shoulder, one arm across my chest, one thigh resting heavily on my own, her breasts against my ribs, and I pressed my hand into the small of her back, pulling her even closer to me.

"You know I have never thought about that before? But I have an answer. It would be Ghilly. Ghilleadh. Do you know him?"

Her voice came from somewhere in the region of my right armpit now. "No, you are the only one of the King's knights I've ever met. But it surprises me that you would choose him, over all the others. I have heard his name mentioned several times, but never in any way that seemed … admirable."

"Hmm. Well, take it from me, my love, as you would from no one else. There is nothing about Ghilly that is *not* admirable. But he is a strange man, on first acquaintance, I'll grant that. When I first met him I didn't like him at all, didn't think I ever would. He's been with Arthur since boyhood, and he's a gruff, grumpy sort of fellow who never says much, but I soon discovered he never says *anything* that's not worth listening to. He has no time for fools and he can't suffer incompetence, and he's difficult to approach, at first. Gives the impression of being distant … cold and aloof. But yet I could see that Arthur thinks the world of him and trusts him completely, and so I decided to make an effort to become his friend. It was the most worthwhile task I ever undertook. Ghilly is simply … Ghilly. He's unique. And when I think about it, here like this, with you, he is even comely. He has little truck with women, but they find him attractive, I think. But as a friend, a companion and a brother in arms, he's simply the best: unendingly generous, courageous, utterly loyal, and not a false or devious spark in his entire soul. The others are all fine, too, barely a flaw in all of them, but Ghilly's head and shoulders above us all, me included. Now, why would you ask me that?"

"I was curious about how you see your friends, that's all." She heaved and squirmed against me, and I turned my attention to other, more immediate things as she whispered, "I really do have to leave … soon."

Within the hour we were both up and dressed, and I accompanied her to the stable, where I hitched her horse to the wagon, then stood for a long time, kissing her as I fretted about the coming day and the moment she would leave me. Outside, the night sky was just starting to grow paler with the first dim hint of dawn, and I felt an almost physical pain in the hollow emptiness of my gut at the thought of losing her. She moved against me, breaking my hold on her, and started to turn to mount the wagon, but I seized her again and pressed her close, begging her not to leave me. She pushed me away, however, with more strength than I could ever have summoned to do the same to her, and stood looking up at me, raising her hand to anchor my chin where I could not avoid her gaze had I wanted to.

"I have to go," she said. "I have a life awaiting me out there, and so do you, and there is nothing we can do to change our destinies without hurting a lot of blameless people, including ourselves." She drew her head back slightly and stared fiercely at me. "We have done nothing wrong here, you and I, but we have lit a beacon that must soon burn itself out. I know I have set your soul alight, and I am glad of it, but mine is burning just as fiercely and as painfully, and the burning is a pain that we have to bear until it dies away. It will, Clothar. I promise you that. It will, if you allow it to. All you have to do is throw yourself into your duties, as I will into mine, and stay away from me. It will be difficult, but by the love you say you have for me, I beg you to be strong for both of us. Stay away, Clothar, and remember who you are.

"You are Seur Clothar of Camulod, Clothar of Benwick, Clothar of Auxerre, Clothar of Gaul. Your men call you the Gaul and the Lancer. And the King himself calls you Lance. You are a paragon, the King's champion, the finest rider among all the riders of Camulod and the finest spearman, able to throw a lance unerringly from the back of a speeding horse. And you have become a legend among your own soldiers. They walk in awe of you and would do anything and everything to please you, simply to earn your regard. They fear your discipline and your displeasure, I have been told, and yet they would happily follow you to death because you inspire them, simply by being who you are, and showing them the strength within you."

She tilted her head again in my favorite gesture. "That strength is what will enable you to stay away from me, Clothar. Use it, in God's name and mine, remembering that in all the time I have known you, since the day you saved my life and my father's, I have seen very little of the man Clothar that everyone talks about with such awe and admiration. The man I have come to know is gentle, kind, soft-spoken, courteous, often shy and unsure of himself, and I find that lovable. I have no doubt that the other man is there, inside you, the warrior and stern wielder of fierce discipline. I have never met him, but I need him to be more righteous than ever from this time on, until the pain fades away."

She laid her fingers flat against my lips, forbidding me to speak as she went on. "You think yourself in love forever with the woman you think you see in me. But you are wrong, Lance!" A tear trembled on her lashes and she wiped it away before I could reach out for it. "I swear to you, my dear man, the love you feel for me now is a passing thing. It is an image in a pool, and a scattering of raindrops will dissolve it. It has no true depth, no substance other than wishful imaginings. In time, a very brief time, it will fade and vanish, and someday you will find a woman you can truly love."

"I don't believe that."

"I know, and I bless you for it, but I *do* believe it. Farewell, and may God be with you always, close by your side. Speak to Him, for me, and ask Him to distract you with some task that will make all of this simpler and easier to bear. I have to go now."

I helped her up onto her bench and she gathered up the reins, weeping openly now, but I made no further move to touch her or to interfere with her leaving, for it was plain even to me that there was nothing more to be done. I had tried to keep her, and I had failed. I walked to the stable doors behind her wagon and stood there as she turned southwards, and only when the last sounds of her passage had faded into the darkness did I saddle my own horse and lead him out into the grayness of dawn. I closed the stable doors securely and rode away from there, knowing that neither one of us would ever visit the log house again, for Elaine had made it clear to me that, by creating new memories of me within the house, she had finally managed to free herself of her older, more distant memories.

5

I rode back to Camulod that morning without even being aware of the new day being born around me. I followed the route I had taken the day before, but I left the navigation entirely to my horse, who picked his way slowly and methodically back the way we had come while I sat slumped in my saddle, wrapped in my heavy cloak against what felt like icy air, and thought about all that had happened to me since the previous morning. My thoughts were in chaos, constantly veering between the wonder and magnificence of what I had found so unexpectedly and the magnitude of the loss I had suffered since, but I remembered Elaine's last wishes and prayed as she had asked me to, begging God to have mercy upon both of us and give me the strength, and the time, to overcome the temptation that was tearing at me even as I prayed.

How easy it would be, I thought, to simply turn around and ride back to the Villa Varo on any excuse that sprang to mind. I did not yet have official verification that Dougald was almost fit to return to his duties, and I owed it to the King to complete the task he had set me, down to the final detail. But then I saw Elaine's eyes in the predawn gloom, and the tears streaking her cheeks, and I knew I could not do that to her, not so soon. And so, fastening my thoughts upon the appallingly sparse memories I retained of making love to her, I moved through the growing daylight with no sense of where I was until I heard myself being greeted by one of the guards at Camulod's main gates, and I was astonished that I had mounted the steep, winding road to the fortress without even noticing.

I made an effort to collect myself and headed directly to the stables, where I left my horse with one of the grooms before marching to the day quarters of the officer on duty, knowing I would find Perceval there. He was sitting at the duty table, reading, and he looked up as I entered, one eyebrow rising as he scanned me from head to foot.

"You look remarkably fit, for a man missing in action," he drawled.

"What are you talking about?" I was in no mood for levity.

He shrugged, looking down again at the scroll spread out in front of him and held open by his dagger on one side and his open palm on the other. "You were reported missing last night, right after dinner."

"That's ridiculous. I was off duty, on my own time. You know that."

"I know, and I knew when I heard the report, but Lectis didn't know. It seems you neglected to inform him when you left the castle."

"*Inform* him? That idiot! I hope you put him in his place." Lectis, an unpleasant, too-officious garrison clerk, had been put in charge of ensuring that no personnel on duty tour were ever to leave the castle premises without good reason—a legitimate concern, since many of our men had women outside the walls and saw little wrong in slipping quietly away for conjugal visits from time to time. I was incensed, however, that he should extend his attentions to me, particularly when I stood guilty as charged.

Perceval was smiling. "Put him in his place? Not at all. I encouraged him to take you to task for your dereliction of duty, pointed out to him that rank gives you no special privileges in breaking rules and suggested that he present himself in your office as soon as you got back, to remind you of your responsibilities."

"He wouldn't dare. I'll have his guts out if he looks sideways at me ... You didn't really tell him that, did you?"

"Course not. I told him you were officially on furlough, forty-eight hours, and that as his commanding legate, you could swat him like a fly for even noticing what you do. He is a toad, isn't he?"

"Where will I find Arthur, d'you know?"

He shook his head. "Your guess would be as good as mine. He still isn't back from wherever he disappeared to yesterday, with Merlyn and the Eirishman."

"Did Lectis report *him* missing, too?"

"No. Apparently he's not *completely* brainless."

I was suddenly aware of how little real sleep I had had since leaving the previous day, and aware that I needed to be alone with my thoughts of Elaine, no matter how painful they might be. "Is there anything important happening that I should know about?"

"Nothing. You're still off duty until noon tomorrow. If anything comes up by then, I'll tell you in the morning."

"Good, then I'm going to get some sleep. If anyone asks for me, I'm still missing in action."

"Rough night, then?"

"Ursus, my friend, you could not imagine it. I'll see you later." I left him gazing at me strangely. I had not called him Ursus in years.

I actually slept, soundly and dreamlessly, for the remainder of the day, rising only in the late afternoon, when I rode down to the bath house at the Villa Britannicus and lounged in the hot pool and the steam room for a long time before submitting myself to the masseur on duty. He was merciless, knowing that I had not been there for many days, and as he pummeled the aches and stiffness out of me I was grateful for the distraction from the images of Elaine that were waiting to haunt me as soon as I let down my guard. By the time I got out of there, dressed in fresh clothing and free of armor, it was time for mess call, and between the two of them, although it must have been hard work, Ghilly and Bedwyr kept me talking and entertained until we were the last people left in the refectory. And once again, despite all my fears of a long and sleepless night, I fell asleep instantly and slept until morning.

I relieved Perceval before noon, leaving him free to enjoy his own forty-eight-hour rest, and sat down to review the rosters he had drawn up and assigned in my absence, and I was still working on the minutiae of garrison details when Merlyn arrived back, midway through the afternoon. I would not have known he was back at all had he not stopped by the duty room to say hello.

That struck me as being strange, for while the two of us were friendly, we were not exactly intimates and I had never known him pass by my door before for the simple pleasure of exchanging greetings. I fancied there was something in his eyes that I could not identify, but I had no way of knowing whether or not I was right, and he gave no indication of having anything particular on his mind. I asked him where I might find Arthur, but he shrugged and told me

he had come back to Camulod alone. Arthur had sailed north with
Connor Mac Athol and would not return home for at least a week
and probably longer. He offered no explanation, and I did not think
it fitting to ask for one.

As it transpired, Arthur remained away from Camulod for
twenty-two days, and on the twelfth of those days, Dougald himself
turned up from the Villa Varo, fully recovered—save that he still
wore a bandage on his face to cover his empty eye socket and raw
scars—with word that his daughter, Elaine, was to be married in
seven days to Jonas, the headman of the village that was Camulod's
closest neighboring community. Everyone in the fortress who was
not tied by duty, from the King himself downward, was invited to
attend the celebrations.

I do not know how I was able to listen to him in front of all the
others without betraying my thoughts or the pain his announcement
caused me, but I managed it without anyone noticing anything.
Merlyn, as Arthur's direct representative, explained the King's
absence, but assured the old farmer that the day would be declared
a holiday in Camulod and that everyone else, himself and the King's
knights included, would be there for the festivities.

I was a foul-tempered bear in the days that followed, gnawing
at my own hidden wounds as though trying to render myself unconscious through the pain of them, and although most people avoided
me completely during that time, no one seemed even to come close
to guessing what was bothering me. I had decided I would not—
could not—attend the wedding, but I changed my mind a hundred
times, and each time had to convince myself anew it would be folly
to go near the place.

In the end it was Merlyn who made sure I would be there. By
sheer coincidence, I was scheduled to be on forty-eight-hour leave
again at that time, and so I had made arrangements to defer my own
time off so that Perceval could attend in my place. Merlyn found out
about that somehow and flatly refused to allow me to do it. I was
one of the King's closest friends and advisers, he told me, and had
served as Arthur's personal envoy to the Villa Varo after Dougald's

encounter with the bear. Were I not to attend the wedding in the King's absence, it might be taken as an insult to the bride, and to all at the Villa Varo, construed as being an indication that I did not think the event worthy of my attention. It was a direct reminder of my duty, and I gritted my teeth and told him I would go.

And on the appointed day, I rode to the Villa Varo with all my friends, trying vainly to mask my anguish, the only mourner in a crowd of revelers.

The bride was beautiful—shining like a full moon, I heard someone say—and the bridegroom looked as proud and happy as a bridegroom is meant to look. Dougald could not have been prouder had Elaine been bred from his own flesh and being wed for the first time, and the entire occasion was a gala affair, the grounds of the Villa Varo more crowded and more festive than anyone could ever remember having seen them. There were musicians and tumblers, acrobats and jugglers, and more than sufficient food and drink to feed the laughing, singing multitudes. It was the most miserable, self-pitying morning I had ever spent.

The lowest point in the entire day was when I had to meet the bridal couple, immediately after the simple ceremony. Elaine and her new husband stood hand in hand within a bridal bower that was decorated with evergreen boughs, for it was far too late in the year to find blooming flowers, and the principal guests stepped forward in procession to wish them well. Several times, when I found myself drawing too near to the head of the line, I slipped to the rear on one excuse after another, but I could not continue doing that for long without someone noticing, and so eventually I steeled myself to do what must be done and moved forward in my turn to the front of the line.

Elaine knew I was there, and that I was putting off stepping forward. I had seen her look at me at least three times, after each of which I broke away and moved backwards again, out of her sight, but when I reached the front and stood facing her and Jonas, she smiled at me in a way that twisted a broad blade in my heart, although there was nothing but pure, radiant pleasure in her look.

I knew I could not speak a word to her without betraying both of us, and so I forced myself to look only at Jonas. He was a tall, amiable-looking man, broad and well set up, with blond curling hair that was starting to turn gray, and guileless blue eyes, and as I met his friendly gaze, thinking he must be at least fifteen years older than I, I was astonished to find all the bitterness I had borne him vanish as though it had never been.

I clasped him by the arm as an equal, closing my other hand over his and wishing him well in his new life, while a small, rueful voice in my mind told me that only Elaine and I knew him in fact to be more than my equal, my superior in this, at least. His eyes had widened at my conferral of such honor on him when we two had never met, for only men of equal rank in life greeted each other in such a way, and I knew I had no option now but to acknowledge my reason for doing so. I glanced at Elaine, and then looked quickly back at him. "Look after this woman," I said to him. "I have come to know a little of her worth in recent weeks, and trust me when I say I believe you have found a jewel beyond price."

The words had emerged naturally and without strain, and I found it easy now to turn to Elaine and incline my head in deference to her beauty. "My lady Elaine, I shall pray Heaven to keep you safe and well in your new life and your new home. May God be with you wherever you go."

I had spoken clearly and confidently, and several of the people standing nearby, Ghilly, Bedwyr, Bors and Sagramore among them, applauded my words. I heard other voices, too, behind me, raised in shouts of approval, but as I bowed and began to step back to clear the way for those behind me, Elaine held up her hand and stopped me.

"Seur Clothar," she said, smiling radiantly at me. "Everyone here knows that you saved both our lives and my father's, and made this marriage possible, and for that we can never adequately thank you. But even after that, your constant attention to our family's needs and welfare placed us further in your debt, so I can only thank you for your strength and fortitude, for the support you have provided to us by simply being yourself. You will live forever in our gratitude … to the gratification of our memories."

Now the shouts around us rang out loud and long and I found my face growing crimson. There was something about the words she had used, and in the emphasis she used, that had reminded me forcefully of the last time I saw her. She had used the same words then—her gift of gratitude and gratification—and then I saw what she was wearing: the same pale green outer robe she had worn on that occasion, but now she was idly pulling the edges together in front of her, and the girdle of rich, dark green wool that had tied it about her waist was no longer visible. My heart missed a beat, for I had no doubt she had conveyed a message to me. I bowed deeply from the waist and stepped backwards.

When the festivities and drinking began in earnest later, I pleaded an aching head and the need to be alone, and made my way back to Camulod by myself, taking the longer route that she had taught me. The small log house was still shuttered when I arrived, but the spring lock on the door was open, and the heavy wooden door swung inward at my touch. There was enough light to show me the bed, stripped now of mattress and coverings, but the soft, thick rope of dark green wool lay on the center of the table in front of the fire, carefully coiled and tied with a yellow ribbon, waiting for me. I picked it up and raised it to my face, imagining that I could smell the scent of her, clinging to its fibers, and then I tucked it into my breast, against my skin, and made my way homewards, feeling better than I had in many days.

6

Arthur returned home three days later and threw my life into a turmoil that would last for years. I was out with Perceval and Bors, inspecting our perimeter guard posts, when he arrived, and I was summoned to join him as soon as I rode back through the gates, before I even had time to dismount.

He was in the duty room with Merlyn, behind closed doors but waiting for me, and when I knocked Merlyn himself opened the door and waved me inside, then went out as I entered, leaving me alone with the King. Arthur stood by the long work table in front of a roaring fire, his head bowed over an open book of cut vellum pages, covered in writing and bound with heavy boards. He seemed unaware that I was there.

"My lord, it's good to see you safely home. You sent for me?"

He looked up, blinking in surprise, then grinned and came quickly towards me, throwing his arms wide to embrace me and make me welcome, after which he moved to a well-stocked tray on a table against the wall. He picked up a jug and poured wine into two cups.

"I know you don't like wine, Lance, but this time I insist you have some, to share the celebration."

I took the proffered cup dubiously and raised it in salute. "Then I'll drink it obediently, my lord … but what are we celebrating?"

He drank deeply, then wiped his mouth with the back of his hand. "Our friendship, Lance, and your Gaulishness, and the fact that this is almost the last jug of wine left in all of Camulod."

I took a sip, feeling the instant tartness that I despised flooding the hollows beneath my tongue. "The last of it," I said. "Is that something we should be celebrating, my lord?"

"Of course not. But the idea of a fresh supply certainly is."

"A fresh supply? How so? From where? Forgive me, but I don't follow you."

"I know you don't, but you will. And since when am I your lord when there is no one else around? Sit down, sit down. I have much to tell you."

I moved to obey, unfastening my cloak and folding it over the back of a chair before setting my helmet on the floor and sitting across the table from him. Even from there, on the far side of the table, I could feel the welcome heat of the fire behind him, for the first snow of the year, wet and chill, had fallen that afternoon and I was cold to the bones.

"Pelles, King of Corbenic, what do you know of him?"

"King of *Corbenic*?" I set my wine cup down on the table and shrugged. "I've heard of Corbenic. I believe it's a region in the northwest of Gaul, along the coast, but I've never been there and I've never heard of a king called Pelles. Where did you hear the name?"

"I didn't hear it, I read it, in a letter from the Bishop of Auxerre, a man called Ludovic."

"Ludovic? The same man who was secretary to Bishop Germanus? Surely not. He was an old, old man when I left Gaul, and a self-effacing one. I can't conceive of him as being a bishop now."

It was Arthur's turn to shrug. "Perhaps not, but the Bishop of Auxerre is now a man called Ludovic. Would you recognize his writing?" I nodded, and he reached out to retrieve a letter from the tabletop. "Then see for yourself, and tell me."

I recognized Ludovic's scholarly lettering instantly. "That's him. Dear God, he must be close to ninety."

"Well, he has not lost his faculties. He writes very convincingly, and that is the third letter I have received from him."

"Convincingly of what?"

"Of the need for an alliance between us and this man Pelles."

I sat back in astonishment. "An alliance? Between us and someone in *Gaul*? Surely we have enough trouble forging alliances here at home without attempting to establish one in Gaul. What would be the point of that?"

"It makes sense, from some viewpoints …" He sipped at his wine again, less deeply this time. "Have you ever noticed how, from time to time, ideas will come together from differing sources and make perfect sense when you combine them? That's happening now, and having considered everything that's going on, I think I would be irresponsible to ignore what my mind is telling me is right. Come over here and look at this— No, on second thought, stay where you are and I'll explain it to you. The exercise might serve me as well as it does you. Let me think for a moment."

He set down his cup and raised one foot to the tabletop, levering his chair backwards until he was balanced on a fulcrum, his fingers laced behind his head.

"First came the letters—or the first letter from Ludovic. He knew who I was, and he knew who Merlyn was—obviously through his association with Germanus. But he wanted to know if I would consider an alliance with King Pelles of Corbenic, one that would offer us mutual advantages. I was curious, so I read on. It was a very long letter, written in several hands, so I presume he dictated sections of it to others, but I read it often enough to notice that none of those sections contained sufficient information in itself to betray the overall content of what he was saying to me."

"He spent long enough with Germanus to have learned that trick well." I sipped at my wine again, but it had not improved in taste and I set it down once more. "So what *was* he saying?"

"That Pelles is a worthy man—a Frank like you—and a fine ruler who shares common problems with us here in Britain, namely sustained and increasing raiding of his territories by fleets of Outlanders, most particularly Danes. He called them by a different name, but there was no mistaking who he meant."

I nodded. "Then bishops and clerics are clearly still crossing the seas between him and us in numbers, carrying information. But how could an alliance with us help this Pelles against marauders in Gaul? That makes no sense."

"It does, if you consider his Frankishness, and our advantage over him. He has Frankish horsemen aplenty, but they are not cavalry, like our troopers. They have no formal discipline, no organization. And that means they are practically worthless as an effective defense against sea raiders. He wanted us to consider lending him a contingent of our forces, as teachers. Not to fight, necessarily, but to teach his people how to fight as a cohesive force— heavy cavalry. Bishop Ludovic told him about us, apparently, and the king was most impressed by what we have achieved. Besides, he has other concerns, this king, distant at this point but easily capable of becoming far more threatening and dangerous than the Danes, if what we are hearing from the far northeast is true."

"What's that? And northeast of where?"

"Northeast of Gaul, Lance, along the Rhine, and the Danube River. Have you ever heard of the Hungvari?" I shook my head, mystified, and he went on. "I am told they are the soldiers of a man who has been terrorizing the world beyond our horizon, the latest conqueror in the broth of upstart barbarians from beyond the northern reaches of the Empire. Bishop Ludovic spoke of the fellow in his last letter to me, and of how mothers are using his name to terrify their children and make them behave themselves at night. His name is Attila, and he calls himself the King of the Huns, and many of the stories about him simply seem to me to be too outrageous to be believed, like the reports that assert that he has several armies, operating independently of each other, and each has warriors numbered in the hundreds of thousands. That is plainly impossible, and because of the wildness of such reports, many people doubt he even exists, claiming the tales of him are but a device to keep folk loyal to the idea of the Empire as Protector.

"But Ludovic warns that he has heard too many reliable reports of this Attila to ignore, and Pelles of Corbenic fears him. To this point he has come nowhere near the west coastal regions of Gaul, but his armies appear to have overrun all opposition in the north and east, and have swung down into the central and southern regions. They have conquered the Burgundians, according to some reports, and even the Alamanni and Alans, according to others. Pelles and Ludovic do not really believe that he will come their way, but their desire to build a cavalry force is founded upon their apprehensions that he might. And so they look to us for alliance."

I contemplated what he had said, and the flaw seemed obvious. Arthur, however, was impatient for my response and asked me what I thought before I had had time to think the whole thing through.

"Well, first of all, that's not an alliance, Arthur, it's ... it's an accommodation, a favor. What benefit for us would lie in that? And if these tales of this king of the Huns are true, he could move west-wards immediately, from wherever he is, and set all our work to naught." And then I raised my eyebrows and lifted a hand dramatically. "Wait! Don't tell me! Let me guess at what we might gain ... a new source of wine!"

"Aye, and of olives and olive oil, too. Some of the finer things in life that we too frequently lack." But there was no trace of humor in his tone, and I felt my jaw sag open in disbelief at the thought of trading wine for cavalry, but he had been waiting for exactly that and laughed, bending his knee to allow his chair to fall back into place. "Horses, Lance! New breeding stock for our herds! That's the benefit we would gain, and my horse masters tell me it's one we sorely need. The stallions you and Perceval brought with you from Gaul when you first arrived were the first fresh bloodstock we have had in Britain since the Romans left. And I now believe, because our breeders have been crying about it to me for years, that the need for fresh stock is a reality we have to think about."

"Aye, but even if we set aside this threat you speak of, from the lands beyond the Rhine and the Danube, and think only of assisting your new friend against the Danes, we have no *ships,* Arthur. We can't *swim* to Gaul. Does this Pelles have sufficient ships to send to us in order to transport our stock?"

"No."

I threw up a hand in exasperation. "Then it can never work. It can't be done without ships. It's wishful thinking and a waste of time."

"I agreed with you until last month. I had said exactly the same thing to Merlyn months ago, while you were away in the north. Can't be done, I told him, and we don't have the time to waste in wishing it might. So I had Merlyn himself write a letter back to the bishop, explaining why we couldn't do anything. But two more letters have arrived since then, each of them offering to supply us with anything we want, if we can make this matter work. I read them, and responded, but by then I had dismissed the idea as being impractical.

"And then last month Connor Mac Athol came a-visiting, out of nowhere, with a strange request that caught my attention as soon as he opened his mouth. Do you know Connor's history?"

I smiled. "Aye, he's Donuil's brother, and he holds the title of admiral, in their people's new island kingdom, off the coast of Caledonia."

A tic of annoyance reminded me how Arthur eschewed all things Roman. "Alba, the natives call it," he said quietly. "Caledonia was the name the Romans gave it. Today it has returned to being Alba, just as Eire has ceased to be Hibernia. But you're correct, he is the king's admiral up there, and the king, like Donuil, is Connor's brother, Brander by name. Now *there* is a man who has ships at his disposal. And on top of that, he has a difficulty that he wishes us to help him solve." He stopped then, picking with the nail of his little finger at something lodged between two teeth.

"A new island kingdom, you said. That is exact, and you have outlined Connor's problem without needing to name it. They call their new home Dalriada. A new kingdom, composed entirely of islands, less than three decades old, still being born and struggling for its life, yet dreaming already of expanding to the mainland of Alba, if for no other reason than to control the coast from which their enemies can sail against them. Brander Mac Athol needs weapons, Lance. Weapons and armor. His people need them. They have a few smiths among them, but none of them with the skills to make fine weapons, and not enough of them, even if they were that good, to make them in sufficient numbers for their needs. They can produce crude armor of boiled leather, beaten and bossed with metal, and they can make axe heads and simple iron flails, but what they need is tempered blades and mailed coats, and strong metal helmets and cuirasses."

"From Gaul," I murmured, seeing where Arthur was going. "But why do they need help from us in that? Why not go directly to Gaul and buy them?"

"Because Brander has no funds—no coinage, no bullion. And so he came to us, not in search of help in Gaul but in the hope that

Camulod might be able to supply at least a part of their needs. He knows we have been making the best weaponry in Britain since the days of Publius Varrus, and he hoped we would have stockpiles he could purchase from us."

"With what? You just finished telling me they have no funds."

"Right. But they are not completely without resources of other kinds." He pushed himself up from the table and stirred the burned-through logs in the hearth with a heavy iron poker. He stood watching the sparks vanish up the wide chimney, and then he set about replenishing the fire from the large basket of cut logs beside the hearth, pushing the fresh fuel into place with the sole of his hob-nailed riding boot.

"They are artists, in their own way, Brander's island folk," he said eventually, speaking over his shoulder, and then he turned back to me. "Look at this."

He lowered his chin and carefully began to unfasten a heavy green and golden brooch that I had noticed as he came to embrace me when I entered the room. It was large and ornate, with the dull gleam of polished gold, a round-edged, scalloped oblong with gracefully fashioned leaf-like spaces forming a floral pattern at its center. The connecting spines of the design were inlaid with some kind of reddish mica, while a circular yellow gem formed the hub of the flower. Its backing pin had been securing a long, shawl-like length of bright, soft-looking green cloth that was wound about his breast, beneath his right arm and over his left shoulder to hang down behind his back.

The brooch came loose and he palmed it, then tossed it to me, and I held it up to my eyes, admiring the way the light reflected off the inlaid patterns, which I now recognized as being a form of enameling, much like similar objects I had seen in Gaul, but infinitely finer and more elaborate.

"Have you ever seen anything quite like that? That's solid gold, as you can see, but they've made it better—more valuable than simple gold. They make wondrous jewelry—both gold and silver when they can find enough of it—but most of what they make is copper and bronze, and they decorate it with melted glass. It sounds strange, I know, but you can see it for yourself. How do you melt glass and make it do that? Whatever it involves, their work is wonderful.

"They're wondrous weavers, too, and the cattle, sheep and goats up there in their islands produce a superior wool to anything we have down here. That's what this thing is made of." He shrugged the woolen shawl over his head and tossed it to me, too. "See for yourself. It's thicker, softer and far warmer than any wool we have."

I rubbed the garment, warm with his body heat, against my cheek and felt immediately that he was right. I laid it down on the table and untied Elaine's woolen rope girdle from about my waist, and rubbed it between thumb and finger as I compared it to Arthur's garment. The rope girdle was thicker, firmer and more dense than the northern material, and yet there was no denying the difference: the stuff of Arthur's shawl was warmer and softer. I saw Arthur raise an eyebrow when I first drew the girdle from about my waist, but he offered no comment and asked no questions, and I felt grateful once again for his unfailing tact.

"You notice the difference between the two?"

"Like night and day. The very fiber seems different. I've never felt anything quite like this."

The King nodded. "Aye. No more have I. And they have no lack of it. Connor told me that every woman and child in their kingdom spends every spare moment of the day spinning wool. I thought he was exaggerating when he told me that, but I have been there since, among their islands, and I have seen it with my own eyes. Women and children everywhere, spinning wool. They do it day and night, every one of them, walking about with a hank of teased, raw wool under one arm and dangling a revolving spindle in front of them, just as our own farm women do. But they do it all the time, without rest, day and night. Think about that."

"I'm thinking," I said, half smiling. "Why so much effort? And are there many of them, women and children? If so they must produce a deal of wool."

"They do. Incredible amounts. And then they weave it into cloth. They have storage buildings everywhere, full of bundles of woven cloth. That's what Connor offered us in return for weapons. Cloth for blankets and warm clothing."

I sat staring at him, trying to fathom what he was telling me. I could grasp the gist of it, but the connections were not falling clearly into place. "So," I said, "you told him we did not need his wool. Is that what you're saying?"

"Why would you think that?" He was clearly surprised by my assumption, and my frustration got the better of me.

"Because it's evident. Had you believed we could use it, you would have agreed to his bargain. But it's obvious you didn't."

"No, no, not at all, Lance. We could use all of it they could supply. It would solve our winter uniform troubles. That kind of cloth, warm and water resistant as it is, could make our troopers' lives more comfortable. No, I told him the truth—that we can barely manufacture weapons and armor for our own needs nowadays. For no matter how our smithies grow and expand, our need for equipment outstrips their capacity. Even wanting to, we can't supply him."

"Oh. I didn't know that." I knew we had few weapons smiths, but I truly had not known that our demand for weapons had outgrown our ability to meet it, and it was now my turn to move about, to absorb all that he had been saying and try to make sense of it. And then a light flickered in the darkness and everything began to come together.

"I have it now," I said, pacing the room. "You told him he would have to go to Gaul to fill his needs, since there is still sufficient Roman production there to meet them, and you were thinking that while he is going there, he can transport your horses, am I right?"

"You're right."

I shook my head. "I might be missing something, Arthur, for I still can't see that working. His fleet consists of galleys, if I'm not mistaken. Am I?"

"No, but go on."

"Galleys are warships, built for speed, slim and narrow, made for fighting and for nothing else. You can't ship horses in galleys, Arthur—not large numbers of them, anyway, and I suspect you are thinking about large numbers, several hundred at least. And besides, Connor's brother, the king … what's his name, Brander? Brander must need his fleet at home if he's being attacked from the mainland regularly, as you say."

Arthur was grinning broadly, showing his startlingly white, even teeth. "Right, right and right," he said. "Every shaft on target, as usual. But you don't yet know all the facts." He held up one hand and began to tick off the points on his fingers.

"Numbers," he began. "Not too long ago, when Connor first came to Camulod, the Scots had two fleets, not one. Connor had command of the southern fleet, based in Eire. His brother Brander, now the King of Scots, was admiral of the northern fleet, responsible for transporting their entire populace from Eire to their new home in the islands to the northeast. But now that they have no base in Eire to maintain, their needs have shrunk. Their entire fleet is home-based in their islands, and it's half the size it used to be. But these Scots are seafarers, and they waste nothing. So the portion of their fleet that's not in use is still there, stored carefully on land above high water and constantly tended.

"Now, bear in mind what I said about transporting their entire populace. Many of those stored vessels are for transport, built to carry cargoes of people and possessions. And many of them are flat bottomed, too, perfect for moving horses, although they were built for cattle and livestock. They even have a couple of Roman biremes, huge things that Connor captured during the war against Carthac in Cornwall. And they are all in prime condition, Lance. No leaks, no rot. That's why I went up there with Connor—to examine them. They're perfect for our needs, and Brander and Connor will make them available to us."

"In return for what?"

"In return for weapons from Gaul." He was still holding up his hand, its fingers spread, and now he hooked his other hand over his little finger. "We provide them with trading goods valuable enough to buy weapons, and they provide us with their ships for transporting our horses."

"Trading goods ..." I thought about that for a few moments. "Don't you think that might be difficult, considering that we trade nothing? Unless there's something else I don't know about. What kind of trading goods?"

"Hard ones. Merlyn spent much of the year traveling through Cornwall, looking around and taking note of what's going on, now that the land down there's at peace again, and he made some interesting discoveries. The people there have started mining again, the way they used to in the old days. They're producing tin again."

"Tin?"

"Aye, and silver, lead and some copper."

"What's tin?"

"You don't know what tin is? Then you must have another name for it where you come from, because you certainly use it over there. It's a metal. It's the main reason the Romans came to Britain in the first place. There's more tin here than anywhere else, and you can't make bronze without it, so it's very valuable for trading purposes. The Gauls will happily trade weapons and armor for it, Merlyn says. So, we can take Connor and his people into Gaul in safety, when we go to deal with Pelles of Corbenic. Otherwise, he would have to go from port to port, looking for one that won't attack his galleys at first sight. In addition to that safe passage to a friendly base in Gaul, we'll supply him with the metal ingots he needs to trade, and in return he will ferry our men and horses—in both directions—and supply us for good measure with woolen cloth for winter uniforms. What think you of that?"

I nodded slowly. "It sounds ... impressive. When will all this start?"

"It's begun already. Letters are on their way to Bishop Ludovic in Auxerre, and he will pass the tidings along to Pelles. Connor's people have already begun to prepare a fleet of trading vessels for all of us to use, and Merlyn has already sent out foragers to buy all the metal ingots they can find the length and breadth of Cornwall. We still have bars of gold and silver left in our coffers—not much of it, but enough to serve our purpose, cut up and doled out in small pieces. If all goes well, everything should be in place by late spring, perhaps early May, as soon as the spring gales have blown themselves out."

"Very well, that all sounds excellent. But what will you do if these Huns are real, and decide to come visiting while we're there?"

He looked straight at me, his face expressionless. "We will face that when it happens. In the meantime, the odds strike me as being favorable to our venture. We need the benefits this arrangement—or alliance—will provide for us, and the apparent risks, as they stand now, seem negligible. If the circumstances change with passing time, we will hope to be sufficiently strong to withstand them by the time they do so."

There was nothing I could add to that without sounding surly, so I merely nodded. "It looks as though you have thought of everything," I said, making no attempt to hide the fact that I was impressed.

"I think I have. I *hope* I have. The only detail that remains—the only one that I can think of, anyway—is appointing a leader for the entire exercise."

"A legate, you mean? That's an important detail, Arthur. Not the sort of thing you would leave to the last moment. Who do you have in mind?"

"You need to ask? I want you to do it."

"Me?" I felt my dismay flooding my face. "But I can't. I have to be back in the north by then, to check on Connlyn and his friends from beyond the Wall. You know that—it was your idea."

"Aye, but that was before this matter came up. Ghilly can go up there in your place."

"But that's madness, Arthur! Ghilly doesn't know the territory or the people. Why not send *him* to Gaul? He's the perfect man for the job, training new recruits starting from nothing."

"Ghilly, in Gaul? Lance, Ghilly barely speaks our *own* language, when he speaks at all. He would be a liability in Gaul. His training and disciplinary skills are great, I know, and I love and trust him absolutely, but our Ghilly's personality is not his greatest gift when it comes to dealing with strangers ... and Gaul is full of strangers. Ghilly has never been beyond these shores. But first and above all else, he does not speak the *languages* of Gaul. You do, and you are the only one to whom I could entrust a matter of this gravity and complexity."

I was now close to squirming with discomfort, seeing insurmountable difficulties fast approaching, and evaluating and condemning them ahead of their arrival, spurred by my own selfish concerns. Despite my change of mind on Elaine's marriage, I had been looking forward to riding northwards in the spring and removing myself physically from the temptation to visit her. But now I saw that Connlyn's northern territories were still in Britain, even though many miles away from Elaine. The thought of leaving the country, and her, altogether, to travel beyond the seas, was quite another matter.

"What are you thinking about, Lance?"

I sighed and mentally threw up my hands. Elaine had told me less than a month before that my life was not my own to dispose of, and here, already, was the truth of that. My life and my duty were to my King, first and forever, and any attempt to deny that truth would strip me of both honor and integrity in my own eyes. Searching for appropriate words with which to answer him, I stood up and walked around the far end of the table to approach the fireplace on his side, and he turned his head to watch me as I approached. When we were separated only by the width of the powerful fire, I stopped and took a step backwards, away from the heat, raising my hand as if to ward it off.

"How can you sit so close to this?" He said nothing, waiting, and I twisted my face into a grimace of distaste. "I have to tell you I am not enthused about the idea of going back to Gaul, Arthur."

"Why not?" I could see that I had shocked him. "I thought you would be happy to go back. You have unfinished business there."

"What d'you mean?"

"Clodas. Isn't that the fellow's name? Have you lost interest in bringing him down?"

My father, Childebertus, my mother, Elaine, and my grandfather King Garth of Ganis in northern Gaul had all died at the hands of a treasonous creature called Clodas, who usurped Ganis and my father's kingdom after their murders. I was raised thereafter by my aunt Vivienne and her husband, King Ban of Benwick, and avenging my family's deaths had been a task beyond my reach ever since.

"Of course I haven't! And I never will. But that has nothing to do with this. You are handing me a task here that will be all-consuming while I am in Gaul. I would have no time to tend to my own personal concerns."

He kept his eyes fixed on mine. "You're wrong. You would. Plenty of time. This fellow lives in northern Gaul, does he not?"

I nodded. "Aye, in Ganis."

"Is that far from where you will be, in Corbenic?"

"I don't know. I've never been back in Ganis since I was a baby. But it can't be too far away, I suppose."

"No, it can't be. Look, Lance, your function in Gaul will be to act as my factor and factotum, supervising the training of Corbenic's new cavalry and keeping an eye on the comings and goings of Connor's ships. But that doesn't mean you'll have no time to spare. On the contrary, you should have ample free time. Certainly enough to ride to Ganis and find out what is happening there, and what you might need, in the way of men and resources, to put this creature Clodas to the sword and reclaim your throne."

"Aye, and were I able to do that, where might I find those men and resources? I don't know a soul in Ganis, and Benwick lies four hundred miles and more to the south. Even if my cousin Brach is still alive and ruling there, the odds against him lending me an army to travel that far away from home for as long as it would take are probably no less than they were in King Ban's time."

"Here!" He stretched across the table to reach my long-abandoned wine cup, and held it out to me. "Drink. I will not have this wasted."

That won him a rueful smile from me. "When I drink wine, my lord, it *is* wasted."

"Drink anyway, and think upon this … a minor matter you appear to have overlooked. You will be in command of half a Camulodian army group while you are there. Not all at the outset, of course, but you will have time for nothing more at the start than setting up your operations, anyway. By the end of the summer, on the other hand, after Connor has made a few crossings, you should have a very substantial force at your command. At your *command,* Lance. At that time, should you wish to ride to Ganis, purely to look around, you could do so with a formidable escort. And it occurs to me that should this upstart murderer be as unpleasant as he ever was, you might find far more support rallying to your armed presence than you anticipate. Think about it. I mean the offer sincerely. You will be my sole commander in Gaul, and should you decide this Clodas presents a threat to our venture in any way, you will have full authority to deal with him as you see fit."

I had to sit down, stunned by the magnanimity of his offer. "Arthur," I said, once I had found my tongue, "I don't know what to say … how to thank you … but if I were to accept that, then I would be bound to stay in Ganis, as king there."

"Aye, that had occurred to me. It would mean that when your tasks are over and Corbenic has its own force, you would send our people home again and I would have two allies among the kings in Gaul, one of them the staunchest I could ever hope to have." He stood up and looked down at me. "Think about it, my friend. I need you there in Gaul. Once you are there, I will rest content, knowing these matters could not be in better care. We will establish trading customs, permitting our own people to work gainfully on their own behalf. We will also gain fresh bloodstock for our herds, earn the goodwill and cooperation of Corbenic and its king, and show the Danes that they may no longer raid the coasts of either north Gaul or Britain without dire peril. But more than that, and perhaps the most important part of all of this, because of the way word of such things spreads, is that it will soon become known throughout Gaul that Camulod stands for Britain.

"Go now and bathe and eat, and sleep on what I have said, and on my request, for I will not command you to do this. You have other, pressing concerns here, I think, although I know not what they are. We will talk again tomorrow. And now I have to find Merlyn again."

I stood up, too, nodding in acceptance of what filled my mind. "No need to think or sleep, Arthur. I'll go. How could I not? Deny the chance to take Camulod to Gaul? I would have to be mad to do that. I take it I can bring the others with me, Perceval, Tristan and Bors?"

"Perceval, certainly. He's your second in command. But I'll need Tristan and Bors here. You're only taking half your strength, remember. Tristan will command the remainder while you're away."

"And Bors?"

"He'll be a knight within the month. Time for him to start learning his own responsibilities as a field commander. I'll assign him to Ghilly's group for the journey north in the spring. Next to yourself, he could not have a better teacher."

"I agree, but I'll be sorry to lose him."

He grasped my shoulder and shook me gently. "You won't be losing him. By the time you get back, he'll be a legate in his own right, and your friendship with him won't suffer from that. But sleep on your decision anyway, Lance. Then tell me the same thing tomorrow."

I bowed, wordless, and made my way to my quarters in a daze.

SIX

1

I was cold, wet and miserable, and this was a far cry from the home-coming I had anticipated, because in my mind, Gaul had always been a place of sunshine and warmth, far removed from the damp-ness and chilly misery of rain-swept Britain. But of course, my memories had been of southern Gaul, where I grew up, and the reality was that northern Gaul, where I sat that day, was only a day's sea voyage from the coast of Britain. The rain came blowing in off the water in icy lancets, its individual needles relentless, numbing exposed skin and penetrating every open seam and joint of armor and cloth to trickle down chillingly between warm flesh and supposedly protective clothing; even my crotch was cold and damp, soaked to the skin as soon as I threw my leg across my wet saddle. And yet I knew I should not complain, even to myself, for I was fortunate. All I had to do was sit here on my horse, wrapped in my heavy cloak, an ample hood over my head and shoulders, and supervise the work that everyone else was doing. The others had to work in the driving downpour, and none of the tasks they had to handle were as easy or pleasant as mine.

Below me, at the foot of the headland on which I sat, the tiny harbor of the fishing hamlet we had reached was thronged with shipping, a dozen vessels lashed together side by side, three deep, against the single narrow stone jetty. The small bay beyond contained four times as many vessels again, all of them bearing shipments of various kinds and all waiting their turn to warp against the jetty and discharge their cargoes. Behind them, the entrance to the bay seemed like a forest of masts as Connor's fighting galleys patrolled the approaches, protecting their charges in this, the most important and vulnerable stage of our venture. The jetty itself was chaotic, for there was not room enough along its narrow spine to hold the numbers of men crammed onto it, all of them working feverishly to unload skittish and frightened horses from the ships. The tide was rising, but it was not yet high enough for the ships to discharge the animals directly from the decks onto the land, and so a number of Connor's seamen from the first few vessels to arrive had erected four simple hoists of ropes and pulleys on the pier, and crews were now busily slinging halters beneath the horses' bellies and hoisting the bridled beasts one at a time from slippery decks to crowded jetty, where they were quickly led to the beach and roped together in strings. Once that was done, the animals were brought up the steep slope to the open ground where I sat now.

There were more than two hundred battle-trained animals to be unloaded, sufficient, including spares, for the three full forty-man squadrons I had brought with me on this first excursion, as well as for the score and a half of Pendragon bowmen who were here to serve as scouts, under the command of Griffyd Strongarm, a distant cousin to Arthur and the eldest son of Huw Pendragon, one of the King's closest friends among his own Pendragon people of Cambria. Behind me now, a squad of my troopers were hobbling the horses together in rows as they came up from below. I knew without looking back that we had thirty-seven animals ashore now, because I had been counting them as they passed me. I could see about twenty more being marshaled on the shingles just off the end of the jetty, and the hoists were still working busily and would continue for hours to come, since all of the horses had to be safely ashore before the rest of the cargo vessels could discharge their loads— loads without which the horses and their riders would be hamstrung. I had spent more than two months preparing for this expedition, working with the finest planners Camulod and Connor could provide, and the logistics involved in this single operation, merely the first of many, were more intricate than I could ever have imagined.

Organizing things had been complex from the outset because we were traveling to an unknown land, to attempt something that had never been tried before: beginning from the most basic fundamentals and lacking any pre-existing infrastructure, we would create and train a completely new cavalry force. Aware as we were of that, it followed that we could not afford to presume that we would find anything where we were going that would fit our specific needs, apart from untrained horses and men. Everything else, every item of gear and equipment that we might need in Gaul for the duration of our stay, had to be identified in advance and assembled, packed and stowed on board ship, and that single aspect in itself, the distribution and stowage of cargo, was a task worthy of Hercules, for people who work and live—let alone ride and fight—on land have no idea of the paucity of space on board a ship. Every item of cargo, from wagons to tent poles, to bundles of weapons and missiles, had to be measured for length and bulk and then accommodated according to its nature and requirements; the horses had to be loaded in carefully chosen batches, since each had to be accompanied throughout the voyage by someone it knew and trusted; bulk loads of saddlery and weaponry had to be combined and assigned to specific vessels; and in every instance a strict inventory had to be recorded, detailing exactly which pieces of gear were on any given ship.

It had been an all-consuming task, and there had been many times when I thought it would be impossible to achieve, but the months had flown past and the pieces had all come together steadily and without insurmountable problems. We had even made use of the old abandoned Roman river port of Glevum as our assembly point, resurrecting it briefly as a living community and using its piers and loading docks for our embarkation, and on the day appointed, Connor had emerged from the western reaches of the river in a gray dawn, leading a fleet of galleys and variously sized ships that choked the waterway, a spectacle the like of which no one in Camulod had ever seen.

And now, twenty-two days later, having sailed uneventfully and in fine weather along the entire southwestern coastline of Britain, we had crossed the Narrow Seas at their narrowest point and made landfall on time and on target, to see the three beacon lights of the bonfires that were our signal burning on the heights above the prearranged landing point, half a day's voyage to the north of the little port from which I had set sail for Britain years before. We had done it, and we were here! I felt a great rush of satisfaction that overcame my present discomfort, and took a moment to look around me.

Stretching to my right and left along the edge of the cliff, for more than a hundred paces in each direction, stood a line of silent, heavily armed and watchful horsemen, the Gauls of King Pelles's welcoming force, ostensibly sent to ensure that we arrived in safety, but in reality dispatched to guard against the possibility of hostile vessels being attracted by the signal fires. No one from Camulod would have called them soldiers, for they lacked all the discipline we associated with soldiers, but they were warriors none the less, and each of them wore the yellow stag's head blazon of Pelles of Corbenic somewhere upon his clothing. One of the first and most pleasant surprises of that morning was that I had recognized their leader, Quintus Milo. We had been students together at the Bishop's School in Auxerre. Milo's surprise had been as great as mine, for he had not expected to know anyone from Britain, and so he was unable to conceal his delight at finding an old friend leading the newcomers. He was now one of Pelles's senior advisers, he told me, and knowing him to be a fine horseman, I assumed he would be among the first to join the new cavalry corps.

Now, as I thought of him, Milo appeared at my side, having approached unseen from behind, the sounds of his coming muffled by the heavy woolen hood that covered my helmeted head and shoulders above my cloak. He reined his horse to a halt and pointed to the activity below.

"This is quite an undertaking," he shouted over the wind. "Do you have to remain here all day until it's finished?"

"No," I shouted back. "Perceval, my second officer, is down there supervising things, and Connor Mac Athol has charge of everything afloat, so I can leave, for a while at least, if the reason's sound enough. What do you have in mind?"

"Getting out of this damn wind and rain, to some place where we can talk." He glowered up at the sky. "This won't last. It never does, at this time of the year—the clouds will blow apart and disappear by noon. But in the meantime it's damned uncomfortable. Come with me."

I turned in my saddle and beckoned to the nearest trooper, and when he reached me, snapping to attention, I ordered him to find Seur Perceval and tell him I had gone with Quintus Milo, the commander of the Gallic guard.

As we swung away and kicked our horses to a canter, Milo called to me, "Do all your people salute you like that?"

"Aye, and soon yours will, too, else you won't have a cavalry force. Where are we going?"

He pointed to where a stone-walled cottage sat alone on a hillside, smoke streaming from a covered vent in its roof. "It's no palace, but it's the best this region offers. It belongs to the village headman. Apparently he feels too superior to his people to live down on the beach with them. But it has a fireplace, sound shutters to keep out the wind and a stout roof. I've kicked him out for as long as we need the place, and a couple of my men have lugged in firewood and prepared some food for us."

A short time later, he led me into a large, bare room with whitewashed stone and plaster walls and a high, peaked roof. A fire was blazing in an iron basket, and a plain scrubbed-wood table against the wall held several platters of breads, meats and cheese and two plump wineskins. As I began to strip out of my hood and cloak, Milo stepped across to the table and cut a thick slab from what looked to me like a side of roasted pork. He sprinkled it liberally with salt and took an enormous bite, chewed it a few times, then pushed it into his cheek and spoke around it as he reached for a wineskin and a pair of horn beakers.

"That's good. I haven't eaten a bite since last night. Wine?"

I lifted off my helmet and shook my head. "I would rather have water, if there is any."

He looked at me as though I had lost my senses, then picked up a jug from a shelf close to him and went to the door, where he summoned one of his men and sent him to the well for fresh water.

"Why not wine?" He settled himself into one of the two chairs by the fire, clutching his slab of meat in one hand and his wine in the other.

I sniffed, wiping my cold nose with the back of my hand. "Don't like the taste of it. Never have." I cut myself a thick wedge of meat and salted it, then carved a slice of bread from a loaf with my dagger and wrapped the meat in it. "I've tried a hundred times to form a taste for the stuff, but I always end up thinking I'd rather be drinking piss."

I took a bite and turned to face him. "It's good to see you, my friend, after so long a time. It's been almost six years since I left Auxerre. How long have you been here in Corbenic?"

"About five. I was born close to here. My father's barony is less than thirty miles from here."

"Your father is one of Pelles's barons?"

"No, he's no man's anything, that one. He's duke of his own territories, which lie directly to the south of here, sharing a border with Corbenic. My father's grandsire and the king's were close friends, and our families have always been amicable since then. When I left school my father sent me here, to serve with Pelles. I've been here ever since."

"Your father's still alive, then?"

Milo grunted. "Oh, aye. He's alive and just as foul tempered as he ever was. That's why I stay here."

I let that pass without comment, remembering that Milo and his father had never been able to agree on anything. "What about the others? Do you ever see anyone else from the Bishop's School?"

"Not a soul. For all I know, they might all be dead."

The door opened quietly and Milo's man came in, carrying the jug of water, and I thanked him before filling my beaker from the jug. Milo watched me in silence, his face expressing his disapproval of anyone choosing water over wine. I took the chair across from him.

"Is the school still there?"

"Aye, although I've heard it's not the same without the Old Man. How could it be? Germanus *was* the school, and it was him."

"What about Tiberias Cato?"

"That old centaur? Last I heard, he was still there and more miserable than ever, but that was years ago."

"I wonder how old he is now."

"The old whoreson was never young, but he must be truly ancient now, if he's still breathing. I haven't heard a word of him in close to four years, so he could be long dead since then."

"Hmm … I wonder if he would come here, if he is still alive."

Milo's eyebrows shot up. "Come here? Why in the name of the lame, limping god would you want him here, Legs? He'd make all our lives miserable from the moment he arrived. He was always best at that."

I grinned, not having heard my own nickname since I'd left the Bishop's School, and spoke around my own wad of half-chewed pork. "Don't ever call me that in front of any of my men, or I'll have you demoted to scullion. Cato never made me miserable, and he never called me Legs. You were never one of his standout favorites, Milo, so I can see why you would think that way, but he was always *my* favorite. The best teacher I ever had, and I'm sure he was more than half equine. I have never known anyone who was better with horses, or who knew more about them … everything about them. If Cato's alive, I need him here. *You* need him here."

"I'll be an old white-bearded man before you convince me of that, my friend. But we should be able to find out easily whether or not the old sodomite is still around. It's not that far from here to Auxerre—a couple of days' hard riding, four or five at a canter." He cocked his head. "You really believe he's as good as you say he is?"

I nodded, and he spread his hands. "Fine, then. I'll send someone to find out for you."

"Before you do, let me know, and I'll tell your man exactly what to say and what to ask for. Otherwise Cato will throw him out."

"Right. Now, what do you intend to do here, exactly?" He saw my astonished expression and hurried to explain himself. "No, I mean, I know what you're supposed to do, what you've come for, but how do you intend to set about it?"

I finished the last of my handful of bread-wrapped meat and was still hungry, so I waved a hand at him to wait, then rose and cut myself another wedge of meat and a fresh slice of bread. It was dry, but delicious, and I chewed slowly and swallowed before I spoke again.

"I intend to carry out my commission to create an army, Quintus, an army of horsemen, out of nothing."

He frowned, and I felt a tiny worm of apprehension wriggle in my gut. "We already have an army of horsemen, Legs. The finest in the western Empire."

"No, you have a mass of fine horsemen, with the size of an army, but they have no slightest trace of what it will take to form an army of cavalry."

He stiffened. "How dare you say that, and you a Frank! Have you forgotten your pride after such a short time in Britain? Our horsemen are invincible."

"No, my friend, you are wrong. Your horsemen *could* be invincible, and I am here to *make* them invincible, but I won't be able to do it if you don't change that attitude of yours."

He started to interrupt me, but I silenced him with a wave of my hand. "Listen to me, Quintus, and believe me, for I am telling you the simple truth. I am at this moment, as you have seen, landing one hundred and fifty men and two hundred and twenty horses on the beaches below this house. Now let me tell you something, and believe me before I say another word: I am not boasting, and I am not exaggerating. When my cavalry are ready, safe ashore and fully equipped, we could engage a thousand of your best, outnumbered ten to one, and beat them in any fight, anywhere, at any time. No, let me finish!"

Again he had been on the point of interrupting me hotly, but now he sagged back into his chair, his face a study in angry disbelief as I continued. "You have never seen Camulod's cavalry in action, but I know you're familiar with the fame of Rome's German cavalry, because we learned about it together in the same class at school. The backbone of much of that cavalry was Frankish, from the Rhine lands. But Rome's German cavalry were skirmishers, Quintus, and they were magnificent, two and three hundred years ago. They rode light horses and attacked in waves, riding apart and throwing lances or shooting arrows when they came in range of their enemies."

"So?" He was still glowering. "Nothing has changed since then. Speed and maneuverability are still what count, and we have that."

I shook my head. "It's no longer good enough, Quintus. Arthur Pendragon's cavalry is something utterly different, utterly new. There is nothing like it in the world. *Heavy* cavalry—big, heavily armored horses trained to move and act in unison, fighting as a living wall of horseflesh and mounted men. *They* are invincible, simply because nothing can stand against them. A full frontal charge by them will simply overwhelm and destroy anything in its path, including other, less-disciplined horsemen." I could see the incredulity in his eyes.

"*Discipline,* Quintus. That's the difference between your horsemen and our cavalry, in one word. And it should not surprise you, if you think about it logically instead of seeing insults when no insult is implied. Rome conquered the entire world because of the discipline of its legions. Six hundred years before that, in Macedonia, Alexander conquered *his* world because of the discipline of his heavy cavalry. There's no new, startling truth in that, is there?

"The truth is this: our cavalry is modeled after Alexander's and our discipline is Roman. But our world is Britain and we're not set to conquer it, although we could. King Arthur has no dreams of conquest. He dreams of a peaceful realm, where there are no regional warlords or tyrants and ordinary men can live in unthreatened freedom, underpinned by a powerful army that ensures that peace. He dreams of uniting all the people—all the clans and tribes of Britain—under one monarch, for the first time in history. And I know you have noticed that I include myself when I think of Britain as 'ours.'

"But now, because of what *he* knows is happening over there, your king has brought me here to Corbenic, with my men and at his request, to teach his horsemen—your Frankish horsemen of Corbenic—to be cavalry like ours. What do you know of these Huns we have been hearing about in Britain?"

Milo's face registered astonishment, quickly followed by scorn. "Not much. We hear rumors and reports, but they are sparse and lacking in detail, so no one pays them much attention. Word has it that their king, Attila or some such outlandish name, is the greatest general since Mark Antony, and that his armies are countless, measured in the hundreds of thousands, but that could all be nonsense. I myself have met people who swore to me that this Attila was warring against some empire of yellow-skinned barbarians ten years ago, in lands far beyond the eastern borders of Rome's farthest territories. Others have him conquering the Medes in Persia. Still others will tell you his horsemen cover every inch of the world, blocking a man's view of the ground. It's all nonsense and fearmongering, if you ask me, because I've never heard a word of anything outlandish ever happening where Huns are involved. Goths of all kinds, yes, and Germans and Suevi, but Huns? What else do they call them, Hungvari? What kind of name is that? It is certainly not frightening."

"So be it," I said, having heard enough to convince me that Milo lacked a healthy sense of curiosity. "I was simply interested in what you might think. But to answer your first question beyond misunderstanding, I intend to train your warriors as cavalry, and I intend to start at the beginning, putting some fundamental rules and arrangements in place right from the outset. From that point, I'll work my way outwards as developments evolve." I saw his eyes narrow again, whether in skepticism or cynicism I didn't know, and I picked up my drinking cup once more.

"I said I'll work my way according to developments, Quintus, but that doesn't mean I don't know where I'm going, so don't be tempted to think that's the case. I know exactly what has to be done, and exactly how we will achieve it. The only thing I cannot be precise about is the timing of each phase, because that depends on an unknown factor: the caliber of your men. Again, no insult meant, but we will be tied to their willingness to learn new skills and attitudes, and their eagerness to change their ways and adapt to new techniques."

I drank from my cup and left him to absorb what I had said, and after a moment he rose up and began to pace the floor, his chin sunk on his chest and his hands clasped behind his back. I said nothing more, content to let him reach his own conclusions, and finally he stopped and faced me, scowling.

"When did our king first contact yours, do you know?"

"Early this year or late last year. I don't know for certain."

"How was the approach made?"

I felt he ought to know that kind of thing. "By letter," I said. "A letter from the Bishop of Auxerre."

"Ah," he said, as if that explained things entirely. "Yes, that would be it. Those two are close. Pelles spent a deal of time in Auxerre last year. Even so, he's been close-mouthed about all this. None of us knew anything about it until a month ago, and even then we weren't told much, other than that a body of horsemen would be coming to us by sea from Britain, and we were to make you welcome. It's only been in the past week or so that we've begun to discover there's more behind your arrival than a simple visit between kings. I didn't know you were from Camulod until you told me."

I did not like what I was hearing. "What are you telling me, Quintus? That we went to all this trouble and came all this way without anyone making preparations to receive us?"

"No. I'm here with my men, am I not? And land has been cleared and set aside for you to use, free of any guard. But Baldwin told me nothing of any plans to start a new army."

"Then what arrangements have been made for us to trade our metal for weapons?" I saw from his blank expression that he didn't know what I was talking about. "Damnation, Quintus, I have a trading fleet out there in the harbor, with holds full of tin and copper ingots, and an admiral who is going to start looking very soon for the weapon traders he was told would be here waiting for him. That was part of the agreement for our coming here at all."

Milo spread his hands. "I know nothing about that. I thought you were here to show off, to demonstrate your cavalry."

"To *show off*? Do you people take us for fools, to come so far simply to parade ourselves for your amusement?"

Now his voice took on an edge of anger sparked by my own. "Don't shout at me, my friend. I had forgotten your very name until this morning. This mess, whatever it is, has nothing to do with me, nothing at all. I had no hand in anything that was supposed to happen here."

That was true, but I was angry at the situation, not the man facing me. "You mean to tell me no metal traders are coming here? No word went out that we were coming? This is outrageous. What about your friends and fellow advisers, or the king's generals? Had none of them any suspicion that there might be more to this than a simple visit?"

"Why should they? Nothing like this has ever happened before." He stopped, aware of my deepening frown. "What? What are you thinking?"

I threw the uneaten remnants of my food onto the table. "I'm thinking I should stop unloading my ships right now, turn my people about and sail straight home again. That's what I'm thinking."

"You can't do that! I might ..." He floundered, looking away into some unknown distance, then concluded, "I could be wrong about all this." His voice had faded almost to silence at the last, so that his last words had emerged as close to a whisper, revealing his own uncertainty.

"Could you?" He lifted his head and gazed at me, apparently having nothing more to say. "Come on, Quintus, remember who you're talking to."

"What d'you mean?"

"This is me you're trying to cozen, Clothar of Benwick, your old friend Legs. You and I never lied to each other in all our time at school. We were too close for that. Let's not change things now. You told me you are a senior adviser to the king. How senior are you?"

He shrugged, still plainly ill at ease, and then I saw his brow clear. "Until about a year ago, I had free access to him all the time. Now I deal mainly with Baldwin."

"That name again. Who is this Baldwin?"

"A former friend of Plotius."

"And who is Plotius?"

"*Was,* not is. He was Pelles's father, long since dead."

"I see, so Baldwin was his friend. But no more than a friend, eh? Not kin, related by blood?"

"No."

"Then I don't understand something: why is he still with Pelles if he was his *father's* friend? That is … unusual, is it not?"

"He is senior adviser to the king now … but he has also been a true friend to Pelles and his family since Plotius died."

"You told me you were senior adviser to the king."

"I was, and am … one of them. But Baldwin bears the title of King's Counselor."

"Who are the others?"

"There are several, but the principals are the seven chiefs of the clans of Corbenic."

"Seven principal advisers, plus you and Baldwin. Are there more?"

"Aye, a few … four more."

"But Baldwin is chief among them and when he talks, you listen, am I right?"

"Not always, but most of the time, aye."

"Why didn't your king come to greet us, to welcome us to Corbenic?"

Milo looked uncomfortable. "Your king didn't come either, did he?"

I bit back the angry words that sprang to my tongue and managed to keep my tone civil. "My King is in Britain, Quintus, governing it. We are on your king's doorstep here, at his invitation. Had it been the other way around, Arthur Pendragon would have been on our beach to greet you. Why didn't your king come to welcome us?"

"I don't know. He may have meant to come but found himself detained by other things. He sent me in his place."

"He sent you? In person?"

"Well, no. Baldwin sent me. I'm in charge of the outer guard this month, so the task fell to me."

"I see. So how was this *task* defined for you?"

He looked more uncomfortable than ever. "Duty, Legs. It wasn't defined at all. It's simply duty, assigned as duties are. I was to welcome you, help you unload if need be, and keep you here until I heard from Baldwin."

"Keep me here … That's what I suspected." I stood up, so that I loomed above him. "I want to see Pelles. Now. Today."

"You may have to talk to Baldwin."

"Be damned to Baldwin. I will speak with Pelles himself and with no one else. If I don't speak with him, I'll be beyond yon horizon and well on my way back to Britain by this time tomorrow. Will you take me to him?"

"Aye, I will, if that's what you insist upon."

2

I left the house and made my way to find Perceval, to let him know about my new intentions. It had to be nigh on noon by then. Below me, arranged in tethered rows, I could see upwards of three score of our horses, and beyond them organized parties of armored troopers moved about purposefully, some of them piling cases and bundles of equipment neatly in a pattern being supervised by three mounted officers, one of whom held a tally board angled against his side, while others were busily erecting tents on the designated camp site on my far left. My own command tent was already up in place, towering above the others, the red and gold banner of Pendragon raised high above it on its own white pole. Everything appeared to be unfolding on schedule and without mishap, and I looked towards the line of Franks along the cliff top. As many were gazing now at the work being done up here as were staring down at the activities in the small harbor.

I felt in the tightness of my chest that something was sorely wrong here. Pelles should have been there to meet us when we arrived—that was a given—but I was much more concerned with Milo's inexplicable ignorance of what was happening, of why we had come at all. If Milo didn't know why we were here, who else was unaware? And if he was, as he said, one of the king's senior advisers, even disregarding the fact that his access to the king had been restricted recently, how much less might the other Franks of Corbenic know about our purpose here?

I found myself inclined to trust Milo, slightly to my surprise. He and I had been close friends in school and I had always found him honorable, trustworthy and smart. But he was out of his depths here, I suspected, and he was intelligent enough to know it. That would explain his evident unease over what I had told him. He plainly felt he was being used in some way, manipulated and deprived of information.

Perceval was still supervising the unloading of the horses down at the harbor. He chanced to look up and saw me making my way down the hill, and he promptly handed his tally board to the officer by his side and waited for me at the end of the jetty.

"Grim face you have there. What's wrong?"

"I'm not sure. Perhaps nothing, perhaps everything." I glanced around, but no one was close enough to hear what we were saying.

"I have to go inland, to meet King Pelles. By the time I get back, I'll be able to tell you what's up or what's not. But I need an escort."

"How big?"

"Impressive. A full squadron, if we can manage that. Can we?"

He grinned at me, a quick flash of white teeth. "You expect me to say no? We've been unloading for more than four hours, Legate. Counting that last batch of horses, we have more than two full squadrons ashore by now. Saddles and tackle came off separately, from the end of the dock, and it's all up there with the horses. I'll have a suitable escort for you in half an hour … impressive enough to strike the fear of God into any little king."

"My thanks." I started to pull my horse around again, then hesitated before the reins could tighten. Another horse whickered and stamped a hoof nearby, and as I looked over at it my hesitancy vanished.

"Is that yours?"

"No, it's young Tom's."

"Borrow it and ride with me for a bit. I need to talk to you and there's too many ears around."

The men were in high spirits, I could see that now as Perceval rode up the slope with me from the beach. I had been unaware of it on my way down, immersed in my own concerns, but now I saw men grinning at us from all directions, some of them shouting greetings, others waving. None of them saluted us formally, and that pleased me, telling me that if they were feeling this well now, soaked and cold as they must be, then that boded well for our future venture. Providing, I added immediately, that my concerns over Pelles and his intentions proved unfounded.

When we reached the relatively flat land above the harbor I kneed my horse towards the three officers I had seen from the window earlier. One of them, Lucius Genaro, our regimental master-at-arms, saw us coming and came to meet us. I asked him to muster two full squadrons, the Reds and the Whites, in full parade gear and to have them ready for Legate Perceval when we returned, and then I led Perceval out onto the open heath of the slopes, to where I could speak freely. He rode by my side, silent as he had been since we left the end of the jetty.

"I think I want you with me in this," I told him first. "Can your subs handle the unloading with you gone?"

"They're doing it now. Where are we going, and why?"

"To visit Pelles unannounced, to see how he reacts."

"What d'you mean, reacts? What's going on, Clothar?"

"We'll find that out when we get there. There's something in the air here that makes me feel uncomfortable, Ursus, and I can't tell you what it is. But it's not the smell of animals or flowers. Something feels wrong."

I filled him in quickly then on my discussion with Quintus Milo and the disturbing gaps in the man's knowledge, as well as the disturbing inference I had drawn about the unknown Baldwin. We had stopped riding by then, and when I finished talking, Perceval merely nodded.

"You're right. Something stinks. So what d'you intend to say to Pelles?"

"I've no idea, but I'll know as soon as I'm face to face with him. I only wish I knew more about the man."

"And this Baldwin?"

"I don't know about him, either. He might be perfectly fine. But I do know the importance of first impressions, so I want these people's first sight of the Camulodian cavalry they brought to Gaulish soil to be one they won't quickly forget."

"Oh, I think you can rely on that, my friend. Two squadrons of our best, in tight formation, fully armed and armored, should achieve that effect, especially alongside what they think of as their own cavalry. I'll talk to the men before I bring them up to the house for you. By the time they arrive, they'll all know that no inspection or parade they've ever had will hold up a candle to what they have to achieve today. Will you want any of Griffyd's scouts to go with you?"

"Aye, ten of them. I always feel safer, knowing their bows can reach out farther than anyone else's. Bring Griffyd himself. Now, is my parade armor unloaded?"

"Aye, and in your tent."

"What about Arthur's gift to Pelles?"

"It came off the ships first, with you. It's in your tent with your armor."

"Excellent. We'll take it with us. Send someone to collect it and to tell young Rufus to have my armor ready for me, if you will. I'll wear it for this. We'd better send word to Connor, too, telling him where we're going and how long we'll be gone."

"How long *will* we be gone?"

I shrugged. "Two hours there, two hours back, but we don't know what we'll find when we arrive, and I don't know how much time we'll have to talk with Pelles. That all depends on him, but I'd rather it were longer than short. Better say we'll be away overnight, returning by noon tomorrow."

He nodded. "Done. I'll have your escort ready for you half an hour from now."

"Right, but then you'll have to wait for me while I change armor. Come for me when you're ready. I still have things to discuss with Milo."

3

Milo was still sitting by the fire drinking wine when I returned, although I saw from a glance at his flushed face that he had replenished both the fire and his cup. As I stopped to remove my helmet he hooked a foot behind the other chair and sent it skidding across the floor in my direction.

"Bring that over here and sit down. There's lots of water in your jug. I promise you I haven't even taken a sip from it. I was just sitting here thinking about the fireplace in Germanus's quarters. Remember that? He actually burned coal, dug up from the fields. That was the first fire I had ever seen inside a fine house." He looked around the bare room. "This isn't a fine house, but the fire's a welcome addition in weather like this. Sit down, Legs, I've been thinking."

I walked to the table and picked up one of the wineskins. It sagged limply in my grasp.

"Thinking and drinking. How much of this have you had since I left? I've only been gone for half an hour."

"Long enough, my sober friend, long enough. I may have had two cups since you left ... perhaps three ... It's good wine, Pelles's best, filched from his personal stock. But wine sets the thoughts free, a magical fact that Germanus never taught us, and I now find I have thoughts that need to be set free."

I poured myself a beaker of water and sat down across from him. "Free them, then. Let them out. What are you thinking about?" I threw my cloak back from my shoulders.

"Baldwin, the sullen, tight-lipped whoreson, and Ludovic of Auxerre. He was Germanus's secretary, you know. Do you remember him?"

"Aye, very well. But you mentioned him and Baldwin in the same breath, and that surprises me. I don't know Baldwin, but I'm already set to dislike him, simply from listening to you. On the other hand I do know old Ludovic, and he is as straitlaced as an armored cuirass. I think I might see him and Baldwin as strange companions."

"Aye, and if you ever did see them together they would be. They detest each other ... Well, Baldwin detests old Ludovic. For his part, Ludovic simply acts as though Baldwin doesn't exist, and that really crushes Baldwin's balls."

"Why the hostility?"

Milo sniffed and hawked, then spat into the fire and rinsed his mouth with wine. "They just don't like each other. That's what I would have said this morning, had you asked me then. But you've been showing me things today that I ought to have seen long since ... things that Baldwin should have told me months ago. And so I've been thinking, since you went away and left me here, that perhaps there is more to this whole situation than I've thought about before."

He bent forward and placed his cup on the ground, but it over-balanced and spilled at his feet. "Shit!" He left it there and looked up at me, narrowing his eyes. "I know you think I'm half drunk, Legs, but I'm not, believe me. On the contrary, I'm seeing things very clearly at the moment, although all unexpectedly. None of the things I'm seeing are new, but they're bothering me, because until today I've never put them all together in my mind and looked at them as one piece ... Does that make sense?"

"Aye, it does, so don't stop. What kind of things?"

He sniffed again and glanced down at the cup by his feet, as though thinking about picking it up again. "That's hard to explain ... but I suppose they're things I've been avoiding. We all have thoughts we don't want to examine too closely, Legs ... you must have some of your own ... and we won't face up to them because the truth is that they frighten us. You know what I'm talking about: the kind of things that used to bother us in school, when we were boys and couldn't do anything about them, the kind of things we tucked away and never talked about, except when we were just the two of us alone, you and me with no one around to overhear us. You remember that? Like the way Brother Anthony used to love to beat us until we were bruised and bloody? Everybody knew he was a monster, but no one ever talked about it." Milo was staring at me in surprise. "You've no idea at all?"

"No, but I remember the school law: *You never complain and you never, ever carry tales.*"

He sucked at his teeth, then looked away, into the fire. "Well, maybe it's time that some things were said out loud, no matter how unpleasant. Baldwin ... Baldwin's what I'm thinking about, and the more I think, the less I like what's in my head. There's something ... I don't know how to describe this, but it's almost as though he has some kind of hold over Pelles, some knowledge or some power he uses to dominate him."

"He dominates him? You mean he tells him what to do?"

"Oh no, it's not that obvious. Whatever it is, it's not obvious at all. But it's there to see, if anyone really wants to look closely enough. The strange part is that no one—including me, until today—ever seems to really look, or if they do, they ignore what's there."

"What *is* there, Quintus? That's what I need to know. Tell me more about this Baldwin. How did he manage to become so close to Pelles? He must be much older than him, if he was his father's friend."

"He is. Old enough to *be* his father. He and Plotius were life-long friends and allies, with Plotius the stronger and more powerful of the two, and Baldwin his lieutenant. Both of them fought with Germanus against the Burgundians thirty years ago, when Germanus commanded the Roman armies in Gaul, and Plotius was killed just before the war ended. When Baldwin came home, he saw to it that Plotius's widow, Catalina, was well provided for, and that her son, Pelles, would come to the kingship in due time. He then married Catalina to his eldest son, Marius Marco, for her protection … no great sacrifice on either side, since Catalina had been much younger than Plotius—his third wife, in fact—and besides being comely was of an age with Marius."

"Did none of your own nobles object to that?"

"Why should they object? Catalina was no longer the queen, and as a woman, even the widow of a dead king, she had no claim on Corbenic. Her only son did, and he was already confirmed as Corbenic's next king. Were he to live, he would have sons of his own and power would pass to them."

"But what if Catalina had sons in her new marriage?"

"No matter. Under our law, the claim to land and kingship flows only through the father's side. Any son of Marius's would be heir to his own father's lands and title, but never to Corbenic."

"Ah, that's right. I remember now." It was true. I had been brought up among the Ripuarian Franks of southern Gaul, but I was a northern, Salian Frank by birth, and I remembered King Ban of Benwick, my adoptive father, telling me about how my own people differed from his people and all others. Since time out of mind, even before the Romans came from Italia, Salian tradition—Ban called it Salic law—had decreed that inheritance could flow only through the male side of a family. No woman could ever lay claim to land as a birthright, which meant that Baldwin could have nothing, no claim to future kingship of Corbenic, to gain from the marriage of his son to Catalina. "So," I continued, "Baldwin's actions were honorable and beyond suspicion."

"Aye, they were. Never any question of that. And they were appreciated."

"So what went wrong? Something must have changed, if Baldwin has gained this mysterious power you speak of. And after all these years of noble service, the change must have sprung from within Baldwin himself. Am I correct in believing that this has only happened—this power and influence over the king—in the past year, since you lost your access to Pelles?"

"Aye, that's about right. And the change was only gradual, not sudden enough to be noticeable. It just grew from time to time, from month to month."

"So when did you last see the king, meet with him in person I mean, as an adviser?"

He turned down his lips, thinking. "Three months ago? No, four months ago, just after the equinox."

"Hmm. So what happened a year ago to change things? Something must have occurred."

Milo shook his head. "Nothing that I can think of."

"There must have been *something,* Quintus. Some event, some occurrence, some change in the way things stood at the time. Think harder. It was only a year ago."

He seemed to be on the point of saying something when the door swung open to Perceval's knock and he leaned into the doorway. "We're ready, Magister."

Magister. I thought again that I might never grow comfortable with that title, but then realized that I was being wrongheaded and that the title was appropriate, since we were out of Britain now and I was Arthur's representative. I beckoned him inside.

"Seur Perceval, meet my old school friend Quintus Milo, now an adviser to King Pelles. Quintus, this is Seur Perceval of Montenegro, legate of Camulod, my friend and deputy commander." The two greeted each other politely and I led the way outside, pleased to hear Milo's startled hiss of indrawn breath when he saw the glittering, rigidly ordered phalanx of eighty mounted men awaiting us. The effect was quite spectacular, even to me, for not even a single horse moved a head or a tail to break the effect of utter, perfectly disciplined stillness.

"Wait here for us, if you will, Legate." I turned my head to where Milo stood stunned. "Quintus, will you come with me? I have to change my armor. It won't take long."

He nodded, speechless, and climbed into his saddle to ride with me across the short distance to my tent, where young Rufus, my new squire, appointed to fill Bors's place, had my magnificent parade armor laid out and ready for me. As the lad busied himself about me, stripping off the armor I was wearing, I spoke to Milo in the tongue we had been using, the language of my boyhood.

"The lad can't understand a word we say, so pay him no attention. What were you about to say when Perceval arrived at the house? Did you remember something that happened?"

He glanced at the boy, and then at the magnificent armor Rufus had laid out for me, and shook his head. "Not really, but it was about that time that Marius Marco died ... Baldwin's son, Catalina's husband. He died several months before anything changed, actually, but that's the only thing I can think of. Soon after his death, and that would have been about a year ago, perhaps a little longer than that, Catalina went to live with Baldwin's people. His kingdom's to the north and east of here. She took her two widowed daughters with her, Lena and Serena."

"Full sisters to Pelles, or half sisters?"

"Full sisters, both of them older than he is."

"And is Pelles close to them, fond of them?"

"Aye, he is, although they have not been back here since they left. He goes to visit them, from time to time."

"In Baldwin's kingdom …"

Rufus had begun fitting my parade armor by this time, and I stood thinking about what I had just been told, my arms raised obediently as the boy struggled with the straps and buckles of my cuirass.

"Let me ask you something outlandish, Quintus. Is it even remotely possible that Baldwin might be holding Pelles's mother and sisters as hostages against his behavior? Does Pelles think enough of them to fear for their lives should he defy Baldwin?"

Milo twisted his mouth and nodded. "It could be possible, I suppose … but only *very* remotely. Earlier this morning, once again, I would have said no. But the way I am thinking now … I have to admit, it could be remotely possible."

"Well then, supposing it were true, why wouldn't Pelles try to rescue them?"

His answer was immediate. "Because he couldn't, no matter how badly he wanted to. Baldwin's kingdom is too mountainous, and his army is too strong, their positions too heavily fortified. His primary stronghold is a Roman fort, and the garrison there are all mercenaries, from beyond the Rhine."

"His *primary* stronghold? How many has he?"

"Three. And his armies are all Roman trained. Foot soldiers."

That stunned me for a moment. "Then what is he doing here, advising another king? How extensive are his territories?"

"Large. They border us on two sides, east and north."

"With the sea to the west."

"Aye, and my father's duchy to the south."

"Damnation, Milo, the more I hear, the less sense I can make of anything! It sounds to me as though this Baldwin could crush Corbenic like a nut, if he felt like it."

"No, he could not. Our armies are all horsemen. His armies could never beat us in our lands, and we couldn't take them in theirs."

"So he's a strong king, playing adviser to a lesser one. By the Christus! What nest of snakes have I stepped into? And why are we here, all the way from Camulod, when no one seems to want us? None of this makes any sense."

"It does if you take Ludovic into account." There was no trace of the red-faced drinker in Milo now. His eyes were narrow, his cheeks suddenly gaunt. "Those men of yours, out there waiting for you … are those your cavalry?"

"Two squadrons of my cavalry, aye. Why?"

"Well …" He clearly did not have words for what he wanted to say. "Are they all like that? The armor, the equipment, the training …?"

"The discipline, you mean. Aye, they are all like that. I have a thousand of them in my army group, backed up by another thousand and a half of infantry. And Camulod has six other army groups. But I will only have five hundred cavalry here in Gaul, and no infantry."

"Well, Legs," he said quietly, "if what I saw outside the house up there—your cavalry—is what you came to bring to us, it would change our whole world. Ludovic obviously knows that, and it's clear that Pelles knows it, too. Unfortunately, Baldwin will know it, too, as soon as he sets eyes on your people. If Corbenic had cavalry like yours, the entire balance here would be completely altered. I think Pelles kept the knowledge of this from Baldwin for as long as he could, but somehow Baldwin found out about it. And since then he has kept the knowledge to himself, shutting the rest of us out, probably wondering all this while what he could do to stop you. And already he is close to succeeding."

"What do you mean?"

Rufus had finished with me, from top to bottom, and now he silently held out my gold-encrusted helmet. I took it from him with a nod of thanks and tucked it beneath my arm before waving to Milo to accompany me.

"If you sail home tomorrow, he will have won."

I stopped at the entrance to my tent, on the point of opening the flap. "Aye, he will, if we are right. But what will he have won, and how, and to what end? I have only six score of men with me right now and I don't want to put them at risk without knowing what I'm facing. In five months I will have four times that strength here, were I to stay, but between now and next month the men I have today

could all be dead, wiped out in ones and twos by stealth and treachery. If Baldwin *is* up to something underhanded—and I'm well
aware we can't be sure, one way or the other, at this stage—then it's
a safe wager that he'll have been planning, ever since he caught
wind of it, to counter whatever threat he sees in us. Who commands
his own kingdom in his stead while he is here in Corbenic, and
what's the damn place called?"

"We call it Baldwin's Land. It has no other name I've ever
heard. It's just Baldwin's kingdom, cobbled together these past
thirty years out of bits and pieces, some ceded to him by Rome for
his services, others taken by conquest or simple occupation. But
there's no real name for it. No need of one. Everybody knows what
it is and where it is."

"And in charge there now is ...?"

"His eldest son, Culric. Eldest now that Marius Marco is dead.
And he has three younger brothers to assist him—Marcio, Thesso
and Karel."

"Tell me, is anyone in Corbenic unquestionably loyal to Pelles?"

He drew himself to his full height. "I resent that. We are all loyal
to the king."

"Who are 'we all'? Who has the right to command in Corbenic,
aside from the king himself? Who are his lords, his battle
commanders and generals?"

"The same seven chiefs I told you of earlier. Some call them
barons, but they are all clan chiefs, and versed in war."

"And who has the responsibility of guarding the king's person?"

"The chiefs take turns, each clan mounting guard for a month."

"How many guards?"

"Sufficient to protect the king, and he has never been threatened
with harm. Not by anyone. Not in years, since he first won his
crown." He fell silent and looked away for a moment. "Bear in
mind, Legs, you started me thinking this way, but all I have is
thoughts ... newfound suspicions with no real substance. Baldwin
has done nothing anyone can see as wrong, nothing even to give rise
to suspicion. He has shown no hostility, uttered no threat. He has

behaved as what he is supposed to be: the king's counselor. And I must admit his aid has been remarkable. Pelles could not have done what he achieved ten years ago without Baldwin's help."

"And what was that?" I was still holding the tent flap, but made no move to open it.

"A victory. He won a war against some interloper who had killed his grandsire—Catalina's father—and usurped his lands. It was a vengeance affair, but I don't know much about it, other than that Baldwin threw in his armies on the side of Pelles, and Pelles absorbed his grandsire's lands into his own, albeit they were separated by Baldwin's holdings."

I felt a surge of irritation and could not disguise it. "Damnation, Quintus, that's the kind of thing only a close and loyal friend will do. It tells me Baldwin is a man of honor and integrity, not some scheming plot hatcher."

"Aye, but that was ten years ago, and some men can change within ten years. What worries me most about all this is that Pelles has had little to say of any note at all—and has barely been seen by any of us—this past half year and more, and that's not like Pelles. That's the main reason—the only reason—for my being so suspicious now."

I threw open the tent flap and led him outside, guards snapping to attention as we approached our tethered horses, and I swung myself up into my saddle before Milo did.

"Accepted," I said, acknowledging his last point. "How many of his own men does Baldwin keep beside him?"

Milo curbed his horse, reining it in tightly as it tried to resist him. "He has a small corps of personal guards, thirty of them."

"Mounted or on foot?"

"On foot."

"And do they stand duty within the king's household?"

"No. Never. They have separate barracks, outside the castle walls."

"Well, that's something, at least. Thank God for that." I glanced around at the extended line of horsemen watching us from the cliff tops. "Your men, all of them?" He nodded. "All loyal to Pelles?"

"Of course."

"Aye, of course, but do you trust them, Quintus? Would you trust them all, without question?"

"Of *course* I trust them. They're my own men, kinsmen for the most part. I brought them with me when first I came here. I know every one of them."

"How many did you bring with you today? I counted two hundred before I lost the tally."

He dipped his head in acknowledgment. "Close enough, for what you could see. Two hundred and more. But I have another hundred in reserve, behind the crest up there, out of sight." He made a face, in response to my raised eyebrows. "What would you have done? I didn't know who you were, and you brought an entire fleet with you. I wanted to be sure there was no trickery or treachery involved."

I nodded. "You want to bring them with us? It might not hurt our aims."

He considered that briefly, then stood up in his stirrups and made a circling motion with his hand, a signal I knew well. Within moments, his entire line was on the move, converging towards us.

4

For the first half hour after leaving our disembarking fleet behind us, I rode alone in silence at the head of my men, my mind a squirming mass of doubts and uncertainties. Directly at my back, Milo rode beside Perceval, followed by the officers of our two squadrons and then the squadrons themselves, riding side by side in tight formation, each five abreast and eight deep. Behind them, straggling in a ragged fan like a woman's trailing skirts, came the horsemen of Corbenic.

I was aware of the spectacle we must present to anyone watching from a distance: my Reds and Whites, I knew, were as clean and square edged as a pair of bronze bricks, moving together in perfect unison, whereas the men of Corbenic showed no discipline at all and merely rode behind us, offering no threat, content to stare at us in wonder. But far from taking the pleasure I would normally derive from such a situation, I paid it no attention, utterly caught up in the knowledge of my own impotence.

Of all the realities that can beset any leader of men or expeditions, there is none more frightening or debilitating than the admission of helplessness and ignorance, unless it be the simultaneous awareness of not having a plan and being incapable of forming one because of circumstances. As I rode, not daring to look at anyone near me, I had visions in my mind of struggling through a dark and fetid swamp, losing ground constantly and being increasingly threatened by the mud and water surging and gurgling up towards my mouth. I was absolutely lost in an ocean of uncertainty, with nothing to guide me but insubstantial suspicions, and I felt myself breaking out in a hot, nervous sweat that quickly soaked my scalp and began to trickle down my face under the stifling heat of my helmet. I reached up and pulled it off, and shook my head violently before attaching the helmet to my saddle by hanging its chinstrap over the hook made for it.

The culminating moments of my panic and indecision came to me when I realized that Pelles of Corbenic might not even be at my journey's end when I arrived. That thought, breaking over me unexpectedly, almost unmanned me completely, so that I drew rein and sat my horse stock-still. How could I not have thought of that before I made such a public commitment to moving my men so blatantly into a gesture of defiant arrogance, thrusting my armed strength into the presence of the king without warning of any kind? And he might not even be there! If that were the case, I would have brought my men all the way from the beaches for nothing, duplicating the folly of having brought them all the way from Camulod for the same purpose. I rejected that thought at once, however, recognizing it for what it was—self-doubt for its own sake—and knowing that Milo would have told me immediately had the king not been at home.

Directly behind me, Perceval and Milo had swung their mounts apart when I stopped, to avoid riding into me. Now both of them reined in beside me, looking at me in curiosity, and for an awful moment, nothing happened in my mind. I sat there like a witless mute, unable to speak or move. But then my reason flooded back and I spurred my horse quickly, surging away from them before the red flush of shame and confusion rising to my cheeks could betray me, and as I went I shouted back over my shoulder something to the effect that I had been daydreaming.

But in that surging leap of terror, spurring my horse ahead of my friends, I found unexpected sanctuary. From out of nowhere, clear in my head, I heard the voice of Tiberias Cato telling me to trust my instincts, and I had a sudden, crystal-clear memory of him sitting in front of me, hunched forward to bring his face close to mine, holding one ankle over his other knee with both hands. I immediately reined in again, pulling my mount back to a canter and then to a walk, letting the memory of that moment with Cato wash over me.

Instincts were real, he had told me that day, and never to be ignored. We all had moments when information came to us, mainly in the form of warnings, from deep within ourselves, without logical explanation. Hunches, he called them; deep-seated, spontaneous sensations that rang true, all too often in defiance of reason. No one had ever been able to explain how such things happened, or where they sprang from, he said, but only a mortal fool ignored them, and always at his peril. Wise men, he said, paid close attention to these warnings, and clever, educated, well-trained men experienced more of the phenomena than dull and sullen clods ever could. He claimed to know why, too: the more you learned, the more you absorbed and the more you disciplined your mind, the greater was the chance that all your knowledge and training and discipline might combine, deep within your mind, to engender great leaps of reasoning and deduction that defied normal processes. No one could anticipate these things, no one could rely upon their occurring at any particular time, but no intelligent person could deny that such things happened.

Trust your instincts, he had said. *Trust your training. Trust yourself.*

There and then, between one moment and the next, I decided to do that—to trust myself—and the decision calmed me immediately, as if by magic. But if I were to trust myself, I would first have to look closely and very calmly at all the conflicting elements that were shaking me, setting aside both the panic that had unnerved me and the crawling, demoralizing fear of being wrong and therefore looking like a fool. And so I set myself to listing, in my mind, all the formless and vague suspicions that had swarmed upon me that day, convinced now, beyond argument, that one of Tiberias Cato's "hunches" lay at the root of all of them.

Prime among them was the lack, not of a formal welcome, but of any suggestion of an organized reception based upon a clear understanding of what we were expected to achieve here in Corbenic.

The fault in that, I had first thought, must lie with the king, Pelles, who had been so insistent that we come here. But then had come the first intimation that another king, Baldwin, counselor to Pelles, might have some form of power over the younger king, and reasons of his own for not wanting us to be made welcome.

Suspicions only, but now, as I examined them more coolly, they took on form if not substance: this Baldwin was a king whose holdings were more extensive than Pelles's own, abutting Corbenic on two sides, and so it made no sense that he would spend his time "advising" a lesser king. But there was no evidence that Baldwin himself sought dominance in Corbenic; no one, not even the seven clan chiefs of Corbenic, viewed him with any suspicion at all on those grounds. And yet there was the tenuous possibility that Baldwin might be holding mother and sisters as hostages to Pelles's behavior … that power over the king that Milo had mentioned. If that were the case, to what end was it intended? Even should Pelles die, Culric could not succeed him to be king of Corbenic, at least not without a long and costly war that, according to Quintus Milo, neither side could win.

I now considered Milo's motives in bringing such a topic to my attention. He had lost his full and free access to Pelles since Baldwin had come into his current prominence a year earlier. Might he then be moved in this, I wondered, by simple jealousy, hoping to bring Baldwin down and regain his own former position? He had been impressed by the strength in what he saw of us, but he had raised his misgivings about Baldwin—and emphasized that they were no more than misgivings—long before he saw my cavalry, and that gave him credibility in my eyes. Had he seen my forces first and then brought up his fears of Baldwin, I might have viewed his words very differently.

All my attention kept coming back to Baldwin, to the possibility that, for reasons of his own, the man did not appear to want us here in Corbenic, or to let anyone know why we had actually come. And those reasons, considered logically, could only be based upon our capability to affect the balance of power between Corbenic and Baldwin's lands, in whatever was happening here between the two kings.

At that point I felt—I believed—that I was right, and as Arthur's emissary, I was entitled to approach the king of Corbenic as an equal and an ally to demand an explanation of what was going on and of why matters were not developing as I had been led to expect before I left Camulod at my King's express instructions. And if the king was not in residence when I arrived, I would settle in and wait for him to return, demanding the courtesy and consideration that Arthur himself would have expected as his right.

As for Baldwin, I would meet him in a frame of mind he could not possibly expect of me, and I would watch him like an eagle eyeing a hare a mile below. But for the time being, I was content that, for the first time since setting foot again in Gaul, I knew where I was going and what my objectives were.

I swung around and rode back to where Perceval and Milo followed me, noticing something out of the ordinary as I rode that short distance. Up on the hill slope to my left as I approached them, I saw a large party of mounted men riding parallel to our route, keeping pace with us. I waved a hand towards them as I swung my mount around to ride between my two friends.

"Quintus, that group up there, who are they?"

"On the hill?" He didn't even bother to look up at them. "The seven chiefs we talked about, with their guards."

"All of them? Why don't they come down?"

Milo shook his head. "They won't, not until they've seen the king himself receive you."

"Then why are they there at all?"

"They're curious. Wouldn't you be, in their place?"

"I suppose I would," I muttered, and decided to ignore the distant party. "Will they try to interfere when we approach the king's place? Where is his place, by the way, and what is it? I'm trusting you to take me to Pelles, but for all I know, you could be leading me to meet your aged grandmother."

"It's a walled villa, directly north of here, and we're about a third of the way there. There's a castle nearby, too, in case of threat, but Pelles prefers the villa."

I rode without speaking for a while, digesting that, and then I grunted. "Well, that's another piece of information in favor of the hostage theory about the mother and sisters."

"What d'you mean? Why would you say that?"

"Knowledge of human nature, Quintus. Give three women the choice of living in a comfortable villa over living in a mountain stronghold, and they'll choose the comfort every time. Ergo, the women had no choice."

"That's nonsense. Baldwin's villa is ten times more splendid and comfortable than Pelles's is."

"What?" I almost stopped again, but jabbed my horse in the ribs before he could react to my involuntary jerk on the reins. Perceval was listening now, I saw, his attention captured by my one-word outburst. "You said they were being held in Baldwin's main stronghold."

"No, I did not." Milo was indignant. "You asked me how many forts he had, and I told you three, the principal one having a garrison of mercenaries."

"I asked you why Pelles would not try to rescue the women, and you said he couldn't, because—" I bit off my words and took a deep breath, recognizing that nothing would be gained by an "I said, you said" squabble. I nodded an apology. "Forgive me, I misunderstood what you were telling me. So, am I now correct in believing that—what's her name, Catalina?—she and her daughters are being held in a villa?"

"Aye. Baldwin lives like an emperor when he's at home, on a huge estate rivaling anything you might ever have seen. It would take you two full days to ride across the extent of his vineyards. The grapes are poor, and they produce foul wine—thin, bitter stuff—but he sells it and buys good wine to drink himself."

"You've been there?"

"Aye, twice, the last time with Pelles when he rode to visit his mother, in the spring."

"Is it fortified?"

"No, I told you, it's a villa, on an estate."

"Garrisoned?"

"No! It's well guarded, but it's not *garrisoned*. One of Baldwin's forts is less than five miles away, up in the hills overlooking the estate, and all three of his strongholds are within an easy day's march of the place. At any sign of a threat—be it invasion or attack—the fort above them could have a force at the villa within the hour."

I looked at Perceval, who was listening intently, but I said nothing, and once again we rode in a companionable silence as I mulled over this latest information. It was Perceval who spoke next.

"What's your plan on meeting Pelles? Have you thought any more about it?"

"Aye, and I still don't have one. I'm no further forward on that."

"And what about this Baldwin fellow? D'you think he'll give us any trouble?"

"What kind of trouble could he give us, short of declaring war on Camulod? I stand in the place of Arthur, High King of Britain. If the man offends me, I'll deal with him. If he accommodates me, I'll deal with him. I have no concerns over that. And for now, there's nothing to be gained by fretting over what might be. Within the hour, we will know, one way or the other. At least the rain stopped, the wind died down, the sun is shining, if only from time to time, and this countryside is beautiful."

I turned again to Milo. "One more thing. The chiefs there, do you have their trust?"

He glanced over this time, to where our satellite party rode on the slope. They had drifted closer, and now I could see the brightness of fine clothes that stood out from the throng, although they were still too far away to make out individual forms or faces.

He grunted. "Aye, they trust me. That's why they're being so … respectful."

"They're showing us respect?"

"Of course they are, simply by not being intrusive. This is their country. Pelles rules it as king, but those seven men out there rule the people. Have no doubt of that."

"Hmm … Well, I don't want to offend them unwittingly by behaving in any way that they might not like, and that includes riding right up to Pelles's gates unannounced, so would you object if I asked you to ride over and pass the time of day with them?" I saw by the nod of his head that he had no objections. "My thanks for that. Greet them cordially for me, if you would, and explain I have no wish to compromise them by intruding upon them, and then inform them what we are about, and that I ride to offer greetings and a gift from King Arthur to our host, King Pelles."

"Happily," he said, "but I'll do more than that. I'll let them know, quite confidentially and quietly, that you are, as you say, the official emissary of King Arthur of Britain and that you have no intention of letting Baldwin block you from meeting Pelles. That will not displease them, since every one of them has been blocked in the same way in recent months. I'll be back." He broke away from us and spurred his horse towards the distant group of watchers.

"Well, my friend," I said to Perceval, "we've cast a die, one way or another, and I have two things for you to bear in mind. The first of them is signals. I have no idea how close you will be to me at any time, so I am giving you two signals to remember. If at any time you hear me say the word 'Caledonian,' no matter who I am talking with, it will mean that I have decided we are in danger and may have to fight our way back to our ships. The word will be your signal to get us out of there. The second signal I will use only if you are too far away to hear what's being said between me and whoever I happen to be talking to, and it will be my new green woolen belt. You know the one I mean, because I know you've been wondering where it came from ever since you first saw it. If we have trouble, I will retie it so it hangs visibly by my right side. It means the same as the word 'Caledonian'—Get us out of there.

"But I really don't think either signal will be necessary. For the rest, whatever else you may see or hear me do or say, I want you simply to follow my lead. If you hear me offer to fellate this man Baldwin, look away if you wish but don't look surprised." I returned his broad grin. "I mean that—don't look surprised at anything I say or do, because I have no idea of what might happen after we reach Pelles's villa, and I'll be reacting as I see fit to anything and everything that comes along. So be prepared for anything. Understood?"

"Aye, but I'd really like to watch you fellate him."

"Fall on your sword, you idiot. But before you do, ride back and let the Reds know you know they're still alive back there, and have young Tomasius ready to bring me the King's gift as soon as we come in sight of the villa. I'll talk to the Whites."

Arthur had sent Pelles a magnificent gift, an exact duplicate of the long two-handed swords owned only by Knights Companion to the King, save that this one was adorned with a gold pommel rather than a plain silver one. It was a gift truly worthy of a king, crafted by our finest smiths in Camulod, not quite as finely specific as the others, simply because each knight's sword was expressly measured and weighted to its owner's size and the length of his arms. In some respects, however, Arthur's gift to Pelles was even finer, for its blade, covered in a sheath of the finest polished leather adorned with gold wirework, was etched with Pelles's name, and the name, along with

Pelles's personal emblem, was repeated on the pommel—a heavy disk of gold bearing the words "Pellesus Rex" encircling a stag's head. It was a gift I could present with confidence, for nothing of its like existed in Gaul, and its magnificence ensured me of the right to insist upon presenting it to Pelles in person.

5

I really do not know what I had expected Baldwin to look like, for Milo had offered me no iota of description of the man, but because I was prepared to dislike him on sight, I suppose I must have anticipated some kind of grossness or unpleasantness in his appearance.

Nothing could have been further from the reality. The man who was waiting to meet us on our arrival at Pelles's villa was a king from head to foot, and dressed as regally as any Caesar. I had time to look carefully at him as we approached, because he stood alone in the center of the portico, backed by a semicircle of six attendants, one of whom, standing in the center of the group, was clearly, from his elaborate uniform, a high-ranking soldier. Even had I not heard Milo mutter Baldwin's name on first seeing him, I would have recognized him purely from his age, for his hair, still full, perfectly groomed and trimmed to shoulder length, was a startling silver white. He was tall and haughty looking, broad shouldered and straight as a sword blade, and he wore no beard but a full, flowing mustache of the same rich whiteness. As he watched us approach he stroked it gently, smoothing it almost reflectively, running the tips of thumb and forefinger from his nostrils to his chin time after time.

We were less than thirty paces from Baldwin when Perceval muttered from the corner of his mouth, "I'm not really surprised Pelles isn't here. Who would want to stand beside that whoreson and look like a turnip?"

There was no need to ask him what he meant. Baldwin was wearing a flowing garment that was almost toga-like, made of some shining fabric that rippled like water and was edged with a broad border of gold brocade, the garment itself only a shade or two lighter than the imperial purple in hue. Beneath this impressive cloak, he wore a quilted, knee-length tunic of the palest blue-green silk I had ever seen, and his legs were covered by trousers of a slightly darker shade, wound with silken gold bindings. His feet were bare beneath fragile, gilded sandals. He was splendid, and I could find no other word for that, other than daunting, which merely complemented the splendor. I ruefully remembered my own earlier comment on the importance of first impressions, and glanced casually around towards my escort, but I need not have worried. They were riding in perfect symmetry, radiating a unique and daunting splendor of their own. And then we were face to face with Baldwin, less than five paces separating us from where he stood smiling up at us.

As Perceval rapped the order to our men to stand fast, I dismounted slowly and approached the steps of the portico, and the ensuing few moments passed in a blur of impressions and the commonplace inanities of greetings. I was highly aware, however—having looked around me carefully as I swung down from my saddle—that Quintus Milo had not dismounted to come forward with me, and that Pelles's seven clan chiefs were still horsed, too, ranged in a semicircle inside the main gates to the villa courtyard. Baldwin ignored all of them completely, concentrating his attention upon me, intent on making me feel welcome. This was no formal occasion and could not be construed as one, with Pelles absent. Baldwin could merely welcome me as an intermediary on the king's behalf; an adviser here, in Pelles's home.

He expressed his regrets at the outset that the king was indisposed and could not greet us in person, and I accepted that without demur, focusing all my attention upon my own reading of the man facing me, analyzing his every move and expression as I searched for an understanding of the kind of person I was dealing with. I had already formed some conclusions on the way here, but I knew they might be faulty, based on hearsay as they were.

He was very polished, welcoming us warmly and inviting me to bring my officers into the villa for some refreshment, but from the very outset something intangible about his effusive reception set my teeth on edge. And then, listening and watching carefully, I realized that there was no singular element of his behavior to which I could take exception. The falsity lay in his entire demeanor, and although I couldn't identify the substance of it at first, I soon recognized it, and it brought my hackles up: there was the merest suggestion in his tone of compassionate regret, as though he pitied us somehow, perhaps for our foolishness in coming here, much as if we were a group of distant relatives turning up inconveniently and expecting hospitality as an entitlement. It permeated everything he said and did, even to the looks he cast at our troopers, as though he were constantly on the point of shaking his head ruefully and tutting to himself in commiseration with our difficulties. But at that time no difficulties had been mentioned, and apart from the one brief mention of Pelles's supposed indisposition, no word of explanation had been offered to us for the casual, nigh on insulting reception we had had on our arrival that morning, or for the lack of any preparation here in Corbenic for our visit. These impressions kept coming at me with increasing clarity, until, soon after our arrival, I found myself thinking, *This is an arrogant whoreson, and he's toying with us, laughing at us, thinking we know no better than to accept his every word.*

It was at that point that I decided to appear to be the fool that he evidently expected me to be, for it had become clear to me that, as things now stood, we could expect nothing from this man in the way of cooperation. Now, however, in one flash of insight—or perhaps it was no more than wishful thinking—it occurred to me that I might learn far more by pretending to be willing to leave and return home to Britain immediately than I ever would by a steadfast pursuit of my mission here. I knew I would have to play the fool as though born to the role.

My decision made, I drew myself up to attention and saluted him as I would a superior officer, calling him my lord king and thanking him for his courtesy before I turned to Perceval and asked him to summon our two squadron commanders to join us for a cup of wine and to bring the King's gift to King Pelles with them when they came. Baldwin turned to the soldier at his back and ordered him to wait for Perceval and my other officers and bring them to us when they were ready, then he led me into the villa, followed by the other five men of his party. He had offered no acknowledgment of any kind to Quintus Milo or the clan chiefs assembled in the background, and now as we walked inside he waved away my fawning deference, protesting that there was no need for me to think of him or treat him as a king here, that he was merely a friend and adviser to poor young Pelles, who had become increasingly unwell these past few months.

I watched carefully for armed guards as we entered the villa, but saw none until we reached the main reception room, where two stood flanking the double doors that evidently led into the main part of the house. They were both tall, thick set and swarthy of face, looking like no Franks I had ever seen, and they wore plain black tunics and heavy black leather armor and helmets. They held unsheathed swords, long-bladed, heavy-looking things, and the left breast of their cuirasses bore a blazon I had never seen before, a solid black, equal-sided triangle in a square of white. Baldwin dismissed them immediately upon entering, and they left through the doors they had been guarding.

"My own guards," he said to me when they had gone. "Occo, their commander, is my master-at-arms. He is the one waiting outside now for your officers." He coughed to clear his throat. "I decided only last week to use my own men to guard the king, thinking it might be better for none of the clansmen to see his true condition nowadays. I may be doing nothing more than postponing the inevitable, but I think the time has not yet come to stir up people's passions. Now, let me offer you something to eat and drink."

He clapped his hands and another door opened in the far wall to admit a line of servants carrying large amounts of food and a variety of jugs and drinking vessels. They came in silence, and as soon as they had set their burdens on the tables scattered among the half score or so of comfortable armchairs in the large room, most of them left again. Only three remained behind, standing against the wall, to replenish plates as they were emptied, and as they took their places, Occo swept in, leading Perceval, Griffyd and Tomasius, the latter carrying the case containing Pelles's sword. There were eleven of us assembled there now, and the tables held enough for five times more.

For the next quarter of an hour I sat wide eyed and rapt, touching neither food nor drink, deliberately hanging visibly on Baldwin's every word as he explained the situation into which I had arrived. About three months earlier, according to his report, Pelles had fallen seriously ill and had, from there, slipped into some kind of decline that had alarming aspects, not merely with regard to the king's physical health but also in the matter of his mental health. He had become erratic in his demands and habits, and had betrayed an increasing tendency towards forgetfulness, to the point at which he would forget completely what he had talked about when he was lucid. Furthermore, these periods of lucidity and forgetfulness were now fluctuating more and more rapidly.

Genuinely alarmed by what I was being told, despite my earlier skepticism, I asked him what was being done to treat the king, a question that caused Baldwin to sigh deeply and shake his head. His finest physicians were all here in Corbenic, he told me, indicating the grave-faced group of men who had accompanied him. Several of them had been Roman trained, in Constantinople and Alexandria, but they confessed themselves powerless in the face of Pelles's rapid mental degeneration, even though they appeared to be making steady progress with his physical ailments.

It was Perceval who asked how much the king's nobles knew of all this, and once again Baldwin's brow furrowed with concern. He had seen fit, he said, to keep the king's condition closely held, fearing to say anything that might cause alarm and create unrest among the clans. Pelles had no heir, and no brothers to whom the rule might pass in the event of his death. He had no surviving family but his mother and two widowed older sisters, and so the kingdom would need a new monarch upon his death—God forbid that such an event should come to pass any time soon. Unfortunately, there was more than one claimant in line to the kingdom among the Corbenic clans. Three of the clan chiefs held legitimate claims to the kingship, but none of the three had a claim stronger than either of the others. Therein, Baldwin hinted darkly, was cause for grave concern and great caution.

He had made no mention of Pelles's mother and sisters being in his own lands, and I had to bite my tongue against the urge to ask him about them; I was playing the fool, but it would be folly indeed to ask a question that might arouse suspicions about the true extent of my knowledge of such things. Instead, I asked about something else.

"But surely," I interjected, trying my hardest to appear as gullible as I had chosen to be, "people must have suspicions concerning Pelles's health?"

No, I was told. Apparently not so. Baldwin had felt a duty of loyalty to Pelles and his people, under these harsh and perilous circumstances, and so had taken great pains to ensure that the king was highly visible during his lucid periods. At such times, Pelles met with the chiefs and talked with them openly and convincingly of many things. Only in the past few weeks had the king been physically unable to do even that, and so Baldwin now felt he would not be able to withhold the information from the clan chiefs for much longer. And that, he added with a great sigh, placed him in a very delicate position concerning our presence here. Civil war, should it break out, would involve every living man in the land, pitting clan against clan and brother against brother. There could be no neutrality for anyone in Corbenic, and while he intended to remain here for as long as need be, trying to keep the peace, he would, should his efforts fail, return immediately to his home territories.

Aye, I thought, *to marshal your own armies and come back in strength when everyone here is exhausted. Sweet Jesus, this man really believes we are idiots.* But I had set myself a role to play and it was time to play it. I stood up abruptly and ordered Perceval to take the two squadron commanders and return to their troops to wait for me there. I had certain matters to discuss with King Baldwin, I told them, that were not for their ears. Perceval stared me in the eye, his face expressionless, and for a moment I thought he might object, but he snapped a crisp salute that was echoed by the two junior officers and turned away immediately. Baldwin at once dismissed his people, too. The servants slipped out noiselessly and Occo and the physicians disappeared into the body of the house. Within moments, Baldwin and I were alone in the enormous room.

In the short time it had taken my men to stride out, their booted heels ringing on the marble floor, my mind had been racing, trying to remember what I disliked most about two junior officers in Camulod, the one an obsequious, sniveling toady who would spend his life handling minor administrative tasks because no one liked him or would ever trust him with anything of real importance, and the other the embodiment of everything dull and lackluster in the term "a simple soldier." Paul Signus, the latter, was brave enough, and loyal, but he lacked even the slightest spark of initiative, imagination or passion and would absolutely never go beyond what he perceived as the letter of the law in carrying out an order. He would do as he was told, but no more, and would incur no risk that had not been specified in advance, and thus he would never be entrusted with the safety of troopers. This was the man I needed to be now, with elements of the other thrown in to bolster my mummery.

Now, alone with Baldwin, I launched myself into my playacting.

"You mentioned civil war, Lord Baldwin, and I find that most distressing, since that would entail a situation far outside of and beyond the limitations of my instructions governing my behavior here. Do you really think that is likely to happen? That war might break out?"

"It is a real possibility, from what I have seen. You must bear in mind, of course, that I am merely interpreting signs that are there for anyone to read … and I may have interpreted them wrongly."

"Aye, perhaps. I ask only because I was appointed to head this expedition by our King, Arthur himself, which is a great and signal honor. But I have no wish to overstep my authority, or to draw the King's anger by exposing my men—the King's men—to needless danger by permitting them to be caught up in the affairs of another kingdom that is no concern of Britain's."

"It seems to me that you have more than that on your mind, Legate Clothar. You appear troubled. Will you not tell me what your difficulty is? I may be able to assist you."

"Aye, well … It is not so much that I am troubled, my lord King, not really troubled in the sense that I suspect you mean. But I am … perturbed. Long months of careful planning went into the preparations for this expedition to Corbenic. Planning and enormous effort. But from the lack of preparedness I have seen here to this point, it seems plain to me that our venture has already suffered severe damage, thanks to this illness afflicting King Pelles. Am I to believe, my lord, that you really knew *nothing* about our arrival?"

"Nothing at all, Legate Clothar. I had not the slightest indication that you were expected. Until barely two months ago, mind you, I was absent from Corbenic most of the time, seeing to the affairs of my own territories and possessions. I came back only in response to an urgent summons from the king's physicians. I knew nothing, until today, of Pelles's dealings with your masters in Camulod."

I took note of that not-too-subtle reminder of my subservient status, but refused to allow any awareness of it to show in my vacant expression, merely nodding in encouragement to him to continue, and he did.

"The only thing I knew about your arrival—the only hint I could have had about your being expected—came to me only two weeks ago, and it was something I overheard almost by accident. It was incomprehensible at the time, for I had nothing against which to measure what I had heard, and Pelles, sadly, was in no condition to explain himself. He was delirious that day, raving wildly, and although I heard him mention Camulod, I knew nothing of what that meant. Only today, when you introduced yourself and your men, did I recollect hearing the name before."

"But what about Bishop Ludovic? Had he said nothing to you?"

"Bishop Ludovic? You mean the bishop from Auxerre? Why would he say anything to me? I only ever met the fellow once, and we did not admire each other. Mind you, I know he and Pelles were friends, but the friend of a friend is not always necessarily a friend to me, and I am sure you must know people about whom you feel the same way. But I have no idea how extensive the old fellow's involvement might have been in whatever plans Pelles made with your people in Camulod. I do know, however, because Pelles talked of it several times, that the bishop is an old and feeble man with onerous and taxing duties that keep him traveling the length and breadth of his diocese, very much to his peril. Knowing that, it seems to me that while his intentions of aiding King Pelles might have been the finest, he may have acted only as a go-between in this matter, contacting one friend, in England, on behalf of the other, here in Corbenic, with no actual knowledge of what was involved."

I was only half listening to this last part, cursing myself for not having read any of the letters from Ludovic to Merlyn. No one had seen any need for that at the time, and my instructions from both Arthur and Merlyn had been distilled from Ludovic's proposals. Nevertheless, had I read any of them, I now realized, I would have been more able to filter the real and the self-serving from the web of lies and half-truths I felt sure Baldwin was spinning here.

I nodded repeatedly, hoping to give the impression of agreeing with everything he had said, and then, concentrating on my "simple soldier" model, Paul Signus, I returned to the topic of endangering my command and the penalty that would surely lie in wait for me were I to do the wrong thing here.

"Aye," I said. "It is very difficult, sometimes, to know what to do for the best. I'll tell you plainly, my lord King, I am a soldier, a battle commander, and I seek no greater station. I am an adequate tactician, but I'm no great strategist, and these matters here, I'll freely admit to you, are far beyond my capabilities. My instructions, and the responsibilities assigned to me concerning this expedition, Camulod and King Arthur, contain nothing relevant to this situation, this civil war of which you speak. I am facing circumstances that no one envisioned before I left to come here."

"So what will you do? What *can* you do?"

"I can return to Britain, now, before matters here become ungovernable. Part of me is saying, deep in my head, that that might be the best thing I could do. Except ..."

"Except what?"

"Isn't that obvious? Except that nothing has happened yet to justify such an action. There is no civil war. Not yet. And I cannot leave before such a war breaks out. To do otherwise would leave me open to charges of cowardice. It really is too bad. I want to do what's best for everyone, for my men and my superiors. And the fact that nothing is happening here—no one waiting for us, no traders assembling, no merchants expecting us—that makes me feel even more strongly that the best thing I could do would be to turn around right now and return to Britain."

I almost winced at the sound of my own voice saying such things, but at the same time I was pleased that I sounded as Paul Signus would have, and I knew I had captured the petulant, put-upon tone I had heard him use many times. Encouraged by that thought, and by the way Baldwin was staring at me, a vulpine half smile on his lips, I forged ahead.

"Truly, my lord King, I think it would be better by far to exercise discretion and salvage what I can from this disaster, knowing it to be no fault of ours, than to linger here too long and risk turning the entire expedition into a catastrophe if hostilities break out. Our alliance, as I understood it, was to have been with King Pelles, but if Pelles dies, we could be stranded here while his would-be successors, all of them probably hostile to us, fought over his kingdom."

"You may be right, Legate Clothar. Your logic seems sound." The voice was liquid honey, deep and seductive, promising sympathy and empathy while it preached despair and sedition. I nodded yet again, as though thanking him for his support.

"Besides," I continued, almost growling now with the discontent I was injecting into my voice, "I have fewer than two hundred men—three squadrons and a few archers—but I have all their horses and gear to think of, too. Two hundred men is but a minor force in any large-scale conflict and it would be a dangerous liability in this, if what you said earlier is true—that no man will be neutral in this war. I would not know where to turn to safeguard my command. I know nothing about any of the people here, and I have no understanding of the politics involved. And then there's the fleet. I had forgotten that."

"You mean the ships you came in? What had you forgotten?"

"It's not ours. Camulod's, I mean. It belongs to an ally, a king in Alba, the land to the north of Britain, beyond Hadrian's Wall. He agreed to lend us his ships upon the understanding that we would enable him, once we were here, to set up trade with Corbenic, exchanging valuable metals mined in his lands for Roman weapons made in Gaul. That's clearly not going to happen now, and Connor, the admiral commanding the fleet, is not going to be happy to find his ships under threat, atop being unable to conduct his trade. He'll leave immediately, irrespective of what we do, and we'll be stranded here."

Baldwin had been staring intently at me all the while, his mouth curved in a smile of unctuous sympathy, and nodding his head increasingly in agreement from the moment he first realized where I was heading. I felt like a posturing fool, and yet at the same time I could see that Baldwin was convinced of my self-doubts and my agonized inability to arrive at a decision. Finally I threw up my hands and twisted my face into a grimace, turning to look all around the room before facing Baldwin again.

"I don't know what to do," I said, trying to make my voice plaintive and sincere at the same time, "and I can't involve any of my subordinates in this. I'm sure you understand that, my lord King, and why it would be demeaning. This is my decision. I must make it alone and I must make it soon—today. I have heavily laden ships and innocent men for whom I am responsible. If I am to stop the cargoes being unloaded uselessly, only to be reloaded later, I have no time to waste." I heaved a deep, long breath and expelled it loudly through my nose, allowing my shoulders to slump. "I am not used to being indecisive, my lord King, but in this instance ..." It was as close as I felt I could credibly come to asking him outright what I should do, and fortunately he recognized that.

He walked away from me to the table laden with refreshments and poured a large glass cup of yellow wine with his own hands, then brought it to me. I took it wordlessly and drank, surprised to discover that it was light and delicious.

"I believe, Legate Clothar, if you will allow me to contribute to your deliberations, that you have assessed this matter with great clarity, and your concern for your ultimate responsibilities does you great credit." He spoke slowly, affecting great *dignitas* and pronouncing each word clearly, as if in love with the sound of his own deep, sonorous voice. "It is beyond dispute that your expectations upon landing here have not been met, and that I regret deeply. But the underlying reasons are straightforward and, unfortunately, could not have been foreseen. The arrangements were made by King Pelles in good faith. I have no doubt of that. But they were also made while he was sound of mind and body. Now he is neither, and the situation here in Corbenic will soon become volatile, at best ... I know you have not asked for it, but my opinion supports your own. I believe the best thing you could do would be to follow the promptings of your legitimate concerns: sail home and report what has happened to your King."

"Aye, but our ally's trading venture ..."

"That can resume in time, in my own lands, if not in Corbenic. My armies are all infantry and much of my land is mountainous, no place for cavalry, but my smiths need a new and reliable source of ingot metals, for raw ore is in short supply nowadays. You may tell your ally in Alba that I will be glad to treat with him, once the situation here in Corbenic has been resolved."

I nodded, permitting myself to appear convinced, then hesitated, looking at the long case of polished elm that Tomasius had placed on one of the tables before leaving. "But what about this?" I crossed to the table and laid my hand on the case. "This is a gift especially designed for King Pelles, sent by King Arthur himself." I opened the lid and showed Baldwin the sword that it contained. "See, it has King Pelles's name and emblem on the pommel."

He stepped forward and stood gazing down at the sheathed weapon. "It is magnificent."

"Aye, it is, but …" I drew myself up with a sharp, indrawn breath, as though a thought had just occurred to me. "My lord King, I dare not go home without delivering this in person, and it strikes me now that neither can I return home without having seen King Pelles with my own two eyes. Would it be possible … would you permit me to visit him, to look upon him and verify his condition? That will permit me to return to Camulod with a clear conscience, able to report that I have seen the king myself and made my decision based upon the evidence I saw in person."

I was prepared to argue long, hard and obsequiously to the point of nausea, playing the hapless, indecisive buffoon until I wore him down, but he surprised me. He looked at me with narrowed eyes, then nodded. "Of course. I'll take you to him now. Come." He turned without another word and walked towards the doors that had been under guard when we came in, and I tucked the long sword case beneath my arm and followed him. He led me along a wide, marble-floored passageway to where the same pair of guards now flanked another doorway.

"The King's Chambers," he murmured as the guards opened the doors.

6

Poisoned! The word leapt into my mind at my first unimpeded sight of the wretched figure propped up on pillows in the bed, and I knew all my suspicions had been justified. There was evil in this room, tangible in its stink, and King Pelles's face and hands bore the visible stamps of it: black and brown blotches standing out starkly against the fish-belly white of his skin and hollow, purple bruises beneath his sunken eyes.

At the sound of the door opening, a man who had been stooping over the bed straightened up and turned towards us indignantly, until he saw who we were. I recognized him as one of the nameless physicians from earlier and noticed he was holding a spoon and a bowl, from which he had been feeding or about to feed the king. The room was windowless, lit only by flickering torches, its walls heavy with dark wood paneling, and it was fetid with the stench of sickness: a mixture of vomit, sweat and feces. But dim daylight was spilling in from an open door in the far corner of the room, to the right of the large, wood-framed bed.

As soon as he became aware of Baldwin, the startled physician stepped back to stand against the wall by the head of the bed, still clutching his bowl. The floor seemed to tilt beneath my feet as a flood of recognition and irrevocable decisions swept over me.

The sleeping king's lips were dry. I noticed that immediately, so I knew that none of the potion in the bowl had yet been administered. But I instantly recognized the blotches on the death-pale lips, face and hands. The previous year, one of the minor kings in the region to the south of Camulod had been poisoned by his wife. I had been horrified by the sight of the dead man, for he had clearly died in great and sudden agony, his lips and teeth stained blue and his mouth, even in death, twisted into a rictus of pain and terror.

On my return to Camulod, I had had a long discussion with Merlyn about poisons and poisoning, and he had told me that there were two kinds of each: the sudden, violent poisons that killed quickly and were obvious; and another, slower, more insidious type that could take long months to effect their purpose. This second kind had to be administered slowly and cumulatively, over a long period, and they were difficult, sometimes impossible, to detect, so that the resultant lingering death of the victim frequently raised no suspicion of anything more tragic than incurable illness. Black and brown skin lesions, sunken, hollow eyes, pallid skin and rotting, discolored teeth were unmistakable symptoms of what Merlyn had called chronic poisoning. All poisoners were evil, he had said that day, but slow poisoners were irredeemably malevolent and malignant, possessed of a callous and deliberate wickedness beyond the understanding of ordinary men.

One of those creatures stood before me now, clutching his devil's brew, and another even more malign, the man who had commissioned his atrocity, was now bending forward over the form on the bed, reaching out to touch the pallid, sleeping face. I had no idea where my conviction sprang from, but it carried its own imperative and I never thought to question it. I quickly placed the sword case on a nearby table, drew my ceremonial dagger, the only weapon I had with me, and stepped forward quickly, raising my arm and smashing the hilt's pommel ball down with all my strength to strike Baldwin on the nape of his neck, beneath the right ear. The force of the blow sent him sprawling across the legs of the sleeping king.

The physician beside me, stunned by the swiftness of my attack, stiffened in horror, pressing himself back against the wall and opening his mouth to shout, but I slashed my dagger across his throat before the sound could emerge, drowning his cry in a spray of gurgling blood. He stood gazing at me wide eyed, then fell forward onto his knees, his eyes already glazing as his nerveless fingers released the bowl he had been holding. It shattered loudly when it hit the floor, and the metal spoon went clattering under the bed, sounding as loud to me as the brazen trumpets of Joshua at Jericho.

Something flickered at the edge of my vision and I swung towards the open doorway in the corner to see the shape of another man outlined against the dim daylight from the other room. He was leaning into the room, peering about him with no idea of what had happened, aware only that he had heard an unexpected noise. I reached him before he could react, closing the distance between us in two strides and recognizing him as another of the five physicians, a sullen, beefy, corpulent lout who had scowled at me ever since he first set eyes on me. I doubt he even recognized me before he died, but my hard-thrust blade struck to the heart and he dropped like a felled ox, the weight of his body ripping the dagger from my grasp.

I bent forward into the lighted room, thinking to pull my weapon free, but I was diverted immediately by the array of tools and implements spread out on a large, long table by the single window. Mortars and pestles and apothecary's measures sat among boxes and vials, bottles and jars, and on a smooth, flat stone in the center of the table, the dead man had been preparing a paste of varying ingredients.

As I gazed at this scene, knowing it was evidence of what had been going on, the main doors to the bedchamber crashed open and I spun to see the two guards from the outer door charge into the room. They hesitated just inside the door, assessing what they saw, and then they charged straight at me, blades already drawn, but in the moment of their hesitation I had already run back towards the table where the king's sheathed sword lay in its case. Even so, I had no time to fumble with the box, for the leading man was already within striking distance. I snatched up the case in both hands and sprang backwards, kicking out at the heavy table to send it toppling towards him, and by luck the solid stone edge hit him hard on the knee and sent him twisting to one side, clutching at his leg. But his companion was already striking at me from within arm's length, a hard, straight stab with a heavy, wickedly pointed sword. I pulled the wooden case against me instinctively, thinking he had killed me, but his blade thrust hard into the wood and pierced it, striking the blade inside the case and jarring the thick container out of my hands as the force of his blow sent me reeling back. As though time itself had slowed down, I saw the hinged lid of the case spring open and the sword inside flew up into the air, spinning slowly as it rose and fell towards me. Still off balance, I snatched at it left handed and managed to seize it by the scabbard, pulling it out of the air until the hilt slapped solidly into my right hand and I leapt to my left, pivoting as I landed on my right foot and bringing the long blade scything around in a lateral slash that sent the loosened scabbard flying off an instant before the razor-edged blade took my assailant in the neck and severed his head. Still in its helmet, the head toppled to the floor, where it bounced and rolled across the room.

This had all happened so fast that the injured man was still down on one knee, and his eyes flew wide as they followed his companion's disembodied head. Before he could rally, I killed him with a single stabbing thrust that took him just above the rim of his cuirass.

For long moments, I stood in the sudden silence, listening for sounds of others coming, but I heard only my own heart, thudding as though it sat inside my head. Neither of the guards had uttered a word, I realized now, and in their arrogance they had probably thought they could handle me alone, one single, unarmed man, and an Outlander, to boot. Still, I stood motionless, straining to hear something, anything, that spoke of alarums raised and running guards, but I finally accepted that, thus far, I seemed to have been fortunate.

And then, from the bed, Baldwin groaned. Moving swiftly, I retrieved my dagger from the corpse in the doorway, wiping it clean on the dead man's clothing, and then ran to strip the belts from the two dead guards. I used the leather straps to truss the now half-conscious Baldwin, binding his ankles tightly and pinioning first his wrists and then his elbows behind his back. Knowing he would begin to shout as soon as he was fully conscious, I took my dagger and cut a length of cloth from his magnificent shimmering purple cloak, and then I waited for him to open his eyes and look at me. As soon as he did, and before he could speak or shout, I stuffed the wadded cloth into his open mouth and bound it in place with another strip from his cloak, allowing him to watch me as I destroyed the precious and, I hoped, irreplaceable garment. I finished by dragging him off the bed and dumping him on the floor behind it, where he would not be seen by anyone opening the chamber door. That done, I hurriedly dragged the two dead guards out of sight, too, pulling them into the apothecary's room and shutting the door behind me when I came out. The detached head, still in its helmet, lay in the corner behind the door, where it could not easily be seen by anyone coming into the room. There was nothing I could do about the blood that lay everywhere, but the room was almost completely dark now, the torches guttering low in their sconces. Someone would be coming in soon to change those, I knew, but in the meantime I would require little time to do what had to be done.

Only as I was on the point of leaving the room did I become aware that I had not even checked the man in the bed for signs of life, and I stopped at the threshold, one hand on the door handle, and looked back at him. His eyes were open, looking back at me, and I felt a chill shiver of gooseflesh run from the nape of my neck to the base of my spine. I walked slowly back to his bedside and stood gazing down at him, his bloodied gift sword clutched in my right hand. The tip of his tongue appeared between his lips as he tried to moisten them, and I moved quickly to where a water jug sat on a stand close by. I loosened Elaine's green woolen belt from about my waist and dipped one end in the water, and I used it to wet his lips, wiping them clean of crusted mucus. I wondered whether everything he ate or drank might be poisoned.

"My thanks," he whispered, close to inaudibly, and I bent nearer to him as he went on, "Who are you?"

"Clothar, my lord, Clothar of Benwick, come from Camulod and King Arthur to meet your needs."

One of his fingers moved on the covering of the bed. "Baldwin?"

"Baldwin has been poisoning you, my lord. I have arrested him." I nodded to where Baldwin lay listening, his face red with fury and disbelief. "He's lying on the floor beside you, for the time being."

The pale lips actually smiled, a hesitant, tremulous twitching. "Am I to die, then?"

"No, my lord King, not if it is in my power to prevent it. Do you feel likely to die?"

"I have felt … stronger … but I am alive."

"Yes, you are, and you will grow stronger daily, now that we have stopped the poison they've been feeding you. From now on, you will eat and drink nothing that has not been prepared by my own men."

His head dipped slightly, the merest suggestion of a nod, and then he whispered, "Where are your men?"

"Nearby, my lord. But now I must go and bring them to guard you, and to clear out this nest of rats that swarms around you. If you will pardon me, I must go now, before anyone else comes in here and seeks to stop me."

He flicked a finger, which I took as permission to leave him, and I nodded and strode away to the door, binding Elaine's bright green belt about my waist as I went, leaving the ends of it free to hang down by my right side. I opened the door cautiously, and carefully checked the rooms on both sides of the passageway beyond, making sure they were empty of any threat before I went to the doors at the end of the passageway, in front of which the guards had stood earlier. They were ajar, and I closed them slowly behind me as I stepped through, looking left and right. Nothing moved in either direction, and I made my way directly towards the distant pair of doors that led to the main reception room, aware but uncaring that blood was dripping from the end of my sword onto the marble floor, and knowing that my men were mere paces beyond those doors.

They swung open from the other side when I was less than ten paces from them, pushed by a pair of Occo's guards who stood bent sideways, one hand each on the handles and the spears in the other upraised, allowing Occo himself to pass between them. He stopped short when he saw me, taking in my appearance and the long sword in my hand in a glance, and then he growled a single, quiet, sibilant command in a language unknown to me. The two guards began sidling towards me instantly, leveling their long weapons, and I saw Occo reach out and swing the double doors shut again behind him and lean back against them as he watched me with narrowed, angry eyes.

I backed away cautiously, sudden fear roiling in my guts. I had
no advantage here, neither in surprise nor in weaponry, and there
was nowhere to run or hide. The long spears reaching for me were
conti, the favored weapon among those elements of Roman cavalry
known as contus cavalry, named after the very spears they carried.
Fearsome weapons, they were long shafted, with great double-
edged heads that were flanged and barbed, sharp enough to rip a
man to pieces on the withdrawal, even after missing the stab. The
long, metal collars that secured the formidable head to the shaft of
each spear extended backwards for fully one third the length of the
weapon, making it almost impossible for an opposing swordsman to
cut through it.

I continued to back away as the two men approached me slowly,
taking their time and measuring me for signs of weakness, the
points of their weapons making tiny circles in the air, not from any
fear or nervousness, I knew, but in search of the best target area on
my armored body. They held their conti with authority and confidence, the butt ends higher than the points, their right arms bent
upwards to provide thrust, while their left hands, held lower, would
provide stability and accuracy in aiming. Neither man spoke, and
neither looked at the other. All their attention was focused upon me,
and for the second time within half an hour I felt Death hovering
above me.

The man to my right lunged suddenly and I leapt backwards,
barely escaping his extended point, and as I did so the other man
bounded forward, thrusting hard and hoping to catch me off
balance. I had anticipated that, having seen these weapons used
before, and I swung my long blade to hammer his point aside with
a ringing clash of metals, then slashed my own point up and at him
in a blur of speed, hoping to strike his face. It was plain to me that
he had never encountered such a long-bladed sword before, because
I almost caught him, but he bent his knees and dodged backwards,
narrowly avoiding my point, and skipped away beyond my reach as
his companion attacked again, running right at me. That was an
error, for I had known he would come at me and had already begun

to sidestep his charge at the moment he launched it. His point drove past me, almost touching me, but I had already planted my right foot and dropped my right shoulder and was changing direction by then, moving to close with him before he could jerk his point sideways and hook me with the barbs. With my sword hand down by my right hip, I stabbed upwards, short and hard, aiming the point of my blade at the soft skin under his chin, but the fellow was fast and leapt away, arching his body and lowering his chin, and my point pierced his eye instead, penetrating his skull and killing him instantly, so that he fell backwards, releasing his hold on the deadly spear and dropping it at my feet.

I went down on one knee and snatched at the shaft with my left hand, jerking it forward to slide along the floor and propelling it behind me as hard as I could. I had no time to do more, because kneeling as I was, I presented a perfect target. I threw myself hard backwards, rolling on my shoulder and hearing the other man's point clang on the floor where I had been, and then I was up on my knees again, gripping the heavy contus in both hands and lunging to my feet, leaving my sword behind me on the floor as I crouched to meet my assailant now on equal terms. Behind him, I saw Occo start forward, drawing his sword, and then the doors flew open at his back and Perceval came charging through, followed by Griffyd Strongarm with an arrow already nocked to his long yew bow. Before Occo could turn around, Perceval hit him with his shoulder and sent the guardsman whirling sideways while he threw himself in the other direction, and as soon as the way was clear Griffyd launched his arrow.

My opponent had not even known he was in danger. The hardshot missile hit him between the shoulder blades, lifted him off his feet and threw him facedown in front of me. I did not even glance down at him, for I knew he was dead and my eyes were already fastened on the fight developing between Perceval and Occo, who were circling each other warily, swords extended, when a second arrow smashed Occo into death, dropping him in an ungainly sprawl against the base of the wall at his back.

Perceval straightened up, gave Griffyd a nod of thanks, then came towards me.

"How did you know?" I asked him before he could say anything.

"I didn't, until I heard the noise in here, but I came back in because I couldn't sit outside while you were in here alone." He flicked a finger towards the green belt hanging by my side. "Couldn't see if you were wearing that thing inside or outside, from where I was, and decided I didn't like that. I brought Griffyd with me because we were talking when I decided to come back in." He nodded towards Occo's body. "This clown was in there when we arrived, and he wasn't too pleased to see us. I asked him where you were and he said you'd gone with Baldwin to see King Pelles. He didn't seem happy about that, either, so I asked him what he was frowning about, and he said you'd been gone too long. That's when he came in here, and when I saw the guards come in with him I came and listened at the door. The rest you know. Now tell me what's going on."

I told him, and by the time I finished he was grinning. "Five of them? You've killed *five* men since you came in here? Where's Baldwin now?"

"In the king's bedroom, trussed up like a bundle of hides. He'll be safe enough there for a while. But you and I have work to do. Baldwin had thirty men in his personal guard, not counting Occo there. I want them rounded up right now, before any of them get wind of this and make a run for home. Set thirty of the Reds to see to that, and send Quintus Milo in here with a score of his own best men and the remainder of our Reds. I'll meet with him in the reception room—there's no blood there and that should make things easier. Use the Whites to cordon off the entrance and let no one else in. Milo's men can turn this building inside out, looking for any of Baldwin's cronies that remain, but our Reds will guard the king while I talk to Milo about what we need to say to the clan chiefs. Send our two medics in here, too. Pelles is in a bad way and needs the best care we can give him. Oh, and round up the other three members of Baldwin's crew of physician poisoners. The quicker we hang them, the better for everyone."

Perceval nodded and turned away to carry out my orders, but then he hesitated and turned back. "You know," he said, "you might want to wait before you hang the physicians. They might not all be guilty. I mean, why would Baldwin bring in five murderers? Seems to me one would be enough—two at the most, to work in concert. But the other three could be completely innocent, doing their best to keep the king alive and never knowing that two of their number are working against them. That makes sense to me."

I gazed at him, considering what he had said, and then I nodded. "I'll think about that. Bring in the others now."

7

A short time later, I was standing against a wall in the reception room, having just listened to Quintus Milo address the seven assembled chiefs and their principal associates. The chiefs, three of whom were much younger than I had expected, had listened in stony silence as Milo related everything that had taken place in the past two hours. He had told them about the king's condition and about my attack on Baldwin and its aftermath, and he had explained the arrest of the three remaining physicians and the remaining members of Baldwin's personal guard and retinue.

I braced myself for the storm of pent-up outrage and protest, and I was surprised when no one jumped to his feet to denounce us. Instead, every eye in the assembled group turned towards one man, a fellow whose name I knew was Cortix, and I knew that only because he was the one to whom Milo had gone directly after hearing my story, and his was the voice that had stilled the swelling unrest in the villa courtyard when the rumors of what we were about had sprung up out of nowhere, in response to the sudden activities of my men and Milo's. Other than his name, however, I knew nothing about him.

Now this man Cortix stood up slowly, appearing to tower over his peers although he was not a big man; he was broad shouldered but wiry, of medium height and radiating strength and great self-confidence. He stood glowering in thought for a while, and then he turned his head to look at me, staring until I felt the blood beginning to rise to my cheeks and had to check myself against the urge to move. Before I could become too uncomfortable, however, he spoke in fluent but accented Latin.

"We are a cautious people," he began, "unaccustomed to giving thanks to strangers, after hundreds of years beneath the Roman boot. But you have earned our thanks." He glanced at his other listeners and then his eyes came back to me. "We knew something was not right, but none of us knew exactly what it was. And we've been loath to act too quickly, perhaps without good reason. Baldwin has been clever in this. His past actions in support of us and our king have left us in his debt, and that has caused us to hang back, in the absence of hard proof, instead of demanding answers as we clearly ought to have. Now that's all changed, thanks to you."

I answered him smoothly in his own tongue, enjoying the effect that I created. "Changed, aye, but not yet finished." I spoke now to all of them. "I am Clothar of Benwick, a Salian Frank like you, born here in the north but raised since infancy in the far south. I went to the Bishop's School in Auxerre, with Quintus Milo here, and traveled to Britain six years ago, sent by the Blessed Germanus. Now I'm back here representing Arthur of Camulod, at the request of your king, to train your people as heavy cavalry. But we have a problem that needs to be solved now."

I gave them a moment to absorb that, and then I continued before anyone had a chance to point out that they already were cavalry. "It's too soon to tell whether or not Pelles will recover from whatever they've been feeding him. Whether he lives or dies is in the hands of God. But if he lives, that's both good and bad, as things stand now: good in that you will still have a king, and we in

Camulod will still have an ally. The bad part is that Baldwin has sons who will succeed him when he does not return, and they have hostages—Pelles's mother and sisters are already in Baldwin's Land, of their own free will, I understand. That will change as soon as word of this event today gets out. Those women will be seized and held prisoner, and Pelles will be forced to negotiate for their release."

"But only if he lives." The speaker was one of the older chiefs, a grizzle-haired veteran with a long, yellow-stained mustache. "I hope he will, even if that should bring us troubles, but the women are useless to anyone if he dies."

"No, they're not," another growled. "One of them has a son— the elder of them, Lena. She wed some Rhinish fellow from the Wetlands, when she was just a chit of a thing, but he fathered a son on her. If Pelles dies, that boy will be the rightful heir to Corbenic, the only direct male relative that Pelles has. *There's* a ball of fish bones for us all to chew on."

It was bad news to me, for I had not known any heir existed. Milo had not mentioned it, but when we spoke of the women we had known nothing of Pelles's true condition, and I had not asked that question. No woman could claim the Salian succession, I knew, but the son of a king's sister certainly could, if the king had no sons of his own. I spoke into the silence.

"We can resolve all of that if we act quickly now. My men are ready to move out, and they are trained for exactly this kind of thing. We can hit the villa where the women are being held and bring them out before any word of what has happened here today reaches Baldwin's Land. All I'll require is a guide, someone who knows the shortest route to get us there without being seen."

That set off the storm that I had been expecting earlier, with everyone talking at once and the gist of their protestations being that they were more than capable of rescuing the women themselves, without help from any Outlanders. The only person who did not take part was Cortix. He stood watching me with a thoughtful expression, ignoring the chaotic shouting all around him, and then he turned away and silenced everyone with a few loud shouts. When it was quiet again, he turned back to me.

"What makes you think your men can handle this better than we can?"

"Think about it," I said. "What's needed here is hard, sudden action, carried out at speed and in secrecy. You all rode out here with us. You've seen my men, their discipline. We ride in formation, fast and straight, in two tight blocks, like bricks—small and easy to see, if you happen to be looking directly at them as they move, but easier to hide and more suited to mounting narrow-fronted attacks against organized defenses than a straggling herd of individual riders could ever be. It's not a question of bravery. Bravery has nothing to do with this. We need results. We need speed and accuracy, training and discipline. My men can punch a hole through Baldwin's Land that its defenders will never even see, and they can be in and out and back here again before word arrives there of Baldwin's fall."

He almost smiled, yet succeeded in looking doubtful. "Are you that sure of yourself?"

I nodded, smiling at him. "Of myself, aye, and of my men. I'm sure of something else, too: you need to see what cavalry like ours can do. When you've seen it, you'll want it. And that's what we came for, all the way from Camulod."

He didn't hesitate. "Right. I'll come with you myself. I've been where you need to go, been there a score of times and know every fold in the ground between here and there. If there's a way to slip a hundred mounted men past Baldwin's guards without being seen, I want to see it done. Brad and Getorix and Luthor will come with us, too. They're our main battle commanders."

I nodded at each of the three named men as they stood up, and they were all the younger men I had noticed earlier. "So be it," I said. "We'll leave within the hour. My men have food enough for tonight. Can you arrange extra rations for them in that time? How far do we have to go?"

Cortix said it was a three-day ride northeastward—two if we rode hard and were lucky with the weather.

"Rations for four, five days, for a hundred men," I said to Getorix. "Can you handle that?"

"It's done," he said, and left the room, but Cortix was eyeing me dubiously.

"For five days? You'll need more food than that."

"Aye, but not going in. How far is it from here to the border of Corbenic and Baldwin's Land, and how far from there to Baldwin's villa?"

He shrugged. "A day and a half to the end of our territory. Less than a day from there to the villa, riding hard."

"We'll be riding hard on the way out, and carrying women with us. They'll send mercenaries after us from the fort in the hills above the villa, and if they're as good as I suspect they might be, they'll be moving fast, so we'll have to ride hard to stay ahead of them. Will they follow us across your border?"

"For a certainty, if they think we're running away from them. But I'll have people waiting in the forest on our side to discourage them."

"Good. That's what I was hoping you would say. Can you have those people bring wagons with them, for the women? They'll all be sore and stiff, after spending a day on galloping horses, so they'll be glad of cushioned wagons when they cross into Corbenic. That's when we'll need extra rations, too. And one more thing." I waved a hand towards the outer door. "These men are two-thirds of my entire landing force. Taking them away means I am placing a heavy burden on my remaining squadron, leaving them alone to supervise the unloading of our fleet and guard the goods once they are on shore. Will you send a party of your men to assist them? Just to stand guard with them and make sure they don't have unforeseen … difficulties."

He hesitated only briefly before grinning and agreeing to everything I had asked for, and I felt a sense of relief, as though someone had removed a burden from my back.

Within the hour I made arrangements for Milo to ride back to our landing point to inform our people what was going on and where we were going, and to carry my instructions to Lucius Genaro, my master-at-arms, to continue unloading the fleet. I also instructed Genaro to send our two best physicians—we had brought four with us—to tend King Pelles. Genaro should also split the White Squadron into double watches, rather than triple, for now, thanks to Cortix, I had no further fear of treachery. All of these instructions I based upon my own expectation that King Pelles might yet live, but even so, looking beyond the uncertainty of that, I saw strength in Cortix, in the stolid certainty and the certain hope he extended, within his being, to his people's welfare and continuing expectations of prosperity.

By the end of the hour, when I could think of nothing else that needed tending, and although my men were already mounted in their formations and waiting for me outside, I went to pay my formal respects again to King Pelles. I found him sleeping peacefully, and gazing down at him, seeing the livid discolorations of his skin, I wondered if he was aware that his would-be murderer was now in isolation in a tiny cell, chained and under constant scrutiny by guards whom I had personally charged with their duties. I did not yet know what the men of Corbenic would do with Baldwin, but I had ensured that no further harm would come to him while he was my prisoner.

I turned and walked away from the sleeping king, wondering if he would be alive when I returned with his mother and sisters, and when I walked out into the courtyard I wasted no time before taking my place and leading our strike force towards Baldwin's Land.

SEVEN

1

We were back within ten days, having taken two days to reach Baldwin's estate, where the women were being held, and three more to return with them in our train. Among the first things that I heard upon crossing back into Corbenic was that Pelles had been alive and his condition improving the day before. Even so, by the time we reached the villa, the change in his physical condition was startling, and he was far more alert than I had expected him to be. The lesions on his skin had faded noticeably and the sunken pockets beneath his eyes no longer held the degree of ghastly discoloration that had so upset me when I first saw him. He was still extremely weak, but he appeared to have lost none of his mental faculties, for he recognized me and greeted me with a tremulous smile, and he was touchingly glad to see his mother and sisters restored to him.

Our physicians, however, were guarded in their prognostications. Only the passage of time, they told me privately, would tell the real story of how much he would recover. Baldwin's report on his degenerating mental condition had been self-serving lies, but the king had been subjected to large amounts of poison for a long time, and none of them was willing to guess whether or not his mind might have been damaged by the abuses he had suffered.

In spite of all that, however, now that he was being tended by his mother and sisters and was eating only foods that had been carefully selected and prepared, Pelles improved daily.

Our raid on Baldwin's villa had unfolded perfectly. Thanks to Cortix's knowledge of the terrain and the excellence of Griffyd's scouts who ranged in front of us the entire way, we were able to penetrate Baldwin's supposedly formidable defenses and ride right to our target without being seen by anyone. Four times we were warned of danger by our Pendragon scouts, but on each occasion, thanks to their vigilance and skill, we were able to ride around the threats—three of them manned watch posts and the fourth a well-armed hunting party.

We had arrived in sight of the villa by mid-afternoon of the second day, riding downwards from a high ridge that we had crossed by following a deep fold in its crest. The upper slopes of the hillside fronting the ridge were thickly forested, and Cortix led us down through them, along a tapering arm of woodland that extended almost to the upper edge of the tailored vineyards that covered the hillsides below. We were all impressed with the richness of the carefully cultivated valley extending from right to left below our vantage point, and the villa itself was less than a mile from where we sat, so we decided to stay where we were until dusk and attack under gathering darkness, since there was no slightest chance that we could cross the vineyards in the afternoon light without being seen, and we wanted to avoid even the possibility of someone's escaping with word of our attack to the fort in the hills on the opposite side of the valley.

The villa was built around a central quadrangle, the main house forming two sides and a variety of outbuildings, some connected, others self-contained, making up the other two. A high stone wall, pierced by only two gates on opposite sides of the compound, surrounded the entire complex, evidently the relic of a time when there was greater need for defenses than anyone expected today. We struck at dusk, as planned, making our way slowly down between the rows of vines on foot, using the lush new growth, sparse as it still was, to conceal our movements and leading our horses by their halters until less than two hundred paces lay between us and the main gates. There were guards on duty, but very few, two flanking the main entrance, and two more by the corners of the outer walls. Griffyd came to me and waved a hand wordlessly, indicating that his men could deal with all of them quietly, and I nodded for him to proceed, then sent word for everyone else to remain where they were.

We heard no sounds and saw no movement, but within moments, it seemed, the guards went down, one after the other, in absolute silence. I waited for a count of ten, listening for any alarum, and then gave the signal to mount and ride. My first squadron, the Whites, went in through the main gates and directly into the central quadrangle, and they were there before anyone in the villa even knew they were being attacked. The Reds of the second squadron split into two groups and rode around the outer perimeter to enter by the far gate, and they, too, found no opposition.

Ironically, the greatest difficulty we had was with Catalina, Pelles's mother. She was an old woman, but she was no weakling, and she did not take kindly to being attacked in what she considered her own home. She seized a sword from one of her hapless guards and came at me, swinging the weapon up and plainly intending to split me in half from skull to crotch. Cortix may have saved my life by throwing himself between us, shouting her name. At the last possible moment she recognized him and stopped in confusion, lowering her arm.

Wasting no time, he informed her of what had happened in Corbenic and of her son's grave condition, and within moments she had turned all of her formidable energy towards making ready to return home, issuing orders to servitors and attendants, bidding them gather up her things immediately. I was content to leave it to Cortix to explain the urgency with which we had to leave and to tell her that she could bring nothing with her but the clothes she was wearing. No time for wagons or baggage, he told her, since we would be pursued by Baldwin's mercenaries as soon as word reached the fort up in the hills. Each woman would have to ride double with a man of our party. There would be wagons waiting for us in the safety of Corbenic, but between there and here we— meaning she and her daughters—had to move quickly.

Catalina made no demur once she had grasped the reality. But there were eight women here, she said, not three, and she would leave none of them behind.

Within an hour of attacking the place, we were back on the road. None of Baldwin's men had escaped in our initial attack, but only the guards on duty had been killed. The others had been captured in their barracks without bloodshed. My men stripped them of their weapons and held them until we left. We knew they would run at top speed to raise the alarum as soon as we were gone, but they would have to run uphill for an hour before they could deliver their tidings, so I estimated that we had twice that long to distance ourselves from whoever they sent after us.

The women proved to be resilient and uncomplaining for all the discomfort we caused them, riding silently and stoically behind, and sometimes in front of, my troopers and changing horses every half hour, when we stopped to rest our mounts. The first sign I had that we had crossed the border into Corbenic was when Cortix waved me down in a grassy clearing in the forest and swung his arm about his head, and within moments we were surrounded on all sides by his own horsemen. We were a mile inside Corbenic, he told me, and the women could now ride in comfort in the two wagons his people had brought for them. Anyone trying to pursue us beyond this point would have his men to deal with first.

I was anxious to return to the coast as soon as I had delivered Pelles's mother and sisters, but I could not do so without first taking leave of the king himself, and I had to wait until all the others had spent time with him, his mother and his sisters most of all, although Cortix, too, claimed precedence and spent a half hour in privacy with his monarch. By the time I was admitted to the regal bedchamber, I knew the king must be in good spirits and improved in health to be able to tolerate such a flow of visitors, and indeed he received me graciously when my time came, and quickly let me know that Cortix had made a good report about my men and me.

I observed him carefully as he spoke, looking and listening for I knew not what, but hoping all the time that his mind was clear, and he appeared and sounded perfectly lucid. He expressed his gratitude to Arthur, Merlyn and myself and told me he was looking forward to cementing our alliance, both by meeting his trading obligations and by attacking our mutual task here in Corbenic. He was still weak, he confessed, but he hoped that, in the meantime, I should begin my preliminary work by dealing with Cortix as though he were the king himself. Cortix and Milo, he said, would be the primary commanders of his new cavalry.

I took note of his eagerness, but also of his own ready admission of his physical weakness, and decided both were good omens for a full and swift return to mental health, and by the time I left him I was feeling better about him than I had in many days. Cortix wanted to return to the coast with me, but I told him that I needed to speak first and forthrightly with my senior commanders about everything that had happened, and his presence at that first gathering might be more of a hindrance and a detraction than a help. He understood, and pleasantly agreed to visit us the following day.

I found the grassy heights above the beaches transformed into a neatly ordered town of leather tents and fenced enclosures for our horses. The men Cortix had sent to assist ours had been more than willing to join in and help with the hard work, it turned out, and that surprised me, but Milo, who had been talking to some of his own people, explained that, intrigued by our people's goodwill and discipline, the Franks had watched closely as the preliminary tasks of unloading Connor's ships were carried out, and then they had volunteered to help cut, trim and transport the saplings for the fences that now edged our paddocks, and even to join in collecting the wagonloads of stones that our builders had just finished using to erect a simple bath house for the camp. It held a cold pool and a *sudarium,* or sweat tent, fueled by an outside furnace.

The Blues were glad to see us return and showed it with jeers and jibes that we had gone riding off on a venture and left them behind to do all the hard work. I dismissed my raiding party, setting them all at liberty for the remainder of the day, and then went to my command tent to meet with my officers. Connor and his fleet master, Angus the Bald, joined us there, as eager to hear my report as to deliver their own tidings of what they had achieved while I was gone. Everything was in even better condition, both with the fleet and with our arrangements on land, than I had expected—and my expectations had been high—and I was glad to be able to deliver them a full report on my own activities and the progress that I had made since leaving them. When the formal reporting was over, however, the real business of our gathering began.

We had two priorities to deal with, and the first of those was the trading portion of our expedition. I told Connor exactly what Cortix had said when he and I discussed the need for weapons and armor for the King of Scots, on our way back to Pelles's villa after the raid. Weaponry was available, he had told me, but no effort had yet been made to assemble it. That would change quickly now. There were a number of commercial smithies and manufactories within a few days' ride of Pelles's villa, all of them built up over hundreds of years to sell their products to the local Roman garrisons. Now that the last remnants of the Roman occupying forces were withdrawing from the region, the demand for their weapons and armor had all but disappeared, and many of the manufactories had shut down. The work force still lived there, however, working mainly now as farmers, blacksmiths and plowrights, and the forges and buildings were all still in good condition, some of them now being used for other purposes. Cortix believed that production could quickly resume once Connor's bona fides had been established. He had dispatched messengers to all these places, inviting their proprietors to gather here to meet with Connor, and had sent his assurances with me that the first of these meetings would take place within ten days.

As for Camulod's portion of the trade in recognition of our presence here in Corbenic, Cortix had delegated one of the other clan chiefs, the likable young warrior called Brad, to begin culling their herds for their finest stallions and broodmares, from which we would be able to take our pick, and yet another chief, Getorix, had undertaken to amass a cargo of wines, wheat and other grains, olives and various oils that were impossible to find in Britain, along with dried, durable cheeses and smoked spicy sausages of several kinds that were unknown in Camulod.

The quid pro quo, of course, was that we must now launch ourselves on the second of our priorities: establishing the training program we had devised before leaving Camulod. Everyone among my listeners knew the elements of what we planned to do, but having seen and evaluated the status quo here for themselves, there were more than a few of my men who wondered aloud whether we could have much success, given the military slackness and the native arrogance of the people we had come to teach.

Changing that attitude, I told them, would be my first task, and I would introduce them the next day to Cortix, who was to be King Pelles's new commander of cavalry. Cortix was the man, I assured them, who would work the magic on his Frankish warriors.

2

After meeting with my officers, from Lucius Genaro, the master-at-arms, to Junius Merkat, our youngest officer trainee, poor Cortix was as bewildered as any of his countrymen would be over how and where we would proceed.

In the year ahead of him he must choose and train his first intake of men, and among those would be his first officers, of incalculable value to the future army of Corbenic, so that the importance of choosing none but the very best was inestimable. His immediate task would now be to select the finest hundred of young warrior horsemen—his future cavalry—from among all the clansmen at his command. One hundred of our troopers would train his hundred, for as long as it took. Initially, each recruit would have to provide his own mounts—two per man—but once the breeding program began, they would be able to replace stock from their own herds. We would provide a Master of Horse for the undertaking.

In Camulod, basic training for recruits took three months, but with everyone new to the discipline and hampered by their own ideas of how wonderful they had always been as warriors, it might take longer, so I was setting aside four months to learn the basics. By the end of this year we would have my entire contingent here, five hundred troopers, plus officers and fifty Pendragon scouts. After that we would be able to train as many of his people at one time as wished to join.

Cortix had mentioned two abandoned forts on the coast that would be suitable to our needs. We would base ourselves at one of those and set up a system of signals to warn us of approaching ships.

Before Cortix left that day, I led him to my work table and opened the large box that sat on one end of it, and I began removing bound books by the handful and piling them up on the table. By the time I had finished, more than a score of books, many of them large and thick, were piled in front of him in two stacks. I slapped one hand on the topmost of one stack. "You're looking at your new army," I said, smiling at the incomprehension on his face.

"Explain" was all he said.

"What you see here is the distillation of more than sixty years of creating, out of almost nothing, what we will create here in Corbenic within the next three years. Even before the decision was made to send us here this spring, Merlyn Britannicus assembled a team of clerics in Camulod last year—a large team—and charged them with compiling these documents, and then he brought in every experienced person in the kingdom, from King Arthur himself right down to our master of the garrison kitchens, to describe everything that is involved in the maintenance of an entity such as Camulod. These books contain all of that lore, Cortix, laid out in the form of plans and instructions, advice and recommendations on every aspect of creating a functional cavalry force. There are books on the breeding and care of horses, on the requirements for military hygiene, on the feeding of large groups of men, from twenty to a thousand. There are books on the military laws of Camulod, on discipline and punishments for malcontents, transgressors and deserters, and on the requirements for promotion and the scale of rewards and recognition of outstanding performance and prowess in any field. There are plans for laying out a basic cavalry camp of the kind we use throughout Britain. There are instructions on everything from setting a guard watch schedule to inspecting outposts and policing barracks. There are standards and policies on the care and maintenance of saddlery, weaponry, armor and, of course, each man's own horse. There are even rules in here governing the conduct of officers towards each other and towards the men in their command. Nothing has been left out, and I show you these only to demonstrate to you that we will not be fumbling in the dark, hoping for divine inspiration in what we are attempting to achieve."

Cortix sniffed loudly. He opened the book I had been touching somewhere around its middle and began to read aloud. "Formations. The basic operating unit shall be a squadron, containing forty troopers under the command of a Squadron Commander. Each squadron will contain two squads, each of twenty men, commanded by a Squad Leader, and each squad will contain two patrols of ten men each, commanded by a Senior Trooper, distinguished by a white tuft on his helmet crest." He closed the book and laid it down where it had been before, then drummed his fingers on its thin wooden cover.

"So, when do we begin?"

"We've begun already. This was the beginning. Now I would like you to take me to look at the nearest fort. Is it far from here?"

"Eight miles north, perhaps ten. And the other one is five miles beyond that. Come, then."

"In a moment. We are not quite finished here. As soon as we've looked at the forts, I will come back here and begin making arrangements to move to whichever is more suitable, and you must return to Pelles and tell him what we have discussed. In the meantime, keep us informed on anything you hear about the weapons traders for Connor, and concentrate on finding your first hundred men. Will a month be long enough for that?"

"A month? Aye, it should be."

"Good, then make it three weeks, if that is possible. Now we can go. It's barely noon and the sun won't set until the ninth hour, so we have plenty of time."

"Wait." Cortix was frowning. "You haven't yet told me. Who will be my Master of Horse?

I smiled, but my response did not seem to put Cortix at all at ease. "I have someone in mind," I told him. "Whether it works out or not remains to be seen, but if it does, you will not be unhappy."

3

"Magister?"

"Come in, Lucius."

We were in the throes of breaking camp and Connor had just left me to return to his ship, since he would be staying here until the gathering of weapon makers that was to take place in three days' time. The Reds and the Blues had spent the previous four days cleaning up the nearer of the two abandoned forts, a mere six miles away from our present camp, working like common legionaries instead of elite cavalry troopers. They had spent the entire four days laboring under the stern gaze of our master-at-arms, Lucius Genaro, clearing away the refuse and detritus of twelve years of neglect, scrubbing and repairing stonework and woodwork, and generally making the place fit for habitation again. They had returned to camp the previous night, and I had given the order to prepare to move immediately to our new permanent quarters.

I had been expecting Lucius Genaro's call as soon as his men were ready to dismantle my command tent, but it was not Lucius who stepped into the tent. It was young Peter ap Fell, one of the two squad leaders of the Blue Squadron and commander of the guard for the day watch. He stopped inside the tent flaps, eyeing me warily and evidently unsure about what he was to say to me.

"What's wrong, Peter? Have the Danes appeared?"

"No, Magister. There's a man … Down in the paddocks … My men arrested him. Found him among the horses and took him for a spy, or a thief. But he's too old to be either one. He … he asked for you. Knew your name. Said we should bring you to him …"

I had felt a leaping sense of excitement as soon as ap Fell began to talk about the fellow they had arrested, and now I told young Rufus, who had been packing our precious books, that if Lucius Genaro should come while I was away, he was to ask the master-at-arms to come back again later, after I had returned. I turned then to the guard officer.

"Take me to him."

I followed him until we came in sight of the paddocks below us, between our camp and the cliffs, where I called out to him to halt and stood beside him, looking down to where a small group of his guards stood diffidently in front of an old man dressed in a military uniform from decades earlier.

"Peter," I said quietly, so only he would hear, "you're a good lad and you'll make a fine squadron commander one day, and I know this is your first time away from Britain, but you are going to have to learn to tell the difference between a thieving spy, a spying thief and an honorable veteran officer of Rome's former legions."

He looked at me with wide, troubled eyes, only now beginning to suspect that the error he had made might have been far greater than he had imagined.

"When Germanus of Auxerre was supreme legate of all Gaul," I continued in the same quiet voice, "commanding upwards of six hundred thousand men in a ten-year war against the Burgundians, that old man down there was his Master of Horse. Unsurprisingly, therefore, he has a great interest in horses. That man taught me to ride, to fight and to throw the lance. In fact he gave me the bamboo lances you so admire. Your men have arrested Tiberias Cato, my oldest living friend, teacher and mentor." I took great care not to look at him, but I knew his face was horror stricken and I was barely able to contain the grin that wanted to break out on my lips. "Come with me now, and let us try to make amends and greet him properly, as an honored guest, and ask for his forgiveness."

Even as I approached him from behind, I could see that the old man was standing in the way I knew so well, leaning forward slightly, one foot ahead of the other, his arms crossed on his chest and his chin stuck out defiantly, ignoring the people around him in favor of gazing at the horses ahead of him.

"Magister Cato," I shouted as I approached. "Welcome to our camp." I could see the disbelief and consternation on the faces of the guards surrounding him when they heard me call him by my own title, Magister, for they immediately began to imagine what their punishment might be for the insults they had offered him. Cato turned towards me, and for a moment I thought he might smile, but his self-control was as strong as ever and all I saw was the suggestion of a sparkle of pleasure in his eyes.

"Magister Clothar," he called back in response. "You have a few fine mounts here. And a herd of zealous guards."

I reached him in two strides and threw my arms about him, feeling him stiffen immediately in protest and then submit reluctantly to my embrace. The elation that overcame me sprang directly from seeing him as he had always been, ageless and bright eyed as ever. Now I pushed him away to arm's length, gripping him by the shoulders.

"Tell me, why would I be surprised that you'd come to see the horses first, before approaching me? By the living God, Magister, it is good to see you again."

Cato nodded, his face unyielding. "I am glad for you then, but I am old and thirsty and I have not eaten since last night. Will you keep me standing here all day, while these fellows threaten me? Or do you have a tent where we might sit and talk in comfort?"

I dismissed the guards, who marched away shamefaced, and led him to my tent, which was now the only one left standing. As soon as we arrived I sent Rufus scampering to the cooks in search of food and wine for our guest, knowing that both would be difficult to provide with the camp almost completely dismantled. As soon as the boy vanished through the tent flaps, Cato, disdaining small talk as he always had, waved a hand towards the tent walls.

"Where are you going?"

"Moving, Magister, to a Roman fort six miles from here."

"Magister, eh? Aye, well, as one Magister to another, you may call me Cato. I'll call you Clothar, as I always have."

I had to grin at that. "Not so, sir. You called me boy most of the time."

"Well, that was what you were, was it not? But that time is long gone. Now you are in command, but of what, and why? I thought you were in Britain, with the Pendragon fellow, Arthur."

"He's Riothamus now, High King of All Britain."

"Hmm, Riothamus … now there's an *alien* word. High King of All Britain, eh? And does he reign over all Britain?"

I shook my head. "No, not yet. But he will, someday."

Cato, however, had already dismissed that topic because he had seen my knight's sword hanging from its peg on my armor tree, and now he stepped closer to examine it. "Yours, I presume?"

"Aye," I said, "but I still have your spatha, the one Stephan Lorco won from me that day in school."

"The one you let him win, you mean. Did anyone ever find out what befell his father?"

"No, we never heard another word about him, where he went or how he died."

"Huh!" He unsheathed the sword and swung it tentatively, then held it up to examine its blade. "Tell me about this," he said.

"It's a cavalry sword, from Camulod, modeled after the King's own sword, Excalibur."

"Excalibur? You are full of grand names since you went away. But this is a fine weapon. Compared to this, yon old spatha of mine is a toothpick. Do all your soldiers own such swords?"

"Troopers," I said, standing beside him now. "We call them troopers, to set them apart from foot soldiers. No, they all have long-bladed weapons, similar to that, but that's a knight's sword.

There are fewer than two score of them at this time, one for each of Arthur's knights, designed to each man's size and strength."

He raised one eyebrow. "Another new word? Who and what are knights?" He slid the sword back into its sheath, then slowly lowered himself into a chair. He held the sword point down on the ground, leaning on it with both hands on the cross guard as he waited for me to reply.

"It's a term for the King's closest and most trusted commanders. Father Germanus wanted Merlyn, and through him Arthur, to form a new order, to the greater glory of God, but not even he knew what that order might be, what shape it might take. He told me that himself, and said that God would provide the answer when He saw fit. Well, it is now the Order of the Knights Companion to the King. Membership requires conscientious preparation and involves great trust, and the ceremony of bestowing knighthood is a solemn one, performed by the Riothamus alone. Each new knight swears a sacred oath to behave honorably and with dignity and strict obedience to the Riothamus, and in return he is granted a title, Seur, and a sword, made especially for him, to mark his membership in the order."

"So you are now Seur Clothar? Is that correct?" I nodded. "*Seur* Clothar? That's a common word. It's not a title."

"No, not over here in Gaul, I agree, but the word was unknown in Britain before we chose to use it, and we chose it for that very reason. Now it is known and recognized for what it means. It is a mark of high honor."

"So what are you doing over here again, with your outlandish troopers? Very few of them, too, I might add."

I told him in great detail, but mentioned nothing of what I was hoping for from him, and he listened closely. When I had finished he sat silent, chewing on his lips in a manner I remembered well.

"So, is Baldwin dead?"

"Not yet. He is being held under close guard until we gauge his sons' response to what has happened."

He jerked his head with a scornful grunt. "You'll get no response. I've been in Baldwin's Land and met his sons. The only decent one he ever had was the dead one, Marius Marco. The others are but whelps and they won't dare march against you. Your friend Milo is right. Their armies, strong as they might be, are infantry. No match for Frankish horse."

I asked him why he had come here.

"You sent word to me," he said, looking at me as though I were still a snot-nosed boy.

"Aye, sir, I did, but I did not expect you to come here in person, all this way. I thought you would send word back, and then I would have gone to you. Had I known you were coming to me instead, I would not have broken camp."

He gazed at me for a spell, his head tilted back, his lids slitted. "You were always a clever lad, young Clothar, clear thinking, ever inclined to take the shortest route to anywhere ... What do you want from me? And don't waste my time pretending that you don't want anything but the pleasure of seeing my frowning, wrinkled face. As I told you, I'm an old man now, which means I *have* no time to waste. So spit it out. What do you need?"

"Horses," I said. "Big horses, suitable for heavy cavalry. The local horses here are nowhere near as big as those we've brought from Camulod, and when we start training Pelles's men, they're going to be at a disadvantage over that."

"Big horses for heavy cavalry. That's what I was looking at when your guards came to arrest me. Saw them as soon as I rode in here. Couldn't believe it, nigh on two hundred of them. Biggest horses I've ever seen. Where did you find them?"

"We bred them in Camulod. The horse masters there have been breeding stock for more than sixty years. We have thousands of them, but we don't have enough ships to bring as many as we'll need."

"You breed these beasts in Britain? Hmm, I should go and see this Camulod of yours. It sounds interesting ... But of horses here in Gaul, you're right. They are not big enough for your purposes, not if those armored men of yours are to ride them. So how would you expect me to help you with that?"

We had come to the crux of my hopes. "I remember those Germanic forest horses you had. The big blacks with the flowing manes and tails and feathered feet. Do you still breed those?"

His eyes narrowed to slits again. "They are called Friesians and I do. What's in your mind?"

"To buy them from you."

He jerked straight upright in his seat as though I had shouted at him, but it was he who shouted. "*Buy* them from me?" He lowered his voice instantly, glancing towards the open flaps of the tent. "Do you think me a fool, Seur Clothar? You have not wealth enough to buy them. Those animals are beyond price."

I raised both hands in surrender. "I agree with you, they are, if they are still as magnificent as I remember them to be. But the price I had in mind was not one of coin or specie."

"What are you talking about, Magister?" He emphasized the title heavily, his voice oozing sarcasm.

"About a price you might be prepared to accept. But this is not the time or place to speak of it. How is the Bishop's School nowadays? Are you still happy there?"

He sank back in his chair and tucked in his chin, frowning up at me from beneath lowered brows. "No," he growled, "I'm not, not since Germanus died. I'll tell you straight, lad, you wouldn't recognize the place. Ludovic tries hard to keep it going, but Ludovic's the bishop in name only, as far as the school is concerned. He was Germanus's *secretary*, in God's name! How he ever let them talk him into taking up the bishop's post is beyond me. So there are fewer than half the students now than there were in your day, and none of them are interested in learning how to ride or fight, although I blame that on their tutors."

"Have the tutors changed that much?"

"Changed? They're all new. All the old ones either died or left after Germanus died. And what's there now is a mealymouthed collection of whining hypocrites that Germanus would not have let within the gates, let alone teach in the school …" He stopped, then continued more temperately. "But the truth is that times change, and tastes change with them. Every trace of interest in the military arts in the Bishop's School died with Germanus, rest his shade." He drew a great, deep breath. "So, when will the time and place be right to talk of this price of yours?"

"After you eat and drink something. That should be soon."

"I'm an old man. I don't need food, I seldom drink and I don't enjoy waiting. Tell me your price now, and I'll tell you why it's not good enough."

"You say it's not good enough without knowing what it is?"

"I told you you were a clever lad, didn't I?"

This was the old acerbic Cato I remembered from my youth, but I had no slightest fear of him now, and had had none since long before I left his tutelage. I merely smiled at him again and shrugged my shoulders. "Very well then, I will not insult you by offering it." I stood up and walked to the tent's entrance. "Where has that boy gone? Bread, cheese and wine should not be hard to find, even in chaos." As I opened the flaps I saw Lucius Genaro standing nearby, watching a group of men loading a cart but obviously waiting for me to summon him. He saw me in the doorway and half turned to me, but I held up a hand, mutely asking for his patience, and he nodded and turned away just as Rufus returned, carrying a heavy basket covered with a cloth. I waved the boy inside and told him to lay whatever he had out on the table, and then to go and see to his own belongings.

By the time young Rufus left again a short time later, Cato was standing by the table, looking down at what the cooks had provided.

"You really are a Magister," he said, picking up a round of soft, white cheese and tearing it in half before doing the same to a long loaf of crusty bread. "Smoked ham, roast fowl, smoked fish, cheese, olives, fresh bread, salt, oil and sweetened vinegar. And all in the middle of a breaking camp. I am impressed, but there's more here than I can eat."

"Or I," I said. "But we have the basket, so we can take the remnants with us. Still, I had hoped you might take it as an earnest of my price … had I offered it, I mean."

"What?" He had just taken a bite of bread smeared with soft cheese, and the word was muffled by the food.

I gestured towards the food-laden table. "It was to have been part of my price offer for your horses."

He swallowed with difficulty, the food only half chewed, then poured a cup half full of dark red wine, gulped a mouthful and swilled it around in his mouth before swallowing. Then he spoke slowly and clearly. "I think I might have misheard what you said."

"No, you heard correctly. I would have offered you food … and drink … in return for your Germanic horses, your Friesians. How many of them do you have now? You had something under a score when I left, I believe."

He shook his head slowly, but his voice remained calm. "No," he said quietly. "When you went away six years ago, I had twenty-eight, seven of them foaled that year. I have seventy-eight now—twelve of those new born, and three more still to be dropped, which will bring the total to four score and one. The finest horses in Gaul, and you would offer me *food* in exchange for them?"

"Aye, I would. Food, and drink. Plus a sound roof over your head … and an army of cavalry to create, train and equip, starting with nothing."

He stared at me for a count of five heartbeats and then landed hard in his chair, his cheese-smeared bread in one hand and his wine gripped tightly in the other, wordless for perhaps the first time in many years.

"I need you, Cato," I said. "And I don't care how old you are. Four times now you have told me you are an old man, and I can see you're not as young as you were when first we met. But there's no one else in all of Gaul who can do for me what I need to have done. I need a Master of Horse for an entirely new kind of army, the like of which has never been seen in Gaul. Heavy cavalry, trained to ride and fight together in tight formation, in perfect discipline. Heavy cavalry that could engage and beat the finest Rome could field in her days of power. That is my price for your blacks—a challenge for your skills: the chance to create a new phenomenon."

I stopped there, letting him digest what I had said, and for a long time he sat utterly motionless, his face vacant of all expression, his eyes staring into some distant place only his mind could see. But then he looked down absently at the bread and cheese he was still holding in his hand. He heaved a quick little sigh and bit into the food, and I watched him chew for a few moments longer, but I could not contain my own eagerness.

"What say you, Cato? Will you join us? There doesn't seem to be much holding you in Auxerre, from the little you have told me. Here you can have your own domain, even a house or villa of your own, for the asking, with all the room you'll ever need to breed your stock. Pelles will grant that happily."

"I will tell you one more time, Clothar," he said quietly, looking at me directly. "And this time I mean what I say. I am *truly* an old man, and I have begun to doubt myself in recent times. I *feel* old. Even if I were inclined to accept your offer, I would be afraid for you … for fear I might let you down by dying before the job is finished."

I rose and poured myself a half cup of wine, and held it up in salute to him. "I loathe this stuff," I said, "but I sometimes use it to signify a pledge. So I will pledge you this: you feel old because you feel useless, because you believe you serve no purpose nowadays. I would be willing to swear that you will lose that burden immediately. From the moment you decide to start feeling useful again, you will start feeling youthful again. Ludovic will make it easy for you to leave Auxerre. How can he do otherwise? He is the man who first thought of this venture of ours, so it will put him greatly at ease to know the most important part of equipping Pelles's new army is in your hands."

He sat staring at me for a while longer, and then he slowly began to smile, his eyes sparkling. "What use would I have for a villa at my age? I've lived in stables for so long, I have forgotten the feel of marble floors beneath my feet. But a solid stone house, with a fine kitchen and a cook … that might be tempting."

"Done. We'll build you one exactly to your wishes. There's a belt of rich grazing land a mile deep and more than ten miles wide behind the fort—perhaps much more, for I haven't seen all of it yet. You can pick your own site."

"I would need help."

"You can have anyone and anything you require, but if you tell me you have no able assistants at the school, I'll be disappointed."

"I have, and they are more than able. I trained them all myself, four of them. They know my ways."

"I'm sure they do. Bring them with you."

"I will, if they'll come."

"Do you doubt it? You think they'll choose to remain behind when you leave?" I drank down my wine, wincing at the sharpness of it, then offered him my hand. "Welcome, Magister Cato, welcome to the armies of Corbenic."

He did not move to take my hand. "That title, Magister, can there be two of them? I have grown used to it."

"Of course there can. I am Magister of the troopers of Camulod. You are Magister of Horse of Corbenic."

"Then I will shake your hand on that." He stood up and stretched his arms, as though awakening from a long sleep, and gripped my arm firmly, and it seemed to me I could see years falling away from him.

4

Cato's decision to join us was the catalyst that threw everything into motion, for from that moment on I had no time to be frustrated and no time to waste in waiting for anything.

He traveled with us to our new home that afternoon and spent an hour exploring on his own while I worked with Perceval and my other officers in making arrangements for quartering our men and storing the gear we had brought with us, and by the time I rejoined him again he was standing in the smithy of the fort, looking about him critically. Knowing what he was going to say, I told him we had brought all the tools we would need for the time being, and that we also had detailed plans for building additional forges and smithies, including the most recent form of bellows developed in Camulod. Supervising the expansion of what was here now would be among his first priorities, since the prime purpose of the smithies would be the care of our horses and gear. We would use local stonemasons to build whatever more he required and would purchase the tools and equipment for the new installations locally, while they were being built.

Then, knowing that stabling would be his main concern after that, I showed him how the existing stables in the fort—designed to hold no more than twenty horses at a time—could be expanded to accommodate twice that number by knocking out the end wall and annexing the empty building next door, which was larger and had been used for storage of some kind. That, too, would fall under his supervision, and I could see he approved, although he said nothing. The paddocks would be built close, and the new log rails were already being brought by wagon from our old camp site.

He left the next morning, with a full squadron and ten scouts as escort, promising to be back within the month, estimating that he would need six days to travel the two hundred miles to Auxerre and twenty to return with his herd and wagons. He would borrow the carts and wagon he needed for the journey from the Bishop's School, and would bring the teamsters with him, so that they could return at once with a much smaller escort for the empty wagons.

As I stood beside Perceval and watched Cato and his party leave, heading southwards shortly after dawn, Quintus Milo arrived in camp from the north with Cortix and all six of his fellow chiefs, accompanied by their escort parties. I dismissed the others in our party to resume their duties, and nodded to Perceval to come with me to greet the newcomers. Aware of their scrutiny, I was thinking as I walked of the deep and fundamental changes that would have to take place here if the plans that Pelles had for his people were to come to anything—enormous changes in the perception these people had of their own lands. They were going to have to abandon all their old ways of doing things and start thinking of Corbenic as a realm—a country with a king and a loyal people—rather than as home to a collection of tribes who placed their own clan interests ahead of all others. I had been wondering for months whether or not they would prove capable of making the leap to a new threshold.

I had never met the three oldest chiefs, although I had heard all their names. Chilperic, the eldest of all of them, was a dour-faced man from the southernmost parts of Pelles's kingdom. He ruled the Bear clan and he greeted me gravely and with courtesy, but made no effort to engage me in conversation. Next in age to him came Clodio, chief of the Raven clan, in whose territories we were now residing, and he, like Chilperic, nodded courteously but maintained his *dignitas* in silence. The last of the three, the leader of the Mistletoe clan, was called Ingund, and I estimated his age to be in the region of fifty, about halfway between Chilperic and the three younger chiefs, Brad, Getorix and Luthor, who ruled the Oak Leaf clan, the Wolf clan and the Aurochs clan, respectively, and were all much the same age, in their early thirties. Ingund was the one who greeted me and thanked me for our presence here and our assistance in what they hoped to achieve.

Cortix handled all the introductions, and when he had finished he looked at me with the hint of a smile. "Now tell these people what you told me, about how and why they must send their best men here, to live in a Roman fort."

I told them, as briefly as I could, touching upon all the major points that I had discussed days earlier with Cortix: the benefits of a centralized location as a base of operations, entailing keeping all the men, horses and equipment in the same place and the same state of readiness, prepared to move together at a moment's notice. I talked to them about the kind of discipline we needed to develop, and the exhaustive training that must be involved, and about reshaping the men they would send to us, breaking down their personal, individual pride and remolding it into pride of place and pride of belonging to an elite force.

These were men accustomed to responsibility and leadership, and they had all grown up together under the influence of Rome and its legions. But the kind of discipline I was describing was alien to them, because Rome itself had not known that strictness of discipline for hundreds of years, its armies grown corrupted and effete as the Empire itself grew ever weaker. They listened to me with stone faces, but they did not scoff, for they had seen our Camulodian discipline with their own eyes, and being pragmatists, they were prepared to take the risk entailed in giving me the opportunity to prove that I could do what I said I would.

I must have talked for half an hour, and then I spent another hour answering their questions until they had no more to ask, and when I had finished they left me, to return to their home territories and begin selecting recruits.

The day after that, the first of the weapons merchants arrived for their gathering with Connor, and within twenty-four hours there were nine more of them, all from towns within a day's ride of the coast, and several of them sharing two nearby towns as competitors. All of them had felt the pinch of the Roman withdrawals in the past decade and a half, and all were eager to discuss commerce. By the end of the first session with them, Connor and his people were happily haggling, and I felt free to turn my mind to other things.

The men of Red Squadron had already transported most of the fence posts and rails for the new paddocks and were laying out the enclosures less than two hundred paces from the fort, slightly downhill and closer to the tops of the cliffs. In the interim, pending the completion of the work, our herds were kept hobbled and secured in temporary horse lines at the back of the fort, watched over by a collection of boys from nearby farms and hamlets.

Blue Squadron had been assigned the duty of first finding suitable sites for warning beacons and watch posts along the coast from north to south of us, and then building them, and that project, too, was proceeding smoothly.

Inside the walls of the fort itself, the small crew of clerical staff who had sailed with us were busy setting up their operations, establishing the administrative center that would enable us to keep accurate and painstaking records of our activities here in Corbenic from the outset, and forced to work for the time being amid the noise and activity of a small army of local carpenters and stone-masons who were repairing everything that required repairs, as well as extending the smithy and the stables, building new stalls, constructing a bigger forge in the smithy and refurbishing the existing one, which had been in continuous use for more than a hundred years. I saw constant movement and industrious activity everywhere I looked, and for the first time in weeks I permitted myself to feel cautiously content.

The fort that I had selected as our headquarters was the larger of the two available choices, but it bore little resemblance to any of the forts I had seen in Britain, for it was enormous and ancient, built four hundred years earlier, according to Cortix, and enlarged and improved constantly since then by untold generations of occupying garrisons. It was a castle now, although it had begun its life as a simple marching fort during the Gallic wars of Julius Caesar, defended by a simple ditch and earthen walls and built to house a cohort of six hundred men. Now it would easily accommodate and feed upwards of a thousand men in comfort, and comprised a massive central tower of stone, three stories high, surrounded by a large array of buildings, many of them stone barracks blocks with solid, sturdy roofs. The entire fortification was enclosed by high siege walls, pierced by two main gates at front and rear. There was everything here, in the way of storage, work and living space, that we would need for the next five years, and if ever the need arose, we could expand into the other fort, five miles away.

I had chosen this location rather than the other because it had most recently been occupied by a small cavalry contingent in addi-tion to its regular garrison. Hence the existing smithy and stables. But other considerations, too, had swayed me. When the place had been abandoned in the Roman withdrawals some fifteen years earlier, the departing troops had taken most of the fittings and furnishings with them, but they had left many large items behind, probably because they left in haste and the largest and most cumbersome pieces had proven to be simply too much trouble to transport. Apparently the local Franks had had no interest in looting them, and so they had lain undisturbed ever since. There were massively heavy, magnificent wooden desks and tables in the praesidium, the former administrative center, a welcome and unexpected bonus for our immediate use. Thus, as it had been for hundreds of years, the entire ground floor of the central tower became once again the administrative headquarters of the fort, its inner walls lined with offices and cubicles surrounding the vast open space of the main clerical area. This place was the domain of Dynas, my quartermaster. In the arena of the praesidium, Dynas ruled supreme and I deferred to him.

The upper two floors of the tower contained the living quarters for staff officers and senior warrant officers, and despite having lain unused for more than a decade, they were as luxurious and well appointed as one might expect after hundreds of years of continuous occupation by fastidious imperial officers. I had chosen my own quarters and my own offices on the main floor, as had Perceval and the other officers, and as our command cadre grew, the place would take on a new life.

It had been some time since I had last seen or spoken with King Pelles, and it occurred to me now that I had eight days available to pay my respects to him before the new recruits began arriving, for I knew that once they did, I would be hard pressed to organize them properly before Cato returned from Auxerre with his stock and all his equipment. I knew that if I were to visit the king at all within the next few months, it would have to be now. And so I left Perceval in command and headed for Pelles's villa, where I found far more military readiness in evidence than had been visible the first time I arrived.

The two physicians I had sent to care for the king were still attending him, and I sent for them before seeking audience with Pelles. They told me that he was doing far better than expected. He was out of bed much of the time now and moving around, although he was not yet strong enough to walk far or quickly, and the ugly lesions on his face and hands had faded to mere shadows and would soon vanish completely. They assured me that he would improve more and more rapidly now, simply by being able to move around the villa and its grounds as the summer progressed, and that the benefits of fresh air and exercise would become increasingly obvious with the passage of time. Their major fear, they were happy to tell me, had been laid to rest, for it appeared that the king's mind had not been noticeably affected by his ordeal. By summer's end, they predicted, Pelles would be a different man—still physically weakened, but as intelligent, incisive and articulate as he had been before Baldwin's treachery.

The first thing I saw when I entered the king's receiving room was the sword I had brought him, hanging by its belt from the back of the regal chair in which he was sitting. He received me warmly and graciously, and there was no doubting the pleasure and gratitude in his greetings. He put me at my ease at once and offered me food and drink, which I refused politely, since I had eaten on horseback between our fort and the villa. He was as alert and inquisitive as I had been told, and had an endless supply of questions for me, all of which I was able to answer forthrightly and without having to stop and think, because the matters he addressed were precisely those with which I myself had been preoccupied.

We talked about the refurbishment of the new base fort, my relocation there with my forces and our ongoing preparations to receive the new recruits, and he told me that he had already informed the Council of Chiefs of his intention to take possession of both castles in the name of the realm, as I had suggested to Cortix, thus ensuring that our tenancy there was legal and could not be disputed at some later time. He asked me what he could do to assist with the work on the castle, and placed the entire resources of his people—their skills, crafts and trades—at our disposal, requiring only that I should inform him of my needs before moving to implement them, since his approval would be required before any of his people would respond to me. He also asked me for a complete description of what the clans were doing in the matter of recruitment, although I suspected at the time that he knew perfectly well what they were doing and was merely curious about my perception of what was happening. In return, I told him about my successful recruitment of Tiberias Cato and made much of the old man's background and capabilities, subtly making sure that Pelles knew beyond a doubt that he had acquired a valuable asset through my own good graces.

Suddenly he fixed me with a strange look and asked, "Have we met before?"

I felt my stomach flip queasily and I wondered if the physicians had been too eager in pronouncing him mentally sound. He must have seen something of what I was thinking in my face, because he grinned widely at me.

"Do not be concerned about my mind, but please do answer my question."

"I am not in the least concerned about your mind, my lord King. But no, I do not believe we ever met until the night I felled Baldwin."

He continued gazing at me for a while, then shook his head. "Strange," he said. "From the first time I set eyes on you, you have looked familiar. Surely we could have met or seen each other some time in the past?"

It was my turn to shake my head. "No, my lord, I think not. Unless you came to Auxerre while Father Germanus was the bishop there. I was a student in the school, with Quintus Milo."

"No, I never met Germanus and I have never been in Auxerre."

"Then we could not have met, my lord. I spent my boyhood in the distant southwest, in the kingdom of Benwick, by Lake Genava, and I never traveled north until I was ten years old. I remained in Auxerre for six years, and then Father Germanus sent me to Britain just before he died, on a mission to his old friend Merlyn Britannicus, and I have been there ever since, serving King Arthur."

"You are close to Arthur, are you not? Closer, I mean, than a mere servitor and senior officer."

"Aye, sir. I am fortunate to enjoy the King's friendship. He and I are close. He calls me Lance, because of my throwing skills."

"Lance. And what do you call him?"

I smiled. "I call him my lord King, when other people are around us, which is most of the time. But when we are alone I call him plain Arthur."

"Then you are just the man I need to speak to." He straightened in his chair and looked about him. "One of the excellent physicians that you sent me, either Alecius or Padraic, will be coming in at any moment now to tell me I must rest, and I have learned to heed them, so I will retire and sleep for an hour. But I am greatly curious about your king. He seems to be a paragon of sorts, but all that I know of him is what I have been told by others who have never met him. You would give me great pleasure, Seur Clothar, if you would consent to be my guest here tonight and to dine with me, alone, so that we can speak of him without fear of our words being repeated elsewhere."

He had barely finished speaking when the doors opened and the physician Padraic appeared, coughing apologetically as he reminded Pelles of the time. By my estimation it was no later than mid-afternoon, but the king immediately rose to his feet, bringing me to mine. "Will you oblige me?"

"Of course, my lord."

"Excellent. Go you then directly to Pierre, my steward, and inform him that you are to be my guest. He will provide you with rooms for your use and see to any requirements you might have. And I will see you later. Until then, my house is at your disposal."

5

Being a guest of the king in Corbenic was considerably more comfortable and luxurious than being even a preferred guest of the king in Camulod, simply because of the wealth, antiquity and continuity of Roman Gaul. Pierre the steward ushered me to a suite of marble-walled, sumptuously furnished rooms that contained, of all things, a private bathing suite with a small, deep, cold pool, a warmer *tepidarium* or hot pool, and a leather-curtained steam room serviced by an external furnace. By the time I emerged from there, feeling cleaner than I had been in months, a masseur was waiting for me and led me to a folding wooden plinth that had been concealed upright behind a door. I lay on it with a sigh of deep contentment and for the next half hour submitted myself to a merciless but wonderful pummeling the like of which I had seldom experienced.

Then, swathed in an enormous towel, I entered my sleeping chamber to discover that my armor and clothing had all disappeared and had been replaced by the richest garments I had ever worn. I dressed myself in silk, fine linen and brocade, and then sat by the open window, reading and thinking, mainly about what I could tell Pelles concerning Arthur, Riothamus. I was still sitting there when two of Pierre's staff returned my armor and clothing, the former burnished to perfection and the latter freshly cleaned and pressed, and I had dozed off in my chair by the time Pierre himself arrived to tell me that the king awaited me.

I found him in fine fettle, rejuvenated by his afternoon sleep, and we enjoyed a magnificent meal together, just the two of us, attended by something in the region of half a dozen servants. We spoke little while we ate, too intent upon the excellence of the food for anything else, but as soon as the remnants of our meal had been cleared away, Pelles called for a flagon of some kind of wine that he identified by name, and dismissed all his attendants.

Alone with him, and waiting for him to speak, I picked up the wine, which had been served in heavy, clear glass cups, and sipped at it cautiously, expecting the usual acrid bitterness, but to my astonishment, the beverage was rich and sweet, smelling of ripe pears and dried grapes and delicious on the tongue. I held it up and looked at it in the glass cup, noticing that it was almost yellow in color, and Pelles launched into a paean of praise for it, telling me it came from the hillside slopes above one of the rivers in lower

Germania, and that he had it imported by the barrel for his personal use, and from there our conversation slipped into a discussion of the difficulties of bringing wine to Camulod, since none was grown in Britain and until now we had had no regular commerce with any region of Gaul.

That quickly led to Arthur himself, and for the next few hours I underwent a pleasant inquisition about everything that could be told, guessed at or anticipated with regard to Arthur and his status as Riothamus. There was no hardship involved for me in speaking of Arthur. It had been more than a month by then since I had last seen him, and I found myself growing nostalgic and more than a little homesick for Camulod as I talked. I described my fellow knights and the order to which we now belonged, and then I went back and described the origins of the colony that had become Camulod. I then progressed to Arthur's quest, as he himself termed it, to unite all the tribes of Britain under one ruler for the first time in history, and for a time we discussed the sheer magnitude of that task and the odds against his ever being able to unify the huge diversity of the chiefs and their chieftains, the petty kings and their satraps, and the warlords who claimed no kingship other than their dominion over the lands they occupied—and those, of course, I pointed out to Pelles, were only the Britons involved. Beyond those lay the invading Outlanders who occupied the undefined sprawl of territories known as the Saxon Shores. We had no means of gauging their numbers or their holdings at this stage, but we knew that for all intents and purposes, the entire eastern half of Britain was now occupied by aliens including Danes, Saxons, Jutes, Anglians and the sullen, flaxen-haired madmen who called themselves Northmen and sought no other fate than to die gloriously in battle.

Pelles interrupted me occasionally to pose a question, but he was otherwise content to simply learn all that he could about his new ally. Eventually, however, after the fire in the hearth had burned down and been replenished several times, I had told him everything I knew, and we both fell silent, sharing the warmth and comfort of the fire in the gathering gloom of the approaching night.

It was he who broke the silence, simply being courteous in asking me if I had anything I might like to ask him, since I had been doing all the talking to this point, answering his questions, and from that point onward our conversation altered my entire world, much to its eventual betterment.

I began by asking him about the clan system in Corbenic, and he surprised me by telling me that it was relatively new, adopted only after his own ancestors moved into these territories from north of the Rhine, less than a hundred years before. Independent and rebellious, migrating in defiance of imperial laws, they had refused to conform to the rigid and corrupt Roman social system they had found in place and had reverted to their ancient customs, forming their own localized governments. Each of the seven major tribal groups who had settled this region, formerly known as Belgica, had reinstated its own ancient clan emblems, and the seven clans of Corbenic had come into existence. The traditional inhabitants of the territories, the Belgae, were still to be found throughout the region, but they had adapted quickly to the Frankish ways once they saw that Rome had neither the time nor the inclination to try to stem the Frankish infiltration from the north, and they had caused no trouble since then. The nearest major town was the former Roman administrative center of Brugis, and it still governed itself as a Roman *civitas,* or city state, with its own council, mayor and city officers, and although the city lay squarely within his kingdom, Pelles had opted, for reasons of his own, to leave its inhabitants to live as they wished, providing they accepted his dominion outside their walls, permitted his people to trade in their markets, and otherwise made no attempt to interfere with Corbenic's affairs.

His mention of Corbenic's affairs prompted me to ask him if he had heard any further word on the activities of the Outlander called Attila, the one who styled himself King of the Huns. I myself had heard nothing of these Huns since landing in Gaul, other than the arrant collection of nonsense that Quintus Milo had spewed out when I asked him what he knew of them, and in truth I had thought little of them since then, having too many other items of urgent interest to concern me.

King Pelles gazed at me with narrowed eyes and nodded his head slowly, then turned away and busied himself in gathering a few small logs and adding them to the fire on his own—something that his servitors would have been horrified to see him do. He was thinking so deeply, however, that I doubted he was even aware of what he had done, and he returned to his seat, leaning heavily on the arm of his chair for support. He told me then that he had, in fact, heard tidings of the Huns, and that he was afraid to permit himself to dwell too deeply upon what he had heard. Here on the northwest coast of Gaul, he said, they were fortunate indeed to be isolated and out of the way of greater things.

"We might gull ourselves into believing that the things we do in our small region are of great import," he said, "but in the grand unfolding of the world at large, our lives and petty problems are insignificant and obscured by distance and direction, tucked out of sight, for the time being, in a quiet backwater that offers no one anything worth stealing. And for that," he added, "we should be thanking God."

Elsewhere in Gaul, he said, according to a report he had received only very recently, chaos and pandemonium were being loosed upon the populace in the east and in the lands to the south, as the countless hordes of Attila's Huns came pouring down from the lands beyond the Rhine and the Danube, sweeping southwards through eastern Gaul and towards the southern territories of the Visigoths, a vast tract of land ruled now by King Theodoric, the son of the great warrior Alaric, whose forces had been the first to sack Rome. Theodoric, now a Christian king and an ally of Rome, ruled all the lands stretching south from the great Liger River, now being called the Loire, to the northern part of Iberia, and his holdings, allied with his reputation, had attracted the malevolent attention of the Hunnish king, who had sworn to crush Theodoric first and then to turn his fury against the last feeble remnants of the Roman Empire. Unfortunately, the report Pelles had received came to him at third or fourth remove, and he had no knowledge of how new or old its content was, nor of how accurate or exaggerated it might be.

When I asked him where these Huns had come from in the first place, and how long they had been in Gaul, he could only shrug. But then he remembered someone—one of the bishops who criss-crossed his kingdom regularly—telling him that long before Attila had decided to invade Gaul, he had fought a long war in the eastern Empire, but had dispatched an exploratory army into Gaul to recon-noiter the terrain and form some kind of understanding of the lie of the land. I immediately remembered the strange invading army Perceval and I had encountered when we first met, an enormous force that we had assumed to be Burgundian and had gone to great lengths to avoid … the same army that had swallowed up and oblit-erated every trace of Duke Phillipus Lorco and his men. Now, think-ing back on those events, I found my skin crawling with the knowledge that I might have actually encountered that first exploratory Hunnish expedition.

I attempted to press Pelles further, hoping to learn more, but he really had nothing to add. And so I was left, not for the first time, wondering vainly whether there was anything at all to these rumors and whisperings.

"Do you truly think, my lord," I asked, "that we would ever have trouble with these Huns here in Corbenic?"

"I doubt we would." The king watched the dwindling fire for a while, clearly considering his next words. "If the Huns do come to Corbenic, I do not believe they will come in overwhelming strength, and I am hopeful that by the time they did appear on the horizon, whenever that might be, we might have a homegrown force here in Corbenic that could meet them and discourage them."

My first thought upon hearing that was that if the numbers being rumored were anywhere close to being accurate, then the Huns could swallow Corbenic whole, without the slightest discom-fort, but there was little point in saying that aloud. I was enjoying the intimacy of the conversation I was sharing with the king far too much to risk depressing him by describing potential disasters. Encouraged by his openness and informality, I changed the subject of our talk then, putting the Huns and their threat behind us, and asked him if he was familiar with a kingdom called Ganis. He gave me a half smile and scratched his chin gently with one finger.

"Ganis," he said eventually. "Of course I know Ganis—or I used to, years ago. How do *you* know of it?"

"I was born there," I said, "but I have no memories of the place. In fact I know nothing about it now ... not even where it is. But it must be close to here, and I would like to visit it someday, when we have this training program well under way."

His face still bore the same inscrutable expression as he asked, "Why on earth would you wish to visit Ganis? It has changed much in recent years, and by your own admission you have no memories of it. Have you a reason in mind?"

"Aye, a good one."

"And may I ask what it is?"

It occurred to me only at that moment that I knew nothing of Pelles's background and, for all I knew, he might be on friendly terms with Ganis and its king, and so I answered his question with one of my own.

"There was a king there once, by the name of Clodas. Do you know the name, my lord?"

"Clodas? Clodas of Ganis?" He sat up straight and leaned forward in his chair, all signs of pleasure gone from his face. "That name is never spoken here, Seur Clothar. What business could you have with Clodas of Ganis?"

Unable to decide whether or not I had placed myself on dangerous ground, I decided to be circumspect, risking his displeasure.

"Purely a personal interest, Lord Pelles," I said, reverting to formality. "It has nothing at all to do with my mission here to you in Corbenic."

"Let me be the judge of that, if it please you, and I will ask you again, what business could you have with Clodas of Ganis?"

"Vengeance," I said, and watched an entire range of surprised reactions flit across his features. "He killed my father and usurped his throne. He killed my mother, too, and my grandfather, King Garth of Ganis."

The color drained from the king's cheeks as I watched, and he rose to his feet and walked slowly to the side of the fire, where he leaned against the stone pillar and looked back at me. His next words shocked me to my soul.

"By the living Christus! I *knew* you looked familiar, but I was not looking back far enough. You are Childebertus's *son*! I never knew your name, but I knew you had been born. I thought you dead, murdered at the same time as your parents."

Chillbirtoos! Hearing my father's name spring so easily to his lips confounded me, so that it took me long moments to find my tongue again. "You knew my father?"

"Knew him? Of course I knew him, he was husband to my aunt Elaine, your mother ... although she was not truly my aunt, more of a cousin of some kind. I met your father several times, and worshipped him as a hero. I must have been five years old, the last time I saw him, and he was killed soon after that, but I remember him so well that seeing you now, and recognizing you, is like seeing a ghost. You are his living image."

"But—" It was hopeless, trying to find words to meet this situation sensibly. I stammered and spluttered, and finally managed to say, "My mother was your *aunt*?"

"Aye, she was, and your grandfather, King Garth, was my grandfather, too ... my great-grandsire, in truth." He saw the question in my eyes and answered it before I could ask. "Garth was first married when he was a youth, barely seventeen, long before he was a king. It was a tragic affair. He wed for love, against his father's wishes, and his young wife died in childbirth within the year. The child survived. Her name was Gertrude and she grew up to marry Thorbec, who was the second king of Corbenic. My father, Plotius, was their son, which made King Garth of Ganis my great-grandsire. I was not yet six when he was murdered, and before my own father could exact vengeance, he too was killed ..."

"Where is Clodas now?"

"In Hades, these ten years and more. I had to wait until I was sixteen before I could command action against him, and even then

I would have been hamstrung had not Baldwin come to my support. He lent me an army and fought beside me and I sent that black-hearted devil down into death knowing who had killed him. He hadn't known I was alive until then and thought he was secure on his stolen throne."

I found myself pacing the floor, with no recollection of having risen to my feet, my mind a seething storm of contradictory emotions. All these years spent dreaming of vengeance, and the usurper had been dead through most of them. A sudden, clear thought struck me and I stopped in mid-stride.

"Who rules in Ganis now, then?"

Still leaning against the pillar of the fireplace, Pelles crossed his arms upon his chest and smiled at me, a tight-lipped little smile. "I do. *This* is Ganis, where we stand right now. Or more accurately, Ganis is now a part of Corbenic, its most easterly province. It has not been known as Ganis since I cleaned out Clodas. The people welcomed me, for they had hated and feared Clodas, who acted as the usurping thief he ever was, and when I arrived in Ganis and cut him down they made it clear they wished me to be their king. They saw it as my right, but in truth it was not. I was great-grandson to King Garth, but through the female side. And so, since I could not be legal king of Ganis, other than by conquest—which I had already achieved—they chose to align themselves with me as King of Corbenic, and they changed the name of their domain. But I am looking at the rightful King of Ganis now. Is that not so, Cousin?"

"What? Me, King of Ganis? No, by the Christ, not I! You are their king, by their acclaim, Pelles, and they have no need of me, a stranger to them in every way. Besides, I have no wish to be a king. I have a king of my own to whom I owe my entire allegiance, by my own free choice. I have no wish to change that."

"You may yet change your mind," Pelles said quietly, "once you have seen the place. It is a beautiful country, small, but lovely. You could be seduced."

I was watching him closely, trying to read what lay behind his narrowed eyes, and feeling strangely buoyant, as though some great weight had been lifted off my shoulders, but I judged that, ambivalent as he might be, he might stand prepared to cede Ganis to me were I to insist. I was its lawful king, by right of birth. But even as that thought came to me, it was accompanied by the certainty that I really had no wish to press my claim.

"So you and I are cousins," I said, searching for a way to make my wishes clear.

Pelles nodded, slowly. "Cousins of some kind. Close kin. So where does that leave us now?"

"Believing that I might be seduced, apparently. That was the last opinion you expressed." Now I found it easy to smile, for I had found my words. "Had you ever spent one single day in Camulod, Pelles, or one single hour in King Arthur Pendragon's company, you would know why I could never be seduced away from being who I have become … not by a kingdom, and not by a people. I am now Clothar of Camulod, legate commander and Knight Companion to the High King of All Britain. That sounds very grand, and it is. But I enjoy being that man. And I could not be better suited to being he. My duties are clear, my tasks and my responsibilities are all that I could wish for or require, and I am now profoundly content to know, in addition to all that, that I have found a cousin of whose existence I knew nothing, and with whom I share much in common.

"Clodas is dead, at your hand, and for years I have been feeling guilty, thinking he yet lived. That guilt is gone now, finished and over with, absolved by your actions."

I waited for him to respond, but he said nothing.

"I have been here in your domain of Corbenic now for what, a month, perhaps longer? I have not been idle, Cousin, and I have not been blind to how things really are here. You are an able king, abler than I could ever be or wish to be, and you have the respect and admiration, even the love, of those you rule. I saw that plainly on the night I struck down Baldwin. So let it be, Pelles. And accept what I am telling you, for I have no need to lie. I have no desire to change or influence anything in your domain, least of all in this matter of claims to kingship. You and I are the only people who know, or even suspect, my true lineage. Let us make a pact, then, you and I, between the two of us alone, to keep it that way. We can be cousins openly, without specifying how, and we can be friends because of who and what we are, sharing the knowledge that is ours alone. But worth far more than all of that, we can be allies in mutual trust and kinship, working together for the good of everyone associated with our union, ourselves included. I will build and train for you an army that will make your kingdom safe against invasion from this day on, and you will provide a solid, secure trading base for me, for my King, Arthur, and for Camulod, here on the mainland of Gaul. And we will say no more—either of us, ever—about this nonsense of my claim to Ganis. What say you?"

Pelles stepped away from the fireplace and picked up my empty glass cup. He carried it to the table and refilled it along with his own, then brought it back, and as I took it from his hand, he tipped his own cup sideways, deliberately spilling some of the contents onto the floor in the ancient libation to the pagan gods, then stood there, evidently waiting for me to do the same. I did, and he lifted his cup and drank from it before moving back to the fireplace.

"You *are* a king, by birthright," he said. "But you have never *been* a king …" He paused and I waited again. "There are … difficulties … attached to kingship. Difficulties that ordinary men may never experience." He sipped at his cup delicately and sucked the wine between his teeth. "No man who is a king may ever fully trust another man—"

He stopped abruptly, evidently considering what he had just said. "No, that is not correct … not accurate … He may trust another man completely, yet be betrayed in simply doing so, as I was in my trust of Baldwin. That is human folly at its most vulnerable. But how can a man live a sane and healthy life without ever fully trusting anyone? Ambition is the most invidious of traits, almost impossible to see if a man chooses to conceal it, and it is the undoing of trust. One man's ambition will turn another's trust to folly, and a king can seldom trust another strong man to be without ambition to succeed him or replace him." He looked me directly in the eye. "I believe you when you say you have no wish to rule here in Gaul. I believe you even though experience has taught me that the finest-seeming wishes of another can lead to poisoning and to attempted murder.

"Baldwin was the one man in all the world, I would have sworn, who bore me no ill will … and yet he tried to kill me. Who can say why? Had he succeeded, he could not have claimed my kingdom. The chiefs would never have tolerated that. Looking back at the situation now, it becomes clear—or it appears to be clear—that he thought somehow to control my nephew, who is a foolish, empty-headed boy without sufficient sense to keep from fouling his own clothing but is, none the less, my heir. Perhaps Baldwin thought he could dominate him completely, marry him off to some ambitious wench and somehow grasp the throne of Corbenic through him for his heirs, if not for himself. I can not claim to understand his thinking, but it must have involved some such scheme … I have kept him alive, even if he should be long dead according to my best advisers. He is alive because I need him alive, at least until I find out what his sons intend to do … and for the time being, it suits me to keep him breathing, perhaps only for the pleasure of looking at him and reminding myself never to trust another man as closely as I trusted him." He fell silent then, and stood looking at me.

I cleared my throat before responding.

"I see … at least, I think I understand … You are saying that, regretfully, you cannot trust me?"

"No, not at all, Cousin. I am saying that, despite all lessons to the contrary, I am not yet prepared to go through life distrusting everyone. We two are kin, and I believe you when you say your whole concern is Camulod today, and that you have no wish, or any need, to live in Gaul for longer than your present task will take. And so I accept your offer of mutual alliance and support, and give you this commitment. It shall be as you describe, and my home here will be your own henceforth, whenever you wish to use it. I will instruct Pierre on that, and the rooms you are using today will be set aside for your use alone in future. Now stand up and embrace me, Cousin

Clothar, and then let's both to our beds. This night has flown by and the dawn will come early, and we have much to arrange when it does."

I lay awake for a long time before sleep came to me.

EIGHT

1

The weeks that followed my visit to Pelles were chaotic but productive, and our new home fortress—Pelles had told me that the Romans called it the Capitol, because of its placement atop the cliffs—rapidly took on an air of crisp, military efficiency as our troopers grew accustomed to their new quarters and to the routines we were adapting to fit every conceivable eventuality. The barracks buildings within the castle walls had been allocated from the day we arrived, so that every trooper had a personal billet, bunk, equipment tree and foot locker where he could store his gear, and the former garrison baths were back to full working condition, fed and serviced by furnaces and hypocausts that provided heated water throughout the day and night. The original smithy was operating fully, the first of what would be several new ones was well advanced in construction, and our carpenters were finishing the new stalls in the extended stables.

Beyond the walls, the enormous horse paddocks were already complete, designed to hold more than six times as many horses as were currently lodged there, and the rectangular drill square in front of the main gates had been reclaimed from the grass that had encroached upon it in the previous ten years and had been made more than twice as large, to accommodate cavalry instead of infantry. Now, morning and evening, in addition to the scheduled chores of the day, our troopers were revisiting the familiar discipline of drills and practices that had ruled their lives in Camulod.

The meeting between Connor's people and the weaponry suppliers had been a great success, and although the first of the newly ordered weapons had not yet arrived, several supplies of stockpiled spears, swords, daggers, axes and armor were already in transit, and work had begun in several surrounding towns and villages to manufacture more. In addition to that, my master-at-arms, Lucius Genaro, had contracted with three smiths in the regional capital of Brugis to purchase as much ring-mail armor and leggings, manufactured to our own specifications from samples provided by us, as they could produce, beginning immediately, and with the understanding that they and their workers would take up permanent residency in our fort as soon as family quarters and smithies could be prepared for them. Once here, they would work full-time making armor for the new army of Corbenic, in return for safe housing and full support for themselves, their families and their skilled workers.

The first contingent of Corbenican recruits arrived on the appointed day, and it fell to me to welcome them and try to give them some idea of what would be expected of them. Most of them were young and eager, but there were many who were veteran warriors, no less eager but far more inclined to be set in their ways.

Corbenic had no army tradition because it had never been Roman. Its men were independent Frankish warriors, with all the virtues of warriors but absolutely no tradition of disciplined soldiering. When Corbenic took up arms and mobilized its men, they rode as individual members of a host, and they prized individual valor and prowess above all else. We had to change all that, and we had to do it with an entire intake of men who regarded us with at least some disdain as Outlanders who did not even speak their tongue. Somehow, with the assistance of our own troopers and the grace of God, we had to make them accept and admire us before we could shape them into an elite and self-sustaining fraternity that would take pride in itself and its ability to shape others of its ilk in its own image.

Perceval and I had decided that he would function as primary commander of the Corbenican trainees, handling all of the day-today matters of discipline and training and thereby leaving me to maintain my *dignitas* as our King's envoy and as overall legate in command of our entire operations.

When the appointed day came and they all arrived to join us, we marshaled them on the parade ground outside the gates, and I talked to them, describing in detail the life-altering changes they were about to undergo, the rigorous, four-month basic-training program that lay ahead of them, and the support they would receive from our own troopers, all of whom had undergone the same programs in qualifying for their present posts.

That done, I spread them around the perimeter of the parade ground to watch as two of our three squadrons, the Blues and the Whites, equipped with oval shields and twelve-foot-long ash-shafted lances modeled on the Roman contus spear, offered them a long demonstration of intricate close-formation drill, winning more than a few murmurs of amazement in response to the complex maneuvers they carried out in complete silence and apparently without effort, the only noise being the creaking and jingling of harness and the thumping of heavy hooves. When the two squadrons brought their demonstration to a close with a full frontal attack on the reviewing stand where I stood with my senior officers, the onlookers broke into spontaneous cheers, as well they might, for the spectacle of a solid wall of mounted men, twenty riders wide and four ranks deep, thundering towards us to slide from a gallop to a full halt less than ten paces from us made even my own heart speed up.

Within the space of ten days, the general chaos of the first few days of awkward hesitancy had largely disappeared and the recruits were showing the first signs of beginning to understand the basic drills.

During that time Cato also returned from Auxerre with his train of wagons and his magnificent herd of glossy black horses, augmented by several splendid stallions and broodmares of differing breeds. He immediately set about devising a master breeding plan that would permit him to develop the best elements of cross-bred stock.

We put our coast-watch system into effect soon after that. It was complex, but not cumbersome, and it would be strengthened as time passed, but initially it comprised a line of beacons tended by teams of old men and young boys supplied by Clodio's local Raven clan. The watch points stretched between the farthest ends of the coastline of Corbenic, thirty miles to the north and twenty-two miles to the south. Every fifth beacon was a fixed relay point from which distances were counted. As soon as enemy craft were sighted, the watch point that had seen it would light a single beacon, and each relay point beyond that, towards the castle, would light one more beacon than it had spotted. That meant that a final count of four beacons at the castle indicated an enemy force sighted between twenty and twenty-five miles north or south, depending on the direction of the beacon fires; a single beacon meant a sighting within five miles of the castle. We hoped it would work efficiently, and young Junius Merkat, who had been charged with responsibility for the lines' maintenance, had spent several days instructing the volunteer watch crews in their duties.

In the middle of the second week in August, the Frankish goddess of fortune granted us an opportunity to put all our planning and hard work to the test. On a golden summer's afternoon, a guard on the top of our walls saw the first smoke spring up from the nearest northward watch beacon and raised the alarum immediately. By sheer chance, I was directly below him at the time, crossing the main castle yard, and I hurried to the top of the wall, where I found him pointing to the hill in the distance. Sure enough, there was no mistaking the signal, two distinct fires burning apart from each other and belching pitch-fed oily smoke into the clear air.

Two fires meant that the sighting had come from between the ten-mile and the fifteen-mile watch posts. I went to the edge of the parapet and called down to the guard commander to sound the general assembly, and our entire force, now five squadrons strong, was gathered and ready to ride out well within the quarter of an hour allotted for the delivery of the second set of signals, which would indicate how many vessels were in the attacking force.

This second signal set was numeric: one fire denoted three vessels or fewer, two indicated four to six, three meant seven but no more than ten, four fires meant more than eleven ships, and five meant an invasion fleet of more than twenty vessels. Since each attacking ship was crewed by any number from thirty to fifty men, ten vessels could land three hundred to five hundred fighting men, and any number greater than ten raised the possibility of an all-out invasion. On this occasion, two fires were lit in the second set of signals, telling us that we would be facing a group of four to six ships, carrying anywhere from a hundred and twenty to three hundred men.

In theory, those numbers suggested that we could be outnumbered three to one, but the reality was far different. The enemy would land in single boatloads and they were raiders, undisciplined and without horses, intent upon striking inland as quickly as they could travel, to attack some hamlets, farms or small towns and carry their booty back to the beaches without waste of time and without having to fight for their plunder. Our strongest advantage would lie in reaching their attack point on the coast before they could fully disembark, for then we could take them while they were most vulnerable.

Perceval, in his Ursus persona, was determined to ride with me on this outing, and so we left Lucius Genaro in charge of the castle with two squadrons, the Reds, who had the duty that day, and the newly formed Golds, and we struck out to the north with White, Blue and Pied Squadrons, the last of those newly formed with the Golds and its recognition standard a maxilla, or banner, divided into four opposed quarters of black and white. All five squadrons now comprised veterans and recruits together, and with two of their three months of training now completed, the recruits were ready to be tested in precisely the kind of situation this promised to be. We could cover five to six miles in an hour, riding in tight formation, so I estimated that we had two hours to go before we reached our contact point, and I had much to occupy my thoughts in that time.

I called Cortix and Quintus to ride with Perceval and me, and questioned them both on their knowledge of what we might expect ahead of us: the shape and configuration of the coastline, and the proximity of towns and villages to the area being threatened. My only certainty was that the search area for which we were headed extended for five miles northward of the ten-mile relay post. The enemy had been seen from somewhere within that stretch of coastline, but they might continue to travel north or south from where they had first been seen until they found a suitable landing point, since they were unlikely to attempt to land at the base of beetling cliffs that would have to be scaled going and returning.

Quintus was from the south and knew very little of the territories to the north of where we were, but Cortix was intimately familiar with our target area. The cliffs receded there, he told us, and fell down to the level of the sea. There was a fishing hamlet just beyond the eleven-mile watch post, and from there a road ran inland to the small market town of Lugubria, a focal point for the surrounding area and one that had been raided several times in the past, although not for at least five years. That made the town, in Cortix's estimation, a tempting target for the incoming raiders, especially if anyone among their number had been there on previous raids. His logic appeared sound, and so we began planning our attack immediately, predicating it upon the existing road and the high probability that the raiders would use it.

We had two possibilities to consider, the first being that we might reach the coast before the enemy had had time to land. If fortune remained with us, and we were in time to be there when they landed, we would hit them as they left the beach and before they began to move inland. The second possibility was that the enemy might already be coming ashore and we would be too late to stop them at the beach. In that case, we would need to strike inland to intercept them along the road, and for that to work in our favor we would need a suitable point for an ambush, and reliable information on the enemy's exact whereabouts. I called to Griffyd and had him send six of his most reliable men to ride ahead of us along the coast, taking extra mounts with them for speed, to locate the original sighting and find out where the enemy was now, then send word back to us. We ourselves would follow the coastline, keeping out of sight from the sea, and be ready to move towards the shore or inland as soon as we received the scouts' report.

At that point I began to discover the disadvantages of our signaling system, first among which was the visibility of the fires, not only to an approaching sea force, demonstrating that they had been seen, but also to anyone watching from inland. Our activities in setting up the watch posts had been closely observed, and the people of coastal Corbenic were as curious as we were about how effective the system would prove to be. Now, as we rode north following the line of the coast, I began to see other people converging on us from inland. There were no massive numbers of these people, for this was a largely uninhabited part of Pelles's domain, too close to the coast itself for safety or peace of mind among the people who had no other choice than to live there, but they came in twos and threes, and sometimes in larger groups that had met along the way, and before we had ridden the first five miles from the castle, we had a train of attendants and curiosity seekers. By the time we reached the ten-mile post, they numbered close to sixty and were now posing a very real threat to our ability to travel unobserved, since many of them chose to ride between us and the sea, often traveling along the very tops of the cliffs, in plain sight of any raiders who might be out there looking for activity.

When I mentioned my concerns to Cortix, however, he merely laughed at me.

"What did you expect, that they would stay at home and hide beneath their cots? These people live here, Clothar, and they are accustomed to being raided, so they always turn out in force—or as much force as they can muster within riding distance, which is seldom much. But if the raid is a small one, a single boat or two, they may sometimes be able to drive the raiders off. The raiders know that, too, my friend, and they expect them, so don't fret over it. It will work to our advantage, you wait and see."

"I don't see how it can. Perceval, do you agree?"

Perceval merely shrugged, and Cortix looked from one to the other of us with raised eyebrows.

"How can it not? Think about it! These people are like auxiliaries. The raiders expect to see them, and they expect to deal with them as part of their raid. And from where we sit, that can only be to our advantage. If the raiders are watching the locals, they won't be expecting us, so all we have to do is stay out of sight until the time comes to attack."

I found myself grinning sheepishly. "I hadn't thought of that."

"How could you have? Theirs is not your kind of warfare. You think in terms of troopers and deployments. These people think only of defending their homes against marauders."

A short time after that, one of our scouts returned with word that the enemy was almost a mile offshore and headed for the beaches Cortix had identified as their likeliest landing point, now slightly more than two miles ahead of us. I passed the word back and spurred my horse, my mind now filled with the possibilities suggested by Cortix's comments about the local warriors, and we covered the remaining distance quickly, arriving within sight of the grassy plain behind the beaches while the enemy ships were still a half mile out on the water. Our spectators were lining the cliff tops, staring out to sea and brandishing their weapons in full view of five approaching vessels that were sweeping towards the shore under full sail and with their crews rowing mightily. I removed my helmet, covered my ring mail with my cloak and rode up with Cortix to join them. There, with a clear view of what lay beneath us as the cliffs on our right fell away to the beach, we made our final arrangements, Cortix ordering the clansmen to ride down and take up positions across the hard ground between the beach and the roadway leading inland.

There were approximately fifty fighting men in the group, all of them mounted, and Cortix pointed out that they were outnumbered at least three to one by the incoming raiders, so they should not attempt a direct attack but should ride steadily forward in a single line as

though undecided on how, or even whether, to attack. Our cavalry
would remain behind them, out of sight of the Outlanders, and the
clansmen's task would be to entice the raiders to abandon the shield
wall they would form on landing and to charge forward. Some of the
clansmen—and Cortix named each one of those he wanted to obey
him—would then turn and flee as though in panic, while the remainder would bunch up into two tight knots and threaten to engage the
enemy, before breaking away and fleeing the beach, too, ahead of the
advancing raiders. The first group of fugitives would ride right past
us, leaving our way clear to advance, and the last groups would split
right and left on leaving the beach, clearing the way for us as we
charged to meet them. We would advance in a wedge of three arrow-
head-shaped formations, led by the White Squadron, with the Blues
and Pieds to left and right of the point, and pierce the center of the
enemy line, splitting it in half and scattering what was left of it. The
Whites, followed closely by Griffyd's ten mounted bowmen, would
then advance at full speed straight to the water's edge in the hope of
capturing any Outlanders guarding the boats, while the Blues and
Pieds wheeled left and right, respectively, to come back in on the
enemy's flanks in what should be a crushing blow.

It worked perfectly—far better, in fact, than the most sanguine
of us could have hoped for. The clansmen behaved absolutely as
Cortix had bidden them, and the enemy response was as predicted.
By the time they saw our cavalry approaching them at the full
charge, they were extended in a running rabble, already tasting the
blood of the fleeing clansmen. They had no opportunity to react or
regroup in any way other than to scatter to avoid our approaching
mass, and that was the worst thing they could have done. Our initial
attack decimated them, the sheer weight of our horseflesh and our
long, extended spears shattering their nerve and their confidence
and leaving dozens of inert bodies on the sand. The White
Squadron, first through the shambles of the enemy ranks, thundered
directly to the water's edge, where they cut down the score or so of
men guarding the landing boats, and the Pendragon bowmen
formed a line and began picking off those raiders who had remained

on board to crew the five waiting ships. Plainly, none of the Outlanders had ever confronted bows with such superior range and accuracy, for they underestimated their own danger and exposed themselves recklessly and fatally.

In the meantime, the two remaining mounted squadrons had wheeled and re-formed themselves from wedge formations into solid lines, twenty wide and two deep, with only enough space between individual horses to allow the horse of the troopers coming from the other direction to pass between them, and they charged back into the flanks of the enemy from both sides, ten horse-lengths apart, so that the reeling survivors of the first charge were still disoriented when the second surge hit them. It was utter carnage, and it was the finest example we could have provided of what our cavalry tactics could achieve. The slaughter—for no one could really call it a fight—was over in mere minutes, with only one man, one of the Corbenican recruits, accidentally lost to us when he broke his neck falling from his rearing horse.

We counted eighty enemy dead on the main killing ground, twenty-two more by the water's edge and an unknown number aboard the five ships, which had hurriedly withdrawn out of range of our bowmen. We rounded up more than sixty survivors, many of them wounded, and none of them with a spark of fight left in him. Glassy eyed from shock, they huddled on the sand watching us with fear plain on their faces, expecting to be killed out of hand. As they watched us, I ordered my trumpeter to sound the recall, and our three squadrons assembled silently in their formations and then sat motionless, facing the sea and the huddle of prisoners in front of them. I then held them there in silence while I rode towards the prisoners, flanked by Perceval, Milo and Cortix, and ranged behind them my three squadron commanders and six squad leaders. No one moved or spoke.

Finally, when I judged the prisoners' trepidation to be at its peak, I pointed at the one among them I had guessed to be a leader and waved towards their ships. He looked back at me blankly, and I repeated the gesture, more urgently this time, waving them away.

The fellow blinked, looked uncertainly from me to his nearest companions, and then slowly, hesitantly, unbelievingly, and without turning their backs to us, they began to edge away from us towards the sea, clearly expecting to be slaughtered at any moment. I waited to be sure they were well on their way, and then, with a word to my officers to follow me, I wheeled my horse and trotted back to sit in front of my men.

Only then did the prisoners believe they were to escape with their lives, and they turned and surged towards the water's edge, waving to their waiting ships. But the ships made no move to approach closer to land, evidently cautious about exposing themselves to further danger from our bowmen, and so I issued orders to withdraw to the very edge of the beach and re-form there in an extended line of two ranks. As we were preparing to do so, however, one of the prisoners broke away from his fellows and ran back towards us, stooping to snatch up a heavy, two-bladed war axe. He may have intended to rejoin his men, but he died before he could straighten up, pierced in the space of an eyeblink by two Pendragon arrows. His death marked the last vestige of resistance, and we sat and watched as the ships finally drew close enough to allow the survivors to wade out to them and be pulled aboard.

"I knew you were going to let them go," Cortix murmured from behind me. "But why?"

I kept my eyes on the marauders. "Those are our messengers, Cortix. Had they simply disappeared, people might easily have suspected they were lost in a storm at sea. Now everyone they meet will know where they went, and what they found when they arrived. Those five ships will not come back here, and because of that, who knows how many more will heed their lesson? Tell your people that, my friend, because I don't doubt they will be asking you. They may see little benefit in setting wolves free to kill again, but that's only because those wolves have savaged them before. Once you point out the reasons for releasing these people, I think your clansmen will see the sense of it." I turned to Perceval. "I think we're finished here. Sound assembly and let's go home."

"What about the bodies?" This was Cortix again. "You intend to simply leave them here?"

I looked around the beach. "What else do you suggest? Bury them in the sand? They'll be washed up again by the first high tide. And I doubt we have the tools to dig a pit large enough to hold them, up here above the beach. Nor is there enough wood around here to burn them. Four score dead men would require a small copse of dried tree trunks. Best to leave them here, I think, where the tides can float at least some of them away. They'll stink for a few weeks, but the birds and animals will make short work of them, and your fisher folk can skirt around them when they come and go this way."

Cortix looked at the corpses one last time and shrugged. "You're right. Let's go back home."

2

I received a summons from King Pelles the following afternoon, inviting me to dine with him the next day, to discuss the raid and to accept his gratitude for having demonstrated the soundness of his original idea of fostering cavalry in Corbenic. The raid had, of course, been the focus of all interest since our return, with the Reds and the Golds avid for details of all that had happened, and the others, most particularly the Corbenican recruits who had been there, eager and willing to tell them. There was a new spirit of excitement among the men now. Their training had been proved sound, and their first success against a real enemy had been full acknowledgment of, and reward for, the months of work they had endured to this point. All of the command personnel, from senior troopers to squadron commanders, remarked that day on the change in attitude of even the best students.

I told Perceval about Pelles's invitation and asked him if he would like to join me, but he declined, as I knew he would. He preferred to spend his time with his men, rather than wasting it in what he saw as a needless obligation to behave himself in formal company. I sympathized with him, but I had an obligation to attend the king, and so the following afternoon, as soon as my duties for the day were completed, I set out on the two-hour ride to Pelles's villa.

His mother and two sisters joined us for dinner that night, an intimate occasion with only the five of us and a horde of servitors, and it was the first occasion I had had to meet these women in normal circumstances, when neither they nor their king was in peril. I found them to be pleasant company at table, although the matron Catalina was something of a forbidding figure, with a biting and acerbic wit. Soon after sitting down to dine, however, I found myself warming to her, despite her initial, disconcerting air of intolerance, and I was soon relieved to discover that beneath her stern exterior lay another personality altogether, an amusing, perceptive and highly intelligent woman who could turn her mind and tongue to almost any topic, revealing herself as intuitive, provocative, forthright and more than slightly cynical about men and their motivations. Her barbed wit, in that persona, was if anything even more caustic than it had been earlier, when she was merely being formal.

Of course, she liked me openly, principally because of my services to herself and her family, and secondarily because I was now known to be blood kin, with no ambition to rule here in Gaul. She evidently accepted her son's judgment on that score, and for that I was grateful, because I had the feeling there might not be too many other people with an easy claim on her good graces. In consequence, my initial awe of this formidable woman waned quickly, and I soon found it easy and stimulating to talk with her about the plans her son and I had for the defenses of his realm, and even to ask for her opinions and to listen respectfully as she expounded upon them, showing a grasp of the realities of life in Corbenic that many of her son's own officers did not yet appear to have achieved. Engrossed as I was with Catalina and her opinions on everything, I found that the dinner passed quickly and pleasantly.

Her two daughters were molded from different clay altogether. Lena, the elder, was withdrawn and taciturn to the point of being ill mannered, whereas her younger sister, Serena, was sufficiently friendly towards me to make me think at several times that she was being almost, although not quite, flirtatious. I had the strong sensation that she might have been far more forthcoming towards me had her mother not been present, and I noticed certain frowning looks being cast by Catalina over some of the comments made by her daughter in what seemed like smiling innocence. One such, and it truly was the only one I noticed as being anywhere approaching obvious—although it was also the first and the one that set me watching and listening more closely thereafter—was to the effect that she had heard great things about my lance and would look forward to seeing it in action. That earned her a glare from her mother that would have seared stone, but Serena blithely ignored it, merely giving me a charming, dimpled smile.

Both sisters were older than their brother, who, I noticed, had sat silent throughout most of the meal, listening to the conversation between his mother and me, without making any effort to interrupt or to participate in our discussions in any way. I looked at him several times when his mother was speaking, and finally decided he was quite content to be simply sitting there among us, enjoying everything we had to say, and I reflected that it might have something to do with his own conviction, mere months earlier, that his mother and sisters were lost to him forever and he himself was slipping towards death. I had estimated him to be five years older than I was, which would have made him twenty-seven, and so now I guessed that his sisters might each be anywhere from five to ten years older than him, but I had always had great difficulty in divining the ages of women with any accuracy, because of the artifices they so often use to disguise their age. Lena I gauged to be at least forty years old, judging from the fact that she had a son of seventeen and had, I had heard, married late. Serena, on the other hand, I estimated to be anywhere from thirty-two to thirty-six. She had a single daughter of seven, and she had been widowed for the past six years. I was twenty-two at that time, and I remember that I thought her old.

When the dinner ended, the women withdrew, and Pelles immediately poured us both a glass cup of his favorite wine before pushing two chairs close to the fire and motioning for me to join him. He was very excited about the outcome of our first foray against the Danes—although I was not at all sure the raiders had been Danes—and wanted to know everything that had gone through my mind since the moment I first heard of the sighting. I did my best to tell him everything I could recall, and when I had finished he wanted to know everything I could tell him about the progress of his recruits and the potential officers we had identified among the first draft. We talked long into the night, disturbed only occasionally by servants coming in to replenish the fire, and it must have been nigh on midnight when we retired.

I found a young man dozing in my chambers when I arrived, and he leapt to his feet, startled awake, to tell me he had been waiting to help me undress and prepare for bed. I thanked him and sent him off to his own bed, telling him that I was perfectly capable of undressing myself, and as soon as he had gone I stripped myself of my silken robes and crawled into bed, heavy eyed and bleary. But this was to be one of the nights when Elaine, or a spirit sister of some kind, seemed determined to stop me from finding rest. Three times I dozed and started awake again, restless and physically aroused, before I finally fell asleep. And then I awoke again to what I thought was a living dream, with gentle fingers cradling my swollen manhood and soft, warm flesh pressed against me, a heavy thigh across my own. It was Serena, of course, and I suppose I could have resisted her and sent her quietly away, had I not been so ready to accept what she offered me. But I was ready, and I accepted eagerly and wordlessly.

Serena rose and slipped away some time before I awoke, and as I bathed and dressed, I found myself wondering how badly I had erred in accepting her favors, and feeling more than a little guilt about my reactions to finding her there in my bed. We had not spoken at all, I recalled, during the entire episode, merely grappling with each other for fulfillment and then holding each other in silence, moving voluptuously and lazily in unison, caressing and fondling each other until sufficient time had passed for us to be able to begin all over again. I had lost count of the number of times we coupled, but I felt sated and rejuvenated, and my only fear was that Serena herself might betray, even unwittingly, what had happened between us. Only when I was fully dressed and preparing to head towards the king's suite did I begin to wonder how I might be expected to behave towards her now.

I need not have worried. Serena was there when I entered the king's receiving room, and she greeted me perfectly naturally, as though she and I had never laid hands on each other and had certainly not rutted like stallion and mare for most of the night. I responded in kind, and our relationship was established from that moment on. It was one that would be seldom pursued, since I spent very little time in the king's villa, but whenever I did stay, Serena came to me at night, and we learned to speak to each other honestly and openly as we lay in each other's arms. She was a large woman, not fat, yet generously fashioned, with large and ample breasts, a soft, rich belly and full, heavy thighs, and her skin was wondrously soft and pink, glowing with vitality.

"Were you afraid I might betray you?" she asked me the next time she came to my bed, and I propped myself up on my elbow to answer her. I had left a lamp burning, hoping that she would come to me, and she had not kept me waiting. Now she lay beside me, smiling up at me, her lovely body sprawled in sensuous relaxation, the lamplight casting golden shadows in the hollows of her shape.

"Not afraid," I answered. "Perhaps ... unsure?"

"Hmm." She moved lazily to bring her lower body into contact with my hip. "Well, my lord of the lance, you can be at ease, because despite what you might believe after my forwardness at dinner that first night, I can be discreet."

"Your mother didn't think so, after that comment of yours about my lance. I thought she was going to choke when you said that."

"I know, I thought you might choke, too. Your face was a delight, because you clearly didn't know if you had really heard what you thought you heard. But I had to gauge your mettle before coming to your bed. You might have thrown me out, and then where would I have gone? Spurned by the first man I had chosen in years?"

I had my doubts about that last statement, but said nothing. Serena did not strike me as being the kind of woman who would go deprived for years, but I was astute enough to recognize that that was no concern of mine. I was more concerned that her mother might be suspicious enough to check into her activities after the villa was abed.

"Does your mother ... Is she likely to suspect that we are ... doing this?"

Her fingers drifted to my belly, probing and poking. "Mother? Of course she is. She knows her daughters and she is no man's fool, and for that reason she will say nothing, even if she finds us together. I am her youngest daughter, but I am also thirty-six years old and a respectable widow, and my dear mother is no stranger to what drives a woman. If she were twenty years younger she might well be here in your bed herself."

I did not know how to respond to that astonishing information, but Serena was not waiting for an answer, her fingers seeking a response of another kind altogether. "I wanted you from the first moment I met you," she said, her voice husky again with desire, "when you rode to rescue us from Baldwin's villa. You were the first man I had met in years who did not stink like a goat. And now that I have enjoyed you several times, I have no wish to endanger what I have found, so I shall treat you as a welcome family guest each time you come, so be it you are willing to treat me as a welcome source of satisfaction when you retire. What say you?"

I grinned at her. "Are you saying you want me only for my clean body and the pleasure you can gain from it?"

"I am, precisely, and I hope to gain much more in future from the same font ... much, much more ..."

"Are we being incestuous? We are cousins, you know."

She laughed at that, and pulled my head down to her breasts, thrusting a nipple into my mouth. "Distant cousins, Cousin, distant in all but closeness …"

For a long spell, there was no need to speak again, and I lost all awareness from that time of any need to wonder about the two of us. We became close friends over the ensuing months, without ever meaning to. Serena had a sparkling, mischievous sense of humor and could make me laugh even in my bleakest moments, and our conduct with each other by day, away from the bedchamber, became so natural and unfeigned that even Catalina's suspicions were eventually lulled, although I suspect she might have wondered at the sudden increase in my visits to the villa. Fortunately, to counter any suspicions that she might have entertained, I found more and more genuine reasons for visiting and conferring with Pelles until he grew strong enough to ride out again, after which my visits dwindled again to respectable, unsuspicious frequency.

3

Connor Mac Athol's returning fleet was sighted on the second day of September, and I rode immediately to the harbor, only to spend an entire day fretting impotently as his ships fought towards land in the teeth of a contrary offshore wind. Watching from the top of the cliffs as his heavy vessels labored against intermittent gusts and squalls that frequently blew them backwards out to sea again gave me an entirely new appreciation of the difficulties mariners faced in dealing with the vagaries of weather, and while I was impatient to have Connor come ashore, I had the partial satisfaction of knowing that his lack of speed had nothing to do with the amount of effort he was exerting to reach me.

Most of my frustration was rooted in my need to know whatever tidings he would bring me from Camulod. It had been nigh on half a year since I left home, and my mind was reeling with possibilities, real and imaginary, of all that might have happened in my absence. I could believe in none of them, since they were all rootless imaginings, but together they combined to bring me close to fever pitch with anticipation. Young Bors, commanding the new intake from Camulod, was out there on the water somewhere, but I knew I would see nothing of him until he had finished supervising the unloading and disposition of all his men, horses and gear, and that would take the remainder of this day and most of the next. I had already left word for him with the squadron leader of the Reds, who were guarding the beach that day, that I would be expecting him at the castle late on the following afternoon. For the moment, my concern was for Connor, who, until the fleet was safe in harbor and completely unloaded, would remain, nominally at least, in command of this operation and therefore unable to abandon his appointed tasks.

Despite that, I knew that as soon as he could do so in conscience, he would hand over responsibility for the entire gamut of tasks to his fleet master and that worthy's remarkable crew of assistants. "I'm an old man now and I only have one leg," he had said to me before leaving to return to Britain in June, "and it pains me when I have to stand on the stump too long. So I have trained Shaun Pointer to be everything I need to be at both ends of a voyage, and he has trained a kennel of his own young dogs to do his bidding the way he wants things done. I leave him to it and I'm glad to be able to. He only has the one hand, so we're a crippled pair, the two of us, but he only needs one hand to point with, and the gods all know he has the lungs he needs to shout with, so no one ever doubts who he is pointing at or what he is saying. He's my faithful, trusted hound, is Shaun, and so I let him do the hunting on both ends of a voyage, while I watch and say nothing. It makes life easier for both of us."

Finally, late in the afternoon when the sun was already low in the western sky, Connor's own galley tied up to the wharf, and I watched as he was swung ashore on the end of the hoist that had been built onto his ship for precisely that purpose and then stood teetering for a moment or two until he regained his balance after weeks aboard ship. He had long since seen me waiting for him, and he greeted me with a massive hug, cheerfully cursing the capricious winds before he turned away again and began to marshal his forces for the unloading that would continue late into the night, to begin again with the dawn and the berthing of new ships. I withdrew again to the cliff top above the tiny harbor, where I sat gazing disconsolately and impotently down at the ever-growing activity below me, knowing that I had no other choice than to wait until Connor felt he could safely turn over the remaining arrangements to Shaun Pointer and his gang.

By the time he did so, it was almost fully dark, and I felt like laughing in dismay as I saw him being led up the ascent from the beach by two of my troopers, each of them carrying a blazing torch. Connor, the one-legged seaman, had never been a rider of horses, and because of his wooden leg he was never at his best when tackling steep inclines, but I had a comfortable and well-sprung two-wheeled cart waiting for him at the top of the slope, and he threw a set of bulky saddlebags into the rear of it before pulling himself smoothly up to the driver's bench. I tied my own horse to the rear of the cart and drove him the six miles from the beach to the castle myself.

"That's all stuff for you, from Camulod," he grunted, indicating the bags. "Mostly from Merlyn, although he said there was a letter in there for you from the King himself. They've been waiting to be read now for weeks, some of them probably for months."

"The ink won't fade overnight," I said. "It's news I'm hungry for, word of mouth from any place other than here for a change. How was your voyage home? You're back on time, so you can't have had too much trouble. Were your people happy with what you found on the first voyage?"

"Aye, happy enough, but there wasn't enough of anything to make them really smile. I knew that when we left here, and I had warned them not to expect miracles. But they were still expecting more than what I delivered. Isn't that always the way things are?

People stay home, doing nothing, and then expect the impossible from those who go out and try to achieve something."

"You sound disgusted."

"Well, I was, but I wasn't surprised. Anyway, the important thing was that we had made a solid landfall here, laid the groundwork for better things, this time and in the future. Now I'm back with a clearer understanding of what we really need. And the main thing we need is to save time, overall, by cutting down on the amount of traveling we do and the time between offloading one cargo and reloading the new one. We took far too long last time, and lost almost a month. Can't afford to do that again. Now, have the smiths here been producing for us while we've been gone?"

"Aye, they have, and impressively. There's weaponry and armor piled up everywhere, above the beach and out of the way so they won't interfere with your unloading, but they're ready to be loaded immediately after that. Lucius Genaro has been dealing with the suppliers, and he seems well satisfied. If he had any complaints he would have told me."

"Aye, that armor's another thing I want to change. I'll take what's there because I asked for it, but I decided on the last voyage that metal armor isn't worth the trouble it takes to carry it. What we need, above all else, is to fill our holds with more cutting weapons: swords and daggers and spear and axe heads. And cattle hides, which is something I hadn't thought about before, for armor. We can make all that ourselves, breastplates and leggings and helmets, out of leather, boiled and hammered in layers and then dried. Well made, it's every bit as good as iron, but to do it properly we need more leather than we have at this point. We need all our own cattle alive and breeding. And so I'll be buying hides this time, for our next visit, dried and cured and baled. They'll be a whole lot easier to stow aboard than iron armor. Shields we can make at home, too, as well as spear and axe shafts."

I was nodding as I listened to him, impressed but not surprised by his grasp of the priorities he had to meet, and only when I was sure he had no more to say for the time being did I move on to appease my own curiosity.

"So, tell me, if you will, what was the situation in Camulod when you were there?"

Connor sniffed, and stretched his arms and spine. "Much as it always is ... Donuil and his wife, Shelagh, are in charge there for all intents and purposes whenever Merlyn's away, and they had everything ready and waiting for me as promised. But Merlyn was actually there this time, for a change—although he turned up only on the day I was to leave. Arthur was campaigning in the north and had been gone for more than a month, Merlyn told me."

"Campaigning?" I had not expected to hear that, and hoped that this did not involve the warlord Connlyn. "Against whom? How long ago was this?"

"Fifteen days ago, when I was there, but you'll have to ask elsewhere for more information. Your man Bors will know all that. I didn't stop in Camulod at all on the way back from here to Dalriada. Didn't have the time. I landed all the Camulod cargo at Glevum and sailed on north from there with my own stuff. Didn't have time for anything while I was there this time, either, except for marshaling cargo and loading it all on shipboard. All I know is what I heard other people talking about: there's trouble somewhere in the north, on your side of the Wall. I heard some names, but none of them meant anything to me, and so I didn't pay much attention. Arthur got wed, you know."

I was dumbstruck. The casual delivery of his announcement took my voice away from me, leaving me floundering as I tried to absorb what he had told me. I understood what he had said, but the words had fallen from his mouth as though they had no particular significance. I was aware of a rush of pain, and even jealousy, that Arthur would have taken such a step without my being there to share his pleasure in such a major event, and that, after all the confidences he had shared with me and all his protestations that he had no wish to wed, he had not even informed me about his intentions. But then my common sense blanked out that foolishness, leaving me feeling shamed that such thoughts could even have occurred to me. Arthur Pendragon was my King first and my friend thereafter, and any obligations between the two of us were purely one-sided, owed by me to him. He was under no requirement of any kind to consult me in anything or to inform me of his slightest thought.

Despite that, however, and try as I would to absorb the conflicting thoughts and emotions that swarmed in me, a deep-seated pain, which I was forced to acknowledge as grief over what my innermost self perceived as betrayal, threatened to close up my throat. I was aware that time appeared to be passing very slowly and that Connor seemed ignorant of what he had done to me with that one short statement. *Arthur got wed, you know.* I managed eventually to calm my breathing, astonished that he had not noticed anything amiss, and forced myself to sound as casual in my response as he had been in his statement.

"Married? The King? That was … sudden. When did it happen?"

"Springtime, I gather, while we were here on the first voyage. Don't ask me when in the spring, for I don't know. I only know that when we arrived back at Glevum to unload, the word was waiting that the King was wed."

"Then the marriage must have taken place within weeks of our departure … in April or May." I forced myself to laugh. "That sounds like Arthur, never one to let the grass grow under him. But where did he find a bride so quickly? Not that there has been a lack of candidates, this past year and more."

"She found him, from what I heard. Or her father did. Some king from the northwest, far out of Camulod and probably closer to us in our islands than to Arthur's holdings. The old legionary fortress up there, the big one … what's it called?"

"*Deva*? Are you talking about Symmachus's kingdom, Chester?"

"Aye, that's the place, and that's the man. Symmachus. What kind of name is that?"

"It's Roman. By the Christus, so he married Cynthia. I warned him about that one."

Connor was looking at me strangely now, one eyebrow cocked. "*You* warned him about her?"

"It's a long story, Connor, but I met her once and we did not like each other … I can't believe Arthur would marry her. The woman has no love in her for anyone but herself."

"Aye, well, that's how you see it and you may be right, but you're only a glorified spear carrier, like me. The Pendragon is a king and a king will marry a cross-eyed hunchback with chin hair and warts if it's necessary for the good and the protection of his kingdom. And I would gauge, if it happened as quickly as I was told, that your man Arthur had good and proper reasons for it … love being the last and least of them, if it had any part at all."

"I know, I know, you are right, but by the sweet Christus, he has taken on a burden with that one. We talked about her once, and I warned him to avoid her—that she would either be the death of him or her self-love and bad behavior would drive him to be the death of her. Cynthia of Chester! I can't believe it …" I realized I was saying too much and in risk of betraying a confidence, and changed the topic of our conversation. "How many men did you bring with you this time?"

"Camulod men for you, you mean. Two hundred troopers and officers, plus all the usual hangers-on … cooks, grooms, carpenters, tent makers, six stonemasons and a few smiths. All counted, the roster came to two hundred and forty-three souls, plus all their horses, baggage and kit. As you might have seen, we brought a bigger fleet this time. Twelve more big cargo vessels." He straightened on the bench and peered around at the blackness. "Where are you taking me? We've been traveling for hours and I still can't see a damned light out there ahead of us."

"It's there, hidden behind the brow of this slope. We'll be there soon."

"Not soon enough," he growled. "I'm used to riding a ship on water … my bony old arse feels every stone we rattle over in this thing."

He was impressed when we finally breasted the shallow ridge and saw the castle in the distance, and I was too, since it was the first time I had seen the place from a distance at night. It was a daunting and intimidating sight, even in the darkness, with the glare of the numerous watch fires creating pools of light that emphasized the massive walls and battlements. I heard him grunt in surprise when it came into view, but he said nothing else until we had been challenged by the guards and allowed to enter the main gate beneath its flanking defensive towers. Once inside, I helped Connor down, waiting for him to plant his wooden limb firmly on the cobblestones before I handed the cart and animals over to the grooms on duty and led him into the main administrative quarters. I threw the saddlebags on my work table and waved an arm about the room.

"As you can see, we don't lack much now. It's a far cry from the hillside tents we pitched when we first arrived, five months ago."

"Aye, I'll grant you that." He was still taking everything in, and as I followed his gaze I began to appreciate for the first time just how much progress we had made within a very short span of time. The huge space was brightly lit, with two large fires burning, one at each end of the main hall, a series of bright torches mounted in cressets around the wall, and a profusion of candles and tapers on the central array of tables where a few of Dynas's crew of clerics were still working, even this late. The central tables themselves were backed by high partitions lined with shelves and cubicles already close to being filled with scrolls and record books, and we stood watching for a moment as one of the scribes rearranged some books, making sure that they were all properly in place.

"Come on, I'll show you the officers' dining room, and then one of our troopers will take you to your quarters and from there to the bath house, if you would enjoy that." He nodded and accompanied me into the cavernous but well-furnished quarters that were the common off-duty gathering place for the staff officers, and when he had seen everything there, he nodded again. "They don't have anything this grand in Camulod," he said, and I grinned at him.

"No, they don't, but seventy years ago Camulod was a barren hilltop ruin. This place has been in constant use by garrison troops for more than four hundred years, and garrison troops always see to their own comfort, over time."

Later that night, once Connor had bathed and changed his clothing, I introduced him to my staff officers at dinner—both Camulodian and newly appointed Corbenicans—and we sat long into the night as he regaled them with tales of his youth, detailing how as admiral of the Erse King Athol's fleet, he had first met Merlyn Britannicus and become involved in the affairs of Camulod. It was after midnight by the time I finally found my cot, and I fell asleep knowing that my first duty in the morning would be to read the dispatches from Camulod.

4

My sleep was short lived and restless, and I was astir long before dawn, emerging from the officers' bath house steamed and massaged even before the sun broke the horizon. The castle was alive by then, with troopers moving everywhere around me and the voices of senior troopers and overseers echoing from the walls as they chivvied their men towards the day's chores. I made my way directly to my day room, shutting the door behind me, and filled a candelabrum with fresh candles, then lit all of them and carried it to my work table. My senior clerk had watched me in silence and knew from my behavior that he would be permitted to disturb me only upon pain of death.

I upended the saddlebags Connor had brought me, spilling their contents out haphazardly before I sat down to sort them into some kind of order.

Most of the documents were manifests of one kind or another, detailed lists of the officers, men, animals and gear sent out from Camulod, together with equally explicit lists of the goods and cargo, from ingots of tin and lead for Connor's trading, to lists of construction tools and chests and barrels of supplies. All of the cargo laden aboard the fleet was accounted for, but only after Shaun Pointer and his people had disgorged all the fleet's contents onto the landing by the village would these documents I held make any specific sense to me or any member of my staff.

Working quickly, I separated the documents into two piles—one of them for future use and one for immediate action—and then into three, dividing the latter pile into administrative matters that could be handled by others and personal pieces that were for my attention alone. There were four of these last: three large packets, each wrapped in a square of soft, tanned leather, from Merlyn himself, numbered in the order in which they should be read, and the fourth addressed simply to me, Seur Clothar of Benwick, in Arthur's own emphatic hand. Naturally, I wanted to open Arthur's immediately, but I set it aside and applied myself to reading Merlyn's three missives in sequence.

They were thick with information and richly detailed, reporting not only Merlyn's thoughts on our first expedition and the increasing preparations in Camulod for its return but also his arrangements for this second expedition and an exhaustive background to the composition of the personnel dispatched with it.

It was the additional information that fascinated me, however, for in writing these long letters, Merlyn had included all the details of the most significant occurrences in Arthur's realm since my departure in April, and by the time I had finished reading all of them, going over a number of them several times to ensure that I had fully understood everything I was being told, it was mid-morning and I was exhausted, overwhelmed by the mass of unwelcome information I had absorbed.

Looming above everything else, from the outset of Merlyn's first epistle, was the confirmation that his initial suspicions about Connlyn, the warlord of Southwall who had been our voluntary "ally," had been accurate. The man was all that Merlyn had feared him to be: treacherous, duplicitous and ambitious, intent upon bringing all of north Britain under his own rule while pretending amity and solidarity with Camulod. Ghilleadh, who had replaced me in leading the spring expedition of two army groups to investigate Connlyn's activities, had proceeded directly northwards, following the Roman roads, and he had made much faster progress than had I the year before, for I had taken a circuitous route, visiting other territories and kingdoms along the way. Ghilly, on the other hand, had followed the road due north to Luguvallium on the western end of Hadrian's Wall and had swung east there, following the line of the Wall itself until he reached the territory that had formerly belonged to Ushmar, Connlyn's neighbor on his western border. There, leaving his main host behind him as planned, Ghilly had advanced with a token force and found Ushmar's former kingdom firmly under the command of Connlyn's people and heavily garrisoned by forces that were clearly not from Britain. Undetected, Ghilly had skirted around the Outlanders, seeking more evidence of treachery, and had found a place where the Wall had been permanently breached to permit traffic to flow freely between north and south of the barrier.

Waiting to see no more, and convinced that he had seen more than enough evidence of treachery to justify a full call to arms, Ghilly rejoined his main force and sent word back immediately to Camulod. Merlyn was careful to note that, suspicious and ill at ease on the way north, Ghilly had taken elaborate precautions to provide for speed, in the event there should be need for it, by leaving a group of four men at every tenth milestone along the route they followed. After his departure, each foursome had split into twos and placed themselves five miles apart, then made camp far enough away from the road to remain out of sight while they awaited whatever might come.

Now, when the word was passed, it moved as fast as a man on a galloping horse could carry it, all the way from Luguvallium to Camulod, in five-mile stages, day and night, and the journey took less than two days. No one had any doubts about the accuracy or the veracity of Ghilly's report, and a punitive force was assembled within two days of the receipt of his tidings, and two thousand cavalry under the command of Bedwyr, with Gwin as his deputy, supported by three thousand infantry under Sagramore and Gareth, set out northwards.

Merlyn's fears, however, extended to more than Connlyn's planning an invasion from the north beyond the Wall; he was convinced that the man's treachery extended eastward, too, and must involve the Saxon forces there. He was also concerned about the security of the entire northwest, and his attention focused upon the single greatest weakness there: Arthur's continuing inability to secure a treaty with Symmachus, who controlled the great fortress of Deva in northern Cambria and thereby held the key to security or chaos in that region. Arthur was determined to ride north with the army against Connlyn, but Merlyn had convinced him that his true duty lay in forging an alliance with Symmachus before he did anything else, and so Arthur rode with the others only as far north as Deva itself, where he remained behind with a strong contingent of horse and foot while the others marched onwards towards Luguvallium.

For all his reluctance to make the attempt, and notwithstanding Symmachus's own unwillingness to commit to the support of Camulod, Arthur had managed to conclude a treaty between the two, but it was predicated upon stringent conditions set out by Symmachus, who had, he maintained, far more to surrender and lose by this treaty than had Arthur or Camulod. Arthur must marry Symmachus's daughter immediately and must name their firstborn son as his heir and successor to the status of Riothamus.

Arthur, torn on the one hand between the need to ensure peace and support at his back, with the formidable resources in men and weaponry that Symmachus could field, and on the other by the urgency of seeing for himself what was happening in the far north, had had little room to maneuver and no real negotiating strength with which to bargain. He agreed to Symmachus's conditions and signed a formal treaty to that effect, sending a sealed and duly witnessed copy of the document back to Merlyn in Camulod, bidding him have it written into the annals of the realm. The wedding between Arthur and the king's daughter took place the very next day, Merlyn reported baldly, and was consummated that night, leaving Arthur free to depart for the north the following morning, since which time Merlyn had heard nothing more of the progress of whatever campaign might be unfolding.

The second package, compiled in the two months that followed, contained little more factual information than the first, but it did contain another packet, which Merlyn referred to only briefly, saying that it had arrived some time earlier by unknown means and had been brought to him by the officer of the guard who had received it from a man on duty at the gates, who had in turn received it from a wandering priest. It was signed clearly to me, as Clothar, King's Knight, and while Merlyn had no knowledge of its provenance, he had decided it might be important to me, and so had included it with his own documents. Something in the words he had written convinced me that he suspected, as I did myself, that its writer was a woman. There was a certain delicacy to the writing on the heavily sealed packet that was unmanly, for the want of a better word, and my heart leapt with excitement when I saw it, since the only woman I knew who might write to me was Elaine. I wanted to tear it open and read it as soon as I saw it and knew it for what it was, but my sense of duty would not permit me to be so self-indulgent, and so I lobbed it onto a nearby table, swearing to myself that I would not open it until I had read everything else that was here for my official attention.

There was little noteworthy in the remainder of that letter, despite its thickness. Merlyn told me everything he knew of developments elsewhere in Britain, but he was as impotent as I in the face of the silence coming back from the north, and he could not afford to deal in rumors. Anything with the weight of real tidings would come directly to him for his personal attention, he knew, and therefore he treated everything else as hearsay based upon rumor founded on gossip and imaginings. But no word came from the north, and time passed slowly while he fought the constant urge to ride up there and see for himself what was happening.

He had, however, received communications from Symmachus in Deva, or Chester, as the local people called it, and he had estimated from the tone of those that the recent treaty was being regarded with respect and all due attention by Symmachus, for the communication advised that the Kingdom of Deva (these words underlined by Merlyn) stood prepared to assist Camulod in its northern war, with a five-thousand-man army fully equipped and ready to march upon Arthur's summons. He made no mention at all of Arthur's new wife or her whereabouts, leaving me to surmise that she must still be residing in Deva with her family.

His final commentary in that letter was on a pair of offers received from the two kings Kilmorack and Einar. The first of these was the king in central Britain whose holdings were abutted on three sides by Saxon territories. All of us in Camulod had warmed to Kilmorack as the most personable, and most able, of the five kings who had come to Arthur the previous year offering their daughters— the sixth had been King Pelinore, a well-known and respected friend—and we had agreed that Kilmorack was a natural ally for us to foster. His problems were similar to our own in Camulod but far more precarious, surrounded as he was on three sides, and his goodwill would be well worth preserving through any investment we could make in supporting him. Now he had come to us, it appeared, not in search of aid but to offer it should we need to call on him.

The offer of aid and alliance from the other king, Einar, was even more surprising, for Einar was an Anglian, not a Briton at all. He and his people were the descendants of invaders who only a hundred years earlier had invested the territories he now ruled. But Einar's people had come in the beginning looking for land to farm, and having found it, they had worked industriously at it ever since, never seeking to expand their holdings or to make war on any of their peaceful neighbors. They would fight, and fight fiercely, if they had to, but only to protect their families and their holdings, and the truth was that we in Camulod did not really know how extensive those holdings, or even those families, had become in more than a hundred years, for they lay far inside the unknown territories of the

region called the Saxon Shores, that massive area of eastern Britain
that had fallen long since to the invasions from across the sea and
had always been *terra incognita* to us in Camulod.

Merlyn saw great significance in Einar's offer, from that viewpoint in particular, because, as he pointed out, it was the first
concrete indication that Arthur's objective of unifying the entire
country was achievable and that the soundness of the King's logic
appealed not only to the indigenous Britons but to the more solidly
established Outlanders who now made their homes there and
wanted peace and order just as much as anyone else did.

The lack of any reference to Arthur's new wife was still uppermost in my mind when I had finished reading this letter, and while
it did not cause me any great or direct concern—since I believed
that Cynthia was not the proper wife for Arthur in the first place—
it none the less reminded me of Elaine and the letter from her that
sat close by on the neighboring table where I had thrown it, and
once reminded of it, I found it impossible to ignore any longer. I set
aside the other material and stood up, then crossed the short
distance to where the letter lay, and picked it up and stared at it,
already aware that all my good intentions had been undermined and
laid waste. It was heavily sealed, with no less than three blobs of
wax, but there was no imprint on any of the seals, and the missive
itself was light in weight, confirming me in my suspicions of who
had sent it. Elaine would have no seal with which to imprint the
letters that she sent, and would probably have had little opportunity
to pen anything at length without arousing the curiosity of other
people, among them her new husband. I looked more closely at my
name, scrawled on the outside of the packet, and it seemed to me
the hand in which it was written appeared more feminine than ever.
I deliberated a few moments longer, then returned to my seat and
ran my thumb beneath the seals.

I had read several lines before I began to realize that the letter
was not from Elaine at all, and it took me several moments longer
to read on far enough for the truth to dawn on me, bringing me
upright in my seat. The missive was very brief, but so troubling that

instead of destroying it after I had read it, as I normally would, I kept it among my personal papers for a long time and found it still among them when I came to live permanently in Gaul, years later. And reading it again then, after all the developments that had arisen because of it, both directly and indirectly, I experienced the same shiver of dread.

> *Seur Knight:*
>
> *I warned you of my brother when we met, several years ago, and events of which I have learned now cause me to hope you heeded my warning. I have tidings to impart to you, concerning my brother and certain grievous matters pertaining to your king, whom I know you love and admire greatly. I dare not write such things herein, lest they be seen by others, for what I have to impart is for your ears alone, to be passed on by you to your king. Therefore, if you are able, I pray you will come to me as soon as may be. I would come to you myself, but I grow weaker as the months fly by and my physician tells me that a journey of such length would surely be the death of me, so I must hope you will be able to come to me. I live in what you think of as the Caledonian land called Gallowa, where my son is king. If you can make your way thus far, it may help you, northward of the great Wall, to let it be known you have business with King Tod of Gallowa, but stay far from my brother's bourne in your traveling. I lied to you once, telling you my name was Judith. I will not lie to you again, now or in future. Ask for Queen Morgas and the castle of Tod of Gallowa. I trust God will permit you to come soon.*

That was all. A short, terse and troublesome message that took my thoughts in a greatly different direction than the one in which they had been traveling moments earlier. Merlyn's memory had been accurate. The woman Morgas, he had said, had married a king of Gallowa called Tod, so the Tod referred to in this missive must be their son and the woman Morgas the same one of whom Merlyn had spoken. But what knowledge could she possibly have that might be so important to Arthur that she would write to me about it? She had not even known who Arthur was until I told her about him, and she had scoffed at the idea of his being Riothamus. Why then this sudden urgency to meet with me? I had no doubt that the urgency was there. The mere fact that she had taken the time to write this missive and then send it to Camulod demonstrated that she, at least, believed the tidings she possessed to have great import.

I wondered how long it had been since the letter was written. It might have traveled quickly and directly to Camulod, which meant it might be only three or four months old, but it could also have taken months or even years for the person who was carrying it to travel overland from Gallowa to Camulod. And Morgas was evidently not in the best of health—or had not been when she wrote the letter. She had been a very old and frail woman even when I met her, and three years and more had elapsed since then. She might be dead by this time, in which case the information that she possessed would probably have perished with her.

I did not know what to do. Had I been in Britain, I might well have gone to her, for I would have been campaigning in the north with Arthur, and the distances involved from there to Gallowa would not have been so great. But here I was in Gaul, half buried in administrative duties and about to be inundated with as many more again within the next few days.

I knew the only thing I could do was write to Merlyn and inform him of the contents of the letter. He would know what to do and whom to send north in my stead, if anyone would serve. I looked again at the letter where she had said the tidings were for my ears only, and remembered the little I knew of Queen Morgas. She was not a woman to be trifled with, and she would not be bullied into speaking to anyone she had no wish to speak to.

I paced the floor for a long time then, trying to arrive at some kind of solution, but writing Merlyn was the only course I could see open to me. I might accompany my letter to him with a letter to

Morgas, to be passed on to her by whoever was sent in my place, but that was all I could do. I decided to set the matter aside for the remainder of the day and to sleep on it overnight before making any commitments, but I knew that we had no time to waste before responding to Morgas.

It was almost noon by then, and I took a brief walk outside to clear my head, then drank a large mug of cold water and went back to work, chewing on a handful of fresh bread.

Merlyn's third letter was as uneventful as the one before it, full of speculation and wonderings, save that he had heard at least one set of good tidings. Arthur's forces had won a large battle in the northwest, at a place the locals called Badon and the Romans had called Mons Badonicus, or Mount Badon, after the high hill that dominated the place. Arthur's army had apparently encountered a large force of Caledons there, reinforced by a rabble of marauders from the eastern kingdom of Northumbria, once Vortigern's and now ruled by Horsa the Dane. The numbers had been approximately equal on either side, but Arthur's cavalry had performed brilliantly, smashing the enemy into chaos before the Camulodian infantry could even engage them, and the rout that ensued had left dead men—very few of them ours—scattered across miles of the bleak northern landscape.

That was heartening news, but there was nothing more of any substance to follow it up. There had been no further word of Arthur or his progress in the north. The news of the victory had been brought back by a squadron dispatched for that purpose, and the messengers had been in good spirits. They had brought no requests for reinforcements, and Merlyn took that to be a positive sign that Arthur's campaign was progressing smoothly. The distances were simply too great to permit the easy transmission of information in either direction, and so Merlyn, like everyone else, was forced to rely upon hope and upon his own interpretation of whatever tidings came his way.

It was plain to see, from the very restraint that he used in expressing his opinions, that he was both perplexed and frustrated,

but he wrote not a single word of complaint about anything.
Unfortunately, from my perspective, he wrote not a single word,
either, in all his outpourings, about Arthur's marriage.

5

I finished reading everything from Merlyn before I finally allowed
myself to reach for the letter from Arthur, noticing, as I broke the
single heavy seal on the shaved vellum wrapping, that the dragon of
Pendragon lay coiled in the center of the red wax blob. His, too, was
a strange and unsettling letter, much longer than the missive from
Morgas, and I read it several times, carrying it once out into the
open courtyard to where I could perch on the edge of some steps
and read it in bright light. In it, he addressed me initially as his dear
friend Clothar, but once he became embroiled in his thoughts, and
his hand and mind relaxed slightly in the exercise of writing, he
called me Lance thereafter.

He had begun writing it in a roadside camp at the end of a full
day's march northward from Deva towards Luguvallium, by which
time he had been a married man for three days, of which he had
spent one night with his new bride, and his new situation was
evidently preying on his mind, shutting out even the dire thoughts
of what he might find when he reached his destination at the end of
his long march. He spoke briefly of receiving Ghilly's report and
the preparations he had launched immediately, and he described the
composition of the force dispatched ahead of him into the northland. He added nothing, however, about what he intended to do
once he himself arrived there and had had time to evaluate the situation in force—and that was natural enough, I realized, since he
could not anticipate what he would find.

The main tenor of what he had to say in writing to me was born
of the discussion he and I had had months earlier about the duties
facing him and the likelihood that he would be forced, sooner or

later, to choose a wife for purposes that had nothing to do with his own personal preferences, and he was still in shock over how quickly those circumstances had arisen, and how powerless he had been to influence them. Now he was legally married in the eyes of God and men, and he had not yet begun to come to terms with the responsibilities imposed upon him.

His wife, however, was not the self-centered Cynthia of Chester but Symmachus's younger daughter, the one called Gwinnifer, whom I had known as Maia. The elder one, the virago, had long since been married to another king, somewhere in the east, close by the Saxon-occupied territories. Arthur remembered quite clearly my talking about the younger daughter, telling him that I had liked her and calling her "a young girl trying hard to be a boy," and now he told me that she remembered me very well and with some fondness, referring to me as *her* Spearman, her *Hastatus*. Apparently, he informed me, I had made a strong and lasting impression upon her.

That information made me smile, trying to visualize the transformation that must have taken place to convert the gangly, long-legged child I remembered into a woman now old enough to be wed to the High King of Britain, but try as I would, I could recall only the tall, thin, childish grace of her, focused with intense concentration as she aimed and cast my javelins. And now she was my Queen! Despite the strangeness of that thought, I was grateful that it was she who had wed Arthur, and not her dreadful sister.

Arthur, however, was less sanguine about the matter than I was, and as I read on I began to see how unhappy he was. He had not wanted this match at all, he told me, but the acceptance of it had been thrust upon him when he had no option but to accept it and make the best of it, and he was far from happy with his newly formed relationship with Symmachus. He recalled my summation of the man's character, the previous autumn, in astonishing detail, remembering exactly what I had said about being able to expect without question that the northern king would be attentive to his own needs and requirements above and beyond all else, and that he appeared to be completely lacking in consideration for anyone else's welfare, problems or concerns. Now that he had met Symmachus and formed his own evaluation of the man, he agreed with my assessment entirely, and yet he was incapable of walking away from him and defying him to do his worst, because Symmachus's worst at this time, thanks to the invidious threat posed by the upstart Connlyn, could destroy all the work Arthur had done to this point, and might even be powerful enough to threaten Camulod itself.

And so, with great reluctance, he had accepted the need to compromise and had agreed to Symmachus's terms in return for the dubious privilege of having him and his fortress of Deva in nominal support of his rear.

He had no current fears, he said, that Symmachus might renege on his promise of support. The die was cast there and he expected the Devan king's loyalty to be forthcoming, along with the support he had pledged, however limited and diluted both might prove to be when the time came. Symmachus, Arthur was convinced, had his eye firmly set on the long-term goal of having his grandson— Arthur's firstborn son and heir—become High King of All Britain. There was no question in Arthur's mind that the ambitious Devan accepted the impossibility of ever having his own ambitions gratified in becoming Riothamus, but he was well aware that Symmachus was a relatively young man and in good health, and as Arthur's most powerful ally—which he would be, beyond dispute, should he ever field his thousands of warriors on Arthur's behalf— it would be only natural for him to anticipate serving as regent to his grandson should anything unfortunate befall the child's warrior father.

For that reason alone, Arthur wrote, he had determined never to sire a child upon Symmachus's daughter. The mere thought of permitting his own fleshly pleasure to expose his beloved Britain and its people to the domination of Symmachus or anyone like him was sufficient to render him impotent, and that, he swore, was unlikely to change in the years ahead. He had no ill feelings about or towards the young woman who had been his bride, he told me.

On the contrary, he found her to be as pleasant and personable as I had led him to believe she was, and he knew that she had been just as much a victim of her father's ambitions and opportunism as he himself had been. He stated plainly that in the brief time he had spent with her he had become convinced she was far from enamored of Symmachus and that she saw him clearly for what he was. He had never heard her speak a word to her father from the moment his Camulodian party had arrived in Deva, and throughout the wedding ceremony and the celebrations that followed it, he had not seen her cast as much as a glance in the king's direction. He noted, too, however, that Symmachus had been sublimely unconcerned by all of that and might, in fact, have failed to notice anything amiss.

In truth, he wrote, his new queen had looked him straight in the eye as soon as they were alone in the privacy of their chamber on their wedding night and asked for his forgiveness for this outrage of a marriage, telling him forthrightly that she had not sought it or wished for it, and had been powerless to prevent it, since an outright refusal to take part in it would have enraged her father and placed certain people, whose lives she cherished, in real danger of death. She stood prepared to be Arthur's wife and queen, she said, because of the ceremony they had shared and the vows they had undertaken in the sight of God, but she would neither be offended nor surprised if he chose to have her as a wife in name alone.

It had been an astonishing speech, and it had impressed Arthur greatly, so that in spite of his anxiousness about being up and astir and on the road northward the following morning, the two of them had then talked long into the night, discussing Symmachus and his ambitions and their own roles in furthering or thwarting those ambitions. Gwinnifer was still less than eighteen years old, but Arthur had seen that she was a real daughter of her father and already his equal in her impersonal, dispassionate consideration of the realities and options facing her in life. The upshot of their talk was that they had consummated the marriage, Gwinnifer's virgin blood providing the necessary evidence of having accepted her husband's approaches, but at the last moment, with Gwinnifer's consent and in defiance of God's law and the expectations of the world, Arthur had withdrawn and spent himself outside her. They had made a pact, he told me. As long as Symmachus lived, they would breed no child to feed his ambition.

The intimacy of that revelation stunned and chastened me, bringing me close to squirming with shame over my initial, selfish reaction to the tidings of his marriage. In imparting that information to me and sharing such a personal confidence when he had no need to do so, Arthur Pendragon had paid me the greatest tribute of my life. And yet despite that awareness, I was deeply troubled by what he had told me. The fact that Gwinnifer herself chose to be complicit with him in achieving the ends he had set for himself was neither here nor there, as I saw it. As Riothamus, Arthur was duty bound to sire an heir. Neither he nor I had been in any doubt of that when we spoke of these things, and now the thought that he was deliberately choosing to circumvent that duty upset me profoundly. But then I recalled, and went back and reread, the actual words that he had written: *as long as Symmachus lived,* they would breed no child to feed his ambition.

That made me feel no better. Did Arthur intend to kill the man or have him killed? Either one would involve murder, and I refused to believe Arthur capable of ever having such a thought. But the meaning was plain: as soon as Symmachus was dead, Arthur would have children. And then I thought of Symmachus's supposed plan to be regent to his own grandson. That plan, too, involved the death of a rival, in this case Arthur himself. That the death could be anticipated and planned for because Arthur was a warrior fighting to forge a kingdom might be morally reprehensible, but it was acceptable in logical terms. The odds were high that Arthur would eventually die in battle, and if he did, there would be no one strong enough to gainsay Symmachus's claim as regent.

The situation bespoke great cynicism on Symmachus's part, but there is no sin in being a cynic, and from Arthur's viewpoint, and incidentally my own, that same cynicism might be the undoing of the Devan king's own plans. Distrusting and disliking the man as deeply as he now did, Arthur would be watching closely for any sign of treachery from the fortress of Deva, particularly after several years had passed without his fathering another Riothamus, and at the slightest sign of duplicity or betrayal, he would descend upon Symmachus like a thunderbolt, breaching Deva's walls by whatever means he could achieve and meting due justice to his devious and unfaithful ally.

Thus I supposed Arthur and his new bride, Gwinnifer, to be united in hoping that her father would prove to be as deceitful and untrustworthy as they expected him to be. It was not a pleasant consideration, and I took it outside into the clear afternoon air, tucking Arthur's letter securely under my cuirass.

As there was nothing demanding my attention then, I saddled my horse and rode out into the countryside, where I galloped for a mile or two and let the wind blow through my hair, wishing it could do the same to my thoughts.

6

I had been waiting for him all afternoon, but it still took me several moments to recognize the man who strode confidently to meet me that evening. There was a group of other officers behind him, but he stood out clearly as their leader, with the great hilt of his knight's sword projecting up over his left shoulder from where he carried it slung at his back as I did my own. Bors had grown enormously, it seemed to me, in the months that had passed since I had last seen him. That had been in January, shortly after the knighthood ceremony, when as a newly raised legate and Knight Companion to the King, he had been immediately dispatched to Cambria to serve his first year as a field commander under Bedwyr's tutelage.

The events in the north had curtailed that Cambrian duty tour, however, and he had been summoned back to Camulod with Bedwyr to form the home garrison when the main strike force left against Connlyn in June. Now, almost nine months after our last meeting, he was taller and broader, and had developed the upright, straight-backed bearing of a confident and self-reliant commander of men. And he had grown a very respectable and surprisingly thick Gaulish mustache that swept from his upper lip all the way down to frame his square, deeply cleft chin. His voice, too, had changed radically, dropping to what was now a deep, growling but melodic basso.

He came straight to me and we embraced as friends. Then he stepped smartly backwards and saluted me before turning to introduce the members of his entourage, most of whom I already knew, although there were a couple of faces that I could not remember having seen before. They all greeted me as Magister, and while they were doing so Perceval himself joined us, having attended to whatever tasks he had set himself before coming inside.

Knowing they must all be hungry and exhausted after spending days at sea and then two grueling days disembarking their command, I had arranged for dinner to be served immediately upon their arrival, and so we ate in the impressive officers' dining room within the castle, in luxury that visibly impressed all of them, including Bors, who, as a native Gaul and a former student at the Bishop's School in Auxerre, was more accustomed to the creature comforts of civilized Gaul than were the newcomers from Britain. Connor joined us for that meal, and I won gratitude from everyone by stipulating that there would be no talk of official matters until the remnants of our meal had been cleared away.

I waited until everyone not on duty was assembled, and then I asked my own officers to stand and welcome the newcomers, inviting each of the latter to stand individually in turn and introduce himself, and as wine was being served liberally, the evening was well launched in an atmosphere of relaxed conviviality.

I seated Connor at my right and Bors himself on my left at the Magister's table, and spent most of the dinner quizzing Bors about what was happening in Camulod nowadays, but there was disappointingly little he could tell me that I had not already gleaned from the letters from Merlyn and Arthur. He had not met Arthur's new Queen and in fact knew less about her, and of the circumstances of the hasty marriage, than I did, and so instead of listening all evening as I had intended, I ended up telling everyone what I knew of Gwinnifer, going into detail about how I had met her years earlier and how she had proven to be the finest, indeed the only proficient and naturally talented thrower of my bamboo lances that I had yet met.

That earned a round of applause for their monarch's new wife, but led to my being asked about the circumstances surrounding the marriage, and so I moved on to talk about the situation in which Arthur had found himself between Connlyn and Symmachus, with the one threatening him from the north and the other, in possession of the great fortress of Deva, necessary to the protection of his rear in the northwest of Cambria. Although everyone listening to me knew of the threat from Connlyn and his allies, few of them knew much, if anything, about Symmachus, and I found myself being naturally diplomatic in what I said, casting no aspersions on the Devan king and making absolutely no reference to what Arthur had told me of his own thoughts and reservations.

Some time in the course of the first part of the meal I overheard a comment from a neighboring table as one of the middle-ranking officers wondered idly what surprises would be coming next to stir the pot in Camulod, and the question, unspecific as it was, reminded me unpleasantly of the letter from Morgas, so that I sat lost in my own thoughts, unintentionally neglecting my guests until someone brought me back to the present by asking me a question.

When the dinner was over, I called the senior officers into conference with me in my command quarters, and we quickly went over everything that had to be reported and dealt with, because as the evening wore on it became more and more obvious that they were all tired and in need of a solid night's rest. I dismissed them as soon as we had dealt with the few necessities to be taken care of and made my way back into the officers' common room, where I found

Connor at the center of a group of entranced young men listening to his tales open-mouthed. My arrival broke the group up, however, and Connor and I were left alone mere moments later.

"Something grave is on your mind, my friend, to make you so serious on a night like this, when you should be celebrating. Would it help to talk about it?"

I knew I should not have been surprised by his directness, but the spontaneity of his question prompted me to respond forthrightly, something I might not otherwise have done, considering the nature of what was troubling me.

"Aye," I said, "it might, since you know nothing about it and have no reason for being other than open minded and honest about it. Something has happened unexpectedly—concerning Arthur— and I don't know what to do about it. Let's move closer to the fire and I'll tell you about it."

Without further ado, I launched into the tale of meeting Morgas three years earlier, and Connor listened in silence until I had finished the whole story, at which point I produced the letter from her, which I had been carrying on my person, and handed it to him.

"Do you read? Forgive me, I had not thought to ask."

He sat holding the letter, eyeing it dubiously. "Aye, a little. I can read a manifest list, and I can follow a navigation chart, but I've never been much of a reader of long scripts. I'd rather spend a day untangling fouled rigging than spend an hour untangling this mess of letters. Read it to me, if you will." He twisted in his seat and peered around. "There's no one here, but you can lower your voice anyway. I'll listen closely."

When I had finished reading the letter he sat mum, tapping his pursed lips with the tip of one finger. I made no move to interrupt his thoughts, merely folding the letter up and tucking it away out of sight again, and he watched me as I did so, his eyes following the movements of my hands.

"Hmm," he muttered when I was finished. "That sounds too important to ignore. Plainly the woman has things to tell you she considers to be of great interest ... and that interest extends to

Arthur and, I would think, to Camulod itself. What have you decided to do about it, or are you still swithering?"

The word was unknown to me, but I took it to mean trying to make up your mind, and I nodded. "I've been swithering, but I've decided the only thing I can really do is send word about this to Merlyn and leave him to follow it up."

"That could take months. What if she dies in the meantime? She's an old woman, as she says. Older than I am."

"How could you possibly guess that?"

He shrugged. "Because I know her ... know who she is, anyway. I never met her, but she was wed to Tod of Gallowa—old Tod, I mean—and her younger sister, Salina, was wed to my brother, Brander. Salina has been dead these five years, and she was not young when she went ... and as I recall, she was full five years younger than Morgas, perhaps even more. So if you are to speak with Morgas, you had best make it soon."

"How can I do that? I have no control over things like that."

"Don't be a fool, boy. You command here, don't you? You could go and see her, as she wants you to."

"That's silly, Connor. From Gaul to Caledonia, leaving my post?"

He was unimpressed by my sense of duty. "How important d'you think this letter is, really?"

I thought for a moment before answering, "It must be important, at least to Morgas. And if she is, as she appears to be, the same Morgas Merlyn learned about, the one who knew and apparently bedded Uther, God alone knows what she might have to tell us."

"That's what I think, too, so why don't you simply come with me?"

"Come with you?"

Connor shook his head in disbelief and said, with exaggerated patience, "I'll be sailing home within the week, lad. And this time, as I told you last night, I'll be sailing directly to Dalriada, splitting the fleet when we reach north of Cornwall, so that the vessels bound for Glevum and Camulod can go there while we sail on northwards with no time lost."

"Aye, I remember you saying that."

"Aye, well, my route will take me within a league of the coast of Gallowa. It's a coastal kingdom, and you can see Tod's stronghold from the sea. You didn't know that, did you? I could drop you off there and go on, and you would then have seven days, perhaps ten, to conclude your affairs with Morgas, if she is still alive, and be back waiting for me when I return from Dalriada on my way back here. You would be gone from here less than a month, returning in late October, and your man Perceval is perfectly capable of looking after things while you're away ... Or don't you think so?"

"Aye, of course. He is more than capable. But—"

"But nothing, Clothar. If that letter is as full of import as you think it might be, you have no choice. I'm here, prepared to transport you directly to Gallowa. We'll be away from here in four days—less than half the month of September behind us—and given good winds, we'll be back within forty. It's the best of all possible solutions. What else is there to think about?"

He was perfectly correct, and my decision was made there and then.

The following morning, I announced my plans to Perceval and to Bors, who would now serve as his second-in-command, in charge of the new arrivals and the new intake of Corbenican recruits, and they accepted my decision without discussion, leaving me free to return to the king's villa and inform Pelles, and incidentally Serena, that I would be gone from his kingdom for the next month. I stayed in the villa for one night, then returned to the castle to complete the few arrangements that had to be made for my coming absence, and in what seemed like the blink of an eye I found myself standing at the stern of Connor's flagship, watching the shoreline of Gaul diminish behind us shortly before the white cliffs of Britain rose from the waters ahead of us.

I was still not at all convinced that I was doing the right thing in sailing off to Caledonia like this, but there was no denying that the elements that had come together to force this decision upon me had all been too significant to misinterpret.

NINE

1

"I'm glad we weren't trying to surprise them." The cliff tops ahead of us were swarming with people, all of them staring out towards our ships and looking distinctly hostile, even from as far away as we were. We had approached with the morning tide, and although none of us could accurately tell when we had first been seen from land, the word had obviously spread quickly, and soon lines of people could be seen on the sloping hillside, running down from the gates of Tod's massive stronghold—no one I knew would have called it a castle—like streams of ants whose nest has been disturbed.

Beside me in the prow of his galley, Connor Mac Athol grinned. "You'll never surprise Tod's people from the sea, my friend. That's why they built their defenses up there in the first place. Living as close to the sea as they do, they live in fear of who might come visiting at any time, and so they make sure they can see and be seen far in advance of any attempted landing on the coast. They turn out to watch us, lining their cliffs like that, every time we pass by, coming and going, so I've no doubt they'll have recognized us by now. The difference is that this time, we're going to land … at least, one of us is." He raised his voice to Shaun Pointer, amidships behind us. "Make ready the boat, Shaun, and take us in, but mind you make sure that no one else tries to approach with us. One ship alone will be a curiosity; two would be seen as an attack. Bring us as close as you can to shore without exposing us to bowshots, then launch the boat."

433

He turned back to me. "You're sure you don't want to wear your armor? I don't know these people at all, and this is the closest I've ever been to them, save once, many years ago. They have no reason to trust us. There's no guarantee they won't open fire on you as soon as you draw within range."

He and I had been through this discussion several times, and I knew he was concerned for my safety, but I had long since made up my mind, for what seemed to me to be logical reasons, to make my approach as simple as possible. I was here in response to a request from the former queen of these people, Morgas, who might now be dead, for all I knew, and since I could not bring a horse ashore with me, I saw little point in hampering myself with heavy armor when I had to walk. Accordingly I had chosen to wear only light armor: a leather corselet over a knee-length tunic of miraculously light and strong ring mail, given to me years earlier by Bishop Germanus, and the only weapons I would carry would be my spatha, my dagger and a quiver of throwing lances. Connor had wanted me to take my knight's banner with me, too, but I had opted not to do even that, content to leave it safe aboard Connor's galley with my knight's sword. I intended to visit Queen Morgas as a simple guest.

Now, as the galley surged forward under the thrust of its massive oars, I wondered fleetingly if I might have erred in that decision, and whether it might have been better to appear in this alien king's domain with a little more visible splendor to announce my *dignitas*. No sooner had the thought occurred to me, however, than I dismissed it with a rueful grin. *Dignitas* was something you either had or lacked, and it was intrinsic. It could not be gained from mere clothing and impedimenta.

Suddenly, with an abruptness that startled me, the bottom shelved steeply upwards and became visible beneath us. I heard Shaun Pointer's voice raised in a series of rapid commands. The right bank of oars rose from the water in a shower of spraying drops, and the left bank spun the galley within its own length, leaving it broadside to the shore as some of the crew rushed to unlash and launch the boat that would take me to the edge of the land. I turned again to Connor, who was watching me with an expression I could not read, and grinned at him, hoping my expression showed no apprehension of what I was about to do.

"Well, I can't change my mind now … I suppose I have to go …"

"Aye. And God go wi' ye … your Christian God or any other of your choosing. If the queen is dead, show her son your letter. Even if he can't read, he should recognize his mother's work, and their laws of hospitality should keep you safe. Be back here on the strand seven days from now, and every day after that until I appear. Stay well, my young friend, and be careful what you eat up there, among those savages."

Moments later, after cautiously negotiating the climb from galley to boat, I was sitting in the stern of the small craft, being rowed towards the shore by four of Connor's men, and people were already streaming down onto the beach, whether to welcome me or to make a prisoner of me I was not yet sure.

My rowers cast off again as soon as I was over the side, and I waded to the beach alone, wet only to the knees, and then stood and waited until the first of the throng from above reached me. They were talking loudly among themselves as they came, showing no fear of a single man alone upon their strand, and I could not understand a syllable of the gibberish they were speaking. I had thought their language might resemble the tongue spoken by Connor's folk, but everything I heard sounded utterly alien to me. They crowded around me, evidently demanding to know who I was and what I wanted there, and I began to grow slightly apprehensive when several of them began fingering my mail tunic and one of them made to snatch at my sword. But as I sprang backwards and away from him, bumping into someone behind me, I heard shouts from the rear of the crowd, and it parted to admit four men mounted on sturdy little garrons, their finery and bright colors, as much as their mounts, showing them to be chieftains or leaders of some description. These four did not dismount, but sat staring at me, not bothering to conceal their hostility.

I spoke to them first in the language of Arthur's people, then in the trading language known as the Coastal Tongue, and finally in Latin, hoping that one, at least, among them might be able to answer me. Nothing I said brought the slightest glimmer of understanding to a single face, and I felt my heart sink, knowing that my own mother tongue and even the name of my people would never have been spoken here.

In the end, despairing of anything else, I drew myself up to my full height—taller than any man there—and jabbed at my chest with my thumb, saying my name aloud and repeating it before I pointed towards the fortified hilltop at their backs and uttered the name of their king, praying within myself that Connor had been right and that this was, in fact, Tod's kingdom of Gallowa. "Tod," I said. "Tod of Gallowa." Stony silence and sullen suspicion greeted that, and so, my heart beginning to flutter in panic, I tried again. "Morgas. Morgas. Your queen, Morgas." I repeated the dumb show with my thumb and pointing finger. "Clothar ... Morgas."

"Morgas." Finally one of the four had spoken, and although all he did was repeat the name, I focused on him immediately, nodding my head and going through the motions again. "Clothar ... Morgas?"

It may have been the interrogatory note at the end of my statement that made the difference, I had no way of knowing, but the fellow to whom I had spoken beckoned me to follow him, turned his mount around and set off up the hill. I followed close behind, surrounded by the now silent but still curious crowd, and as we mounted the steep slope I began to be thankful that I had not, after all, worn my full armor. It was a long, slow climb.

We eventually reached the top, and I found myself confronted by a huge example of the kind of stronghold that Camulod had been hundreds of years earlier: a vast, circular defensive position of successive earthen ramps separated by great steep-sided ditches, each of them more than three times the height of a man. The place would be easy to defend and almost impossible for an enemy to capture, no matter how determined the assault, because the defenders could merely withdraw from one ramp to the next, leaving the attackers to climb into and then out of each ditch in succession, while under constant attack from above. There was one opening in the massive outer wall, a broad tunnel of a gateway protected and defended by side ramps and overhead bridges, and my guide led me through it as the accompanying crowd magically faded away to continue whatever activities its various elements had been involved in before our ships were sighted.

When we emerged from the tunnel I found myself on a draw-bridge that spanned the chasm of the first interior ditch, and we progressed from there over a succession of similar bridges, from rampart to rampart across the intervening ditches. I counted six rings of defense, each with its own retractable bridge, and beyond the final ring was the central area, perhaps a hundred and fifty paces in diameter, that was the central command post and the focal point of all life in the stronghold. It was almost completely filled with buildings, most of them simple round or oblong huts, dug into the earth itself and roofed with a low thatch of reeds. Two buildings, however, much larger than all the others, were of post-and-pole construction. My guide led me directly to the smaller of these and barked something unintelligible to one of the three guards at the front entrance, then turned to me with an upraised palm in an unmistakable signal to stand and wait.

A short time passed before a truly remarkable figure emerged from the dark doorway and stood looking at me, leaning casually against the wall by the entrance, arms folded over an enormous chest. The man seemed gigantic, but not so much in height as in sheer bulk. His head was bald, but he was clean shaven, too, which surprised me, because every other man I had seen since landing here was wildly bearded. Mere moments later, however, I realized that he was, in fact, completely hairless, lacking even eyebrows, and I had to force myself not to stare at him in open curiosity. For all I knew, if this were the king himself, he might be easily offended by any recognition of his obvious difference from other men, and so I schooled my face to reveal nothing of my thoughts, silently thanking both Germanus and Merlyn for the many lessons they had given me in the need to remain inscrutable when dealing with strangers.

Whoever this man was, his stare was direct and slightly disconcerting, even although I knew what he was seeking to achieve. A prolonged, silent appraisal can be an intimidating weapon against anyone who has not learned to deal with such things. Fortunately, I had used the same technique myself on many occasions and so was able to withstand its being used against me. I smiled at him, and he immediately began speaking in a deep, rumbling voice to the man who had led me here. Their conversation was brief, and when it ended the bald man came towards me, his arms still folded across his chest, and circled me several times, examining me from head to foot. Then, after his third time around me, he stepped back, looked me in the eye and spoke in fluent Latin.

"My man Cyrgus here tells me you speak outlandish gibberish, looking down your nose. I presume it is Latin?"

"Thank God, an educated man," I said, unable to contain my relief. "Yes, it was Latin, although I also tried the Coastal Tongue and several others. Where will I find King Tod of Gallowa?"

"I am Tod. Who are you?"

"My name is Clothar, and I come from Camulod, far to the south of here in Britain. Your mother wrote to me and asked me to come here to talk with her."

"My mother wrote to you?"

"Aye. Your mother is Queen Morgas, is she not? I trust she is well."

"Aha! I remember now. You must be the fellow she met in Connlyn's country. The Frankish knight, she called you. But I did not know she had written to you, let alone asked you to come here. She was very ill for a long time."

Something in the way he spoke the words chilled me, because beneath them I sensed the underlying and unspoken phrase, *before she died.* I coughed, uncomfortable with having to ask, and glanced around me.

"Is she … is she well?"

He laughed, to my profound relief. "Oh, aye, she's well now, but she's not here. Why would you think she would be here?"

"I—" I was completely at a loss for words. "She—I thought … She wrote to me, asking me to come to her here, at your castle. She said she lived with you."

He laughed again, and I found myself liking him in spite of my ignorance of what was happening here. "She does, she does, but this is not my castle, merely one of my coastal strongholds. This is Cyrgus's place, the fellow who brought you up here. He commands here on my behalf, and you have only found me here by accident. I come this way no more than once in every few months, to see that everything is as it should be. He told me that you asked for me by name, but mine is a common name hereabouts and he paid it no attention until you mentioned my mother's name. Fortunate for you that you did. There is only one Morgas in Gallowa. Come inside and talk to me, for you are the first man I've met in years who can speak to me in Latin. Come, come inside." He unfolded his arms and reached out an enormous hand to grasp me surprisingly gently by the shoulder and urge me towards the doorway.

It turned out that his castle was a full day's ride from the coast, directly inland, and that he would be returning there in three days, after he had visited one more stronghold to the north of where we now were. That news dismayed me, and I quickly explained to him that I had but seven days before the ships that had delivered me would pass this way again to pick me up and take me back to Gaul. No matter, he said, he would dispatch an escort to ride inland with me in the morning and see me safely to his mother, and with any kind of fortune, he and I might meet again before I had to return to sea. In the meantime, he insisted that I dine with him that night.

We enjoyed a private and surprisingly civilized meal. I learned that he was a practicing Christian and had received his Latin education from a series of visiting priests throughout his boyhood, all of them students and disciples of an Eirish missionary called Padraic, whose teachings they had spread throughout the islands off the coast and through much of the Caledonian—he called it Alban—

mainland itself. He had a fine mind and an amiable personality, and he loved to talk, and so we talked throughout the entire day, he hungry for conversation on any and all matters that were not concerned solely with hunting, fighting, fishing or farming, and I happy to oblige him, since he was such an engaging and mercurial character. I told him about Arthur and his dreams, and about Camulod and its armed forces, about our expedition to Gaul at the invitation of King Pelles, and even about Connor Mac Athol and his people's new kingdom in the islands to the north.

Tod knew all about that last topic, as I had expected, and he told me ruefully that the Scots of Dalriada were the main reason why he kept his coastal strongholds so fully manned. He knew his mother and the queen up there were sisters, and while he had never had reason to doubt the goodwill of King Brander Mac Athol, he yet held little hope of ongoing amity between his people and the contentious Islanders, once King Brander was no longer there. He was convinced that, sooner or later, the Scots of Dalriada would descend upon his holdings, seeking conquest. They had made no hostile moves to do so to this point, he said, but they were plainly an industrious and ambitious people, and he doubted that they would long be satisfied with living solely in the cramped confines of the isles.

I tried to reassure him that such an outcome was unlikely, but even to myself, my arguments lacked conviction. Connor and his crews were the only Scots I had met, and I had never seen their home, but I knew the people there were arming themselves to strike into the mainland. They might not come this far southward, but once on the mainland and established, who could tell how far they would range, or in which directions?

I left at dawn in search of Morgas with an escort of ten mounted warriors, and Tod lent me one of his own horses, not a garron, for the journey. I had to ride bareback, since the saddle with stirrups did not appear to be known this far north of the Wall, but that was a minor consideration and I enjoyed the comparative freedom of riding an untrammeled mount. It was indeed a full day's ride, and the sun had sunk in the west long before we saw the pile of Tod's castle on the horizon.

2

"I can hardly believe you are here, young man ... that you really came. In truth, I never thought to see you again at all. Had anyone asked me what I expected of you, after reading my letter, I would have said I expected you to be too much a man, involved in other things—*any* other things—to pay the slightest attention to the ravings of an old woman whom you had met but once and briefly. And yet here you are, and all the way from Gaul, no less!

"I should have my slovenly servants beaten for not awakening me the moment you arrived ... but they have all been with me these many years—too many years—and their concern is all to make my final days as restful as they may be. Even so, notwithstanding, I should have them whipped for being such dullards, for not knowing that just seeing a strange face and talking with its owner would brighten my days and shorten my nights. Nights can be too, too long when you grow old, young man. Remember that. Now, what was I saying?"

I was smiling at her easily, marveling about how I could ever have found her unpleasant or demanding on our first meeting. Now, she was utterly delightful, mainly because she was pleased and flattered that I should have taken the time and trouble to come from so far away to visit her, merely on the strength of her cryptic invitation.

She had been asleep when I arrived the previous night, and her stern guardians, all of them women and none of them young, had been instinctively mistrustful of me, so that they had not only refused to rouse her merely to greet me but had warned me that, because of the queen's advanced age and frail condition, I might not expect to see her before noon the following day.

She had not been informed of my presence until after her midday meal, and she had sent for me immediately, furious at the presumptuousness her wardens had shown in daring to decide for themselves whom she might and might not see. She summoned all of them and then apologized profusely to me for their misconduct and arrogance before dismissing them all angrily, sending them off with hanging heads that would mark their contrition at least until they rounded the nearest corner.

I settled down to converse with her after that, and to try to satisfy, at least partially, her insatiable curiosity about everything that was happening in Britain, south of Hadrian's Wall. It was several more hours, however, before she referred in any way to the topic of her letter and the portentous tidings she had hinted at so mysteriously. She had to sleep for an hour every afternoon, she informed me, and the time had come for her to do that, but she and I would dine alone that night, and when we were well fed and comfortable by the fireside, she would tell me everything I had come here to discover.

There was nothing I could say in response, other than to promise to be ready whenever she should summon me, and I stood respectfully while her attendants ushered her away in the direction of her personal chambers. Then, with time on my hands again, I went to the stables and found my horse, after which I rode around Tod's castle in a great, sweeping circle, examining it from every aspect. This truly was a castle—a square-sided edifice designed purely for defense and protection—built of stone and sited strategically at the top of a long, low ridge that offered clear sightlines for miles in every direction.

I found the place disconcerting, however, because it was clearly Roman in origin, and yet I had been taught that the Roman legions had never penetrated this far north into Caledonia, beyond the long-abandoned Antonine Wall that lay north of Hadrian's great barrier. It was clear, however, looking at this castle, that they had not only penetrated this far but, contrary to all my teachings, they had remained here for long enough to erect the imposing stone battlements at which I was now staring. How long the castle had stood there I had no means of knowing, but it must have been hundreds of years.

The exercise of riding around the place had filled up the time between mid-afternoon and dinner, but I was greatly disappointed to learn on my return that the original Roman bath house had been unused for so long that no one nowadays even knew what it had been used for. Despite that, or perhaps because of it, I had plenty of time to cleanse myself with hot water from the kitchens and to make myself presentable before the queen summoned me to her table.

The dinner we shared that night was delicious, although it had evidently been expressly prepared in acknowledgment of the lady's great age, for it was a wonderful offering of stewed meat, so tender that it required no strenuous chewing, in a thick, wondrously flavored gravy full of vegetables and herbs, and served on thick rounds of bread still warm from the ovens. There was no wine, which pleased me mightily despite my having formed a tolerance for the stuff in recent months in Gaul, but instead enormous flagons of rich, yeasty and wonderful beer that they brewed right there in the castle. Then, as Morgas had promised, the meal was cleared away, the fire stocked with fresh fuel, the servants all dismissed, and she and I were left alone to enjoy the firelight and the warmth, and to talk together to our hearts' content. I was almost beside myself with curiosity by then, having to fight the urge to ask her outright whence all this secrecy sprang, but she kept me waiting no longer, and as soon as she began to speak I sat back, enthralled on the instant by the tale she had to tell, and grateful that I had made no attempt to rush her before she was ready to tell it in her own way.

"I wouldn't say I was ever Uther Pendragon's mistress," she began, "but I shared a bed with him on several occasions, for a period of several weeks." She saw me sink back into my seat, and she laughed, a surprisingly high, girlish giggle. "I shocked you! You never expected to hear such a thing from an old woman, did you?"

"No," I protested, throwing up my hands. "No ... Yes! Forgive me, but you are correct. I was shocked, at the speed of ... I mean, right at the start of ... You certainly know how to capture a listener's attention, my lady."

"And so I should, at my age. Besides, it was the simple truth. As I said, for a while he shared my bed ... or I shared his. We deceived him, you see. We lied to him."

"Pardon me, my lady, but I don't understand. I have heard Merlyn Britannicus speak of these events, but he was not there when what he was describing took place and so he was reporting only what he had heard, seen through different eyes than yours, so forgive me for asking, but who do you mean when you say 'we'?"

"Us, of course. Ygraine, and the rest of her women ... Oh, very well, I'll have to start right at the beginning, since you clearly know nothing of such ancient history. You're too young, so there's no difference in your mind between what happened a mere fifty years ago in my lifetime, and what happened five hundred years ago, in Julius Caesar's. Let me think now ...

"Ygraine was the queen of Cornwall, originally from the place the Romans called Hibernia, and she had been wed to create an alliance between her father, a powerful chief over there, and Lot, the King of Cornwall. His full name was Gulrhys Lot, and although he could pretend to be pleasant when it suited him, which was not very often, he really was an abominable creature, and completely mad. And the older he grew, the worse he became.

"There was a war going on at that time, between Lot and the northern forces of Camulod—any place north of Cornwall was 'northern' to the people down there—and the Camulod armies were commanded by Uther Pendragon, whom we had been led to believe was a ravening beast. Of course, it was Lot who was doing the leading there, and you couldn't believe a word from his mouth. In any event, the queen, accompanied by a group of us, her ladies attendant, had spent the winter that year at the home of Lot's old supporter, Duke Herliss, and we had to travel back in the spring-time, to Lot's stronghold at Golant. It was a journey of some thirty Roman miles, but we were accompanied by Herliss himself and an entire train of men and supplies bound for Lot in Golant, and it was deemed to be too early yet for any serious penetration of our territories by Pendragon's armies.

"As it turned out, it was not so at all. We were ambushed and captured—our entire party, men and wagons of supplies—by a part of Uther's army. It was a terrifying experience for the queen, and for us, but she was more resilient and resourceful than I had thought she was, and she immediately ordered me to take her place and assume her identity, pretending to be Lot's queen while she presented herself as a mere servant, hoping to avoid detection. And the ruse worked, for a while. I was taken away and held separate from the other women, although they were allowed to visit me each day, and Ygraine remained unidentified.

"I don't really know when I began to notice it, although I suspect now it was evident from the outset and we simply did not want to grant it credence, but Uther Pendragon was as different as he could possibly be from the animal we had been told he was. He was clean, for one thing, and so were most of his men, and they took cleanliness seriously … far more than Lot and his followers, most of whom stank like rancid goatskins. He was soft spoken, too, never raising his voice in my hearing, anyway. But most of all, he was considerate of my person, and I had not expected that. He was my captor and I was his prisoner, his chattel … and supposedly the wife of his greatest enemy. He could have used me like the most common strumpet, in front of his men, or thrown me to them for their sport, and no one would have raised an eyebrow. But he did not. He held me in his own command tent, certainly, and under guard at all times, but I had a screened-off section of the tent for my own use, and he never sought to enter it uninvited, not once."

She was quite wrong about that, I was sure, for I was having no difficulty at all in seeing her as she must once have been, decades earlier, and I was utterly captivated by her recital, trying to imagine the response that her beauty must have provoked in a young Uther Pendragon at the very peak of his powers, less than a year before his death. I had no need to protest this time, however, for she was already moving on, lost in her own memories.

One eyebrow quirked upward. "You notice that I said 'uninvited'? Well, I invited him several times, and he came to me willingly. Of course he thought I was the queen, Ygraine, and I did not disillusion him. Indeed, I encouraged him, believing it would mold him better to our intent, which was all a strategy to divert his attention away from the real Ygraine." She paused for a moment, and when she spoke again her voice was wistful, tinged with what might have been regret.

"It was flattering to be chosen to impersonate the queen, and I accepted the duty knowing that I might have to bed our captor, but what never crossed my mind was that I might enjoy doing it. His enjoyment of me was taken for granted by all of us women, for he was but a man and I was beautiful in those days, hard as you might find that to imagine. I was tall and wide shouldered, with a slim waist and full, heavy breasts that turned the head of every man who saw me, and I had long, golden hair. I was very proud of my hair … of my breasts, too, for that matter … Anyway, I was also young and healthy, with the lusts of any healthy young animal, and I enjoyed men. In fact I had a reputation among the queen's women—undeserved, I must point out—for being too easy, too willing. And Uther was attractive, admirable and appealing. And now you are almost certainly wondering why I am telling you all this and challenging you to imagine me as a young, proud, long-haired beauty. Well, be patient for a little longer.

"The most astonishing part of this entire tale to that point, at least in my own mind, is that Uther Pendragon had known right from the outset that I was not Ygraine of Cornwall. He had known from the very moment of our capture that we were attempting to gull him, and he gulled us, instead, using our own stratagem against us and allowing Ygraine to think herself safe, while his men kept her under constant watch, listening to her every word. But he soon discovered that Ygraine had no grand secrets to disclose concerning Lot, and that in fact she loathed and feared the man. And then, on a mild spring afternoon, he called me to him and told me he knew I was not Ygraine.

"I thought he had just found out, and I was terrified at first, for I thought he must be furious and would have me flogged, at the very least, for deceiving him. But he was not even slightly angry. He told me then that he had known all along who Ygraine really was, recognizing her at first sighting by her bright red hair, which he had heard described in Camulod by one of her own brothers. Then he asked me who I was and where I had come from, and I told him the truth this time, that I had been born above the Wall, one of seven daughters of a small local king who had once been a famous warrior, and that I had been sent to Cornwall by my father, who had known Lot's father well in their youth.

"He asked me, too, if I was content with my life in Cornwall, and what prospects I had of a good marriage, and I told him the truth again. I had none at all, since all the men I knew were either toadies to Gulrhys Lot or else were dead by his hand. I might have considered marrying some of those who died, but I would never lie with, let alone wed, any of the disgusting creatures who had bought their survival with the sacrifice and betrayal of everything they had been taught to believe in. I had no wish by that time, I told him, to live anywhere else but in the place where I had been born, here in the north.

"He sent me away that same day, taken under guard towards the sea, where his soldiers, after only a few days, hailed a small fleet of galleys from the north that had been sent to meet with them. I sailed back here aboard one of those craft and found my father's home and was made welcome. I have never been back in Cornwall since then, nor have I felt an urge to go there. I never heard another word of Queen Ygraine and her women … probably all dead now, long since. Nor did I hear the name Pendragon again until I met you, on that visit to my … brother." The hesitation in her voice was minimal, but there was no missing it. Queen Morgas was less than comfortable acknowledging her brother, and she returned immediately to her monologue as if glad to be able to dispose of him.

"You told me then that Uther Pendragon had fathered a son, this Arthur, whom you named as King of All Britain … what was the name you used?"

"The Riothamus."

"Aye, that's it, the Riothamus. But I could not see then how that could come to be, and I confess I still do not. Uther Pendragon was no king, he was a chief in his own land, Cambria. And Camulod was no kingdom, it was a place. I heard it described once as a village on a hilltop." She stopped short as I muttered something to myself, and suddenly she was once more the querulous, humorless old woman I had first met in Ushmar's stronghold, years earlier. "What did you say? Have I said something amusing?"

I wiped the beginnings of a smile off my face and cleared my throat. "Forgive me, my lady, but I was amused by your description of Camulod as being no more than a village on a hilltop."

"And what, tell me, is amusing about that?"

I held up my hand in submission. "Nothing, my lady, nothing at all. It merely crossed my mind that Rome began its life in the same way, as a village on a hilltop. Forgive me, I had no wish to offend you."

Her face cleared and she nodded. "You are perfectly correct and I am not offended. Rome was once a village on a hilltop. But since when has Camulod become a kingdom?"

"It has not, my lady. It is merely the home of the High King, and he has been King only since the assembled bishops of Britain placed the crown of Riothamus on his head in solemn conclave, less than five years ago. But he comes of royal blood, none the less. He has the blood of the kings of Hibernian Scots in his veins, through his mother, Ygraine, and—"

"Of course ... Ygraine was his mother." Her face twitched with the racing of her thoughts, and then she nodded, accepting whatever she had seen in her mind's eye, and even beginning to smile gently. "Aye, that would be inevitable, given time and opportunity. Ygraine's had been a bleak and loveless life, married to Lot. She would have been ill prepared to resist Uther's attractions ... if she ever tried at all. And they were never wed?"

"No, my lady, they never were. From what I have heard, Uther and Lot and the Lady Ygraine all died on the same day. Uther had sired his son upon Ygraine, and they had been together for a year, so the boy was three months old when they all died in the final battle of that war. Merlyn Britannicus arrived too late to save the life of the child's mother, and as he himself had been married to one of Ygraine's sisters, he was now both cousin and uncle to the babe, whose mother called him Arthur just before she died. The child was the only survivor of that entire debacle, and Merlyn found him only by accident, floating in a boat. He took the child home with him to Camulod and raised him as his own son, the heir to a long and distinguished blood line …"

As I fell silent, Morgas moved as if to speak again, but then she, too, lapsed into silence, lost in her own thoughts for a long time. Eventually she said, "So Uther died in Cornwall … I never knew that … had no way of knowing … but I always believed that he survived that war and married, to breed other sons and daughters."

"No, lady," I replied quietly, "he did not survive." And then her words finally registered in my awareness and I straightened up. "What do you mean, 'other sons and daughters'? Other than whom? You knew nothing of Arthur until I named him to you, so what other—? By the sweet Christ! You bore a child to Uther Pendragon! You did, didn't you?"

"Yes, I did." Her face was a picture of utter tranquility. "I was quickened by the time I left him, his child already growing in my womb, although I would suspect nothing of it until I missed my second menses. The first one I disregarded. My body never had been regular in its cycles and I had several times missed an entire showing. And by then, two months had passed and I was safely home, and had attracted the attention of the man to whom I would be wife for many years. He had a son of four years old, also called Tod, who had never known a mother's love and who now reveres me as he would his own mother—the girl child who died birthing him—and we were to be wed. Tod was eager to have it so before he returned south to his own kingdom here in Gallowa, and when I discovered the truth of what was happening within me, I confessed my condition to him, fully believing that he would put me aside. He did not. He knew I had been a prisoner, and he decided I had been used against my will, and so he told me to say nothing more, and he never mentioned it again. We were wed immediately, and I left my own father's kingdom forever and came here. And in the course of time, I gave birth. My husband never told anyone that the child was not his, and you may be sure I kept the knowledge closely guarded in my heart."

"So you are saying, are you not, that Arthur has a brother, a rival for Uther's bloodright?"

"No, not a brother. Uther fathered me a daughter."

"A daughter." Somehow, that surprised me and was anticlimactic. A daughter would provide no threat to Arthur's situation. In fact a daughter, a sister to Arthur, might be a joy rather than a threat of any kind. "Uther had a daughter? And you never tried to find him, to tell him?"

She smiled at me, a tender, wistful smile. "What good could that have done? The very attempt could have brought nothing but grief to everyone concerned. I bore Uther no malice. He had treated me humanely and with dignity, and he had given me back my life. His child, our child, was accepted by my husband, Tod, immediately and he became besotted with her, and she grew up loving him as her father, loving him more than any man on earth throughout her childhood years. She had no idea of her true paternity, and I had no slightest wish to cause distress to either her or Tod by telling her. Better, I thought, to let it be, to change nothing and carry the truth of it to my grave without hurting her."

"I see. And I can appreciate your reasons for doing that ... But why change now? Has she learned the truth about her father?"

"No, and she is dead ... my lovely child is dead ... has been for ten years now ..." She sighed deeply. "As to why I should break my silence now, there are several reasons, one of them overriding all the others. The one that made me write to you.

"I was convinced for years that I had told no one the truth, but I had forgotten, because I trusted her completely and had never seen her since, that I had told my sister Morag, right at the very outset, when I first discovered my condition and did not know what to do. Morag and I were friends as well as sisters. We were the two eldest daughters, and we shared everything. She was far closer to me than any of my other sisters, who were all much younger. Morag was no more than a year older than I was, but it was she who urged me to tell Tod the truth about my being with child—I was already more than two months quickened by then, and she convinced me that I could never conceal the truth about the dates and timing of such an event. It was a terrifying thing to do, but it turned out to be the right thing, and I have always been grateful to her for that, although I never saw her again after I left, and when my child was born, I named her Morag, too."

"And …?" I could not see where this was leading, but her next words struck me dumb.

"Morag told our brother, Connlyn. He was just a little boy at the time, spoiled beyond belief by a crowd of doting elder sisters, so that he learned early how to manipulate people … and he never forgot what she had told him. I have no idea when or why she did it, but I have no doubt she did, because Connlyn himself told me about it."

I sat quiet for a moment, pondering that, before I spoke again, spreading my palms in bafflement. "So Connlyn knows that Arthur has, or had, a sister. Where is the harm in that? Your brother has proven himself to be a treacherous liar and a devious, dangerous enemy, but this knowledge of a dead sister … I can see nothing in it that might endanger Arthur, or Camulod."

"I know you can't. But there is more to tell."

A distinct chill swept over me, bringing my skin up in a rash of goose bumps, and I knew that I would not like what I was about to hear next. "What more?"

"Much more. I told you earlier that I had six sisters. One of the youngest was called Salina, and she was the most beautiful of all of us. I barely knew her before I married Tod, for there were eight years between us, but I met her again years later and we became friends. Well, through a long tale which you don't need to know,

Salina, from her very early childhood, lived in the islands of Orknay, in the far northeast, where she became the adopted daughter of the king there, after his son, who was to have been her husband when they came of age, was taken and killed in a raid.

"Years later, when the Scots who now rule the islands west of here made contact with the Orknay king, Salina met and wed their king, a man called …" She was plainly searching for the name, and I supplied it.

"Brander Mac Athol."

Her eyes widened. "How come you to know that?"

"I know his brother, Connor Mac Athol. It was he who dropped me ashore here. He told me your sister had been his brother's wife."

"Well!" She made a snorting sound, expressing her bafflement at the ways of the world, and then her eyes narrowed and she returned to her story. "Connor Mac Athol was the name of the man who first brought me tidings of my sister Salina, in a letter. He rowed ashore alone, watched by our guards, and left the package containing it lying on a rock, to be delivered to Tod. In the letter, Salina told me about her life, and invited me to travel north to Orknay, to witness her wedding to this Brander fellow, who called himself King of Scots."

She fell silent again for a while, gazing into nothingness. "I could not go," she began again. "Tod had fallen sick, for the first time, of the pestilence that would kill him two years later, and I could not leave him sickening abed while I ran off to meet a sister I had never known. But Morag was fourteen that year, and well grown, for her age, tall and beautiful and as innocent as a flower. I thought it would do her good to be away for a while, to see other parts of the world, and to be free of the heartbreak of watching her father grow ever sicker. And so we made arrangements for her to travel north to Orknay, aboard one of Brander Mac Athol's galleys, to witness in my stead. And so she did, and remained there for almost a full year, breaking hearts wherever she went." She smiled, wistful again, and then turned to me and looked me directly in the eye.

"When they brought her home again, they stopped first in Brander's kingdom, and then set out in Connor's own galley to come here, but a storm blew them off course and they were swept far to the south, to take shelter in the bay of a town called Ravenglass, very close to a place called Mediobogdum, an abandoned Roman fort ten miles from Ravenglass and high in the hills, where one of Connor Mac Athol's dearest friends had chosen to live. Naturally enough, finding themselves so unexpectedly close, they went to visit him, and there, ten miles from nowhere, Morag met and fell in love with a young man her own age, whose name was—"

I had caught my breath so sharply that I inhaled some saliva and choked, throwing myself into a fit of painful coughing. By the time the paroxysm had died away, my mind was still reeling with the implications of what Morgas had told me.

"She was his sister," I gasped, still straining for air. "Sweet Christ, she was his sister! And he loves her still, his lost, true love … His own sister …"

"Half sister, but that makes no difference. This was the ancient gods at work … those who delight in confounding mankind's hopes and plans. The tragedy lay in the fact that Destiny itself had decreed what must happen—even to sending the storm that blew them south to Ravenglass. It was not the fault of the children. All they did was to react naturally to each other. Neither of them could have known anything was wrong, for none of the people present there knew anything other than that Morag was the daughter of King Tod of Gallowa."

"But they lay together …"

"Aye, they did. And their union bore fruit. There are people who will tell you lightning never strikes twice in the same place, but where the name Pendragon is involved, I choose to believe otherwise."

"Great God! What did you do?"

"All that I could. Even before Morag came home, she had a suitor waiting for her, a young Norweyan prince called Haakon, who had met her in Orknay, and I had been amused to see him come, and to see how smitten he was with my beautiful child. But then Morag came home, full of joy over this other boy she had loved, whom she swore she would marry one day. His name was Arthur, she told me, from a place called Camulod, and his father had been a great warrior chief from Cambria, called Uther Pendragon."

Once again a stillness settled over both of us, and I sat staring at her while she gazed off into some far-distant corner of her memories. Then, after a time, she sighed, shuddering. "You cannot possibly imagine, young man—first of all because you *are* a man—the effect that name had upon me when I heard it from my daughter's lips. Within the space of a single heartbeat, all the pain and grief and shame I thought I had avoided came crashing down on me, and I saw what I had done ... what my years of silence had brought about. I could not cope with it, and for the first and only time in my life, I collapsed, senseless.

"When I awoke, I was in my own bed, and Morag was sitting on it beside me, holding my hand, distraught. She had thought I would be happy with her announcement, and instead I had fallen down in a swoon of horror.

"I cannot really tell you why I behaved as I did immediately after that, because it makes no sense. You must bear in mind that, at that point, there was no suspicion in my mind that she might be with child. She was a mere child herself and that never even crossed my mind until much later. No, I was simply overwhelmed with grief because all the happiness I had sought for her—and all the lies of omission, all the silence I had undertaken to protect her and shelter her from the truth—was not now merely set at naught, it was shattered, destroyed by the tragic folly of her having fallen in love with the only person in the world who was forever forbidden for her: her own brother."

She sighed again and plucked absently at something on the fabric of her dress. "I began to weep with her, and once I had begun, I could not stop. I wept for two days ... I who had never been seen to weep before. I knew I was being foolish and full of self-pity, but I was powerless to control myself, to simply stop the tears. And of course, no one knew why I was behaving that way. My man was dying, everyone knew that, but he had been failing steadily for two years and incapable of rising from his bed for the past six months, so that everyone, including me, had long accepted that his death would be a benison when it eventually came. But that is finally what they blamed for my condition ... grief. They were right, of course, but wrong in thinking to know why. I was grieving for my daughter, and the loss of innocence she was about to undergo, for throughout all that time when I was inconsolable, my mind was working, working, working, and I had come to know what must be done."

"You told her."

"Yes, I told her. What else could I do? I took her away with me, to visit a dear friend who lived half a day's walk from here. Morag loved going to visit her, and she and I would often ride over there on garrons, all by ourselves, for there was never any danger of raiders in these parts. The ride took about four hours, so we could leave after dawn and be there before midday. On this occasion, however, I had arranged for my friend to be away from home when we arrived but expected back within the day. And so we settled in, supposedly to wait for her, but really to give me time and privacy for what I had to say to Morag.

"She refused to believe me at first, told me I must be mad, or mistaken, or both ... But there was no avoiding the truth of it for her, once I had begun to tell her my story.

"She took it very badly, far worse than I had imagined, and for a month she would not speak to me at all. Not a word, not even a look. And then she missed her monthly flow. She had been of age for that for two, almost three years by then, so we knew she did not suffer from the irregularities that had always plagued me. Morag was as predictable as the moon itself in her cycles, and when she missed, knowing she had lain with the boy for several nights since her last time, she had the good sense to come to me and tell me. And of course that put an entirely new aspect on the situation. But it was Morag herself who solved the problem, for by then she had spent weeks thinking about the story I had told her, and without asking me, she approached the young prince from Orknay, who was still haunting our harbor hoping to catch a glimpse of her. She made no attempt to cozen him or to lie to him. She told him she had met a young man and been foolish enough to fall in love, and that she now regretted it, but she was carrying the young man's child. She had no wish ever to see the young man again, but her child would need a father. She would become his true wife, she said, if he could bring himself to accept her in the condition she was in.

"It must have been humiliating, having to abase herself like that and throw herself on his mercy, but he was insanely in love with her, sufficiently besotted to accept her terms as the only way he could ever hope to have her, and so they were wed, quickly and without fuss, and he carried her away to Orknay as his wife." She lifted her chin towards the fire. "The fire's almost out. Better put on some more peats now, before it's too late."

I crouched in front of the dying fire and stirred up the sunken husk of glowing peat coals into a last tiny inferno, and thrust fresh bricks of the dried fuel into the glowing embers. I moved back to my seat, rubbing the peat dust from my hands. Morgas had sat watching me as I rebuilt the fire, and seeing that her thoughts were elsewhere, I prompted her quietly.

"You stayed here, when she left."

"Of course I did. How could I do otherwise? I had a dying husband to attend to. But I had spoken with young Haakon before he left, and he promised to send a ship for me in half a year, by which time, we believed and hoped, Tod should be long dead and free of the constant pain he had suffered for two years ... Long dead was correct. He died the month after Morag left, and young Tod, who was a man nearing twenty by then, became king in his stead. The rest of that half year passed very slowly, but eventually a galley came for me and took me off to the north, for a long, long way. Do you know how far away Orknay is?"

I shook my head. "No, my lady, I don't even know *what* it is."

"It is a group of islands, far to the north and east, isolated and bleak. They are almost as far away as the Norweyan lands, which is why the Norweyans rule there. No one on the mainland here cares about them."

"But you arrived there in time to help your daughter with the birthing?"

"Aye, I arrived in time, but she was not to be helped. She died, delivering her baby. She had always been a healthy, beautiful child and she was a beauty as a woman, too, but when I arrived in Orknay, I could scarcely recognize her as my daughter. She had lost far too much weight and she looked terrible, and her pregnancy had not been an easy one. Something, some spark, the very will to live, it seemed, had gone out of her when she discovered that your Arthur was her brother. She felt betrayed—soiled, too, I suppose—and she simply lost interest in living. There was nothing I could do to change that, because I was the one at fault. She believed that I had been the author of all her grief, and she was right. Had I been honest with her from the start, had I told her the truth about her birth, she would have known her brother by his name when they met, and all of this would have been avoided."

I waited, but she seemed to have no more to say, and so I cleared my throat gently and asked my next question. "And the baby, my lady … was it boy or girl?"

"It was a boy. We named him Mordred. He is your king's son … his son and his nephew at the same time, since his mother and his father were brother and sister. A pretty pickle …

"You will hear people say, from time to time, whenever a case occurs, that the offspring of incestuous couples are born deformed or demented, living symbols of their parents' guilt and sin. But that is not the case with Mordred. The boy is beautiful, with large, gold-flecked eyes that any young woman would love to possess. He is ten now."

"And is he still in Orknay?"

"No, he is here with me, in Gallowa. I brought him back here as a babe in arms, as soon as he was weaned from the wet nurse

who fostered him. Haakon had no objections, since the boy was
not his and had cost him his wife. I grieved for Haakon, poor man,
almost as deeply as I did for my lost child, but I came to thank
God for the boy, for he gave me back a reason for living. You will
meet him tomorrow. He has been out on his first hunting trip, with
one of his uncles."

"Does he know about …?"

"About his father? Aye, he does. I had to tell him sooner than I
thought to, when I learned what my demented brother had in mind
for him. I would have told him eventually, however, having no wish
to make the same error twice."

"And what, precisely, did you tell him?"

"I told him who he is … the heir of Camulod's king."

"Camulod has no king, my lady. The High King of All Britain
merely lives there. But that high kingship is what the boy might be
heir to … High King of All Britain."

"I knew that. King of Camulod was just a simpler way of
explaining things to the child. But my brother Connlyn knew it,
too … I know not how."

I could not sit still for another moment. I rose quickly to my feet
and began to pace the room from end to end. "How could he know
that? How could he have learned of it? Who could have told him?
And what did he think he could gain by the knowledge?"

"He *thinks* he can gain a kingdom, Master Clothar. He is
convinced of it. That is why he had sent for me on that occasion
when you rescued me, and even although I knew nothing of what
was in his mind, I would not have gone to him had he not threatened
my grandson. It was a subtle threat, but unmistakable to one who
knew Connlyn's ways of old. I had never liked or trusted him,
even as a child, and I would not trust him now. And so I traveled
south, wearing a false smile of familial friendship, to find out
what he truly wanted.

"Well, he wanted me to know that he knew the truth of things,
and he wanted me to bring the boy to him. He was full of grand
ideas and plans, and while I thought him mad at first, I came to see

that he was intent upon making it happen. I had always known him as a self-centered, manipulative creature, with no thought of anyone else in his head at any time, save when he needed them for reasons of his own, but I had never known how grasping, ambitious and ruthless he really is. I managed, fortunately, to keep all signs of my loathing for him hidden. I listened with what I hoped appeared to be enthusiasm, and told him I would gladly bring the boy to him. Then I returned here and told Tod everything, and that was when I wrote the letter to you. That was nigh on two years ago, and nothing has happened in the meantime, probably because my grasping brother has had his hands full, fighting off Arthur's armies. Word comes through to us from below the Wall from time to time, so we know what is going on. But we expect Connlyn or his allies to come searching for Mordred very soon now … So your arrival is well timed."

I had stopped pacing by then and stood frowning at her, my arms crossed on my chest. "How so, my lady? What mean you by that?"

"The boy needs to meet and know his father. He is merely curious now, because he has never known a father, and I have told him the truth, that his father knows nothing of him and does not even suspect that he exists. So there is no malice in the child, no ill will, and he will go to meet the Pendragon openly, as who he is. But all of that could change if my brother lays hands on him instead. He would turn Mordred against his father very quickly and he would use the boy as a bargaining tool—Arthur's son, the legitimate heir to the High King's legacy. And eventually, when Arthur dies in battle or from illness or by treachery—Connlyn cares nothing how he dies, only that he does—then he will thrust the boy into power and himself into dominance as Mordred's uncle and regent."

I stalked away from her towards one of the narrow, shuttered windows that kept out the night air and flung the shutters open, feeling the cool breeze flow in instantly. I spoke to her over my shoulder. "I still do not understand how your brother could have come to know all this, my lady … Unless you told him."

"Do not be foolish, Master Clothar. He knew from my sister that Morag's father was Uther Pendragon, and none of the other people in the party that was with Morag when she met young Arthur saw anything strange or remarkable in their attraction to each other. The two were of an age, and both were beautiful and full of life. Their escort talked of it openly and with enjoyment, thinking they had control of everything and that the two of them were too closely watched to permit anything improper to occur. Connlyn has spies everywhere, and any one of them could have stumbled over what he saw as this useless but intriguing piece of information—Tod of Gallowa's daughter, Morag, and the young Pendragon. He would then have sold it to Connlyn, and all my brother would have needed was the merest hint of what had happened. And when word came to him that Morag was wed to Haakon of Orknay so soon afterwards, he, being Connlyn, would have added the results in his own mind and drawn his own conclusions.

"But he would probably have thought it merely amusing and of no value to him, until Arthur Pendragon became High King of All Britain. Then Connlyn's devious, scheming mind would have begun to see the possibilities underlying what he knew." She had been speaking into the space between us, her eyes fixed on some point above my head, but now she looked directly at me. "And so we come to the point of all of this. How do you think your king will react to the announcement that he has a son?"

I could only shake my head, trying to visualize myself breaking the news to Arthur. I truly had no idea of how he would react, and I told the queen so. She pursed her lips and sat nodding her head gently.

"Will he receive him, think you?"

"Oh, Arthur will receive the boy, have no doubt of that. And once the shock of knowing that he has a son wears off, he will probably acknowledge him openly as his heir. And he will treat him as he should be treated, with deference to his rank and in honor of his mother, whom Arthur still reveres after ten years … And yet the boy is the fruit of incest, no matter how innocent of knowledge or intent it was. I have no way of predicting how that might influence the King. I simply do not know."

"But you will take the boy to Camulod now."

"Now?"

"Yes, now," said Queen Morgas. "When you leave here to return to wherever you are going. Otherwise he may not be here when you return, and if Connlyn has possession of him, the gods alone know what grief will come of it, for all concerned."

She was right, beyond dispute, but she had given me far more to chew on than I thought I could accommodate, and I lay awake yet again until the very middle of the night, agonizing over another session with this old woman before I finally drifted off to sleep.

3

Connor's ship was easier to board at sea than any other I ever saw, because I had the privilege of using the device they called the Admiral's hoist, a swiveling crane built into the ship for the sole purpose of moving Connor on and off the vessel, since his wooden leg made it almost impossible for him to do so by any other means, save when the ship was moored at deck level alongside a wharf. I tightened the rope beneath young Mordred's arms and signaled to the seamen to heave away. The rope tightened and the boy swung up into the air, his eyes wide with concern until he disappeared safely into the well of the ship. Moments later, the rope came back for me, and I quickly placed one foot in the loop at the end of it and held on grimly as I, too, swooped up and outwards to board the galley. Land creature that I was, I detested being swung out over heaving waters that I knew could swallow me alive, never to be seen again.

Connor was waiting for me on the deck, one hand on the boy's shoulder. "Found something of value then, did you?"

I winked at the lad. "Mordred, this is Admiral Connor Mac Athol. Connor, meet Mordred, a prince of Orknay."

Connor inclined his head as the boy bowed deeply. "Orknay, eh? You are a long way from home, young man."

"No, not so. His home is here in Gallowa. He is a prince of Orknay but has no memory of Orknay, since his grandmother brought him here as a small child, after his mother died."

"Hmm." Connor reached down and ruffled the boy's hair. "I've been to Orknay, but that was many years ago, when my brother, King Brander, wed the Princess Salina. That was before you were even born. So you are to travel with us, are you? Well, we had best see to it that you learn your way about the ship. Have you been aboard a ship before? No, well, you will enjoy it, but there is not much room aboard a fighting galley like this, and so there are places you may go, and places you may not. Shaun! Shaun Pointer, to me."

When Shaun had taken the boy away to show him the ship and its crew, Connor turned to me. "Who is he?"

"Queen Morgas's grandson."

"I know that, from what you said. And I know his mother is dead, too. Who was she?"

"The queen's daughter."

He fixed me with eyes narrowed to slits. "Wonderful. I might never have guessed that … Then that leaves us only to establish who the father is. Is he dead, too?"

"No."

"No. That's all you have to say? You're going to make me pry it out of you, aren't you?"

I stepped close to him and spoke quietly into his ear. "No, I'm not, Connor, but it's not for the ears of others. The boy was in danger here in Gallowa. He has an uncle who would use him as a weapon. Morgas asked me to take him away for his own safety."

"Use him as a weapon against whom?" He, too, spoke quietly now, keeping what he said from being overheard.

"Against us—against Camulod. The uncle is Connlyn, the same man Arthur is fighting in the north. The warlord."

Connor's head jerked back. "The same man?" He looked at me suspiciously, then nodded his head. "Very well. I'm prepared to accept that, but I'm no great believer in coincidences. If this Connlyn seeks to use the boy as a weapon against Camulod, then there's more here than meets the eye. Who else but Merlyn or Arthur himself could be threatened by an unknown child? By-blow brats are a fact of life. It happens all the time. And why would either one of them care about such a witless thing? To threaten the place itself, in any way, you would have to threaten one of those two. But nothing makes sense there, except that the boy's father has to be one of them. So which of them is it, Merlyn or Arthur? I find myself thinking that it would have to be Merlyn, because this boy is ten years old and Arthur would have had to sire him when he was fourteen or fifteen. Am I correct?"

"Yes, you are correct."

"So it's Merlyn?"

"No, it's Arthur. He was fifteen. Fell in love with a young woman and sired the child on her without anyone's knowledge— including his own. He has no idea the boy is alive."

Connor drew himself upright in a way that reminded me of a hostile cat arching its back at a threat. "A young woman, you say, when he was fifteen? What was this young woman's name, d'you know?"

"Aye, Morag."

"And Arthur sired a brat on her!"

"You sound as though you know who she was."

"I do know who she was! It was I who took her to Mediobogdum, the place where she met Arthur, when we were blown off course in a storm. But there was nothing between her and Arthur. And she was in my charge, so you may believe I was watching her closely. I would swear nothing happened between the two of them."

"Then you would swear in vain, because it was Morag's own mother who told me the truth. The girl was with child when she returned to her home, although she herself knew nothing of that. All she knew was that she had fallen in love with a young man called Arthur Pendragon and that she would be his wife. When the mother discovered her condition, she wed her off to some Norweyan lordling from Orknay, and Morag went sailing off to the north with her new husband. But she did not go happily. She was heartbroken, and she died birthing the boy."

"Then why would her mother do such a thing to her?" Connor's voice was growing louder, and I tugged at his sleeve, warning him to keep his voice down.

"Because she had no other choice."

"There is *always* another choice."

"Not so, Connor, not when the alternative is incest."

His head jerked up as his eyes flew wide. "What?"

"Morag and Arthur were brother and sister, Connor, both of them sired by Uther Pendragon, although neither of them could have known of the other. Neither of their mothers knew of the other's pregnancy. The children grew up hundreds of miles apart, and their father died before either one of them could come close to a first birthday. There is no possible way either one could have known of their real relationship to each other, and so the incest involved was guiltless and innocent, but it was real, none the less.

"It was all a mystery, shrouded in secrets and in silences … Queen Morgas herself said to me that this was a scheme of the ancient gods, who revel in confounding the hopes and yearnings of mankind, and I am inclined to take her at her word on that. Goings-on like this certainly have no place in the plans or activities of the one, merciful God I have been taught to worship."

Connor turned away from me and caught hold of one of the ropes that secured the swinging chair from which he had commanded his galley and his fleet for many years, and he lowered himself carefully, but with the ease of long practice, into the securely anchored and suspended seat, and raised his artificial limb to rest it on the bench that extended outwards from his chair. He said nothing for a long time after that, but then he sniffed and spoke again, quietly, as though to himself.

"Well now, at least I can see why this whoreson Connlyn thinks to have found himself an opportunity—" He broke off as one of his mariners approached and stood waiting to be recognized. "Yes, Tearlach. What is it?"

The man growled something that I did not understand, and Connor rattled off what I took to be a string of instructions, then dismissed the fellow and turned back to me. "Forgive me, Clothar, but the fleet will not take care of itself, and my people seem to insist on having me make decisions for them. What was I saying? Connlyn, the treacherous whoreson, and his eye for a quick profit. I think he has miscalculated gravely, and it will cost him dearly. But the boy ... does the boy know who his father is?"

"Aye, he does. He knows he is Arthur's son."

"And how does he feel about that, about his father? Is he angry, feeling abandoned and abused?"

"Not at all. As far as I can judge, he has no misconceptions about any of this. He never knew who his father was, but no one ever suggested to him that he had been abandoned, or that the father had neglected him. The boy appears to have grown up happy and well loved among a close family who, while not British, and really more Pictish than anything else, have managed to breed him properly and appropriately. I have great hopes for the lad."

"Based upon what," Connor growled, "other than the fact that you have a natural liking for the boy? I'll grant you that he seemed pleasant enough in the few moments that I spent with him, but how can you hope to know what lies in his heart?"

"Because he has a wondrous sense of humor, Connor, and he is only ten years old. He knows how to laugh at himself already, and that is a marvelous thing. He can thank his uncles and cousins from his mother's family for that, I know now, because having met many of them, I cannot remember ever having met an entire clan I liked so strongly and immediately."

"What d'you mean, he knows how to laugh at himself? That sounds like stupidity to me."

"Well, it isn't, and you ought to know how important it is, because you share the same gift with him. A man who cannot laugh at himself can never see the humor in anyone or anything else, and that is a tragic flaw, no matter who it may involve. For in the lack of humor lie all the seeds of evil and destruction. People who see themselves as being worthy of admiration, and who cannot conceive of themselves as ever being a cause for laughter, are far too serious for their own good, and even worse, they generally believe they have a calling to impress the importance of their beliefs on others. God save us all from humorless men, for they are also merciless and implacable."

I saw Connor's shoulders straighten slightly as I said that, but he did not look at me.

"Connor, I like this boy. Mordred is a gentle and trusting soul, entirely lacking in evil or in discontent."

He heaved a great sigh then and twisted in his seat to look at me. "So be it," he said. "I believe you. But what will you do now? Why did you bring the boy with you?"

"Because I have to take him to Camulod, to meet his father."

Connor shook his head. "Bad reason. His father's not even in Camulod, for all you know. You told me a few moments ago that he's fighting somewhere in north Britain, against the boy's own uncle. So what good will it do to drop the lad off in Camulod and simply leave him there? You know how people are ... the word will get out on him, and Arthur will find out about him before he ever gets close to home. And knowing Arthur, I doubt it would please him to have his family affairs providing the talk of the land before he even knows about their existence. Besides being ill considered, that way of handling this affair would be grossly unjust for both the boy and his father. Better to take him back with you to Gaul."

"To *Gaul*? Now that *would* be stupid. Why would I do that? I want to take him to Camulod, to Merlyn. Merlyn will know what to do with him."

"Aye, mayhap he will, but you'll still be leaving the boy stuck there like a toad in a mud hole, and he'll be the talk of the entire place. And Merlyn might *not* know what to do with him, despite what you think." He pointed a peremptory finger at me to silence me before I could begin to interrupt him, and his voice grew more incisive as he went on to explain.

"Merlyn's no longer the man he used to be when I first met him—he is human, like all of us, despite what silly, ignorant people mutter about him and sorcery. He has grown old. I first met him more than thirty years ago—before you were even born—and just like me, he is growing older and less agile than he was, both mentally and physically, with every passing month, let alone each year. He and I are almost of an age, and I know what age does to a man. He is not as resilient or as ... what's the damn word I'm looking for? He's not as ... *adaptable,* mentally, as he used to be. Believe me, it were better by far to write to Merlyn from Gaul, spelling out what you have learned from Queen Morgas, with all the goings-on behind it and underlying it, and let him work out some plan of response on his own. Merlyn takes his responsibilities very seriously nowadays, and my own brother Donuil is constantly at pains to make the old man's pathway smoother and less rocky. But every time I see Donuil, or hear from him, he sings me a plaint of grief about how difficult it has become to keep Merlyn in Camulod and focused solely on Camulod's affairs. Too many things demand his attention, and too much of his energy goes to waste nowadays in trying to deal with matters that really should not concern him. He has taken it upon himself to be Arthur's representative to the clans in Cambria and Cornwall, and now he travels constantly, north Cambria to south Cornwall and back again, visiting in Arthur's name and keeping the King abreast of what his people are thinking and saying. He's too old for that, but too stubborn to stop. But when Arthur is away from Camulod, Donuil says, Merlyn spends most of his time there in his stead, and he speaks with the King's voice and has become his seneschal, just as Donuil became Merlyn's adjutant."

"I know that," I responded, "but surely this matter of the boy contains its own priorities? When he comes face to face with the boy, Merlyn will—"

"Merlyn will react as he sees fit at that particular time, Clothar, and if he is beset with problems, as he usually is nowadays, with

Camulod at war, he may refuse to recognize the urgency of this particular situation."

It was on the tip of my tongue to say that Merlyn would react promptly to this news, but I realized that Connor had his mind made up, and nothing I could say was likely to change it. Besides, he was already talking over me.

"He doesn't even know you've left Gaul, does he? How do you think he might react, then, to seeing you standing in front of him in Camulod, when you have grave and genuine responsibilities to look after in Gaul? Think you he might be angry? Seems to me he would be, and with good reason, as he would see it."

I sat mulling over what he had said, and the more I thought about it, the more convinced I became that Connor was right. It would be both foolish and intemperate to drop the boy into Camulod unexpectedly and then abandon him there to whatever might occur. But the sole alternative open to me now was to take him back with me to Gaul, and I could not see how that might work to anyone's advantage. And so finally, in frustration, I asked the question that had been in my mind for some time.

"What is to be achieved by taking young Mordred to Gaul?"

"Opportunity, lad ... and breathing space. Once you have the boy safe in Gaul, you will know that he cannot be abducted, seduced or suborned by his whoreson uncle, so that will relieve you of a great cause for concern. Then, free of that concern, you'll be able to sit down and take as much time as you need to write to Merlyn and explain what you have discovered, and describe everything that has happened in the past twenty-five years, far from the ken of anyone in Camulod, to bring matters to the condition in which they now stand. I will then take your letter with me directly to Britain when I next return, and it will be in Merlyn's hands in Camulod within days of my leaving here. Merlyn will take the time to fully understand what you have told him, and he'll be able to come up with some civilized way of dealing with the situation and of breaking the news to Arthur.

"In the meantime, while you are waiting to hear back from Merlyn and perhaps even from Arthur, you will have time to expose the lad to the way things are done in Camulod, and to teach him whatever you decide he might need to know—how to behave, how to dress, how to present himself when he finally comes to meet his father. He's a Pict, an Outlander, whether you like it or not, and he *looks* like one. You'll have time to change that, once you have him in Gaul. Cut his hair properly, teach him to wear your style of clothing, teach him the basics of good manners and civilized *Roman* behavior—and I'm only being half sarcastic there. I mean the other half in all sincerity. Hell, you can even teach him to ride a horse the way your people ride, and to fight the way they do. You'll have the time, and all the old gods know the boy won't suffer by learning new skills."

I heard the sound common sense in everything he was saying, and the die was cast. I nodded in acceptance and told Connor to take us directly back to Gaul.

4

I set out to befriend the boy Mordred on the voyage to Gaul, knowing that he must be confused and perhaps even a little frightened by the suddenness with which all this had happened to him. I remembered very clearly my own panic and confusion when, as a ten-year-old boy like him, my life had been disrupted and set at naught within the space of mere hours and I had been shipped away from my home in the care of Bishop Germanus, whom I would grow to love but who had been a stranger to me—a stranger who had been given complete control over my life.

Mordred was wary of me at first, courteous enough in his acceptance of me as a participant in his new life, but none the less reluctant to concede anything to me in the way of goodwill before I had shown him my true mettle. That amused me and it pleased me, both at the same time, for it suggested that the lad was level-headed and would be nobody's fool. But I made a point of being pleasant to him at all times during the first few days aboard Connor's galley, and soon enough, once he learned that I knew his father as a friend and was willing to talk about him, he became eager to know everything I could tell him, so that we frequently ended up talking to each other for hours in the very prow of the long, narrow boat, where we were least likely to hamper the functioning of the vessel and its crew.

The boy's appetite for information about his father was insatiable, but it was his lack of rancor over his status that I found most intriguing and most admirable. He asked me directly, very early in our discussions, if I really believed that his father the King had genuinely known nothing of what had happened after he was separated from Morag, and I responded openly, telling him that Arthur had known only what he had told me: that Morag had died within a year of leaving him in the abandoned Roman fort at Mediobogdum. That was all he had been told. He had known nothing—and still knew nothing—not only of what had happened to Morag but of anything else that had taken place since then, including Mordred's own birth in Orknay and his mother's death that same day. Arthur, I swore to the boy, had absolutely no knowledge of Mordred's existence.

I could see from his face that the lad believed me, for he nodded, wide eyed with that gold-flecked gaze that marked him so unmistakably as Arthur's son, and then shocked me by asking me if I believed Arthur would welcome him and acknowledge him, seeing that he must be a constant living reminder that Arthur had lain with his own sister. It was the kind of question I would have had difficulty dealing with had it come from a grown man, but to have it presented for my consideration by a ten-year-old boy was an unexpected twist that left me floundering, looking for words that would be neither offensive nor too adult and esoteric for his understanding. He waited patiently, however, his eyes fixed on mine until I had managed to bring my thoughts under control and to formulate an answer to his question, and then he listened carefully to what I said, nodding his head occasionally.

I made no attempt to prevaricate. As soon as I had adjusted to the shock of hearing him ask the question, I admitted that I could not guess at the correct answer, for in truth the only person who could answer it was Arthur himself, and even he would be incapable of responding truthfully until he found himself confronted by the truth of the situation. This was one of those things, I told Mordred, to which an easy and high-principled answer would always be positive before the fact, but when the harsh realities of the truths involved had to be assessed, and the life that must be lived as the consequence of those truths had to be faced, it would take a man of courage and moral determination to accept all that was entailed, and to proceed openly and in honesty and good faith. I told him I believed that Arthur was such a man.

But what if I were proved wrong, he wondered. And what if his father the King decided not to believe he was who he claimed to be? In spite of everything he or I or anyone else might believe, his grandmother's story and the supporting evidence were all subject to denial were Arthur to determine that a conspiracy had been brought to bear upon him, fomented by Connlyn and abetted by Queen Morgas. Would Mordred's life then be placed at risk?

That question was far easier to answer with conviction and authority, and I was able to set him at ease in the belief that his life would be in no danger from his father or from any of the King's associates.

He appeared to accept that, too, with an astonishing degree of equanimity, and I marveled again, as I would so often in the future, at his composure. I had never known anyone so young to possess so much quiet self-confidence, and yet I thought there must be something more fragile underlying it ... perhaps fear, perhaps doubts that he was keeping well concealed. And so I sought to distract him with talk of more pleasant things—things that I considered more suitable for a boy his age.

I told him about Camulod and the Order of Knights Companion to the King, and then went about the system of training that had recently come into being there, with young boys like him, known as squires, entering into an apprenticeship to an individual knight, a program that would teach them all the skills and disciplines, both moral and military, that were required by an aspiring knight. That caught his imagination, as I had hoped it would, and he was eager to know what he would have to do in order to enter into the squires' training program. I told him that as soon as we were safely returned to Gaul, I would introduce him to my own young squire, Rufus, who would begin teaching him his basic tasks and duties, and he could work for me and share Rufus's responsibilities until such time as we decided upon a knight from Camulod to whom he could be permanently attached. That way, I said, when Mordred finally returned to Britain again, to meet his father in Camulod, he would be well versed in the disciplines practiced there among the King's knights.

From the moment of that discussion, he wanted to know everything that I could tell him about what the task of squire entailed from day to day, and by the time we came within sight of the coast of Gaul, I was confident that I had won his trust and respect. He was a sunny lad, tall and broad for his age, with a ready grin and a sharp wit, and there were times, looking at him, when it seemed to me that no one could ever have a moment's doubt about whose son he was, for he had Arthur's own coloring, from the dark hair streaked with strands of dark golden yellow, to the large and lambent yellow eagle eyes.

On landing in Gaul, I let it be known that he was Mordred, a prince of Orknay, the nephew of King Tod of Gallowa and the grandson of Tod's mother, Queen Morgas, and that I had undertaken to see to his education as a favor to the queen herself. No one thought to question me any further, which pleased me greatly. I knew I could trust Connor Mac Athol to keep his mouth shut, and I had already decided that I would inform Perceval, Bors and Tristan about the truth of the matter as soon as I had decided upon the best course of action facing me. In the meantime, however, it was late October and winter was looming over us. Connor was already fretting about the weather, scanning the horizon constantly for the first signs of the approaching winter storms and haranguing his seamen mercilessly in his efforts to get the new cargo safely stowed quickly enough to let him off the shores of Gaul before the winter gales arrived to keep him in harbor. He had no slightest desire to spend the winter in Gaul, no matter how restful the sojourn might be.

The work schedule awaiting me on my arrival back in Gaul was a hectic one, and I plunged into it without delay. Within a day of our landing, young Mordred had been put to work with Rufus, who was a mere two years his senior, and I had my hands full with those particular tasks that had awaited my personal attention since the moment I set sail for Britain. There were few of those, fortunately, and I attended to them promptly, grateful that Perceval and his fellow officers had handled the mass of everyday tasks and drawn up all the necessary rosters and training schedules for the new intake of recruits. That would have been my responsibility had I remained here in Gaul, and I was genuinely grateful to have been relieved of it. But throughout all that I was doing in those first few days, I was thinking constantly about the letter I must now write to Merlyn.

The new batch of Corbenican recruits, the Second Sons, as they proudly called themselves, were already well on their way to completing their second month of basic training, and they were shaping up far more quickly than the first intake had, already developing what Lucius Genaro spoke of as a unit pride. That was to be expected, for the first intake had been the pioneers who demolished the mysteries of group discipline and the fears of the unknown that had faced them as traditionally independent, individual warriors, and they themselves were now helping to train the men who followed them. There was no longer any *terra incognita* in cavalry affairs for the incoming warriors of Corbenic. The men of the first intake had effectively cleared the way for all their countrymen to follow in their footsteps. Now, on the first opportunity I had to inspect the Corbenican troopers and the new recruits, I saw the change in all of them immediately. They had a confidence about them that was strikingly evident, and even the newest of the recruits already showed signs of being real cavalrymen, riding as members of a team of comrades, rather than as the self-reliant individuals they had always been in the past.

Pelles was glad to see me back in Corbenic—as was his sister Serena, who was waiting in my bed to welcome me when I retired on the first night of my visit to the villa. The king's health had improved almost beyond belief, and he was more physically active and more enthusiastic about our joint plans and the growth of his new cavalry force than I would have thought possible mere months before. The success of our venture with his first intake of warriors had been largely responsible for the spectacular improvement in his health, and since my departure for Britain he had taken to spending at least half of his time in our new castle, in the quarters set aside for his use. He had developed a close friendship with Perceval, and was on first-name terms with Bors and Tristan.

During my absence he had even dealt with the problem of the murderous and unpunished Baldwin. I was intrigued to hear that, for Baldwin had still been held prisoner in the cells attached to the villa's stables when I set out for Britain and I had been half expecting Pelles to have him quietly killed as he so richly deserved, but my cousin was neither that bloodthirsty nor that stupid. He had taken Baldwin, under heavy, mounted guard, on a tour of the training activities and facilities attached to the castle we had appropriated. Baldwin, no man's fool at any time, had taken note of the activity, the organization, the discipline of the new Corbenican recruits and trainees, all working eagerly and diligently under the supervision of their Camulodian trainers. He had also been shown the training programs themselves and the number of personnel and cavalry mounts involved, and he had seen that, as he had correctly feared, Corbenic's new military strength had already surpassed any power that he might ever have intended to bring against it from his own lands.

Then, at the end of the tour, Pelles had accused Baldwin again of foulest treachery and attempted murder of a particularly slow and heinous nature, reminding him that he had well and truly earned death at Pelles's hands. Instead, the king had released him and told him to return home to his own holdings under threat of invasion and death should he or any of his people ever be found again in any part of Corbenic. Manacled and bound to his saddle, he had been accompanied to the edge of his own territories by a heavily armed cavalry escort, and turned loose there, weaponless and dressed in the clothes he had been wearing since his arrest on the day of our arrival.

I was not sure, when I first heard this story, that Pelles had done a wise thing in releasing such a man, and I told him so, but he merely smiled and waved away my concerns, telling me calmly that he had thought the matter through well in advance of doing what he did, and that both he and Baldwin knew, with absolute conviction, that Corbenic would never again be threatened by Baldwin or any of his people. I said nothing after that, accepting what Pelles had done, because it was done and there was no way now of undoing it, but I had lingering doubts about the wisdom of it.

It was Perceval who set my mind at ease the very next day, when I asked for his opinion. He was full of admiration for Pelles's farsightedness and immediately pointed out the main benefit of releasing Baldwin, one that had not yet occurred to me. By releasing the father, Pelles had defanged the sons, none of whom had believed that their father would ever return home again. Convinced that he had vanished from their lives for good, they had started bickering and posturing among themselves in anticipation of the time that must soon come, when the old man died in captivity and his "kingdom" would be split among them. The truth was that each of the brothers believed that, after a certain amount of negotiating, he himself would rule Baldwin's Land in its entirety, and tensions had already risen high, with bands of armed men in each of the brothers' employ riding all over and squabbling with each other, not yet come to open warfare but escalating steadily in their open hostility to one another.

Pelles knew all of that from his own spies, and he knew, too, that if civil war broke out so close to his borders, his territories would inevitably be invaded and his people caught up in the war to some extent. He also knew that his cavalry force was nowhere close to being ready for full action against an invading enemy;

they had not yet had sufficient time to work off their rough edges, and every day, week and month that could be gained for extending their training was priceless. And thus he had decided to release his prisoner, sending him home to restore order among his restive sons and to re-establish peace and whatever prosperity he could recapture. Baldwin would warn his sons of the threat they would now face from Corbenic, and it was likely that the sons themselves would then attempt to upgrade their readiness. But that would take time and more expertise than they had at their disposal, and in the meantime, Pelles's people would continue training and expanding their activities and their recruitment, going from strength to strength.

By the time Perceval had finished his poetic praise of Pelles's long-headedness in this matter, I was smiling broadly and nodding in agreement, believing finally that Baldwin alive would do far more good for Corbenic than he ever would have had Pelles simply executed him.

Time was passing quickly, I found, and my letter to Merlyn remained unwritten, mainly because I felt no great sense of urgency about writing it. The other half of Connor's fleet had not yet returned from Camulod and was expected daily, but until it arrived and its cargo was disposed of, I saw no need to tackle the physical writing of the letter and was content to let the elements of it simmer in the back of my mind.

I had miscalculated, however, for Connor had no intention of waiting around for the rest of the fleet to arrive, late as they were. He was content to leave the Camulod-to-Gaul traffic to be handled by the people to whom he had delegated that responsibility, and he surprised me by sending word to me, after what seemed no more than a few days, that he had purchased and collected most of the material available for him on this expedition and he expected to have his fleet laden and on its way home again within the following four to five days. That precipitated some intense activity on my part, for I could not permit him to leave without the crucially important letter I must write to Merlyn, and I knew that when he was ready and the tide was right, Connor would sail, with or without my letter, so I retired to my quarters and issued emphatic orders that no one was to disturb me for any reason. And then I sat down to write.

I cannot remember how many false starts I made in composing that letter, but there were more than merely a few. I would stop to read over what I had written, and would then decide that I had not made the proper introduction, or the right connections between vital elements of what I had to describe, or that I had not approached it from the best viewpoint. And so I would start again, the rejected pieces of handmade paper littering the floor around my feet and piling ever deeper. Finally, however, I began a version that did not decry itself on first inspection, and I kept working at it until I discovered I had exhausted my fund of information and had no more that I felt obliged to say. The letter was nine pages in length and covered in my small, densely packed writing, and when I finished it I knew I had worked through the night and dawn could not be far away. I dried the ink of my signature with sand, and then I folded the missive carefully, burned all the drafts, and took it with me when I went to find whatever sleep I could.

In the morning, feeling remarkably well despite my all-night marathon, I read the letter over again in the light of the new day and was pleased to find that nothing in it struck me as being inaccurate or wrong. I wrapped it securely in soft, supple chamois leather, tied it and sealed it with wax, and slipped it into a heavy leather cylinder for Connor to take with him to Britain. And then, enjoying a remarkable feeling of achievement, I went to the kitchens in search of something to eat.

5

Two days after Connor left for Dalriada, on the last day of October, the other half of his fleet arrived from Camulod, bringing the next-to-last contingent of our cavalry force and increasing our numbers in Gaul to somewhere in the region of four hundred fully trained Camulodian cavalry. Once again, they brought their own trained mounts with them, and I made a point of taking Tiberias Cato with me when I went to inspect them upon their arrival, since I knew he was anxious to examine the new bloodstock sent out on loan from Camulod. He had already begun breeding some of our largest stallions with his own black German forest horses, and his enthusiasm for the task had infected our troopers, who were wagering among themselves on the size and birth weight of the anticipated crop of cross-bred foals.

Our officer corps was enlarged by the new intake, too, which meant that Pelles's recruitment and training programs would expand yet again, this time passing the point beyond which his new cavalry army could become self-sustaining even were our forces to return to Britain immediately. The senior officer in the new intake was an old friend and a fellow Knight Companion, Sagramore, whom I had not seen for nigh on two years, and his arrival was a pleasant surprise. But as he had brought letters with him from Merlyn, the celebration of our reunion would have to wait until I had read whatever tidings were contained in those.

As before, however, lengthy as Merlyn's letters were, they contained little in the way of hard, factual information about what was happening with the campaign against Connlyn in the far north of Britain, and absolutely nothing concerning Arthur's new wife, or her whereabouts. There was information aplenty, however, about domestic affairs in and around Camulod, including a specific mention that Elaine had been delivered of a boy child some months previously.

The strength seemed to drain from my legs so that I had to sit down quickly when I read that. Fortunately no one was there to notice my sudden distress, for had anyone questioned me about it, I know not what I might have said. As it was, I sat perched on the edge of a hard chair for some time, and I have no idea whether it was for a short space or for half an hour. I can only remember thinking that Elaine—my beautiful and wondrous Elaine—had

had another man's child. It mattered nothing that the man was her legal husband, formally wed to her in the eyes of God and man. The anguish that I felt was purely self-indulgent, born of self-pity, and my mind was filled with the image of her radiant face, smiling at me.

My reverie was broken when Bors leaned in through my doorway to tell me that King Pelles had arrived and was looking for me. I quickly tidied Merlyn's letters into a pile, weighing them down with a rusted, centuries-old dagger that someone had found in the bowels of the castle months earlier, and then I shook my head hard, as though I could dislodge all selfish and extraneous thoughts, as I strode out into the afternoon sunlight to attend to my duties and to greet my guest, who was standing in the sunlight, laughing with Perceval, Bors and a small group of our senior officers.

I had met with Pelles three times since returning from Britain, but on this occasion he took me aside from the others immediately and told me he wanted to talk about something important that we had not talked about before. I was of course intrigued, because I could tell from his demeanor—and from the cautious, almost apprehensive look on his face—that he was far less than comfortable with whatever it was that he was about to say to me. I glanced back at the others, who were paying no attention to us, and suggested that we take his cart and go for a leisurely ride together out into the countryside where we could talk at length and in private.

Pelles had made great strides in his physical recovery, but he was still not fit to ride a horse for any length of time, and so he traveled in a fast, light two-wheeled cart that had been specially built for him and was drawn by a beautifully matched pair of geldings. He agreed, and I sent a runner to the stables to bring the king's cart, and another to the kitchens for a flask of wine and a basket of food that we could take with us. I took the reins myself, and we were soon well away from the castle and riding easily along the cliff-top path that ran parallel to the beach far below. My regal cousin, however, remained much quieter than he would normally have been on such a day and such an outing, and so I decided to tackle him directly—him and whatever was causing him such obvious concern.

"You are unhappy, Cousin. What's troubling you?"

He flushed and looked away towards the sea on our right. "I'm not *unhappy*, Clothar, not at all. Uncomfortable, perhaps, but not unhappy ... I have something to ask you, and I'm having difficulty with it."

"Why?"

"I ... I suppose I'm afraid you'll think me preposterous and foolish."

I kept my tone light and bantering and my eyes firmly fixed on the rutted pathway ahead. "Preposterous *and* foolish ... I see, both at once. Well, Cousin, I might, once I know what you are talking about, but even if I should think you so, both at once, what would you suffer by it?"

Even without looking at him, I could tell that he was watching me closely, probably frowning a little as he tried to determine whether I was being serious or facetious, and I gave him no help, keeping my face expressionless as I continued. "This time last year you did not even know I was alive, and had anyone told you then that I thought you foolish you would have paid no attention, because my opinion on anything you did would have been meaningless to you. Now you know who I am, and I am flattered that you would be so unsure of my approval, but it really is no more necessary to you now than it was a year ago." Only then did I turn to look at him. "Did you understand a word of what I have just said?"

He was gaping at me, and his face broke into a grin. "No," he said, "but that's nothing new. I seldom understand anything you say."

"So be it, then, and let's get on with it. What is worrying you, and why would you think I'd find you foolish?"

"Because you might think I want to move too soon."

"Move to where? And why?"

As his story spilled out I saw at once why he was so ill at ease, because although what he had to say to me was straightforward and easy to understand on the most obvious level, it quickly became clear that there were depths and eddies lurking beneath the surface, unseen and unsuspected, that might be gravely dangerous for the unwary traveler.

While I had been away on my brief visit to Queen Morgas, he told me, he had received several approaches from other kings whose territories lay nearby, kings with whom he had never had previous dealings. About three weeks after my departure, he had had two envoys quartered in his villa, one of them from the self-styled king of the Parisii, who had given their own name now to the old Roman station of Lutetia on the Seine River, calling it Paris, or Parisia, depending upon who was giving the report, and the other from the king of an ancient kingdom that extended along the coast to the south of the Parisians' territories.

I listened to this without commenting, fully aware that it had been hundreds of years since either of the tribes he was speaking of had known any real power, and that I could not recall having heard either one of them, ever, mentioned by name throughout my entire boyhood. Rome's presence had driven the lesser tribes of Gaul into oblivion. Now that the legions were gone from Gaul, however, sucked home to Italia to try to stem the invasions of the Huns and the Goths, the vacuum left by their departure was rapidly being filled by other power seekers—warlords and other ambitious men calling themselves kings, and all of them in need of an appearance of legitimacy—and it seemed only natural, Pelles said, speaking as a reigning, legitimate king, that most of these should spring, or be said to spring, from the ancient ruling clans of pre-Roman Gaul.

What was most important here, however, he pointed out, was not that the claims to power being made by these newborn kings were flimsy and spurious. That was irrelevant. They already held the power, so justifying their claims to it now was mere affectation. Nor was it relevant that Pelles of Corbenic was an established and respected king, whose legitimacy had never been questioned. To nakedly aggressive and ambitious men like these upstarts, all such

considerations were trivial and unimportant beside the urgency of
their own agendas.

The crucial relevance of their visits to Corbenic lay in the fact
that these men—kings, warlords, call them what one might—had
come in person, not caring or daring to send envoys, to talk with
Pelles. That could only mean one thing: that word of Corbenic's
new military strength was abroad, no doubt as the result of our
victory over the fleet of raiders a few months earlier. There were
rumors out there, and these people wanted to see for themselves just
what Pelles had in mind, and in hand, with his new army of cavalry,
and to assess the level of threat that this development might present
to their own plans.

"I hear what you are saying, Cousin. They are wondering how
strong your strength really is."

"Aye, they are, and some of them are none too subtle about
their wonderings."

"Think you they would dare to test you?"

"No." His denial had not the slightest trace of hesitation, but he
had more to add. "I doubt that any of them is strong enough to try
us on his own, not at this stage, because our potential—and our
actual strength, for that matter—is still unknown and their own
forces are all infantry troops. Some of them, no more than a few,
have horsemen at their disposal, but those are wild and undisciplined, just as we were before you came. They are not cavalry ...
not as we know cavalry. But upstarts or not, these men are arrogant
and prideful, and it is not beyond belief that two or more of them
might combine their forces, for a while at least, to lure us into battle
and try to get the measure of us. More worthy of note, however, is
the consideration that they may be afraid of Attila and his Huns. If
that is the case, and I suspect it is, then these kings may be looking
for allies, purely with an eye to their own welfare. I cannot fault
them for that. The Huns are out there. Only a fool would doubt that
now. Theodoric is no imaginary king, and all the talk is of Attila's
rage at him."

"Did either of these kings ask you about alliance?"

"No, but they came together here by accident and neither one would care to show weakness of any kind to his neighbor. Had they come alone, at different times, I believe the outcome might have been different."

"Hmm … How much did you show them while they were here?"

"Very little. Next to nothing, actually. They saw what they could see with their own eyes and I made no attempt to hide anything from them, but I laid on no demonstrations for them, either. They saw whatever was happening here while they were here, and so they will have some idea of how our troopers move and function as groups, rather than as single fighters, but they can have no conception of how devastating our cavalry would be in battle."

I rode for a spell in silence before adding, "I am glad to hear that. So, disregarding everything you have said about your visitors, what is it, in your mind, that makes you afraid I'll think you foolish? What you have told me to this point makes perfect sense and I see nothing foolish about it. But you want to stage some kind of demonstration, don't you?" He said nothing, but I saw his eyebrows shoot up in astonishment. "Well, am I right?"

"Umm …" His thoughts had obviously been elsewhere, but his gaze sharpened quickly and he nodded. "Aye, I do. I believe we need to do something … but I'm unsure now what would be best. I thought at first of taking a strong force with me and introducing myself to all my brother kings around these parts, but then I realized I might simply be asking for trouble doing that. They are kings, but they are not my brethren by any stretch of logic or imagination. Besides, that would be a long and strenuous exercise, and I am not yet strong enough for anything that demanding. It would mean weakening our own position here at home, too, while I was away traveling, and depriving our recruits of the teaching they could receive from the veterans I would have to take with me. So I rejected that idea. And then this morning I decided I would ask you for your advice. I'm convinced I need to do something, but I can't make up my own mind on what would be best. That's why I feel foolish."

"No need, Cousin." I had been looking about me, searching for a place to stop and eat, and now I steered the wagon off the path towards a copse of trees on the sloping side of a small knoll. "There's no foolishness involved in this. You have defined a problem clearly and it needs to be addressed." I looked back at him, grinning, but quite serious. "What you really need is a minor war ... not a full-scale, years-long event, but a short, sharp affair that would allow us to tackle an enemy superior in numbers and to crush them quickly and thoroughly, demonstrating our far greater strength clearly enough that only a suicidal fool would ever dream of attacking Corbenic thereafter.

"That would be the best possible solution, but it's one that's unlikely to occur any time soon. As you say, these kings you're talking about are too newly come to power to make alliances. They can't afford to trust their own associates yet, let alone their rivals. One of them might attack you someday, but I doubt that any would be foolish enough to try it now, before they know your new capabilities. So, what we require is something else, some other form of demonstration that will show, peacefully but unmistakably, that Corbenic is not to be trifled with." I hauled on the reins and stopped close by the trees, pleased to see a tiny stream meandering through the grass at the bottom of the little hill. "Here, let us climb down, cushion our bony backsides on soft green grass for a while. We can eat and drink while we await the dawning of inspiration."

It was a full day later when a possible solution came to me, seemingly out of nowhere. I had been working all morning on a task I detested—preparing duty rosters for the coming month—and as soon as I was done with it, sometime towards noon, I made my way outside and up to the top of the walls, where I stopped to lean against the parapet and let the breeze clear my head. Directly below me, outside the walls, two ten-man squads of recruits were battling each other afoot, wearing full armor, and although I could not see their faces, I could imagine them frowning with concentration as they sought to hold formation and fight as single units of five men each, under the watchful eyes of a group of their senior trainers. The heavy clacking and clattering of their wooden practice swords carried clearly up to where I watched, and the scene suddenly reminded me of a day from my boyhood, at the Bishop's School in Auxerre, when I had been involved, with all my classmates, in a contest of skills for an unknown prize.

An unknown prize. The phrase triggered an entire series of reactions. The mere suggestion of a prize implied a reward of real value, there for the winning; that the prize was unknown added mystery; and the combination of the two had meant that every entrant had competed against all comers with everything he had. I still remembered the excitement of that afternoon, and my heartbeat quickened as I realized that it had all been staged by a man who was here with me today—Tiberias Cato. I swung away and almost ran back down the stairs from the battlements to the castle yard.

A short time later, I was sitting in Cato's work area, less than a quarter of a mile outside the castle gates, perched in reasonable comfort on a wooden stool as I waited for him to finish the notes he had been compiling when I arrived, and enjoying the familiar and evocative smells that surrounded the old man in his living. Predominant among those were the odors of dung and horse sweat, mixed with the sweetness of hay and the dusty, distinctive aroma of old straw, all of these augmented by Cato's own peculiar, familiar and far-from-unpleasant body scent, and the aromatic mixture transported me effortlessly back to when I was a boy in school, bubbling with enthusiasm for everything that I was learning.

Now he sat up straight, threw down the pen he had been using and rose to his feet, beckoning me to follow him. He led me out of the cramped cubicle he used for his records keeping and across the cobbled stable yard to the front door of his cottage, where he ushered me inside and poured a mug of frothy beer for each of us from a wooden keg set up against the wall by the window. That done, he produced two small knives and a couple of wooden platters from a low shelf, and laid out a wedge of strong cheese, a fresh loaf of bread and a bowl of sun-dried grapes that he took from a lidded wooden box on the table. We ate and drank in companionable silence for a time, and then the old man set aside the heel of bread he had been eating and drank down the last of his beer before belching loudly and asking me what had brought me knocking on his door so unexpectedly.

As briefly as I could, I told him about my discussion with Pelles the previous day, describing the visits of the other kings and the motivations we had ascribed to them. He sat listening intently, his mouth pursed in thought, and when I began to talk about the contest at the Bishop's School, he raised a hand abruptly.

"You want to set something up … something of that kind, eh? A contest, here in Corbenic."

I nodded. "Aye. But for all comers, and not simply here in Corbenic … I think here, at the castle, where our walls can speak for themselves. A contest of arms, open to anyone from the region who wishes to compete, with prizes of sufficient value to attract the best of the best."

"What kind of prizes?"

I barely hesitated. "Horses, for one thing. We have the finest anywhere, the biggest and the best trained, any one of them worth six to ten of any other herd. And weapons, too. We would offer fine weapons to be won, weapons of the highest quality. And purses— both gold and silver. We could make the contest highly attractive."

"Aye, you could, but if I am not wrong in my understanding, the objective in staging this event would be to demonstrate Corbenic's strength and superiority in cavalry. Is that not so, or have I erred here?"

"No, Magister, you're correct, but what are you suggesting?"

Cato's eyebrow quirked at my use of his title, and he returned it immediately, shrugging his shoulders, his voice heavy with irony. "Nothing at all, *Magister* … not really. But you might not be doing yourself much good, arranging such a thing. Seems to me, for this idea of yours to work the way you want it to, your own people would have to win *all* the prizes, against *all* comers. *All* of them. Otherwise, it's a waste of time and effort, because if you don't do it right—if your victory is less than overwhelming, less than total, with outsiders winning any of the major events—then the message you'll be delivering won't really be saying what you want it to."

"What will it be?"

"What you'll be saying, in the event that some of your people get beaten, is that you might be formidable, with all your elaborate, high-and-mighty cavalry, but you might not necessarily be *invincible*. Right?"

"No, I don't think so." I was hedging here, suddenly uncomfortable with what Cato was saying because part of me recognized the truth of it. "I don't think so, because throughout the tournament, we'll have our cavalry on parade at all times. They will dominate the event. They'll—"

"Horse turds." His tone was flat and unequivocal. "Who cares how they look? Who's going to pay attention to any of that? There's nothing magical about cavalry, Clothar. There's been cavalry quartered in these parts now for hundreds of years. German cavalry, the best that Rome ever had. They were right here, in Corbenic, more than a hundred years ago. Of course, they were different from yours—no comparison, in fact. I know that, and you know it and your people know it, but nobody else knows it, or cares. A man on a horse is a man on a horse. Some are bigger than others, but they're all basically the same. They're cavalry." He waved away my protest before I could utter a word. "I know you don't like it, and I know it's not even true, Clothar, *but it's what people think!* It's what they believe, and you can like it or lump it. They think your new cavalry is just another updated version of an old idea—and one that will never last, because it has been tried before, right here in their own region, and it failed then because it flies in the face of everything we know, which is that if God had wanted horses to behave like herds of sheep, he would have given them long, wooly coats.

"Besides, your troopers are Corbenicans. They're local. They live here. That means everyone else who lives in these parts knows what to expect of them—they expect them to fail, because that's what people always expect of people they live with. People fear and detest new ideas. They *want* them to fail because if they don't fail, they'll succeed. And that means that, willy-nilly, things will change—things that have no need to change. So don't delude yourself with talk of expectations and perceptions, Magister Clothar. What you have to concern yourself with is how your new Corbenican cavalry will *behave*, if you do this thing—how they will *perform*. It will be what they do, what they are *seen* to do, that counts, and if one or more of their champions gets himself bested in fighting against an outsider, that's the image the people watching will take away with them. It won't be, 'Did you see the beauty of the Corbenican formations and the size of their horses?' It'll be, 'Did you see the way the Parisian champion, What's-his-name, unhorsed that prancing fool of a Corbenican?' People are nasty, Clothar, and they love to sneer at people who set themselves above others and then take a fall. You need to avoid that, my young friend, and at all costs."

I realized that I had never before heard Tiberias Cato become so excited about anything other than horses, nor had I ever heard him say so much at one time, but more than anything else, his words made me recall a similar conversation I had had a few years earlier with Arthur Pendragon, about the strength and power of people's perceptions. I stood up from the table and went to stand at the window, thinking about what Cato had said while I looked out towards the neighboring paddocks. Then I turned to look at him again. "Are you saying it won't work? That I should abandon the idea?"

"No, damnation! I'm not saying that at all. I'm saying that if you intend to take this route, you'd better make sure that the people you select to do your fighting for you are the best of all the men at your disposal, and that they all know you'll cut off their balls if they let you down. Don't think, even for a moment, that you can rely on volunteers for this. All the volunteering will come from outside Corbenic. Your most important job will be selecting the best of your own men for each and every contest. You can't afford to have anyone less than the very best in each category fighting for you, and you'll have to have all of them training full-time, and at top capacity, for at least a month in advance of the event, because you can't afford to leave anything to chance. Chance will always play a part in contests of skill, but not too great a part if your people are trained and rehearsed to the point of perfection … or as near to it as is humanly possible."

I found myself grinning. "Some might call that cheating."

Cato did not return my smile. "We are discussing war here," he said, reverting to the same flat, emphatic tone he had used earlier. "I pray you, do not lose sight of the realities involved in this. You have, after all, just pointed them out to me. They amount to warfare, Clothar, and there is no *cheating* in war. There is planning, and subterfuge and blatantly contrived deception. Any ruse is legitimate in the pursuit of victory. If you pursue this plan, you will be staking everything, including the future of Pelles's kingdom, upon your men's ability to win a total victory. Large stakes, Seur Clothar of Camulod. Large enough, I would suggest, to make you ask yourself if this commitment can be worthwhile.

"If you decide it is, then we had better start working on it immediately. We will need to start making solid decisions very quickly: where and when these Games will be held, the kind of contests that will be involved, the way they'll be structured, the layout of the various testing grounds, the weapons to be used, all the rules of procedure and the criteria to be applied in rendering judgment on the results. And I can tell you now, it's already too late to do anything this year, because it will take more time than we have left. You're going to need a year to do this right. It will take months to plan everything, so you'll be working on that throughout the winter, and all the planning will have to be completed before we send out the word that the Games will take place. Doing that alone—getting the word out there and spread properly—will take months, and we'll have to be ready to announce it in the spring.

"And if we do this at all, we should do it in conjunction with a major festival, the vernal equinox or the summer solstice, and invite everybody to attend, the common folk as well as the contestants. And all of them, attendees and contestants, should be invited to bring their wives and consorts with them. And if you're going to have that many people gather, you're going to need to be able to entertain them all day, every day, dawn to dusk, and to put them up in comfort and feed them amply for as long as will be needed." He plucked at his lower lip and half smiled as he quirked one eyebrow at me. "You have much to think on for the next few days, I believe."

I grinned at him. "Aye, I do, but the decision is not mine. I have to take this to King Pelles and await his pleasure on the matter, but I would like to be able to tell him you'll help me with the planning. Will you?"

The old horse master grinned back at me and nodded. "Aye, with the planning, but not with the donkey work. I am too old nowadays to go shoveling dung."

TEN

1

"Well, my friend, I hope you'll judge, when all's been said and done, that this was worth all the sweat and tears thrown into it. Because no matter how big a success it is with our own lads, and with the women and the common folk, you're going to have a lot of angry contestants moaning and complaining about the rules being biased."

"Let them complain, Sag. I don't care." Sagramore had been made master of the Games months earlier, one of the first appointments Pelles and I had made after our decision to proceed with the Games, and since then I had almost grown immune to his fretting, telling myself patiently that, right from the outset, he had failed to see the reality of what I was trying to do here. Sagramore was a fine soldier, an exemplary knight and a true and loyal friend, but he had not been gifted at birth with great intellect or with the ability to theorize at length. Tactics came naturally to him in the face of action, but strategy and long-term planning were forever beyond him.

As Magister Ludorum, master of the Games, he had focused all his energies single-mindedly upon fulfilling his magisterial duties and making sure that the Games would be as close to perfectly organized and run as he could make them, and it troubled him deeply that I seemed to be going out of my way to make the task of winning easier for our own men than it would be for the visiting contestants. The idea that these Games had been designed as a political tool dedicated to only one purpose was beyond Sag's comprehension. He believed, on one high level, that my honor would never permit me to do anything shameful, but none the less, he remained uncomfortable with some of the decisions I had made and with some of the directives I had issued, and he believed that the visiting Franks were not going to like what I had done to undermine their chances of winning. Even more worrying to him was the possibility that if the rumors we had heard were true and Burgundians were coming to take part in our Games, they would be likely to be even less pleased and more hostile than the local Franks.

"Let them cry, Sag, let them cry. And I hope the Burgundians do come, although I'll be surprised to see them. They're no more popular in these parts now than they were when I was a boy. Franks or Burgundians, though, or whoever else might join us for the entertainment, they will all be in the same small boat ... by the time they realize what's happening it will be too late and the lessons will have been taught. I would rather have them angry at me after the Games, and aware of what will happen if they provoke me, than I would have them go away victorious and feeling superior, so that we have to ride out and teach them bloody lessons on a battlefield."

Sagramore was standing beside me on the castle wall, arms folded on his armored chest and scratching at his chin with one thumbnail as he squinted down at the enormous enclosure that had been created in front of the main gates. It was square in area, two hundred paces to a side and enclosed by railed fences. Beyond it, two hundred paces farther north and easily visible from where we stood high above the castle gates, the edge of the cliffs that formed the precipitous coastline angled gently from southwest to northeast, a hundred feet and more above the breakers at their feet.

I was proud of the arena we had built to house King Pelles's Games. The steeply ramped banks of seats on the northern and eastern sides of the enormous *campus*—the ground on which the contests would be played out—had taken our carpenters more than a month to build, and were designed to provide ample vantage points for the crowds we expected to attend. Behind the eastern block, concealed from view, was the encampment for the visiting contestants, built with full stabling facilities and exercise yards for both men and horses. Access to the contestants' encampment was provided by the roadway that lined the south side of the great square, running along the base of the castle wall at our feet. As well, the entire western side of the square was fenced in removable sections, permitting variable access to the immense sprawl of buildings and paddocks—far larger than the main enclosure—that comprised Tiberias Cato's stables. No one knew who would be coming from the ranks of the new nobility in northern Gaul, or even from the old nobility, but grounds and facilities had been set aside for their use, too.

I had grown tired of waiting for Sag to respond to my last comment, and so I was surprised when he finally grunted and nodded. "That's as may be, Lance, but none the less, were I a champion of any rank who had traveled a hundred miles or more to take part in these Games, only to discover that the whole affair had been set up to make it impossible for me to win, I would not be pleased. Were I such a man, I think I might be tempted to go looking for the fellow responsible." He turned and grinned at me. "The master of the Games."

I laughed at his sally, but refused to accept his point. "That's horse apples, Sag, and you know it," I told him. "We've been through this before. There's nothing impossibly difficult about winning any of the contests. All we've done is to make sure that it's as near to impossibly difficult as we can make it, in order to ensure that everyone who wins is worthy of the victory and has earned it. And so certainly our men, our very best men, have been training hard for the event. Where is the fault in that? It has been six months since the word went out that Pelles of Corbenic is to host a Festival of Games for the Vernal Equinox, a contest of the best against the best, with valuable prizes to be won. Are you suggesting that there might be champions out there who intend to take part but are not training for whatever events they intend to enter? Are you?"

"Well, no, but—"

"No buts, Sag. I will grant you that we have certain advantages that others do not possess. But try not to lose sight of the primary purpose of these Games. It is to set an example of how good we truly are, Sag, to demonstrate exactly how much better and stronger and more versatile we are than anyone else is. And we're ready." I waved my hand to indicate the massive square below. "Everything is looking excellent. I don't even think we need to go down there at all today. We can see it all from here. Can you think of anything we need to check at close quarters?"

"No, Magister. Nor could Bors and Perceval, when I asked them earlier. It's all done, they think."

I was happy to hear him say that. There were three weeks left before the Games were scheduled to take place, and I was astounded that we had been able to finish everything ahead of our planned completion date. I was unstinting in my praise of the prodigious work that had been done by everyone involved.

At our backs, out of sight beyond the rear walls and between the castle itself and the mile-distant edge of the inland forest, an entire town had been laid out in a grid of large, carefully measured blocks, in preparation for the arrival of the multitude of visitors we expected. The lines of the grid were clearly marked as thoroughfares and streets, and the blocks between them were divided into spacious sites to accommodate tents, wagons and livestock. Each block had a water station with ample fresh water for everyone's needs, and in what I believed to be our most spectacular achievement, we had even built an elaborate network of communal, partitioned latrines. The latrine sheds were sited over a series of enclosed pipes that were sluiced by the waters diverted from a nearby stream to carry the waste away from the inhabited area and down to the cliffs above the beach. The system had been designed by a team of engineers Pelles had brought at his own cost from the nearby city of Brugis, where they were responsible for the city's water system. It was the very first project we tackled in preparation for the Games and it had taken weeks to design and months to build. It would accommodate, its builders estimated, upwards of a thousand people, each using it three times a day. The most surprising thing about the sluices system, from my viewpoint at least, was that when the festivities were over and everyone had departed, it would be left in place for a month to dry out, and then it would be dismantled and its constituent parts put to other uses, leaving no sign that it had ever been there.

We had sent out messengers months earlier, with instructions to leave no town, castle, outpost or hamlet in northwestern Gaul, between us and Paris, uninvited, and we had been receiving reports ever since then that people would be coming in large numbers.

Pelles and his family—even his mother, Queen Catalina—were all highly excited about the forthcoming events, for nothing of this magnitude had occurred in Corbenic before, and they all knew how important the outcome could be to their entire future. All in all there was an atmosphere of anticipation throughout Corbenic, a sensation of being perched upon the threshold of great events.

I ran my fingers through my hair and Sagramore turned to look at me, his face wrinkling in a smile. "What are you thinking?" he asked me. "I can't tell if you are scratching your head or pulling your hair out."

I smoothed my hair down with both hands and laughed in spite of myself. "I think it's a little of both, Sag. We've finished all the hard work of getting ready, and any day now people will start to roll in—visitors and travelers, soldiers and knights, kings and dukes and all their entourages, merchants and traders, peddlers and scavengers and whores and musicians and tumblers and jugglers and cutpurses, thieves and mummers and vendors of food and drink and everything else imaginable. And once they start to come, the tide will swell and grow until our very land is transformed beyond recognition. And somewhere around that point, we will all be wishing we could recapture the peace and quiet of the past few, frantic weeks. But by then you will be master of the Games in fact, and I will be relegated to being garrison commander again. And so I think you and I should stroll over and talk to the cooks, right now, this moment, while we are still ourselves, and prevail upon somebody to feed us and give us something to drink. What say you? Come, then, and walk with me."

2

The visitors began to arrive within the week, the first contingent of them being a troupe of traveling entertainers who had set out north-ward from the town of Luguvallium, southeast of Auxerre, as soon as they heard of our forthcoming festival. Originally from Massilia, the oldest trading port on the warm southeastern coast of Gaul, they had been traveling incessantly for five years, presenting their offer-ings for the entertainment and amusement of audiences throughout the southeastern areas of Gaul, but they told us how the incursions of the Huns had shut them off from their traditional routes and forced them westward, in search of new audiences.

They told us they had heard mention of us first in Luguvallium, almost four hundred miles away, and that information shocked us profoundly, an object lesson in just how quickly matters can get out of hand. Until that moment, we had not even dreamed that the word of our activities would travel so widely or so quickly and effectively, and the realization that it had soon set us to scratching our heads over the arrangements we had put in place to handle visitors. These people had traveled more than twice as far as any we had expected to attend. If their arrival was any indication of what we might expect in the coming month, then our accommodations and logistics were already overtaxed.

Late in the afternoon of the day the first visitors arrived—they had come into view from our battlements around mid-morning—Pelles sent word that he needed to meet with me immediately, and I was on the road within a quarter hour of receiving his summons, aware from what his messenger had told me that he knew about the newcomers and was already fretting. I knew my cousin well by that time, and had learned that he was one of those people who, while normally placid and unexcitable, disliked intensely being taken unawares by events he could not control. Sure enough, I arrived to find him already surrounded by his Council of Clan Chiefs and senior advisers.

In the council that followed, Pelles and I talked long into the night, discussing the opinions of his advisers, and a number of them rode back with us to the castle the following morning, where our entire officer cadre was waiting to meet with us, summoned by a messenger sent ahead of us. That afternoon we conducted a thorough review of all the arrangements we had in place to deal with the expected influx of strangers, and three officers on our quartermaster's staff, who had already shown a facility for such things, were set to work developing additional ways to cope with unexpected demands, should such a need arise. There was really nothing more that anyone could do by that stage, but the mere exercise of addressing the matter had a soothing effect on everyone, creating at least an illusion that everything was well and in hand, and Pelles was able to return to his villa content that his chiefs would carry the appropriate word to their people.

The fact that we had dispatched several bodies of troops in strength to guard the approaches to our lands against intrusion by unwelcome troop formations was recognized but went unacknowledged among our senior personnel.

Three days after the arrival of the traveling troupe, the next arrivals came in, a small train of wagons carrying four families of merchants and accompanied by a twelve-man retinue of guards. They had barely begun settling in to the new camp site when another group arrived, this one a band of more than half a score of warriors, all of them come to compete and already well launched into a mood of gaiety. The trickle grew to a flood, and the population of the makeshift town behind us grew bigger every day, so that by the time the opening of the Games arrived, we had lost sight of who had come from where but were aware that upwards of three thousand visitors were living around the castle—approximately the number we had planned for. Only long afterwards would we be sure that the traveling players had been the only group to come from more than two hundred miles away. In addition to our three thousand visitors, we had our full complement of cavalry troopers and our normal garrison force, as well as several thousands of Pelles's own Corbenicans—the resident clans themselves. All in all, our quartermasters were housing and feeding in excess of ten thousand people a day, and would continue to do so for nigh on a month.

Once under way, the Games developed swiftly into something even greater and more satisfying than we had imagined. The spirit of competition among the contestants was ferocious from the outset, and the spectators soon began rooting for their chosen champions, and with growing enthusiasm came wagering, with people betting on everything and anything that could be bet upon, and factions emerging from nowhere in support of whatever champion or group of champions came into prominence on any day. The competition was fierce and uncompromising in every event and in every category of skills, and there was no lack of numbers in any of those, since the best minds in Corbenic and much of Camulod had bent themselves towards building a program of tests and contests that would plumb the very depths of capability for everyone involved in them.

Foot soldiers wrestled in singles, pairs and groups, using bare hands and even leather *cestes,* the gladiatorial fighting gloves so beloved of the Romans for centuries; others used wooden practice swords and shields, while still others fought with short, heavy wooden clubs simulating daggers and axes, and with headless spears and long, heavy practice staves. As the Games progressed, these large, well-equipped groups dwindled steadily in numbers as umpires and judges culled the ranks of "vanquished" men, until one clear victor emerged in each category. In other parts of the great, square campus, men competed with spears and javelins, slings and other missiles, including bows and arrows. And always, in one way or another, at all times, horsemen were visible everywhere one looked.

The horsemen were, of course, the sole reason for the gathering, and more planning had gone into the equestrian elements of the

Games than into any other aspect of the event. The Franks had always been proud of their horses and their horsemanship. According to their own legends, they were the first people ever to acknowledge a man and his horse as a working partnership of anything approaching equals. The Romans, on the other hand, had never been known as horsemen, and they had begun conquering the world before the Franks ever became known. Their legions had been infantry, and the only cavalry they had used were light skirmishers: bowmen or javelin throwers who used their speed and agility to create a mobile, protective screen in front of the Roman armies while the legions were massing into their invincible battle formations. Hundreds of years after the days of Julius Caesar, the Romans had relied heavily on their famed Germanic cavalry—ferocious warriors who rode into battle with both hands free to fight, controlling their mounts with their legs alone, and among those troops, the Frankish elements had considered themselves *primi inter pares*—first among equals.

Here and now, however, in Pelles's territory and in the brief course of Pelles's Games, we had to show our Frankish neighbors—and show them convincingly—that their day had passed, and that the new cavalry of Corbenic had come into its own. It was not a task to be lightly approached or easily completed, and thus everything that happened in the main arena was designed to draw attention to cavalry performance. All escort duties to and from the field were performed by groups of cavalry, every horse and every man perfectly groomed, flawlessly turned out and accoutered, and moving in perfect synchronization, as though bound together by physical welds. All presentations of prizes and awards within the arena were made within or in front of a formation of cavalry, even although most of the formations were spread far enough and the individual riders positioned with sufficiently painstaking care to ensure that they blocked no one's view of what was happening on the field. The awards ceremonies in the middle of the field were always simple and dignified, satisfying in their own right and perfectly attuned to recognizing the achievements of the victors, but they were always highlighted in a setting of military readiness, with the entire arena seemingly carpeted in disciplined ranks of vigilant and brilliantly caparisoned cavalry.

The show of strength was not subtle, but neither was it offensive. It merely reflected the realities of life in Corbenic nowadays, where everything revolved around and was dependent upon the new cavalry imperative. Everyone in the crowded stands knew about Baldwin's treachery against Pelles a mere two years before, and about the subsequent changes that had taken place in Corbenic since our arrival from Britain, and they understood that Pelles had taken the steps he had in order to protect himself and his kingdom in future.

The equestrian events in the arena had been designed to emphasize the differences between Corbenican cavalry and all others. We had to ensure that from now on, whenever men spoke of cavalry, they would envision large, tightly disciplined bodies of mounted men moving and fighting as a single entity, so huge and overwhelming in its irresistible weight and force that it could and would obliterate any less disciplined force drawn up against it.

We had to show that, and we had to prove it, and so we designed trials involving teams of horsemen working together to win points for timing, coordination and cooperation. The difference between our troopers and all the other contestants became obvious immediately. Throughout their history the Franks had been intensely proud of their prowess as equestrians, but they idolized individual excellence and individual performance, and they had no slightest understanding of the idea of working together as an integrated group. They fought as single warriors, and on the very few occasions when circumstances dictated that they had no other choice than to combine to fight together, they most frequently dismounted and fought together side by side as a static block.

From the first events of the opening day of the Games, the opposing values of the two sides became painfully obvious as Corbenican cavalry teams obliterated their Frankish opponents in every category, from relay races to team jousts. The Franks were incredulous and even scornful at first, scoffing at the elaborate-seeming maneuvers and methods of the Corbenicans, but after their tenth successive defeat they stopped scoffing and began to concentrate on winning at any cost, and the harder they tried, the less success they had. They also paid attention to the unavoidable truth that as the size of the groups involved in any contest grew larger, so did the margin by which they were defeated. Singly, in individual events, they fared quite well, and we sent our best horsemen and competitors into those encounters, determined to win against all odds. But in larger groupings, five against five or ten against ten, the coordination and density of our cavalry blocks made them impervious to the Franks' attacks, no matter how high-spiritedly they assailed us or how doggedly they strove to outmaneuver us.

It was in one such encounter, at the end of the second week of the festivities, that the most troubling event of the Games took place, during a bout that had pitted a score of our men against an equal number of the visitors, who had banded together and had spent several days practicing the skills that would be required in the competition. They had done better than any of us had expected, losing, admittedly, but losing less severely than had become normal, when they suddenly drew together, grounded their weapons and changed the rules of the encounter. They had lost eight men to that point, as opposed to five men lost on our part, and tempers were growing short as frustrations mounted. We were using wooden practice swords and long, headless spears, but the blows being dealt and traded were far from harmless, and several of the men on both sides who had been "retired" were real casualties. The umpires, most of whom were local Frankish warriors, had been doing a splendid job, risking their lives and limbs among our swirling, swinging weapons as they sought to keep track of every blow that landed, and to gauge whether or not it would have been lethal or crippling to the man receiving it. And then, without warning, the Frankish contestants had stopped fighting, lowered their weapons and grouped together in the middle of the field, leaving our men to ride helplessly around them, unsure of what was happening.

Before any one of us had time to regain the initiative, one of the Franks stood up in his stirrups, raised his wooden sword above his head and shouted a challenge in a voice loud enough to be heard all over the arena and the stands surrounding it.

"Hear ye, all and everyone! I propose an end to this nonsense. A challenge, issued to all Corbenic from all of us who have come here to fight. Let Corbenic put forth a champion ... a single man ... to meet with one of ours. And let the outcome of that fight decide the victor here."

There was a palpable silence after he had finished, as people thought for a brief time about what he had proposed, and then a swelling chorus of agreement broke out among the visiting crowds. Single combat between two champions was an ancient and honorable tradition, not only among the Franks but among all the ancient peoples that the Romans had named Barbarians, and it was a practical and admirable one, at that. Many a battle had been decided thus, in the open space between opposing armies, when their leaders had conceded that there was little point in decimating their entire armies when a single display of strength and superiority could demonstrate the ascendancy of one side over the other. This spokesman of the Frankish group was saying the same thing, and now he began shouting again, his voice silencing the last vestiges of discussion.

"One against five, they say. One of them—*any* one of them— can better five of us. Well, we have heard enough of that. Time now to show the truth. We have grown sick of Corbenic's boasts, and now we challenge them to prove their claims—if they can. Let one of them—any one of them—come forth now against me ... one to one, man to man, using the weapons of his choice."

Some said afterwards that we should have anticipated such a thing, but in truth I do not believe we could have done so, simply because the contestants facing us were not an army. They were not even related geographically and most of them could make them- selves understood to others only with great difficulty, using limping, hesitant forms of the Coastal Tongue, the cobbled-together language used among traders. That they would combine to defy a group they had commonly perceived to be an enemy was something that no one could have anticipated.

My mind was racing, weighing the dangers and deciding on a course of action long before the enemy leader had finished, and the gist of what I was thinking lay in the fact that he *was* their leader and his challenge had to be met, which meant that this fight was mine alone. There was no possibility whatsoever of my stepping aside and leaving it to a subordinate. At that instant, an image popped unbidden into my mind—the face of my young squire, Rufus—and I thrust it aside, annoyed at its irrelevance, because I was already thinking about the terms of the fight and the weapons at my command. I had only my long wooden practice sword and a light shield with me and I could see that my opponent had a long thrusting spear in his hand and what looked like a pair of light throwing javelins slung in a quiver at his back, plus a long wooden sword much like my own. Again I saw young Rufus in my mind, his eyes wide, staring at me as he waited for me to answer a question, and again I thrust the image aside, but even as I did, understanding came to me of what I had been seeing: I could use whatever weapons I chose, my opponent had stipulated that very clearly and bore a sufficiency of weapons to illustrate it. I would have preferred to use my lances, but they were lethal.

Young Rufus, however, in his enthusiasm to copy me in every-thing I did, had made amazing and almost perfect replicas of my bamboo throwing spears. He had no bamboo—no one had—but his weapons, and he had six of them now, were all made from flawless aged and turned ash wood, fashioned with the willing assistance of an old Frankish craftsman whom Rufus had befriended soon after our arrival from Britain. They were longer and slightly thicker and heavier at one end than my missiles were, blunt ended but cleverly balanced to compensate for the missing weight of the metal heads that crowned the real weapons, and the gentle taper of the shafts at the butt end enabled him to affix the same kind of throwing cords that I used on my own lances. Rufus went nowhere without his beloved spears nowadays, and I had seen him less than an hour earlier, while I was in the paddocks preparing to ride out for this competition.

I stood up in my stirrups but I could not pick him out among the throng of boys lining the railed fence that separated the paddocks from the arena. I waved my shield to attract the attention of Quintus Milo, who had turned out to be one of the best of Pelles's cavalry officers and a doughty fighter.

"Agree, Quintus. Take the challenge. Tell them I'll do it, but that I need to go and find a weapon. But don't tell them my name … simply say I'm a squad leader. And talk to the umpires for me while I'm gone. Tell them what's happening and have them announce the details for the crowd. I'll be back."

I set the spurs to my horse, but just before swinging him around to gallop away I reined the animal in hard before he could react to the spurs. I had just been filled with an outrageous idea and now I felt myself grinning. I was angry, but I was also cool and clear headed, my decision firmly made in absolute defiance of good sense and the laws of logic.

"I hope you realize that these people just called us liars, Quintus. You do, don't you? You heard what he said. They're laughing at us, daring us to take them one on one. Well, we're going to feed them back their bile. We may not be better men than they are, but we have better weapons and far better skills, and that's what this is all about. So accept the challenge … *all* of it. One against one, five times. Me against their five best, one after the other."

"But Clothar—"

"Do it, Quintus, and don't debate with me. And don't mention my name aloud again, either. The fight is mine and I've no intention of losing it to some swaggering braggart from the far side of some river that no one has ever heard of. And now I have to pick up some weapons. I'll be back by the time they've made the announcement."

I made my way directly to the elaborate pavilion in the south-western corner of the field that housed the king, and Pelles himself, knowing something strange had happened, came forward to meet me as I approached. I told him quickly what had come up and what I had decided to do. To his credit, he did not blink an eyelid, even although he knew, as did I, what might happen afterwards were I to lose the challenge. He trusted me without question or comment and I was grateful. He summoned a messenger to carry his approval to the heralds, he and I exchanged salutes, and I swung away again in search of my weapons.

I saw young Rufus as I rode along the western edge of the field, right where I had expected him to be, perched on the top rail of the fence closest to the action, in the middle of a group of squires wearing the colors and devices of the knights they served. Rufus was wearing a plain light brown tunic, and his eyes were fixed on mine even before I found him among his friends. As soon as he decided that I was, in fact, looking for him, he jumped down from the fence and came running. I leaned down, my hand outstretched for him to grasp, then swung him up to sit at my back.

"Your practice spears," I asked over my shoulder. "Are they here, and will you lend them to me?"

"Of course, my lord!" I could hear the wonder in his voice that I would even be aware of his spears, let alone wish to borrow them.

"Good. They have cords attached?"

"Already wound, my lord. They're in Magister Cato's hut, over there."

"My thanks, then. I'll try not to break any of them. Fetch them for me, if you will."

He ran and brought me the weapons, and I spent the next few moments checking their readiness, although I knew there was no need. They were the boy's pride and joy and were in perfect condition. I nodded my approval, slung their long quiver over my shoulders, picked the lad up bodily again and carried him back to where his friends were gawking at us, then kicked my horse back towards the large knot of horsemen in the center of the arena.

The heralds were just starting to make their announcement as I got back: the captain-at-arms of the Blue Group, currently in the arena, would fight in single combat against the captain-at-arms of the

Red Group. Should the Blue captain be successful in his challenge, the Red Group would concede defeat and leave the arena. Should the Blues fail to win, however, the captain of the Reds would remain in the arena and fight the next Blue challenger in line, until either he was vanquished or he had beaten five successive champions.

The crowd erupted in a frenzy of cheering and jeering, and I imagined I could hear the levels of wagering escalate as I rode to the far southwest corner of the field to await the signal for the start of the fight. Behind me, I knew, my first opponent would be doing the same thing, moving northeastwards. I reached the corner of the field and turned my horse around, shutting my mind to the spectators and concentrating only on the arena and what lay there for me. Ahead of me and to my left, my own men and all but five of the enemy were leaving the arena and entering the paddock area. In the corner opposite me, almost a quarter of a mile from where I sat, my five opponents were clustered together, watching me, their leader in the center, slightly ahead of the others.

I knew nothing about the man I was about to fight, not even where he came from. I knew that he was tall and lean, his limbs long, clean lined and well muscled. I also knew that his hair was long and pale gold in color, because locks of it had escaped the confines of his helmet. I knew he favored a spear over a sword, and I suspected he might be a skilled javelin thrower, simply from the way he carried the two missiles slung at his back, but I doubted that he would be able to throw as accurately as I could from the back of a galloping horse, and that was the tactic I intended to use to bring him down quickly.

A single horn blast signaled the start of the bout, and I kicked my horse forward immediately, taking him smoothly from a walk to a canter and into an easy lope as I reached behind me and pulled a lance from my quiver, then wrapped the end of the throwing cord comfortably around my fingers. Across from me, bending forward over the neck of a horse far smaller and more wiry than my own, my opponent still grasped his thrusting spear, holding it out and away from his body, the point angled slightly downwards yet still roughly parallel to the ground as he advanced more and more swiftly to meet me. I waited until we had closed half the distance between us, and then I leaned forward, pressing my weight down into my left stirrup and feeling my horse responding beneath me, veering to my left. My opponent veered to intercept me and I kicked my mount to a full gallop and started to circle away from him. He countered instantly, swinging hard left and committing to the chase, so that by the time he realized I had merely feinted and turned in a tight little circle to head back towards him, he was too late to do anything effective. I galloped flat out towards him then veered to pass in front of him, fully ten horse-lengths to his left, and as he swept by me I raised myself in the stirrups and unleashed my lance. It hissed across the distance separating us and struck him hard and high on the left shoulder before being deflected upwards to clang against his heavy, visored helmet. The impact, completely unexpected and far more crushing than he could possibly have expected, lifted him clear of the saddle and sent him flying.

I ignored him after that, knowing that he was effectively dead and could not possibly get to his feet and remount after such a fall. I broke away and charged back at full speed towards his four remaining companions, controlling my horse with my knees as I reached behind me for another lance and prepared it for throwing.

Ahead of me, the second of the Frankish champions belatedly spurred his horse into motion, kicking wildly at it as he fought to bring it to fighting speed. This one carried no spears at all that I could see. He had a light shield and a long wooden sword and he rode crouched in his saddle, presenting me with the smallest possible target as he came sweeping towards me. He did not even last as long as his leader had. My first cast hit him full on his lowered head, right in the middle of his helmet's dome, as he came charging towards me like a dart from a ballista. He was still unconscious, I learned later, when they came to carry him out of the arena.

The third man approached me more slowly, having learned from the swift fate of his two companions. He, too, carried a wooden sword and a light shield, but he was more cautious and probably more intelligent than his predecessors. I rode circles around him for some time, and he was content to allow me to do so, merely turning his own mount to keep me in sight, and keeping his shield raised protectively in front of him at all times. It was soon plain to see that he was hoping I would tire my horse and make his life a little more simple, and so I stopped circling and instead sat facing him for a time, hefting my lance and gauging the distance between us and the time it would take him to swing his shield and block my throw.

When it became clear that he was prepared to sit there all day, defying me to make the first move against him, I made it. I charged straight towards him, rising high in my stirrups and throwing hard and straight, and sure enough, just as I had expected, he swung his mount sharply to his right and brought his shield arm scything sideways to send my weapon whistling off, over his shoulder. By the time he had seen my cast, however, and begun to pull his horse aside, I had already closed half the distance between us and was pulling my long, heavy wooden sword from my saddle bow. I was within striking distance of him before he could recover from his defensive shield swing and I caught him in the angle of neck and shoulder with a crushing overarm swing that sent him reeling, clutching reflexively at his saddle bow as he toppled sideways and crashed to the ground almost beneath his horse's hooves.

My friends told me afterwards that the crowd was screaming in delirium by that stage, but I was unaware of anything beyond my own priorities as I slipped the leather loop of my practice sword off my wrist and hung it over the hook on my saddle. I had begun to reach behind me for another lance, my eyes sweeping the far corner of the field for my two remaining opponents, when I realized that neither one of them was there. My heart leapt in alarm and I wrenched hard at my mount's head, yanking it down hard, sideways and to the left, just as I heard the thunder of hooves at my back. My fourth opponent was in full attack by the time I began to look for him, and now his first heavy blow landed on me before I had a chance to prepare for it.

My sideways lunge, however, tightening as it did into a miraculously narrow turn by my magnificent horse, was neither instinctive nor intuitive, no matter how it might have looked to an observer. It was the result of deliberate and intensive training, developed over months of wearying, repetitive drills and designed to go against the instincts of man and animal and to thwart any attacker by doing the unexpected at a time of great stress. It was the best move I could have made in this instance, because this attacker was left handed, and the angle of my hooking movement to his left took me sufficiently inside the arc of his swing to throw off his aim. The long, heavy cudgel that was his practice sword landed high on the rear edge of my helmet and clanged down from there to skip across my shoulders. The glancing blow did little damage to me, for I was still turning into it even as it fell, but I felt the long blade of the hard-swung weapon catch against the quiver hanging at my back, snapping the shoulder strap and sending the quiver flying, along with the three spears it still contained. Then, knowing that another blow, this one back-handed, was already coming at me, I kicked my right foot free of its stirrup and let my body slouch forward until I fell sideways from the saddle, my left foot securely braced in the stirrup while my right hand found and grasped the peak of my saddle, ready to pull me upright again.

As soon as it felt me drop like that, with my head down below the level of its own, my horse responded as it had been trained to do, wheeling abruptly to its right in a rearing turn, to bring the protection of its body between me and whoever my attacker might be. I felt the concussion of a blow landing on the bare saddle, but I was already scanning the ground ahead of me, searching avidly for the quiver of spears I had lost. It was almost within my grasp, tantalizingly close but beyond my reach until my attacker struck again, his horse striking my own as he leaned forward to hack at my hand on the saddle horn. I can but presume that is what he did, because I could see nothing of him and the blow never hit me, but that is what I would have tried to do had I been

him. Whatever his intent, he aided me, because my mount shied
in protest and sidled far enough away from his attack to allow me
to snatch up the quiver of spears without his being aware of it,
and I immediately straightened my left leg, thrusting against the
stirrup for leverage as I kicked upwards with my right leg and
hauled myself back up into the saddle as my horse responded
perfectly, bearing me away and to the left of my opponent in a
long, looping circle.

As soon as I was back in my seat, I set about preparing a new
lance, controlling my horse with my knees and ignoring the surge
of galloping hooves closing quickly again from behind me. I
wrapped the end of the throwing cord around my index finger, took
the reins again in my left hand and this time swung around to my
right, still turning tightly and aiming as I went. The fellow barely
saw the missile before it took him under the arm on his right side,
passing beneath the edge of the shield he had thrown up too high
and too quickly, and slamming into his side between armpit and
waist. It would have been a killing strike, even though it failed to
unhorse him, and he was finished.

I turned my attention to his last surviving companion, who had
been riding close behind him all the time, not participating in any
of his attacks on me but ready to move at once should I win again.
Now he sat gazing at me, he and his horse both motionless, and
although I could not see his face behind the visor, I knew what he
must be thinking. He had stood fifth in ranking among his peers
and I had beaten all four ahead of him. Now that he was left alone
to face me, he should have had the advantage, since I ought to have
been exhausted by the fights against his fellows. But that was not
the case. All I had done was throw spears, lethally and skillfully,
outmaneuvering all of them. And now I sat waiting for him to bring
the fight to me. I found nothing surprising in his hesitancy, and in
fact felt a pang of sympathy for the fellow, so I threw away my two
remaining spears, one after the other, then drew my practice sword
and leaned backwards to kick my right leg high over the front of
my saddle and slide to the ground, where I slapped my horse on the

rump and told him to move away. Only then did I hear the noise of the crowd, as they released a great susurration of pent-up breath and then fell silent.

The man fought well, once he realized that he had a straight-forward chance of besting me on foot, man to man, blade to blade and with no strange missiles involved, but he was not accustomed to swinging the immense weight of the practice swords we used every day, and so he tired quickly. When it became visibly agonizing for him to keep his point clear of the ground, I finished him quickly, smashing his blade aside and tripping him easily, then pressing my own point to his unguarded throat.

At that moment, standing over the last of my five opponents that day in one corner of the arena, facing the ranked seats ahead of me and hearing the shouts and cheers of the spectators there, I felt nothing but a fleeting sense of satisfaction that was amplified when one of the umpires approached me carrying the six javelins belong-ing to my squire. As I thanked him for his considerateness, however, I became aware of a change in the tenor of the sounds surrounding us. A formless feeling of unease sprang up in me, and I turned to look behind me.

The Corbenican cavalry were advancing into the arena from the paddocks beside the field. Their decision to come out, I knew, must have been spontaneous, and yet they moved in their units, following each other wordlessly in the disciplined formations that had become second nature to them. Gauls and Britons together, they came forward in sequence and in silence, forming up wordlessly until the entire armed cavalry strength of Corbenic sat motionless in front of me, their eyes fixed on me, making me feel both proud and humbled. The only sounds that came from their ranks were the occasional snort or whinny of a horse and the thud of hooves as an animal stamped its feet or shied at a fly bite. I saw King Pelles himself riding among them, surrounded by his clan chiefs and heading towards me, and I was aware that the edges of the huge field were lined with ranks of watching Franks who had spilled out from the visitors' encampment behind the stands. There was no need for words. A message had been delivered for all to see and it had been understood.

Moments later Pelles was stretching out his hand to me, and I walked forward, took it and bent over it. When I looked up again he was smiling at me.

"Well done, Cousin," he said. "You may dismiss your men now. This day's events are over, for who could improve on what you have already shown us? Come you now and dine with us."

My commanders were watching me, aware of King Pelles but waiting for my signal. I gave it, they passed it along, and still in silence, the cavalry troops thronged in the field began to disperse, still in formation and still in disciplined sequence.

That single episode, spontaneous as it was, marked the effective end of the King's Games, for the spirit seemed to have gone out of the visiting competitors as a result of it. The Games had been successful, nevertheless, for the lessons they presented had been well observed and taken to heart. From that time forward, all over northwestern Gaul, the warrior peoples began to pay close attention to Pelles's cavalry and its fighting techniques. No great, sweeping equestrian movement was born of the lessons learned, however, for the only sources of capable cavalry teachers were Camulod in Britain and Corbenic itself, and even when interested parties attempted to lure high-ranking officers away from Pelles with rewards of money and position, they were doomed to fail because they lacked the infrastructure that had emerged from Camulod and was necessary to the successful undertaking of such a venture: the hundred-year-old cavalry background and the established blood lines and breeding programs.

The story of my five-champion challenge survived, too, although in a form that was considerably altered as years passed by. When I heard it repeated many years later, I was already an old man and I laughed at it, never thinking that such a silly piece of fabrication could be true in any sense, but some of my younger companions took great delight in telling me that it was my tale, and that I was the hero knight in it. I was astonished, and even quite ashamed, to be remembered in such an exaggerated tale, notwith-standing that my name was mentioned nowhere in it. It was a ludi-crous distortion of what had really happened, embellished time and again until not a grain of recognizable truth remained in it.

Rather than living in the castle above the sea, I was a visitor in this tale, a stranger from outside, seeking to overthrow the evil lord of the castle and constrained to deal, time after time, with the implacable champions he sent against me, until I had overthrown his entire complement, at which time I entered the castle, claimed it as my own and slew the king.

3

I had been in Gaul for more than two years now and our entire complement from Camulod numbered in excess of six hundred souls, with nigh on five hundred of those being officers and troop-ers. Pelles's cavalry army was firmly founded by now, with its own bloodstock and horse farms, armed camps and garrisons, and sound, solidly supported recruitment programs, and the advisory and supervisory capacities fulfilled by myself and my officers had become redundant. Pelles's own army staff, headed jointly by Chief Cortix and Quintus Milo, was now every bit as competent as my own. Cortix and Milo, between them, commanded four complete alae of approximately two hundred and eighty men apiece, includ-ing officers—we had originally called them squadrons, but Milo, on assuming command, had chosen to go back to the old Roman name for cavalry regiments—and although they were barely over half strength when their Camulodian members were subtracted, they would be at full strength within half a year, once the next full intake of recruits was trained. As they had been from the outset, the alae were called the Reds, Whites, Blues and Golds. Our original Camulodian troopers—the trainers of the new army—now consti-tuted the Pied Squadron, with black-and-white banners and maxillae, and they had become a self-contained and self-governing entity nowadays, little more than auxiliary troops.

As the days passed by in the aftermath of the Games, I found myself thinking more and more about that, and about the need to return to Camulod, where the war against Connlyn in the north had become a bleeding ulcer in the side of Arthur's vision of Britain.

My concerns came to a head one night when I was at table with Pelles, in his main dining hall, attending a celebration dinner in honor of his two newest squadron commanders, a brilliant young rider called Serdec, who sprang from Getorix's Wolf clan, and one Gaius Balbus, a half-Roman warrior from Chilperic's Bear clan whose mother was Chilperic's own daughter. The two new officers had been inducted into the Brotherhood of Corbenic, the grand-sounding name that Pelles's officers had awarded themselves less than a year earlier, upon being judged capable of surviving as caval-rymen without our Camulodian input, and the celebrations were reaching the point at which the king and his personal guests would be permitted, and indeed expected, to quit the festivities and leave the younger subalterns to their own amusement.

Already tired of the loud and drunken antics of my subordi-nates, I had been idly watching young Mordred approach one of the tables, carrying a large and obviously heavy jug with extreme care, biting his tongue with the effort of concentrating upon not spilling a drop. He reached the table, which was occupied by a group of the most senior soldiers, and craned forward, stretching out his arms to place his burden on the table, but I could see he was not strong enough to lift it as high or as far as was required. Before he could drop it, however, one of the men turned and took it from him, swinging it easily to the table with one hand and ruffling the lad's hair with the other. I saw the boy's face flush with pleasure even as another man turned with a grin and a wink and passed him a large wedge of soft bread stuffed with a generous slice of roasted pork. Young Mordred grasped it, his eyes shining, and nodded his thanks before scuttling away, grinning broadly and already tearing hungrily at his prize. As one of the castle "boys"—squires, pot boys, stable lads and apprentices—he would not normally be fed until everyone in the Great Hall had eaten his fill, so this beneficence from the senior soldiers' table was high privilege indeed.

Now, the mere sight of the lad scuttling happily away between the tables of officers and ignored by all of them reminded me with surprising force that he was the son of Arthur Pendragon, High King of Britain, and that his father still knew nothing of the boy's existence. That ignorance on Arthur's part meant that I had not yet performed my duties to the full, and had become culpably delinquent in failing to do so, since I had known the truth now for nigh on a year. That, I now realized, was the basis of all the growing discontent I had been feeling for weeks and even months. It had been plain to me now for some time that Merlyn had said nothing to Arthur about the lad, having decided for reasons of his own that the information I had sent him in my letter was not sufficiently important for the King's attention, and although I had no knowledge of his reasons for thinking so, I decided that he was wrong and that it was high time for me to take young Mordred home, in defiance of Merlyn if need be, to meet his father. And his stepmother.

It was high time, in fact, for me to take my troopers home, all of them. Their task here in Gaul was done, and Pelles's kingdom could now survive without them.

My train of thought was interrupted when Pelles stood up, bringing the entire group at his table to their feet, but as I filed out of the hall in the king's wake, nodding to smiling faces here and there as I went, I made up my mind to broach the subject to him later that same night if opportunity presented itself. Pelles was more of a king nowadays than he had ever been and he seemed constantly to be surrounded by envoys and supplicants of one stamp or another. More than half of his table guests that night had been complete strangers to me, although I had been introduced to all of them at one time or another in the course of that day, and even as we walked from the hall, he was clustered about by four richly dressed men, two of whom I had earlier dismissed in my own mind as prating idiots but all of whom were intent upon capturing his full attention.

I watched them ruefully, knowing that I would have little chance of sequestering Pelles that night, and in fact it was three more days before I was able to speak to him with no one else around. I managed it then, too, only with the collusion of his sister Serena, who arranged it by the simple expedient of summoning Pelles to her presence—he dropped everything and came to her immediately, as he always did—and telling him that I needed to talk to him, after which she left the two of us alone.

It was obvious from the moment I began to speak of what was on my mind that the possibility of my leaving with my troopers to return to Camulod had simply not occurred to him until then. He was profoundly shocked to hear what I had to say, and some of the confidence appeared to drain visibly out of him as he began to consider the ramifications of what I was suggesting, because the first and most evident result of our departure would be a gaping hole in the defenses he had built for his kingdom. Even the removal of our horses and breeding stock would cause Corbenic's paddocks and stables to look far larger and far more empty than they actually were, because when we removed ourselves from his domain, we would be taking upwards of a thousand trained war horses with us. I spent the following hour trying to reassure him that our departure would be very gradual, spread over the same amount of time as our incremental arrival had been, and that by the time the last of our men and horses boarded the departing vessels of our final fleet of transports, his own people would have had ample time to replenish their herds and to train replacement cavalry mounts for their cavalry troopers.

Pelles came around to my way of seeing things, eventually, but he was still a chastened man, a king with much on his mind, when the two of us finally parted.

ELEVEN

1

The period that followed my decision to return with my men to Camulod is one of those times, which I am sure must occur in the life of every man, that I remember as being completely beyond my control. I recognized it, even during its passage, as a lesson in humility, brought to bear upon me specifically to demonstrate to me how completely powerless I was in the face of events that were thrown at me by an uncaring world. It was a time of chaos that challenged my deepest beliefs, and of hurtling events that defied me to impose any kind of sanity or order upon their occurrence; a time when everything that might arguably have happened anyway seemed to happen all at once, with events and developments coming hard and fast, falling over each other, one atop another in a concatenation so sustained and disruptive that I sometimes lost awareness of the passing of time and of the importance of any one individual occurrence.

The upheavals began almost immediately after my talk with Pelles, sending me rushing home to Britain long before the first elements of our withdrawals strategy even began to approach completion, and I went accompanied by a few of my own men and a large contingent of purely Frankish cavalry, dispatched by King Pelles of Corbenic as a visiting honor guard, to convey his thanks and appreciation, along with an offer of military assistance, to King Arthur of Britain.

The reasons underlying these unexpected developments were simple: word came to us with the next arriving fleet from Camulod, in the early spring, that Arthur had been severely wounded in a skirmish with some of Connlyn's Outlander allies. Merlyn's anger and disgust were palpable even in letter form, plainly discernible in the slashing lines of his furious scribblings. He went to great pains not to dignify the encounter as anything more than a disastrously inopportune squabble—certainly not a battle lost by Arthur's armies—but his graphic and alarming description of the encounter was enough to sicken me and send me scurrying to Pelles, to inform him that I would be returning to Camulod aboard the next ship to sail from Corbenic.

According to Merlyn's account, Arthur and Ghilleadh had been taken by surprise while riding together just a little way ahead of the main bulk of Ghilly's mobile strike force. They had met earlier that day, after not having seen each other in more than a week, and were on their way from Arthur's main camp, where Ghilly had shown up unexpectedly, back to Ghilly's outlying frontal position, about two miles to the north, and having things to say to each other that they did not wish to be overheard—all armies, everywhere, are manned by rumormongers with long, insatiably curious ears—they had ridden ahead of their men, with only a nominal escort of ten troopers, widely dispersed around them.

It should have been an uneventful ride, for Ghilly had combined his mobile strike force with Gareth's infantry more than a week previously, and their combined strengths had swept the enemy out of that entire region, leaving the surrounding countryside firmly in Arthur's hands. Someone, however, had forgotten to tell Connlyn's allies that to go there again after such a serious reversal would be insanity, and hence a roving band of more than a hundred blue-painted Albans, the Picti or Painted People of Roman legend, had crested a hill while making their way southwards into Britain from their own territories north of the Wall, and found themselves looking down on a small mounted party that was coming towards them along a narrow pathway hedged in by trees. The Albans attacked without hesitation, seeing only mounted men and knowing them as enemies, and, taking the newcomers by surprise, overwhelmed them. They killed the horses first, as they always did, bringing the animals down with a hail of spears and arrows, and then they attacked the unhorsed riders before they could regroup themselves.

Ghilly, Merlyn told me in his letter, was the first man killed, shot in the face with an arrow and then beheaded when he fell from his horse. Arthur's horse, which had been right beside Ghilly's, was also killed instantly at the start of the attack. Pierced through the eye by an arrow, it went down so quickly that the King had no chance to kick his feet free of the stirrups. He crashed down still astride it, stunned by the impact with the ground, his right foot pinned beneath the horse's deadweight, and while he squirmed there, helpless, he took two spear thrusts, either one of which might have killed him. The higher thrust deflected off his cuirass and gashed him deeply beneath the armpit, cutting through the heavily layered muscle there and drawing sufficient blood to make it look as though he had been killed.

The other spear point did far more serious damage. Aimed at his belly as he sprawled there on his back, kicking uselessly with one leg at the deadweight of the horse on his other, the weapon glanced off Arthur's ring-mail-covered knee and found a gaping seam in his armored leggings, just at the fork of his groin. The long, tapering spearhead went in at a high angle and plunged deep, entering the right fold of his groin and sliding beneath his pubis to thrust upward into his pelvis before lodging there, and had not the man wielding it been killed before he could twist the shaft or throw his weight on the weapon again, Arthur would have died there and then. But Ghilly's main force had been riding close behind their commander, although tragically not close enough, and had come spurring when they heard the first sounds of fighting. They were there within moments, but even so, Arthur and one young trooper were the only two men left alive by the time the others reached the scene.

The young trooper had died of his wounds several days later, and, by the time of Merlyn's writing, which was three weeks after the attack, Merlyn was not completely sure that the King would yet live, and that fear communicated itself to me with utter, despairing clarity as I read his description of the incident.

In the week that followed, Pelles and his sister Serena did everything in their power to soothe and divert me in order to take my mind off what had happened to my King and my closest friend, but it was a thankless task they undertook. I had no way of knowing Arthur's condition, or even if he was still alive, and I must have been insufferable in my frustration, subject to all the agonized extravagances of a fevered imagination. I saw the King constantly in my mind, in varying situations ranging from raving delirium to lingering, pallid decline, his eyes sunken in his head and his wounds suppurating and gangrenous, his destiny denied him by the sheerest accident of circumstance and his presence in the wrong place at the wrong time. Time after time, all day and every day, I wondered how he really was and I cursed my inability to do anything that might make a difference to any slightest part of what was happening. Was he alive, or had he died of his wounds since I had heard these tidings? And if he was alive, was he improving or declining, healing or growing sicker?

My agony was made worse by knowing that I would never be able to forgive myself if Arthur were to die before he set eyes on his son. He needed to see Mordred, but even more urgently, *I* needed him to see the lad, and to hear him acknowledge that the boy was all I believed him to be, despite the tragic circumstances of his parenthood. I had never felt so impotent, and I knew that I had to return to Camulod by the fastest possible means, which meant taking ship on one of the vessels in Pelles's harbor as soon as it was ready for sea. And so I waited and chafed at the bit as the ships, too slowly, prepared themselves for sailing away again.

The news of Ghilleadh's death was a personal violation to me, and I simply refused to believe it. Ghilly could not be dead, especially not in such a mundane, tawdry, inglorious fashion; it was unthinkable, defying belief. He and I had far too many things yet to do together, too many achievements to share and too many things to tell each other.

There are times in life when the truth is simply unacceptable. I woke up one night, calling his name and smelling his familiar scent close by me in the darkness. I hunched there, up on one elbow and blinking my eyes against the pitch-blackness of the room, and I remembered lying in Elaine's arms, my head pillowed on her breasts, while she asked me to name my favorite among all Arthur's Knights Companion. Ghilleadh. He was, and had been from the earliest days of our friendship, the personification of my vision of what Arthur's new knights were supposed to be: strong, yet generous and gentle, upright, forthright, straightforward and trustworthy to the death, a faithful friend and a relentless champion of rightness, incapable of lying and totally free of corruption, cowardice or calumny. Had I been a boy in need of a hero, my friend Seur Ghilleadh would have fulfilled my every requirement. And now he was dead, knocked from his horse and beheaded by a blue-painted savage.

I believe it may have been Serena who originally had the idea of sending an honor guard of Frankish knights back with me to Britain. Pelles and she had been willing to attempt anything that might distract my burning impatience from wanting to commandeer a ship—any ship—and go sailing off to Britain in haste. Pelles seized upon the idea and promptly issued a call for volunteers, knowing that every qualified trooper in his ranks would leap at the chance to journey to Britain as a member of an elite honor guard, and that sent his entire military establishment into a frenzy of activity, reviewing and selecting the most qualified applicants. Naturally enough, since I was the overall commander of Pelles's cavalry forces, both in Corbenic and nominally in Britain, the final decision was left to me—a clever ruse that did, in fact, succeed in making me forget, sometimes for hours on end, the problems that were bedeviling me.

Accompanied by Mordred, I boarded the returning fleet with my forty-man honor guard escort and a small number of my own men. I took Bors with me, as my only Camulodian officer, and six of Pelles's best, including Quintus Milo, who made no secret of his desire to meet Merlyn Britannicus face to face. Pelles himself came to see us off, knowing that we would be back within the year, all things being equal, and that I would be writing to him regularly, keeping him apprised of what was happening in Britain.

Standing on the tiny rear deck of my ship, watching my friends receding slowly into the distance, I knew I should be feeling worse than I did, leaving them there, but too many uncertainties awaited me in Britain to permit me to fret over leaving my friends for a few months. They were more than capable of handling anything the gods might throw at them in Gaul. I could only wish I had the same certainty about what might happen to us in Britain.

2

The spring gales had blown themselves out by the time we left Gaul, and we had an uneventful crossing back to Britain, where we proceeded northwards, up the western coastline to the old river port of Glevum. The port had taken a new lease on life since we had begun using it as a disembarkation point, repairing and revitalizing its old wharves and warehouses. We landed without incident and wasted no time in deploying our formations. I had had a long discussion with Shaun Pointer, the shipmaster, concerning the High King's condition and the word that we ought to send back north with Shaun to Connor and King Brander. The upshot was that Shaun agreed to remain in Glevum for five days, awaiting the latest word on Arthur's health, information that I promised to send back in letter form as quickly as I could.

We left the ships safely moored along the riverbank and struck out for Camulod by way of the great road to Aquae Sulis, traveling quickly enough to be sure that no one could outstrip us. No one had known we were coming, but I was unsurprised to be told, even before we reached Camulod, that Merlyn was waiting for me. A single rider approached us at a walk as we came into sight of the hilltop fort in the distance, and it took me only a few moments to recognize the slouched posture of my old friend Gwin. He was a natural and brilliant commander of infantry, and when he needed to be, he was a gifted and versatile rider, but in spite of that, he always appeared to be ill at ease on the back of a horse. When he saw me wave to him, he reined in and waited by the side of the road for us to reach him, at which point he kicked his horse forward and clasped hands with me, welcoming me home with a quiet smile before casting a quizzical eye over my Frankish escort, who were resplendent in bronze ring mail and burnished cuirasses, with helmets of the same metal. He grunted a wordless greeting that was somehow heartening despite everything, and then raised his eyes to the blazoned banner that swayed above their heads.

"A stag's head? That must be the emblem of yon Frankish king, am I right?"

"Yes, as usual … If you are talking about King Pelles of Corbenic, I mean."

Gwin was looking at me now, waiting for me to say more, and I asked the question he was plainly expecting.

"How is Arthur?"

He pursed his lips and looked away. "Can't say," he muttered. "Know how 'e is, I mean, but Merlyn told me to say nothing, just to get you to meet with him before you go anywhere or talk to anyone else. You know Merlyn, he dun't often make demands, but when he wants to be sure 'bout something, you never go away in doubt about what it is. He's waiting for you now, in his own place."

"But the King is alive, is he not?"

"Aye, course he is." Gwin's eyes showed his surprise that I should even ask the question, and that made me feel better than I had since first receiving the news of the ambush.

"How did he know we were coming—Merlyn, I mean—in time to send you out to meet us?"

Gwin looked at me and raised an eyebrow. "Now there's a foolish question, Lancer, even for a Frank! You're asking me to tell you how Merlyn knows what Merlyn knows? I don't think even 'e knows that …"

I nodded again and kicked my horse back into motion. It had been more than two years since I had last seen this place, and my eyes moved constantly as we approached the base of Camulod's hill and then made our way up the steeply winding roadway to the main gates. For the duration of the climb, however, passing a constant procession of people going in both directions, I saw not a single face that I recognized, and that, plus the fact that none of these people paid any attention to our passage, made me think about how accustomed the inhabitants of Camulod had become to seeing strange warriors moving among them. Our Frankish riders were all armored in bronze ring mail, which identified them clearly as being foreign, and yet no one among the throng of passersby paid them the slightest attention.

It occurred to me that they were far too complacent, smug with the certainty that no one who was not a friend of Camulod would ever dare to come here among them. It was perfectly clear that they believed implicitly that the King's cavalry would guard them against incursion by any hostile force, but the truth was that since we had landed less than a day earlier, no one had challenged us or made any attempt to identify us.

There were more buildings among the trees surrounding the drilling ground than there had been when I left, but I found nothing surprising in that. Camulod had been growing as a community for nigh on a hundred years, and much of what had been farmland and dense forest surrounding the central fortress had long since been given over to housing for the troopers and colonists who now swarmed everywhere in sight.

We were greeted at the top of the approach road, in the area facing the main gates, by the assembled fortress guard under the command of the officer of the day, Seur Gareth, another of Arthur's Cambrian Knights Companion. He saluted us with great formality, welcomed us home and greeted our Frankish visitors with grave courtesy before indicating the open gates at his back and assigning a squad of guards to accompany them as guests to the stables. For me, however, his message was more direct: Merlyn Britannicus awaited me in his quarters. I dismounted and dropped my reins to the ground, and headed without delay towards the central administrative building, accompanied by Rufus, leaving my horse to stand there, ground tethered, until young Mordred could collect it and take it to the stables.

It seemed that everyone in Camulod knew I was back in Britain, for I received a welcoming smile, completely lacking in any signs of surprise to see me, from everyone who saluted me on my way to Merlyn's quarters in one of the log-built barracks buildings. As soon as I arrived in the tiny vestibule fronting the door to his day room, I removed my helmet and shrugged off my heavy traveling cloak before raising my arms to let Rufus undo the awkwardly placed buckles beneath my armpits that held my cuirass firmly in place. Rufus set the armor gently behind the door where he could return for it, then turned back to help me remove my ring-mail tunic and heavy, belted leggings. He piled the ring-mail pieces by the cuirass, and I instructed him to take them to the temporary quarters that had been assigned to me, and then to find Mordred, who was probably in the stables, and to tell him to stay there until I came to collect him. He listened carefully, then saluted and went out, carrying my belted sword over his shoulder and my long cloak carefully folded over one arm.

I watched the door swing shut behind him before I turned back to Merlyn's heavy wooden door, my hand raised to knock. Before I could do anything, however, the door swung open and I found myself being waved towards the interior by a man I had never seen before. He nodded to me as I passed him in the doorway, and then he left, closing the door behind him.

The room, which seemed larger than I remembered, was filled with flickering light, but equally with shadows, and the small windows high in the end wall did little to illuminate the darkness, especially this early in the springtime, when the sun still hung low in the new year's sky. Merlyn's voice came to me out of the deep, gloomy shadows that filled the corner beside the fire basket on its bed of stone.

"Come in, Master Clothar, sit down and be welcome. It has been a long time since we two last met." He was wrapped from head to foot as always in voluminous black, and he stood up to welcome me as I moved towards him, although he made no attempt to reach out to me. I returned his greeting as warmly as I could, but was aware of him looking beyond me, as though expecting to see someone at my back.

"Where is the boy? Did you not bring him?"

"From Gaul, yes. But I thought it might not be appropriate to bring him to this meeting."

"How so?"

I shrugged. "Because I like the lad and have no wish to see him hurt. I had no way of knowing what your treatment of him might be. You did not respond to the letter I sent you concerning him, and until I discovered your feelings on his being here, I saw no purpose in exposing him needlessly to the risk of pain. Nothing of this situation in which the boy finds himself is of his making. He is utterly blameless. And, as I said, I like him too well to see him suffer needlessly. Time enough for suffering if his father rejects him. How is the King, and does he know about the boy?"

Merlyn made no attempt to prevaricate. "Not as well as I would have him, and no, he does not know about the boy. He improves daily, but he came close to death and it will be a long time before he is fit to ride or fight again. That, fundamentally, is why I chose to say nothing to him about the boy. I simply did not know how the information might affect the King in the condition he was in at that time, and I did not wish to take the risk of causing even greater harm than we were grappling with. And quite honestly, nothing there has changed." He turned away from me and spoke into the fire so that I had to strain to hear what he was saying. "There were times when he was so far consumed with fever that I believed we would— must—lose him, but each time, he rallied and fought through the crisis." He paused again, and I could tell, from the movement of the cowl that enveloped his head, that he turned his face slightly towards me. "Were I inclined to be a Christian believer, I might have sworn the hand of God himself was involved in fending off death on several occasions ... five, in fact, that I can recall.

"He lay unconscious for much of the first three weeks follow-ing his injuries, not sleeping constantly, but tossing and turning and raving and gaining no rest at any time. The weight fell from his bones, so rapid was his descent into oblivion. We have some fine physicians and surgeons here in Camulod, as you know, but none of them was able to do any more than watch and wait, and the same was true for the visiting healers who came to offer their skills."

"What about the Queen?"

"What about her? She barely left his side, save when she was too exhausted to remain. Between the two of us, we made sure that he was never left alone in three full weeks. And then the fevers finally faded and he began to mend. But he is still bound to his bed and only now beginning to eat solid food."

"So the Queen showed genuine concern for him? It surprises me to hear you say that. You have never said, Master Merlyn, and I have never asked, but do you like the Lady Gwinnifer?"

He answered instantly. "I respect her greatly, and that grows more true as I come to know her better. I admire her, too. She has a ... a strength of character that is refreshingly different ... and she has courage and faith in her own self-sufficiency. She is the only person I've told about the boy. I believed she ought to know and so I told her, not long ago, and her reaction justified my faith in her. You will have no difficulties with the Queen over the boy. She understands completely and her sympathies are with the boy."

"Will she meet with me, think you?"

"She has already bidden me bring you to her as soon as you and I have finished here. Please, sit down by the fire and rest. You must be tired, I know, but we have much to discuss, and so I have had food and drink brought in for you. Serve yourself, if you will. It is over there on the table in the corner."

"Thank you, I will, in a while. But first I have a need to talk, and to ask questions. What of the war in the north? Who is in charge there now that Arthur is not? And are we making headway against Connlyn?"

"Hmm. Fairly asked. The war in the north has gone on far too long, as you are well aware. Recently things have started going more our way, probably because we have an enormous number of men in the field up there now—nigh on five thousand, all told, and a thousand of those are cavalry. As long as we stay by the Roman roads, we can move quickly and the enemy can't withstand us. Unfortunately, they know that as well as we do, and they are sticking to the hills and highlands, well away from the roads.

"Bedwyr has overall authority, and Pelinore is his second-in-command. Under those two, there's a warrior king from northern Cambria called Rience. You may not have met him before, but he's an old friend of Arthur's. They were boys together. Rience commands the infantry forces, and Balan, one of the last-raised batch of Knights Companion, has the cavalry command.

"Are we making headway against Connlyn? I believe we are. If we could ever bring him to battle, we could crush him. But he is too cautious—or too well advised—to be enticed into a battle where he could be outnumbered and outfought."

"What do you mean, too well advised? You have suspicions about his advisers?"

Merlyn inhaled sharply through his nose, the mere sound expressing his disapproval. "I have … more than suspicions, but not quite sufficient certainty to issue any orders that would change the status quo. But I have people digging, and one of these fine days I will have the proof of my suspicions. And the moment I obtain it, Connlyn's sources will narrow rapidly and permanently."

"A spy? You suspect someone in particular?"

"I do. But as I say, I have no proof. Not yet. Apart from that, this alliance that Connlyn has cobbled together is a strange one … As well as his own people from south of the Wall he has Alban Picts, Norweyans, Saxons of varying kinds, Anglians and even some Eirishmen from the west. A large host, but one made up of alien groups. They all fight differently, their beliefs differ from group to group, they speak different tongues and they behave differently, and that leaves our men feeling as if they are fighting half a dozen enemy armies."

He went on for some time about the situation in the north, and when he had finished, I told him everything I had to report about the honor guard I had brought with me from King Pelles and apprised him of the situation in Gaul—how I considered Pelles's cavalry army to be well enough established to be self-sustaining henceforth, and how I had begun preparing my troops for their eventual return to Camulod.

Merlyn listened carefully to my entire discourse, and only when I spoke of returning to Camulod with my battalions did he raise a hand to silence me. When I paused in obedience, he merely suggested that I might wait before committing my men to a departure from Gaul. Arthur, he said, had been talking about other Gaulish matters shortly before he was ambushed.

I was intrigued, but before I could ask any questions, he began to question me closely about the boy Mordred. He was fully aware of the background, for I had left nothing out of my letter about my visit to Morgas, so his questions were all about the boy himself: his character, his temperament, his attitude towards his father, and anything else Merlyn thought might be important to know. Some of his questions were surprising, dealing with things that had not occurred to me before, but I answered all of them openly and ended up by asking him if he would like me to send for the boy so that he could meet him and draw his own conclusions. He demurred, however, and said he would prefer to wait until after I had met with Queen Gwinnifer, at which time he and she could meet the lad together.

I never did consume any of the food or drink he had brought in for me, for he told me then that the Queen was waiting for me in the Villa Britannicus, on the floor of the valley below, and I excused myself to hasten to her. Merlyn made no attempt to invite himself along with me, but told me simply that he would walk with me to the stables to collect my horse for the ride down to the villa, which lay about a mile from the main fortress gates. There the Queen herself would conduct me to the King, he said, providing Arthur were awake and strong enough to receive me.

Seeing the curiosity in my expression, he explained that the newly wed regal couple had taken up residence in the old Villa Britannicus soon after Gwinnifer had come south from her father's home in Chester to live in Camulod. Arthur had decided that the living conditions in the hilltop fort were ludicrously primitive compared to the luxurious accommodations offered by the old villa, which had been in continuous use by the Britannicus family for almost two and a half hundred years, although in recent years it had been given over to farm management and the accommodation of visiting guests and dignitaries. He had ordered the old house to be completely refurbished, then moved into residence with his new wife.

That single commentary told me more about the changes that had occurred in Camulod during my absence than anything else could have. Before my departure for Gaul, access to Arthur had been effectively controlled by Merlyn, whenever the King himself was not directly involved. Now, Arthur's wife held that position of power, and that made me rethink the entire matter of the new Queen, whom I had grown accustomed to remembering as a large-eyed, slender, long-legged wisp of a child. Clearly, that could not be the case today, for now I was in her domain, where even Merlyn Britannicus deferred to her as the castellan of Camulod and wife to the High King of All Britain.

We had barely left Merlyn's quarters on the way to the stables when I saw another sign of Gwinnifer's importance. Two junior officers passed by us, saluting us in silence, and each of them wore a flash of bright blue fabric on his left breast. The men were members of the Queen's Guard, Merlyn told me, a personal body-guard formed for Gwinnifer's protection by Arthur himself, soon after his marriage, when he realized that he would be gone from Camulod and from the Queen's company much of the time, at least until the war in the north was won. Membership in the guard, and the right to wear the bright blue flash, "the Queen's Azure" as it was called, had quickly become a much-sought-after appointment, Merlyn assured me, suggesting the high esteem the troops held for their Queen.

The two boys, Rufus and Mordred, were waiting for me at the entrance to the stables, and as soon as Mordred saw me, he stepped forward to where I could see him.

"The dark one is Mordred," I said to Merlyn, and sensed him straightening imperceptibly as we drew near the boys. I knew he was absorbing every detail of Mordred's appearance and demeanor. Mordred appeared to realize that, too, for he suddenly grew still and the smile faded from his face. But then it occurred to me that this was the first time either boy had set eyes on Merlyn Britannicus, and Merlyn, featureless and inimical beneath his long black robes and heavy cowl, could be intimidating even to me.

When we reached the boys I introduced both of them by name to Merlyn and they bowed from the waist as they had been taught and greeted him respectfully as Magister Merlyn, although both of them were wide eyed and pale with apprehension. Merlyn responded only with a silent nod and then ignored the boys, bidding me present his respects to the Queen before he walked away and left me alone with Mordred and Rufus.

"Well, now you have met Merlyn and lived to tell of it." My attempt at humor failed to impress them, and I realized they thought I meant what I had said. I shook my head and waved them away with one hand. "Saddle up, we're going for a ride. I'll saddle my own mount. You two look to yours, and be quick. I have an appointment with Queen Gwinnifer and I have no wish to keep the lady waiting because you two are too slothful. Quickly now!"

3

The Villa Britannicus had changed greatly since I had last seen it, and I knew it was not for the first time in its long life. The last time I had seen the place, it had been under attack by a hapless and incompetent band of raiders, and I had saved Arthur's life and nearly lost my own in that encounter. Now there was no sign anywhere that the attack had ever occurred. The burnt outbuildings had all been rebuilt or replaced, and the grounds of the villa, which had featured edible crops of vegetables at that time, had been given over once again to flowers and shrubbery and stretches of green sward bordered by hedge-lined pathways. The guards on duty at the main doors snapped to attention and challenged me as I approached, eyeing me with a mixture of indifference and suspicion. None of them reacted to my name, and I was actually relieved when their squad leader emerged from the house and recognized me, for I had begun to think I might have to go to some lengths to identify myself before gaining admission. But they passed me through and the squad leader directed me to the Queen's quarters, which Arthur had once proudly pointed out to me as the former home of his father's grandparents, the Lady Luceiia Britannicus and her husband, Publius Varrus.

I must admit that as I approached the regal chambers, I was curious. In the very brief time I had known Gwinnifer before, she had been a child of twelve, and the main impression she had made upon me was of unformed but lissome, fluid gracefulness. She had reminded me of a young deer or a well-bred foal, all eyes and legs and seeming awkwardness, yet destined to become a creature of great and elegant beauty.

The guard outside her doors had challenged me again, quietly this time, and then opened the doors respectfully and announced me. The Queen was writing at a table in front of the fire when I entered, but she stood up and looked at me immediately, and the impact of her wide, bright blue eyes struck me from clear across the space between us. They were the precise shade of the Queen's Azure. A thick fringe of black hair framed her forehead, the long, rich tresses concealed now beneath a white veil that was wrapped, like a shawl, around her head. Her cheekbones were magnificent, high and slanted, and although the veil concealed her long, slender neck, I now remembered her swanlike, regal look.

Arthur's Queen was, quite simply, the most beautiful creature I had ever seen, and she appeared to have absolutely no awareness of that beauty or of the power it gave her over men. Before I could even collect my thoughts sufficiently to allow me to open my mouth and greet her, she was on her way to meet me, moving smoothly and

with great speed, her face wreathed in a radiant smile of welcome.
I had only ever seen her smile on two occasions as a child, neither
of them inspired by me, and in consequence I had always thought
of her as a solemn, humorless kind of person who would take little
pleasure in anything. Now, with this smile of glorious womanhood,
she welcomed me back into her life.

"Seur Clothar of Benwick, the King's Lance," she said, her eyes
dancing with pleasure. "Finally, finally you are here. No, you will not
kneel, Seur Knight," she said, reaching out to me with both hands and
restraining me, "not here and not to me. I will not permit it. I have
always known you as Clothar, since our first meeting at Saint Alban's
Shrine, and have thought of you as my *Hastatus,* my spearman, thereafter, wondering at times where you were and what had become of
you. But Arthur's name for you is perfect. Lance. I shall claim it as
my own name for you, too, if that would not displease you." Clasping
both my hands in hers, she tilted her head back and looked at me
through narrowed eyes. "You have changed, grown ... older, but not
older, if you know what I mean. More graceful, more ... capable.
My husband speaks more highly of you than of any other man."

"And how is he, my lady?" I asked, before her flattering words
could bring the color flooding to my cheeks.

"Better with every day that passes. I will take you to him soon.
But first I have things I wish to say to you ... things I want no one
else to hear, including Arthur." I must have shown my astonishment,
for her eyes narrowed again and her gaze sharpened. My face was
flaming, I knew, but as I stood there tongue-tied, she smiled again
and spoke, her voice softening, surprising me with its depth and
warmth, for she was still a very young woman, with a full year yet
to go before she would see twenty. "You have no need to be afraid
of speaking openly to me, my friend. You were the only one of all
the people at Saint Alban's Shrine who spoke to me when first we
met ... the only one to recognize me as a person and to offer me
kindness and a word of praise when I was sore in need of those
things. You were my friend, without hope of gain or reward. Why
then would you be in awe of me now, simply because I am a queen,

wed to a king? Especially since the King is your true friend, and I would be, too, if you would grant me that."

With those words, my shyness and confusion melted away and I found my voice, and from that moment on we never knew a moment's strain between us, Gwinnifer and I.

I thanked her for her welcome, and as she turned to lead me into the room, still holding me by the hand, I was astonished to see that other people were there, watching us. They were all women—the Queen's Ladies—and Gwinnifer pointed them all out to me, one by one, naming them in turn. I greeted each of them, finding it easy to smile now, and when the last one had been named and had returned my bow, the Queen dismissed them to work at the far end of the room, where they could not overhear what she and I were saying. She then ushered me to a seat by the fire and sat across from me.

"Will you have wine, Seur Clothar?" When I shook my head politely, she smiled and settled her clothing about her. "Now, you and I have much to talk about. Where would you like to begin?"

"With your husband, my lady. How is he faring, truly?"

"Improving daily, as I said … I can sleep now, at night, knowing he will not slip away and die while I am not there with him. On other fronts, however, I am less sanguine. He is the very soul of loyalty, as you know."

"Aye, Lady, he is."

"Too much so, and I know whereof I speak. I am my father's daughter, irrespective of my will in the matter, and I have learned well from him, more by observation, be it said, than by tuition. Arthur trusts my father as an ally. In that, and in that alone, my husband is foolish. He will hear no ill of my father, not from me, nor from anyone else, and until he has absolute proof to the contrary, he will insist on treating my father as an ally and an equal. But my father is betraying him to Connlyn."

The sound of her words was like a dousing with cold water, for it took my breath away even as I connected it instantly to Merlyn's suspicions. And yet I confess my first reaction was one of discomfort and disbelief at the speed with which she had denounced Symmachus. How, I asked myself, could any child condemn her own father so chillingly? But then I remembered the man we were talking about, and the terms governing Arthur's wedding to Gwinnifer. Symmachus had grand plans for the grandson he presumed Arthur and Gwinnifer would produce for him. Nevertheless, I felt constrained to murmur at least a word of objection on his behalf, and so I said something inane about the lady's judgment being perhaps a trifle harsh.

The skin on her brow tightened perceptibly, and the light in her eyes hardened to an incandescent blaze. "Harsh?" she said. "Have you no memories of my father from your time at the saint's shrine? As I recall, he gave you scant reason to think fondly of him or to sympathize with him." She paused, tilting her head to one side and looking gravely into my eyes. "Arthur told me he had confided in you about the pact we made between us, he and I, to thwart my father's dreams of laying hands on the title of Riothamus. You did know that, did you not?" I nodded, and she continued. "Well, my father now suspects, after two years of nonperformance by me as a wife and mother, that I may be barren—incapable of breeding. In his eyes, that would constitute disloyalty on my part, absolving him of any need to consider me in seeking redress for what he perceives to be my dereliction. And so he has turned to seeking a secret alliance with Connlyn."

"You have proof of that, my lady?"

"No, I have not, but I know my father very well. He will always choose the course of most advantage to himself. I believe absolutely in my father's capacity for treachery, having seen it demonstrated all my life in the name of politics and expediency, and I do not need proof to know what I know." She paused, pursing her lips as she gazed at me. "Merlyn knows, too, but he requires proof. Has he mentioned it to you?"

"Aye, but in terms of treachery only. He did not name your father."

"No, he would not." She hesitated, searching my face. "You have a question. What is it?"

I shrugged. "Not a question, my lady, not really. It is more of an observation … What possible advantage could your father see in allying himself with Connlyn? The man has proven himself to be a nuisance, and longer lived than most of his ilk, but he is yet no more than an upstart northern king. Connlyn's armies will never defeat Camulod."

"No, probably not, but they could bleed Camulod dry, draining its resources in a long, debilitating struggle far from home, and when my father judges the time to be right, he could then attack with his own forces, taking advantage of Arthur's back being turned." She held up one finger. "Don't look so shocked, dear Lance. I have known my beloved sire do far, far worse. You might call it treachery, but he thinks of it as survival. But there is a random element in the mix now, is there not? Mordred changes everything … Symmachus does not even suspect that he is alive, and you may be sure that Connlyn will never tell him, because both he and my father have the same idea: to rule as high king after Arthur's death. While Connlyn sees himself as regent for Mordred, my father dreams of being regent for my unborn son … unborn and unconceived! Connlyn does not know that Mordred is here in Camulod, or that he was in Gaul with you, but if Arthur acknowledges Mordred as his son, he will have drawn Connlyn's teeth and my father's at the same time."

"And will he acknowledge the boy?"

Gwinnifer shook her head. "I have no idea. He still does not know of the boy, and that has been at my insistence. By the time the word came to us here, Arthur was in the north again, and then after he was wounded, I considered that he had enough to be concerned about, simply in staying alive, so I forbade Merlyn to say anything to him. As for how he will react when he does find out, your guess would be as valid as my own. Why are you smiling?"

"You said you forbade Merlyn to say anything to him. I found that impressive, and amusing. Very few people I know would dare to forbid Merlyn anything."

She grinned at me, the flashing, mischievous grin of a happy young girl, revealing a wider-than-expected mouth filled with sparkling teeth. "Ach, that's because they are all men. Merlyn is as sweet and docile as a child's pony, if you treat him properly." Her face sobered again as quickly as it had wrinkled in the grin. "But it is true that I have no notion of how Arthur will respond to being told he has a son. In his weakened condition, these tidings, and the thoughts they might stir up, could damage him severely, perhaps even kill him. I will not take that risk, and therefore I must include you, too, in my interdiction concerning word of the boy. Can you understand that?"

I sat blinking at her for a moment and then nodded. "Clearly, my lady, but for how long will this condition of silence last?"

"Perhaps a week, perhaps longer. I cannot say at this point, nor can the doctors. But he continues to gain strength daily, and yesterday he had his first solid food since he was wounded. That is usually a good sign of returning health, and my physicians tell me I should see miraculous changes taking place from day to day from this time on. I promise you, however, that as soon as he appears to be strong enough to withstand the shock of knowing what you have to say, I will accompany you myself to tell him."

"And what of you, my lady, regarding the boy? Will you wish to meet him?"

"Of course I wish to meet him, as soon as it may be arranged. And it may please you to know that I am prepared to like him, because from what Merlyn has told me, it seems clear that you yourself like and admire the boy."

"I do. I find him delightful. He's a strong lad, upright and straightforward, with nothing of the schemer in his nature. Exactly the kind of boy I would like to have as a son someday. I thank his family for that … his mother's family, I mean. I met several of his uncles while visiting Queen Morgas, and I liked all of them. They have taught young Mordred admirable values."

"That is good to hear." The Queen was smiling slightly as she spoke, almost musingly. "Of course, his disposition and good nature might also have something more directly to do with his parentage, his father being who and what he is. And I am quite sure his mother had some admirable qualities of her own, judging simply from the effect she had upon my husband."

"Does Arthur have to know the entire truth?" I had not known I was going to ask the question, and it came blurting from my mouth before I could control it.

Gwinnifer stared at me wide eyed. "Does he have—? How can he not? What are you suggesting?"

"I don't know," I said, admitting my own bafflement, "but I've been thinking of little else for months now, and it seems to me that everyone who knows about what happened agrees that there was no fault attached to what went on—no blameworthiness and no sin, even although incest is the greatest sin anyone can imagine."

The Queen immediately waved me to silence and looked nervously across the room to see if any of her women had overheard.

"Be careful, Seur Clothar. That is not a word to be lightly spoken aloud, especially here. Yet I agree with you. I see no blame attached to anyone in this, merely a tragic ignorance."

"To the best of my knowledge," I continued, "you and Merlyn are the only two people in Britain who know—with the obvious exceptions of myself and young Mordred." I cleared my throat, then said what had been on my mind. "Perhaps there might really be no need to tell Arthur the entire truth at this point. I mean, not immediately, not while he is abed and not yet fully equipped to cope with it. But we could tell him most of it. He needs to meet Mordred, and the knowledge of who Mordred's mother was, properly presented, should please him greatly, giving him good reason to welcome the boy and honor his mother's memory—" I broke off, suddenly aware of what I had said and how its tenor might be misconstrued by a young bride who, from what I already knew, could be less than certain of her status in her husband's affections. Gwinnifer, however, was nothing if not intuitive.

"Aha! His mother's memory," she said. "You thought I might be angry at that. Well, I am not. The King and I have talked at great length about that, Lance, of how he lost Morag, and of how the partnership we two have come to share—from highly inauspicious beginnings, be it said—is of a different kind and nature."

I nodded and smiled, greatly relieved that she was not upset, and her reaction increased my regard for her, but I held my peace for a spell after that, aware for once that anything I had to add would be superfluous.

Gwinnifer sat silent as well, her brows knitted in thought, but finally she shook her head. "No, Lance, that is a risk I dare not take. The potential for disaster afterwards is too great. Besides, the boy knows the truth, and he is only … how old is he now, eleven, twelve? He could say the wrong thing at any time and the affair could unravel, with far worse consequences than those that will spring from telling the truth at once, from the outset."

I knew as soon as I heard her words that she was right. The boy knew the truth, and he saw nothing shameful in his situation, so I knew that were we to change our presentation at this point, Mordred might be the one to suffer the most, from confusion, if nothing else. I nodded, feeling misery well up in me as I agreed, and we sat in silence yet again until the matter of King Symmachus came back into my mind. Treacherous he might be, but when his daughter had begun to speak of him earlier, I had received the impression that she knew how to handle the situation. Now I went back to it.

"Your father, my lady. Given that what you say is true, and given equally that no one here is prepared to act on the knowledge—or the suspicion—without proof of wrongdoing, it seems to me he must be at liberty to do whatever he so wills at this point. Have you any thoughts on how we might put a stop to that?"

"I have one thought … Had I a skilled hastatus at my command, such a man might resolve the issue to everyone's advantage with a single javelin cast."

The suggestion was so matter-of-fact that it took my breath away, but I countered quickly: "Aye, such a man might, but acting without clear and verifiable evidence of falsity on the part of Symmachus, that man might be accused of unprovoked murder."

The Queen's response was hard edged and clear. "My husband, your King, is lying near here, barely removed from the point of death. He is there through treachery."

"Your pardon, my lady, but I was told the encounter with the enemy was accidental. Neither party knew the other was there until they met."

"Aye, but had it not been for treachery, foul and unforgivable, they need never have met at all. Connlyn and his rabble should have been wiped out a year ago ... half a year ago, at least. That he was not was only because Arthur could never bring him to bay. Each time we moved against him, he was gone, vanishing ahead of us and evading our armies, and eventually Arthur and Ghilly and the others were so aware of that that they spent inordinate amounts of time planning in secret and then executing their plans with great caution and secrecy, moving in stealth and in the most serpentine maneuvers. And still Connlyn eluded them with ease. It became impossible to doubt that he was receiving detailed information from a trusted source close to Arthur. That was as obvious as the snout on a pig to anyone who cared to look, and it was equally obvious that whoever was supplying the information must be very highly placed, for no underlings were ever privy to the details before the plans were set in motion.

"I made my own observations and deductions from the facts as I knew them. There were only nine or ten people who could possibly pass along such detailed and sensitive information. One of those was Arthur, another was Merlyn, then Ghilleadh—I still can't believe him gone, God grant him peace—then Bedwyr, Gareth and Gwin, and the three kings Arthur believes to be his strongest allies: Pelinore, Rience of north Cambria and Symmachus of Chester. Among them all my father stands out like a suppurating boil."

"I see. Then tell me why you could not convince the King to see that?"

"Because of his nobility. Symmachus, Arthur was quick to point out to me, was seldom physically present when the plans were being prepared. Therefore, the argument went, he lacked the opportunity for treachery, even had he had the inclination. Useless for me to point out that my father employs an entire range of vile people who specialize in ingratiating themselves to other, more trusting folk and effortlessly sucking them dry of everything they know. Arthur simply refused to believe that this was what was happening. And that is why I referred to him as being foolish in this one single but crucial thing."

"So, you wish me to kill your father, my lady?"

She drew herself erect in her seat as though startled. Her face was blank with astonishment, perhaps seeing for the first time the reality of what she had been suggesting. I watched her eyes grow larger and then slowly fill with tears before she shook her head slowly, allowing the tears to spill down her cheeks.

"No," she whispered. "I do not. It would solve many problems, but I cannot bring myself to ask it of you, or of anyone else, including myself."

Gazing into her face, seeing her tears overflow, I realized that I would have ridden off to find and kill her father without a second thought had she answered otherwise. And only then did I understand that all the duty, and all the loyalty, love and devotion I had dedicated to Arthur now applied to her—his wife and my Queen— in equal measure. I drew a deep breath. "I think I know a way to clear out this whole nest of rats and obtain proof, one way or the other, of your father's role in this." She blinked away her tears. "I believe Mordred will be the key to this … Mordred, his uncles, my Frankish honor guard and our good friend Connor Mac Athol, whose galleys brought us here and still sit in Glevum, awaiting word from me on the King's condition. If I can get back up north of the Wall to Gallowa, and if I can conscript some support from King Tod, to back up my Franks, I believe I can win close enough to Connlyn to capture him or kill him."

She was frowning at me now. "You would never find him. Have you not heard a word I've said? He has spies everywhere. My father may be the largest and foulest of them, but he has legions of others, reporting on everything that happens and everything that moves along the roads the length and breadth of Britain. Connlyn is intangible, insubstantial. He is a wraith, a ghost. And even when he does appear somewhere, he is seldom himself. He uses men who look like him, to confuse his enemies."

"He might be able to do that with most of his enemies, but not with me. I know the man. I have spent time with him, before he broke faith with us. I will know him when I see him. As for his spies, let them spy all they want. We won't be using the roads. Our route will take us north to Gallowa, out of sight of land. Connlyn's spies will all have their eyes and ears pointed southward, and his listeners won't understand a word they overhear from my Franks, for they don't speak their language, and the only plans I make aloud will be in Frankish. And only yourself and Merlyn will know what they are.

"I'll make my way to Gallowa, take the boy home for a visit, then send word to Connlyn, through his sister, Morgas, that Mordred is there and will be coming south to join him. With Tod of Gallowa's backing and support, and my own guardsmen, we'll ride south, through the Wall, to meet with Connlyn, and when we do, I will deal with him. And if I am fortunate to take him alive, I will enquire about his sources. If your father has provided him with any help at all, I'll find out what it was and when. And then Arthur will have his proof."

"Can you really do that? Won't you be placing the boy in danger? What if you find yourself in a situation where you cannot win, no matter what you do? Then you would have delivered Mordred into Connlyn's hands."

"True, except that I'm not that foolish. Connlyn has never seen young Mordred, so he won't be able to tell him from my squire, Rufus. I'll leave Mordred safely with his grandmother—she will be glad to see him again—and I'll take Rufus to the meeting with Connlyn. That way, if everything goes wrong, Mordred will still be safe. I could, of course, leave the boy here in Camulod in perfect safety, but I suspect his kinsmen, seeing him there and well, will trust his word about our treatment of him far more than they would accept my unsubstantiated word that I had left him safe in England."

"And you believe this King of Gallowa will help you?"

"King Tod. Yes, I think he will, especially if he believes he will
be helping his nephew win respect and position south of the Wall.
Which means, I suppose, that it would be greatly to our advantage
to have the King acknowledge Mordred as his son before we leave
for the north."

"I can see that, but when would you expect to leave?" She was
looking at me intently, a tiny frown puckering between her brows,
and I shrugged.

"As soon as may be. Perhaps the day after tomorrow, although
tomorrow would be better."

"That soon?"

"The sooner the better, my lady. You appear to have a problem
with secrecy in Camulod nowadays, so the faster I can leave, the
better I will feel about my plans being close guarded. Besides,
Connor's fleet will not wait longer than five days in Glevum, and
one of those days has already passed."

"Does Merlyn know you intend to leave again so soon?"

"No, my lady. I didn't know myself until you and I were speaking of it. But it feels like the right thing to do."

"Hmm." Gwinnifer's tone was distant, her thoughts evidently
racing as she stared sightlessly into the distance beyond my
shoulder. "I doubt there will be time to tell Arthur about the boy
and have him acknowledge him, even as who he is, let alone as
the heir to Camulod, if not the Riothamus name itself." She held
up a peremptory hand even although I had made no move to
speak. "I shall have to do this ... by myself. If he hears of it from
me, he will accept it more readily than he would from you or
Merlyn. With you two, he would argue. With me he will be more
inclined to listen and consider." She sat drumming her fingers
against the arm of her chair, her mouth pursed and her eyes
thoughtful. Finally she nodded. "He knows you are here and is
expecting to see you, but I think you should postpone meeting
with him until tomorrow morning. Leave him to me this evening.
I know my husband and he will want to be alone to think once

I have told him these tidings. He always elects to be alone when-ever he has to adjust to ill tidings or to absorb a setback, that is his nature. He will spend the night thinking over everything I tell him, and will probably send for you early in the morning. In the meantime, you may spend the evening preparing your men to ride out again tomorrow."

"And what exactly do you intend to tell the King, my lady?"

"Exactly what you have told me—about the boy Mordred, his background, his parentage, and Connlyn's plans to use him. And then I will tell him of your plan to sail north to Gallowa and to use the lad's presence as a means of making contact with Connlyn."

"I see." I was greatly impressed with the speed with which this young woman grasped things. Many of my own officers would not have been so incisive. "Then may I ask your opinion on how he might react to what you tell him?"

She smiled, fleetingly. "You may ask, Seur Clothar, and I will tell you what I believe, but I might be very wrong. It seems to me, however, that the King might welcome your idea of an approach from the north. We are in dire need of something that might turn the recent tide of reversals. Now, take me to the boy Mordred."

"No need, my lady, he is nearby. I brought him with me, just in case you should decide you wished to see him, so if you would remain here, I will bring him to you."

She stood up and I rose with her, but before she could move farther I held up a hand and she paused, one eyebrow rising in a query.

"Forgive me," I said, "but should we not tell Merlyn what is happening ... how you intend to approach the King?"

"You may tell him, if you wish. He will accept what you say." She saw the dubious look in my eyes and added, "You have been gone for two years, Seur Clothar, and Merlyn Britannicus is no longer ... well, he is no longer the warrior Merlyn Britannicus who led his armies against Cornwall. He is become an old man nowa-days, and although his counsel is no less valuable than it ever was, his role is less involved and more analytical. Arthur's is the most important voice in these matters, and Merlyn will agree to whatever Arthur decides, in this as in everything else."

I could only bow my head and accept what she had said, and then I left her with her ladies while I went to fetch young Mordred Pendragon for her inspection.

4

Arthur sent for me late that evening, just as I was thinking about going to bed, and the fellow who came to find me was not inclined to be friendly. He growled to me that the King desired my presence, and then led me through the small maze of passageways connecting the King's Chambers to the quarters that had been assigned to me earlier by the Queen's chief steward.

I expected Gwinnifer to be there in the sickroom when I arrived, but there was no sign of her. Merlyn was there instead, much to my surprise, but I had no time to consider the ramifications of that. I had to school myself to betray nothing of my real thoughts when I came face to face with Arthur for the first time, because he was frighteningly altered from the friend I knew and loved. Ever since my first encounter with him, I had thought of Arthur Pendragon as being massive, rather than simply a large man. In a society of tall, strong, muscular men, he was a phenomenon, larger in every respect than those around him. He stood taller than any other, and his shoulders were nigh on half as broad again as were my own; his chest was broad and deep and his legs long and heavily muscled. Yet in the interim since he and I had last met, all of that had changed. He now seemed tiny, lying in a massive bed, because he had shed both weight and muscle mass in alarming amounts, and his face was gaunt and haggard, deeply lined and discolored by pain and sickness. Fortunately, as I discovered almost immediately, his mind was still working with its customary ease and precision.

He made no secret of his delight at seeing me, smiling and beckoning me to approach his bedside. I found that both flattering and encouraging, and when I reached out my hand to him, in response to his beckoning, he seized it in both his own and held it tightly. His voice was weak, with a distinct tremor, but he could still smile and make light of such things, pointing out that a mere week earlier, he had been unable to move without assistance and had been incapable of speaking aloud.

I was having difficulty at that moment with my own voice, my throat swollen with emotions that threatened to choke me, but I forced myself to swallow hard and spoke in a voice that emerged far more lightly and confidently than I would have thought possible.

"I am glad to see you looking so well, my lord, but it was not necessary to go to such extremes merely to prove me wrong."

I saw his eyes widen as he recognized the raillery in my voice and understood that I was twitting him, but he asked me in a whisper what in Hades I was on about.

I turned down my mouth and shrugged, flipping my hands outwards, my elbows pressed against my sides, and dipped my head, knowing the sheer Gaulishness of the gesture would make him grin. "Don't you recall?" I asked, looking down at him owlishly. "I distinctly remember having an argument with you one afternoon, when you were in one of your foulest and most churlish moods, about invulnerability. I had said Excalibur, and the circumstances under which you received it at your coronation, endowed you with an air of invulnerability, and you grew most obnoxious, denying that you were invulnerable in any sense of the word." I took a single step backwards and spread both hands again towards him, indicating the bed. "You were correct, obviously, and I was wrong, but I would have admitted it gladly, after a while ... You didn't have to go out and *prove* it."

He glared up at me in disbelief for several moments, and then he began to giggle, whimpering and squirming with the effort of clutching his own ribs against the pain caused by his laughter.

"Damn you, you Gaulish fool," he wheezed eventually, "it's worth all the regrets I've had about not executing you, just to have you back. Help me to sit up higher."

As soon as I had made him comfortable again, he asked about our venture in Gaul and wanted to know all the latest details of what we had been doing over there, and I brought him up to date with how well Pelles and his new army were progressing, and the success of Pelles's recent Games. I also spoke of my own feelings that we should be considering starting the preparations to bring our troopers home. He nodded at that and waved a hand in a gesture that told me unmistakably to set that aside for the time being and go on to other things, and I recalled what Merlyn had told me earlier that day about his having other plans concerning Gaul. It seemed to me then that Merlyn had not been talking about Pelles or Corbenic, but when I glanced at him now, hoping for a sign of some kind, I saw nothing but the grim, black shape of him and I could not imagine what else he might have meant. I told Arthur more about Pelles and his new troopers, describing the honor guard that the Corbenican king had sent to accompany me and convey his gratitude and respect to his esteemed friend Arthur Pendragon, High King of All Britain.

I do not know how long it took me to exhaust my store of Gallic material, but when I eventually ran out of words, Arthur lay looking up at me for some time, then gestured with one hand towards a chair close by his bed. "Sit. And think."

I glanced again at Merlyn, then moved to obey, and when I was seated I bent forward. "Think about what, my lord King?"

"Think about my name, for one thing, and speak to me as a friend. And think about your answer to my questions … the ones I'm going to ask you now." I said nothing, wondering what was coming. "My wife tells me I have a son, Mordred, and that his mother was my beloved Morag. You know of Morag, Lance. I've told you about her, and about how I lost her, more than a decade ago when I was a mere boy. Now I discover that I was more of a man than a boy at the time, and that when Morag left our fort up there in the northern mountains, she was already carrying my son.

"As I'm sure you can imagine, I was caught unawares by the story, for I had never suspected anything of the kind." He closed his eyes, then inhaled deeply and opened them again. "I have been lying here thinking ever since. And I have questions, which is why I summoned you two here to me."

Once again I looked over to where Merlyn's shape sat in silhouette against the fire's light at his back, but I received nothing in return.

"What are your questions?" I didn't want to ask that, but in the face of Merlyn's silence, I had no option.

"Well, I believe that Gwinnifer is glad for me. But for some reason, I feel *I* should feel better than I do about this." He paused, and I could sense him choosing his words carefully. "You went up into the north, Lance, summoned by a letter from the Queen of Gallowa, Morag's mother, who is also Connlyn's sister. Once there, you discovered the reason for the summons—the fact that I had a son, and that his uncle Connlyn wished to use the boy to undermine me and to lay claim to Camulod. So you took the boy back with you to Gaul. And there lies my problem, Lance. That happened nigh on a year ago. Now I have been asking myself, what possible reason could you have had for keeping the boy's existence from me? You would have written to Merlyn, in fine detail. Merlyn, is that not so? Did you receive such a letter from Clothar?"

"Aye, I did." The words seemed to echo from within the cowl.

"Then tell me, if you will, what was the impediment that hindered the boy from being sent here from Gaul on one of Connor's returning ships? He could have come directly into your charge, from Clothar's, and you could have informed me of who he was. Why did that not happen? And why had this Queen Morgas made no prior attempt to inform anyone of the boy's parentage?"

"She—"

Arthur looked at me. "She what?"

I silently cursed my impulsiveness. "She didn't know about it." That, of course, was a lie, for Morgas had known about Arthur's involvement since she discovered her daughter's pregnancy and the disastrous truth behind it. The only thing she had not known was that Arthur Pendragon had since become High King of Britain. That was the only time I ever lied to Arthur, but it was a lie born of desperation, since I could not tell him the truth at that point without bluntly and brutally exposing the incest involved.

"Bear in mind," I continued, "this is an aged woman who lived in the wilds above the Wall and had no contact with Britain and no knowledge of what was happening here until her brother Connlyn summoned her to visit him. You may recall that Queen Morgas was on her way to visit Connlyn when I first met and rescued her, as you'll recall. Well, during that visit, Connlyn told her what he had discovered about the boy's parentage, and as it transpired, he knew much more than she did. It's a long story, but he had learned of it himself almost by accident, years earlier, after Morag returned home and had her baby. His elder sister—Morag, after whom the child was named—had told him about it at the time, and he had tucked the information away, because that's the kind of man he is—he never forgets or neglects anything that might work to his advantage someday—but it really meant nothing to him until he heard your name again, years later, and learned that you had been made Riothamus. Then it became really significant that you had a son who was also blood kin to Connlyn. That is when Connlyn's ambitions sprang up and overwhelmed him. When Morgas visited him after we rescued her, Connlyn told her he wanted her to send the boy to him, and he thought she would be glad to know her grandson might become high king of Britain someday. He was wrong. He miscalculated badly, and the queen wrote of it to me. She had never liked or trusted her brother and she feared for her grandson's welfare, and so she wrote to me because I was the only person from Camulod she had ever met."

"I understand that. I do *not* understand why it took so long for me to be told what she told you."

There was no way for me to avoid the question this time, and so I nodded, squirming with discomfort. "I could have brought Mordred home when I left Gallowa again with Connor, on my way back to Gaul, but Connor dissuaded me. He pointed out that there was no guarantee that you would even be in Camulod when we arrived—and he was correct, for you were fighting in the north at the time, as it turned out. He also made it plain that if you were not in residence, since I would have to leave again for Gaul immediately, I would have to leave the lad behind, stuck among strangers and isolated like a toad in a mud hole. That struck me at the time, I remember, as being not a particularly clever thing to do … announcing the boy's status—particularly to the Queen—as the son you did not know you had, then leaving him there without support, and without your even being aware of his existence … So I kept him with me, awaiting a better time."

"That makes no sense, Lance. That was a year ago. Am I to believe there has been no better time than that in an entire year?"

Before I could respond to that, Merlyn stepped closer to me and lowered himself cautiously to perch on the edge of the King's bed, taking care not to jostle his monarch. "Tell him, Clothar," he said, his voice deep and sonorous. "You can tell it more accurately than I can."

And so I told my King the whole tragic tale of his unwitting misadventure with his sister, missing out no detail of the background complexities and relationships, and emphasizing, to the best of my ability, the total lack of knowledge that had beset and confounded everyone involved.

I was aware of a terrible stillness settling over Arthur as I spoke. His head seemed to settle back farther and more heavily into his pillow, as though it had suddenly become too heavy for his neck to support. The rise and fall of his chest became imperceptible and his face gradually settled into a masklike rigor, empty of all expression and unrelieved by as much as the tic of an eyelash. I was aware, too, throughout all this, of Merlyn's presence beside me, and of the growing impatience and frustration threatening to overwhelm me because although he was there in person, he was providing me with absolutely no visible or audible support. I carried on, never the less, and regurgitated the entire sorry tale, and when I fell silent at the end of it, Arthur continued to lie motionless, ignoring us.

The silence stretched and grew and I lost track of time until Merlyn reached out and touched me on the knee, telling me quietly to go to the Queen and leave him alone with Arthur. Obediently, I stood up to leave, fully expecting that the King would take notice and detain me, but he did nothing, and I felt greatly saddened as I closed the heavy doors of his chamber behind me.

The Queen had already retired for the night, they told me, and so I debated with myself for a while over the merits of attempting to find some sleep while I had the opportunity—although I strongly suspected I would be unable to sleep at all that night—or of waiting fruitlessly for a summons from Arthur that would probably not materialize before the following morning, if it came even then.

5

I opted for sleep, and to my own amazement I discovered before dawn that I had slept soundly and could not even recall going to bed. I must have fallen asleep immediately, in defiance of all my concerns, and I awoke well rested and ready for anything the day might bring. I bathed in the villa's excellent bath house and found fresh bread and a hot porridge of oats with fresh milk in the kitchens, and after that I presented myself, still well before sunrise, at the King's Chambers again, just in time to intercept the man that Arthur had sent to find me mere moments earlier.

Arthur seemed calm and self-possessed when I entered his room again. He looked, if anything, more rested and at ease than he had the previous night, and I found that mildly surprising, recalling his situation when I had last left him.

"Come," he said the moment I entered. "Sit." As soon as I had seated myself he nodded to me and cleared his throat. "My thanks, my friend. That was a difficult task you faced last night, and you acquitted yourself well. I myself would not have enjoyed having to tell me the tale you told. I thought about it for a long time, and then

Merlyn, after he sent you to bed, led me once again through the full set of circumstances in force at the time I first met Morag. I now accept that there was nothing anyone could have done differently, since no one at the time knew the truth of what was occurring. I accept and agree, too, that the boy, my son, is utterly blameless and innocent of any fault in any of what has happened, before or since his birth. He should not, therefore, be made to suffer in any way for events that were completely beyond his knowledge and control. Here, take this." He held out a closed fist and I reached for his hand, then felt a hard and heavy object drop into my palm. Before I could look to see what it was, however, Arthur's fingers spread farther, to close over mine, and his other hand came up beneath it, and his hands enclosed my fist.

"Give this to the boy, for it is his. Merlyn and my wife both tell me you like the lad immensely."

"Yes, my lord. I do."

"Good, for if you do, the chances are good that I will like him, too. Go you now and give him this, then bring him back here to me, as soon as you wish." He released my hand.

"May I look at this, my lord?" Seeing his nod, I unclenched my fist and looked at what it contained: a signet ring of solid gold, with a red enameled dragon sunk into the flat lozenge of its head.

"It was his grandfather's … Uther Pendragon's personal seal, signifying his status as chief of the Pendragon clans of Cambria. I have had it since I was a boy. Merlyn gave it to me, and because it was all I had of my father, other than his name, I was fiercely proud to own it and have cherished it all my life. Now it appears my own son has never known his true family name, nor known he has an inheritance awaiting him as chief of Pendragon. Time now that he should know, so give him the ring and bring him to me, but let him marvel over the gift alone … its value and its beauty … tell him nothing of what it really is or what it means. That will be my task. Kingship of the Pendragon Federation is an appointment, not a hereditary right, and I have no knowledge of what process will apply to the creation of the next Riothamus. But the rank of chief of Pendragon passes to my firstborn son. So bring him to me, if you will."

In the decades that have elapsed since that morning, I have several times heard wild and fanciful rumors of Mordred of Britain and the role he supposedly played in his father Arthur's downfall, and I have treated all of them as nonsense spawned by self-important, pompous, petty little men who know nothing of the truth and vomit up whatever spiteful, bilious pap they have been fed by the last person to whom they spoke. One even said, although not in my hearing, that Mordred had suborned the Queen and used the King's great love for her to destroy Camulod. I was angry when I heard of that, but then I laughed, for I had heard but a short time earlier that I myself had done the selfsame thing, betraying my best friend for the love of his false wife and thus destroying Camulod. It made me realize that when great events are undone by mundane things, people often feel constrained to make the failure larger and somehow more significant by lying about what truly happened, as if what actually occurred were too ludicrously petty to have brought about such awe-inspiring and cataclysmic results.

I have never forgotten what I saw that day when Arthur, Riothamus of Britain, first met and welcomed his only begotten son, Mordred Pendragon, and so I could never be brought to believe any of the envious tales men tell about the boy nowadays. Such malice simply could not have existed within the boy I knew.

The meeting between him and his father was a private one, witnessed only by myself, Queen Gwinnifer and Merlyn Britannicus, and the only person there who was not moved to tears by what transpired was Merlyn—and of course I cannot even be sure of that, since his face was completely concealed by the deep hood of his robe, as it always was in those days. I know that I myself was blinded to the point where I had to scrub at my eyes and swallow hard to dislodge the great lump in my throat, and as I did so I could hear the Queen's sobs from where she stood close beside me on my right.

Arthur himself set out strongly, welcoming the boy formally and then going on to explain the significance of his father's great signet ring and the reasons for his passing it along to Mordred that day, as Uther's grandson, but then he asked the lad to approach him, and as Mordred leaned over the bed, the King reached up and traced the outline of the boy's face with his fingertips. "Morag," he said then. "I see her in there. You have your mother's nose, boy, and her eyes." That realization was his undoing, and he hugged the boy to his breast, both of them weeping and shuddering convulsively. The Lady Gwinnifer, unable to restrain herself, moved forward and embraced them both, and for a moment they formed a tableau of three.

By the time the tears had dried up and order had reasserted itself, Arthur was tightly focused on what needed to be done next. He questioned me closely on how I saw the unfolding of the plan I had proposed to the Queen the previous evening, and then he asked Mordred if he would be willing to take part in this, to the extent of returning home to Gallowa with me and persuading his uncle to support me in my attempt to come to grips with Connlyn. The boy did not hesitate, and his enthusiasm was self-evidently genuine, so Arthur gave me permission to take my honor guard of Franks, all of whom were slavering at the thought of seeing some real fighting, and to make the attempt on Connlyn. He agreed that my small striking force might have a better chance of making contact, although admittedly in desperate circumstances, than any of his larger forces had had in the past. The only condition he imposed upon me was that I should take half a hundred of his indefatigable Pendragon scouts with me, under the command of Gwin, who had grown up among their mountains, adopting their ways and their laconic language, so that now, even as a Knight Companion to the King, he enjoyed their liking, in addition to their respect and admiration. I accepted happily, since Gwin was one of my favorites among Arthur's friends, and the fearsome Pendragon longbows with their lethal arm-long arrows would offer us an advantage that the enemy could not match—most particularly so in areas where our Frankish cavalry might not be able to function to full effect.

I set about making my final arrangements immediately after that, and Merlyn went away to write a letter for Shaun Pointer to carry north to Connor and King Brander in their island kingdom after he dropped us off in Gallowa. In it, he included a full description of the King's condition, his imminent return to health, and our immediate plans for closing with Connlyn from the northward.

And while Merlyn was occupied with that, I went looking for Gwin, to tell him about his new orders and get him started on assigning the fifty scouts he needed to take with him. He was happy to be coming with us, and slyly curious about my Frankish guards, offering to wager—at odds that favored him greatly—that none of them would be able to pronounce his name properly, so that it sounded more like Gwain. I grinned and waved him away, and he laughed as he went off to select his men, knowing he would have won his wager had I been foolish enough to accept it. I had the same problem with *Gwain* that I did with sounds like *kill, will* and *sill*. That unique vowel sound that I still think of as Briton left me constantly frustrated in those days, because try as I would to make the sound they demanded, they emerged upon my tongue as *keel*, *weel* and *seel*. Even Gwinnifer, now that I think of it in that light, was always Gweeniffer to me, although I addressed her mostly as "my lady" in those days.

I spent the remainder of that morning organizing my Frankish guards and preparing them to move out again, back to Glevum and our waiting ships.

TWELVE

1

We arrived in Glevum several hours before sunset on the day after we left Camulod, loaded all our horses and bowmen with their gear, ammunitions and supplies onto Shaun Pointer's ships the day after that, and were clear of the river estuary and well under way with the evening tide of the third day.

The weather was kind to us on the short overnight journey north, and we anchored just below the cliff-top fortress that I had once mistakenly thought to be Tod's castle. It belonged to a chieftain called Cyrgus, whom I remembered well, and we waited there in plain sight until his people began to make their way down towards the beaches to meet us. They were familiar by now with the sight of Connor's galleys passing in the distance, and now, since this was the third instance of his ships stopping by their beaches without ill effect, I saw no weapons being brandished and no evidence of threats. I called Mordred forward to join me at the prow of the lead vessel and appointed him interpreter to our mission, for I remembered well the embarrassment I had felt at being unable to communicate with Cyrgus and his people the last time I had landed here.

We beached our dinghy safely beneath the cliffs, and Mordred went to work immediately, asking for Cyrgus by name and saying we were on our way to visit King Tod and would wait on the beach until Cyrgus came to us. Cyrgus, of course, was already there, biding his time until he felt it appropriate to make an appearance, and as soon as he realized that we had an interpreter with us, he came striding forward. He did not recognize Mordred, however, until he was standing right in front of him, and then his fierce-looking eyebrows shot upward in surprise. Mordred greeted him casually, with an air of absolute serenity and certitude of his own rank—prince speaking to chieftain—and informed him that we would need to find a place suitable for off-loading livestock and cargo, a thing that turned out to be easily achieved, since the locals had built a very serviceable wharf less than half a Roman mile farther up the coast, in a deep, narrow inlet that was invisible from the seaward approach.

We spent that night camped on the hillside close to the fortress walls, for Cyrgus's was a community without horses and therefore lacked even the most basic amenities for large animals. I had explained to him, through Mordred, that my companions were Frankish knights, sent by King Arthur to bring greetings and honor to King Tod, and although I truly believe he had no knowledge of what I meant by "Frankish," he accepted my explanation with as much graciousness as he was capable of showing, then offered us food, which we declined in favor of our own rations, knowing that the laws of hospitality in these northern parts decreed the offering of food and lodgings, no matter how scarce food and lodgings might be. I knew, from my previous visit, that food was hard to come by in these parts, and that Cyrgus would be appreciative of the fact that we were self-sufficient. I invited him to dine with us, instead, but he refused, equally politely, unwilling to be seen to dine in relative luxury while his own people were unable to do the same. Soon after that, he took his leave of us and left us to our own devices.

We were up and heading into the interior by sunrise the next day, and because we were all mounted, we came in sight of Tod's great square Roman castellum by mid-afternoon. Mordred's grandmother was delighted to see the boy, for she had not expected him to return to Gallowa in her lifetime, and she quickly spirited him away with her, to drain him of every vestige of memory he retained of all he had done since leaving her more than a year earlier.

Her son Tod, the giant, hairless King of Gallowa, was equally delighted to see me, for he had not spoken a single word of Latin, he told me, since my departure, but when he heard my answer to his initial question of what it was that had brought me back to Gallowa, he frowned and held up an open palm, warning me to silence, and invited me to ride with him. The last time I had been there, he had lent me one of his own horses, his dearest personal possessions. This time, on the spur of the moment and knowing it was exactly the right thing to do, I made him a gift of one of our finest mounts, a magnificent, fully trained bay gelding cavalry horse, with a deep chest, long, beautifully proportioned legs and a white blaze in the shape of an equal-armed cross in the center of its forehead. The gift silenced him for a spell, something that I had discovered at our first meeting was not easy to achieve, for Tod was a lonely and highly intelligent man with few people to whom he could really talk on equal terms. Now, unable to find words to express his gratitude, he merely admired his new horse. I mounted my own horse in silence and waited for him to climb up, and then I led him out of the gates and across the open heath that surrounded his stronghold.

A long time later we drew rein together on a low ridge from which we could see his castle in the distance, and I asked him if the place had a name.

He frowned at me, then grinned. "The Romans built it, you know, but if they had a name for it, they forgot to tell any of us. My people call it what the Old People called it—the people the Romans called the Picti, the Painted Folk. They called it Glenlochar in the Old Tongue, and so it remains today. So," he said then, dismissing that topic, "have you admired my new horse? He's the finest I've ever ridden. Tell me again about all those ring-mailed riders you brought with you. You say they're from Gaul? Then what are they doing here, in Gallowa?"

I told him exactly why they were here with me.

"I see. So you are here to ensnare Connlyn … with thirty mounted men and two boys against his thousands. That's very …

well, I'm unsure what it is, my Frankish friend, but it is very … something. Very brave, possibly. Very admirable, perhaps. Very stupid, almost certainly. The search for just what it is makes me appreciate the richness of the Roman tongue, however—its breadth and subtlety. Try to explain that kind of inexactitude in my language. Hah! The very thought is sickening.

"So what you are not saying, but clearly hoping I will guess, is that you need help in this venture. You want me to take up arms against my own uncle, my own blood relative."

I looked him straight in the eye. "Aye, I do. And if you can see through the kinship, to the man beneath the reflection, you will see why."

"Hmm. You are not lacking in audacity, friend Clothar. But then, neither is my uncle Connlyn, and his audacity has been annoying me and causing me grave concern for some time now. I really have had no interest in what he is attempting to achieve down in his part of the world, south of the Wall. That's in another land … in Britain. This is Alba, and the Wall, to this point, has kept the contagion of the southern lands away from us. But now my uncle has surrounded himself with allies I wouldn't let into my lands, and those allies increasingly consider themselves to have the freedom to do whatever they want in my domain, and to my people. It began about a year ago, just after you were here last time, and it wasn't much, at first, merely a few bands of Outlander marauders drifting into our territories on their way south. But within the month of that first occasion, it happened again, and then, on the occasion after that, they killed some of my people. We went after them, but we couldn't find them and I complained to Connlyn. He ignored me, and when I sent word to him again, his response was that he was not to be held responsible for the misdeeds of a few passing strangers, and that I should keep silent and stop making a nuisance of myself." He stopped talking and pointed to where a large hare was loping towards us, unaware yet of our motionless presence. It saw the raising of his arm, however, and froze in the ground cover, only its ears remaining visible.

"Well," Tod continued, once it became clear that the hare would come no closer, "I have kept silent, and only days ago another report reached me of two families burned out and slaughtered by white-headed Outlanders, so it's evident to me that not being a nuisance is no solution. I had recently decided, three days ago in fact, to become a very large and annoying nuisance to my uncle Connlyn, and I sent the word out for my people to rally here within the week and bring their weapons. So instead of me helping you and perhaps feeling guilty afterwards, you may be in a position to help me and soothe my conscience at the same time." He glanced sidelong at the light quiver of bamboo lances that hung, as always, from a hook on my saddle. "Think you could hit that hare with one of those? I came out without my bow, and that beast would feed us well tonight, could we but take it. My man Iain, who cooks for me, can make a fresh hare taste like food stolen from the table of the gods."

I selected a lance and prepared it, wrapping the throwing cord around my index finger, then spurred my horse towards the hare, which bolted as soon as I began to move. Its long, muscular hind legs propelled it in great bounding leaps, and it changed direction every time it touched ground and leapt again. I watched it go, gauging how far it leapt and how it varied its direction from jump to jump, and then I braced myself, rose in my stirrups and sent my blade whipping towards the animal, taking it at the apex of a leap and piercing it through the chest, transforming it in the blink of an eye from a thing of leaping beauty into a tangle of quivering, dying limbs on the end of a stick.

I saw rather than heard Tod grunt beside me as he jerked upright, and then he kicked his horse forward to where the dead hare lay, no longer quivering, and slid to the ground, where he picked up the beast and carefully extracted the long needle point of the tapered spear head before wiping the blade on the animal's fur. Then, grasping the hare by the ears in one hand, he held the javelin out towards me, butt first. He climbed back into his saddle as I rewound the thong and replaced the lance in my quiver.

"That was impressive, and it obviously wasn't accidental. How often would you miss a shot like that?"

"It depends on distance, terrain and speed. But at that distance, and on that shot, practically never. Perhaps once in a score of throws, but only perhaps."

"Hmm." He busied himself slipping the hare into one of his saddlebags. "How had you intended to contact Connlyn?"

"By sending him word that I have Mordred and would bring him to meet with his uncle."

"And of course you believe Connlyn will agree to that, simply because he wants to have the boy close to him."

"Wants it and needs it, because the boy is his key to Camulod and thereafter to the regency of the young Riothamus. Of course, we would not take Mordred with us. My squire, Rufus, would come with us in Mordred's place. They are almost of an age and Connlyn has never set eyes on Mordred, so he'll know no different. He'll accept the boy we offer him, and he'll do so at face value."

"So you believe Connlyn can kill Arthur?"

I had to fight the urge to say that he had already come frighteningly close to doing it. "No, but he *thinks* he can kill him, and he believes—and needs to believe—that Arthur will hesitate to kill his own son."

"And you, do you think the same?"

"What, that the King would hesitate? Arthur would never even consider such a thing."

"Why do you think Connlyn would respond to you? He knows who you are and he knows you're loyal to Arthur. Why would he trust you, one of Arthur's own knights?"

I shrugged. "He would not … not at all, under any circumstances. That's why I was hoping to enlist your support for your nephew, at least, if not your armed assistance. A letter from you to Connlyn would do the trick."

"Aye, or better still a trusted messenger, one of my own chiefs, known to Connlyn. I'll tell him the boy has been in the far north with my mother, visiting his Norweyan kin, and has but recently returned. Connlyn will know no different, and will accept what he wants to hear. But I'll tell him, too, that we have been having trouble with his allies again, and will demand safe conduct through his territories—which I consider to be hostile—to wherever he may choose to meet with us. And I'll play the fool—the safe conduct I demand will be in the form of escorts chosen from his own body-guard. Believe me, his territories are swarming with Outlanders of every kind, and I'll make it plain I fear for my people and their safety in transit, since I have already lost entire families to his allies. A letter of safe conduct would be useless. We need people with us—strong people and recognizably his—who can vouch for us and brandish the threat of his anger and displeasure should we come to harm."

"And what about my thirty horsemen? Don't you think some of these bodyguards you're talking about might wonder who they are and whence they came? Cavalry of our kind is something of a rarity outside Camulod."

Tod grinned, his strong, even teeth flashing in his hairless face. "Of course they might, Clothar, of course they might—and they would, absolutely, the moment they set eyes on them. But your cavalry will not be there for them to see. We will cause all the fuss when we are passing through their lands. You and your force, with a few hundred of my own clansmen, will move parallel to us out of sight and away from the commotion we will generate, and within a day or so, some of my men will acquire whatever recognizable armor or trappings Connlyn's own men use, so that they'll look like Connlyn's safe passage warrantors, too. As soon as we discover where the meeting is to be, I'll let you know, and we'll join forces close to the spot. Then the hunt will be on, and the old gods will feast on the laggards. Let's go back now. My people should start arriving tomorrow, and they'll all be here within the week. In the meantime, however, Iain should be getting this hare ready for the pot."

"How many men have you called out?"

"Eight in every ten—damn near all I have. We should muster nigh on two thousand by the time the shouting is over."

"Two thousand! And will you take them all?"

"Ah, well, there's the thing ... Once you've called them out, it's difficult to send them home unblooded. These are prideful men, warriors all, and they don't like being made to look like fools and they don't like being mishandled and they don't like being slighted. So yes, we will take them all, perhaps a quarter of them with me and the remainder with you, moving beside us unseen and unsuspected until it's too late to make a difference."

2

Two memories remain with me of that journey southward from Tod's castle into the territories to which Connlyn laid claim in north Britain. The most immediate of those is the enormous defensive bastion called Hadrian's Wall, and the effect it had upon me when I saw it from the north side for the first time. I had seen it several times before, but always from the rear, from the side of the defenders, where everything—pathways, approaches and stairs—was designed to simplify access to the defensive ramparts at the top. The view from the side facing the attackers was radically different and profoundly intimidating. We had left Tod's castle and struck straight south for the estuary called Solway, then followed the coast road eastwards all the way to the abandoned Roman town of Luguvallium and the western end of the Wall. We skirted northeastwards around the town, taking pains to remain concealed, and then headed south until we came upon the Wall suddenly, in a place that let us see at first glance what an intimidating barrier it really was. The sight of it chastened me, however much I knew the bastion had been abandoned decades earlier and was now unmanned.

The first and most impressive difference I noticed from this northern side was that the Wall was high and blank, a flat, featureless wall, three times the height of a tall man, that stretched away beyond view to right and left and was fronted by a deep, weed-filled ditch—a classic Roman *fossa*—with high, steeply banked sides that made the wall above seem even higher.

We had emerged from a thicket of heavy brush at the top of a long, sloping ridge and found ourselves confronted by more than we had been anticipating. We knew, of course, that the Wall would be somewhere in front of us, but we came to it at the point where one of the original gate towers had been added to allow the Roman garrison free access to the lands to the north. The high tower added an additional six feet to the height of the already impressive wall, and in the stonework beneath it was the clear shape of the doors the tower had originally protected. Those doors had proven to be more of a curse than a benison, however, and they had been sealed with masonry soon after being built. Now the blank face reared above us, surmounting a deep ditch that had obviously been carved with great pains from the bedrock fronting the Wall. The ditch was approximately twenty-seven paces wide and nine deep, a standard measure throughout the entire length of the Wall, and although grass had rooted in this particular section in the progress of hundreds of passing years, the raw stone of the bedrock on the side of the ditch facing us looked as unyielding as it must have looked to the unfortunates who had dug it in the first place.

We had been struggling uphill on foot, leading our horses individually since it was impossible to ride through the dense thickets of hawthorn that covered the terrain thereabouts, and the effect of the first sight of all this, coming so unexpectedly after a hard climb, was literally breathtaking. I heard Bors grunt close behind me, and then saw his hand, from the corner of my eye, as he reached out to grasp my saddle horn.

"Sweet Jesus," he breathed, "is that the Wall? It's bigger than I expected."

"What, you expected to jump over it?" Aware that others were crowding close behind him, I raised my voice and switched from Latin to Frankish for the benefit of our companions. "The Emperor Hadrian built this wall hundreds of years ago, my friends, to keep the northern barbarians safely out of Britain. This was the northern boundary of the Roman Empire, and this Wall one of the greatest construction endeavors of all time. Seventy-six miles in length, it stretches all the way across the top of Britain. It stands eighteen feet in height and is fronted by a ditch from end to end. It has a fort every six miles along its length and a smaller defensive castle every mile. The gates you can see outlined in the stonework were to let the legionaries come out to raid on this side, in Caledonia, but they worked in both directions and so they were filled in. Now it simply sits there, in our path, empty and undefended but still formidable because we have to pass it."

"How do we do that?"

I did not look to see who asked the question. I merely raised my hand and pointed forward. "We send some people to climb over it, with pry bars and pickaxes, and then we wait for them to dig out the rubble blocking the gateway, and knock out those stones there. I'm going to need volunteers."

It took an entire afternoon to penetrate Hadrian's Wall and pass beyond it, even without having to deal with defenders, but we had planned for it and had left Tod's castle three full days in advance of his party, allowing one full day to get through the Wall and two more for the additional difficulty of our journey to the south on a parallel route to his. And that is the second memory I have of that journey.

There are but two roads to the north of the Wall, one in the east and the other just to the west of Luguvallium, and both of them are in very poor condition. Both continue south of the Wall, but there is nothing but fifty miles of bitter wilderness between them there. That may not seem a very pertinent observation, but that is merely because few people ever take the time to think about roads and what they signify. Rome built long, straight roads for the sole purpose of moving its armies as quickly as possible from one place to another, and then it built defensive camps to allow its legionaries to patrol, defend and maintain those roads for future use. And eventually, around each one of those camps, towns sprang up and grew into cities, and traffic moved along the roads that stretched between them, and trade and commerce flourished as populations grew. But all of that changes as soon as you pass beyond the bounds of the Empire. At that point, immediately and all-pervasively, the importance of roads makes itself blatantly and ludicrously obvious. Because where roads exist, people travel, and in their travels they will frequently leave the road, venturing into the lands that border them, so that their presence and their passage, over the course of centuries, will cause a thinning out of the wild, natural growth on both sides of the roads. Haphazardly tended campfires will regularly start wildfires that thin out the underbrush and consume the piled-up debris of times past, and eventually the stone-built roads themselves will be paralleled by wide swathes worn by passing herds of soft- and cloven-hoofed cattle and livestock.

Where there are no roads, on the other hand, the undergrowth merely accumulates and thickens, burned off occasionally in places, during the summer months, by destructive conflagrations caused by lightning. Lacking roads of any description, people seldom travel beyond the place where they were born. Hamlets and small settlements spring up, and within and around those, fields are cleared for crops and trees are felled for timber and fuel, and the cleared woodland is farmed or used as common pasture. People develop skills and share them with their neighbors, and thus local commerce develops, but there is seldom any contact between neighboring settlements, because in the absence of roads every journey, even the shortest and most mundane, becomes an enormous task beset with dangers and difficulties. Animals and livestock cannot move freely through the choking undergrowth of the surrounding wilderness, where every tree that dies and falls, and every limb those same trees shed before dying, crashes to earth and remains where it landed, overgrown by moss, rank grasses and new saplings, until it decomposes back into the soil. That makes it nigh on impossible for any man on horseback to move safely, because a horse can break a leg at any step.

In consequence, our southward trek into Connlyn's country was the stuff from which nightmares are born. On a flat Roman road, my mounted troopers could have covered eight miles in a single hour. In the roadless forests south of the Wall, interspersed with tracts of unpredictable and rocky terrain, with treacherous bogs and swampy marshes in the bottoms of many of the valleys between low ranges of hills, there were places where we were sometimes fortunate to travel a single mile in four or five hours.

We did make headway, nevertheless, and Gattric, Gwin's second-in-command as leader of the Pendragon scouts, knew exactly where we were at all times, and how far we had traveled. When Gwin came to me with word from Gattric that we had traveled thirty miles straight to the south and should now be dispatching scouts to make contact with King Tod to the east, I agreed without demur and ordered him to do so, and to have his people find a clearing where the rest of us could set up camp until the scouts returned. That was no small request, for our group was a large one, comprising as it did my own forty Frankish knights, and their seven senior officers including Bors, myself and the four Corbenican officers under Quintus Milo's command, all of them with horses, plus Rufus masquerading as Mordred, Gwin and his fifty Pendragon scouts, and something more than a thousand of Tod's own Gallowa men.

Despite our numbers, however, I had been sinking further and further into despondency since we left the Wall behind us. Much of the great barrier ran over open hillsides, and on each side, front and rear, a belt of land one hundred paces wide had been cleared along the entire length centuries earlier and kept clear of growth for as long as the Wall was garrisoned. These cleared belts both permitted swift access from the rear to the Wall for the defenders and offered a clear field of fire on the side facing the enemy. It would have been effortless to follow this belt eastwards along the base of the Wall for as far as we had to go, but it would also have been sheerest folly, for its accessibility and lack of clutter guaranteed that it must be in constant use by Connlyn's forces in their comings and goings. We had to cross the open space quickly and move deep into the dense forest on the other side of it, traveling through a trackless wasteland for thirty miles, and throughout that entire journey I found myself beset by two realizations that defied all of my training, all of my enthusiasm and all of my expectations: cavalry and bowmen were both useless in the kind of terrain we were traversing, and I had been completely unprepared for that. Here, in badly broken, rock-strewn terrain, my cavalry could not function and my bowmen could not see far enough to take unrestricted aim at any targets they might see. The only kind of fighting that would be effective in such surroundings was the face-to-face, brute-strength hacking of King Tod's Gallowans, and I was not enthralled by that prospect. I had spent too many years learning how to fight to relish the thought of being struck down by a ravening savage because I couldn't find enough room to swing my own weapons.

I need not have worried, for when the Pendragon scouts returned, they brought King Tod with them, accompanied by half a score of his personal bodyguard. He was single-mindedly intent upon what we had to achieve, and he set about issuing orders to me as though I were one of his newest recruits.

"I came myself because I had to," he began. "This thing is too important to risk fouling it up because of some hapless middleman's well-intentioned misinterpretation, so I wanted to look you in the eye as I tell you what I know, and to hear your reactions with my own ears. Connlyn is in a stronghold, an old ring-fort on a hilltop, unreachable unless he wants to be reached. He comes and goes, from time to time, always heavily guarded, but my people tell me that for the past month and more he's been wrapped up in there tighter than a babe in swaddling and there can be no getting through to him without his own say-so. Otherwise, he's walled in—no contact with the people of the surrounding countryside, and no access permitted to his fort. Even my envoy Liam had a hard time reaching him, under a white flag and bearing letters from me."

"Have you spoken with him?"

He raised an eyebrow, as though impatient with my interruption. "With Connlyn? No, I haven't. How could I? Didn't you hear what I just said? Liam, one of my chiefs, went in and spoke to him on my behalf, told him I was on my way from Gallowa with the boy, Mordred. The whoreson told him to have me wait until he summoned me."

"Which whoreson was that?" The questioner was Bors, but Tod kept his eyes on mine.

"My whoreson uncle, the whoreson Connlyn. The warlord who expects kinsmen kings to wait upon him like lackeys." He was squinting at me now, and I was unable to read the strange expression on his face. Then he said, "Do you know a fellow called Lanar?"

"It sounds as though I should know it," I said, "but I have no face in my mind to go with it."

"He's one of Connlyn's folk."

Hearing that, the name and the face that went with it came back to me immediately. Lanar was the man who had told me that Morgas was Connlyn's sister, the man Connlyn himself had lent me as interpreter when I first met him, and he had ridden with me on the raid against Knut One-Eye. I remembered thinking that Connlyn had treated him harshly for doing what I considered a fine job, and I had paid him well, banking on his goodwill in the matter of finding the meaning of the word *morgas*.

"I remember him now. He rode with us for a spell, interpreting for us the first time I came up here. What about him?"

"He asked about you … or about some Frankish warrior he knew. Liam thought it could only be you, since he has never heard of any other Frank around here."

"But … How could he ask such a thing? Why would he? He knows me from the southward, from Camulod, not from Gallowa."

"No, he knows you know my mother, and he knows about Mordred. I don't know the exact connections, how he found out or how he managed to tie them together, but he told Liam he wanted to talk to you. Then he vanished."

"Vanished? You mean he was made to vanish, by Connlyn?"

Tod shrugged. "I don't know. I only know that Liam said the man looked afraid, and once he had said what he had to say, he disappeared." He cocked his head. "What's going on here? D'you think this fellow might be willing to help us tackle Connlyn?

Because I'll tell you, if he does not, then we have no hope of achieving anything against the whoreson ... not as long as he stays in that stronghold. Liam says it can't be taken, and he's taken half a score like it in the past few years. He's my best commander and he knows what he's talking about."

"Hmm. Then I had best talk with this Lanar. Where is he?"

"He's in Connlyn's stronghold, two days' march from here."

"You mean two days' real march, or two days through this forest?"

"Through the forest."

"Then when do we leave, and what do we do with my main force?"

"We leave now. We'll take some of your bowmen. The others will follow close behind us, with Bors. Before we leave, however, we should at least talk over the possibilities of what might happen once we reach Connlyn's stronghold. As I see it, there are two possibilities, and both of them might depend absolutely on this fellow Lanar." He broke off and cocked his head again in that inquisitive gesture of his. "If we can reach him again—because it's not certain we can—would you be willing to trust him?"

I pursed my lips and considered that. "From what I know of him, from what I recall of him, yes, I think I would be willing to trust him. I remember being impressed with the way he handled himself in dealing with Knut One-Eye's people. He's cool under pressure, and although he is not a fighter, he is not a man who will be easily intimidated. Yes, if he's there and has something to offer us, I'll trust him."

"Good. So be it, then. So when we get to where we're going, our first task will be to find this Lanar. I'll have to send Liam back into Connlyn's stronghold, give him some reasonable tale of woe to relate, and make sure he knows what to tell Lanar if he meets him. Then, given that Lanar comes out to talk to you, we'll see what he has to say and we may or may not act upon whatever he tells us. One way or the other, you're going to have to hold your people out in the forest, Bors, until we find out what the possibilities may be. It's frustrating, I know, not to be able to plan anything with any certainty at this point, but that's the way it is. We have to wait and see. There's no other choice. Does anyone want to say anything?"

"Aye," I responded. "You said there were two possibilities of action once we reach Connlyn's stronghold, and that both of them might depend on the man Lanar. What are they?"

He looked at me wide eyed. "Why, we'll either fight or we won't. If Lanar can help us, give us some advice or advantage, we'll fight, and with any kind of good fortune, we might win. If he can't help us, on the other hand, then we'll have no other option than to sit quietly and wait for Connlyn to come out from his hill fort, in the hope that we can catch him by surprise outside the walls. I don't like the odds against that, but I can't see any other possibility open to us." He looked about him, from man to man, then nodded. "Anything else? Does anyone have any more questions to ask?"

No one did, and it was not yet noon, so we made our preparations to move out within the hour.

3

"Lanar, well met! It has been a long time since you and I last were face to face."

He looked considerably older than he had when last we met, although it had been little more than three years, and he was no better dressed now than he had been then. He had always tended to be stoop shouldered, but the bow in his back was more pronounced now and his hair was grayer and thinner, the lines about his mouth and eyes etched more deeply. Lanar looked as though he had suffered in the years that had elapsed since I crossed over into Gaul, and I wondered again about his relationship with Connlyn. It had always seemed to me that Connlyn held too much sway over the man for their relationship to be merely one of warlord and follower; Connlyn held the interpreter at his beck and call, and he treated him with less consideration and humanity than he showed to his hunting dogs.

I waved him towards a folding chair by my fire. We were in camp, deep in the forest and far from Connlyn's stronghold, and Lanar had been traveling half the day to come to me, after reading the letter I had sent to him with Liam.

"Sit, sit, Lanar. I left word for someone to bring you food and drink as soon as you arrived, so it should be here at any moment. You must be starved." I made no mention of what I had been thinking, which was that he appeared to be truly starving, but even as he settled himself close by the fire I saw young Rufus coming towards us, balancing a wooden platter heaped with steaming food in one hand and carrying a heavy jug in the other. Lanar took the jug from him and drank thirstily, and I watched in admiration as he swallowed more at one draft than I could have.

"I regret that it could not be beer," I said. "But when you travel without roads, you must travel without wagons."

"No matter," Lanar growled, picking up a plump leg of fowl and eyeing it appreciatively. "The gods made water to be drunk, long before men thought of beer." He sank his teeth into the meat in his hand and tore off a mouthful, sucking it noisily into his mouth, and I watched in awe as he demolished the entire piece in several greedy bites. Rufus had been watching, too, his mouth hanging open, and I waved to attract his attention.

"Bring more."

As the lad scuttled away, Lanar grinned at me and wiped his fingers on a piece of thick bread, then wiped the bread on the juice on the wooden platter and stuffed the morsel into his mouth. It took some time for him to finish eating, for he consumed three portions of meat and half a loaf of bread, but I was content to wait and to admire his appetite, and eventually he straightened up and leaned back, wiping his hands on his robe.

"That," he said, and belched softly, "was excellent. I thank you."

"No need, but it looked welcome. You wish to talk with me, I've been told, and I confess I am curious. Can you talk now, or would you prefer to wait a little longer?"

"No, we'll do it now, because we have no time to waste." He

used the back of his hand to wipe away some grease around his mouth. "My sister is dead."

"Your … sister …" I did not know how to respond, because I had not known he had a sister.

"Aye, my sister. Her name was Martha. She was my only relative, and my closest friend. She reared me when our parents died.

"She was his wife … Connlyn's, I mean. But not always, not in the beginning. Our father ruled these lands when we were children, and when he died, his place was taken by Martha and her first husband, whose name was Alisan. I used to travel widely as a younger man, and while I was away on one long journey, Alisan was killed. A hunting accident, they called it. Within the year, Connlyn was wed to my sister, mainly because she needed a strong man to rule with her. I came home the following year, by which time Martha had fallen sick of some mysterious and apparently incurable illness, and when I started asking questions I was hit over the head by some of Connlyn's men and dragged before him. He had not taken the title of king, for there was no kingship in our lands, but he was king by then in every respect. Most of those who might oppose him had been removed from contention by one means or another, and I was but the last of them. For some reason, however, he thought he needed me, to give himself some semblance of legitimacy … I don't know why. But he informed me, without any possibility of misinterpretation, that he held my sister's life in his hands, as hostage to my behavior, and that if I did not do everything he said, as soon as he said it, Martha would die, unpleasantly …

"I cared nothing about my own life, even then, but I could never do anything that would cause my sister pain, and Connlyn made it very clear to me that, should anything unfortunate happen to him, Martha would die immediately and agonizingly. I believed him, because he surrounded himself with some of the most debased and evil creatures I have ever known. That was eight years ago.

"Then, less than a month ago, I discovered that Martha was very sick—some wasting, fatal illness—and not expected to live much longer, and I determined that, as soon as she was dead, I would kill

Connlyn. But the Gallowan chief, Liam, appeared at Connlyn's gates soon after that and I learned about what was happening, and that the boy Mordred would soon be coming to join his uncle. I remembered you then, and that you had been on friendly terms with the old queen, and I devised a plan that I thought would serve my purpose better and more satisfyingly than simply killing Connlyn. I decided to try to contact you and make it possible for you to bring Connlyn down. It was a long chance, but if nothing came of it, I knew I could fall back on my original plan of killing the swine myself. And then Liam said he knew of you, and that you were back in Gallowa again. I knew that the gods had heard my prayers, and I was content to await their pleasure after that. Then Liam returned, the day before yesterday, with your letter and instructions for finding you, and Martha died a few hours after he arrived."

"The day before yesterday? Forgive me, my friend, for my ignorance. You must be distraught."

He shook his head, turning down his lips. "Not so, not at all, strange as that may seem to you. I am not at all unhappy. I grieve for her, and I mourn the loss of her love for me, but I am truly grateful that she is out of her misery at last, for she has had no pleasure in her life these past years …" He gazed off into the middle distance, then shrugged. "Connlyn was not there at the time of her death, of course. I doubt the whoreson will know she is gone, even now. But she is gone, finally beyond his reach. I took her remains and carted them away with me, then buried her safely in a spot I had found weeks earlier, a place I knew she would love, and after that, I came seeking you. I took care, however, to let his people know that I had gone to bury Martha, so they will not be too concerned when I fail to return for a few days. They think me a useless thing, anyway, too much of a weakling to be worthy of their notice. Still, Connlyn will probably arrange to have me killed, now that his hold over me is ended."

"And will you let him kill you?"

Lanar smiled at me and spoke quietly, shaking his head. "I think he may have too much other on his mind when next we meet. He may not think of killing me at all."

"Aye, well, here we are … I assume you have something in mind. What is it?"

"An end to this war. And to Connlyn the Devious … My name for him. We end the war by putting an end to Connlyn."

"But how do we do that? I have been told he's unassailable, sitting up there in yon stronghold of his. Liam says the place is a thousand years old and has never been captured by anyone."

The look that Lanar threw me was one of pure scorn. "And who would have told him that? Someone a thousand years old? That stronghold fell in the time of my great-grandsire's grandsire, whose name I bear today, and I know that is true because the tale of its capture is part of my family's lore. Before that time, it was held by a bloodthirsty madman who terrorized the entire land until he attracted the wrath of the Romans and brought about his own destruction. My grandsire's grandsire, who became known as Lanar the Wise, captured the place and killed the madman. And because he was a wise man in truth, he ensured that what he had done might be done again, should ever the need arise."

"And what did he do?" I was fighting an urge to smile at what sounded like a fantastical tale, but his next words soon cured me of any skepticism.

"He dug a hole and gave us the greatest family secret we have ever had. It is passed down from son to son, and now I am the last to know it. He was an old man at the time, my ancestor Lanar, but he was Roman trained and had served his full years of duty as a legionary officer with a tribune's rank. He was an engineer, specializing in the movement of water. The word I heard used to describe him, when I was a boy, was 'sapper.' "

"A sapper, by the ancient gods! He was a tunneler!"

Lanar dipped his head, delighted. "Aye, he was, and that was how he took the place. First, because this was a local struggle, very close to his own home yet far removed from any large garrison, he used his former military connections to secure a commission authorizing him to take the fort and execute the mad rebel king. He then set siege to the hill fort, working his tunnelers for months on end. I have heard that it took them eight full months to complete the assault. They dug a long tunnel clear up through the hill beneath the fort, through the ramparts of the place and into the first inner ditch. Once they were there, the fort fell within hours."

My heart was thumping in my breast, excited by memories of the King's Caverns beneath Ban's castle in Benwick. "Eight months of tunneling! And what became of the tunnel afterwards?"

"Nothing. It is still there, although today no one remembers what it was a hundred years ago, when it was first dug. I've been inside it. It looks now like a simple excavation dug into the flank of the first defensive rampart of the fortress to be used for storing heavy tools and implements. But the rear wall is a mere ten paces thick, and behind the smoothed clay surface, it is made of loose rubble. Behind that lies the tunnel. It slopes down sharply to the base of the hill, then runs for almost two and a half hundred paces beneath the ground, before ending in another cavern, to the west of the hill in an old quarry the Romans used for mining paving stones. The entrance to the tunnel there is concealed, too, and will have to be dug out, but once the attack is launched, our family's belief is that an entire assault, recapturing the hill fort, can be completed in half a day ... or half a night."

There was nothing prophetic in what he said; he simply stated a known truth upon which we decided to act immediately. I summoned my own commanders and Tod's to a hurried council, at which Tod himself served as interpreter to his own men, and we drew up a very simple plan that, if it worked—and I could see no reason why it should not, given a modicum of good fortune—would produce an apparently miraculous result: the end of the war that had been draining Camulod for nigh on three years.

Tod would send word at once to Connlyn's hill fort, announcing that he would be arriving the following day with Mordred, but that he would not present himself unless he knew for certain that Connlyn would be there in person to greet him and to meet and welcome the boy. It would be a truculent and angry message, delivered, once again, by Liam and reflecting the offended dignity of a visiting king who felt he was being slighted and consigned to deal with inferiors and intermediaries. Its content would not necessarily surprise Connlyn, for he must be fully aware that his treatment of his sister's son to this point had been high-handed and patronizing, but we needed it to be strong enough, even offensive enough, to convince the older man that failure to comply with Tod's wishes would ensure the king's return to Gallowa, taking his young nephew with him.

In the meantime, while Tod's message was being delivered and Liam was awaiting Connlyn's response, Tod's Gallowans, in concert with my Frankish horsemen, would be moving closer to the bottom of the hill that housed the fort, keeping themselves concealed from above and taking full advantage of Tod's information that the countryside around the hill fort's base was deserted.

While they were doing that, I myself, accompanied by my Pendragon bowmen and a score of Tod's strongest men, all armed with pickaxes and shovels, would be mounting a determined assault on the blockages sealing the tunnel in the hill. If Lanar's calculations were correct and the tunnel was at least a hundred years old, that in turn indicated a distinct possibility that there might have been cave-ins and some subsidence over the course of years. If that were the case, we would have to dig our way through whatever debris we found and hope that we could, in fact, win through. Failure to do so, however, would mean we would have to resort to waiting for Connlyn to emerge from his retreat, and with Tod's new promise to arrive with the boy the following day, that option was looking less and less attractive. I forced myself to dwell on the fact that the Lanar who had designed and carved out the tunnel had been a professional military engineer, willing to dedicate eight months to the project, which suggested that he had progressed carefully and with much forethought and attention given to safety requirements. But as I led my men towards the quarry as the sun began to sink in the afternoon sky, I was in a sweat of nervous anticipation.

Lanar's tunnel, we were excited to discover, was virtually pristine, dry and remarkably well aired, so that our men were able to work in relative comfort, without fear of suffocating, and our illuminating torches burned brightly and without smoke. We discovered later, when we examined the tunnel more closely in the aftermath of the fighting, that Lanar had added air shafts before sealing and concealing the tunnel ends, and in consequence of that our own "sappers," working a hundred years later, were able to make short work of removing the debris that blocked our access.

When we were certain we had reached the thumb-thin coating of glazed mud that sealed off the cave on the other side of the wall, I ordered the last of our lights extinguished—we had come too far by then to risk being discovered because a glimmer of light had been seen shining through a chink in what was supposed to be a solid hillside. I found myself standing in pitch-darkness sometime towards the darkest hour of the night, listening for any sound from the more than half a hundred people who surrounded me. I could hear, perhaps feel, my own pulse throbbing somewhere inside my head, but not another sound. I drew a deep breath, and then spoke.

"So be it, then. Break it down."

The silence lasted a few heartbeats longer, and then came a sudden blow and a clatter of falling material, too light for rock and, I hoped, too quiet to be heard from any distance away. Another blow came, this one quieter, and then I began to see shapes ahead of me as a pale glow appeared beyond the newly opened threshold of the tunnel's end. And still we waited, holding our collective breath and straining our ears for sounds of alarum. I finally allowed myself to breathe again.

"Let's go, lads. Move out, and keep quiet." I knew even as I said the words that there was no need for them. My Pendragon scouts were as silent as wraiths when they moved, for their very lives depended upon their stealth, whether by day or night. Now, as their silhouettes moved ahead of me, between me and the minute amount of light in the sky, I counted them as they passed and still marveled that, even although I could see them, I could hear no sounds. I myself was in no hurry to leave the shelter of the tunnel mouth, not because I had any fear of going outside, but simply because I was wearing armor that created noise by its very substance, and until the silence was broken and an alarum was raised by the defenders here, my presence out in the open would be an unnecessary liability. And so I remained where I was and waited for the first shouts and the sounds of weaponry that would signal our discovery.

I waited far beyond the time when I had thought we would be seen or heard, knowing by now, although scarcely daring to believe it could be so, that every moment that passed enhanced our chances of complete success in this daring raid. And still the silence stretched and I wondered how it could be possible for us to have been inside the fort for so long without being detected. Men were dying close by me, I knew, but men were notoriously difficult to kill and almost impossible to kill in absolute silence. I knew, too, that Connlyn's people thought themselves perfectly safe and in no danger of attack here, in what was supposed to be an impregnable fortification. They had no knowledge of our presence in the region, and they were expecting the arrival of the King of Gallowa the next day, with Connlyn's sister's grandson in train, so they were complacent about their security. There were still enough of them here, however, to stamp us into nothingness if they were given the chance to rally before we had completed our advance, but the odds against that improved with every moment of extended silence, and with every guard killed without noise.

I saw Gwin, accompanied by Gattric, the leader of the scouts, gliding back towards me, and I realized that dawn was close. Gwin held up a finger to his lips as he approached, as if warning me to silence, but even as he made the gesture, a long, gurgling scream made nonsense of it, and he straightened up quickly, looking around him and nocking a fresh arrow to his longbow.

"Now it's dancing time," he growled. "I thought for a while we'd kill them all before a single one took note." He flicked a thumb in the direction of the main curtain wall at his back. "Gates are all open, guards are all dead. Nobody alive on the outer ring or on the next two in from that. We have the causeways under control up above, so our people can cross without much trouble, and anyone

alive and awake when we came in is dead now. Most of the enemy
are in the very center, where we expected them to be. We'll have
some tough fighting ahead of us, trying to get in there, for all that
we're more than halfway through the place already. Tod's
Gallowans should be coming through the gates any moment now,
and I've left men in place to guide them up onto the causeways,
where they can cross the ditches. Bors and his cavalry will have to
wait outside and clean up any group that tries to break out."

I nodded to him, acknowledging his report, and he grunted
impatiently.

"I have to get back. We're almost out of arrows, and after that,
it's blade to blade. Are you coming now?"

"Aye, lead on. I'll be right at your shoulder."

I have only hazy memories of the tussle that followed, for it was
the kind of fight that left me in the role of an observer, to which I
was not accustomed. The fort was built, like all its kind, as a series
of large concentric rings—high, steep mounds of earth and rubble
separated from each other by wide, deep ditches—with the central
ring being a flat, filled area that served as the living quarters and last
rallying point of the defenders. It was a defensive formation that
was virtually impregnable unless treachery was brought to bear
against it or, as in our instance, superior knowledge of weaknesses
in its construction was used to gain a surprise entry. We had
achieved that, and had been able to take possession of the causeways, light, strong, removable drawbridges that allowed the defenders
to run from crest to crest over the defensive ditches while their
attackers struggled to fight their way up every slippery slope. Once
on the first ring of drawbridges, our bowmen had been able to
sweep the others clear of defenders and prevent them from being
destroyed or thrown down into the voids below.

Now, standing on the last defensive crest before the central flat,
mere paces off one of those causeways, I watched our Pendragon
bowmen use the last of their long, lethal arrows to kill effortlessly
from a distance the enemy could not match, and I wondered what
would happen when the missiles ran out. There would be nothing

then to stop the enemy from rallying on the central flat, and our men
would then have to approach them along the narrow and suddenly
flimsy-looking drawbridges. Many of the enemy had bows of their
own, I saw now in the gathering light. Nowhere near as long or
strong as the Pendragon longbows, they would be lethal none the
less when properly used against men approaching in single file
along a narrow bridge.

I heard a swelling roar off to my right as the arriving Gallowans
began to swarm in through the gates, and then I saw a group of
men—perhaps half a score or even more—come running towards us
along the causeways from the outer ring, each of them carrying
several heavy quivers of long arrows slung about his person.
Gattric, just ahead of me, waved them forward, and I went to stand
beside him.

"Gwin told me you were running out of arrows," I said.

He kept his eyes on his men. "Aye, but what he meant was
running low," he growled from the corner of his mouth, as though
sharing a deep confidence. "We try hard never to run out, because
when we run out of arrows, we tend to die. We'll only use these now
defensively, because they're almost the last of our supply—no more
spraying them like sea foam, because we can't afford to waste a one
of them. We have to keep the causeways as safe as may be, until
Tod's lads are safely over and bearing the brunt of the fighting.
They're big, those boys of Tod's, and they fight well—that's what
they're bred for." We watched as his men began doling out fresh
quivers to the bowmen nearest them, and as each man took one, he
and a companion hurried away to find a vantage point from which
they could shoot. I started to move forward.

"Where are you going, Frankie?"

I had not heard Gwin approaching from behind me. I glanced
around at him, my hand already resting on the flimsy handrail of
the causeway beside me, and pointed towards the central flat.
"Where else?"

"Then you're a fool, and you are about to be a dead fool. You
won't last a minute out there. Those bows they have are no long-

bows, but they can still reach you here. They're paying us no attention now, but if you step out onto that bridge wearing that fancy
armor you'll be begging them to use you as a target. Best wait here
with me until Tod's people cross the bridges, then follow them.
You're a fellow knight and you're commander here, and I need you
alive when this is all over, 'cause if you're not, then I'll have to take
charge and I have other things to do … Besides, I've come to like
your foreign ways."

I was about to respond with a gibe of my own when there came
a sound of splintering wood and a chorus of screams as one of the
narrow drawbridges crashed down into the ditch beneath it, taking
its living cargo with it. But the attack was over quickly after that,
because as Tod's Gallowans began to make their way across the
final bridges the defenders surged forward to meet them, lulled by
the recent absence of deadly arrows. Their newfound enthusiasm
withered as quickly as it had flourished when the arrows began to
fly again, not in showers this time but in ones and twos, carefully
aimed and terrifying in the power with which they struck from such
short range and pierced even the heaviest armor. And then one giant,
golden-haired warrior with a massive belly ran forward, threw down
his axe and held his hands high, his fingers spread to indicate that
he was no longer a threat. His example was contagious, and within
moments men were throwing down their weapons and sitting down
in groups, evidently determined to fight no more.

I looked again at Gwin and found him watching me, his
eyebrows high. "They're finished," he said. "Do you believe that?"

I found it easy to smile as I replied, "Aye, I do. Their options
seem to be limited, and life almost always seems preferable to death
in the eyes of most people." I looked back to the center of the fort,
where more and more men were simply sitting down. There were
hundreds of people over there, far more than I had expected to see,
with women and even children among them. It was a large area,
however, much of it crowded with huts and rough stone buildings,
and I could not see all of it, or what was happening beyond the
section that lay directly in front of me, although I could see clearly

that many of our own people were now moving among the enemy and experiencing no trouble. "I think I might cross over now."

"Aye, and I'll come with you. But where's Connlyn? He's the whoreson we came here to find and I haven't seen a sign of him. Think you he's here, or has he slipped away from us again?"

"He has never slipped away from me before, Gwin, and I doubt he will this time." We stepped off the narrow causeway and onto the central island of the fort, where our people were already herding the enemy survivors into lines, stripping them of their weapons and placing them under guard, and as I did so I heard my name being shouted. I spotted Bors and Quintus Milo waving to me from the next drawbridge on my left. "I'll see you later," I told Gwin. "I have to start imposing some kind of order here, and I need to talk to Bors and Milo."

Less than an hour later, order had been established. The majority of the prisoners were being guarded, for the time being, in one of the steep-sided outer ditches, but still there had been no reports of Connlyn being sighted anywhere. Tod was livid with fury, thinking himself slighted by his uncle again, and although I was equally unhappy, something in his anger, and in the way he was glaring about him, stirred my curiosity and prompted me to ask him if he would recognize his uncle, face to face.

"I would not," he said to me, fuming. "And that is what is making me so angry. I have never met my whoreson uncle."

I laughed at that, I remember, my laughter louder and harder than it had any right to be, but as I turned away from him, I saw a man emerge from behind the wall of a building, less than ten paces from where we were standing. He was dressed in a long, drab robe and carried a walking staff, and he walked steadily towards the nearest causeway. He had not seen me standing there with Tod, and the shock of recognizing him—for I knew him immediately—affected me even more profoundly than it might have otherwise, because of what Tod had just been saying.

I drew my sword quickly and ran to catch up to the robed man just before he reached the bridge, leaving Tod staring after me.

There were two guards there, one on each side of the entrance, and they both began to frown as they saw me hurrying towards them. I pointed and waved for them to stop the man, and they crossed their spears in front of him just as I reached out and laid the blade of my sword on his right shoulder.

"Connlyn," I said. "I wondered where you had gone."

He turned very slowly and deliberately, clearly prepared to brazen this out, and saw Tod before he saw me. It was clear he had no idea of who his nephew was. He looked him up and down, coldly and dismissively, and drew himself up to say something withering and scornful, but in the next instant he saw me and recognized me as swiftly and surely as I had him. The skin on his forehead tightened and he dropped to one knee without warning, slashing out with the heavy walking staff to crack me painfully on the side of my right knee, and even as I was falling I saw him swing the staff around in a great, scything sweep and take the legs from one of the two guards before Tod could even begin to react. The guard fell into the chasm behind him with a shout that was echoed by his companion, but by that time Connlyn was already on the causeway of the drawbridge, running hard and shrugging out of his long robe as he went. Half blinded with pain as I was, I remember admiring the speed with which he ran, for he was not a young man, but the shouts of the guards had been heard and someone must have seen me lying on the ground, for suddenly the snapping, hissing sound of hard-shot arrows was in the air again. The first one to hit took him high in the back, beneath his right shoulder blade, and knocked him forward to fall on his face, so that at least one more arrow hissed harmlessly over him.

An utter stillness had fallen all around us at the sudden outbreak of renewed violence, and it persisted as we watched Connlyn reach up, grasping for support, and then struggle to his feet, to stand swaying, his head hanging. Slowly, but doggedly, he turned himself around to look back at me, and as his eyes found mine, he wrestled a knife, left handed, from his belt. I knew he had a reputation as a deadly knife thrower, but I had forgotten that he was left handed, and I knew, too, that he could not possibly have the strength left in him to reach me with a throw from where he was. As he raised his arm to throwing height, two more arrows struck him, one hitting full in the chest, piercing his heart, the other striking him almost simultaneously in the left temple less than an eyeblink later. The first impact threw him up and back, and the second picked him cleanly off his feet and spun him over the side of the bridge and down into the ditch below. His disappearance was followed by a long silence and then by a collective sound, almost a sigh, and people began to move again.

Later that night, when we were sitting around the fire talking about the day's events, we found some of what had happened hard to believe. We had lost only ten men in the entire affair, three of those bowmen, the other seven Gallowans, but Connlyn's people had lost no more than half a hundred, most of whom were killed in the earliest part of the assault. Once the hand-to-hand fighting had begun, it had been short lived, and we had ended up with several hundred prisoners who had decided that Connlyn and his cause were not worth dying for. And that had, of course, left us in turn with the problem of what to do with them.

It was Tod of Gallowa who suggested that we should simply release them, and although the initial reaction he drew was one of disbelief and outrage, his logic eventually convinced us that his might be the best solution. He and I had talked freely about the situation in north Britain, and I had told him about the doubts many of our people had concerning the loyalties of Symmachus of Chester. Now he reminded me of what I had said, and at the mention of Symmachus's name, Lanar sat up straighter and asked if we were talking about the king from the great fortress stronghold in the far west. He had never met Symmachus, he told us, but he had somehow befriended one of the king's envoys to Connlyn, an envoy who liked to talk about how important he was and how essential his services were to King Symmachus. Naturally enough Lanar had fed the man strong drink and drained him gently but thoroughly of everything the fellow knew about the dealings between his friend the king and Lanar's own friend and brother-in-law, Connlyn.

Lanar's recollections provided all the proof I would ever need of Symmachus's perfidy. But when Tod had heard all that Lanar had to say, he grinned at me and pointed out that his unlamented uncle's death had resolved Camulod's dilemma over Symmachus as well. It was now quite evident, from what Lanar had told us, that Connlyn had been the buffer protecting Symmachus and his seat at Chester from the rapacious horde of assorted Outlanders the dead warlord controlled, and that his payment for such a valuable service had been privileged and highly detailed information about all Camulod's plans to deal with him and his allies.

With Connlyn now dead, nothing could stop those allies from striking westward in full force, towards Chester, forcing Symmachus to go to war to defend himself and his territories. Neither party had any choice in that, Tod pointed out. The west was the only direction open for expansion to Connlyn's former host, now leaderless and vulnerable because it had no other strong man who could combine its elements as the dead warlord had. They had penetrated southwards into Britain to the maximum limit of their capabilities by this point, and everything that now lay to the east and south of them was already controlled by newcomers, invaders like themselves, who would be vigilant in defending their newly won possessions. Only to the west was there room for expansion, for the conquering of new territories, and their major obstacle there, the single catalyst that might frustrate and even defeat them, was Chester, the great legionary fortress formerly known as Deva, that was now home to Symmachus and his army … an amorphous and mysterious army that, to this point, had never had to fight, secure behind its great walls and smugly confident that its own formidable reputation would keep it safe from attack.

Once Symmachus was involved in fighting for his own life— and I saw the truth of that as soon as Tod drew my attention to it—he would have no more time to plot against Camulod. In fact, not knowing what we had discovered, he was likely to demand assistance from Camulod, under the terms of his alliance with Arthur, his son-in-law, and that knowledge gave me a deal of selfish and rather spiteful satisfaction. Now that I would be returning to Camulod with Lanar's evidence—and indeed with Lanar himself willing to present that evidence—Symmachus's alliance would be declared null and void, leaving him with no claims on Camulod, unless he wished to declare war and fight both us and the invading Outlanders on separate fronts. My satisfaction sprang not so much from that, however, as from the knowledge that the dissolution of the alliance and the proof of Symmachus's perfidy would free Arthur and Gwinnifer from their pact to breed no heirs.

I went to sleep that night with the pleasure of knowing beyond a trace of doubt that we had done a good day's work, and that the joyous and surprising tidings we would bear south with us the length of west Britain would delight everyone who heard them.

4

Before we could travel south, we were forced to travel north again, simply because of reports, too numerous to ignore, that the forest to the south of us was even more dense and trackless than what we had traversed on our way to Connlyn's fort. And so we released our prisoners, having stripped them of their weapons and armor, and retraced our steps until we reached the Wall again. The news of Connlyn's death did not travel ahead of us, because we had contained the force he had with him in the hilltop fort, and that meant that we were riding north into enemy territory where the enemy knew nothing of the death of its leader and commander. Lanar had told us, however, that the enemy could function in the field for weeks and even months without direct word from Connlyn, who was notoriously uncommunicative to his allies, spending no time on niceties but exacting absolute obedience and compliance through savagery and fear, using an utter and implacable ruthlessness the like of which men like us—Lanar's description of all civilized Camulodians—could not imagine. Dealing constantly with savages more akin to animals than the kind of people we knew, Connlyn had long since decided, according to Lanar, that his only means of dominating them and forcing them to do his bidding lay in outdoing them in savagery.

In the aftermath of the fighting in the fort, my men had discovered the cache where Connlyn had stripped himself of his armor and any symbols that would have identified him. Connlyn had been more imaginative and resourceful than I had expected, at least when it came to broadcasting his own presence. His personal armor was larger than life and had been built with a double purpose in mind: to make its wearer appear larger than he was, and to make his identity unmistakable. It was made of multiple layers of thick bullhide, boiled and hammered into the shape of his muscular body while it was still wet and malleable, and then it had been dyed or painted a bright and virulent green, the yellowish, vibrant green of new spring oak leaves. The helmet, in particular, was cleverly made, its domed top surmounted by a high, narrow four-legged pedestal of sorts that bore a green-painted human skull rather than the standard plume of horsehair. For lack of a better place to put it, and because I had no slightest notion at that time of what to do with it, I had my men carry the armor back to our encampment and leave it in my tent, where I found myself contemplating it that night, after everyone else had gone to sleep. It may have been the greenness of the thing, its immediate and highly obvious recognition potential, that led to my eventual decision to make use of it, but whether it was that or not, the decision absolved me of a need to do something that had been troubling me deeply.

I cannot remember who it was who had pointed out that no one besides ourselves yet knew Connlyn was dead, but the observation had led directly to discussion of the need to furnish proof of some kind that the warlord *was* dead, and to the suggestion that the best means of doing that was to sever his head and take it with us, pickled in brine, as we rode north. I had several difficulties with that, the first of them purely personal and unmilitary: my entire education and upbringing had fostered a horror of such things. Violence in war was justifiable, given just cause and sufficient provocation, but barbarism never was. Civilized Christians did not indulge in barbarism, and pickling a head was barbarism, plain and simple. It mattered not at all to me that others did such things, and I was unimpressed by arguments that sought to point out the efficacy and immediacy of such methods. I had been involved in fratricidal civil war by the time I was sixteen and I had seen more atrocities than most people would in an entire lifetime. I knew from experience that one severed human head is indistinguishable from another, once drained of blood and life and stained with dirt and gore. And since I knew that few of his own people had known the warlord Connlyn well enough to recognize his face in life, I doubted that few, if any, would know him by the shape of his severed head.

His bright green armor, on the other hand, with its mounted skull as a crest, was another matter entirely. Any of his people would have recognized Connlyn by that, even seeing him from a great distance away, and even those who had never seen him before would recognize him from reports they had heard about his wondrous armor and the fearsome green skull it flaunted. For those reasons, therefore, I determined that since no one yet knew Connlyn was dead, his living presence, or the appearance of his presence, might do a great deal to ensure us safe passage through the territories occupied by his armies.

Pleased by that thought, and mildly titillated by its whimsy, I crossed to where the armor lay and took up the helmet and placed it on my head, only to find that its rim was so small that I could not even begin to seat it in place. Astonished, I looked at the thing more closely to see whether there was some way of loosening the leather liner and making the opening larger. There was none. The helmet, which looked to be of normal size, had been especially made to fit Connlyn, and Connlyn's head was apparently far smaller than mine was. The outer shell of the helmet had been thickened to conceal the smallness of his head.

Intrigued, I went to the door of my tent and called one of the guards inside, where I asked him to remove his own helmet and try on the green one. His head must have been even larger than mine, and the green helmet looked ludicrous perched atop his shaven pate. That led to further experimentation, and it soon became clear that no one in our entire camp had a head small enough to fit the warlord's helm: Everyone was making fun of the smallness of the great villain's head.

Hours afterwards, Gwin came back into camp after spending the evening by himself exploring the old hill fort. Upon being told what all the fuss was about, he picked up the helmet and put it on effortlessly, silencing much of the hilarity. No one was in any hurry to risk offending one of Arthur's most renowned knights.

From that time on, Gwin wore the green armor whenever we were on the road, and a group of our scouts accompanied him, wearing clothing salvaged from a group of dead men who had clearly been of a different quality from those who surrendered and threw down their weapons. These men, a score and a half in number, had tried to fight their way clear of our trap and had fought until the last of them fell to Pendragon arrows. Lanar identified them later as Connlyn's personal bodyguards, famed for their brutality and distinguished by the green tunics they wore.

I had explained the importance of the green armor to Gwin, together with what I hoped to achieve with it, and he raised no objection whatsoever to wearing it thereafter and riding a horse, even although I knew he would have been more comfortable and more at ease on foot, among his scouts. The scouts, for their part, and to my astonishment, took an almost gleeful delight in pretending to be Connlyn's bodyguard. Normally silent, dour and notably humorless, the solemn Cambrians, finding themselves faced with an opportunity for mummery and self-distraction, threw themselves wholeheartedly and with enthusiastic hilarity into their new role. Most of the tunics they had now to wear had been pierced by arrows, so they were not badly torn or damaged by anything other than bloodstains, but the scouts had gone to the trouble of washing them, over and again, until the worst of the stains had leached out. Seen from but a short distance, marching with their longbows unstrung and leaning on their shoulders like spears, they looked like what they were pretending to be.

Thus it came about that we encountered three large groups of the enemy within four days and had no dealings with any of them. They all recognized Connlyn's highly visible green armor and the green tunics of his guard from afar, and they swung away and left us to our own devices.

When we finally reached the Wall again, I led my men eastward for about twenty miles, passing the former holdings of King Ushmar, dead now these four years and more, without stopping until we came to Connlyn's home stronghold, the place where I had first met him. Once again, our passage went unchallenged, the mere sight of Connlyn's armor and his green-clad escort being accepted everywhere as proof of his identity. Our advance scouts reported that the stronghold was almost deserted, with only a few guards on duty and all the inhabitants plainly secure in the knowledge that they were safe here in the very center of Connlyn's home territory. We waited in the surrounding forest until night was falling, and then, leaving our Frankish cavalry in concealment there, and followed by Gwin's "bodyguard" and the main body of Tod's Gallowans marching in columns of five men across, I rode side by side with Gwin as we approached the main gates in the last light of the afternoon. Lanar followed close behind us, prepared to perform yet again as interpreter and going over in his mind the comments that we had practiced along the road. The remaining daylight was still strong enough to let people see our bright green colors, but the encroaching darkness at the same time helped to conceal our real identity.

We entered the stronghold without difficulty, Gwin clattering through the passageway between the manned gate towers and then allowing me to lead as we proceeded directly to the main parade ground in front of Connlyn's villa.

People were assembling to welcome us even before we reached the place, and the Pendragon scouts, their deadly bows now strung, fanned out quickly into a half circle and threatened them, stunning them into silence and confusion. At the same time, the incoming Gallowans, led by Tod and his own commanders, broke formation and swarmed up onto the walls and throughout the enclosure, making short work of those few defenders who dared to object.

Gwin and I sat silent, facing the assembly in front of the villa, until one man, clearly the senior custodian in Connlyn's absence, stepped forward and spoke to Gwin, his face creased in puzzlement.

"My lord Connlyn—"

Gwin held up his hand, cutting the man off in mid-sentence, and pointed to me. As all eyes in the group turned to me, wondering who I was, I reached down into my saddlebags and pulled out a tightly rolled bundle, which I threw to the speaker. He caught it in both hands and then wordlessly, his eyebrows rising ludicrously, he shook it open to reveal what it was: a tightly coiled belt of green leather with an ornate silver buckle, and an equally elaborate silver-hilted dagger in a sheath of dyed green leather. As he held it up, bemused, showing it to everyone around him, I drew my long knight's sword and held it upright.

"That was Connlyn's," I said in their own tongue, loudly enough for all of them to hear, and as they stood frowning, trying to absorb what I had said, I reached out sideways with my sword's blade and rapped it hard against the green-armored man at my side. "This armor was his, too. But the man inside it now is not Connlyn."

I had used up my entire store of their language, painstakingly learned from Lanar during the ride here, but they had understood me and their eyes were fixed on Gwin as he reached up with both hands and pulled off his helmet, and at the sight of him a strange and strangled gasp rose from the watching men. He settled the helmet comfortably against his hip and looked over the crowd, allowing the silence to stretch out until I raised my sword again and Lanar rode forward into view.

They knew him instantly, there was no mistaking that, but no one uttered a sound, and Lanar took his time looking at each man before he spoke, his words clear and slow enough for me to understand them.

"My sister, your true queen in all but name, is dead. So is the animal who called himself her husband but was, in fact, her jailer. That means that I am now your chief." He stopped, his gaze moving from face to face among the men who stood before him. Some of them stared back at him, defiant; others looked away, unable to meet his eyes. For myself, I merely tried to hide my own surprise at Lanar's words, for it had not occurred to me that he might inherit from his sister. But he had not finished speaking, and now scorn dripped audibly from his words. "I never wanted to rule here, even when I was a child. I will not rule here now. Nor will any other. These men behind me hold the power of life and death over all of you. They are Camulod, and I ride with them. Listen now to what they have to say … their words through my mouth."

He turned to where Gwin sat watching him and nodded, and as Gwin spoke out, his heavy Cambrian mountaineer's accent making even the Latin that he spoke sound barely intelligible, Lanar's voice rode over his.

"There might be some of you here who wish to pray for Connlyn. I hope so. He needs prayers. This war is over. Connlyn the Warmonger is dead." He paused, allowing that to sink in. "Connlyn the Whoreson is dead. Connlyn the Treacherous is dead. Connlyn the Butcher is dead. Camulod is victorious, and Arthur Pendragon, Riothamus of All Britain, will be justified in sending his armies here now in full force, should he so wish, seeking reparations for the destruction your foul master has brought about. So those of you who wish to pray for Connlyn, and to honor his memory, may do so and be damned with him. Those of you who have better things to do, and better men to follow, had best be about it. Be gone from here by the time we come back, and spread the word as you go that Connlyn, who was not, after all, much of a warlord, is dead. He is dead and gone, beaten and destroyed, and the victorious force of Camulod will not be withstood."

Some of the faces of the listeners showed understanding of what Gwin had said, but many bore blank expressions of disbelief. I raised my sword arm again and all eyes came back to me. "I am called Seur Clothar," I said, pacing my delivery so that Lanar could translate my words with ease. "I am a Frank, a native of Gaul and a Knight Companion to King Arthur Pendragon of Camulod, High King of All Britain. This man beside me is Seur Gwin, a native of Eire, raised among the Pendragon clans of Cambria. He, too, is a Knight Companion to King Arthur of Camulod, Riothamus. These bowmen are Pendragons, kin to that same Arthur, High King. Seur Gwin spoke the truth to you. Connlyn is dead, as is his wife, Martha. This war is ended, unless you choose to prolong it.

"We are leaving now, as we came. I doubt that anyone here would be foolish enough to attempt to stop us or to hinder our going. You will suffer no punishment for your support of Connlyn to this time, for I suspect you may not have had much choice. But this settlement is now proscribed and will be destroyed. Be warned. We will show no leniency to anyone found here when we return. Get you gone from here and make a life elsewhere. We will come back, and when we do, we will raze this place to the ground and scatter its stones to redeem the foulness of what has been here until now. Fare well."

Gwin replaced his helmet, after which we wheeled in close formation and returned the way we had come.

5

Less than three weeks later, having fulfilled my promise to destroy Connlyn's former nest, and having made my farewells to King Tod and seen him safely on his way back to Gallowa, I had made contact with the army of Camulod in the north, commanded by Bedwyr, with Pelinore as his second-in-command. Under those two, the infantry was commanded by a man I had never met, a king called Rience, from northern Cambria, beyond the boundaries of the Pendragon Federation, and Seur Balan, one of my fellow Knights Companion, commanded the cavalry. They had been alarmed to have us approach them from the north, for they had received no word of us yet from Camulod and so were unaware of our presence in the region. Our northerly approach, plus the failure of their scouts to recognize the bronze armor and alien trappings of my Frankish troopers, had forced them to regard us at first as an enemy force— an enemy cavalry force, which was an unprecedented development—and to react accordingly, sending an expedition to meet us that outnumbered us hugely, five hundred troopers and a thousand infantry against our tiny force of less than half a hundred mounted men and fifty scouts. They made no attempt to conceal themselves, advancing towards us slowly and in full panoply, allowing us to see their strength and be intimidated. And watching them approach, anticipating with enjoyment the forthcoming meeting, I made no effort to identify myself until we were almost within longbow shot, whereupon I stopped then and unveiled my own colors, holding them up to be recognized. Within moments I heard a whooping shout, and Bedwyr himself came galloping towards me, accompanied by Balan and several of his officers.

Our reunion was a joyful celebration from the outset, for Bedwyr and I had not seen each other in years, but when they learned that Connlyn was dead and the war was over, the celebration became even grander and greatly prolonged. Two days later, apprised by Lanar of the entire story of Connlyn's association with Symmachus, Bedwyr handed over his command to Pelinore, with instructions to make no further efforts to contain the Outlanders from the east. Camulod's battalions were to disengage from hostilities and begin the long march homewards as soon as was feasible, leaving the north and its defense in the hands of Symmachus and his armies. In the meantime, taking half of his cavalry force and a thousand infantry with him, Bedwyr joined me on the road to the south, and we detoured together to Chester because neither of us could resist the opportunity of putting Symmachus firmly in his place.

We assembled our force, almost two thousand strong, on the plain before the walls of Chester, and there we raised Arthur's Pendragon battle standard, a great red dragon on a field of green, and waited for Symmachus to come out to greet us. As usual, he chose to insult us by making it plain that he felt no pressing need to acknowledge our presence, but by that time, savoring what was to come, we were beyond caring how long he might keep us waiting, and we issued orders to our men to set up their cooking fires right there on the parade ground. That garnered us a swift reaction, and soon Symmachus himself was coming towards us, reclining on a litter and carried by six large men who must, we presumed, have been slaves.

When he finally arrived and climbed out of his litter to come to greet us, we stood up but did not return his greetings, and his face flushed with anger at the plainness of our insult. Before he could vent any of it, however, I spoke Connlyn's name. His eyes instantly narrowed to slits and flitted from one to the other of us.

"What about Connlyn?" he growled. "Why would you throw up his name to me?"

"Because I've learned that you and he were friends, and I could think of no better reason to throw his name at you, or anything else close to hand. Lanar!" The fellow came forward, his eyes on Symmachus, who glared back at him, evidently wondering who this was and how it reflected upon him. "This is King Symmachus, Lanar. You have heard much about him, and now you see him. Tell the king what you told us ... about how you uncovered the activities between him and Connlyn."

"That is enough!" Symmachus was furious, his voice little more than a venomous hiss as he swung to confront Bedwyr, who had stood silently until then. "Would you insult me by bringing a nameless, faceless liar to confront me in my own domain?"

Bedwyr shrugged, as if totally disinterested, and murmured, "Try this next fellow then, sir king. He is neither nameless nor faceless." He raised an arm high, and in response Gwin, fully helmed and clad in Connlyn's green armor, swung himself nimbly up into his saddle and emerged from where he had been standing concealed among a tight knot of mounted men. I was watching Symmachus's face closely, as were Bedwyr and the other officers

beside us, and all of us saw the blood leach from his skin as he realized what this apparition meant. He froze, motionless, his mouth
opening to speak, then remaining that way, incapable of utterance.
I beckoned, and the green-clad horseman came cantering towards
us, and still Symmachus was as one struck mute.

When Gwin had reined in quietly by my side, I spoke again to
Symmachus. "This is Seur Gwin of Camulod, not Connlyn as you
so plainly thought. You may or may not remember meeting Gwin,
but you most obviously have remembered meeting Connlyn.
Connlyn is dead now, which is why Seur Gwin now wears his
armor. He was shot down by our Pendragon bowmen like the
running cur he was. Stripped now of all significance, his life, his
armor and all his possessions, he has left his former allies and associates leaderless. They will be coming your way soon, Symmachus,
striking westwards now that Connlyn has no further use for the
information you were selling to him, and there is no one now to stop
them doing what they will. We wish you well of them. Look not to
Camulod for help from this day on. Mordred, come forward."

The boy nudged his mount forward obediently, and I introduced him with a wave of my hand. "This is Mordred Pendragon,
Symmachus. He is King Arthur's firstborn son, born of the Princess
Morag, of the painted people of the north, above the Wall, and
reared without Arthur's knowing he had ever been born. But now he
has been united with his father and is the King's acknowledged,
lawful heir, publicly accepted and privately beloved." I smiled,
feeling my lips respond stiffly and knowing there was no trace of
humor or amusement in my expression. "Any grandson of yours, as
yet unborn, would come a distant second in succession to this
young man. And you may rest assured that, should such a grandson
be born someday, unlikely although that may be, he would be kept
far away from you and from your pernicious influence ... not
through the wishes of his father but through the expressed will of
your own daughter, the child's mother. So, there we are, and you
have heard our judgment of your perfidious conduct. You have been
boasting of your wondrous army for years, but none of us from

Camulod has ever seen a man of yours bleed. We have been doing all the work here, all the fighting, and you have repaid us with treachery, lies and disdain. No more. Stay here now and fight your own battles. But should you ever think of coming against Camulod, wear heavy armor, for we will crush you like a beetle underfoot."

I asked Bedwyr if he had anything he wished to add, but he shook his head slowly, gazing at Symmachus through narrowed eyes, the expression on his face suggesting he had either smelled or tasted something foul. I looked back to where Symmachus stood white faced and rigid.

"Well then, we will leave you, in the profound hope of never seeing you again. I never did like you, Symmachus, from the moment of our first meeting at Saint Alban's Shrine. You were devious and unpleasant then. Some things never change, it seems. So now I am going to turn my back on you and organize our withdrawal, in the hope that you will feel tempted to summon your people to chastise us for our ill manners. That would bear out my opinion of your command capabilities and at the same time it would give me great cause for celebration."

When I turned to look back one last time from the far edge of the parade ground, he was still standing there facing us, backed by the six porters who had carried him out to meet us.

No one had any comment to make as we rode away after that confrontation, and I myself, to my great surprise and disappointment, could find no satisfaction in what we had just done. The rebuke we had delivered had been well deserved and Symmachus had earned every word of condemnation we had uttered, and far greater punishment in addition, but the gratification I had expected to gain from exposing his duplicity and betrayals was strangely absent. I pulled myself together and rode on, Bedwyr and Gwin flanking me on either side at the head of our column. My two squires had vanished, as boys always will when they think themselves free from supervision, and I suspected they would be installed in one of the commissary wagons, scrounging food from the cooks and making themselves comfortable on the bags of flour and grain.

For the next twelve days we headed steadily south without incident, making good time and enjoying mild and pleasant weather
until we reached the outskirts of the now massive territory that was
Camulod, after which, in our excitement at being home and at being
privileged to bring tidings of peace, the weather could have done
what it wanted without our ever having noticed. All was well in
Camulod, and God still ruled in Heaven. We were home, we were
safe and alive, and we could rest in peace and sleep at night without
fear, at least until the next threat to the kingdom arose.

6

Arthur, when I saw him on the afternoon of our arrival, looked to be
ten times the man he had been when I had last seen him. He was up
and out of bed, although still not moving around, and I found him
wrapped in warm woolen robes, propped up in a comfortable chair
in front of a roaring fire. Although he still looked haggard, his face
had filled out noticeably, and that gaunt, purple-pouched, staring-
eyed pallor that had made me think of a death mask had vanished.
His shoulders, too, looked wider, although that could have been the
muffling effects of the robes in which he was swathed, but his
hands, curled on his lap, looked strong and capable again.

We were not alone on that occasion, for Bedwyr and Gwin had
accompanied me to pay their respects, and I had brought young
Mordred along to greet his father after his own absence, so the talk
was general and the overall mood was light and joyous, thanks to
our tidings of Connlyn's death and the end of the war, and the proof
of Symmachus's treachery. Merlyn was present, too, as was Queen
Gwinnifer, with her ladies. A small number of senior members of
the Governing Council had joined us there as well, at the invitation
of Merlyn, and the king personally charged these latter, as a mark
of his great satisfaction, with preparing a special day of games and
festivities to celebrate the end of the northern hostilities.

Servants moved among the small crowd, pouring wine and serving tiny, delicious oaten cakes stuffed with chopped, roasted nuts and steeped in honey, and the time passed pleasantly and quickly, until the Queen judged that her husband was becoming overtaxed and should rest for a while, and we all filed out obediently, leaving the regal couple to their privacy.

Later that afternoon, while I was in the stables inspecting my weapons and saddlery with the now inseparable Rufus and Mordred, issuing instructions on how and when I wanted the gear to be cleaned and mended, I was approached by one of the Queen's Guard, who had been searching for me for some time, with a command to attend the Queen in time to dine with her and the King. I left the boys to their tasks immediately and went to clean myself up and change into fresh clothing before presenting myself at the King's Chambers at the proper hour. The guards knew me this time and passed me through, saluting me crisply as I looked them in the eye and nodded to each of them in passing, but I was unprepared for what happened next.

When I reached the door to the Queen's apartment, I found Gwinnifer herself there, evidently waiting for me, and looking very pleased with herself for some reason. I saluted her with a dip of my head, but before I could say a word she said, "You are early," and then beckoned me to follow her into a small antechamber, where she stopped me with an upraised hand and bade me remain there and wait for her. Mystified, I again dipped my head dutifully, and by the time I looked up again she was on her way out, closing the door carefully behind her and leaving me alone to wonder what in Hades was happening.

A short time later, standing staring into an empty fire basket, I heard the door open again behind me and I swung back to greet her, but instead of Gwinnifer, I found the Lady Elaine smiling at me. The sight of her beautiful face sucked the air out of my lungs and left me stunned, hovering on the threshold of the room and incapable, for long moments, of stepping towards her until she spoke my name and held out her hand to me. Her movement, and the sound of her voice, broke the spell, although only partially, and I moved awkwardly to greet her, humiliatingly aware of the stiffness of my posture and my inability to find a smile for her.

In truth, I was in the grip of an overwhelming panic that had destroyed my ability to think in reasonable, logical terms. I was awash in trepidation and guilt caused by the lustful and brutally carnal thoughts that had sprung up in me upon the instant I set eyes on her and saw again the longingly remembered beauty of her body, and the way her clothing clung to it. The images shamed me, for the thoughts that filled my mind were, I believed, far removed from what I ought to be thinking. The woman smiling at me here so guilelessly was a respectable matron, a married woman.

I have been grateful ever since that day that the agonies I suffered then—unbearable and intolerably drawn out—were private and, quite incredibly, invisible. Elaine's eyes showed no awareness of anything amiss, and as I tentatively reached out to take her hand and kiss it formally, she swept it aside and threw her arms about my neck, pulling me down to her and hugging me fiercely, thrusting herself against me so that I felt the shape and softness of her entire body. I did not dare to touch her with my hands, and so stood with my arms outstretched, stooped over and feeling like a fool, but so long did her embrace last that I finally reached up and broke her grip, concerned for her reputation, and looked around guiltily, as though expecting to see someone standing behind me, watching this display.

"There's no one else here," she whispered, apparently fully aware of what I had been thinking.

"Not now, I know, but I am waiting for the Queen herself, and she could walk in at any moment."

She laughed aloud. "No, Seur Knight, I think not. The Queen is being dressed for dinner and will not be returning here. I am to bring you in to dine with her and the King at the proper time."

"She—You—you mean the Queen sent you here?"

"Of course she did. And why not?"

"Why not? Does she know we know each other?"

"Of course she knows. We have talked of you many times, enough to make your ears burn at times, even in faraway Gaul."

"Talked about what? Does she know … about us? I mean, about you and I …?"

She smiled and silenced me with one fingertip on my lips. "I am not going to answer that, Sir Lance. Men have no need to know what women talk about between themselves. The Queen and I are very close. I am one of her favorite companions."

"How so, and since when?"

"How so, because she asked me to join her companions when she first came to Camulod as Queen. Arthur brought her to our village and introduced me to her, and she asked me almost immediately to come to Camulod and join her ladies. She had but two at the time, and I was ready for the change. Come here." She moved to me again, less urgently this time but more deliberately, sliding her hands up the slope of my chest to clasp them behind my neck and pull me down towards her waiting mouth. I kissed her long and deeply, feeling the ripe softness of her beneath the texture of her clothing and no longer caring about the obvious signs of my arousal. Eventually she released me and stepped back, breathing hard, her face flushed with passion.

"Forgive me," she said, smiling, her voice tremulous, "I have been dreaming of doing that for a long time."

"So have I, Lady." Magically, all my awkwardness and confusion had vanished and I was myself again. "Even in Gaul, you have been close by in my thoughts."

Her smile widened, then faded to nothing, and she tilted her head gently to one side. "You looked troubled for a moment there. What were you thinking about?"

"Finding you here, I suppose. It is more than I could have hoped for. I was but remembering the last time we two were together."

"Aye, that was a wondrous time, brief but full of meaning."

"A lifetime in a single day."

Her face sobered and she lowered her voice. "I was sorry to hear of the death of your friend Ghilleadh. I felt your pain, I believe, for I know how much he meant to you."

"My thanks for that, my lady," I answered. "I try not to think about him—I even walk away to look for other things to occupy me when he comes into my mind—for I am not yet ready to deal with the loss of him. That must sound foolish, but it's true. I cannot yet believe he is dead, even although I've slain the man who brought about his death. My friends tell me I will adjust to it, that time heals all hurts simply by passing, but I can't see that. And yet I know he is gone, never to come back."

"I have a son, you know."

The change of topic disconcerted me and forced me to acknowledge her marriage and status, so that I could not prevent the frown that formed quickly between my brows although I strove to erase it. I nodded. "I know. I knew that. Merlyn wrote to me of it ... merely as a matter of interest, since we had all attended your wedding feast. Jonas must be very proud."

"Hmm ... He is ... The child is beautiful beyond belief."

"With you as his mother, Lady, he could not fail to be so."

"Hmm." She raised her head high, almost tilting it back, and looked me in the eye. "He was born ... early. A mere eight months after we were wed."

There was something there, in her voice more than her words, that gave me pause, confusing me because I had not thought to hear—nor was I even sure I had heard—what I suddenly thought I might have heard there, and, because no such notion, no such likelihood, had ever entered my mind, I did not even dare to attempt to examine what it might have been that had alarmed me.

She saw me blinking in my confusion, and she reached up and stroked my cheek softly with one hand. "I named him Galahad."

"Galahad? Your son? It sounds a little like Ghilleadh."

"Aye, it does, I know. That is why I chose it ... In memory of you and your admiration for the man you thought to be the finest of your friends. If my son should grow to manhood with any of the attributes you shared with Ghilleadh, he will be blessed, as will I."

Her admission was now as plain to me as it could be and I felt my heart swell up within me. "Then he is—"

She stilled my lips with her extended fingers. "Hush you now, Seur Clothar of Gaul. The King and Queen await you. Come with me, now." She hurried away, leaving me to follow her, with my heart bounding inside me and the memory of her words warming the depths of my being, so that I spent the remainder of that evening and the sleepless night that followed it in an agonized state of wonder and uncertainty that overrode every other consideration with which I had to deal at that time, and there were several of those, none of them trivial.

Had Elaine really said what I thought she said, or had I misinterpreted her obvious pleasure in seeing me again and in telling me about her son? Was the child mine, and if he was, what should I do?

I knew I had to ask Elaine directly and of course, life being what it is, I had no single slightest opportunity to speak to her alone for the remainder of that night, and so was forced to bite my tongue in silence and to concentrate all my energies on pretending that I was still the man that I had always been, uncomplicated and unchanged.

If Arthur knew anything of the attraction between Elaine and me he gave no sign of it, and neither did Gwinnifer, yet there were but the four of us at table that evening and we spent the next three hours dining together very pleasantly and in great comfort, attended by a legion of servants who worked assiduously to ensure that the King was comfortable at all times. We had supremely delicate fresh-caught fish from a local brook, a succulent goose with a skin coated in herbs and crisped to perfection, and a pot-braised hare, cooked with sweet turnips and carrots pickled in brine, was served upon thick platters of bread, still warm from the oven. The conversation was light and fluent, confined to fairly trivial things in honor of my homecoming. Only once, when Gwinnifer brought up the subject of Elaine's small son, Galahad, and mentioned how beautiful he was, did I think I saw a flicker of something in her eyes, but whatever it was—knowledge, humor, understanding or complicity—it was quickly gone, and I could not be sure it had even been there.

When dinner was over and the remnants had been cleared away, some of the Queen's Guard carried Arthur to a comfortable chair by the roaring fire, and the Queen and Elaine took their leave of us soon after, leaving the King and me alone, seated on opposite sides of the fire, Arthur with a flagon of red wine and a goblet by his side on a small table, and I with a glazed, dew-beaded jug of cool beer and a substantial drinking mug by mine.

When the women left, Arthur made a few very pleasant and complimentary references to Lady Elaine, mentioning that she and Jonas were seldom together nowadays, since Elaine had chosen to be a companion to the Queen and Jonas had his own responsibilities in his village. He also observed that the separation did not seem to inconvenience either one of them greatly, and that on the occasions when they were together, they seemed content with their lot. Once again I found myself listening attentively, searching apprehensively for hidden meanings and nuances, but as before, there was nothing that I could pin down, and I had no wish to draw attention to my own interest in the matter, so I remained silent, and a few moments later he sat back in his chair and tucked in his chin, gazing at me with a speculative look.

"Well, my friend," he began eventually. "You wish to come back to Camulod, with all your men, and so you should. And I understand why you came alone this time, with your Frankish escort. I understood that from the very first, from the moment I heard you had landed: you were concerned for me and you wanted to do something about the Connlyn situation." He looked down into the fire for a few moments before looking back at me. "Well, you did something, and spectacularly so. You achieved within the space of weeks what the rest of us have been unable to achieve in years, and you did it without fanfare and without disrupting anything or embarrassing anyone … except for Connlyn, of course. You did both to him with great efficiency." He stopped again, and I waited, feeling my heart sinking into the pit of my stomach because his face had turned solemn and there was no hint of levity in him.

"I need you to return to Gaul, Lance, and to hold your troopers there." He raised a hand to stifle any protest before I could give it voice, but I made no attempt to protest. I simply sat there, looking at him across the space between us. The silence stretched for so long that he clearly felt he needed to enlarge upon what he had said, because he lowered his hand and added, quietly, "I really have no other choice, my friend. You are my only option in this."

"In what? Tell me what you need me to do, Arthur, and I will do it. You know that."

"Aye, I do, and it galls me that I have to ask it of you. You have never questioned me, never balked or quibbled. Nor have you ever rationalized or sought to modify my opinions or beliefs in any way. You have done everything I have ever asked of you; and now, in this one thing that you would ask of me, I must refuse you."

"Arthur! It's not important that you should be able to grant my wishes. What do you need me to do for you? *That* is important because I know that you are not asking for it for your personal pleasure or on your own behalf. Whatever it is, you see it as being necessary for Britain … for your realm and its future."

I stood up and crossed to where his sheathed sword hung from his armor tree in the corner, its belt looped over the magnificent bronze cuirass of his ceremonial armor with its golden stooping eagle. Feeling his eyes on me, I drew out the sword Excalibur and carried it back to where he sat, extending it to him hilt first. "You can't swing this now, but you can hold it." His fingers tightened on the sharkskin grip and he raised the great sword's point free of the floor, holding it up for a few moments before allowing it to subside, and I nodded. "That's more than you could have done the last time I saw you, my lord King, but I'm glad to see you remember the feel of the hilt. Your main task right now is to focus on regaining your health and mobility. Nothing else has any importance besides that, because until you have both of those attributes back in your control, until you can sit on a horse and swing that sword again the way you always have, you can do nothing else to any kind of convincing effect."

He dipped his head, acknowledging the truth of what I was saying. I returned the gesture and continued. "Of course, that goes without saying. I'm presuming that you have plans to begin exercising and training again as soon as you are fit enough to move around, but even then it will take many weeks, perhaps even many months, to restore you to full strength and vigor, and through all that time the world will continue to turn and people will continue to do what people do. Now, you say you need me to go back to Gaul, so I assume there are people and events in Gaul that you wish me to deal with on your behalf, and there might be a potential for armed confrontation. Correct?"

He nodded again, and I collected the sword from him and replaced it in its sheath before returning to sit again. "Good! Then tell me who and what's involved, and tell me what you need me to do."

I could tell his mind was engaged elsewhere, focused on other things. But then he grunted and straightened slightly in his chair, grimacing as something, somewhere inside him, caused him a twinge of pain. "You know," he grumbled, "every time I think of you and that nonsense you used to spout about me being invulnerable, I start to get angry, but I understand what you really meant at the time, and so the anger grows easier and easier to suppress. You were really talking about a perception that grows naturally and inevitably out of the notion of invulnerability—the mere *idea* of invulnerability creates an impression of *invincibility*. Now all of Britain knows I'm not invulnerable, but they are still unsure as to whether or not I might be invincible. So I agree with you that the first thing I have to do is get back onto my feet, and then climb back onto a horse as soon as I can after that. And you are right, it will take time. But right now, we have that luxury of having time for such things. But I don't want you to waste time sitting here, waiting for me to mend, when you can be doing great things on my behalf elsewhere. You are the one who really seems invulnerable at this time, Lance, and I need—as both a king and a commander—to wring as much support and sustenance as I can out of that aura that surrounds you. That is why I need you to return to Gaul. Corbenic is a tiny place, and it's isolated, if any place large enough to have a king can be called isolated. It is remote, high on the northwest coast of

Gaul and tucked away, far from the sweep of the world's great and momentous events. And in that, I have come to believe, Pelles and his kingdom are highly fortunate. I don't know how much … Well, let me ask you: how much do you know or suspect about what is happening elsewhere in Gaul?"

"You mean about the invaders, the Hungvari?"

"Aye, the Huns. Have you heard anything new since we last spoke of them?"

"Not much. They are there in northeastern Gaul, as you said they were, but they've never come near us in Corbenic, so we only hear snippets about them, bits and garbled pieces, rumors and old wives' tales, most of them unbelievable."

"Such as? What is so unbelievable about the things you hear?"

"Well, this king of theirs, before all else. As you know, his name is Attila and he calls himself the King of the Huns, among other, more grandiose titles. Apparently he has sworn a mighty oath not merely to tear down and overthrow the remaining power of Rome and its Empire but to rip out the Christian Church and destroy it utterly. They would have us believe—whoever 'they' might be— that this is not merely another hungry, angry barbarian from beyond the bounds of Empire, but a conqueror with the stature of an Alexander of Macedon, subjugating all the races and people in the path of his march to omnipotence, a powerful and brilliant king, ruler and commander of armies approaching mythic proportions. I have heard sober reports—and drunken ones, as well—of his army being two hundred thousand strong. Two hundred thousand! Even allowing for normal exaggeration, that speaks of huge numbers. And yet we have never seen a trace of any of those people, or heard of them being anywhere close to our territories in Corbenic."

Arthur's eyes had narrowed to slits. "So, are you saying that, after all you have heard, you really do not believe these Huns exist? That they are mere rumors? The inventions of too-fertile minds?"

"I am not saying that at all. Quite the opposite, in fact. The Huns are there … they have to be there—there can't be this much rumor without substance. But my guess is that what we are hearing is distorted by both time and distance, beyond recognition. The tales we hear in Corbenic have passed from mouth to mouth perhaps a hundred times or even more by the time they come to us, and every telling adds to the distortion. But there is a discernible pattern of truth underlying all we hear, and when you strip away all the unbelievable elements of the stories, what you are left with is that these people seem to have come southwards from the far northeast, from beyond the Rhine lands and far beyond the Danube, and the routes they've chosen have taken them down through eastern Gaul, passing us cleanly by with a margin of at least two hundred miles. They are headed south, into southern Gaul and down into Iberia, and perhaps even over the Alps into Italia itself. And they clearly understand that terror is their strongest and most powerful weapon, so they work hard and long to spread the word that they are not merely invincible but unimaginably savage and merciless. I might be tempted to do the same, I suppose, were I in their position."

"What would you say if I told you that you are totally correct in some ways and utterly, unbelievably wrong in others?"

It was my turn now to stare through narrowed eyes, wondering what was coming next, but I thought carefully about my response before voicing it. "Well, since you are both my King and the Riothamus, I would accept that you have sources of information better placed to inform you of what is going on over there than I have … and I would therefore accept that you might be right, despite your never having been to Gaul, but after that I would listen very closely to what you had to say in explanation."

"Listen, then, and believe, for what I am about to tell you has come to me from many sources, all of them credible because all were bishops, working and living in Gaul, under direct threat from Attila. I know you know from experience how well the churchmen communicate with each other in all things pertinent to their survival and their future. Attila, apart from having sworn to destroy the remnants of Rome and its Empire, made it his mission years ago to stamp out Christianity beneath his rule. He can never succeed, of course, because Christianity is an idea and a way of life, and not even the vaunted King of the Huns can influence, let alone change, the way people choose to think and believe.

"Be that as it may, there has never been a threat to civilization comparable to Attila and his Huns. Never. His full title, self-given and self-serving, is Attila, Descendant of the Great Nimrod, Nurtured in Engaddi, by the Grace of God, King of the Huns, the Goths, the Danes and the Medes, the Dread of the World.

"Take note of that claim 'by the Grace of God.' A strangely Christian claim for a man who wishes to destroy Christianity, would you not say? And then 'the Dread of the World.' It is ponderous, but it is not an inaccurate description, for the whole world, with the exception of Corbenic and Britain, dreads him in truth. Think about those titles, Lance. This man has conquered Persia!

"You disbelieve the claims you have heard about his armies being two hundred thousand strong, and I will admit that does sound outrageous and impossible, but the number that has been given to me—and I do *not* disbelieve it—is *seven* hundred. Seven hundred thousand men, Lance … and at least half of those are horsemen. We could barely raise ten thousand men from all of Camulod, and scarcely as many again from our former so-called allies in Chester. Perhaps twenty thousand in all. But Attila has *seven—hundred—thousand*. Every warrior from every land and every race he has ever conquered has been enlisted in his armies, and he has been conquering for decades, mainly in the eastern Empire.

"Four years ago, however, he turned his attention to the west, beginning on the farthest borders of northeastern Gaul, just below the Rhine River, where he attacked the Burgundians and smashed them like kindling, sweeping them away in front of him like dead leaves. And the year after that, shortly before the time you first ventured into Gaul and Corbenic, he split his forces in two and invaded Gaul itself. One half of his army struck westwards towards the sea, to a place called Arras that still had an occupying force of Romans, and that group must have passed within a hundred miles of Corbenic—it had to, to reach Arras, so I am amazed that no one there knew of its passing … although now that I come to think of it, that was probably the source of the reports you heard of two hundred thousand men. Anyway, that half of his army turned south again after sacking Arras, and the other half—still over three hundred thousand strong—had thrust eastwards in the interim, along the course of the River Marnia, to destroy the last of the Burgundian strongholds there before sweeping straight south again. I am told they regrouped as a single massive army in the vast forests there below Paris—or Lutetia, men seem to call it both these days—and from there they attacked a town called Orleans. Have you heard of it?"

I shook my head.

"The name was new to me, too, when I heard it, but it is a crossing town on the Liger River—or the Loire, depending again upon which tongue you speak there. Its bridge guards the main approaches to the south of Gaul and the territories of the Visigoths, under Theodoric. You know that name, don't you?"

"Aye, if he's the same Theodoric I'm thinking of, his father was Alaric, the first man to sack Rome."

"That's him. He's an old man now, but still a strong king and a Christian, and Orleans is one of the strongest outposts of his kingdom. The garrison were alert and well warned of Attila's approach, with sufficient time to prepare for his arrival so that his armies were unable to overrun the town, and were thus obliged to lay siege to it instead. The siege itself did not last long, but the ferocity with which they raped and despoiled the surrounding lands was apparently so brutal that it surpassed belief. They slaughtered tens of thousands of the local people there for no reason at all, other than that they were unfortunate enough to be there and to be vulnerable … slaughtered and raped and despoiled, killed and burned and ravaged, purely, it seems, to teach people to walk in terror of the Hun. One demented hermit there, apparently seeing the wrath of God in the terrible afflictions laid on the populace, was moved in his madness to address Attila himself as 'the Scourge of God, for the chastisement of the Christians.' Attila loved the name, and adopted it. But his fate was already in the hands of others. Have you heard of a fellow called Aëtius?"

"Aye, I've heard the name somewhere. But I don't know where or when."

"A Roman general, appointed by Valentinian. They call him the last of the great Roman generals, and he has been the senior Roman soldier in the western Empire these twenty years and more. He spent several years raising an army from all over the Empire to challenge Attila, raiding every tavern in Italia and Gaul, apparently, and raising levies everywhere he could find men breathing, even purchasing assistance when he had to and rallying everyone in the surrounding lands who had a reason to fear Attila. But no matter what he did, he couldn't match the Hun in numbers, and so he finally approached Theodoric, suggesting an alliance in arms against the common enemy. Theodoric saw the sense of that, and they combined their forces and marched on Orleans, to raise the siege."

I sat waiting, but he was staring into the fire by then and showed no sign of taking up his tale again. "Well, and did they raise the siege?"

"They didn't need to. As soon as Attila learned of the alliance, and that the combined armies were marching against him from the south, he abandoned Orleans and pulled his armies back into the northeast, to the line of the River Marnia, where he had smashed the Burgundians. It's flat and barren territory there, I'm told, wide plains with few trees and fewer hills—perfect terrain for Attila's cavalry. And there, less than a year ago in a place known to my churchly sources as Chalons, he met Aëtius and Theodoric in a great battle."

"A great cavalry battle? Then why did we not hear of it in Corbenic?"

The King looked at me, one eyebrow rising high. "Lance, you had barely heard of Attila, and you thought his army was merely a third as strong as it really was, and you knew nothing of the siege at Orleans or of the alliance between Aëtius and Theodoric.

Why, then, would it surprise you not to have heard of a single battle, even a great one?"

Of course I had no answer to that, and so he continued with his tale. He knew little of the conduct of the battle itself, he told me, since his informants were all bishops, with no knowledge of warfare, but he knew it was not a cavalry battle, in the sense that we understood the term. Horsemen, yes, in vast numbers, but not disciplined cavalry. He had been told by several different people—some in writing and others in person—that the Huns had almost gone down into defeat on the first day of the fighting, saved only by the onset of night. The Roman Aëtius had commanded the allies' right front that day, King Theodoric the left, and Sangipan, King of the Alans, who was trusted by neither of the other commanders, was placed purposely in the center, and in the very front of the battle.

On the opposing side, Attila commanded his center in person, at the head of his own countrymen, while the Ostrogoths and a people called the Gepidae, whoever they might be, were drawn up on the wings along with the other subject allies of the Huns.

Early in the proceedings, before the actual engagement began, Aëtius had somehow managed to maneuver his troops so that they succeeded in occupying a sloping hillside opposite Attila's left flank, and Attila, approaching the position and recognizing the importance of the high ground, had immediately launched a ferocious attack on that part of the Roman line, detaching some of his best troops from his center to aid his left. Aëtius and his Romans, however, having won the advantage of the high ground, used it well and repulsed the Huns easily.

On the other side of the field, attacking the Ostrogoths who formed the right of Attila's army, King Theodoric, charging at the head of his Visigoth subjects, was struck down by a javelin, and his own cavalry, charging over him, trampled him to death in the confusion. But instead of being disheartened at the loss of their king, the Visigoths were infuriated by their monarch's fall. They routed the enemy formations facing them, and then wheeled right to attack the flank of the Hunnish center, which had been engaged in a bloody but indecisive contest with the Alans.

Seeing what had happened, Attila had signaled his center to fall back upon his camp, and from there his massed archers easily repulsed the charges of the Gothic cavalry, but his battle plan was in total ruin by the time night fell over the battlefield: his right wing had been routed, with the loss of countless thousands of men, and his center had been forced back upon his camp with equal losses, and left with no room to advance again. But his left was still undefeated, facing Aëtius, who for reasons unknown had not pressed the early advantage he had gained on his side of the field.

It was the following morning, Arthur said, that had proven difficult for outside observers like ourselves to accept or even to believe. During the night, the Scourge of God had evidently decided that his chances of being defeated were too great to be denied, and so he had determined that his enemies would not have the satisfaction of capturing or killing him. The dawn revealed that he had repositioned all his armies during the night, in a huge defensive formation around his encampment, and in the very center of the camp he had built a giant pyramid—a funeral pyre— made of the wooden saddles of his cavalry. Upon this pyramid he had spread all the wealth of his enormous treasury, and high upon the very peak of it, prepared to die and be consumed in the inferno with all his wealth and booty if need be, he himself had stood in defiance, surrounded by his wives and concubines.

Aëtius, seeing what his enemy had done, and what he clearly intended to do next, had then made a decision that no one had understood from that day forth. He had decided not merely to spare Attila's life but to make no attempt to blockade the enemy camp or to interfere as the enemy armies began to make ready to leave, and Attila and his Huns were permitted simply to walk away from the place where they should all have died. Aëtius had offered no explanation for his decision, nor had anyone apparently asked for one. The battle had simply ended and Attila had gone home, or so it was believed, as though he had not been defeated.

I was unable to believe what I had heard.

"I know what you are thinking," the King said. "I reacted the same way. Why would Aëtius do such a thing? How could he do it? And believe me, I asked the questions, many times in many letters, without finding an answer. But then I received a letter from a source I trust and whom you once knew, Ludovic, the Bishop of Auxerre. He is a clever and astute man, Ludovic, and I am tempted to believe he has the right of this, for he had questioned many people and dug deeply into the great general's background before forming his opinion. But I will let you judge its value for yourself." He fell silent, collecting his thoughts, then resumed. "Aëtius is no man's fool, and never has been. Nor has he always been an admirer of, or beloved by, our gracious Emperor Valentinian, the third of that name. And thus he walks a cautious line always, with both eyes to his own welfare although he seems to be truly devoted and loyal to Rome—not to the Emperor, you understand, but to an ancient, selfish and archaic vision of Rome itself ... a vision that has been out of fashion for these hundreds of years now. Aëtius saw, where most men in his position would not, that Theodoric, a former and formidable enemy, was a natural ally in this joint cause against the Hun, and so he courted and won the favor of the Visigoths. But Theodoric died in the battle on that first day, and his Visigoths won great glory for themselves, in addition to which the king's son, Thorismund, distinguished himself sufficiently to be acclaimed by his armies on the field of battle not merely as his father's successor but as a worthy successor of his famous grandsire Alaric.

"Ludovic believes that having witnessed that acclaim, and acknowledging the image it raised of another Alaric to frighten Rome, Aëtius might have been sufficiently influenced to prompt him to spare the Huns the following day, out of simple self-preservation—or more accurately what Aëtius, with his peculiar viewpoint on things Roman, might have construed as self-preservation. It is certain that, having permitted the Huns to walk away—hundreds of thousands of them, bear in mind—he then persuaded the heroic and victorious young king Thorismund to return to his capital in the south and to stay there until any threat of a Hunnish resurgence should dissipate. Thus Ludovic came to believe, and I now agree with him, that Aëtius chose quite consciously not to be too victorious, opting to leave a dangerous foe and a potential threat alive and still at large, and thereby keeping a dangerous friend and another potential threat safely confined within his own borders and vigilant against future attack."

I allowed myself ample time to digest that before I spoke again, still unclear on what had transpired there. "So what is happening now in Gaul? Where did Attila go?"

"Where does any defeated king go with that many men still under arms? I have no idea, but the evidence I have indicates that he withdrew whence he had come, and his army split into pieces, all of them formidable. We have no idea how many men he lost at Chalons, but the numbers were in the high tens of thousands, and after the defeat his forces simply dissipated, hither and yon."

"So they are still in Gaul?"

"Some of them, aye."

"Do you fear they might invade Britain?"

"No, Lance, and I never have." His smile was genuine. "This is a land army, this horde of Huns, and we are an island kingdom. Attila has no ships. He knows nothing of such things, and therefore he can pose no threat to us. Besides, I truly doubt that Attila will ever again threaten civilization as we know it. He may make a nuisance of himself, but he has been defeated once in open battle and will be in no rush to suffer the same fate again."

"Then why do you want me to stay in Gaul?"

"To represent me to the kings there."

I do not know what I had expected to hear in response to my question, but it was not what emerged from Arthur's mouth, and I sat blinking at him, feeling a frown gathering on my brow. "What kings, Arthur? The only king I know in Gaul is Pelles, in Corbenic, and you know him only by association."

"Aye, but I know him well in that regard, and he thinks highly of me. And for that I am grateful to you, Lance. I want to come to know this young Gothic king, too, this Thorismund, in the same manner—in open friendliness and goodwill, irrespective of whether we ever meet in person. You can achieve that for me where no one else could hope to. You have the force now in Corbenic, comfortably based and quite at home among your Franks. I'll wager more than a few of them already speak the Frankish tongue."

"Aye, they do. And many of them—almost all of them, in fact—have Frankish women. Others are properly wed to Frankish wives and have started families. We had to think long and hard over that decision, by the way, and I was going to discuss it with you at greater length tomorrow, because it means that when we do return home there will now be men who wish to stay behind in Gaul. But now it sounds as though you are warning me that none of my men may ever be permitted to come home—"

He grimaced, masking a sudden twinge of pain, I thought, and shook his head. He spoke through clenched teeth. "No, I am not ..." He drew a deep, sharp breath and held for a count of three before releasing it loudly. "Not at all." Another pause followed, while he gathered himself and calmed his breathing. "What I am saying is that, from this time on, I want to maintain a presence in Gaul, a small but powerful force that enjoys the goodwill of the local people, personnel to revolve regularly between there and here, in annual tours of duty. What's wrong? Why are you scowling?"

"Because you're evidently in great pain. Can I—?"

"Do nothing. I'm almost done with this."

There was nothing to do but obey. "Annual tours of duty, you said. How are you going to guarantee that for years? The only ships we have at our disposal belong to Connor Mac Athol, and he won't live forever, any more than his brother the king will. And once those two are gone, who can tell what their successors will want to do? We have no close ties with those people today. Our only contacts there are the old guard—Connor and Brander and a few others like them, all old men and likely soon to die."

He nodded abruptly and spoke again, more easily now. "I have thought of that, of course, and I already have people building ships for us, along the southern coast of Cambria. We have a fleet already—a very small one, mind you, only four vessels, but that is four more than we had when I became king. I started working on the project with Merlyn before you and your people left for Gaul, because it was obvious that we would have a need for seagoing ships sooner than later. We live on an island, surrounded by water, so we ought to have the means to cross those waters when we wish or when we need to. They are trading vessels, too—not warships. Those may come later, as our ventures expand. For the time being, however, our major need is for trading vessels that can carry horses."

"Who is building these ships for you?"

"Some of Connor's people, on loan to us until such time as we can train our own."

"And *can* we train our own?"

"Aye, Lance, that we can. We have always had shipbuilders. No, that's not right. We have always had *boat* builders—fishing craft and the like. But now they are being taught new skills by people who can show them how to expand their thinking and their scope. As I said, we have four ships now and our operations are expanding rapidly. Within the year, I'm told, we will have half a score, and within three years, if all goes according to plan, we should be building upwards of a score of vessels each year."

That sounded optimistic, and unlikely, to me, but I was in no position to dispute what the King was claiming and I had no desire to counter his enthusiasm.

"Let's get back to Gaul," I said. "What, exactly, do you have in mind that I might do? You mentioned an approach to King Thorismund, but that might be one of those objectives that's easy to define and impossible to achieve."

"Why would you say that?"

"Because his kingdom is in southern Gaul, hundreds of miles from Pelles and Corbenic."

"Aye, I know that. He rules the territories that the Romans named the Province of Aquitainia, although his Visigoths spill out from there into the upper portion of Iberia. But his northern territories begin in Orleans, and that is nowhere near so far away, is it? It is less than half a hundred miles south of Paris. Is that not so?"

"Perhaps. I don't know how far it is, in truth, but you told me it sits on the Liger River and I know that the Liger is the dividing line between the northern and southern parts of Gaul, so yes, let's say that Thorismund's territories start in Orleans. What then?"

"Then you are already on good terms with most of the people living between you and there, thanks to the recent Games you held."

I could only shrug. "Aye, perhaps, although not all of them were happy with the outcome of the Games ..."

"Unhappy, perhaps, but they were impressed, no? And they might know you well enough by now to raise no objection were you to ask leave of them to cross their lands, providing your own food and fodder and offering no threat to their inhabitants or their crops, would you agree? And once you reach Orleans and send out word that you have come to meet with Thorismund, to discuss cavalry matters, you would receive safe conduct from there to wherever the king might be."

Arthur's logic was irrefutable, and so it was decided that I would return to Gaul and do precisely what he had envisioned, and after that we talked on for a while, discussing lighter matters until he began to grunt in pain again and to shift uncomfortably in his chair and his face began to grow more gaunt looking. This time I summoned his guards as soon as I noticed his discomfort, and they carried him, still in his chair, into his bedchamber, where they were quickly joined by Arthur's physician. Under the physician's scrutiny, they undressed the King gently, taking great care not to disturb the bulky dressings around his groin, and put him to bed.

I remained until Arthur fell asleep, drugged by a potion the physician made for him, and then I made my way back slowly to my own quarters, thinking about all that Arthur had told me about the events that had been going on all around me in Gaul without my knowledge, and about my own concerns regarding Elaine and her son who might be my son, too—our son! And the more I thought about the complications of it all, the more I marveled, bitterly and not for the first time, over how little influence we have, despite all our imaginings of our potency and knowledge, over what happens around us, all day and every day, in the world in which we live. The greatest and most arrant folly in our lives is the belief that we are individually important and capable of affecting the circumstances surrounding us.

THIRTEEN

1

Throughout my life I have heard people say, in different ways, that the most tragic moment in a man's life is the instant when he is first made to see and understand that his body has aged decades ahead of his mind and he is suddenly old. Of course, all the times I heard the hoary old adage, I smiled indulgently, accepting the comment as a fatuous, meaningless pleasantry and failing completely to see the truth of it because I was too young to think that such a moment could ever come to me.

Alas, I now remember exactly when the truth struck home to me, and it does not seem that long ago even now, although I know it was. More than a score of years have elapsed since that ruefully remembered night, and now I really am old, with the wrinkles and the silver-rimmed bald pate to prove it. The moment occurred during a gathering in my home in celebration of the coming of age of my second-eldest son, Thoric. All of my family were there, and all their friends, and although I cannot recollect what prompted the realization, it suddenly struck me that I was not really the host that night: Arturic, my firstborn son, had taken over that capacity quite naturally and without anyone even being aware of what had happened, and he was in his element, directing the proceedings and giving his mother and me the opportunity, as he explained it, to spend some extra time with our own friends and guests.

The moment stood out for me, although I did not yet recognize its significance. I simply acknowledged that his mother and I did have friends who kept slightly apart from everyone else, mainly because of their age, and that we would be glad of the chance to spend more time with them instead of having to oversee the festivities. And it was then that I noticed how the younger people there—the vast majority of those present—were unaware of us, other than as elderly and respected presences at the feast. I had always been the host in my own home, and a profusion of young people had always attended our gatherings, but now I found myself behaving as a guest, my own former capacity as host taken over by my son ... in truth, by all my children. It was not a shattering epiphany, and I did not feel in any way slighted, but from that moment on, forever afterwards, I saw my place in the world diminished by a younger generation who had come of age, with more to give and more to prove and more demands to make upon the world than I had ever had, and I had no choice other than to accept it with whatever grace I could find inside myself.

There are advantages to growing old, I am told, and although I would normally choose to dispute that, I find at times that there is some truth to it. Nowadays, for example, although I often forget what might have happened yesterday or the day before, I can sometimes recall with total clarity events that happened decades ago. Frequently my mind will open unexpectedly and show me episodes, many of them delightful, from years gone by, when I was young and hale. Time, it appears, has little relevance in, or to, advanced age. More than anything else, however, I have come to realize that time is like a teasing woman-child, forever present and underfoot when we are too young and unaware to have any interest, yet elusive and unconfinable once we betray a mature desire to know and enjoy it at length ... The older we grow, the quicker time runs away from us.

The recollections that I have of that visit to Camulod, when Arthur was an invalid and Connlyn newly dead, are fresh and pristine in my memory today, the faces of my friends and loved ones bright and flushed with health, the very air surrounding us vibrant with color and the promise of high summer. All of Camulod's army groups were home in their own bases at that time—even my own in

Corbenic—and there was peace throughout our lands. Everyone knew that could not last, for we were surrounded on all sides by steadily encroaching Outlanders and would soon have to bestir ourselves to stop them in their tracks, if not to drive them back. But for the time being, at least, we were at peace and all was well, and our King was thriving and improving every day, learning to walk again, and full of hope that he would soon be able to ride and fight again. I took great delight in training with him, and seeing him gaining strength from day to day and week to week was one of the great joys of my life, so that I felt blessed and privileged to be there in Camulod at such a time. Until Connor's ships returned to Glevum to collect me, I could not return to Gaul, and since there was nothing I could do to influence the length of time that might take, I had to make the best of things and be patient.

I spent a deal of time thinking about Elaine during the days that followed. In response to my burning question about whether or not the child Galahad was mine—a question I was forced to hold inside me for two whole days before I had a chance to ask it—Elaine was truthful and forthright. She did not really know, she admitted freely, but she suspected that he might be. But whether he was mine or Jonas's made no whit of difference to her, she told me, laughing. Either one was perfect, since we were the two men she loved most in all the world, and her knowing nothing of his true paternity allowed her to imagine the best of each of us in the boy. Jonas, of course, and she added this quickly lest I misunderstand, had no idea that there was any question of the child's sire being anyone but him.

I was less than happy with her explanation, and even less with her attitude when she explained herself, for in her demeanor I saw clearly that I had indeed misconstrued what she had said when she first told me of the baby's birth, and that what I had chosen to see as love for me was indeed love, but not at all the kind of love for which I thought I yearned. I went to bed that night full of self-pity, I remember, but by the time I awoke the next day a profound change had taken place in me, and from that time on I never again thought of Elaine as anything but wife to Jonas and mother of his child.

Jonas himself came to Camulod a few days later and seemed glad to see me and to shake my hand, and try as I would I could see no smallest trace of jealousy or suspicion in him. He insisted on my meeting his son, young Galahad, and I was glad to see that the child, now almost two years old and already walking and learning to talk, was as beautiful as everyone had claimed, with black, thickly curling hair and deep blue eyes.

That afternoon, sharing a pot of beer with me in the open yard by the kitchens, Jonas told me of the arrangement he had made with his wife. She spent one month out of every two here in Camulod, serving the Queen, and the other month at home with him, sharing his life as headman of his community. It pleased them both, for he was as happy as his wife was in knowing that young Galahad would grow up with all the privileges of being a ward of the King and Queen, and his education would begin as soon as he was old enough to reason. In the course of consuming several pots of excellent beer, I decided that I liked Jonas immensely, and that I wished nothing but the best in life for him and his family, and I sat with him on several occasions while he remained in Camulod, waiting for his wife to finish her duties and return home with him.

On the afternoon of their departure, I rode down to the Villa Britannicus with Arthur when he was taken there in a comfortable, well-sprung wagon to be bathed and to have the dressings on his wounds changed in the villa's luxurious bath house. Once there, however, I left him to the attentions of his physicians and surgeons and went directly to my favorite place in the villa, the large room that had been known as the Armory since the days of its founder, Publius Varrus, dead since long before my birth. There, still in place on the walls where he had hung them, was a magnificent collection of ancient weapons, and among them, standing out in their relative newness, were a number of Roman shortswords and daggers, all of them made by Varrus himself.

I do not know how long I had been there, simply admiring the exhibits, when I heard a discreet cough behind me and turned to find Crassus, a captain of the Queen's Guard, standing at my back.

As always, the man was flawlessly turned out, his armor burnished and his colors crisp and almost glowing in their brightness. He apologized for interrupting me and asked me to accompany him to where the Queen was waiting to speak to me. Puzzled, for I had thought the Queen was still up in the fortress on the hill, I followed where he led and was astonished to find Gwinnifer, accompanied by young Mordred, on a long, narrow stretch of grass along one side of the villa's southern wall. Beside them, leaning against the wall, was a quiver of my throwing lances, and some distance away, I estimated it as roughly thirty paces, someone, presumably one of the guard captain's men, had sunk a pointed stake into the ground.

As I gathered my wits, gaping from the Queen to Mordred and thence to the lances and back, Gwinnifer stepped towards me, a smile dimpling her cheek as she took pity on my discomfiture.

"Forgive my boldness, Seur Clothar, but I was talking about you with Prince Mordred earlier today, telling him about how we two first met, and how you became my spearman—my Hastatus— but I fear the Prince did not believe me when I told him how I threw your lance." Her smile widened and she turned to Mordred, whose face flushed crimson. "And so, impulsively, I sent Captain Crassus here to find you and to ask you if you would bring your lances and treat the Prince and me to a display of your skills. Unfortunately you had already left to come down here with the King, but Captain Crassus, meaning no ill, saw your lances in your quarters and thought fit to bring them to me."

I glanced at Crassus and saw he was now red faced too, aware of what he had done and unsure of how to rectify it.

"Of course," the Queen continued, "I would not think of using your weapons without your permission, and so when we discovered you had come down here, we followed, hoping that you would oblige us both. Will you?"

Completely disarmed by her unapologetic smile, I felt myself smiling in return and looked at Mordred. "Is it true you doubted the Queen's word, Prince Mordred? I find that hard to credit, because I know how truthful she is. She truly was—and she still is—the single most naturally gifted user of my javelins that I have ever seen. With no training, having learned only through watching me at practice, she threw my lances almost flawlessly the first few times she ever tried."

"The *only* times I ever tried!" she said with a laugh.

"Forgive me, my lady, you are correct, of course ..." I turned back to Mordred, who was gazing from one to the other of us, his mouth hanging slightly open. "The first and only few times she ever tried. And she was no more than your age now, thirteen at most. Am I correct, my lady?"

"I was twelve that year. You are correct."

"You have not yet tried my lances, Prince Mordred. Would you care to?" His eyes were wide, and when he nodded, wordless, I went and picked up my quiver, then showed him the construction and composition of the weapons and the way the throwing thongs worked. He watched, fascinated, missing no detail of what I did, and the Queen watched over his shoulders, no less enthralled than he. I then walked him through the various steps of preparing to throw a lance, showing him first how to gauge the balance point of the shaft and then how best to attach and wind the throwing cord along the butt end so that it would uncoil evenly and smoothly, spinning the shaft of the weapon as it unwound and thrusting the missile forward, far harder and faster and with much greater accuracy than could be achieved by a normal, unassisted throw. Of course I had to demonstrate each stage as the explanation unfolded, performing the moves at full speed, and then attempting to repeat the performance and slow every individual stage of the exercise down to a speed that could be watched and observed ... a virtual impossibility.

That demonstration took about half an hour, and by the end of it I could see that Mordred was in a fever of impatience to attempt it on his own, and so I allowed him to try it, sharing a smile with the Queen over his bent head as he concentrated, grim faced and biting his protruding tongue, upon securing the throwing end of the cord securely around the index finger of his throwing hand.

His first throw was a disaster, as were his next two, but on his fourth attempt he actually managed to cast the lance in the direction of the stake at the other end of the sward, and his sixth attempt ended up sticking point first in the ground less than two paces from the target. He was completely unaware of the rest of us by then, lost in his own world of computation as he sought to master all that he had learned. Crassus had quickly grown bored here and, seeing that the Queen was perfectly safe with the boy and me, had sought Gwinnifer's permission to take his leave to attend to other matters.

Wordlessly then, while she was watching the boy, I collected another lance and wound the throwing cord carefully around it, then held it out towards her. She gazed at it without expression for long moments, then looked up into my eyes, her face breaking into a smile again.

"Do you think I dare? I'm a queen now, not a twelve-year-old tomboy. Do queens do such things, are they permitted to?"

I dipped my head sideways. "One of your most renowned queens, Boudicca of the Iceni, did it from the back of a war chariot, my lady, and almost drove the Romans out of Britain. I doubt that anyone would think to chastise you for honoring her memory."

"Ah, but what if I have forgotten how to do it with the passing years?"

"Then you will find out quickly. But the skill you showed as a child is not the kind that atrophies. Natural talents endure. Take it and try."

To this day I cannot say whether what she did was warranted by skill, or whether fortune played a part in it, but she would never attempt to repeat it, and I am forced by my own beliefs to accept that her throw was an astounding demonstration of true and innate natural ability. She made the perfect cast. Her lance leapt across the intervening thirty-odd paces and its elongated needle point penetrated the exact center of the target stake about a handspan from the top, the solid weight of its impact thrusting the entire stake backwards and out of alignment.

Mordred, thinking I had thrown, spun towards me, grinning, but his jaw dropped and the grin was wiped from his face as he saw the unraveled throwing cord dangling from Gwinnifer's still-outstretched hand. Blinking, he looked at her face, then at mine, then turned to gaze at the long spear angling upwards from the drunkenly angled stake. "My lady," he said, with the beginnings of a tremulous smile on his lips, "I had thought to be your protector when I grow older, but perhaps you might be mine."

He could not have chosen a better thing to say. The Queen erupted into delighted laughter and I joined in, suddenly and quite absurdly convinced that young Mordred was in his proper place at last, here in Camulod, and that the future would be bright for him and his new parents.

2

Ten days after that episode, word reached us in Camulod that Shaun Pointer was back in Glevum, waiting to take me and my Frankish honor guard back to Gaul. The night before we left to return, Arthur—who by then was walking unassisted for much of the time—summoned all the Knights Companion to dine with him and his Queen, to do honor to the Frankish knights. Merlyn had been absent from Camulod for several days, no one knew where, and no one knew, either, when he might return, so there was little to be gained in waiting for him to appear, and Arthur simply decided to proceed without his senior adviser.

In the course of the gathering that night, he apologized for Merlyn's absence and then paid public thanks to the Gallic warriors, crediting them with the death of Connlyn and the end of the northern war. It was not, strictly speaking, altogether truthful, but the fact was that the Franks had ventured north of the Wall with me and from there had ridden openly into the heart of enemy territory with no thought for their own welfare in a war that was none of their affair. They deserved whatever credit they received, and Arthur went out of his way to ensure that his guests would return to Gaul with high regard for the Britons they had met in Camulod. He knighted the two senior Frankish commanders, Cortix and Quintus Milo, in a special ceremony, and presented each of the other officers and members of the honor guard with a personal memento of their visit, a hand-embroidered blazon of his personal insignia, the red dragon of Pendragon on its field of green, set in a finely made frame of beaten silver and intended to be sewn onto the left breast of the wearer as a signal mark of honor from the High King of Britain. He also presented the guards with a magnificent chestnut gelding as a gift from him to their king, Pelles.

When dinner was over that night, he called me to his chambers and went over with me again all that he had asked me to see to on my return to Gaul. I was to thank Pelles for his continuing support and obtain his permission to ride south to Orleans, and thence to visit Thorismund, wherever he might be in residence. On finding Thorismund, I was to commend my King in Britain to his attention and present the Visigoth monarch with several rich and appropriate gifts from Camulod. The main purpose of my visit, of course, was to explore the possibility of establishing trade of some kind between Thorismund's territories and our own in Britain. Arthur was not even sure what Thorismund's people might have that was worth trading for, apart from wine and perhaps weaponry, but he was certain that I would discover a store of valuable trading wares as soon as I arrived there, in return for which we would offer lavish supplies of solid Cornish tin.

I nodded my head, accepting what he had said, but my thoughts had been shunted aside to other things.

"What are you thinking of? Something new just came into your face."

"It just occurred to me, talking of Thorismund's territories, that I will be traveling close to my boyhood home in Benwick. You once told me I could go there with your blessing. Does that still apply?"

"Of course it does. Go wherever you wish, and take as many men with you as you require. I think it would be wonderful for you to go home again, even for a brief visit. How long has it been since you were last there, ten years?"

"Aye, more or less. I was sixteen when I came here, so ten years would be about right."

"Then it's high time you went back. Your cousin is king there now, I know, but I can't remember his name."

"King Brach of Benwick. At least, he used to be king of Benwick. I don't even know if he is still alive."

"Well, how could you? You have been giving all your time to me ever since leaving there. But you merely prove my point. It has been far too long since you were last there, so you must be sure to go when you return to Gaul. And that reminds me of something else that I wanted to ask you about. You wrote an enormously long letter to me soon after you went to Gaul, in which you told me about Pelles being your blood cousin, and ruling the kingdom that is rightfully yours, in Ganis. You said you were quite content to have it so at that time, and reading your explanation of why you felt that way, I saw no reason to doubt you. But I have sometimes wondered since then whether you might have changed your mind. Have you, in fact, or do you yet believe yourself fortunate?"

I laughed aloud at that. "I couldn't *be* more fortunate! God did not intend me to be a king, Arthur, and for that I am glad, every day. I look at you and see the wrinkles on your balding brow and the crow's feet of concern around your eyes and I thank God that I am left to remain young and carefree." He made as if to stand up in mock outrage and I raised both hands to placate him. "Forgive me, Seur King, for my foreign tongue. I have no wish to be flogged or executed."

He subsided into his chair again, smiling gently. "Then answer my question civilly, you Frankish lout."

"No other answer necessary, than that my mind remains unchanged. Truthfully, Arthur, I am perfectly content with my lot. Pelles is a far better king than I could ever be, and I thank God for having seen to that."

He smiled and nodded, somehow managing to convey an impression of rueful amazement at the same time. "Then so be it, my friend. So be it. I will confess to you, however, that I do not know another man, anywhere or of any age, who could walk away as easily as you have from the thought of being a king. It is a seductive notion, kingship, with all its suggestions of power and influence."

I found it easy to refute that. "I have all the power I require, Arthur. I have the power to command my men, and to command their respect, which is even better. What need have I of more than that?"

We talked about several other things after that, but our conversation was desultory and unstrained, the easy, companionable talk of old friends who have taken care of their priorities and are now merely passing time together for the enjoyment of the moment. Gwinnifer had chosen to leave the two of us alone that night, knowing that it would be the last private time the King and I would be able to spend together until my next return from Gaul, whenever that might be, and I, for one, was grateful to her for the consideration. We talked of Arthur's campaigning plans for the time ahead, once he was fully returned to health, and we talked, although less cogently, about possible contingencies for any dealings he might have in future with his wife's father, Symmachus of Chester. That topic led me, almost incidentally, to Prince Mordred and his inheritance, and the complication of a possible future heir with a secondary claim.

"He's a fine boy, isn't he?" Arthur warmed to his subject instantly, glad of the opportunity to deal with something pleasurable for a change. "He'll make a grand chief of Pendragon, I can feel it in my bones, every time I look at him. I don't know what it is, Lance, but there's something very *familiar* about him, something that reminds me very strongly of someone I once knew."

"His mother?"

"No, not Morag, although I can see her in there, too, in his eyes and in the way he sometimes tilts his head to one side. I used to love the way she did that, and he has it to the life. No, whoever it is he reminds me of, I can't put my finger on it. But it's there. I see it often and it eludes me, but one of these times I'll catch it, and I'll know."

"Will he be king of the Pendragon Federation, as your son?"

"No." He looked at me sharply and then added, "At least I don't believe he will, although that could change between now and when he comes of age, provided he wants to hold the position and succeeds in building a sufficiently noteworthy name for himself. Kingship of the federation is not inherited, Lance. It's an elected position. I've told you that before. The new king is chosen upon the death of the old one by the assembled chiefs of the clans who make up the federation, and not all of those are Pendragon. Even the name of the federation could be changed at any time. It's called the Pendragon Federation today because the last five or six kings have all been Pendragons, but that, too, could change tomorrow."

"And what about the Riothamus name? Might that be his someday?"

Arthur's face clouded. "I can't answer you on that, Lance, because I simply do not know … and believe me, it is not for the want of thinking about it."

"You don't know? How can that be?"

"Because it *is*. The truth is, I have no idea at all what is likely to happen there. No one does." He saw my uncomprehending look, and he spread his hands in a gesture of frustration. "I know it seems to make no sense, since I am the Riothamus and anyone would think I ought to know these things, but on another level it makes perfect sense, once you accept the truth underlying the whole situation. And that truth is that the rank and title of Riothamus are both fabrications, or at the very least, borrowings from legend."

"Legend?"

"Legend, myth, history, what you will. Merlyn resurrected the title from tales told of antiquity. He revived it for two excellent reasons that he believed were ample justification for what he did. He needed something to provide me with an appearance of legitimacy in my quest to unify the remaining clans and kingdoms of Britain so that they can stand against the rising tide of Outlander newcomers. And he needed to rally support for the Christian Church, for its continued existence here in Britain, because he believed, absolutely, that the support of the Church is essential to my being able to do what I must do. The Church offers legitimacy to me and to my mission, and so in turn I must dedicate myself and my allegiance to the Church." He grimaced. "Unfortunately for all of us, however, the Riothamus tales that he used are open to question, because we know of no hard, indisputable evidence that any Riothamus ever actually lived."

I stood silent for a while, disconcerted and dismayed by what I had just heard.

"So are you saying this is all a lie, your kingship and your mission? I won't believe that."

"No, my friend, no, no, that's not what I am saying at all. I am merely saying that none of us—not Merlyn, not me and not my counselors—has any knowledge of what will happen to the title when I die. The rank of Riothamus is a mythical one, resurrected for a specific purpose. There may no longer be a need for it after I am gone. There may not be a man worthy to hold the title, although I still have doubts of my own worthiness. But I know beyond doubt that I do not have the right to hold out the promise of such a rank and title to my son, much as I may love him."

"So what will Mordred's legacy be?"

Arthur turned down the corners of his mouth and shrugged. "He will be chief of the Pendragon of South Cambria. Depending upon what the future holds, he may even be king of Britain, or of Camulod, since the people here seem pleased enough to have a king. But Riothamus?" He shook his head. "That I do not know and cannot guess."

"And what if you should sire another son on Gwinnifer?"

He looked at me shrewdly, his eyes narrowing. "I won't, but what of it?"

"Will Mordred's inheritance hold true?"

His face crooked into a half smile. "Aye. Another son would alter nothing of Mordred's future claims. I have made no secret of the fact that he is my firstborn, and Gwinnifer has no difficulty with that. Mordred will inherit all that I leave behind, whatever that may be."

Those words, with their qualifying uncertainty, struck home to me, because I knew that there was no plan in place to appoint a successor to Arthur if, in fact, he fell in battle or succumbed to wounds or illness. It was an untenable situation, and I found it so incredible that it was seldom far from my mind, threatening to drive me to distraction, but Arthur and his advisers simply refused to discuss it, apparently oblivious to the fact that his untimely death, from any cause, would guarantee the failure of all their plans and ensure their total collapse and defeat through lack of leadership.

Arthur himself had always maintained that any one of his close friends and commanders—now his Knights Companion—was capable of ruling in his stead, and would do so, should the need arise, but even with the support of Merlyn and a powerful convocation of bishops, the resistance to that idea from the existing kings and warlords among Camulod's allies was overwhelming. It was self-evident that the kings were thinking about their own interests, above and far beyond any thoughts they might have of the welfare of the realm against the invaders, and that had always made Arthur both angry and deeply despondent, leading, I had always presumed, to his refusal to discuss the matter of his successor. Now, at least, I saw a glimmer of light in that darkness, if Arthur was being serious about Mordred. And it seemed he *was* being serious, because he had not yet finished speaking of him.

"Besides, Lance," he said, "you know the truth of that son-and-heir situation. We agreed, Gwinnifer and I, that I will be siring no sons with her while Symmachus remains alive. That would be sheerest folly and I would be signing a warrant of death against Mordred, for his life would be worth nothing once Symmachus perceived him as a threat to his designs. But even setting that aside, another child is an impossibility at this point, thanks to this wound I took. Believe me, my friend. It is beyond even thinking about. Perhaps in years to come, if God ever permits me to recover myself sufficiently to be capable of lust again, I might make the attempt, but for the time being, all my energies and all my strength are going into getting me fit enough to ride a horse again."

He stopped, gazing directly into my eyes, and then he smiled and I smiled back at him.

"So, young Frank, no chance of other sons, for now. Mordred, in himself, is all the sons I need at this time, and my only regret is that it took so long for him to find me, but with God's aid I will be able to spend the next few years with him, and see him safely into manhood. Then, depending upon how and when I die, and how he grows, he will at the very least have the makings of a fine king, perhaps even a great one. He has them now, I know. I have seen glimmerings of them even in the short time since he has come here. All he requires now to bring them to maturity is a guiding hand. Given that, and given sufficient time, he will make a formidable leader fit for the formidable task that will lie ahead of him."

I knew exactly what Arthur meant by that, because *formidable* was an appropriate word. He himself had been fighting the growing tide of Outlanders, and beating them, since before I ever met him, but far from thrusting them significantly or permanently backwards, in spite of all his successes, Arthur had found himself defending his holdings against ever-increasing incursions by an enemy who grew ever stronger, with reinforcements arriving inexorably from overseas, all of them hungry for land on which they could live and thrive.

We sat silent again for a long time after that, each of us thinking over all that had been said and all that it meant, and eventually the moment arrived when there was nothing left but for us to retire. I was already dreading the coming dawn, knowing that I would see no rest at all from then until we were safely aboard Shaun Pointer's ships and out at sea again, and so I made my farewells to my King with great solemnity and deep fraternal love, swearing to waste no time in Gaul before I carried out his wishes, and promising to keep him fully informed at all times of what was happening to me there. I had written a long letter to Merlyn, setting out all I needed to tell

him, since I had not known when he left Camulod that I would be
gone by the time he returned, and I left that letter with the King
himself, to pass along to the old counselor. And then, long before I
was ready, it was time to leave.

The dawn broke gray and dreary, the sun struggling vainly to
penetrate a canopy of thick clouds and a mist of drizzling rain, and
we were huddled miserably in our saddles even before we set out
for Glevum, but Queen Gwinnifer was there to wish us God's speed
on our way, and even young Mordred had climbed from his bed to
bid farewell to me and to his friend Rufus. We took our leave of
them all and turned resolutely towards the north, and when I looked
back one final time from the top of a distant rise, the clouds had
already swallowed the hilltop and there was nothing there for me to
see. I turned away again and rode on my way, feeling heavy at heart.

3

Somewhere in the margin of one of the great pages of his tally book,
the Recording Angel in Heaven must have written a notation to
the effect that the Frankish knight Clothar, sometimes known as
Clothar of Benwick and sometimes as Clothar of Ganis, would
never be able, under any circumstances, to like or to befriend King
Thorismund of Aquitaine. I have no idea how or why the Angel
should have ordained such a thing, but no matter how I tried, or how
many times I forced myself to try again, I simply could not warm to
the young king of the Visigoths, and to this day I am not sure why
that was. It would be easy to condemn him by simply saying that he
was unlikable, but that would be unjust, for it was patently not so;
he was a young man, not yet in his prime, and he was comely and
pleasant to look upon. And he had but recently won his kingship to
great acclaim on the battlefield at Chalons, fighting heroically
against Attila the King of the Huns after his own father, King
Theodoric, had been killed, and I had ample cause to accept that

other people liked him. The plain truth was that I did not like him, for reasons inexplicable even to myself, and of course, he did not like me.

I had spent less than half a year with Pelles in Corbenic on my return to Gaul, and had set out for Orleans and the south, accompanied by Perceval and Bors, riding at the head of five hundred troopers and two score of mounted Pendragon scouts, as soon as the first spring buds were greening the trees. Half of our complement were my own men from Camulod, while the other half were homegrown and trained troopers from Corbenic. This had been at Pelles's insistence, because I had originally intended to ride south with my own five hundred, but Pelles, as a responsible and forward-thinking king, decided that he wanted his own presence represented to Thorismund of Aquitaine, on behalf of his people. He wanted the Visigoth king to know that there was a militarily efficient and sophisticated ally available in northern Gaul, should the Visigoths wish to recognize the fact and deal with Corbenic in good faith as allies and trading partners. I was happy to oblige my regal cousin, for the composition of my escort made no difference to me; my Camulodian troopers and Pelles's Corbenicans were indistinguishable from each other to anyone not knowing the subtleties of their colors and visible signs of rank. My sole priority in that regard was to present myself and the men who rode with me as a force to be reckoned with—a disciplined cavalry force.

We moved quickly and experienced no difficulties of any kind on our way south from Corbenic to the River Loire. Our arrival before the walls of the town of Orleans caused quite a stir, however, and the gates were quickly closed against us. The sight of five hundred unknown horsemen riding into view unexpectedly and in tightly disciplined formations can be unnerving to peaceful townspeople, and it quickly became clear that the gates were to remain closed until we retreated the way we had come. That, however, was not an option for us, because the town of Orleans protected the only bridge over the fast-flowing Loire in that region. Bypassing the town in search of a suitable spot to attempt a crossing would entail a detour of many miles through difficult and hostile terrain.

Accepting that I had no other choice than to face whatever might come from behind the walls, I rode forward alone, weaponless save for my knight's sword, which hung in its normal place between my shoulder blades, and carrying a white banner to indicate my peaceful intentions. The gates opened slightly then to permit a party of six spokesmen to ride out to speak with me. Four of the six were representatives of the city's garrison, as might be expected, and the other two were members of the city's governing council. I introduced myself and explained who we were and where we had come from, and that we were on an embassy on behalf of King Arthur Pendragon of Britain and King Pelles of Corbenic, to meet and talk with their lord, King Thorismund of Aquitaine.

Their initial response was ill-concealed hostility, and I had no difficulty in deciding that High Commander Claudio—he introduced himself as the senior soldier there and the commander of the garrison of Orleans—was less than pleased at the thought of passing half a thousand armed, mounted and presumably hungry warriors through his gates and giving them access to the rich farmland of the territories beyond, of which he was, at least nominally, the guardian. He had never heard of Arthur of Britain and made no attempt to pretend that he had, merely sniffing dismissively. He was wearing full armor, this Claudio, including a helmet with closed cheek flaps, which threw his face into darkness and made it difficult for me to read his expression, but I decided to gamble on my conviction that his boorish ungraciousness stemmed from his own uncertainty over his authority in this matter. It seemed logical to me that, in all probability, he had never had to deal with anything remotely resembling this situation, and that he was being more truculent than was necessary because of that, feeling a need to impress his associates with how unfriendly and inimical he could be when the occasion called for such extremes.

I drew myself upright in my saddle and kneed my horse towards him, aware of his eyes scanning me from head to foot and lingering on the large, impressive sword hilt at my back. He was a big man, massive in his armor, but I was taller and heavier than he was, and my armor was finer and more imposing, and that, allied with the fact that my horse was several hands taller than his, allowed me to dominate him, although I took care not to do it too overtly or aggressively, as I drew near him.

"That's close enough," he said loudly when I was almost within a spear's length of him, and I could see him cursing himself silently for having said it. I drew rein and nodded my head deeply before beginning to speak again as though he and I had not exchanged any words until that moment.

"High Commander Claudio, I am sure you noticed from your battlements as we approached that our column is accompanied by ten wagons, each pulled by a matched team of four horses. Those wagons contain our rations—oats for our stock and food for our men. We are a flying column, which means that we stop moving only infrequently and have no interest in anything other than reaching our destination in the shortest possible time, and we are self-sufficient in food, which means that we present no threat to any of the farmers whose lands we may cross. The only foraging we will do along the road—any road—is to send out hunting parties in search of wild game, from time to time, to vary the monotony of dried rations one day in three or four. Our appointed task is to find your master, Thorismund, King of the Visigoths of Aquitaine, in order to offer him—from my master and Riothamus, Arthur Pendragon—access to something that your king will value very highly.

"You may not have heard the title Riothamus before today, for it is a word from Britain. Its meaning is High King—High King of All Britain. You also may not know that Britain, for hundreds of years, was the bread basket of the western Empire. Its crops fed much of the Western world, up to the time when your king's famous grandsire, Alaric, captured Rome itself. When Rome fell to the Visigoths, Britain stopped shipping its crops to Rome. But the huge farms that produced the crops for Rome are still there and still fertile, fully capable of as much production as they turned out in

former times. King Arthur wants to offer King Thorismund access
to that source of food, contingent upon certain trading conditions.
Clearly, however, you have no intention of allowing us to pass
through your gates, and that means we will have to find other means
of reaching your king. I can promise you, however, that the fact that
you turned us away on your own authority and sent us back to
Britain will not go unmentioned when we do meet him."

There was no further argument. Claudio dispatched a series of
fast riders to carry word into the south, advising Thorismund, wherever he might be, that we were on our way to meet with him. He
could have been anywhere in Aquitaine, or even in northern Iberia,
because Claudio eventually confided that the king had traveled his
domain widely since his accession to the kingship, but as it turned
out, Thorismund was in Carcassonne, in the southernmost part of
his domain. And when we arrived there we found ourselves
expected and we encountered no difficulty in gaining access to the
king himself.

Nevertheless, the monarch kept us waiting for three hours in an
anteroom before we were ushered into his throne room, and then,
although he mouthed the proper words of welcome, he failed to
convince us that he set any store by our journey or the message we
delivered. Throughout the course of our audience he was constantly
interrupted by incoming messengers, all of them apparently hag-
ridden with the urgency of their communications, until I reached the
conclusion that he was doing this deliberately, attempting to
impress us with a demonstration of how pressed he was by his
affairs of state, and how his time was so valuable and so restricted
by ever-changing needs that he really could not afford even the little
time it took to extend courtesy to visiting ambassadors from
another, albeit lesser, king.

I took my own instructions from that observation and finally
stood up as yet another hard-breathing courier entered the audience
chamber, ushered in by the guards at the doors. I raised my hand
peremptorily and cut the newcomer off before he could attempt to
speak, and in return he gaped at me, in concert with the king and

his few counselors. Before either king or messenger could recover sufficiently to attempt to regain the initiative I had just snatched away from them, I offered rapid apologies to the monarch from myself and my lord Arthur, Riothamus of Britain. Neither of us had realized, I told the speechless audience, that the Visigoth king was so insuperably beset by time and circumstance. Had we known how helpless the king was in the face of everything that harried him, we would never have presumed to waste his time with the trivia of our visitation. We would depart in the morning, I assured him, and thanked him again for his courtesy in receiving us, saying I would inform my king that Aquitaine stood in no need of extra foodstuffs or commodities from Britain. And with that, we bowed and took our leave.

I will credit Thorismund with sufficient presence of mind to make no attempt to hinder us from leaving his audience. Even if he felt royally insulted by my hubris in daring to insert my opinion into his proceedings—and I have no slightest doubt that he did—he was intelligent enough to recognize that he himself had driven me to behave the way I had, and that were he to attempt to make too much of it, nothing but trouble could ensue. And so he stood silent and permitted us to leave, which we did with many bows and gestures of respect, all of them as empty of true respect as had been his reception of us. We had barely cleared the passageway beyond the audience chamber on our way to the exterior courtyard, however, when I heard my name being called and turned to see one of his senior counselors hurrying after us.

That man, whose name was Gundovald, earned on that single occasion whatever stipend he received from Thorismund for his counsel in the course of a year. Thinking as he walked and clearly improvising as he went along, he assured us of his master's consternation over the way matters had come to a head during the course of our brief audience. It was a confluence of misfortunes, he assured us, an unfortunate combination of circumstances that could not have been anticipated and might never be repeated. As he talked on, his eyes moving from face to face among us, looking for allies and

sympathy, I had a mental image of Thorismund seizing him by the
robe and hissing in his ear, threatening him with ruin if he did not
intercept us, appease us and persuade us not to leave in haste.

I must admit, the notion of a thoroughly rattled monarch
pleased me, and so I allowed myself to be persuaded that I should,
perhaps, delay my departure, and Gundovald guided us smoothly
into a sumptuous and private dining room, wherein we were treated
as honored guests for the next hour or so, at which point the king
himself came in to join us, stripped of his robes and jewelry of
office, and full of apologies and good-natured explanations of all
that had been going on that day. And I sat and watched him and
listened, convinced that he was lying with every breath and that he
would prove to be a dangerous and possibly treacherous ally. He
had a quick and ready tongue, and could raise shouts of laughter in
any room full of men, but I could never make real eye contact with
him, and every time I tried—which I did often, once I became aware
of it—his gaze would slide away in another direction just before I
could fasten on it. As a trading partner, I decided, he would bear
watching, but as a military ally, I feared he would be less than trustworthy, and I resolved to inform Arthur fully about my reservations.

Be that as it may, and thankfully without my personal involvement, the clerks in my contingent successfully entered into trading
negotiations with Aquitaine and the Visigoths, on behalf of both
Arthur in Britain and Pelles in Corbenic, with the understanding that
most of the initial trade ventures would be conducted by sea routes
until mutual trust and goodwill had been clearly established and
sufficient revenue was being generated to justify other, cross-country
travel routes. Everyone involved was greatly elated, and since I
appeared to be the only one suffering from boredom, I left them all
there to work out the details while I rode away alone, accompanied
only by half a score of my own troopers, a handful of Pendragon
scouts commanded by a veteran called Caerfyn, and one Guntram
Redbeard, a Visigoth companion appointed personally by the king to
ride with me, accompanied by a standard-bearer carrying King
Thorismund's banner for our protection. My destination was my

boyhood home of Benwick, just over two hundred and fifty miles to the north and east of Carcassonne and beyond the eastern borders of Aquitaine. I had done some preliminary calculations and felt confident that I could be gone and safely returned to Carcassonne within the space of three to four weeks, given a modicum of good weather and no hostile encounters on the open road.

Guntram, who came by his other name, Redbeard, honestly enough, was an amiable fellow who laughed loud and long when I mentioned my hope of avoiding hostile encounters. No one, he swore, would dare to inconvenience, let alone harass or attack, a party riding under the king's own banner, and his assurance was quickly borne out.

I could see plainly, however, that much of the territory through which we rode showed evidence of having been fought over in the recent past. I asked him who had been involved in the fighting and was unsurprised when he told me that a huge contingent of Attila's Huns, numbering almost one third of his entire host according to some reports, had split away from the Hunnish king's army after its defeat at Chalons and had swung directly southwards, battling and plundering their way down the entire length of Gaul, more than half of that time in Aquitaine, heading towards the Pyrenees in the hope of penetrating to southern Iberia. Thorismund, warned by Aëtius of the likelihood of exactly such a development, had withdrawn from the north almost at the same time and headed south, too, at the forced march, leaving Aëtius to clean up the detritus of the Chalons bloodbath. His southward course had paralleled that of the Huns, but Thorismund had been able to make better headway, since he was moving through his own territories, whereas the Huns found their passage contested at every step. Thus, the Visigoths had been able to lie in wait and strike the Hunnish forces from ambush time after time, wearing the enemy down through dogged persistence and attrition until the hundred-thousand-strong array of attackers had withered, weathered and split into three far smaller and more manageable armies, driven to remain apart from each other by their growing need to find new sources of food and supplies. Every army travels on its stomach, Guntram told me, deriving great pleasure from intoning the old truism, but one hundred thousand souls create a very large and hungry stomach that can strip an entire countryside of food and leave it looking as though a plague of locusts had passed over it.

Using interlinked fortifications built by the Romans and later refurbished by his own father, Thorismund had drawn a reinforced line across the path of the advancing Huns, barring their way from the mouth of the Gironde on the west coast, northeastward along the south bank of the Dordogne River to the old Roman town of Lugdunum, now known to its inhabitants as Lyon, and from there down along the western banks of the Rhône River to the Mediterranean. He had held that line grimly, sparing neither men nor effort, and denying the Huns access to the lands at his back with their rich fields and ample crops, stores of grain and treasuries of fine wine, until the remnants of the Hunnish invaders had finally been forced to retreat east towards the Alps and the northern borders of Italia in search of food and less determined opposition.

I interpreted that as meaning towards the foothills of the Alps and Lake Genava—in other words, towards Benwick—and I grew impatient to reach my boyhood home again, wondering what troubles, if any, beset it nowadays.

Guntram astonished me by refusing to cross the eastern border of Thorismund's kingdom, at least while he was carrying the king's standard, and he gave me a short lecture on the protocols in force now in Gaul between kingdoms. I had never heard of any of them, and I privately thought they were nonsense. I left him there, on the west bank of the Rhône, where he promised to wait for my return, and made my way onwards, with my small escort, towards Benwick.

4

Although I knew the region surrounding Benwick was inundated with units of Attila's splintered army, I was outraged to find Brach's fortress under siege when we arrived. I took personal exception to seeing King Ban's castle, my boyhood home, under attack, especially when a cursory survey showed that the siege had apparently been going on for several months. I found that incredible at first, for two excellent reasons. The rear of the castle bordered Lake Genava itself, which meant that the castle could therefore be supplied by water, rendering a siege ineffectual. The second reason for my surprise was even more compelling, because I knew that the fortress had a secret subterranean exit known as the King's Caverns, the selfsame feature that had alerted me months earlier to the potential of the ancient tunnels beneath Connlyn's stronghold. During the civil war that swept Benwick after King Ban's death, we had used the mile-long system of caverns to spirit men into and out of the fort beneath the noses of our enemies. The exit from the caverns lay concealed in deep woods, in a small cave formation known as the red-wall caves, just over a mile from the castle walls, and I was curious about why it had not been used.

My confusion on both points evaporated as soon as the scouts I had sent out returned with the word that the Huns were everywhere, and were in fact using the red-wall caves as living quarters. I had no concerns about their finding the secret adit there, because it was impossible to find, built centuries earlier by some long-forgotten engineering genius and completely concealed from anyone who did not know exactly where to look, what to look for and what to do with what was eventually found. As for the other reason, Genava was a lake and not a sea. It was landlocked, and the few ships that plied it could be easily captured, given sufficient time, planning and committed resources. It was evident that the Huns had taken the time and made the effort to overrun the entire lakeside before laying siege to the main defenses. With every ship of any size in enemy hands, there was nothing anyone could do to reprovision the fortress and its garrison.

We had reached the lake on the afternoon of the third day after leaving Guntram by the river, but before we could actually breast the hill ahead of us and come in view of it, Caerfyn and his scouts were back, warning of what they had found. The castle was

completely enclosed by siege works on all landward sides, and
Caerfyn estimated the enemy numbers as being somewhere in the
range of ten thousand men, which was a far smaller number than
any I had heard before in talking of the Huns, but none the less
sufficient to give me pause over advancing with ten troopers and six
scouts at my command. I led them instead to a nearby copse of
trees, where we dismounted and sat down to discuss our next move,
although because we were totally lacking in information, there
really was nothing to discuss. I stripped off my armor and borrowed
a plain, dark green tunic and a cloak from one of the scouts, and
then went forward with Caerfyn to see the situation for myself, and
out there in the forest on the hillsides, moving cautiously and taking
pains not to be seen, we spent the next three hours spying on what
was happening in the valley below.

There was one tiny fishing boat working the edge of the lake,
far to the left of the fortress and so far from us that only the height
of our vantage point allowed us to see it at all. I had no idea who its
single occupant might be, although the ease with which he stood
erect and cast his net suggested he must be a local. Apart from him,
however, we could see no signs of any other vessels on the lake, not
even at the long pier guarded by the castle tower at the rear. And a
more accurate tally of the enemy circling the walls verified that
Caerfyn's initial estimate had been close; the enemy did, in fact,
number close to ten thousand, but not more than that. We still
needed information, but this time it had to be hard facts, and that
meant we would need prisoners to question. We went back to our
temporary little camp, where Caerfyn rallied his men and led them
out to capture some Huns. I was well aware that we would be fortunate to find one to whom we could speak and be understood, and
vice versa, but we had to try, and while I was sitting there, waiting
for the scouts to return and fretting over the language difficulty, I
remembered the fishing boat we had seen earlier and recognized its
potential. Not only was its occupant someone to whom I could talk,
but his vessel offered me a means of reaching the castle and
whoever was besieged in it.

I was immediately plunged into a dilemma over what to do next. The people I needed to go and find the fisherman were the Pendragon scouts, and I had no way of knowing when they would be back. The troopers who remained with me had not seen the fisherman—they had not yet even seen the lake—and so they would not know where to begin looking. I could lead them, but that would mean I would not be here when Caerfyn returned with his prisoners. And yet that could not be helped, for the single certainty in my mind was that the fisherman would not remain afloat much longer, with night approaching. Nor would he meekly row ashore when I hailed him … not with the countryside alive with Huns. I knew I had to find him soon, to watch unseen until he headed ashore, then be there to capture him when he landed. He might not even be from Benwick, might be a Hun himself, but that made no difference, ultimately. He had a boat, and I needed it.

I knew that Caerfyn and his men would have no trouble following our tracks, and so I changed hastily back into my own armor, took eight of my troopers with me and left two behind to wait for Caerfyn and tell him what I was doing, and then I struck directly north towards the lakeshore, hoping that when I crested the hilltop the small boat would still be visible. It was, and we played cat and mouse with its occupant for the next hour, dogging his journey along the shore in absolute silence and making sure to remain out of sight the entire time, while the sun set and the long dusk grew gradually darker. I had cause to be thankful for my caution, because before the fisherman came in to land, he stopped his craft and stood silently for a long time, balancing easily and scanning the reed-grown banks suspiciously, time after time, alert for any sign of movement or danger.

We lay motionless, scarcely breathing as we waited for him to reassure himself and come ashore, and it seemed to take forever for him to make up his mind. I could see him clearly from where I lay behind a clump of rushes, and when he eventually committed to coming ashore and began to row again, I held up my hand, warning my men to wait and do nothing until I gave them the signal. The soft sound of scraping signaled his hull touching the shore, and I waited until he had leapt into the water and hauled his boat up the bank before I gave the signal to take him. The only sound he made was a quavering wail as he disappeared beneath two flying, mail-clad bodies, and mere moments after that I was kneeling over him, my hand cupping his mouth to stifle any noise.

"Are you from Benwick?" His eyes were enormous, staring up at me, but when he heard me speak in his own tongue he nodded his head strongly. I gripped his mouth tighter. "I am, too. If I remove my hand, will you stay quiet?"

That earned another nod, and I released him and sat back just as I heard Caerfyn asking me, "What have you there, then? A boatman, is it?"

Caerfyn spoke in Cambrian, which, judging by our new prisoner's reaction, sounded to him much like Hunnish. He heaved beneath me in a panic and I had to stifle him again, quickly, before he could cry out.

"Listen to me. Listen! My friend here is not a Hun—he merely sounds like one. He is from Britain, across the sea. I am from Benwick. My father was King Ban. King Brach is my cousin. My name is Clothar—Clothar of Ganis. Do you know the name?" That earned me another nod, even stronger than the previous one. I removed my hand. "What do you know of me?"

"I know you. I know your face. I was a shepherd as a boy, and you used to come out to the hillside where I kept the sheep ... you and old Chulderic. He liked it out there and he used to teach you sword fighting. I watched you. Dreamed of fighting like you, with a real sword."

"What's your name?"

"Orik."

It meant nothing to me, but I remembered the place he was describing, because it had been one of Chulderic's favored spots, and I had vague memories of a skinny shepherd boy, with enormous eyes and arms and legs like sticks, who was always around there somewhere, watching what we were doing. This must have been he, with the huge eyes. I nodded briskly, called him by his name and then told him what I required of him: that he row me across the lake to the rear of the castle under cover of darkness. He nodded eagerly, not a trace of hesitation in his bearing, then looked around at the group of my companions.

"Can't take all of they."

"No, Orik, only me. Your boat will hold the two of us, won't it?" He nodded. "Then you will take me out across the water, wait for me while I talk with whoever is commanding in the castle, and bring me back here afterwards to join my companions. And in return for that, I will pay you two gold coins, one now, one when we come back." I handed him the gold *aura* I had been holding and he showed me those great eyes of his again, as well he might. That single coin could have purchased him ten fishing boats, all twice as large as the one he owned, had he but known where to go to find them.

Mere moments later, we were afloat on Lake Genava, the shore a thickening of the darkness on our right, but the guard lights on the castle's walls standing out clearly against the night sky.

There came a nasty moment when, once ashore, we had to shout up to attract the attention of the guards on the walls above us, for they had no way of knowing who we were and we had no means of knowing what they might throw down at us, but God was firmly on our side that night and the first man we contacted, on guard directly above our heads, recognized my name and had ridden with me during the civil disturbance we had called Gunthar's War. With three brief questions, asking me to name people involved in specific events, he established my identity beyond dispute and told me to wait where I was. Some time later, I heard banging and thumping noises, and a postern door swung open, its rusty hinges squeaking loudly, and spilled torchlight out onto the ground ahead of us, and in an unbelievably short space of time I found myself being ushered into the presence of the king himself, my cousin Brach.

Brach was bigger than ever, the largest and tallest man I had ever seen, his muscles huge and awe inspiring yet perfectly proportioned to his overall size. He was a man whom women found fascinating, but because of his sheer size and bulk he had always been shy and awkward in their company, as though afraid that his size alone might hurt them by its presence. He gaped at me now in goggle-eyed stupefaction, which was, I suppose, no more than natural, considering everything involved. The last time he had seen me had been ten years earlier, when I was barely seventeen, and I had changed greatly, but he had not heard a single word from me since that time, and he had not known of my sojourn in Britain. And now here I was, sprung from nowhere, in the middle of a full siege when no one ought to have been able to make their way through to him.

There was no doubting the warmth of his welcome, however, or his pleasure at seeing me again so unexpectedly, and once I had survived the experience of being hugged half to death in his bone-crushing embrace, he and I dispensed with the amenities of small talk and fell quickly to discussing the situation in force here.

Benwick had been under siege from the Hungvari for three months, he told me, originally invested by an army numbering between twenty and thirty thousand men, more than one third of them horsed. They had arrived in Benwick with very little warning, approaching from the far northern side of the lake, and they had then split their forces and made their way around the entire lake, capturing and burning villages and hamlets and confiscating or destroying any vessels they found. Brach had been in the south of Benwick with more than half his army when the Huns arrived at his back, and by the time word of the invasion reached him, it had been too late to permit him to take any effective defensive measures—and almost too late for him to scramble back to the fortress before the invaders cut him off from it. They had barely made it safely across the drawbridge and inside the curtain walls when the enemy arrived through the surrounding forest and spilled out in a hopeless charge as the narrow deck of the bridge was raised ahead of them.

Once safe behind his walls, however, Brach's conscience had swiftly been assuaged with the knowledge that his own counselors had acted quickly on receiving the news of the invasion, and knowing what he would have done, had he been there, they had managed to bring almost all of the people living near the castle into the safety of its walls.

Brach had not realized, at the start of the siege, that all the shipping on the lake had been seized and destroyed, nor had he anticipated that the enemy would settle into the red-wall caves as one of the most convenient camping spots in the region. It was several days, therefore, before he realized that he was, in fact, cut off from assistance, and it had only been by sheerest accident that the scouts he sent out through the King's Caverns had been able to jump back inside the exit and close it again without being discovered by the Huns sleeping in the red-wall caves.

Brach had been forced to turn his mind towards finding other ways to break out of the castle and ride to the caves, knowing that as soon as the Huns there turned out to repel an attack from outside, then a coordinated war party could attack from the caverns and take the enemy from behind. To this point, however, he had not been able to develop a plan that offered any great hope of success. In order to break out from the castle in force, he would have to form up his army in plain view of the enemy and then lower the drawbridge, and the painfully slow nature of those arrangements offered as many opportunities and benefits to the enemy as it did to Benwick.

My arrival, however, made everything look very different. I explained that I had a cavalry force of five hundred highly trained troopers less than two hundred and fifty miles away and that I could have them back, ready for battle, within fifteen days, and although he had no concept of the kind of cavalry force I was talking about, Brach grasped the implications of that quickly. Our plan developed swiftly after that, taking less than two hours to put together because it was essentially simple: I would be gone for approximately fifteen days and would return with my five hundred cavalry and forty scouts armed with Pendragon longbows. We would split our cavalry into two groups as soon as we reached Benwick, four hundred troopers in one group and a hundred in the other. I would retain control of thirty of the forty bowmen, leaving ten to accompany the larger group.

On my return, I would hold my troopers outside Brach's borders until the nineteenth day, since we could not assume that I could actually travel to Carcassonne and back in only fifteen days. The journey might take four or five days longer, depending upon a host of circumstances. If we did manage it in fifteen days, that would be well, and my troopers would appreciate a few days of rest after a hard ride. And so we decided that before dawn on the morning of the twentieth day, Brach would quietly form up his men outside the castle walls, under the protection of massed bowmen on the walls themselves, and have them ready to advance as soon as the bridge was lowered. At the same time, he would also dispatch several hundred of his warriors through the King's Caverns, where they would wait until I opened the exit from the inside of the red-wall cave, something I could only do after the resident Huns had been dispatched.

My four hundred troopers, under Bors, would attack the besieging force outside the castle at the break of dawn, as soon as it was light enough to see, and their arrival would be the signal for the lowering of the drawbridge. Brach's waiting men would cross the bridge, deploy in groups and attack and destroy the siege towers before they could be brought close enough to threaten anything. My remaining hundred, under Perceval, meanwhile would attack the red-wall caves, working in conjunction with me and our Pendragon bowmen, who would function as infiltrators, surrounding the caves and killing from a distance that the enemy could not match. As soon as the caves were cleared of Huns, I would open the secret entrance to the King's Caverns, allowing another contingent of Brach's warriors to set about attacking and harrying the enemy while Perceval and I rode to reinforce the remainder of our force in front of the castle. We anticipated—and I felt confident in our projections—that the enemy would have little stomach for the fight once it became clear that their siege was broken and the defenders had been powerfully reinforced.

I was soon back in Orik's little boat, on my way to rejoin my men before the first pale hints of gray began to lighten the eastern sky. Daybreak found us moving quickly back towards the border of Aquitaine, to where we had left Guntram Redbeard, and from there we rode straight to Carcassonne.

It took us five days, thanks to the wonderful roads in that part of Gaul, and as soon as we arrived back I informed King Thorismund, as a matter of courtesy, about what was happening in Benwick and what I intended to do about it. He immediately offered me a thousand men to back up my cavalry force, and had the offer come from any other source, I would have seized upon it with delight, but I could not overcome my instinctive distrust of the Visigoth, and so I refused his offer, claiming a paramount need for speed that my cavalry could supply but which his slow-moving infantry could not. There was something that made me bite down on my teeth at the mere idea of encouraging the Visigoths, with their enormous territories of Aquitainia, now stretching from the Loire River all the way down into northern Iberia, to visit the tiny kingdom of Benwick.

It took only two days to prepare and provision our force and set out again for Benwick, still accompanied by Guntram Redbeard and the king's standard-bearer for safekeeping, and although our heavy commissary wagons cut down the speed we could maintain—our much smaller party had covered fifty miles each day on the way south from Benwick—we managed none the less to travel upwards of thirty miles each day, largely thanks to the roads and the clemency of the weather, with not a drop of rain or a breath of wind to impede us. We reached the eastern border of Aquitaine exactly when I had predicted we would, fifteen days after leaving the castle, and I asked Guntram to provide us with a camping spot where we could pass the next few days before we had to ride on towards Benwick. We were less than a day's ride from Brach's castle, and had five days remaining before we were to launch our attacks. Three of those we spent profitably, training in safety in Thorismund's land, and we traveled on the fourth day, arriving close to our appointed stations unobserved and settling down, concealed in the forest, to wait for the next day's dawn.

The Huns had been in position around the castle just long enough to become disgruntled and bored. They had grown lax in everything, expecting no opposition of any worth and knowing that there was no possibility of their siege being interrupted. They had absolutely no expectation of being roused from their sleep in the predawn shadows by a thundering charge of cavalry, especially by cavalry that moved in solidly lethal, disciplined blocks of armored horseflesh and riders that nothing could stop. The Huns put up no great fight, and as soon as they realized that the bridge was down and the castle's defenders were sallying out against them and in support of the cavalry, they broke completely and their retreat turned into a rout.

A mile away, the same thing was happening simultaneously in miniature. A hundred horsemen under Perceval, attacking in squads of ten, scattered and rousted the sleepers outside the red-wall caves, the men who had not been fortunate enough to find a place inside. The panic and confusion there, and the ensuing results, were greatly similar to what was happening at Castle Benwick, with one significant difference: my thirty Pendragon bowmen had ensconced themselves where they could best see the exits from the caves themselves, and as the bewildered Huns came rushing out, roused from sleep by the commotion outside, we shot them down without mercy. That activity continued for some time before the emerging stream of men dried up, and then it fell to a team of specialists to enter the caves and finish off anyone left inside. It was quickly done, and by the time the scouts came back out of the caves, wiping their blades clean of the blood they had spilled, Perceval had his troopers lined up in formation, with the welcome tidings that we had not lost a single man in the fracas. I saluted them, then ordered my Pendragons to mount and make ready to ride out again, and we made our way, in a thunderous and stirring drumming of hooves, back to Castle Benwick, where we found the drawbridge down and most of the Hunnish siege engines being disabled and dismantled.

No one made any attempt to pursue the fleeing Huns, for it was obvious there was no need. They had seen the dramatic rescue of their prey and had borne the brunt themselves of the rescuers' discipline and tactics, so they would be in no hurry to return for more of the same. Since the day of battle in Chalons, Attila's was no longer a name to be reckoned with, and his Huns knew they had lost their aura of invincibility. Now they had been beaten again, thoroughly thrashed by cavalry the like of which even they, supposedly the greatest horse-borne conquerors in history, had never seen. They would not be back to Benwick.

5

It was two days after the lifting of the siege before my cousin Brach and I sat down to dine together, and I had spent that entire time watching and admiring the way the king administered and ruled his kingdom, which was far smaller and less imposing than its near neighbor Aquitaine, but none the less large enough to tax the abilities of any ruler. Much of my admiration sprang from my awareness of how little Brach had desired the burden of kingship, for he was a modest and self-effacing man, for all his immense size and strength, and he had wished for nothing more than to live a life of peace and quiet. Destiny had decreed, however, that Brach would be King of Benwick, predeceased by his three brothers, and from the moment of being thrust into the kingship, he had set aside everything else in his life to do what he must do, sacrificing himself completely to duty and responsibility. In return for his selfless dedication, his people treated him with undisguised respect and love. Brach's word was absolute law in Benwick, accepted without question and without constraint, and he had spent the two days after the siege visiting far and wide throughout the northern, central and southern regions of his kingdom, accompanied by me and Perceval and an honor guard of our cavalry, explaining to his people that the siege was lifted and that any further incursions of Huns—or any other would-be invaders—would be aborted before they could succeed.

He had returned to his castle at the end of the second day, in order to look after some affairs that would not wait, but I knew that in two days' time he would ride out again, to show his face to his people in the eastern and western regions of the land. We had eaten well together that night, isolated at a table set apart from all the other attendees, and no one appeared to mind that he and I should wish to be alone, simply to talk between ourselves with no listeners to overhear us or offer commentaries. The main meal had been cleared away, and now drinking was the order of the day and the babble of conversation filling the hall was growing ever louder, verging upon the deafening. Brach and I, each nursing a mug of cool beer that was warming noticeably, were probably the two most abstemious people in the entire hall, since neither of us had ever been great drinkers, and thinking that, I turned to find him looking at me and smiling.

"What? What are you smiling at?"

His smile broadened. "I was remembering the time you and I talked about being married. Neither one of us believed he ever would be … I was afraid I was simply too big for any woman and you simply didn't think any woman could interest you. Do you remember that?"

"Aye, I do, I remember it well. And we were right, were we not?"

He snorted a great laugh and then his face turned sober. "You might have been, Cousin, but I was definitely wrong. I met a woman that same year, not long after you left to return to Auxerre and the Bishop's School up there. I fell in love with her as soon as I spoke to her. She was a clan chief's daughter from the lands abutting our southwestern borders, less than three days' ride from here. Her name was Geneviève and she stood taller than most men I know. I married her soon after meeting her, and she bore me three sons, Michel, Aloysius and Clothar."

"Clothar?"

"Aye, the youngest. He's three now."

"And where are they? Why have I not met them?"

"Because they are with their mother's family, in the far west. You will meet them in a few days, when we go there."

"And your wife, the Lady Geneviève?" I had heard his use of the past tense in speaking of her, and did not want to pry.

His face settled into stillness and he answered me in a matter-of-fact voice that none the less betrayed a great conflict somewhere deep inside him.

"Geneviève died birthing Clothar. Childbed fever, they called it. I have never understood it, for the birth was easy, Geneviève suffered little discomfort—she was a large woman, as you might imagine—and the child was perfect in all ways. Everything seemed to be normal, at first, and they were both doing well; but she grew fevered three days after the delivery. The physicians told me something inside her had turned septic or toxic or some such thing. All I know is, I lost my only love, for no reason that I could see or understand …"

I must have looked as stricken as I felt, because he smiled again and reached out to grasp my arm and comfort me. "It was a time ago, Cousin, and I'm close to being over it, but for a while I was very bitter, railing at God and the foul world he had created. I even tried to hate the boy, but his mother's death had nothing to do with him, poor little brat, and so I soon stopped that.

"But life was empty of meaning for a long time after her death, and strangely enough, it was my duty as the King of Benwick that saved me. We had a crisis about a year after her death, a minor invasion by Outlanders, probably Huns, now that I think about it. I threw myself into that, and never stopped working again at being the king I had never wanted to be. I travel constantly nowadays and sometimes feel I know the name of every living soul in Benwick. But being in the saddle and in armor all the time keeps me fit and strong, and the work gives me purpose … too much purpose, I am sometimes told. That's why the boys live with Geneviève's family nowadays. I am too seldom here and they need their grandmother, a woman's hand to guide them. Michel is seven now, close to eight, Aloysius will soon be six and Clothar, as I said, is three years old." He gazed into the distance for a few moments, then sucked in a great breath and turned to me again.

"And what about you? You never found a woman to love?"

It was my turn to smile and then grow sober. "Aye, Brach, I did … At least, I thought I did. But it was not to be."

"Why not? Can you say?"

"Aye, I can say, and very clearly. She was wed to someone else."

"*Was* wed? You mean when you met her, or later?"

"Later. When I met her, she was a young widow, betrothed to an older man than I. Her name was Elaine and I saved her life. She rewarded me by taking me to her bed. But then she went ahead and married her betrothed. I thought I was in love with her and that my life was over, but only recently, before I returned to Gaul this spring, I realized that although she loves much about me, she loves her husband more, and I discovered that the discovery did not kill me. I realized, truthfully, that I did not really love her in the way that her husband, Jonas, loves her, and that even had she felt differently about me, I would still have had to leave her. That sounds shallow, even in my own ears as I say the words, but it is true, none the less. As much as I love her—and I still do, somewhere down deep in my soul—and for all my jealousy over her husband, I have come to accept that I have no tolerance for the domestic stability she represented to me. The thought of settling down in one place and staying there for twenty years to raise a brood appalls me."

I thought about what I had just said, then shrugged. "I am not proud of that, but I have to acknowledge the truth of it. A wise friend once told me that love is inextricably fraught with responsibility—absolutely entangled in it. I believe that, and I have no fear of responsibility, Brach, but I find that my feelings of responsibility extend to something other than a home and a family. I thrill to the thought of carving out Arthur Pendragon's grand idea of a united Britain, free of invaders, but in all honesty I cannot generate the same kind of enthusiasm for the thought of life as a married man and paterfamilias. It is not for me, and had I been foolish enough to pursue it, I would have made both of us, Elaine and me, miserable."

Again I paused, remembering that, and smiled at the thought. "She has a son called Galahad, and she thinks he may be mine, but she is not sure. The thing that amazes me most about that, however, is that she does not care which of us, Jonas or me, sired the child. She loves us both, and she loves the boy. I had difficulty understanding that at first, but as soon as I accepted it, I felt liberated, and I lost the driving need to see her again."

"So what will you do now? And tell me about this Camulod. You like the king there, I gather."

For the next half hour or so, I talked about Arthur and Camulod and the dream of his great-grandsires for a new Empire, built on the principles of the Roman Republic and based on the island of Britain, and Brach sat rapt, absorbing every word.

"So ... This Arthur and his wife do not even try to have sons? They do not ... cohabit?"

I could tell the word was alien to him but that he did not want to insult me or my friends by using the vulgar terms he would normally have used. I smiled and shrugged my shoulders. "That was true in the beginning, certainly, when there was cause for fear of breeding a son for Symmachus of Chester, the Queen's father, to control if Arthur died young. Now, however, I suspect the problem is one of ability. Arthur may never be able to walk properly again, may never be able to ride again. And he may be less able to mount his wife than to mount a horse. Only time will resolve that ... time and God's own will."

"What will you do, then, if your friend the King dies young? Will you remain in Britain?"

That made me think, because I had not anticipated the question, and I sat nursing my beer for a long time before I answered him.

"No," I said eventually, "I don't think I would do that. I really think that, were Arthur to die before he can consolidate all his work to this point, Camulod would break apart. Not even the fear of the

Saxon invaders could dispel the ambitions of the smaller kings and clan chiefs and replace them with some kind of unity. Arthur Pendragon is the only man with sufficient strength and vision to see to that. Without him, Britain would—it *will*—fall back into its ancient pieces and be overrun by the Outlanders."

"Then where will you go, if you leave Britain?"

I tried to read behind his eyes and divine what he was driving at.

"Well, Cousin," I told him, "I am not spending much time there even now, and Arthur has recently entrusted me with missions of sufficient gravity to ensure that I will not return there soon. My men will return, on duty rotation, but I may not. I have the duty of representing Arthur, and therefore Camulod and all of Britain, here in Gaul. He wants me to set up trading ventures with local kings and regional rulers, to take advantage of the fleet of trading ships he is building in Britain. He also wants me to forge alliances of differing kinds with certain powerful individuals, some of them kings, some clerics. And of course, he wishes me to maintain cordial relations with Corbenic and its cavalry. Most of all, however—and no word of this has ever been said aloud—I suspect he needs the reinforcement I supply here in Gaul, the image I suggest of a kingdom, and a King, strong enough and wealthy enough to maintain a force of cavalry like the one I command, outside of his own domain and purely out of goodwill and support for his friends and allies ... But as I say, that's only my opinion, and be it right or wrong, all of those responsibilities combined should keep me here in Gaul for several years."

"He sounds like a formidable man, your King Arthur."

I laughed. "Oh, he is formidable, Cousin, make no error about that. I have never known his like."

I mulled my thoughts over one last time and then continued. "If I absolutely had to leave Britain someday, and that would only be because of Arthur's death, then I would return to Gaul, to my other regal cousin's kingdom of Corbenic." I saw his eyebrows shoot up in astonishment at my mention of another regal cousin, and I grinned and waved to catch the attention of a passing servitor, ordering fresh mugs of beer before I launched into the story of my father's family in the north and the joint kingdoms of Ganis and Corbenic. By the time I finished, Brach was shaking his head again.

"So this King Pelles of Corbenic is kin of mine, ruling your kingdom of Ganis?"

"Yes and no, to both points. He must be a cousin of some description, but not direct blood kin. That kinship extends only to me, on my father's side. His sole connection to you is through the marriage of my parents. As for his ruling my kingdom, there is no kingdom of Ganis nowadays. Ganis became part of the kingdom of Corbenic, by the will of the people of Ganis after the death of Clodas, the usurper who murdered my parents. Pelles is the king of Corbenic, and therefore, by extension, of Ganis. That pleases me greatly, since I have no wish today to be a king."

"Then come back here if you ever leave Britain. If you are still young when that happens, we will have a use for you as a soldier. If you are no longer young, we will still have a use for you as a counselor, and in either event you will have a home here—with a family of nephews, a fine house to live in and sufficient lands of your own to sustain you and yours." He raised one eyebrow and gazed at me resolutely. "I mean what I say, Clothar."

"I know you do, Brach, and I thank you for your kindness, but—"

"No buts, Cousin. You have always served Benwick well, unselfishly and better than you needed to. The invitation is made, and it will stand, because I will have my clerks register my wish and my command in writing, in such a way that it will remain binding upon my sons in the event of my death. If ever the time comes when you want to come home here, to Benwick, there will be a place waiting for you."

I thanked him again and respected his wishes, offering no more provisos, and we moved on to talk of other things, none of which I can remember now. But I have never forgotten that earlier conversation and the rush of affection it stirred in me for the giant king who was my first cousin.

I stayed in Benwick for a month, and before I left I wrote a complete report of the attack by Attila's Huns and the means by which we had raised the siege and freed the garrison. I could not send the report until I returned to the northwest and found a ship that would carry it, but at least the events were accurately recorded and so would not be exaggerated or warped beyond recognition by the passage of time and the vagaries of memory.

We returned after that to Carcassonne, to ensure that everything we had arranged with King Thorismund was still in place and being acted upon, and we discovered that it was, even though the king himself was not in residence there. We struck out northwards after that, following the great trunk road that led to Orleans and the Loire crossing, and from there we traveled on to Corbenic by way of the main crossing of the River Seine at Lutetia, where we discovered that the town's name had been formally changed to Paris by the local people, who called themselves the Parisians. A few days after that, we were back in Corbenic, where Pelles declared a festival to welcome our return, and his sister Serena arranged a smaller, more personal and far less public one to welcome mine.

One week later, to the day, a bright, new-made ship arrived from Britain, its timbers not yet discolored by wind, weather and sea salt. It carried a cargo of ingots of tin and lead and, to my astonishment, a large number of bolts of soft, beautifully woven and brightly colored wool that I recognized as having come from Connor Mac Athol's homeland in the far north. I did not know the man who captained the vessel, but he introduced himself to me and delivered a pair of heavy leather saddlebags, stuffed with dispatches and reports for my attention. I carried them to my work quarters, where I emptied them out onto a table and separated them into piles that could be attended to by others. For myself, I kept three letters from Merlyn and two from Arthur, none of which was very thick or heavy.

The tidings from Camulod were sparse, and I was concerned to note that Merlyn's handwriting was degenerating rapidly, his script often thin and wavering, his point wandering frequently from the normally straight path of his incisive, emphatic fist. He wrote that the King was recovering visibly and steadily but too slowly for Merlyn's peace of mind. He had spoken of it with the Queen, and Gwinnifer agreed, but pointed out that there was nothing they could do but put their joint trust in God and await the outcome. Arthur was walking better nowadays, although not yet perfectly, and he continued to exercise regularly with his weapons, building up his muscles again and increasing his stamina, but as with everything else, his progress was slower and less dramatic than at any time earlier in his life and although he could ride a little, he was nowhere close to being able to ride out and command an army again. In the meantime, Merlyn wrote, the knights were surpassing all expectations anyone, including the King himself, had ever had of them. Among them, Bedwyr, Tristan, Gwin, Pelinore, Gareth and Balan were keeping the kingdom operating as an entity. I made a note, reading that, to pass that word along to Perceval, Bors, Sagramore and the others here. They would be proud of their brethren and the work they were doing.

Arthur's first letter was short and rambling, and in reading it I received a strong impression that he was not saying what he wanted to say, and in consequence was saying nothing of any value, other than admitting that he thought sufficiently highly of me to take the time to write to me at all. His second missive, however, was greatly different. In it, he wrote to me as his friend, baring his heart and asking for my understanding of the difficulties he was suffering in his relations with his wife. His groin wound caused him constant and unrelenting pain and had rendered him impotent for many months, which was only to be expected, and he had been warned by his physicians and surgeons that he might be adversely affected in that manner for even longer than he had already been. But then his body had attempted to function normally again, and the agonies he suffered during arousal were unbearable, to the point at which his body had shut down any sexual urges he might feel. Gwinnifer, he said, professed to understand and sympathize with him, but he was suffering greatly from guilt, and was finding it difficult to spend time in her company, so great was his embarrassment over his own condition.

Reading that letter, and knowing my friend as I did, I could see that Arthur's wounds had affected his mind as well as his body, and it was plain to me that, no matter how chronically painful and unbearable his injuries might be, the agonies he suffered in his mind must dwarf them all, for Arthur Pendragon was not the kind of man to let anyone see him as less than he could possibly be. The notion of being too weak to support even the illusion of looking strong must be destroying him.

I wrote back to him immediately, requesting that he transfer me back to duty in Camulod, where I could at least support him by acting on his behalf and in his name in the performance of his duties.

The next ship to arrive, three months later, carried another letter from him, reminding me of what I had promised to do on his behalf over here in Gaul. He was improving rapidly now, he wrote, and was riding regularly. The wound in his groin still caused him constant pain, but the intensity of the pain seemed to be diminishing gradually, and he no longer limped. He made no mention of his other problems, and I wondered if there had been any improvement there, but I could hardly write back and ask him about it bluntly. I was happy to note, however, that Merlyn confirmed in his single report on that occasion that the King really was doing well, riding regularly and walking without limping.

I fell into a routine, then, of riding all over the northern part of Gaul, establishing relationships and even, in some instances, alliances between local kings and Corbenic, and sometimes even Britain, as well as continuing to coordinate the various trading activities now in place between Connor's fleet and the ports his ships frequented, and I found myself growing familiar with the wines of the different regions, some of them reportedly excellent, others less so, and all of them repulsive to me. I found myself, too, becoming something of an authority on the various tradable commodities available in different towns and regions, including westerly regions and coastal areas of Aquitaine. And all of the time I wrote meticulous reports on my findings and sent them back to Camulod, where they were evaluated by Arthur's army of scribes and clerks.

Perceval made his way back to Camulod eventually, but returned to Gaul, his real home, within the year, filled with information that I drained from him like a thirsty man. Bors, too, went and came back, but Sagramore went home and remained there. My squire Rufus completed his time with me and I was happy to send him back on a returning ship for the annual knighthood celebration, for he had fully earned the honor of his advancement to the ranks of the order. He was posted to Cambria, to Gwin's command, for his probationary year after being raised.

Serena grew plumper, and eventually fat, and although the sexual passion between the two of us declined as such things always do, it did so at an equal rate on either side and our friendship prospered. Arthur continued to improve, and I received a memorable letter from Queen Gwinnifer herself advising me that he was fully restored to physical health and strength and was now as formidable as he had ever been. I remember that the pleasure I felt at reading that, in a letter written personally to me by the Queen herself, was alloyed with the pessimistic thought that he had taken three full years and more to recover, and that should he suffer anything close to such a wound again, it might be the end of him. Still I remained in Gaul, tied by duty and achieving tangible results, but pining to see Camulod again.

Catalina, mother to Pelles and his two sisters, Serena and Lena, died quietly in her sleep one night in the fourth winter that passed, and my friend Quintus Milo, now supreme commander of Pelles's cavalry, developed a lung congestion that same winter and died within three days.

Word came from Merlyn in the spring of the following year that his old friend Connor Mac Athol, once admiral of the western seas, had drowned when his galley was driven onto a shoal of rocks in a violent storm. Several of his crew had survived, but Connor, hampered by his wooden leg, had sunk quickly and been dashed against the rocks. That news saddened me greatly, for although I had never known Connor well, I had heard about his exploits for years. In a clan of remarkable men, he had been outstanding in every respect. To this day I do not know if the two events were connected in any way, but I never received another letter from Merlyn after Connor's death.

And then suddenly, almost without my being aware of it, seven years had gone by and I received an urgent summons from the King himself, calling me back to Camulod. I had not heard a word from Merlyn in more than three years, and when I saw the King's summons I realized just how completely ignorant I had become of what was happening in Britain. I made my farewells to Pelles and handed over my command to Perceval, leaving Bors as his second-in-command, and sailed back to Britain on the returning ship.

FOURTEEN

1

"Well, are you not going to respond at all?"

The King, haggard beyond belief when I had first set eyes on him again after our seven-year separation, now sat across from me, his right leg propped up on a footstool for comfort, his upper body slouched forward to allow him to clutch his right elbow loosely with his left hand, resting the weight of both arms on his raised right knee. He was peering directly at me from close range, his eyes narrowed to slits and his focus shifting slightly as his gaze moved from one of my eyes to the other, and I was amazed to realize that, even after he had just unburdened himself of an appalling litany of woes and tribulations, a half smile played about his lips. Now he was waiting for an answer from me, and I had none to give him, because I had not yet grasped the full significance of what he had been saying to me. I shook my head, slowly, to win myself some time to think.

"Oh, I'll respond. I will respond, be sure ... but not before I get my wind back. May I think for a few more moments?"

"For as long as you wish."

My mind was in turmoil. He had summoned me to join him in the Villa Britannicus immediately upon my return to the hilltop fortress, and I had barely taken the time to instruct my new squire, a Frankish boy called Lanfranc, in where to find my quarters and stow my equipment, before I rode down to report to the King in the villa below Camulod's hill. When I came face to face with him,

however, the mere sight of him had driven the air from my chest. He
was gaunt, his face close to cadaverous in its deep-lined pallor, and
yet his posture was flawless, his back straight and his head held
high. He had walked right to me and embraced me in a hug that
showed me even more graphically than his face had that my beloved
friend and King was far from being the powerful monarch I remembered, and yet his hair was still rich and thick, its deep brown locks
layered with lighter golden streaks, and his yellow, gold-flecked
eyes were no less vibrant than they had ever been. Only when he
moved could I begin to discern the cause of his ailment. He moved
haltingly, holding himself relentlessly upright yet giving the indelible impression that he was upon the point of cringing and folding in
upon himself, crossing his knees in agony. That was merely an
impression, as I have said, but it was a powerful one.

I had referred to his old wound, looking down at his groin and
asking him how much it still troubled him, but he had no intention of
wasting time discussing something that was immutable. He had
waved away my question with a stock answer that was clearly delivered by rote, then dismissed everyone else in the room with instructions that he was not to be disturbed, for any reason whatsoever, until
he and I had finished our deliberations. That done, he had brought me
up to date immediately, with a complete and realistic overview of
what was happening, both militarily and politically, here in Camulod
and elsewhere throughout Britain. I sought to ask questions of him at
the start of things, but he had no patience for questions that sprang
from ignorance. He told me bluntly to be quiet and listen, and to
absorb everything he had to tell me. Once I had done that, he said, the
questions currently in my mind would all have been answered, and I
would have other, more important questions to ask.

And so he talked on, for nigh on a full hour, and I listened
without interrupting. He had come well prepared for this presentation, too, for he had known months in advance that it was coming
and he had assembled evidence to back him up in everything he
said, particularly in those areas where I might have sought to
dispute his findings. He had left no room for disputation. His argu-

ments were crisp and concise, his findings were thoroughly researched and backed by written reports, and, above all, the logic of what he was telling me was incontestable.

It was the content that was unacceptable. The cumulative effect of all that he was telling me left me stunned, my mind reeling and my senses unable to absorb the series of disasters he was foretelling.

I was painfully aware of his eyes watching me, and I was in no hurry to return his gaze. The forefront of my mind was filling up with trivial questions and queries, too, all of them dreamed up to offer me a way of avoiding the confrontation that I knew to be inevitable. Where was Merlyn? Why was he not here? Where was the Queen? I had not seen a single sign of her since my arrival. And where were my fellow knights?

Finally I sat back and crossed my arms on my chest, acutely aware that he was waiting for me to say something. "You've just finished telling me that it's all over, here in Britain, that Camulod cannot stand up to the forces that are being brought against it, that you are beset on every side by treachery and jealous rivals and that you yourself are soon to die. And you want me to add something— some kind of commentary—to that?"

His tiny smile grew wider before dying away.

"No, Lance, that is not quite what I've been telling you. The situation here in Britain is fluid, and it will never be 'all over,' as you put it, for as long as people live here. It will change greatly, however, because the entire world is changing greatly nowadays, since the collapse of Rome. And at this moment, as destiny would have it, the forces aligned against us—meaning against me and my grand designs—are greater than any I can rally in response. Yet that may change, too. Mordred has the potential to change everything, if he can but manage to stay alive. He has grown into a real Pendragon since you last saw him. He will soon be twenty, and he joined the brotherhood of the order last year."

"Seur Mordred. It has a solid ring to it."

"Aye, it does. But my son is more of a hothead than I ever was. Less disciplined in some ways, more rigorous in others, perhaps the

influence of his mother's blood. Mordred does not enjoy being
jostled by anyone and has been involved in several challenges
within the past year."

"Challenges? You mean with steel?"

"No, he is not that rash. He knows the penalty for that too well
to challenge my authority in that matter. His fighting has been
confined to legal weapons … practice swords … legal but no less
lethal. He has thrashed three opponents severely, out of four challenges." Arthur shrugged. "They were but young hotheads like
himself, not a one of them yet exposed to the realities of warfare.
There's nothing like feeling real terror and spilling real blood and
seeing your friends butchered in front of you to make you realize
there are better ways to spend your time than fighting, eh?"

"What about the fourth challenger? What happened to him?"

"He beat Mordred severely enough to put him in sick bay for a
handful of days. Taught him a valuable lesson. Mordred had been
picking several fights a week, some of them serious, some less so,
but after he came to see that he was not invincible, despite being my
son, he changed his ways, became more circumspect in his dealings
with others … Best thing that could have happened to him. Now he
and Lionel, the fellow who thrashed him, are inseparable and will
probably remain lifelong friends."

"That pleases me," I said. "I have known some close and enduring friendships grown from ill beginnings. Tell me, then, about
these forces you claim are being brought against you. You said you
are beset on every side by treachery and jealous rivals."

He shook his head, gainsaying me again. "No, I said I was beset
on all sides, referring to the increasing pressure of the Outlanders
who appear to be swarming into Britain from beyond the seas to the
east, along the Saxon Shores. They never stop coming, Lance, and
because they control the entire eastern coast and we have no ships,
we are denied access to their landing beaches and so can do nothing
to prevent them from landing.

"They've always been coming here, you know. That's why the
eastern coast is known as the Saxon Shores. But the Saxon Shores

have now become the Saxon Lands, and no one knows today how far inward they stretch from the sea. The Outlanders are everywhere today, Lance, swarming the length and breadth of Britain, with the exception only of these lands here, the lands we hold and rule in conjunction with our allies.

"They call me the Riothamus, but if I am High King at all, it is only High King of southwest Britain, and to believe anything other than that is sheer folly. Believe me, for I know the truth of this from a host of traveling priests, were you to draw a line straight south from Hadrian's Wall through the middle of this land today, you would find that the entire area east of that line is occupied by the people we call Outlanders, and that they have spilled over the divide and now occupy much of the land on this side of the line, too, most particularly in the northwest. I think it is safe for us to assume that the entire region south of the Wall, from coast to coast and as far south as Chester, is now occupied by what we think of as the enemy."

I felt my eyes grow wide. "What does that mean, 'we think of as the enemy'? Do you doubt that they're the enemy?"

"No, I do not. But neither do I believe that they are all godless savages like your Attila and his Huns. Certainly there are savages among them, men I would kill on sight and think nothing of the blood I spilled, but there are others, and far more numerous, who are simply people looking for a place to live and rear decent crops with which to feed their families. The Anglians are the most evident of those. Anglians have been living here in Britain for a hundred years and more, and many of them are Christians. Merlyn befriended some of them, as did your friend and mentor Bishop Germanus. I have met some of them myself, and so have you.

"Einar of Colchester is one, and you met him when he brought his daughter here, long years ago, seeking alliance through marriage. Einar is an Anglian, and therefore, strictly speaking, an Outlander, but he is as British as I am, born and raised here, as were his parents, and Anglian or not, he is a fine man and a staunch and loyal friend. He is also strong enough in his own right to hold a kingdom intact and secure in territories that no Briton from our part of the world has visited in half a hundred years. I find hope in that, Lance, in the fact that Einar and I know and respect each other as men and kings and allies, and as friends. He has great influence among his own people, and the Anglians, combined, are far more numerous in Britain than all the other races of Outlanders combined. I believe that Einar and I, working together, could forge a treaty that would permit us, Britons and Anglians, to live together side by side in amity from this time on. I have discussed the matter with him, and we are of like mind, seeing such a treaty as the only peaceful solution to the problems besetting all of us."

I sat open mouthed. "You mean you would forge an alliance with *all* the Anglians and simply give them more than half the country?"

His brows knitted in perplexity. "What country would I be giving them, Lance? We are the ones in peril here. They already hold more than half the country. It's theirs, by right of conquest and occupation, and much of it has been theirs for these past hundred years, since before Caius Britannicus and Publius Varrus founded Camulod. I am merely trying to salvage something for my Britons and their children, attempting to convert the Anglians from victorious enemies to cooperative neighbors.

"Einar is working now—and working hard—to convince his fellow Anglian kings to join with him and subscribe to our ideas, but it is a difficult concept to sell to men who think of us as implacable foes. Nevertheless, he is optimistic that an accommodation can be reached, and if he is correct, and we can achieve alliance, then our combined forces would be strong enough to compel the other Outlander races to make peace and live in amity with us, or quit our shores once and for all."

He drew a deep breath. "But, as I say, the process is slow, and I cannot take part in it. The men Einar is trying to convince to join us have believed for years that I am evil incarnate. And in the meantime, I have Danes breathing down my neck from the northeast and marauding Saxons and Ersemen raiding my shores from the west. That is something I am going to have to deal with very quickly, I fear."

He snorted a laugh that was half amused and half bitter. "And of course, my old enemy in Chester, Symmachus, is thriving. The latest I have heard, in tidings that arrived two months ago, is that he is back at his old tricks, forging alliances with alien Outlanders and apparently promising them all the wealth of Camulod if they will join his campaign to stamp us out. That was the treachery to which I referred. The jealousy is far less serious and I have been aware of it for years. Two kings, both known to you, sworn enemies of mine since I rejected their daughters all those years ago. There's Lachlan from northern Cambria, and Annar of Mann. Both of them are ungracious malcontents, petty louts who are really not worthy of consideration but who have always believed the world should be indebted to them."

"And what about this belief that you yourself are soon to die? What kind of nonsense is that? Of all the people I know, Arthur, you are the very last one I would ever expect to bleat such weak-kneed, self-pitying tripe, so I hope you have some convincing theory to back it up."

Instead of answering, Arthur rose to his feet and walked away to stand peering closely at the colored glass in the magnificent window that brightened the entire room. He reached out then and touched it gently, running his fingertips across the smooth, uneven, translucent surface, and the bright afternoon sun beyond painted him in blotches of bright color, splashing its light across his standing form.

"Do you know the story of this window?" He continued without waiting for an answer. "This room was called the Family Room, the most important room in the whole villa when Publius Varrus and his wife, Luceiia Britannicus Varrus, lived here. It was Luceiia who decided that she wanted more light in here, since she and her family spent most of their time together in this room. So she had this window made, at great expense, to let in the light and keep out the weather, and she knocked a hole in the wall to accommodate it … Her brother and her husband, both dead far longer than she, were the dreamers who founded Camulod, and her grandson was Uther

Pendragon, my father. Luceiia Britannicus has been dead for decades, forgotten by all but Merlyn, who knew her personally, and by those of her family who have been told the tales of her wondrous beauty and great strength."

He turned back to face me, slowly, his face now melancholy. "We all die, Lance. That is the one inescapable cost of being born. We all die. But that is why I summoned you home. I have one last task for you to do, my friend, one final duty to impose upon you."

I felt a deep chill settle into the pit of my stomach and I had to swallow hard to quell a wave of nausea, and I had a sudden, absolute conviction that he himself believed he was about to die. In consequence, I spoke more flippantly, perhaps, than I had intended to.

"There was a lot of terminality in that last statement. Far too much for my liking."

He moved back to his chair and settled himself comfortably before he responded. "And far too much for mine, Seur Clothar. We are as one in that. But there are times in life, and this is one of them, when we must simply accept that certain things exist and have to be accommodated, no matter how much we may dislike them."

I waited then, and when I saw that he would say no more, I nodded. "What would you have of me, my lord King?"

He smiled at me again, that same sad, secret smile that I had seen him use several times during this interview. "Something that I have always had from you in addition to loyalty, honor and integrity, but a thing which I think you may find difficult to accord to me this time."

"Try me, my lord. What would that be?"

"Unquestioning obedience."

Again, in the mere tone of his voice, in the flat, uninflected way he pronounced the words, I sensed a knell, and a rush of gooseflesh stirred the hairs on my arms and on the nape of my neck, so that I had to fight down the physical urge to shiver. "And when have I ever refused you that, my lord?"

"You never have. I merely said I think you might, this time."

"Then you are wrong."

His lips quirked again in the ghost of a smile. "I remember you now, from bygone days. You are the fellow who never learned how to speak to a king civilly and without contradicting him. I never did have you flogged for insolence, did I? You might have been a good man and a noble knight had you ever learned the proper deference and humility to show to your reigning lord. A touch of humility here and there, a bit of groveling, even a hint of sycophancy might have stood you in good stead over the years ... But then again, I tend to forget that you are an Outlander, too, with heathen ways and a foreign tongue, and each time I remember, I elect to show leniency because of it."

I stood up while he was still talking and walked to where Excalibur stood propped in a corner of the room. I picked it up, enjoying the weight and feel of it, and drew the magnificent blade from its sheath, watching the way the light beams flickered and danced along its shimmering length, and then I turned and faced him and held the extended point towards him as he finished what he was saying, aware that I was the only person in all of Camulod who would dare to bare a blade in the King's presence, let alone to point one at him.

"Aye, right," I responded as he fell silent. "I should have spent more time kissing your regal arse. We've had this talk before, many times, my lord, but you are simply going to have to come to terms with the fact that I have never liked you and that I tolerate you only because I was ordered to tolerate you when I first came to your cold, rainy domain." I turned away from his grin and slipped the sword back into its sheath, then replaced it in the corner. "Now tell me, if you will, why I am going to disobey you for the first time in my life."

His laugh was a loud, short bark, reminiscent of the Arthur I had known years earlier. "God, Lance! I wish I had five hundred more like you. We would sweep this country clean of all the ills that plague it. I want you to take the Queen to Gaul with you, to your cousin Pelles's place in Corbenic, and hold her there in safety until it is safe for her to return, although I doubt that time will ever come."

Of all the things he might have said to me, that was the last I could ever have anticipated hearing. Not the part about taking the Queen away, for that I could understand and, to a degree, concur with, but the last part of what he had said, about doubting that it would ever be safe for her to return to Britain, simply scooped the breath from my lungs and left me incapable of speech. I turned abruptly on my heel and stalked away from him, aware of the loud sounds of my booted feet on the wooden floor.

"I can't do that, Arthur!"

"There, you see? I was right."

"No, damn it, you were not right, but this is simply too much."

"How so? D'you not believe she will be safer in Gaul than she will be here?"

"Of course she will, if you go to war as you think you will. But what is too much to accept is your evident belief that she—and therefore I—will never be able to come back. Does Gwinnifer have any notion of what you are planning for her?"

"Of course she has. We have talked of it many times. She was adamant at first, refusing even to address the possibility, but then she began to see the logic of what I was suggesting, and from being adamant, she went to being merely reluctant."

"So how did you change her mind?"

He quirked his lips and tipped his head drolly to one side. "By reminding her of how much she loves her father, Symmachus, and would enjoy the prospect of being reunited with him, particularly if he and his nasty friends had the good fortune to kill me or capture me. That, plus a grudging admission that I myself would be safer and more effective in war knowing that she was far away and in no danger, finally convinced her to agree to my suggestions. But I enjoin you, on your honor, to say nothing to her of the possibility of her being unable to come back here. That would undo everything."

I wanted to scream at him, to vomit out all the frustration caused by seeing him, Britain's paragon and paladin, talking so calmly and

acceptingly of defeat and death at the hands of enemies for whom
he had always had soaring disdain. I had never known, had never
suspected, that he might be capable of such passivity, and yet even
as I thought those things, I knew that he was being pragmatic and
realistically trying to do what was best for Gwinnifer.

"Arthur," I said, hearing the near despair in my own voice,
"answer me this: what's the real reason underlying all this
pessimism? In all the years we've known each other, I have never
known you to be so negative. Why are you doing this?"

"Because I know I am soon to die, my friend. I do not *think* it,
Lance, I *know* it. That knowledge, once accepted, tends to alter a
man's viewpoint." He smiled at the stricken look on my face and
shook his head gently. "As I said a moment ago, we all die."

I attempted to answer him, but the anguish in my throat
prevented me from saying anything on the first attempt. I coughed
savagely to clear my throat and then responded, "Aye, we all die,
Arthur, but in the course of time, and the bishops tell us we can
never know when our time will come. You're telling me you do
know. How can that be?"

"Ah, Lance. Because I know. I have lived inside this body for
years enough to know when it is failing me. I walk without limping
nowadays and fortunately, albeit mysteriously, I ride more easily
than I walk, but too much of my life today is given to the appearance of being well and strong and healthy. Were I to acknowledge
the constant pain that wracks me, or betray how I really feel most
of the time, the effect upon my men, from garrison troops and horse
troopers to Knights Companion, would be disastrous. The ancient
laws of our people decree that a king must be physically flawless
and unimpaired in order to remain in power. I am badly flawed
nowadays and deeply impaired, and I dare not show it, Lance, not
to anyone. But setting all pretense aside, just between you and me,
I live in constant pain from my wound. It never leaves me, not even
in the night, when I should be shielded by sleep. I walk in public
without limping and I hold my head high, but in truth I want to
scream and sag to my knees after only a few steps. I simply do not

dare to show weakness, and it is becoming more and more difficult every day to keep up the pretense. It has been close to eight years now since I took that spear thrust. The skin is whole, and the scar is faded, but the damage done inside will never heal …

"And Gwinnifer has suffered more than me, in some ways. She is a passionate young woman, with strong and natural desires that I am now incapable of servicing. I have not been a husband to my wife in more than seven years, and even before that, I gave her little to remember, thanks to our determination to avoid having a son for Symmachus to control and corrupt.

"Quite apart from that, however, I can feel myself growing weaker with each month that passes. That began about a year ago. Until then, I had been … coping, sufficiently at least to look the king I was supposed to be. But last winter I sickened with a congestion, and I have never been able to regain full health since then."

He stood up again and returned to the window, where he resumed his examination of the glass and spoke to me over his shoulder. "Recently, as I told you earlier, I have begun receiving reports that Symmachus is preparing to move against us. Word is that he has learned of what I plan to do with Einar and the Anglians, and he intends to put a stop to it." He turned to face me, leaning his back against the wall beside the window and crossing his arms on his chest. "He still has his ten thousand men, apparently, and he has allied himself with the Erse king Cyngal, from the south coast of Eire, who has a large fleet of galleys and the warriors to man them. He has also induced Annar of Mann Isle and Lachlan of Snowdonia to join him—no great difficulty there—along with a few other petty brigand kings who share a hunger for Camulod's wealth, and he is inflaming all of them with stories of how I am betraying Britain to the Anglian Outlanders. They believe him, of course, because they are too stupid to doubt him. But one of these fine days, sooner rather than later, they will come calling on us, seeking to test our mettle. When they do, I will be forced to fight—I mean in person—and my weakness will quickly become visible."

He turned away, peering into the translucent glass of the window as if he could see through it. "My two remaining sources of hope are that Mordred will emerge as a strong leader in time to take my place, and that Einar will succeed in bringing the Anglians to treat with us before the hammer falls. In the meantime, however, I require you to see to my Queen for me."

"In God's name, Arthur, think about what you are doing ... and think of what people will say."

He spun to face me, his face tight with anger. "Why should I care what people say? And why would you think I have not already thought, deeply and painfully, about what I am doing in putting my wife away while I am still alive and filled with love for her? People will say what they wish to say, Clothar, irrespective of truth or untruth. They might well say she ran away with you, or that you abducted her. Who will remember, or even care, once we are all dead? Let them think what they will and say what they wish. I want to know my Queen, my wife, my love, is safe from harm—the harm that will surely come to Camulod within the next few months—for when I die, however I die, she will have no life ahead of her here, other than to exist as her father's chattel or as the concubine of some foul-smelling, beer-swilling pig like Lachlan of Snowdonia.

"In Gaul with you, on the other hand, she will live in sunshine, and she will be happy there ... happier than she ever could be here. She is still a young woman, short of her prime. Twenty-six years old, by her own estimation. Plenty of time ahead of her to bear children and raise a family, Lance, once I am gone. I tell you true, I could not wish her any greater joy than to entrust her to your care, for you and she are the two people I love most in all this world." He held up his open palm towards me. "I know! You do not wish to hear any of this. Let me enclose it, then, in better terms. If all goes as I hope it might go, I shall send for you, for both of you, to come home again within the year. Will you accept my word on that?"

"Of course I will. And this is what you would have me do, this is how you believe I can best serve you?"

He hesitated for one fraction of a heartbeat, and then nodded. "It is."

In that moment, seeing that slight hesitation and then the emphatic nod of his head, I knew that there was nothing I would not do for this man or for his lady Gwinnifer, and that I would do whatever I did out of sheerest love, accepting full responsibility for that love in the manner this man himself had led me to expect and accept so long ago.

He saw me nod in acknowledgment, and slapped his hands together. "Excellent," he said, beaming with delight. "So be it."

"What about my men, Arthur, the men currently in Gaul? When will you bring them back?"

"As soon as I can, Lance. But Connor is dead, and I know not who serves as admiral now in his place. If we yet have friends there in the north, then the trading ventures will continue and we can begin the evacuations with the next fleet..."

"But?"

"But the word I hear now is that the Scots have started moving from their islands onto the mainland and they are having to fight every inch of the way. But they now have all the armor and weapons that they needed at the start, and so they have little incentive to trade as heavily with Gaul as they did in the past."

"You believe that?"

"Not fully, no. But it's probably partly true. They will keep trading, though."

"Good, and as long as they do, we will keep sending men and horses home, even if we have to do it one squadron at a time. Some of our troopers might prefer to remain in Gaul—the married ones— but it would be unforgivable to strand the others there."

"It would, I agree, as long as they yet have a home here to return to." He looked at me, his instinct as keen as it had ever been. "There's something chafing at you. Come on, spit it out and let's look at it."

I nodded. "Where is Merlyn, Arthur? I have not seen him or heard from him in several years. Is he alive?"

"Aye, he's alive, but I can't tell you where he is, for I don't know. He is seldom seen nowadays, for his condition is far advanced and he shuns the company of people. But he has much to keep him occupied ... or so he tells me. He is transcribing, or arranging, some very old writings by my own ancestors—journals compiled by Publius Varrus and Caius Britannicus. At least he was when I saw him last, about four months ago. But yes, he is very much alive and as unpredictable as he ever was. He could appear here at any time, so don't be surprised if he simply materializes one day and demands to talk with you. Now let us go and visit the Queen. She did not wish to be present when I was burdening you with the task of looking after her, and she will be happy to know that you have accepted the task."

"I have one more question before we do that."

"Ask away."

"When will we leave?"

"Whenever you wish."

"I don't wish, Arthur, not at all, I have no slightest desire to go anywhere, but I need to know *your* wishes in this. If you have no particular time in mind, that will suit me to perfection. Can we stay here, think you, until war actually breaks out?"

"Of course you can, but you would then have to be prepared to leave between any given moment and the next, and that might be subjecting you and your mission to more risk than would be wise."

"True, but it might never happen at all ... the war, I mean."

"I know what you mean. But I think we would be foolish to live in hope of that. Symmachus is eager to confront me face to face. The war is coming, Lance, and I want you two safely away from here before it breaks. Now, let's go and talk to Gwinnifer."

2

For the next two months, Camulod seemed under an enchantment, even while everyone was training openly for war. The weather was unusually clement and warm, and there were no disturbances or raids in any of our territories to disrupt the peace. Arthur, in commemoration of the War Games that Pelles had held to such grand effect in Corbenic years earlier, organized a similar event in Camulod, with great, serious and highly skilled competition among the Knights Companion themselves and among the various outlying garrisons, as well as the troopers from the different army groups. Gwinnifer was the Queen of the Festival, and she and her ladies took turns in awarding prizes, gifts and honors to the victorious participants. Everyone who was fit enough to attend was there for the festivities, and many of the Knights Companion, thanks to their magnificent armor, swords and accoutrements, and the skills they showed in using all of them, distinguished themselves in the eyes of the spectators sufficiently to make their names well known to the ordinary people. The names of Sagramore, Bedwyr, Tristan, Lionel—he who had thrashed Arthur's son and heir and made him a friend for life— along with Gareth, Mordred and Gwin now became as familiar to the common populace as were those of Arthur and Merlyn.

Then, ten days after the conclusion of the Games, a report reached us that one of our northernmost outposts, manned and garrisoned by our faithful Seur Pelinore, one of the King's oldest friends and a king in Cambria in his own right, had been overrun and wiped out in a surprise dawn attack by a horde of assailants from the north and west. Pelinore had been killed in the fighting, and the survivors had surrendered but been slaughtered out of hand. Four men, all of them wounded, escaped the massacre and made their way homewards together to Camulod. Two of them died on the road, but two won home, and one of those, a veteran of Ghilleadh's campaign, swore under oath that the leader of the raid had worn the armor and insignia of Symmachus of Chester—a Roman corselet emblazoned with the double X of the Twentieth Legion, which had built the fortress of Chester and garrisoned it thereafter for three hundred years.

Two days later, amid chaos and confusion on all sides as Camulod prepared for all-out war, we quietly bade farewell to Arthur and our other friends, and I led his Queen and mine away from the place I had come to love most in this world. Gwinnifer brought no ladies with her. She and I rode off alone towards Glevum, where a vessel waited to carry us to Gaul. I wore only a plain wool tunic and a traveling cloak, and we traveled in a single two-wheeled cart driven by our only companion, my squire Lanfranc. In the cart, beneath our bodies, were all of Gwinnifer's worldly possessions and my own, including my armor, my weapons and a superb saddle and bridle that had been a parting gift from Arthur.

No one seemed to take any notice of our departure, and that was as it should be, since the entire operation had been planned months earlier, and the ship had been moored in Glevum since that time. I had, of course, said goodbye to Arthur the previous night, at a dinner shared by my old companions from the first knighthood ceremony, and Gwinnifer had spent the remainder of the night making her own farewells to him, but even as we slipped away in the morning mist, neither of us truly believed, even in the depths of our souls, that we would never see him again. It was not that kind of parting, somehow, and we both departed believing that this would be a temporary separation and that we would return within the year, once everything had settled down again.

To my great surprise and delight, Merlyn was waiting for us when we reached Glevum, his somber, black-clad figure unmistakable even from a great distance. He did not have much to say, and I noticed when he did speak that his voice was rough and indistinct, as though his tongue had swollen to overfill his mouth, but he spoke slowly, and by listening closely I understood what he was telling us. He wished us well, both of us, and asked the gods, Christian and pagan, to look over us and keep us safe. He would remain near, but not in, Camulod, he said, working on his written history of Arthur's colony from the days of its earliest beginnings. When I asked him where he would stay, he answered, "Where I always have, in Avalon." I smiled then, remembering the tiny, hidden valley among the hills that had been his sanctuary for so long. I had been there several times but had forgotten both its name and its existence until that moment. And then, just before we boarded the ship, he handed me a bulky package that he had concealed beneath his robe. It was my heritage, he said, the documents sent to him by Germanus concerning my family and background. He had kept them safe for all these years, and now he could think of no place safer for them than in my possession. I thanked him, intrigued, and carried the package aboard beneath my arm, intending to read it later.

I never did read it, however. I never even opened the package, and I still have it, intact, because every time I moved to open it and read the contents, something, some warning little voice, stopped me from doing so. I cannot explain that, even to myself, but I never failed to heed that voice.

My last memory of Merlyn alive is of him stooping forward and saying to me, in his strangely thickened voice, "Come back, Hastatus. Come back someday, when all this hurly-burly has died down. I'll be waiting for you in Avalon."

It took me more than a score of years to return, but when I did I found him waiting there for me as he had promised, although nothing remained of him by that time but a few dried old bones and wisps of snow-white hair. But he had left a store of treasures there for me in my old age. His manuscript was written, and when I read it, I found it gave me strength to persevere with my own record. And he left me one more wondrous gift. I have it in my home today and everyone who sees it marvels at its beauty. Of course, I tell them it was mine when I was young, for if I told them it was Arthur's, they would know its name and that would cause nothing but more grief. And so it is no longer Excalibur, the magical sword born of a flashing, fallen star and forged for a great King. It is simply a magnificent sword, fit to be worn by a champion. When I die, it will go to my son Clovis.

We heard word from Britain from time to time, most of it—all of it, in fact—brought out by priests. We heard of a great battle at a place called Graupius, or Grampia, or even Gropus, where Arthur was reported dead, although his corpse was never found, and neither was his fabled sword. And we heard reports that all his knights had died with him. We heard, too, that some of his knights survived and that one of them had stolen the King's sword, Excalibur. And then we heard that the King's wife, Gwinnifer, had proven faithless and had run away with one of the King's own knights. And we heard that the King's son, Mordred, had been killed in battle; and also that he had betrayed his father and survived the battle; we even heard that he had seduced his stepmother, the Queen, and had then been slain by the King's vengeful Frankish knight. On another occasion, we heard a report that reversed that tale entirely, stating that the Frankish knight had seduced the Queen and had been slain thereafter by her vengeful stepson, Mordred.

The most persistent tale of all was of the death of Arthur and the disappearance of his body and his sword, and the story being told among his former people was that he had been enchanted and spirited away by protective gods, to recover from his wounds and regain his strength for times of need ahead. There were many variants of that tale, each newly arriving priest bringing us several versions. But the one thing they all contained in common was that Arthur the King was dead.

Hearing that last tale on one particular occasion, I remembered what Arthur had said about people saying and believing what they wanted to say and believe, irrespective of the truth involved, and remembering my friend that night, I wept for him and for what might have been and should have been.

And then, three years later, by which time all reports from Britain had dried up and Gwinnifer and I had come to know and love each other, we were wed, and I left Corbenic, with my cousin Pelles's blessings, and led her home with me to Benwick, where no one knew she had ever been a queen. Perceval and Bors, the last surviving members of our Brotherhood of Knights Companion to the Riothamus, rode with us and remained with us until they died, and now they are all dead.

I miss them all.

FINIS

ACKNOWLEDGMENTS

Long before I started writing this last book in my saga, I had become convinced from my own researches and analyses of the legend that Arthur Pendragon must have suffered from some kind of physical disability, and most likely from a chronic and debilitating illness. I then went searching to discover just what kind of illness might have produced the symptoms I visualized, and I was fortunate enough to be able to enlist the willing assistance of Dr. David Kates of Kelowna, British Columbia, a nephrologist with a keen interest in ancient medicine, medical techniques and obscure illnesses. David spent a great deal of time delving into what records he could find that detailed ancient instances and symptoms of diabetes and many other illnesses, in a vain attempt to find something that would debilitate my King convincingly, rendering him impotent without killing him. Nothing would fit perfectly. Back in those days, if you caught anything really bad, you died of it quickly. But then one day, in a flash of inspiration, he pointed out that there are probably few things more debilitating than a deep stab wound from a dirty, rusty old blade, be it sword or spear. I have been grateful to him ever since, for that insight was exactly what I needed to make my hero real.

Long overdue thanks to many people who have seen this Arthurian saga through with me since 1990:

To Brad Martin, then a vice president at Penguin Books, who read the original material and decided Penguin had to publish it;

To Cynthia Good, the longtime Publisher of Penguin Canada, and to Kirsten Hansen, my very first editor, both of whom have now moved on to other things;

To Catherine Marjoribanks, who has been my editor ever since 1993 and who has come to know this story better than I do myself, contributing profoundly to its success;

And to Debby DeGroot, Director of Publicity for the Penguin Group (Canada), and all the other Penguins across Canada with whom I have had the pleasure of working now for almost fifteen years;

To Mark Burgess, who designed my "official" website at www.camulod.com and has maintained it for more years now than either of us really cares to compute … Mark approached me very soon after I was first published and offered to run a website for me. I didn't even know, back then, what a website was, and what little I know about such things now, I owe to Mark;

To Ray Addington of Abbotsford, British Columbia, who read my first book in manuscript, in the mid-eighties, then brought me back five copper coins from Bath (Aque Sulis), all of them in use during the time of Publius Varrus and Caius Britannicus, and all of them still sitting in pride of place on my desk;

To my old friend Bob Sharp, of Calgary, to whom I was talking when the Initial Idea came to me, revealing the explanation of the Sword in the Stone. Had it not been for him, and the interest we shared in things Arthurian, that epiphany might never have occurred;

To Alma Lee, Founding Executive Director of the Vancouver International Writers' Festival, who first got me involved and then became a good friend;

To Marion Dingman Hebb, a literary lawyer and stalwart of the Canadian Writers' Union, who helped me greatly in finding a publisher and then graciously declined to push me for her legitimate fee;

To my longtime friend Bill McKay, who could not quite contain his disbelief when I told him I had signed a publishing contract and said "Holy sh—!" five times;

To Mark Askwith of the Space Channel, who filmed a long interview with me, talking about Excalibur, on the campus of the University of Toronto, and then ran it as a filler between shows for years, until it had been seen by everyone in Canada, it appears, except me;

To my friend Mike McCrodan, lawyer and bon vivant, who has been supportive in too many ways for me to count;

To Diana Gabaldon, who said, when I told her back in '92 that I had no literary agent, "Well, you've got one now," and promptly went to work to make it so;

To Perry Knowlton, former President of Curtis Brown Ltd. of New York, now retired but known for decades as the dean of American literary agents, who sent me a signed contract in the mail at Diana's behest, and to Janet Turnbull Irving and Dean Cook, Perry's Canadian associates;

To Martin Gould, who was until very recently the resident Art Director at Penguin Canada, who has worked enthusiastically with me from the beginning to design each of the covers in the original Canadian editions of all my books;

To Aaron Heck, the invaluable computer resource person who recognizes my Luddite inefficiencies and keeps my wheels turning without ever losing patience with me or making me feel dumber than I undoubtedly am in dealing with his computer-world realities;

And, of course, to all the loyal readers who have bought and enjoyed my work.

Thanks to all of you.